Hans Fallada was born Rudolf Wilhelm Adolf Ditzen in 1893 in Greifswald, north-east Germany, and took his pen-name from a Brothers Grimm fairy tale. He spent a number of years in prison or in psychiatric care, yet produced some of the most significant German novels and documentary writing of the twentieth century, including *A Small Circus, Little Man, What Now?, Once a Jailbird, Tales From the Underworld, Wolf Among Wolves, The Drinker* and *Alone in Berlin*, the last of which was only published in English for the first time in 2009, to near-universal acclaim. He died in Berlin in 1947.

HANS FALLADA

Iron Gustav

A Berlin Family Chronicle

Translated by PHILIP OWENS

Completed by NICHOLAS JACOBS *and* GARDIS CRAMER VON LAUE

Foreword by JENNY WILLIAMS

PENGUIN BOOKS

PENGUIN CLASSICS

Published by the Penguin Group
Penguin Books Ltd, 80 Strand, London WC2R ORL, England
Penguin Group (USA) Inc., 375 Hudson Street, New York, New York 10014, USA
Penguin Group (Canada), 90 Eglinton Avenue East, Suite 700, Toronto, Ontario, Canada M4P 2Y3
(a division of Pearson Penguin Canada Inc.)
Penguin Ireland, 25 St Stephen's Green, Dublin 2, Ireland (a division of Penguin Books Ltd)
Penguin Group (Australia), 707 Collins Street, Melbourne, Victoria 3008, Australia
(a division of Pearson Australia Group Pty Ltd)
Penguin Books India Pvt Ltd, 11 Community Centre, Panchsheel Park, New Delhi – 110 017, India
Penguin Group (NZ), 67 Apollo Drive, Rosedale, Auckland 0632, New Zealand
(a division of Pearson New Zealand Ltd)
Penguin Books (South Africa) (Pty) Ltd, Block D, Rosebank Office Park,
181 Jan Smuts Avenue, Parktown North, Gauteng 2193, South Africa

Penguin Books Ltd, Registered Offices: 80 Strand, London WC2R ORL, England

www.penguin.com

First published in German as *Der eiserne Gustav* by Rowohlt Verlag 1938
First published, in an abbreviated edition, in English as *Iron Gustav* by Putnam 1940
First full edition published in 1962 by Aufbau Verlag in *Hans Fallada: Selected Works in Single Issues*,
edited by Günter Caspar, Vol. VI
First published, in this revised edition, in Penguin Classics 2014
001

Copyright © Aufbau Verlag GmbH & Co. KG, Berlin, 2009
Translation copyright 1940 by Philip Owens
Newly translated material copyright © Nicholas Jacobs and Gardis Cramer von Laue, 2014
Note on the Translation copyright © Nicholas Jacobs, 2014
Foreword copyright © Jenny Williams, 2014
All rights reserved

The moral right of the copyright holder, the translators, and the author of the
Note on the Translation has been asserted

Set in 10.5/13pt Dante MT Std
Typeset by Jouve (UK), Milton Keynes
Printed in England by Clays Ltd, St Ives plc

ISBN: 978-0-141-19653-4

www.greenpenguin.co.uk

Contents

ONE
The Good Days of Peace

TWO
War Breaks Out

THREE
The Evil Days

FOUR
Peace Breaks Out

Contents

FIVE
Tinette

SIX
The Old Cabby

THE LAST CHAPTER
The Beer Glass

Foreword

On 12 November 1937 Hans Fallada signed a contract to write a novel 'dealing with the fate of a German family from 1914 until around 1933'. Little did he suspect how much grief this project, which culminated in the publication of *Iron Gustav: A Berlin Family Chronicle* in 1938, would cause him – or how tortuous the path would be that would lead to the first complete English edition in 2014.

The manuscript that Fallada submitted on time in February 1938 was not initially intended for publication in book form. He had signed the contract with the Tobis Film Company, one of whose board members was the German film star Emil Jannings (1884–1950), most famous perhaps for his role in *The Blue Angel* of 1930, in which he had co-starred with Marlene Dietrich. Jannings had been looking for some time for a film script that would offer him an attractive leading role and was delighted with the larger-than-life figure of Gustav Hackendahl. Jannings took an active part in the negotiations between Fallada and Tobis, in the course of which it was agreed that Fallada would submit a novel and that the company's screenwriters would develop it into a film script.

Gustav Hackendahl is based on the historical figure of Gustav Hartmann (1859–1938) who, like his literary counterpart, inherited his father-in-law's coach business, built it into a successful enterprise and became famous for his return journey by coach and horse to Paris in 1928.

Fallada clearly wrote the novel with filming in mind. The physical appearance of Gustav Hackendahl himself, in his dark coachman's coat and white top hat, perched on the seat at the front of his coach with the reins of his horse firmly in his hands, is visually striking. His symbolic status is powerful, too: a man of 'iron' principle who sees the values of order, discipline and obedience, on which he has built his life, crumble in the face of modernity. The episodic nature of the work, the extensive use of dialogue (and dialect), the clearly delineated characters all lend themselves to a film adaptation, as does the wide range of social settings – from brothel to elegant villa, from stables to parliament buildings, from hospital to stationery shop, from a newspaper's headquarters to a tenement building. In this novel, as in *Wolf Among Wolves* of 1937, Fallada explores how the lives of quite ordinary people are affected by the tumultuous events of German history in the first three decades of the twentieth century. In *Iron Gustav* this social realism focuses on the Hackendahl family where the effects of the authoritarian nature of Wilhelminian Germany, in the form of Gustav's 'iron' principles, result in only one of the five children growing into a 'decent' human being. For Fallada, whose view of morality was a decidedly individual one, 'decency' ('*Anständigkeit*') is the key to ethical human behaviour.

When Fallada signed the contract for *Iron Gustav* in November 1937 he most probably knew that Tobis – like all media organizations – had been taken over by the Nazi Party. What he did not know was that Joseph Goebbels (1897–1945), the Minister for Public Enlightenment and Propaganda, was beginning to take a keen interest in his work. In January 1938 Goebbels read *Wolf Among Wolves* and, interpreting the critique of Weimar Germany in the novel as a confirmation of the Nazis' rejection of everything to do with the Weimar Republic, noted in his diary that this was 'a super book' and its author had 'real talent'. What Fallada ought to have known was that signing a contract in 1938 with a Nazi film company to write a book covering the period 1914 to 1933 in German history would mean including a glowing account of the rise of the Nazi Party.

Fallada seems to have had no inkling of the collision course on which he embarked in November 1937. In his defence it must be said that his main aim was to create a role for Emil Jannings and to write a social history around the Hackendahl family. This led to him concluding the novel shortly after Gustav's triumphant return from Paris in 1928.

Fallada expected the screenwriters to make changes to his

manuscript; what he did not expect was the personal intervention of Goebbels, who insisted that the story be continued until 1933 and that Gustav Hackendahl become an ardent Nazi. While Fallada was able to decline Goebbels's invitation for a face-to-face meeting, he could not ignore his instructions about the conclusion of the novel. He suggested to Jannings that a Nazi author would be much better placed to write the sort of conclusion that Goebbels required. When Jannings conveyed this view to Goebbels, the Minister replied that if Fallada was still unsure about his attitude towards the Party, the Party had no doubts about its attitude towards Fallada. Fallada now found himself faced with an unmistakable threat to his life. How would this non-Nazi, whose work since *A Small Circus* had constituted an extended plea for human decency, react?

He capitulated. Like most of Gustav Hackendahl's family he was unable to resist the iron fist of an authoritarian regime. By way of explanation he would later write: 'I do not like grand gestures, being slaughtered before the tyrant's throne, senselessly, to the benefit of no one and to the detriment of my children, that is not my way.'

Fallada's great gift lay in his keen observation of the world around him and his talent as a storyteller. His ability to feel his way inside his characters and convey their hopes and fears, their successes and failures, produced realistic figures such as Otto Hackendahl in *Iron Gustav*, Willi Kufalt in *Once a Jailbird* and Johannes Pinneberg in *Little Man, What Now?*. This, his great strength, was also a weakness, for he was unable to rise above his emotional involvement – in his characters, in his attitude to politics as well as in many aspects of his day-to-day life – to develop an analytical or philosophical standpoint. His 1944 Prison Diary leaves no doubt about his hatred of the Nazi regime but it was an instinctive hatred, not one based on a political philosophy. And this left him defenceless against the bully-boy tactics of Joseph Goebbels. He spent August 1938 carrying out Goebbels's instructions: 'this month [. . .] is marked in black in my diary. The world filled me with loathing, but I loathed myself even more for what I was doing.'

Fallada did the minimum necessary to meet Goebbels's demands. There is no detailed account of the rise of the Nazi Party or the nature of Party meetings, nor is there a celebration of the Party's much-vaunted achievements. In fact, Party activities are reduced to folding leaflets and getting involved in street brawls. There is no discussion of Party policy apart from Heinz Hackendahl's question about anti-Semitism, which is left unanswered.

In order to prepare the ground for first Heinz's and then Gustav's Party membership, Fallada added a small amount of material in Chapters Four, Five, Six and Seven in which he underscores the injustices suffered by Germany in the aftermath of the First World War and sharply criticizes the role of the Communists in the November Revolution. The first major addition is the insertion at the end of Chapter Seven of three new sections that explain Heinz's reasons for joining the Nazi Party: his unemployment (which leads to difficulties in his marriage), his meeting with a former comrade of Otto's (who is a Party member) and the feeling of comradeship and the sense of purpose that Party membership brings. As a member of the Party, Heinz 'becomes a human being and a real man again'. The additions in Chapter Eight pave the way for Gustav to become a Nazi and the new Chapter Nine describes the death of Gustav's wife, Heinz and his family moving into the Hackendahl family home and Gustav's decision to join the Party. The final line of the new conclusion is Gustav's declaration to Heinz and his comrades: 'Well, then: let me join you!'

Heinz and Gustav do not join the Nazi Party because they are convinced by Nazi Party policy. Heinz finds a reason for living and a sense of belonging in his political work (which remains unspecified); Gustav's reasons for joining are rather unclear.

Fallada, who later described these changes as 'stupid tinkering around', expected that they would not satisfy Goebbels. But to his surprise the Minister approved the *Iron Gustav* project and work started on the film. However, it all came to a halt in October 1938 when the Party's chief ideologue, Alfred Rosenberg (1893–1946), declared that Fallada was not the kind of author that a German state could support.

Given Rosenberg's views and the fact that the novel did not constitute a paean to National Socialism, it is not surprising that when the novel appeared at the end of November 1938 it received very negative reviews and was withdrawn from display in bookshop windows.

Despite the outbreak of war, Fallada's English publishers, Putnam, bought the rights to *Iron Gustav* and the first English translation appeared in 1940.

The 1940 English edition was considerably shorter than the one that had appeared in Germany in 1938. In the first place, it was based on Fallada's original manuscript and did not include Chapter Nine, the new sections in Chapter Seven and the other material that he had included at Goebbels's behest. Moreover, Putnam removed an additional eight sections and undertook wide-ranging cuts across the board. They clearly wanted a much shorter book.

Content that was considered repetitive or not central to the main narrative was simply excised. This affected primarily the portrayal of the Hackendahl children: the account of Sophie's application to volunteer for nursing at the Front (Two, X), Erich's visit to Dr Meier (Two, XIV), Otto's experience of Lille (Three, VII) are all simply omitted. A further three sections relating to Heinz are also cut: his visit with Irma to Tutti and Eva (Four, IX), his row with Tutti (Six, XIII) and his visit to his former teacher and mentor, Professor Degener (Seven, XII). Even Chapter Two, section VIII, which describes Gustav's walk with Heinz and the incident with the spies on the day he handed over his horses for the war effort, does not appear in the 1940 English translation.

Besides deleting whole sections, the editor removed much inner monologue and descriptions of characters' thoughts and feelings, such as the account in Chapter Six, section IV of Gustav's reaction on hearing that his grandsons, whom he has never met, prefer to play with coaches and horses rather than with cars. Key scenes that give particular insights into character motivation and plot development are also omitted. A good example is the conversation between Otto and his mother in Chapter One, section XII, in which they consider whether to release Erich from the cellar. Here Otto's character is given depth and the reasons for the decision to break the locks on the cellar doors are provided – a decision that sets Erich on a path of criminality that ultimately leads to his being arrested for treason.

Putnam's editor in 1940 had little time for Fallada's detailed and often humorous accounts of everyday life, such as the conversations in the queue for rations (Three, II) or in the waiting room of the doctor's surgery (Three, XV) during the First World War.

The cumulative effect of these changes was to produce characters that are much less complex and a novel that lacks the colour and vividness of Fallada's original work.

The final set of cuts in the 1940 edition relates to passages dealing with the political and historical background to the events portrayed in the novel. Perhaps the editor took the view that English readers would not be interested in detailed descriptions of recent German history. However, it is likely that the context in which the novel was published also had a considerable bearing on these cuts. The decision to omit Chapter Five, section XVI, which deals with the Treaty of Versailles, and drastically to reduce the account of the occupation of the Ruhr in Chapter Six can be ascribed to the sensitivity of these issues in Britain at the time.

Indeed, Putnam's decision to publish a contemporary German novel by an author still living in Germany in 1940 is unique in British publishing. It was, of course, Putnam that had arranged for Fallada and his family to leave Germany in the autumn of 1938 and it is possible that the original plan was to publish a new Fallada translation to coincide with the author's arrival in London and to provide some financial support for his new life in exile. However, Fallada could not bring himself to leave Germany. For his English publisher he was nonetheless an important enough contemporary German author to be published in translation, despite the fact that he was living in a country with which Britain was at war.

It was not until 1962 that an attempt was made to reconstruct Fallada's original German manuscript in the form it had taken before he made the changes in August 1938. This reconstruction, undertaken by Günter Caspar of the Aufbau publishing house in the German Democratic Republic, who was the editor of Fallada's *Selected Works*, has since become the standard German edition. It ends rather abruptly on the day that Gustav returns from Paris. Caspar did not have access to the 1940 English translation; he was probably unaware that it represented, albeit in bowdlerized form, the structure of Fallada's original manuscript. If he had seen it, he might have retained its last chapter, entitled 'The Beer Glass', in his German edition. This chapter continues Gustav's story until the death of his wife and finishes, in typical Fallada fashion, with an anecdote that portrays Gustav as 'iron' until the end.

The new Penguin translation uses the Caspar reconstruction to reinstate Putnam's original excisions and thus produces a much more complete English edition of the work than that published in 1940. This edition also represents the most faithful reconstruction of Fallada's original manuscript to date. As such it provides an instructive case study of the significant role that translation can play in preserving a foreign text that has fallen victim to censorship in its country of origin.

Finally, the publication of *Iron Gustav* marks an important milestone in reconnecting Fallada with his English-speaking readers, who now have access to all his major critical realist novels from *A Small Circus* (1931) to *Alone in Berlin* (1947).

Jenny Williams, 2014

Note on the Translation

Iron Gustav was first published by Putnam (London) in 1940. Starting with *Little Man, What Now?* in 1933, Putnam had published a Fallada novel every year. Fallada's popularity must be the only explanation for a British publisher bringing out a book by a writer – and one who was hardly known as any kind of dissenter – with whose country it was at war.

In view of the fact that Putnam had already substantially abbreviated Fallada's even longer novel, *Wolf Among Wolves*, also translated by Philip Owens, it is not surprising that its British publisher abbreviated *Iron Gustav* even more drastically, by some two hundred pages. Many of these cuts concern issues – the so-called German Revolution of 1918–19, the Occupation of the Ruhr, and mass unemployment (about which Fallada wrote most powerfully) – which had been used successfully by the National Socialists in their propaganda, and so were considered unwelcome reading during a war against Germany which had just begun.

These cuts mean that the book was substantially misrepresented when first published, and that this edition is more than a reprint with some cuts restored, but rather a completely new edition of this novel.

Philip Owens, born in 1901, was a writer, translator and editor, who formed part of the British literary avant-garde alongside figures like Jack Lindsay, Samuel Beckett, William Empson and Edgell Rickword in the twenties and thirties. Among other works, he wrote an experimental novel, much of it set in Berlin (*Hobohemians: A Study of Luxurious Poverty* (Mandrake Press, 1929)). Little wonder that he was such a brilliant translator of Fallada's low-life ambience.

Philip Owens was killed, serving in the Intelligence Corps, in the Greek Civil War in June 1945. I learned much from him.

More practically, I would like to thank Gardis Cramer von Laue for not only locating everything missing – as discussed elsewhere – from the 1940 translation, from single words and phrases to passages and whole chapters, but also for typing everything out, with its context, for the convenience of the translator. I also benefited from her native German and strong feel for the English language.

N.M.J.

Iron Gustav

All the characters in this book, including Iron Gustav himself, are creatures of the imagination, no living person being referred to in any way. Moreover, the author has used only such material as could be gathered from the daily newspapers of the time.

H. F.

ONE

The Good Days of Peace

§ I

Perhaps it was the grey mare, old Hackendahl's favourite, demanding its feed by dragging the halter chain through the manger ring and pawing the floor of its stable; perhaps it was the dawn replacing the moon, the light of earliest morning breaking over Berlin, which had awakened the old man. Possibly, however, it was neither the dawn nor his favourite grey that had awakened him at twenty minutes past three on the morning of 29 June 1914, but something quite different.

Struggling with sleepiness, the old man had groaned: 'Erich, Erich, you won't do that, will you?' Then he had started up and gazed round the room. Slowly, perception returned to his eyes; over the carved shell of the marriage bed, with knobs on either side, he saw the sabre and helmet, from the time when he had been a sergeant-major in the Pasewalk Cuirassiers, hanging on the wall beneath his photograph, taken on the day he had left the service twenty years ago. He saw the faint gleam of the blade and of the golden eagle on his helmet, bringing memories which made him even prouder and happier than did the big cab-hire business he had since built up; the esteem that had been his in the regiment pleased him more than the respect paid him, the successful businessman, by his neighbours in the Frankfurter Allee. And, harking back to his nightmare, he said, now fully awake: 'No, Erich would never do a thing like that. Never!'

Abruptly he set his feet on the sheepskin rug by the bed.

§ II

'Are you getting up already, Gustav?' enquired a voice from the neighbouring bed, and a hand groped for him. 'It's only three o'clock.'

'Yes, Mother. Twenty-five minutes past three.'

'But why, Father? They're not fed till four . . .'

He was almost embarrassed. 'I've got a feeling that one of the horses might be ill.' And, to avoid further explanations, he plunged his head into the wash basin. But his wife waited patiently until he had dried himself. 'You've been talking all night in your sleep about Erich, Father.'

Her husband suddenly stopped combing his hair, was about to speak, but thought better of it. 'Really,' he remarked nonchalantly, 'I wasn't aware of it.'

'What's up between you and Erich?' she persisted. 'I know something's the matter between you.'

'Yesterday Eva was the whole afternoon at Köller's. I won't have it. People call it the "Café Cuddle".'

'A young girl wants a little life and Fraulein Köller's bought a gramophone. Eva only goes there because of the music.'

'I don't like it,' emphasized the old sergeant-major. 'You keep the girls in order and I'll look after the boys, Erich included.'

'But . . .'

Hackendahl had gone, however. He had said what he had to say and in this house his will was law.

The woman let herself sink back into the pillow with a sigh. Oh, yes, dear God. What a man! Stiff as a poker, and wants the children to have a life like his! He can talk – but I'll see to it that the children get their share of pleasure in life – Eva as well, and Erich too. Especially Erich.

And she was already asleep.

§ III

The father stood hesitantly for a moment in the gloomy hallway. From the stable below, he could hear the grey reproachfully clinking her chain, but he withstood the temptation to give his favourite an extra ration on the sly, and instead softly opened the door to his daughters' bedroom.

The two girls slept on, accustomed to their father making his rounds by day and by night, exactly as he had done in the barracks when inspecting the dormitories to see that everything was in order. When Hackendahl had turned civilian and taken over his dead father-in-law's hackney carriage business, he had given up none of his military habits; drivers, horses and children had to toe the line as strictly as if they had been soldiers. The children were not allowed to have any life of their own, nor the kind of secrets that children love so much. Everything in the chests of drawers and cupboards had to be in its place, for Father was merciless about what he called order and cleanliness. 'Father' – that was the sword that hung over the family Hackendahl. 'Father' meant discipline, criticism, the sternest justice.

'Iron Gustav' they called him in the Frankfurter Allee, a man as unyielding and stubborn as he was upright and irreproachable. Entering late in life a civilian world which seemed to him too soft, he had tried to inoculate his children with the principles by which (as he thought) he had attained success – and these were industry, the sense of duty, and obedience to the will of a superior, whether that superior be called God, Kaiser or the Law.

Old Hackendahl scrutinized the room. Over Sophie's chair hung a nurse's uniform, carefully folded; the starched hood with its Red Cross badge lay on the bedside table. Hackendahl sighed. His daughter, having come of age, had insisted on taking up nursing, although in his view this somewhat pious and anaemic child would have been better suited as a teacher. But Sophie knew how to get her own way.

'If you positively won't give your consent, Father,' she had said in that quiet way of hers, 'I'll have to do without.'

'But I'm your father,' he had stormed, taken aback by such disobedience. 'You're breaking the fifth commandment.'

'Pastor Rienäcker,' she had replied, 'tells me I have a call.'

'God's call' – she hadn't been ashamed to talk like that to her father! And since when did one talk of God, the Omnipotent, as if one were personally acquainted with Him? One was too small to do that. Old Hackendahl regarded this earth as having distinctions of rank that were, so to speak, spatial; that is, the Lord sat on the very top and, far below, sat Hackendahl; everyone in between, whether colonel, judge of the supreme court or emperor, had his appointed place.

'I only want what is best for you, Sophie,' he had said. 'You're not strong enough for nursing.'

'God will give me strength,' she had replied.

All right, all right! Mechanically old Hackendahl adjusted the ribbons of her hood so that they lay at right angles, although tidiness was more probably to seek in the clothes of his second daughter, the eighteen-year-old Eva, who slept on her side, her face hidden by an arm and her long, fair hair. Sophie, quite properly, had done up her hair for the night in two plaits, but Eva would say, 'At night at least I want my hair free from the silly old bun!'

She was taking a liberty, but her father didn't say so. She looked so pretty without it, with her blonde ringlets framing her pale face. It somehow lit up his heart to see her lying there like that – a life in bloom, a mature girl, but still a child.

Still a child! Of course – he knew his Eva.

Remembering the confectioner's shop, that wretched 'Café Cuddle' with its tinned music churned out from a great horn painted pink and gold, Hackendahl frowned. Yes, she had certainly gone there, but only because of the music from this new-fangled apparatus, and not because she was thinking about men or kisses . . .

Feeling his glance she flung herself, with the impetuosity which characterized all her movements, on her back, stretched and gave out a sound of ecstatic joy – just an 'Oh!', but so happy. Then she looked at him. 'Is that you, Father?'

'Good morning,' he said slowly.

'Good morning, Father. Listen . . .'

'What is it? You should be asleep!'

'Never mind, I'll go to sleep immediately. Father, do you know what time Erich came home?'

'You mustn't tell tales, you know that.'

'At one o'clock, Father! Fancy, one o'clock.'

'Shame, Evchen, you shouldn't tell tales.' This was not said very firmly, however, for what he had just heard agitated him very much.

'Shouldn't tell tales! When he's always telling about me! In the Café Köller they said he'd got a lot of money, Father.'

'You're not to go to the Café.'

'But I'm so fond of whipped cream – and we never get any at

home.' She was watching her father shrewdly and saw that he was no longer thinking of her. 'And now I'm going to sleep, I'm so tired . . .'

'Yes, go to sleep. And don't tell tales, it's not nice.'

In the corridor he heard, more distinctly than ever, the grey stamping. It was just on four o'clock, feeding time. But first he would go to his sons' room.

§ IV

Three beds, three sleepers, three sons. They could be regarded as wealth, and so the father had hitherto regarded them. Not now, however, not now! There was something else besides Eva's tittle tattle that made Hackendahl stand on the threshold listening. Listening . . .

He had heard hundreds, thousands of people sleeping. So he was familiar with this oppressed breathing; he had heard it in the barracks, mostly on Saturday and Sunday nights after leave, but he had never before heard it in this room. Eva's words rushed into his mind. 'Erich came home at one o'clock.' But he needed no one to tell him what a drunken sleep sounded like.

Although there was reason to complain about the way in which Heinz, the youngest (nicknamed Bubi), left his clothes lying around, and reason also to make the eldest, the twenty-four-year-old Otto, realize that his father knew he was not asleep – he lay much too stiffly – Hackendahl was now occupied only with his drunken son. Distraught with grief and anger, he stood by the bed of his Erich, his quick-witted boy . . . Erich was only seventeen but he was already in the second highest class at the grammar school; he was his parents' favourite, the most popular boy in his class, a favourite also with his teachers. But he was drunk . . .

The father stood there lost in thought, his foot on the bedside rug, if that's what it was; there was no time to look. He must watch his son's face, this much-loved face, and try to read its expression.

But the light was still dim, so he went to the window and turned back a corner of the curtain, so that the already bright daylight shone full in the face of the sleeping boy.

At the same time, the father's gaze met another's, that of Otto,

who looked at him darkly and a little troubled. Anger rose in Hack-
endahl, as if Otto had caught him doing something forbidden. And
he completely gave way to his anger – you could do that with Otto.
He was a milksop, apparently unmarked by either anger or love.
Raising his fist as though to strike him, the father hissed: 'Be quiet!
Go to sleep at once! D'you hear?'

The son closed his eyes immediately.

For a moment, the father looked again at the pale, weak face with
the thin beard. Then he turned back to his other son. But what had
happened had changed him. Since knowing the eldest son was
awake, he no longer felt alone in the room. The time for quiet con-
templation was over. Anger, complaining and sadness had passed.
Something had to happen.

Something had to happen!

First he bent down. Yes, he hadn't paid attention, but he had
noticed the clothes thrown drunkenly about. It wasn't a bedside rug
he'd stood on. And he began to pick up the clothes.

Something dropped out of the waistcoat pocket and fell with a
clink.

First of all the old man hung the waistcoat in an orderly way over
the back of a chair. Then he picked up the key. It was a completely
ordinary key, a little key, the kind used for cupboards and drawers. It
was still quite new. Even in the dim light the father thought he could
make out the filing of the bit . . . and it was no industrial key but one
made by a locksmith – nothing special.

The father stood absolutely still. As he held the little key in his
hand, he felt he could hear time go by in seconds and minutes. It
fell like heavy rain, obliterating all other sounds – all the sounds of
life. And behind this veil, life itself became grey, colourless and
distant . . .

Only a little key . . .

He no longer looked at his drunken son's bed. He didn't care if
Otto was awake and watching him. When in great pain everyone is
utterly alone. Nothing reached him any more.

With dragging feet and unseeing eyes the father went to the door,
the key in his hand.

A little key!

§ V

In the passage Hackendahl again heard the grey, his pampered favourite, demanding its extra ration. No, things were not right, either with the horse or Erich or the master of the house. He, scrupulously just and conscientious, got up half an hour earlier to give the grey something extra before Rabause the head stableman arrived. His children all meant a great deal to him, but Erich with his coaxing could always in the end obtain what was refused the others. The father had never thought of this as unjust, since no one can command his affections, yet now he saw that it was not the proper way of doing things; it sinned against reason, human and divine. He carried the proof in his hand.

He carried it as though it were a magic key with a power as yet unknown and which had therefore to be handled cautiously. It was a magic key, opening Iron Gustav up to new knowledge. No father's heart can be completely made of iron. It is soil forever newly ploughed, some of whose furrows never disappear.

He stood before his desk. There was no retreat now, even had he thought of it – an old soldier faces the enemy, and attacks.

The massive desk was of heavily carved oak, with brass embellishments representing lions' mouths. He pushed the key into one of these mouths and – there! – the key turned. He was not surprised; it was to be expected that this key would open the drawer in his desk. Hackendahl looked inside. When the children were small, a slab of toffee was always to be found on the right-hand side, in front. Every Sunday, after lunch, the children lined up before the desk where the father, sitting in judgement on their behaviour during the week, hacked off appropriate pieces from the slab. He had thought toffee good for the children; in his youth sugar had been dear and was believed to bestow great strength, and Hackendahl wanted healthy children. Later this belief turned out erroneous, the dentist explaining that sugar actually spoiled children's teeth; Hackendahl had meant well but had acted wrongly. That often happened in life. You mean well and do wrong all the same. You don't know enough, perhaps – had learned too little. With Erich he'd also meant well and done the wrong thing. He hadn't been strict enough, and now his favourite son was a thief, the meanest of his kind – a pilferer in the home, a creature who stole from his parents, from his brothers and sisters . . . The old man's pride was wounded. He groaned. His honour was stained. If the son is a thief the father cannot be blameless.

Standing there, he heard it strike four o'clock. He ought to go downstairs to the stables to superintend the feeding and grooming of the horses – in half an hour the night cabs would be coming back and he had to settle up with them – he had no time to stand there brooding over an undutiful son.

Yes, but first he must count the money in the little linen bag, ascertain what was missing and question his son; then he could superintend the feeding and the grooming, have the horses seen to, settle up with the drivers . . . He did neither of these things. He shook the linen bag which Sophie had embroidered with '10 marks' in red cross-stitch, the little bag that contained gold in ten-mark pieces. But he did not check the contents; he went neither to his son nor to the stable. He was lost in memories.

His life in the army had made a man of him and given him principles; all his experiences in civilian life had their counterpart in the army. He could remember instances of barrack room thieves, incorrigible rogues who repeatedly stole tobacco or home-made sausage from their comrades. In the beginning they would get a good thrashing one night with a belt buckle on their naked backsides, their head muffled in a horse blanket, although even without that precaution no NCO would have taken any notice of a scream. But if the thrashing was in vain – if the man was really incorrigible, an enemy to his comrades – then came degradation before the entire regiment and transfer to a penal battalion, shame and dishonour. And wasn't it worse to steal from a father than from a comrade?

In three hours his son would have to go to school. It was almost impossible to imagine that he would never again go there, he, his pride and hope. And yet it had to be. He remembered a certain soldier with a great big blob of a pale nose facing his comrades on parade. Tears ran down his cheeks as the merciless voice of his officer declared that condemnation of the man and the thief against which there was no appeal . . .

That his own flesh and blood had sinned did not affect the issue – a thief is a thief. They had christened him 'Iron Gustav', probably half in jest because he was stubborn. But one can turn a nickname into an honour.

At last Hackendahl counted his money and when he had ascertained the amount missing he stood aghast. So much? Surely not! But it was true – yet more shame and dishonour. Surely all that money couldn't have been spent in drink, at seventeen! And suddenly the father saw behind his son's pale, intelligent face the leer and grimace of loose women, abominations to any decent man. At seventeen!

Shutting the drawer abruptly, he locked it and hurried back to his sons' bedroom.

§ VI

At his father's unexpected return Otto, who was dressed and standing by the window, started violently, trying to conceal the wood and knife in his hands; a dozen times he had been forbidden to pursue his hobby of carving pipe bowls or tiny animals in wood, his father holding it a ridiculous pursuit for one who was some day to manage a stable of thirty horses. Now Hackendahl took no notice of his eldest son's disobedience but went directly to Erich, clapped his hand on the boy's shoulder and ordered him to wake up.

The sleeper moved, trying to release his shoulder; his eyelids fluttered, but he did not wake up.

'Wake up, do you hear?'

Erich was still trying to escape into sleep, but in vain. His father's hand hurt, his father's voice threatened. With an effort he opened his eyes. 'What's the matter? Time for school?'

Without a word the father gazed at him. Then, grasping the long, fair hair, he pulled his son's reluctant head so close to his own that the two foreheads almost touched, and each saw only the other's eye. In one was fear, in the other an angry glow . . .

'What's the matter?' repeated Erich. But his voice trembled.

The father, his heart beating heavily, read a confession in his son's gaze. For a long time he said nothing; then, suddenly, despite himself, he quietly asked: 'Where did you leave the money?'

The dark, narrow pupils seemed to contract. Was this the son's answer? The father didn't know. He pulled his son's hair and repeatedly hit his brow against his own.

'My money,' he whispered. 'You thief! You key-forger!'

The son's head shook uncontrollably. He didn't even try to escape his father's gruesome hold.

'What are you stinking of?' asked the father once more. 'Drink? Whores? You give them my money?'

No reply. And this cowardice only incensed Hackendahl the more. 'What shall I do with you?' he groaned. 'Go to the police? Send you to prison?'

No reply.

'What do you want?' he burst out, turning angrily on his eldest son. 'Don't interfere, blockhead.'

'I'm going to the stables,' said Otto. 'Shall I give out the feed?'

'You?' barked the father contemptuously. But the distraction had relieved him and he even let go of Erich. 'That would be marvellous! No, you go on – I'll follow presently.'

'Yes, Father,' said Otto submissively and went.

Erich had risen and was standing, very pale, on the other side of the bed.

'Have you anything to say?' The father was trying to whip up his rage again. 'Be quick – you know I've other things to do. I've got to earn money for my fine son to steal and booze and whore with.'

Erich looked up at his father with trembling lips. Now that he was free of that painful grip, and with the bed between them, he spoke. 'I want something from life . . .'

'Want, eh? And what do you *give* to it? If you want something, you've got to give something back. But you're only a thief.'

'I don't want to live like this,' said Erich sullenly, pushing his hair away from his aching brows. 'Only school and homework, and when I want half an hour off I've got to ask you, and you have your eyes glued to your watch to see that I don't take a minute longer.'

'*You* can't live like that? When I was your age I was a farmhand. I had to get up at three in the morning and when I went to bed at nine o'clock at night I was half dead. And *you* can't stand five hours of school, good clothes and good food? – That's too much for *you?*'

'But I'm not a farmhand. A schoolboy doesn't live on a farm. Times have changed, Father.'

'Yes, they have indeed changed. No respect or honour left. Look at the Reds making a row in front of the Schloss, demanding their rights from the Kaiser. Their rights! And you've become a Red as well and want to prove your right to imitation keys and stolen money.'

'You never give me a farthing,' went on the son defiantly. 'Haven't I a right to live like the other boys at school? You brought me into the world and wanted me to study . . . Very well then, give me what's necessary. But you only want to tyrannize, you're only happy when we're all trembling before you. You're just like your Kaiser. He who doesn't obey is shot down.'

'Erich!' The old man was deeply wounded. 'How can you say that? All I want is your happiness. What are you talking about? You've stolen my key and had a false one made, you've stolen my money – and you are trying to defend yourself. Why don't you repent and ask my forgiveness? Have you gone completely mad? A son steals from his father and it's the father, not the son, who's guilty!'

At this point Heinz, awakened by the quarrel, sat up and said, in his cheeky Berlin manner: 'Don't get so worked up, Father. Erich's got a screw loose, he's not quite right in the upper storey. The whole school knows that. Why, he's a Red!'

'A Red!' cried the father. 'My son a Red! A Hackendahl a Socialist! Don't you know that the Kaiser's said all Socialists are the enemies of the Fatherland and that he'll smash them?'

'If they don't first smash your Kaiser,' said Erich angrily. 'He can only rattle his sabre, that's all he's good for.'

'Father!' cried Heinz. 'Don't take any notice of Erich, he's cracked.'

'I'll show him,' shouted the father. 'When my own son . . .'

He reached out but Erich ducked away.

'Quietly, quietly!' cried Heinz from his bed.

§ VII

'Just listen to the row,' wailed the mother. 'And this early in the morning! Father can never keep quiet – he thinks he's still in the barracks.'

Eva sat up in bed, looking almost pleased about the quarrel. Sophie had pulled the blanket up to her chin and behaved as if she heard nothing.

'Sophie,' implored her mother, 'Father listens to you. Go and smooth him down and find out what's really the matter, what's the trouble with Erich – he was even quarrelling with him in his sleep. Sophie, please!'

'I don't want to have anything to do with your quarrels.' Sophie sat up, her face pale and twitching. 'Oh, how you get on my nerves! I can't stand it any longer. Nothing but quarrels and scandal! What does one live for, then?'

'To go to church, of course,' sneered Eva, 'and see Pastor Rienäcker. God, what a wonderful beard he has! You can't get bored with that in front of you.'

'I'm not speaking to you,' cried the elder sister. 'Oh, you're beastly. You think because you . . . But I don't want to speak evilly of you. God forgive me that I should behave like you . . .'

'Children, don't quarrel,' begged the mother. 'We could all live so happily together. We could be so comfortable. But no – only quarrels and trouble . . .'

'I'm sorry, Mother,' said Sophie resolutely, 'but it's not enough, your comfortable life as you call it. You like it, but it's only you old people who do. We, the younger generation – I have to agree with Evchen and Erich about that – we prefer other things.'

'Thanks, Miss Goody-Goody,' interrupted Eva. 'I don't want your support. I can tell Mother what I want myself. But to be like Erich, coming home at one o'clock in the morning, getting drunk and pinching Father's money . . .'

'Oh, God,' wailed the mother. 'Erich can't have done that! If Father gets to know, he'll kill him. He can have money from me.'

'But, Mother,' argued Sophie, shocked, 'you shouldn't give Erich money behind Father's back. Parents ought to stick together.'

'I've never heard such rubbish!' said Eva contemptuously. 'That is so much priggish nonsense. Better for Erich to steal money than . . .'

'What does he want money for?' countered Sophie heatedly.

'I'll tell you what's wrong with you, Sophie. You get out of doing anything here. You'd rather gad about with some dirty little cheat in the private ward than empty Father's chamber pot. You think you're God knows who and that He'll give you full marks . . .'

'Mother,' cried Sophie tearfully. 'Don't let her talk in such a vulgar way, I can't bear it.'

'Yes, you're too refined to listen to the truth but you're not too refined to thrust it down our throats.'

'I won't stand it any longer.' Sophie wiped away the tears with the sleeve of her nightgown. 'And I don't need to. I'll speak with the Matron this very day and I'll move my things to the Nurses' Home this evening.'

'Sophie,' cried the mother, 'don't do that, please don't! Father will never allow it. You're our daughter and we're a family and we should cling together.'

'Yes, so as to quarrel,' said Eva. 'Sophie's quite right, she should get away. And I'll go as soon as I can. Everyone must look after himself, and all that stuff about family and parents and love is only nonsense.'

'But, Evchen, we do love one another.'

'We don't,' said Eva. 'We can't stand one another.'

'I won't listen any longer,' said Sophie. 'Talking like that just shows your lack of faith – both you and Erich. And you only want to go away because you don't want any restrictions. I've seen it coming for a long time without having to meet you arm-in-arm with men. It's shameful. I knew it when you used to go to the fairground. When you were only thirteen years old you let boys pay for you on the roundabouts.'

'You're jealous because nobody ever looks at *you*, Sophie.'

'And you weren't at all ashamed when the wind blew up your skirts so that people could even see the lace on your knickers.'

'Splendid!'

'Oh, children, do help!' wailed the mother. 'Just listen. I believe Father's killing Erich . . .'

§ VIII

'Governor overslept?' asked old Rabause, the head stableman, sitting on the feed chest and kicking his clogs against the sides. 'Time's getting on.'

When Otto entered twenty horses had turned their heads, neighing expectantly. But they knew he was not their master, the one who brought food, and they turned their disappointed heads away. Only the grey pawed the ground with more determination than ever.

'He's coming presently,' replied Otto, sitting down beside Rabause. 'He's been up a long time.'

'Then why hasn't he fed the grey?' wondered the head stableman. 'He never misses.' He laughed. 'The Governor thinks I don't notice.'

'It's nothing to do with us, Rabause. It's Father's horses and Father's corn – he can do what he likes with them.'

'Did I deny it, Ottchen? I only said he feeds them on the quiet and that's true. The boss has his favourites however much he pretends to treat everyone according to merit.'

'I know nothing about that,' said Otto distantly. 'I do what Father wants.'

'Just what I say, Ottchen,' grinned the old man. 'But for all that you're not his favourite either.'

For a while they were silent. Then Rabause cleared his throat. 'Well, Otto, have you carved my pipe bowl yet?'

'I haven't had time. You know I have to be so careful, and not let Father see.'

'Make a good job of it,' begged Rabause. 'I want it like my Ajax. You know – a blaze down one side of his muzzle.'

'I'll do it, as soon as I have time.'

'You see, Otto – you've once again forgotten to remind me that I should use the formal "you" when talking with you. You know the Governor has strictly banned me from being informal.'

'I hadn't forgotten. I just don't like telling you all the time.'

'That's precisely it,' said Rabause hurriedly. 'If you yourself wanted me to be formal, I wouldn't keep forgetting not to be. But you want the informality.'

'Rabause, you've just done it again!'

'See? Your father was quite right. It's of no importance if a chief stable boy uses the informal "you" when talking to the Governor's son. You're not ten years old any more, as you were back then when I came here. You're now twenty-five.'

'Twenty-four.'

'All right, twenty-four.' And Rabause kicked thoughtfully against the chest. 'Well, you may have to play at soldiers again . . .'

'Me? Never! Once is enough.'

'But suppose there's a war?'

'There won't be a war.'

'Didn't you read the special editions yesterday about the Serbs assassinating the Austrian Crown Prince? There'll be war, you see.'

'What have we got to do with the Serbs? Where are they, anyhow?'

'I don't know exactly, Ottchen, somewhere that way . . .' Rabause pointed vaguely across the stable.

'Well, there you are! That's why there can't be a war.'

Both were silent a while.

'If the Governor doesn't come soon I'd better feed the horses . . . The cabs have to go out on time . . . Hadn't you better go and see, Ottchen?'

'Father said he was coming at once.'

'I'll call him myself if you're afraid, Ottchen.'

'I shouldn't, Rabause. Father'll come.'

'What's the matter? A dust-up?'

Otto nodded.

'Again? So early? What's it about?'

'Nothing . . .'

'I suppose there's a saucepan out of place again in the kitchen. The Governor overdoes it; he's killing himself and the others too. You've got no guts left as it is, Ottchen.'

'Oh, I'll stick it for the present. But I wouldn't say No to a war if I could get out of this place. I'd like some peace and quiet for a change, not always to be barked at.'

'But they bark at you in the Prussian Army too, Ottchen.'

'Not as Father does, though.'

'There!' cried Rabause, 'we're in trouble now. Come, Ottchen.' And he ran to the stable door.

'Wouldn't it be better to stay here?' asked Otto indecisively, but then followed Rabause out of the stable.

§ IX

Across the courtyard came old Hackendahl shoving Erich, dressed only in shirt and trousers, in front of him. The women, frightened and curious, were peering out of the windows. The son's defiance had ended in the father getting beside himself with rage.

'So you want to be a student, eh?' the old man was shouting, pushing Erich so that he stumbled. 'Well, you're a blackguard, a thief!'

'I'll not put up with it,' cried Erich, 'I'll . . .'

'Sir! Please, sir, you're waking the neighbours,' begged the alarmed stableman.

'Just have a look, Rabause, at this young gentleman who's squandered eighty marks in one night and says he has the right to do it. Stand still, you, when your father speaks to you. I'll show you who's master in this house. I'm taking you away from school today.'

'You can't do that!'

'I can. I swear I'll do it, and today.'

'Sir, don't upset yourself so . . .' began Rabause.

'Father!'

'Yes, you can call me Father now, when it's too late. But there's an end of fathering for you, my lad; henceforward I'm just your boss – and I'll see that you learn to obey. Quick, into the stables! From today on you're a stable hand here. And I can promise you, you'll have so much mucking-out and cleaning . . .'

'I'll never do it, Father! I'd rather run away than touch a pitchfork!'

'Think about it, Governor – such a good head on him.'

'Good? For what? For theft! No, Erich. Into the stables with you!'

'I won't!'

'At once!'

'Never!'

'You refuse to obey your father?'

'I'll never set foot in the stables, and I'll never lay hands on a pitchfork!'

'Erich, don't go too far! Go into the stables, do the work, obey – and we'll see at the end of a year—'

'A year? Not an hour, not a minute!'

'You won't go?'

'Never!'

His father stood, thinking, almost calm.

'Ottchen, do talk to Erich,' begged old Rabause. 'He must be sensible. It needn't be for a year, your father'll be satisfied with a month, a week even – once he's sure of his good intentions.'

'Erich . . .' entreated Otto.

'Be quiet,' shouted Erich. 'You poor worm! If you hadn't cringed to Father he wouldn't have got like this.'

'Come!' said the old man, as if he had heard nothing. 'Come!' He put his hand on his son's arm. 'Let's go.'

'I won't go into the stables.'

'Come!' said the father, dragging his son along in the direction of the house. 'Bring me the cellar key, Otto.'

Otto ran off.

'What are you doing?' exclaimed Erich.

'Come,' said his father.

They had reached the house. Not to go upstairs, however, but down into the cellar.

'And here you stay till you come to your senses,' said the father, opening the cellar door. 'I give you my word I won't let you out till you knuckle under.'

'Here?' demanded Erich incredulously, looking into the dark cellar. 'You're going to lock me up in here?'

'You'll stay here till you've come to your senses.'

'You can't, you mustn't!'

'Oh yes, I can. Give me the key, Otto. Go in, Erich! Or will you obey me and work in the stables?'

'Father!' The son held onto the door jamb. 'Listen, for God's sake! You give way for once. Perhaps I've been a bit silly. I promise I'll change . . .'

'Good! Change by going into the stables, then.'

'Never!'

'Then in you go!' Abruptly the father pushed his son into the cellar. Erich flung himself against the door. 'Father!'

Hackendahl turned the key. Fists were heard drumming from inside, and an almost unrecognizable voice shouted, 'Tyrant, slave-driver, hangman!'

'Let's feed the horses, Otto,' he said and went.

'You're too hard, Father,' whispered Otto.

'What?' shouted his father, and remained standing (the prisoner continuing to shout). 'What?! As if he wasn't hard on me!' He looked at his son reproachfully. 'Don't you think it doesn't hurt me? Let's feed the animals, Otto.'

§ X

He had walked up the cellar steps like a very old man, but he stepped into the yard with a firm tread. 'Yes, yes,' he muttered, 'and may God help us all!' In what was almost his old domineering voice he called to the women at the window: 'Haven't you anything to do? Get on with your work.'

The faces vanished at once, and Hackendahl entered the stables. 'Everything in order, Rabause?'

'Everything in order here.' The word 'here' was the sole allusion Rabause dared to make to recent events.

There was much to do in the hour that followed – hasty, silent work. By half past six the horses had to be ready for the day trips.

But still, Otto repeatedly found a moment to go through the stable door and listen for the cellar. He heard nothing, but that didn't mean that his brother had been brought to heel. That possibility seemed unlikely – almost as unlikely as that of his father giving way.

Sighing heavily, Otto went back to work again. He noticed that the stableman, Rabause, looked out of the stable door more often than usual – only his father behaved as if nothing had happened.

Only when the night cabs started coming in did old Hackendahl leave the stables. As usual he spoke to every driver, examined the taximeters, reckoned up the moneys and entered them in his book. Business had been unusually good that night; the cabs had hardly waited on their stands at all. With a good deal of money in his possession Hackendahl revived. Not everything was hopeless. Business was good!

Shouting to Rabause that the night horses were to get an extra ration of oats, he turned to one of the drivers. 'And how did you get on, Willem?'

'There was a lot happening. Folks still all hot and bothered about that Archduke's murder. Three times I had to drive to Scherl s where the telegrams are posted up. They've got the murderer under lock and key, Herr Hackendahl. He's a student, I forget his name. He swallowed poison on the spot but spewed it up again.'

'A student, eh? And people stay up all night on account of him? He wants his behind thrashing till it bleeds, that's what he deserves. Hanging's too quick, he ought to suffer a bit first . . . But there's no discipline left in the world.'

The old driver looked up from the blue cushion he was brushing. 'D'you think so, Herr Hackendahl? I think there's too much discipline, too much spit an' polish. A man's not a machine, he's a living creature with feelings . . .'

But old Willem had chosen the wrong moment, for just then his colleague Piepgras drove into the yard. Though it was a mild summer morning he had the hood up and the apron across, just as if it were raining cats and dogs. And it seemed that there was a reason.

'Yes, Herr Hackendahl,' said Piepgras, as he climbed down from his box, puffing and blowing and pushing from his wrinkled brow the top hat bearing his number. 'Will you stand still, Ottilie? The stupid beast won't ever wait for its fodder. Well, Herr Hackendahl, you tell me what was I to do! One o'clock at night they both got in my cab at Alten Kuhstall and he said go past the Lehrter into the Tiergarten and then on and on till I knock. I didn't notice he'd had one over the eight. Well, knock he didn't, so on I went, on and on, and every now and then I'd ask is it far enough now? But no reply, nothing, and when I do stop I see they're both dossing. Talk about sleep! Shaking's no good and shouting's no good, just boozy drivel from the chap. Not a word about his address or suchlike.'

'You're always doing this,' said Hackendahl, annoyed. 'Wake them up! Get the money and see that they clear out of my yard.'

'But, Herr Hackendahl,' said the driver reproachfully, 'they're mere children and it's true love straight from the songbook.' Slowly Piepgras removed the hood of his cab and undid the apron. Quite a lot of people were looking on – drivers tired from the night shift and others arriving fresh for the day's work. Nor were Otto and Rabause inclined to miss anything – old Piepgras was always up to something. Even the women in the house had smelled a joke and were again looking out of the window, thirteen-year-old Heinz between them.

It was no unpleasant sight. Even if they had got into the cab drunk, the pair now slept as sweetly as children and, as was fitting, her head lay on his breast and they were holding hands as though they wished to be together even in sleep . . .

'Well, Herr Hackendahl, did I lead you up the garden path? Does you good, doesn't it? To see this in the Imperial city of Berlin, where the tarts can't help treading on each other's heels. But there's something of everything in Berlin . . .'

Who can say what passed through old Hackendahl's mind at the sight of those two lovers? He too had been young once and saw that this was still puppy love, something light, something happy . . .

But Piepgras had mentioned tarts and Hackendahl may well have recollected how his daughter would sometimes sneak into a café with a very bad name, or thought of his son who had stunk of cheap perfume that very morning. With a bound he was on the cab, shaking the sleepers and yelling: 'Wake up! Clear out of my yard, you!'

It was the young girl who woke first. Starting up, she gazed at the unfamiliar place and the unknown faces looking at them with surprised and sullen expressions; naturally she could not know that this had nothing to do with her but was a result of Iron Gustav's outburst. Seizing her friend's hand she pulled him out of his seat, crying:

'Erich, do wake up. What has happened?' And she was off, picking up her long skirts and running across the yard to the gate, her Erich behind her.

Old Hackendahl, however, quite enraged by the name of Erich, ran beside them, storming, while Piepgras, who had never expected his little joke to end thus, ran imploringly on the other side: 'Herr Hackendahl, what are you doing? The gentleman hasn't paid me yet. Stop, sir! Stop and pay me my fare.'

But the young girl and the young man ran quicker than ever, away from the sullen faces into the fresh, blue June morning.

At first old Hackendahl remained standing. He stood beneath the stone gatepost with the golden ball, wiped his face and looked, wide awake, into all the faces. However, the faces all turned away, embarrassed. Each got on with, or pretended to get on with, his work. Iron Gustav went silently into the yard, shouting at only half-strength as he went, 'Finish up, Otto!' and disappeared into the house.

The yard immediately became a turmoil of secrets and rumours, at their thickest around the now heavily breathing Piepgras, who had just returned. He had not been able to catch the young people. Love that night had got off scot-free.

§ XI

In the Hackendahl household the breakfast coffee always appeared on the stroke of seven, and whatever his feelings may have been this morning, Iron Gustav stood erect at the head of the table at seven o'clock precisely, listening to Heinz saying grace. Then there was a shuffling of chairs and feet and Mother ladled out the porridge.

In the silence they could hear the spoons scraping on the plates, and first one then the other looked at Erich's empty chair. Now and then the mother, thinking of her hungry son in the cellar, sighed and muttered: 'Oh God!' but no one took any notice until she complained: 'You're not eating again this morning. What's the matter with you all? At least you might, Bubi. You've no reason to starve.'

Heinz looked shrewdly at his father and said, his adolescent voice breaking into bass: '*Plenus venter non studet libenter* – a full belly doesn't agree with study. In the interests of my Latin examination restraint is necessary in the consumption of foodstuffs.'

'Oh dear,' sighed the mother. 'That's what one gets for letting one's children study. You don't understand a word they say.' She spoke no further. Her eyes had filled with tears. Everyone could see that she was thinking of her son in the cellar – his studies had come to an end.

'Shut up!' growled Hackendahl at Heinz.

'Certainly, *pater patriae*.' And, not at all crushed: 'Shall I take a note about Erich to school?'

The father flashed an angry look at his son, the others bowed their heads, but the storm passed without breaking. Hackendahl only pushed back his chair and went to his room.

Half an hour later, Heinz had gone to school and Sophie to the hospital. Eva cleared up with the little maid. Frau Hackendahl was washing vegetables in the kitchen, and in the stables Otto and old Rabause were discussing whether or not to remind Father about his private tours.

The cash book was open before him and the morning's takings on the desk, but he did not check or enter them up; he sat there and brooded, telling himself a hundred times that the world wouldn't come to an end because of a thief in the family or because an employer had lost his self-control in front of his men.

No, the world hadn't ended, but his own private world had. He brooded about why his children never wanted what he did, why they were always contrary. He had always obeyed all authority with pleasure, but if his children ever did still obey him, they did so unwillingly, with sulks and objections. But perhaps what had happened today was really not so bad and would be forgotten and buried in a few months or half a year. But it really was bad! Because it was not only house theft, but led to decline, collapse, and completely ignored everything he had achieved.

Frowning, he stared at the money. The amount, large as it was, didn't please him; he had no desire to enter it up – there was another entry to be made first. Yes, he must make it. And, taking up the pen, he hesitated, then laid it down again. Despairingly he stared at the ledger. What he had to do was an offence against order and rectitude.

A thought struck him – perhaps only an excuse for delay: wasn't there a chance that all the stolen money hadn't been spent? He hurried to the boys' room, where Eva was making the beds. He could send her away . . . but . . . was a father to be ashamed before his own children? Almost defiantly he took Erich's jacket and waistcoat, which were hanging over the chair, and hunted through the pockets, finding nothing however but the proof of fresh disobedience – some cigarettes. This did not reawaken his wrath, though; he merely crushed them so that the tobacco was reduced to shreds on the floor. 'Sweep up that filth,' he said, and went into the kitchen. The kitchen was empty.

He cut off a chunk of bread, about the quantity allowed to delinquents in the army, but looked in vain for the kind of glazed jug used for a prisoner's water and, after some hesitation, took an enamel measure and filled it, letting the tap run for some time so that the water should be fresh. Even a prisoner has his rights.

As he turned into the corridor leading to the cellar he heard whispering, listened, coughed and went on. His wife slipped past him. 'No one has any business here,' he said severely, and unlocked the cellar.

The son stood at a window so small that it could be hidden by two hands. He did not turn round. Putting the bread on a box and placing the water beside it, the father said: 'Here's your food, Erich.'

The son did not move.

'Say "Thank you".'

No reply.

Hackendahl waited another moment, then he said more sternly: 'Turn out your pockets, Erich. I want to see if you've any money left.'

Still the son did not move. In a rage Hackendahl went up to him and shouted: 'Can't you hear? Turn out your pockets!' Yes, that was the old steely sergeant-major's bark that had once called a whole company to attention, a voice that struck home to every man-Jack of them. And his son, too, jumped, turning out his pockets without a word. But they held nothing. Hackendahl couldn't believe it. 'All that money!' he cried. 'Eighty marks squandered in a single evening. It's not possible.' Amazed by such laughable simplicity, the son shot a glance at his father. 'I could easily have spent eight hundred,' he boasted. 'What else is money for?'

The old man was thunderstruck; the situation was even worse than he had thought. In these namby-pamby times of peace there had sprung up a generation soft and pleasure-loving, which could squander but not earn; 1870/71 was too far off. And he recollected the murder of the Archduke yesterday. People were speaking of war, not a bad thing perhaps, since youth would then learn that life meant struggle.

'So you would have thrown away eight hundred marks,' he said contemptuously. 'You, who haven't earned eight in your life! Why, without your father you'd die like a dog in a ditch.'

The son shrugged his shoulders.

Hackendahl went, locking the cellar door and, when he got upstairs, he also locked the door leading to the passage – there was to be no more whispering. Disobedience must not be encouraged.

He went into his room. This time he took up his pen without hesitation and wrote in the cash book: '29 June. Stolen by my son Erich . . . eighty marks.'

Well, that was that! He pushed both cash and cash book into the drawer. They could be dealt with later – the most important matter was settled.

Going out, he donned his blue cab driver's coat with the brass buttons and his top hat; in the yard the hackney cab stood ready, Otto holding the bridle of the mettlesome horse.

Hackendahl mounted the box, put the rug over his knees, settled the top hat on his head and took the whip. 'I'll be back at twelve. Take Kastor and Senta to the blacksmith's – the foreshoes are worn out. You should have noticed that yourself. Gee-up, grey mare!'

He clucked his tongue, the horse moved off and the cab rolled out of the yard.

The whole house heaved a sigh of relief.

§ XII

Eva had stood on tenterhooks behind her bedroom curtains waiting for her father to leave, although she had not risked much, as she knew, by sneaking into his room while he was busy with Erich in the cellar. She had not been so foolish as to touch the money on the desk, knowing that the morning receipts had already been counted and that the little bags of money lying in the drawer were also checked of course; but when Father found out that not only eighty but two hundred marks as well were missing, he'd blame Erich. And it hardly mattered to Erich whether he was hanged for a sheep or a lamb.

She shrugged contemptuously, fingering the ten gold coins in her apron pocket – you had to keep your wits about you. Since making up her mind not to stay much longer in this cheerless house she had hoarded cash, as opportunity offered, taking small amounts, secretly pocketing some of the shopping money, pawning articles from her mother's linen cupboard. Slowly but surely she was freeing herself from dependence on her father.

Was she going to be conscience-stricken over stealing from him? Not on her life! Father of his own free will wouldn't part with a penny, always maintaining that he was saving for his children, but he could live to be a hundred and she almost seventy before she inherited anything. No, better a bird in the hand, so far as the cash box was concerned, especially when it stood wide open, as it had done that morning!

Eva pushed the swing-lamp – an old-fashioned oil apparatus converted to electric light – up to the ceiling. The higher she pushed it, the lower sank the counterweight, a brass Easter egg decorated with arabesques; this she took off its hook and unscrewed in the middle. Gleaming, her golden treasure lay in the interior which had probably once been filled with sand or lead.

She stared at it, breathless with happiness, enraptured by those twelve or fifteen large coins. Her father had a good, solid fortune – partly invested in the business and the house, partly in sound government securities – she reckoned it at rather more than a hundred thousand marks. But this wealth had no intrinsic value in her eyes. Father belonged to a generation that willingly earned and grudgingly spent. He amassed money and believed that his children also ought first to earn before they spent. But times had changed, or people had changed, or perhaps it was only the old law of ebb and flow operating – low tide after the high. The new generation wasn't interested in money hoarded up; it was something dead, senseless, ridiculous even. Money was there to be spent; idle money was futile.

And thus the little hoard in the counterweight of the lamp, accumulated by a thousand shifts and devices, enchanted this prosperous man's daughter. Leisurely she dropped the ten fresh coins onto the others, and their melodious tinkle enthralled her. More than sight or sound of money, however, was the thought of what it would buy – freedom and a silk dress, amusement and a new hat.

With a sigh of happiness she replaced the lamp and put on her Florentine straw hat in front of the tiny mirror which was all her father would permit, and went into the kitchen.

'Give me some money, Mother, I want to go shopping.' Frau Hackendahl was sitting in a big chair before the fire, mechanically stirring a long spoon in a cooking pot. Everything about Mother was pendulous – stomach, breasts and cheeks, even her underlip drooped. At the window stood Otto nervously fingering his moustache.

'What do you want to buy, Evchen? We've got everything we need for lunch. But you only want an excuse to go out.'

'Not at all,' said Eva, and her radiant mood changed to irritation at complaints so often repeated. 'Not at all. You yourself said, Mother, we want fresh herrings this evening and potatoes cooked in their jackets. If I don't get the herrings this morning they'll be sold out.'

Neither statement was true. Her mother hadn't thought of having herrings for supper nor would the Berlin market be destitute of them by the afternoon, but Eva had realized for a long time that it did not matter what her mother said – she would always give way if contradicted.

Nor was it different now. 'I wasn't making any objection, Evchen.

For all I care you can go. How much do you want? Is one mark enough? You know your father doesn't like you running around . . .'

'Then Father must engage an errand boy.'

'O Lord, Evchen, don't say that. A strange lad prying about the house! You can't leave anything about . . .' She broke off, looking in embarrassment at the son silent by the window.

Eva spoke for him. 'You mean because of Erich? Don't be so silly. Father'll look after him. He won't let him out of the cellar till he gives in.'

'But he can't do that – it might be days or weeks,' said the mother helplessly. 'Do say a word, Ottchen.'

'Did I take the money?' said Eva and thought herself very clever. 'We all have to swallow our own medicine. I can't help him there.'

'You were always like that, Eva,' complained the mother. 'You only think of yourself. You say that Erich took the money, but how much do you make out of the shopping?'

'I . . .' stammered Eva, thunderstruck at her mother's not being so stupid as she had supposed.

But Frau Hackendahl's slight show of spirit had already died away. 'I don't grudge it you, child. Why shouldn't you have something out of life? But, Evchen,' her tone became cajoling, 'if I don't tell about you, couldn't you do something for Erich?'

'I haven't taken any money,' protested Eva, putting it so to speak on record. 'I don't do such things.'

'You know, Evchen, you're your father's darling. He wouldn't mind so much if it was you who went into the cellar and let Erich out. Otto says the locks could easily be broken with chisel and hammer.'

'Then why doesn't our great Otto go into the cellar and free Erich? Why don't you go yourself, Mother? You're his mother, after all – I'd only be your cat's-paw. And I'm not going to be. I don't care if Erich sits there till he turns blue. That wouldn't worry me at all.' And here Eva threw a triumphant glance at mother and brother. 'You'd better keep out of it,' she said, picked up the shopping bag and slipped out of the kitchen.

The two who remained looked helplessly at each other, then the mother sank her head and began mechanically stirring her pot again.

'And if he gets out, Mother, where will he go?' asked Otto eventually. 'He can't stay here, can he?'

'Perhaps he can stay with a friend for a bit, till Father quietens down.'

'If Erich runs away, Father will never forgive him. He cannot stay with a friend that long.'

'And if he found some work?'

'He's never learned to. And he's too weak for physical labour.'

'So that's why we had children . . .' Mother started up again.

'Perhaps I'll let him out,' said Otto after a pause. 'But if we don't know where he'll go . . . and we haven't any money either.'

'Look here,' cried Frau Hackendahl, upset. 'Here I am, the wife of a rich man, and would you believe that I've never had a single Reichsmark to myself? Never! Not in my whole marriage. But that's your father, little Otto. What was he then – a mere sergeant-major. And it was I who brought him the whole coach business.'

'What point is there in complaining about Father? He is as he is, and you are as you are, and I am what I am.'

'Yes, and that's why you sit there and do nothing, just staring into space. If you could you'd be sitting again at the trough with old Rabause, whittling away at a piece of wood. As far as you're concerned the world could go to the dogs and your brother with it.'

'No one can jump over his own shadow,' said Otto undisturbed. 'Because I'm the oldest, I was first and most in Father's power. That's why I'm as he wanted. I can't change things.'

'And I,' cried his mother, really moved, 'I've lived with Father longer than any of you. Most of his shouting he has done at me. But when a child of mine is in need, that's when I stand up.' (And she did so.) 'And if no one else will help my Erich, then I will. You run, little Otto,' she said, determined. 'Bring me tools I can open the lock with. Then disappear into the stable yourself so that you're not around and don't know anything. I'm also afraid of Father – but not more than that, otherwise I wouldn't want to live any more . . .'

§ XIII

Old Hackendahl had never allowed his fifty-six years to prevent him from occupying the box of his cab day in and day out, summer and winter alike. Admittedly he did not drive all and sundry, having no necessity to do so, but he drove certain regular fares, gentlemen who would use no one else to take them to their offices, banks or consultation rooms.

'Nobody drives like you, Hackendahl. Always punctual to the minute and off at a good trot, no cracking the whip or fuss and, what's more, no rowing with these new-fangled motor cars,' some councillor of the Supreme Court would say.

'Why should there be, Herr Kammergerichtsrat? Why make a row? I don't demean myself with such benzine-stinkers, Herr Kammergerichtsrat. They're nothing but death traps and in ten years no one will care two hoots for them. They'll be out of fashion.'

Thus did Hackendahl speak with his regular clients, and as he spoke so he thought. He detested motor cars if only because, by their hooting, stench and lunatic speed, they made his best horses nervous. His fine grey would fall into a panic, take the bit between her teeth and bolt. And that was the sort of thing his elderly gentlemen fares did not like at all.

So that Hackendahl, arriving this morning at the Geheimrat Buchbinder's villa in the Bendlerstrasse, was far from delighted to see a motor car standing at the door. The grey pricked her ears, grew restive and did not want to draw up at the kerb; indeed, Hackendahl had to get down from the box and take her head.

The chauffeur standing there grinned, of course. 'Well,' he jeered, 'what's up with the fodder-engine, pal? Ignition wrong? P'r'aps you'd like me to adjust the exhaust with a spanner, eh?'

Hackendahl naturally made no reply to chaff of that sort. He mounted the box again, stiffly taking in one hand the reins, in the other the whip, its butt on his knee, and looking as distinguished as any colleague from the Imperial stables.

The chauffeur eyed him critically. 'Swell,' he said. 'First-class. Another ten years, mate, and you'll be received at the Brandenburger

Tor by the mayor as the last slap-up horse cab. And then they'll stuff you and put you in the Märkische Museum. Or rather, in the Natural History Museum in Invalidenstrasse – right next to the big human apes from the jungle.'

Hackendahl turned purple and would probably have stated his views very forcibly had not Herr Buchbinder come out of his villa accompanied by a young man. Hackendahl touched his top hat with the whip.

'Good morning, Hackendahl,' called out the Geheimrat cheerfully. 'This, Hackendahl, is my son, also a physician and . . .'

'I know, Herr Geheimrat,' said Hackendahl reproachfully. 'I knew at once. I drove the gentleman to the Anhalter Station, Easter 1907, to catch the Munich Express, the 6:11.'

'Of course. Yes, my good Hackendahl, there's nothing wrong with your memory. But, Hackendahl, my son has grown into a man and he no longer wishes to have you drive him. He's bought himself a car – my money, Hackendahl – and now he wants to go in it everywhere . . .'

'He'll get tired of it, Herr Geheimrat,' said Hackendahl with a malicious look at the car and its grinning chauffeur. 'When he has collided with a tree or made a few people unhappy, then he'll leave off.'

'Well, Papa,' said the young man impatiently, 'get in and in four minutes you'll be at your hospital.'

'Yes, my boy, I know that. But in half an hour I have to operate and if I get palpitations from your excessive speed, or if my hand is trembling . . .'

'Word of honour, you'll think you're in a cradle, you won't notice the speed. If there's something new in surgery you certainly try it . . .'

'I don't know,' said the old gentleman doubtfully. 'What do you think, Hackendahl?'

'As you wish, Herr Geheimrat,' said Hackendahl formally. 'If I may speak, however, in eight minutes I can get you to the hospital – and nothing ever goes wrong with me or ever did.'

'Well, Papa, if you want to take your cabby's advice about cars . . .'

Old Hackendahl had had a good deal to put up with that morning but 'cabby' was almost too much. By the mercy of heaven the Geheimrat said at once: 'You know quite well, my dear boy, that Hackendahl isn't a cabby. And now I'll make you an offer – I'll go with Hackendahl and you can go in your car alongside us and I'll watch your little craft from my anchorage and if it's not too stormy you may drive me back home.'

Geheimrat Buchbinder had spoken quietly but firmly. The son's tone was somewhat annoyed. 'As you like, Papa.' He turned towards his car.

The old gentleman pulled the rug over his knees and settled down comfortably. 'Now drive slowly, Hackendahl. In any case he'll at once catch us up with his twenty or forty horse-power.'

Hackendahl was glad to get this order because the grey had been indignant for some time about the horror standing just in front, and the chauffeur had begun to jerk the starting handle. Dense little clouds, blue and stinking, issued from the exhaust right in the grey's face.

'Gently, Hackendahl, gently,' shouted the Geheimrat, who had almost been flung off his seat. 'Drive slowly – you're to go slowly, Hackendahl, we don't want any racing here.'

Nor did Hackendahl; but it was a pity the grey did not feel like that too. The excited creature was galloping down the Bendlerstrasse. She turned so sharply into the Tiergartenstrasse that the wheels grazed the kerb. Then, rather less furiously, but still foaming at the bit, she passed the green expanse of lawns.

'You must be mad, Hackendahl,' groaned the Geheimrat.

'It's the grey. She hates motor cars.'

'I thought you only had quiet animals.'

'So I do, Herr Geheimrat. But when something like that is exploding and stinking right in her face . . .'

'Then drive slowly. In no circumstances are you to try to race it.'

Hackendahl looked cautiously round – not a sign of the car. Couldn't get the old tin to move, of course! Well, the Geheimrat should see for himself which was the more reliable – a decent horse or a machine. And he grinned.

At a goodish trot they drove down the Siegesallee.

'Lots of people,' remarked the Geheimrat.

'That's the fine weather.'

'And the excitement! Have you read about the murder at Sarajevo, Hackendahl?'

'Yes, Herr Geheimrat. Do you think there will be war?'

'War! Because of the Serbs? Never, Hackendahl! You'll see, they'll give way. There won't be a war.'

In the distance sounded a horn. Hackendahl heard it and the grey heard it too, laying back her ears.

Hackendahl took a firm grasp of the reins. 'I believe your son's coming, Herr Geheimrat.'

'So he got the thing going after all. Well, no racing, please, Hackendahl.'

Nearer and nearer sounded the horn, almost uninterruptedly, a screech and a warning. But to the horse it was pure alarm. Trotting faster, she flung her head from side to side . . . Slowly the green monster came alongside, reached the driver's box, the grey's hindquarters, her head . . . She reared in the shafts, the cab seemed to stop a moment, and then the horse bolted.

'You're not to . . .' came the Geheimrat's voice.

Parallel with the horse ran the motor car, clattering, honking, smelling. Although Hackendahl looked straight ahead between the grey's ears, keeping an eye open for any obstacle, he was still conscious of the chauffeur's sneering face. That fellow mustn't see a sign of weakness.

They had gone round the Victory Column without disaster when a new danger was sighted in the form of a spike-helmeted policeman, to whom the wild chase and galloping horse were highly displeasing. With a thick notebook in one hand, the other raised aloft, he stepped into the road for the purpose of putting a stop to these breaches of the traffic regulations.

Easy for him to command – Hackendahl was only too ready to obey – but the grey was subject to her instincts alone and raced on, so that the policeman had to make a most unmilitary leap to safety and was left far behind. And Hackendahl, racing onward, knew that particulars were being taken – he would be fined – and ever afterwards he would be a 'previous offender'.

With a desperate effort he pulled the horse to the right into the quiet Hindersinstrasse; outmanoeuvred, the motor car shot past; the horse made another ten or fifteen bounds, fell into a canter, then into a trot . . .

Hackendahl realized that the Geheimrat was tugging at his arm. 'Stop, you fool, don't you understand?' yelled the old gentleman, crimson with rage.

Hackendahl stopped. 'Excuse me, Herr Geheimrat, the grey bolted. The motor car upset her. The chauffeur did that intentionally.'

'Racing like mad!' said the old gentleman, still trembling. 'Old people, racing!' He got out. 'We've driven together for the last time, Hackendahl. Send in your bill! You ought to be ashamed of yourself.'

'But it wasn't my fault. The quietest horse wouldn't stand it.'

A horn sounded. The car, that triumphant monster, had circled the block of buildings and cut them off. Defeated and exhausted, the grey stood with hanging head; she did not move even when the car drew up beside her.

'You blame it on the horse!' cried the Geheimrat. 'But the horse is standing still. No, it's you who wanted to race the car, Hackendahl, you alone.'

Hackendahl said nothing. With gloomy eyes he watched the Geheimrat get into the car with his smiling son. The burden God imposed on a just man was heavy indeed to bear.

§ XIV

For half an hour Frau Hackendahl had worked with chisel, hammer and pliers on the padlock to the cellar door, and had beaten the staple out of shape and bent the shackle, injuring her fingers but not opening the door.

Weary and despairing, she sat down on a stair tread. From the distance, through two doors, she imagined she could hear her imprisoned son calling. But he called in vain – she could not get to him. When she thought of the trouble she was inviting from her husband, and all for the lost labour of a spoiled padlock, she was filled with an ever-increasing despair.

And, as it was now, so had it been the whole of her life; her intentions had not been bad, her courage not less than that of other people, but success had never been hers. The marriage was not successful, the children hadn't turned out as she had hoped, she hadn't broken open the door.

She looked at the lock. Certainly she could have fetched a locksmith but one didn't expose to a stranger the family shames. She could have gone into the yard and listened at the cellar grating, but the neighbours might be watching and laughing. Life was such that you couldn't tell your own husband what you couldn't stand most about him. And if you did tell him, he wouldn't listen, and if he heard, it wouldn't change anything. Life was unbearable anyhow, and yet one endured it.

And now she was getting old and fat (she liked her food), and the faint, meaningless hope she cherished that everything might still be different was the stupidest thing of all. Exactly the same hope as in a young girl still existed in her old, used-up, bloated body. Not once even had it been fulfilled, but hope lived on more stubbornly than ever, whispering: if you get the door open and set Erich free, everything may yet change.

Nothing but this absurd padlock stood between her and a better life, just as it had always been some trifle which had unfailingly prevented her from enjoying existence. Only trifles – that was the worst of it! And it was the same for Erich. Because of a trifling sum, a few marks, he was to be branded as a criminal.

Life was so miserably limited. Absolutely nothing happened. If a local girl had a baby, it was news for years. Little people, little lives! Her body was enormously swollen, but her own soul – who she really was – that was just the same size as when she was a little girl. That hadn't grown.

There she sat on the cellar stairs knowing she could not force the door open, and knowing that, because of it, Erich might be plunged into disaster, perhaps even hang himself. But she would call neither Otto nor a locksmith. She could not change her nature.

She tried to visualize the cellar, whether it contained hooks and ropes, and whether the ceiling was high enough ... Then she remembered reading of someone who had hanged himself on a door handle, and that the tongue of a hanged man protrudes purple and swollen from his mouth and that they are supposed to mess their trousers . . . Overcome by fright she jumped up, shouting and beating on the cellar door. 'Don't do it, Erich. Don't do it, for your mother's sake!'

What she did wasn't conscious. She didn't even hear what she cried out. But her martyred heart suffered, and she danced a kind of grotesque dance of pain. And when Otto and Rabause in alarm rushed down the stairs, demanding anxiously: 'What's the matter?' she pointed and screamed: 'He's hanging himself, he's hanging himself!'

Oh, but life is so complicated! If Frau Auguste had been a little more aware of what she was doing, more alert and intelligent, one might have thought she was acting like this so that the men should break open the cellar door and allow her to reach her goal and not founder on a mere lock. For her weeping and panic prevented all questioning. Without a word the men worked away at the lock while she stood beside them moaning and imploring: 'Be quick, he's doing it now!'

But Frau Auguste Hackendahl was not clever enough to contrive and carry out such a plan. She was genuinely terrified, genuinely in fear, and she herself was the most surprised of all when she saw, after the second door had been prised open, Erich sitting calmly on his box eating his hunk of bread.

'I thought . . .' she stammered, and said no more.

No. No more hanging. But because she had inadvertently achieved her aim, she was overcome by a feeling of happiness. She leaned against the door, looked at her son through half-closed eyes and murmured, 'It's all right, Erich.'

The three liberators looked at the prisoner. Seeing him so calm, they felt almost ashamed of their agitation.

'You're marvellously brave, you three,' said Erich, rising and stretching. 'You, Otto, the model son! Father'll be very upset indeed. And old honest Rabause! Well, Father will sack you at once. And Mother – well, Mother . . .' But at this even he, so cold-blooded, felt a little ashamed.

All were silent. (It is curious. This seventeen-year-old wretch behaves as if he's had far more experience of life than any of you – as if he's the eldest and not the youngest. And they all accept it!) 'Well, and what have you got for the prodigal son?' began Erich again. 'Or has Father already gone to fetch the fatted calf for the merry feast?'

Rabause was the first to have enough of it. 'There's no time to lose, Erich; the chief will be back any minute. And I know who'll come down a peg or two then,' and he went.

Erich gave a forced laugh. 'Well, Mother, what's to be done? You haven't been so silly, surely, as to get me out without having something ready – money, clothes?'

They were both silent. Yes, they had been so silly. They had completely disregarded their brother Erich's cold-bloodedness.

'Mother thought you were doing yourself in,' muttered Otto.

Erich was dumbfounded. 'Doing myself in? But why? Because of this nonsense? Because of a few minutes in a cellar and eighty marks? You're loony!'

'Not because of the eighty marks,' said Otto.

'Oh, you mean the dishonour and disgrace and so on. What does Father's honour and disgrace matter to me? Nothing! I have my own views about honour; what I mean is, I don't acknowledge dishonour. If one's a progressive . . .'

Nevertheless he became a little confused in spite of his youthful self-assurance and therefore looked angrily at them. 'So you've got hold of nothing for me? All right, I'll have to look after myself – as usual.' And he passed them by without another word and went upstairs.

Mother and son glanced at each other, then looked away like conspirators plagued by guilt. Sitting down on the box, she picked up the rest of the bread and, as if to console herself for her defeat, remarked: 'Now he won't have to eat dry bread.' But as she said it another and very distressing thought occurred to her, extinguishing every spark of consolation. 'And what will he do now?' she faltered.

Otto shrugged, perhaps entertaining the same thought as his mother. He looked at the ceiling, as if he could see through it, up into the house.

'Suppose he goes on stealing?'

Otto made no reply.

She sighed heavily. Now that her son was free again her mood changed; he would have to look after himself. It was time to be thinking of her husband. 'He mustn't,' she said. 'Father has his troubles too.'

Otto nodded.

'Please go upstairs, Otto. Stand in front of the door and don't let Erich in. Tell him I'll give him ten marks, no, nine – Eva took one for the herrings . . . With nine marks he can live three days. Tell him that, Otto, and by then I'll get some more money from Father.'

'I've got seven marks.'

'Good, give him them too. Tell him to let me know where he's staying. I'll send Heinz with money now and then. Tell him that, Ottchen.'

'Yes, Mother.'

'And, Otto,' she called after him, 'ask him to come down and say goodbye to me. I can't come upstairs this moment, my knees feel weak with the excitement. Don't forget to tell him. He *must* say goodbye to me. I'm his mother, I got him out of here.'

Otto nodded and went obediently. Otto was the family beast of burden, the one ordered about and scolded, and nobody cared what he thought or felt. His mother was holding Erich's bread. It was good bread. Slowly, with enjoyment, she started to eat it. The chewing, the nourishing flavour, the assimilation of food did her good. The last remains of her excitement passed. She ate, ergo she lived. She no longer thought about the argument which might break out among the brothers upstairs. And she didn't think, either, about the coming conflict with her husband. She ate, she lived.

But, before she had quite finished, Otto returned. She couldn't read his message from his face.

'Well,' she asked, chewing. 'Where's Erich?'

'Gone!'

'Didn't you tell him to say goodbye to me? I particularly asked you.'

'He'd already gone when I went upstairs.'

'And – do tell me, Ottchen – what about Father's room?'

'Everything's all right, Mother.'

'Thank God.' She was relieved. 'I always said that Erich was sometimes inconsiderate but never wicked. No, our Erich isn't wicked.' She waited for confirmation from Otto but that was too much to expect. He spoke at last, however. 'But he's smashed the lamp in the girls' bedroom.'

She was astonished. 'Why should Erich have smashed it? Don't be silly, Ottchen. Doris did that, obviously, when she was cleaning up, but never mind, I'll deduct it from her wages on the first.'

'Heinz told us Eva kept her savings in the counterweight of the lamp.'

'Heinz? How does Heinz know? In the weight? You can't keep anything in that.'

'The weight's hollow. It can be unscrewed.'

'But . . .' Still she did not understand. 'Why did he break the lamp?'

'I have to take the horses to the blacksmith's,' said Otto. 'Erich has taken Eva's money and while he was about it the lamp must have come down and smashed.'

'I'll give it back to Eva,' cried his mother. 'Eva can't have had much, a few pence out of the household money! There's no need to make a row, tell her that immediately, Ottchen.'

'I must take the horses to the smithy, Mother. And Eva had over two hundred marks, so Heinz said . . .'

With that Otto went.

§ XV

Eva had not been in a hurry about the fresh herrings. Past the Schloss, where people were standing in large groups waiting for the Kaiser, she had dawdled along enjoying the fine June morning . . . Fools, decided Eva. Why, the Imperial standard wasn't to be seen; His Majesty was on a cruise in the North Sea – people could stand there till they took root!

Passing down Unter den Linden, she turned into the Friedrich-strasse and sauntered on till she came to Wertheim's Stores. Eva had only the one mark with her, so she had no intention of buying anything there, but she went in and looked round nonetheless. Her eyes shone. This abundance of silk and velvet, this great wealth, intoxicated her. Up and down stairs she went, as her fancy took her. It was all the same whether she looked at dresses or china, at Thermos flasks or hats; she wasn't so much carried away by the sight of any one object as by the profusion and rich magnificence – seven hundred pictures, hundreds of china services.

Finally she wandered into less crowded regions, into the dimly lit Jewellery Department where the contents of showcases gleamed and sparkled. Catching her breath, she leaned over them. The glimmer of gold, the green and blue flashes of diamonds – oh, to possess such things! Rows of gold watches of delicate workmanship – and so tiny! Slender rings set with a single stone larger than a pea, and trays of silver – you could almost see how heavy they were. And she, with all her cunning, could only make twenty pfennigs at the most on the herrings. She sighed.

'Well, Miss,' said an impudent voice at her elbow. 'Nice stuff, what?'

She looked up with the rebuff instinctive to every girl in a large city when unexpectedly accosted. But at once she became uncertain. The young man with the black moustache standing beside her might be a salesman. He wore neither straw hat nor panama, and in 1914 all men wore a hat or at least carried one. 'I'm not buying,' she said distantly.

'What's the matter?' asked the young man in his impudent voice, which repelled her but not altogether unpleasantly. 'Costs nix to look and you get a kick out of it. Miss,' he went on persuasively, 'tell yourself I'm fat old Wertheim – course he's fat – and you're my intended. An' I say ter you: "Choose, my darlin', choose your heart's desire." What'd you choose then, me dear?'

'What's the matter with you?' said Eva. 'How dare you speak to me?'

'But, Miss, I told you I'm fat Wertheim an' you're me young lady. I've got to talk to me young lady.'

'You must have drunk a lot of ginger beer to be gassing so much. What's upset you?'

'Me, upset? Not on your life. It's the others who'll be that. Well, Miss, what about some sparklers, a diamond necklace with a pendant and a diamond clasp?'

'That's for some old trout,' said Eva, amused, although she sensed there was something odd about this young man. 'No, I'd like a dia-mond ring like that one in the case there.' She walked past a salesman who, since it was clear that these two were not going to buy any-thing, was inspecting his fingers in a bored way. 'See, a ring like that . . .'

'Quite nice,' agreed the young man patronizingly. 'But, Miss, if you was my young lady I'd give you something better than that rubbish.'

'Yes, you would,' laughed Eva. 'And you'd have to pay a fortune for it.'

'Oh, would I? Lemme tell you, Miss, you know nothin' about dia-monds. That stone's a dud, it's paste. Get me?'

'Don't talk rot!'

'I'll show you the real goods, Miss. Look here, those are genuine in that case there. Look at this one, the yellow one I mean. When you look at it from the side it turns red. That's seven carats all right and flawless! And this one here.'

'Don't get so het up about them,' said Eva teasingly, but impressed by the young man's enthusiasm.

'And that one – Lord, Miss, if you an' me could get our claws on what's in this case . . .'

'But we can't. And we won't either.'

'Don't be so sure of that, Miss. Things turn out quite diff'rent sometimes . . . You've got a nice shoppin' bag, holds quite a lot, I see. And if you have to make a dash for it, you make it as hard as you can . . .'

'What are you talking about?' asked Eva suspiciously. 'I believe you're tight.'

'You see that salesman, Miss,' asked the man quite hoarse with excitement. 'He'll drop off in a mo. Take a peep at the clock over his head. What's the time by it? My peepers are a bit weak. No, plant yourself here if you want to see the clock . . .'

His excitement was infectious. Almost against her will Eva placed herself as he told her. Actually she couldn't see the clock very well and had to strain her eyes . . . There was a crash and a clatter nearby. She saw the salesman start and she too swung round . . .

'Run, girl, run!' cried the hoarse voice beside her . . .

As in a dream she saw the smashed showcase, the hand clutching the jewellery.

'Run, you fool!' and the young man pushed her against the advancing salesman, who tried to grab her. Without realizing what she was doing she hit out at him and ran. Other people rushed up, she dodged round a showcase, stumbled up five or six steps, threw open a swing door . . .

Behind her voices were shouting: 'Stop thief!'

A bell shrilled.

She was in the crowded Food Department. Startled faces regarded her and somebody tried to seize her, but she evaded him, pushed behind a fat woman, found herself in another corridor and ran behind a stack of tinned goods. Here there was a staircase. She pushed the door open and hurried downstairs – one floor, two floors, lower . . .

She stood still and listened. Were they coming? Was she being pursued? Why had she run away? She hadn't done anything. That loathsome fellow – what impudence to use her of all people as a screen. The thief! If ever she saw him again she'd scream, attract a crowd, and the policeman would handcuff him; then she'd laugh in his impertinent face. To involve her, an innocent girl, in this dirty business! It was unheard of.

A heavy step was coming slowly down the stairs and she fled again, pushing open a swing door, walking as if casually through a department or two and approaching the exit. Suddenly she was overwhelmed with fear. She would undoubtedly be recognized; her description must have been phoned already to every exit and they knew she was carrying a shopping bag of black American cloth. Why was that salesgirl looking at her like that?

She pulled herself together. I've done nothing, she reassured herself. 'Where is the lavatory, please?' she asked the salesgirl.

She went in the direction the girl told her, then changed her mind. The stairs, the good old stairs of the Food Department had saved her once before – and she went back to them. They were thronged with people going up and down but she did not show any hurry. Putting her foot on a tread, she tied and retied her shoelace . . .

When at last she felt she was unobserved she picked up the

shopping bag. She knew, of course, that the name of Hackendahl was written in the lining and that she must tear it out. But she stopped. Something gleamed inside, something flashed and sparkled.

She laid the bag down – that scoundrel had turned her into an accomplice – he had dropped part of his robbery into it. Supposing they caught her! She could never explain it away, never. Oh, if only she had him here, the swine, with his slick talk about shopping bags and making a dash for it!

Somebody was coming down the stairs in a hurry. She peeped; it was a man in the brown uniform of the Stores, and she at once busied herself with her shoelace, having quickly covered the bag with her skirt . . . The man gave her a side glance – was he suspicious? In any case it was high time to leave the building. At least ten minutes had passed since the theft and it was very likely that police were now posted at the exits . . . No sooner had she heard the swing door clicking to below than she stuffed the jewels into the pocket of her white petticoat, spending no time in examining them but smiling when she saw the ring set with the yellow diamond. A cool customer, that chap!

Tearing the name out of her bag, which she left behind, she went through the ground floor past counters whose glamour had waned, walked by a commissionaire and, mingling with the flood of customers, stepped into the street . . .

Stepped into safety and freedom.

§ XVI

When the boys entered the school playground for the eleven o'clock break they saw a smart cab stop outside. Nobody took any notice except Porzig, who could not resist a spiteful, 'See the rival of our beloved Heinz. Hackendahl, decline *equus*, a hack.'

'Don't you start a row, Porzig,' warned Hoffmann.

'As a matter of fact, it's my father's cab,' said Heinz Hackendahl. 'Did you think I'm ashamed of it?'

'Behold!' said Porzig, mimicking the teacher of Greek. 'Forsooth, Hackendahl, and is there verity in the street rumour that the

Imperial stables are negotiating with your honourable father anent the purchase of yon shining steed?'

The grey, old Hackendahl's favourite, looked uncommonly pitiable; after that morning's misadventure she was only the wreck of a horse. The Upper Third boys looked first at the grey and then at the two antagonists. Heinz Hackendahl and Hermann Porzig were sworn enemies, their skirmishes a recurring treat for the class.

'Don't bray, Hermann,' said Heinz calmly. 'The Porzigs are stinking coyotes – on hearing the war cry they hide in the wigwams of the squaws.' (This was a memory from the beloved author, Karl May.)

'We see nowhere the shining pot hat of our *Patris equorum*, the badge of the Cabmen's Guild,' resumed Porzig with assumed apprehension, his imagination greatly stimulated by the circle of listening boys. 'Why does he tarry? Why does he not protect his steed against the slings and arrows of the sausage-makers? Is he putting down, forsooth, a spot of Kümmel in some cheap bar? Speak, legitimate offspring of a cab!'

Current in the school was the never-to-be-forgotten story of how old Fritz, the Great Frederick, had once presented a silver chamber pot to the Court of Appeal as a mark of his annoyance at its judgment against him in a certain case. Hermann Porzig was the son of a magistrate of that Court of Appeal. Hence the reply of Heinz: 'The shining pot-hat of my father pales before the glitter of the silver chamber pot. Is it true that your father has to scrub out this gracious gift every Saturday, and that you, my lord, are permitted to spit on the scrubbing brush?'

A shudder went through the audience on hearing this deadly insult. Porzig, one who bestowed gibes more easily than he received them, turned crimson.

'Retract the chamber pot,' he screamed. 'It's an insult to the whole Court of Appeal.'

'Never!' cried Heinz Hackendahl. 'You insulted my father.'

'But you insulted the entire Court of Appeal. Will you retract?'

'Never!'

'Fight it out?'

'Fight it out!'

'Windy?'

'Not me!'

'To the death?'

'To the death – till one side begs for mercy,' said Heinz, thus completing the traditional challenge. He looked round. 'Hoffmann, you're my second.'

'Ellenberg, you're mine.'

'Let's leave it till later,' suggested Hoffmann soberly. 'We've only got three minutes left.'

'And in one he'll start whining!'

They had already removed their jackets, burning for the fray.

'One – two – three!' shouted the seconds. The combatants approached, tested each other's defence, gained their grip, leaned breast to breast and forehead to forehead – then a moment later were rolling in the dust.

In his study the headmaster was telling an anxious father: 'You mustn't take a youthful indiscretion too seriously, Herr Hackendahl. The saying "Youth and folly go hand in hand" is truer today than ever.'

'Stealing is hardly an indiscretion, it is a sin,' contradicted Hackendahl.

'The youth of today has a craving for amusement, a craving unknown to our generation,' declared the headmaster. 'A long peace has made the young soft . . .'

'Yes, we want a thoroughgoing war,' cried Hackendahl.

'For heaven's sake, no! Have you ever thought of the proportions a modern war would assume?'

'About a small nation in the Balkans? It would be over in six weeks and have done the young a lot of good.'

'The whole world's full of high explosives,' replied the headmaster. 'Everyone's looking enviously at Germany as it grows ever stronger, and at our heroic Kaiser. The whole world's going to attack us.'

'For a few Serbs you can hardly find on the map?'

'No, because we're growing richer and richer! Because of our colonies! Because of our fleet! Pardon me, Herr Hackendahl, but is it not almost sacrilege to wish for a war merely because one's son has committed an indiscretion?'

'He needs military discipline.'

'Within a year he will have passed his final, then you can let him serve at once,' said the headmaster persuasively. 'Don't take him away now and deprive him of a course of study which will open up for him all sorts of opportunities.'

'I'll think it over,' said Hackendahl reluctantly.

'Don't hesitate – say yes now!'

'I must see him first . . .'

'That's just what you mustn't do. If you see him in his present mood of obstinacy you will change your mind again. But why on earth lock him in a coal cellar – do you call that pedagogy?!'

'I wasn't treated with kid gloves when I was young, and I never stole money.'

'Well, are you a criminal judge or a father? You'll have fulfilled forbidden desires yourself at one time or another. We are all weak, and crave fame. You know it very well. Do please agree now.'

'Only if he asks my forgiveness.'

'Herr Hackendahl! Do you think he will say he is sorry the moment you release him? One must ask only for the possible.' From the playground there drifted in the sound of conflict. 'It is within the bounds of possibility that Erich may pass his final at the top of his class – *primus omnium*, we call it. "First of all" – that is a great achievement.'

Hackendahl smiled. 'A bait, I see. All right, I'll walk into the trap for once. The boy shall come to school tomorrow.'

'Splendid, Herr Hackendahl,' said the headmaster, looking pleased and shaking hands. 'You won't repent it . . . What behaviour is this?' He swung round and hurried to the window, where he was met by a roar from the playground.

'*Evoe*, Hackendahl! Go to it, Hackendahl!'

Heinz was victor. Caught in a wrestler's grip, the strangled Porzig could only gasp for mercy

'You retract the pot-hat? The steed? The sausage-maker? The spot of Kümmel? Everything?'

Porzig acknowledged each item with a grunt, while the ring of
boys roared applause.

'It seems' – coughed the headmaster at the window – 'to be the
other Hackendahl boy in a misunderstanding. No, we'd better not be
seen at the window. It's often wiser to appear to have seen and heard
nothing.'

'The rascal has torn his trousers,' grumbled Hackendahl behind
the curtain. 'He's always tearing his clothes and his mother has to
mend them.'

'The talents of your son Heinz lie in another direction to Erich's,'
said the headmaster, 'and I should say he is the more practical of the
two. It might be considered whether a non-classical secondary school
wouldn't be more suitable for him. Both your sons are talented . . .'

'It's extraordinary that my eldest isn't,' said Hackendahl. 'He's
just a nitwit; put him where you like, he stays there.'

'He too is sure to have his special gifts,' said the headmaster consolingly. 'One must just keep searching. Search and support.'

'He's a mere nitwit,' Hackendahl repeated. 'He doesn't bring me
any trouble, but no pleasure either. He's just a cross to bear.'

§ XVII

Otto Hackendahl handed over the two horses to the smith's journey-
man and hurried away, although he knew that by doing so he was
breaking one of his father's commandments, which was to keep a
sharp eye on the smith at his work, since a hoof was so easily cut too
deep or a nail driven in too far.

But Otto had his secret life also and if he was indeed somewhat
dull he was by no means as dull as his father believed. He handed
over the horses to the smith. There shouldn't be any trouble with
nails today.

He hurried down the street and by his manner and the way he
kept close to the wall it was clear that everything was not well with
him. He was a tall, finely built fellow, the strongest of the brothers,
stronger even than his father, but he carried himself badly and lacked
energy, self-confidence, a will of his own. Perhaps it's just as he told

his mother. His father spent a lot of time drilling him, and in doing so broke his will. But it's also probably the case that his will was never strong. A strong tree grows against the wind; a weak one is blown over by it.

He was dangling a small packet in his hand until he noticed what he was doing, when he hid it under his arm as though it were stolen. Looking furtively round, he entered a doorway, crossed a courtyard, passed through another doorway, crossed a second courtyard and climbed swiftly upstairs.

He seemed to know where he was going, for he gave not a single glance at the names on the many doors, nor did the people he passed take any notice of him. Otto Hackendahl had a kind of natural camouflage and mimicry; no attention was paid to one so colourless.

He stopped before a door with the nameplate: Gertrud Gudde, Dressmaker. Once, twice, he pressed the bell. Inside, someone moved, he heard a voice, a child laughing. Otto smiled.

Yes, he could smile now, for he was happy. And he smiled still more when the door opened and a small child stumbled against his legs, joyfully shouting 'Papa! Papa!'

'You're rather late today, Otto,' said a woman's voice. 'Is anything the matter?'

'And' – he kissed her – 'I have to leave in a quarter of an hour, Tutti. I left the horses at the blacksmith's, I've got to return immediately. Yes, yes, Gustäving, Papa's here. Did you sleep well?'

The child was overjoyed; Otto tossed him in the air, the little boy laughing and shouting. The woman too smiled, Gertrud Gudde the dressmaker, with her sharp features, unequal shoulders and that gentle dove-like glance so many hunchbacks have. She knew her Otto well – his weakness, his irresolution, his fear of his father, but also his wish to give happiness.

'What's the matter?'

'I've brought you some carving,' he said. 'Templin will give you about ten marks for it.'

'But you shouldn't sit up half the night, whittling away – I'll manage all right. I had four fittings today.'

'Gustäving, haven't we a wonderful mummy?'

The child shouted in glee and the mother smiled.

'Well, you can sit down for a moment, anyway. I've some coffee left and here are rolls. Come along now, do eat! Gustäving will show you how well he can do his physical jerks.'

Otto did as he was told. She always had something ready for him and he could come at any time he liked, as if they were really husband and wife. And he understood that this was how it should be; he ate what she gave him and never refused it even if he had already eaten more than he wanted.

Gustäving set about his little tricks, of which the mother was even prouder than the son. She, who had hardly known a day free from pain, took pleasure in the child's straight back and strong legs.

'And now tell me what is the matter.'

Slowly and clumsily he told her. But Gertrud Gudde understood him, could read him. And apart from that she knew them all very well indeed – Mother, Erich, Eva and the stern father – for she had been dressmaker to the Hackendahls many years now; that was how Otto and she had become acquainted and had learned to love each other without anyone noticing it, not even the astute Eva. Gertrud's vivacious face mirrored every word he said, she accompanying his story by exclamations of 'Very good, Ottchen!' – 'What you said was right!' – 'And you broke open the door? Splendid!'

He – the man ground between two millstones – had the feeling that he had achieved something. 'And what will Father say now that Erich has gone? And Eva who is so miserly – what a scene she'll make!'

'Eva? She can't say anything – at least not to your father. The money was stolen.'

He nodded. 'But Father – about Erich?' he asked, hoping that she would relieve his mind about this too.

She looked thoughtfully at him, her look as soft as a dove. 'Your father,' she said – and the form of Iron Gustav, who had overshadowed her modest life, towered above them – 'Your father' – she smiled encouragingly – 'he'll be very hurt. He's always been so proud of Erich. Don't say a word against Erich, particularly about taking Eva's money. Your father will be upset enough as it is. Admit quite calmly that you forced the lock and tell him – listen, Otto – "Father, I'd have got you out of a cellar, too." Can you remember that?'

'Father, I would have got you out of a cellar, too,' he repeated awkwardly. 'But that's really true, Tutti.'

'You see, Otto, I'm only saying what you yourself think.'

'But what will Father do then, Tutti?'

'One can't tell.'

'Perhaps he'll throw me out. And what then?'

'But you could always get work, Otto. Overnight you could go in a factory as an unskilled hand or a builder's labourer.'

'Yes, I could do that all right. Yes, that's possible.'

'And we could then live together quite openly. Your father would have to give you your papers and we could . . .'

'No, not that! I mustn't marry against his wish. It says in the Bible . . .' Strange that this weak man is adamant in one respect – he will not get married against his father's wish! At the beginning she had told him many a time that he could get the necessary papers without old Hackendahl's knowledge and that she would put up the banns. What difference would a civil marriage make? How could it hurt a father who was ignorant of it? But Otto would not be moved. From the religious instruction at school, the confirmation course by Pastor Klatt, and the depths of his being arose the conviction that it would be unlucky to marry without his father's consent.

She had understood. She realized that, to the despised son, his father was not only the God of Wrath but the God of Love; this son loved his father more than the other children did. Nonetheless she continued to hope for the marriage, not for her own sake but for Gustäving's who, already named after his grandfather, had still to receive the family surname.

'Couldn't you give your father a hint, Otto?' she had often asked. 'For instance, if you were to speak of me in his presence sometime when I'm working at your place.'

'I'll try, Tutti,' he had replied, yet had never made the slightest attempt.

This question of marriage was the one point on which she was not in agreement with him. She always mentioned it, although she knew it tortured him. She didn't really want to, but it always came to her tongue, just as it did now, entirely without her wanting it to.

So she said quickly: 'No, you're right. Just when Father has so
many other worries, it would be wrong.'

She looked in front of her. His hand came nervously over the
table to hers. 'You're not angry, are you?' he asked worriedly.

'No, no,' she assured him straight away, 'only . . .'

'What are you thinking about?' he now asked, noting her silence.

'I was thinking of the assassination and that people think there
will be a war . . .'

'Yes?' he murmured, not understanding.

'You would have to join up, wouldn't you?'

He nodded.

'Otto,' she urged, gripping his hand, 'Otto, tell me you wouldn't
join up without having married me. It isn't for my sake, you know
that. But Gustäving would never have a father if anything happened
to you.'

He looked at the child. 'If there's a war I'll marry you. I promise
it.' And, seeing the hope in her eyes, he muttered: 'But there won't
be a war.'

'No, no,' she exclaimed, herself terrified by her wish. 'Of course
not. Not at that price!'

§ XVIII

As on any other evening, Iron Gustav had stood in his yard settling
up with the returning day cabs and dispatching those for the night.
Perhaps he had been more taciturn than usual, but nobody paid
much attention to that in the general excitement. For the drivers
were very excited this evening.

Some said: 'There'll be war,' and others: 'Nonsense. The Kaiser
has left Kiel – he'd return to Berlin immediately in case of war.'

'But the Kiel Regatta has been cancelled.'

'Because the Kaiser is in mourning, not because of war. The
Archduke was related to him.'

'The *Lokalanzeiger* says . . .'

'You with your silly *Scandal Advertiser*! *Vorwärts* says we have

110 Social Democrats in the Reichstag and they're in agreement with the proletariat of the world not to go to war.'

'Silence!' ordered Hackendahl.

'We won't vote a penny for a capitalist war . . .'

'Quiet!' commanded Hackendahl again. 'I won't have such non-sense in my yard.'

But the men continued to whisper behind his back, which did not bother him for once though it would have annoyed him at other times. Even the day's takings, unusually large – again because there was much afoot in Berlin – did not please him. People were restless; they couldn't remain indoors but hurried into the streets, driving from the Reichstag to the Schloss, from the Schloss to the War Ministry, from the War Ministry to the newspaper offices, wanting to hear and see whatever there was. But the Schloss lay in darkness – the yacht with the Kaiser on board was sailing towards Nordkap – and only when the guard was mounted, to the sound of drum and fife, were people able to cheer.

Old Hackendahl wouldn't have any of this kind of gossip in his yard. He went on cashing up. The day's takings were plentiful, but one thing annoyed him, and something else displeased him, and war talk interested the old soldier not one bit! He was thinking: my Erich has gone just when I was going to fetch him out of the cellar and tell him he could attend school and that everything was all right.

Silence reigned in the yard. The day drivers had gone home and the night drivers had gone to work. Hackendahl looked up at his house. Outside it was still a little dark, but in their bedroom the light was already on. Mother must already be going to bed. He could go to bed too, but he turned round and went into the stable.

Rabause was handing out the second feed and looked at his chief warily, clearing his throat as if to speak but not doing so. A little further away Otto was rubbing a horse down with a handful of straw; the cabby, so as to catch a train and earn a good tip, had driven it too hard. Hackendahl looked on. 'The belly, Otto, don't forget the belly,' he called out.

Otto glanced dejectedly at his father and then did as he was told.

The vigorous rubbing tickled the animal and it snorted, beginning to dance about.

'Harder!' called the father. 'It's a horse, not a girl.' He spoke in the old sergeant-major manner, and almost automatically. Once again Otto lifted a red, swollen eye, where his father had lashed out at him on learning that he had freed Erich, thus giving him no time to repeat the sentence Tutti had taught him.

Hackendahl looked at his son almost with hatred. Had it not been for this fool's precipitate action he would have liberated Erich himself, and everything would have been all right. As it was, the one occasion on which the fool thought of acting on his own initiative had been sufficient to spoil everything.

The father looked at his oldest son with scorn and hate. 'Lift up the leg!' he shouted. 'Can't you see that you're hurting the poor beast?'

Otto lifted up the leg, placed it over his knee and went on rubbing. 'You're on stable duty tonight,' added Hackendahl. 'I don't want to have you sleeping in my house.'

Otto did not interrupt his work.

'You're to do stable duty,' shouted Hackendahl. 'Did you hear me?'

'Yes, Father,' said the son in the loud, clear voice he had been trained to use.

He wondered if he should say anything more, to make clear how much he despised him. But he decided not to. The lad was far too soft and obedient, always said 'Yes, Father', and was without resistance. He didn't even raise his arm when being hit in the face – a milksop you can do anything you like with. He won't change.

Hackendahl turned round and left the stable. When he passed old Rabause, still carrying his feeding bucket, he told him kindly, 'When you've finished feeding you can go home and sleep. You've got today off, Rabause.'

Rabause looked at him sideways. This time he dared to open his mouth. 'I slept during the day, sir,' he croaked. 'I don't need sleep during the night – but Otto does.'

Hackendahl flashed his eyes angrily at this rebel. He didn't want his son defended. He should defend himself if he's unjustly treated. But he isn't unjustly treated.

'By the way, I helped to break open the locks on the cellar doors, sir,' said Rabause. 'I agreed that it was the right thing to do.'

'Did you indeed?' asked Hackendahl slowly. 'So . . . and now, you old lush, you think I'll hit you in the face, like I did Otto? You'd like that, wouldn't you – so that you can feel big and insulted, eh? But I'm not going to do you that favour. You're just a creep, just like your dear Otto. Both just creeps. You make me sick!'

He looked at the old man, almost shaking with anger. 'I want you out of the stable by ten. Do your sleeping at home. Understand?' he shouted. 'That one . . . that one' – and he pointed backwards – 'he's got to wake up.'

And with a bang the stable door closed behind him.

§ XIX

Night came and the roar of the town died down, but there was no peace in Hackendahl's mind. It seemed that it was not even his own initiative that had made Otto free Erich. That bastard, that drunken sot Rabause showed him how and he simply followed him, just as he's been following his whole life long. And someone like that stayed at home while the intelligent and beloved son ran away and was even now wandering about deprived of any means of support and exposed to all the perils of a large city. What would become of him? Would he end up as a Hamburg cabin boy, a Foreign Legionary, a suicide in the Landwehr Canal? At the best he saw his favourite son on a bench in the Tiergarten, constantly moved on by policemen, since one was not allowed to sleep in the open. The prodigal son and the swine – his situation was poignantly described in the New Testament but not a word was said about the father's feelings during his absence.

Hackendahl turned round, went quickly upstairs, crossed the landing and went into the bedroom. 'Where's Erich?'

His wife started. 'What's the matter with you, Father? You frightened me.'

'Where's Erich? That's what I want to know.'

'I don't know. He didn't even say goodbye to me before he

went . . .' She stopped, fearing she had given herself away, but he took no notice.

'That's not true,' he said gruffly. 'You do know where he is.'

'I don't. I'm worrying about him too. Otto looked for him but he'd gone by then.'

'That's not true. Erich wouldn't run away like that. Did you give him any money?'

'Not a penny,' she moaned. 'I have no money, you know that quite well, Father.'

By now he was convinced she was lying. They had hidden Erich somewhere. He knew Erich – Erich wouldn't run away without money. 'I'll find out. You wait!' he threatened and marched off.

It was dark in the girls' bedroom. Eva had gone to bed. In the last of the daylight she had been playing with her jewels, trying on the rings, pinning the brooches on her nightdress. Oh, they were so beautiful! When she had come home at noon and learned that the hiding place in the lamp had been looted (she had regarded it as an utter secret, and now they all knew about it), she could have burst with fury and had even thought of going to the police and charging her brother.

But now she had these jewels and dared have nothing whatever to do with the police. Trembling, she had read in the newspaper a description of the theft. The authorities were of course convinced that the young man and the girl were accomplices, working together very cleverly. And the shopping bag had been found . . .

No, anything for peace and quiet! Only that morning she had desired her share of the beautiful things of life and now she possessed a good deal already. She heard her father's footsteps in the corridor, his voice scolding and her mother's whining. She hid her jewellery quickly in a little bag, which hung from a thin but strong string between her breasts. She then turned to the wall and pretended to sleep.

Hackendahl was standing in the doorway, listening – it was an old habit of his to listen like this to his children in bed; he knew every sound and could tell at once if they were shamming sleep . . .

'Eva,' he called, 'you're not asleep! Where's Erich?'

'I don't know, Father.'

'You do. Tell me at once where he is.' Then, almost pleading: 'Be sensible, Evchen. I'm not going to do anything to him. I just want to know where he is.'

'I don't know, Father, I was shopping when it all happened. You can be sure I'd tell you if I knew. I wouldn't have let Erich out.'

Yes, his daughter held the same opinion as he did – Erich ought not to have left home. But, oddly enough, the way she expressed this did not please him. 'I don't want to know what you think about it. Keep a sharp lookout and let me know at once if Erich calls or sends a message.'

'Certainly, Father.'

'You will?'

'Of course, Father.'

'Good!'

Hackendahl had turned to go when it dawned on him that the second bed was empty. 'Is Sophie on night duty again?'

'Sophie? Didn't Mother tell you that Sophie has gone too?'

'Gone? What d'you mean?'

'Gone to her nuns. This afternoon she's moved into the hospital for good, bag and baggage. We're not pious enough for her, so it seems. We're always quarrelling, she says.'

'Indeed!' was her father's sole comment. 'Well, goodnight, Evchen.'

For a long while he stood in the passage. Blow upon blow, worse and worse; two of the children lost in one day! And Sophie hadn't said goodbye either. What had he done that they should treat him like this? Certainly he had been strict, but a father had to be strict. Perhaps he hadn't been strict enough. Now he saw how spineless they were, how they took to their heels when things became difficult. They should have been soldiers! Gritted their teeth, without batting an eyelid, and hung on.

He stood there a long time, resentful and accusing, his thoughts flitting to and fro. Nevertheless he did not soften or give way. His children had dealt him heavy blows, but he did not complain of the blows, only that a man's children should become his enemies. He did not give way. He continued his evening round and went into the boys' bedroom with a firm step. Of the three beds two were unoccupied.

'Good evening, Father,' said Heinz.

'Good evening, Bubi. Aren't you asleep yet? It's been bedtime for a long while now.'

'I'll be going to sleep, Father. You're still up and about and you rise three hours earlier than I do.'

'An old man needs very little sleep, Bubi.'

'You're not old, Father!'

'Oh, yes.'

'No!'

'Yes.'

'No.'

Hackendahl crossed the dark room and sat on the boy's bed. 'Have you any idea, Bubi, where Erich is?' he asked, as if he were a friend and not his father.

'Not the slightest, Father. You're not worrying?'

'Well – the others don't seem to know where he is either.'

'Don't they? I'll keep my ears open then. Perhaps one of his pals at school may know something.'

'Will you do that, Bubi?'

'Certainly, Father.'

'And you could go to the headmaster. I'd promised him I'd send Erich to school again tomorrow. That can't happen now. You must explain . . .'

'Oh, Father!'

'What?'

'I'd rather not go to the beak tomorrow . . .'

'Why ever not? Anyway, you shouldn't call him that.'

'Oh, he might be angry with me. Me and a classmate had a bit of a fight today. The teacher put us on report and said he'd tell the beak – the head.'

'So why were you fighting?'

'Oh, only because he had a silly look on his face, asking for it.'

'And did he get it?'

'And how, Father. In spades! He ended up gasping for air and shouting pax.'

'What's pax mean?'

'It means peace. It's what you shout when you're at the end of your tether.'

'So, Bubi, it will be quite all right to go to the head and tell him what I asked. As a matter of fact, he and I saw your fight from the window.'

'OK then. I was just scared that to get bad marks for behaviour would be miserable.'

For a moment there was silence. Hackendahl had been restored to tranquillity. 'Well, all right, don't forget. Sleep well.'

'Sleep well too, Father, and don't worry about Erich. He's cleverer than you and me put together. Erich will always come out on top.'

'Goodnight, Bubi.'

'Goodnight, Father.'

TWO

War Breaks Out

§ I

31 JULY 1914.

Since early morning the crowds now occupying much of the Lust-garten had been gathering before the Schloss, on which flew the yellow Imperial standard, symbol of the presence of the all-highest War Lord. Unceasingly the people came and went, an ebb and flow of thousands who waited for an hour or two before departing to daily tasks half-heartedly dispatched, for everybody was oppressed by the question: would there be war?

Three days had passed since the allied State of Austria had declared war on the Serbs. What would happen now? Would the world intervene? What importance, after all, had a war in the Balkans, a vast empire against a small nation? Yet it was said that Russia was mobilizing, that the French were bestirring themselves and – what would England do?

The weather was oppressive, and grew closer; the crowds buzzed and could not keep still. The Kaiser was said to have spoken that morning from the Schloss – but Germany was still at peace with the world. There was a ferment in the people; a month of uncertainty had come and gone in obscure negotiations, threats and assurances of peace – nerves were on edge with suspense. Any decision seemed better than this terrible uncertainty.

Vendors of sausages, newspapers and ice cream pushed through the crowd, but they sold nothing, for the people were in no mood to eat nor were they interested in news which must have long since been overtaken by events. They wanted a decision. Incoherent and excited, everyone had something special to relate. And then, in the middle of their talk, they would fall silent, forgetting everything else as they stared up at the balcony where the Kaiser was said to have made his speech this morning. They were trying to see through the windows but the glass was dazzling in the sunshine, and nothing was visible but pale yellow curtains.

What was going on inside? What decision affecting everyone waiting there, every man, woman and child, was being taken in that palace twilight? Forty years of peace in the land; people could not imagine what war meant . . . Yet they felt that a word from the silent building could change their whole lives, change everything. And they were waiting for that word. They dreaded it and yet dreaded still more lest it should not be forthcoming, and the many weeks of suspense should prove to have been endured in vain.

Suddenly the crowd became as still as if it were holding its breath . . . Nothing had happened – nothing yet – but the clocks in the steeples were striking from far and near, quickly, slowly, deep-toned, high. It was five o'clock.

Nothing had happened yet; the crowd was waiting breathlessly . . .

Then the great gate opened, opened slowly, very slowly, and out came . . . a policeman, a Berlin policeman in blue uniform and spiked helmet.

They stared . . .

Climbing up on a balustrade, he made a signal for silence.

They were already silent . . .

The policeman removed his helmet, held it before his chest. Breathlessly they followed every movement, though he was no more than an ordinary policeman, the kind to be seen any day in any of the Berlin streets . . . And yet he made an indelible impression. They were to see monstrous and terrible things during the coming years, but they would never forget that Berlin policeman who had taken off his helmet and was holding it in front of him.

The man on the balustrade opened his mouth; every eye was fixed on those lips. What would come forth? Life or Death, War or Peace?

The policeman spoke. 'By order of His Majesty the Kaiser I announce that a state of mobilization has been proclaimed.'

Closing his mouth, he gazed over the countless heads; with the jerky movements of a puppet, he put on his helmet.

For a moment the crowd was silent; then a voice here and there started to sing, and hundreds – thousands – of voices joined in:

> *Now praise we all our God*
> *With hearts and hands and voices . . .*

In jerks, like a puppet, the policeman took off his helmet again.

§ II

Along Unter den Linden motor cars tore along with officers standing up in them waving flags. Through their cupped hands they were shouting: 'Called up! Called up!'

People were laughing and cheering and throwing flowers; girls had pulled off their large straw hats to swing them round by the ribbons, and were shouting, enraptured: 'War! War!'

It was the officers' hour – for forty long years there had been nothing but parades and drills, till men had become heartily sick of life; people had hardly turned to look back at them, they had become so ordinary. Now everyone was cheering them, with shining eyes; they were going to fight and perhaps die for the freedom and peace of everyone.

'That I should live to see this day!' cried old Hackendahl amid the surge of enthusiasm. 'Everything'll be all right now.'

Heinz was clinging to one arm and Eva to the other; they let themselves drift along with the people, laughing. In high spirits Eva was kissing her hands to the officers in the cars.

'Oh, Father!' cried Heinz pressing his father's arm.

'What is it, Bubi?' In the turmoil Hackendahl had to bend down to hear.

'Father!' Bubi was quite out of breath. 'Father . . .' At last he managed to speak. 'Couldn't I go too?'

'Go where?' Old Hackendahl did not understand him.

'Go to . . . the war . . . to the Front. Please, Father!'

'But, Bubi,' said old Hackendahl teasingly and yet with pride, 'you're only thirteen. You're still a child.'

'It would be possible, Father, if you gave permission. If you sent me to your old regiment. They do have drummer boys, I know that.'

'Drummer boys! And you the son of an old soldier! We Germans never have drummer boys – perhaps the Frenchies do.'

'Father!'

'Hold tight, Evchen, hold tight! We've got to get home now, to tell Otto – he won't know yet. If they're mobilizing today, he'll have to present himself tomorrow at the latest. Or even today . . . I don't know. Quick, let's get home, I'll have to see what it says in his papers.'

It was a stiff battle to make any progress at all against the human tide and they had to clutch one another so as not to be separated.

Heinz looked cautiously at old Hackendahl. 'Father . . .'

'Yes?'

'Don't be cross – but won't Erich also have to join up?'

'Have to?' The father answered freely, as if Heinz were an adult. He'd just been thinking about it. 'No, he doesn't have to. He's only just seventeen. But he could volunteer.'

'Erich volunteer?'

'Why not? You mustn't think badly of your brother, Heinz, there's an end to that now. From now on we must all stand together. Everyone feels a new sense of unity – Erich will, too.'

'Yes, Father. I also believe everything has changed.'

'Yes, absolutely. You mark my words – Erich will come back now. He's compelled to, I've got his papers, he needs them. But even so he would have to come back anyhow. Bubi, he'll know now that no one can live just for himself. Each belongs to the other, and all belong together – we Germans!'

'Yes, Father.'

'That we've been looking for him in vain all these weeks had to be the case. He had to learn what it's like to be quite alone, without anybody. Now we all belong together. See how Eva laughs and speaks with that man?! They didn't know each other from Adam a moment ago; and now they've never heard of each other. But now they feel they have *one* thing in common – they're German! You wait, by the time we get home perhaps we'll find Erich sitting with Mother and waiting for us. Well, not a word about the past, you understand, Bubi? All is forgotten and forgiven! It just never happened. And, of course, you'll be so kind as to behave yourself like a brother. From now on we're all . . . Stop, where's Eva? There she is! . . . Eva, we're here! Would you believe it? The girl doesn't see us. Eva!' He shouted with his hands round his mouth. 'Eva . . . Eva Hackendahl! Hac . . . ken . . . dahl! Over here!'

A troop of young men was coming along linked arm in arm, trying as far as possible to march in step through the crowds. They were singing: 'Victoriously we will vanquish France . . .'

One of the marchers laughingly made a grab at Eva, who was battling her way through the people, and she too laughed as she evaded him.

Hackendahl shook his head. 'She's gone, I can't see her. Can you, Bubi? No, you're much too small, of course. Well, come along, Eva will find her way home. We have to hurry. Otto must be told and perhaps Erich is waiting . . .'

§ III

Gleefully Eva mingled with the crowd going along Unter den Linden in the direction of the Brandenburger Tor, away from her home, quite content to be separated from a father and brother who had talked nothing but a lot of boring rubbish about war and unity. So now they were expected to pig together more than ever, a real loving family! Why should there be war, anyway? This was only mobilization – she had managed these last few days to grasp that mobilization did not necessarily mean war.

But if the war turned out to be like the mobilization, then it was pretty magnificent. Never had she seen men in such high spirits, and with such shining eyes. A little fat man, an old boy with a turned-up moustache, forty at least, suddenly took her round the waist. 'Well, my dear, you're pleased, aren't you, I am!' And before she could protest he was gone.

A young man shouted: 'Urgent – war bride wanted to darn my socks,' and everyone laughed.

Splendid, to drift with a crowd in such festive mood!

A hand fell on her shoulder. 'Well, missie, still goin' strong?' a somewhat hoarse voice enquired.

She wheeled round, startled, to meet a face she had once seen for a few minutes and had not forgotten – a dark, impudent face with a black moustache.

'What do you want?' she cried. 'I don't know you. Please let go.'

The young man smiled. 'It doesn't matter; if you don't know me now, you soon will.'

'Leave me alone or I'll call a policeman!'

'Call one, missie, call one. I'll help you. Or what about goin' together, eh? I don't mind the bluebottles meself – blue's my fav'rite colour. You've got a nice blue costume on yourself, missie.'

Eva had always been a real Berlin child, pert and self-confident; it wasn't easy to frighten her. But she was frightened now. Faced with this fellow's assurance her own nerve vanished. The impudent manner in which he was patting her frock, just on the breast! And between her breasts hung . . .

'Please let me go,' she begged. 'There must be some mistake.'

'Of course I'll let you go,' he laughed. 'Going's good for you in this heat. Come on, my dear, I'll go with you.' And without further ado he took her arm. 'Look at this pack of fools,' he went on, 'dying of joy because they've been given a war. As if it wouldn't be a sight easier with a razor in front of a mirror. But no,' he said, finishing, 'that's not for us. We're more for the life beautiful.'

'Let me go,' she implored. 'Let me go, I don't know you.'

'Girl,' he whispered, 'don't you kid me.' His smile had changed into a cold anger. 'A whole month I've been traipsing all over Berlin looking for you and now I've found you, d'you think I'm going to let you off the string again? D'you think I put them things into your ruddy shopping bag, with its photo stuck up everywhere, just to have you keep 'em? No, my girl, I'm not so cracked as all that. You've got to shell out.'

He looked at her and she, against her will, nodded.

'And when you've shelled out, that won't be all. I've been looking for a girl like you for a long while – a girl fresh from home. Be a great help to me. You've no idea how I'll put you up to things. You're going to be something classy an' the cops will put you in a frame at headquarters – that's the girl what started off with a jewel robbery at Wertheim's!'

'Please don't. People . . .' Her brain was working feverishly. Surely she could tear herself free and disappear in the crowd, once his grip slackened for a moment.

'Well, what's your name?'

'Eva,' she said in a low voice.

'Well, and what else, Eva, my pet?'

'Schmidt.'

'Yes, of course! Schmidt! Just what I thought. Meier's too common, I must say. And where d'you hang out, Fräulein Schmidt?'

'In the Lützowstrasse.'

'Ah, in the Lützowstrasse. Posh district, eh? And where d'you keep the stuff, you know what I mean, the sparklers? At home, I bet.'

'Yes,' she said boldly, resolved now to scratch at his eyes with her free hand when the right moment came, and so get away.

'Oh, at home!' he sneered. 'And where d'you keep 'em? Under the pillow?'

'No, in the lamp-weight.'

'In the lamp-weight,' he repeated thoughtfully. 'That's not at all bad. You're smart, I can see that. Don't tell me you thought of that hide-away just for this. You've been pinching things before, eh?'

Furious at her blunder, she did not reply and once again there was the abrupt change from mockery to threat. With his swarthy face close to her pallid one, he whispered: 'And now I'll tell you what's what, Fräulein Schmidt from the Lützowstrasse. Do what you're told – that's what you've got to do. And turn up whenever I whistle, understand? D'you understand? Eh? Look at me, you – whore!'

Trembling, she looked at him.

'You whore an' thief!' he hissed. 'You nice young lady – Eva Hackendahl!' He was savouring her terror now that she realized there was no escape, that he knew her name.

But when he saw her so utterly subjugated, deathly pale and trembling, his rage went. The victor became magnanimous. 'Yes, surprised you, what?' He laughed. 'Well, you shouldn't cart round an old buffer who bawls out your name right across the street. You see, I'm not the sort to pretend I know by magic. That was your father, wasn't it, who called you?'

She nodded.

'When I ask you something, you answer, see. Say "Yes".'

'Yes.'

'Say: "Yes, Eugen".'

'Yes, Eugen.'

'Good – and now where d'you really hang out? But no more lies or I'll give you something to worry about, you can depend on that.'

She was convinced he would keep his word and racked her brain for an escape and found none.

'Where d'you live?'

'Frankfurter Allee.'

'Whereabouts?'

'The cab yard.'

He whistled. 'Oh, that's him, is it, him with the taxicabs? So I'm getting a swell sort of girl, I've clicked somethin' first-class. Fine.' Suddenly he was very good-humoured. 'And now listen, my dear . . . me Evchen. Don't you look so worried, you needn't be afraid of me. I'm the kindest chap in the whole of Berlin. I'm a real mug, I am, if you do what I tell you, that is. Well, you be at the corner of Grosse and Kleine Frankfurter Strasse at nine this evening. Savvy?'

She nodded. But when he made a gesture she said quickly: 'Yes, Eugen.'

'As for the sparklers you needn't bring 'em with you specially – because you've got 'em on you already. Don't be so stupid another time and tell an old friend that they're in the lamp-weight when I c'n see the cord in the neck of your blouse.'

She turned pale.

'But I'm a decent chap. I'll take the swag off your hands. What use is it to you anyhow? You can't wear 'em or you'd get caught. But I'll give you somethin' you can wear, something nice – I got enough for that . . . And anyhow, my girl,' and he pressed her arm affection-ately, 'we're going to have a swell time together. You needn't be afraid. Oh, we'll have some grand times.' He gave a short laugh. Her arm was lying quietly in his. 'There's only one thing. You got to do what I tell you, make no mistake about that – even if I say jump off the roof. Otherwise I'll get mad.'

He let go of her arm and observed her closely. 'Got the wind up, eh?'

She nodded slowly, tears in her eyes.

'You'll get over that, Evchen,' he said brightly. 'At first every girl's frightened, but they get over it. And don't be fool enough to bolt off to the police – or I'll kill you, now or in ten years' time.'

He laughed curtly, nodded, and then: 'Clear off home!' he commanded.

And before she understood what was happening he had gone.

§ IV

In a first-floor room of a house in Jägerstrasse, a swarthy, thickset man in shirt and trousers walked up and down whistling the 'Marseillaise', his leather-shod feet lightly treading the linoleum floor. Now and again he went to the window and looked into the street, which also caught something of the disturbance that reigned on Unter den Linden on this first morning of mobilization. The man shook his head, went on lightly whistling, but continued to walk up and down.

The door was jerked open and on the threshold stood Erich Hackendahl, panting and flushed.

'Well?' enquired the swarthy, thickset man.

'Mobilization!'

The man, taking his waistcoat from the chair and putting it on, continued to look at Erich. 'That was to be expected,' he said slowly. 'But mobilization doesn't mean war.'

'But, Herr Doctor,' cried Erich, still breathless, 'all the people are so enthusiastic. They were singing "Now praise we all our God". I sang as well, Herr Doctor.'

'Why shouldn't they be enthusiastic?' asked the Herr Doctor, slipping on his jacket. 'It's something new. And probably their glorious Kaiser has spoken again about gleaming arms and enemies all over the world . . .'

'But no, no! Nothing of the kind,' shouted the young man. 'You're quite wrong. A policeman came out of his cabin, an ordinary bobby, and announced the mobilization. It was magnificent.'

'He's a great impresario, your hero-emperor. Now he's putting on some old Prussian simplicity, copying Frederick the One and Only. But, Erich, surely you realize you've been taken in – you know his love of pomp and circumstance. And now all of a sudden just this policeman! It's all humbug.'

'But it wasn't humbug when we were singing,' countered the lad.

'And didn't you look at the singers? They weren't the people, my boy, they weren't the workers who create the wealth but the fat bourgeoisie, and when they thanked their God for the mobilization they were really thanking Him for the big profits they smell in the offing, the biggest of all profits, war profits derived from their brother's corpse . . .'

'Shame, shame, Herr Doctor! You weren't present. Those people weren't thinking of business, they were thinking of Germany threatened by Russia, France, perhaps even by England.'

'Just think a bit, Erich,' said the swarthy man. 'You have a good brain and you might use it! If we mobilize now, doesn't it mean we threaten the others, and the workers on the Neva and the Seine feel they're threatened at the same time, but now by us?'

Erich stood perplexed. 'The others . . .'

The man smiled. 'Now you want to say that the others started it – just like children complaining about one another to their mother. But we're no longer children. The worker, Erich, has no other fatherland but that of the working class of the entire globe.'

'But Germany . . .'

'Germany even today is a land where the worker has no rights. "Work and obey" is the password here. The German worker has only one friend in the world and that is the French worker, the Russian worker. Shall he shoot these?' Impetuously: 'There are 110 Social Democrats in the Reichstag – we're not going to grant war credits, we shall refuse. In our persons almost one-third of the German people refuses also.'

'I was standing near the Schloss. I heard them singing, I joined in, too, and the workers joined in. Nothing bad could have inspired us to that.'

'But it is something bad! You're intoxicated, Erich, intoxicated with evil. You don't know what a war means, when one mother's son kills or mutilates some other mother's son.'

'And do you know what a war means?'

'I do. From my youth I have fought for the workers. That's a war, too – every day we have our dead and wounded . . . But I know what I'm fighting for, which is that the German worker and with him the workers of the world should have a little more happiness, a little more comfort. What are you fighting for? Tell me.'

'For the defence of Germany.'

'But what is your Germany? Does it give its sons a home and daily bread, or even the right to a job? Is the worker to defend his bed infested with bugs or the policeman who dissolves his meetings? He can have all that anywhere else in the world, without Germany.'

'What you say must be wrong. I can't put it into words, but I feel it. Germany is something more than that. And if the workers really only had flea-ridden beds, as you say, in Germany they would be happier with them among Germans than in a completely different world.'

They stood silently for a while. In the streets the shouts and the rejoicings rose and fell, rose and fell like waves on a shore . . .

The big man moved as in a dream. 'You must go, Erich,' he said quietly. 'I can't have you here any longer.'

Erich made a movement.

'No, I'm not sending you away in anger. But I'm a Social Democrat and I can't have a warmonger as secretary. That's impossible. When you came to me in such a pitiable state four or five weeks ago, I thought I could help you. You would be one of us, part of the great movement of workers' liberation . . .'

'You were very good to me, Herr Doctor,' faltered Erich.

'You had done wrong, Erich, and you wanted to do worse – lie down in the mud deliberately and perish. I knew your alert, critical mind which made you dissatisfied with a comfortable home, and you seemed to me a rebel – we need rebels.'

Erich made a hasty movement, thought for a moment, and said nothing.

'You want to say you're still a rebel. But you're not one, when you fight to defend the bad existing social order. You want to join up, don't you? A volunteer?'

Erich nodded defiantly. 'I feel that the people want this war, not only me.'

'Really! And I thought we were defending ourselves! Anyway, we Social Democrats didn't want it. We'll vote against the government and the war credits. The workers throughout the whole world will too – and your war will be finished!'

And he snapped his fingers.

But Erich shouted: 'No, war will not be finished – and you will vote for it. You haven't even yet seen the people. You sit in offices and on party committees, but the people, the people . . .'

'But Erich, we don't want to part in anger. You'll be going home now . . . Here,' he unlocked his desk, 'here are the four hundred and eighty marks you brought with you – return them to your sister. And here are eighty marks for your father. You can take them with an easy mind. It is roughly what I intended as your salary, and you have earned it honestly.' And, more quietly, he added: 'I was always pleased to see you here.'

'You're very kind, Herr Doctor.'

'No, I'm not kind to you, I oughtn't to let you go into this . . . adventure. But I've no time to argue and struggle with you. This war has to be prevented – that's my struggle.'

They stood silent for a moment.

'Goodbye for the present, Erich.' This was in a friendly tone.

'For the present, Herr Doctor,' said Erich in a low voice.

§ V

For the first time in weeks the Hackendahl family sat in its totality round the supper table. And old Father Hackendahl had been as mild as he could as he looked round the table. All had been properly for-given and forgotten, and no unpleasant questions asked. What peace had sundered, war now brought together.

Sophie, too, had come home, straight from hospital, to see what changes war had brought to the Hackendahl family.

'So Otto is joining up tomorrow morning,' reported Hackendahl with satisfaction, 'and they'll probably take Erich too when he vol-unteers. Sophie, I suppose you expect to go to the Front even though you're only a probationer.'

'What about me?' cried Heinz. 'You say "No", Father, but I say they'll take me. Every man's needed.'

There was a general laugh and Hackendahl said: 'We should indeed be in a bad way if we needed children like you. Thank God, that's not necessary yet. But what about me, eh?'

'You, Father? What do you mean?'

'Well, I shall volunteer, of course.'

'But you're an old man, Father.'

'Old? Only fifty-six. What you can do I can.'

'But your business, Father! The cabs!'

'What do I care about the business? The Fatherland comes first. No, children, that's settled. I'll join up.'

'Father always said that he couldn't take a day off because the business couldn't manage without him,' wailed Frau Hackendahl. 'And now he's able to go to the war.'

'Well, you'll have to look after the business, that's all, Mother.'

They all laughed.

'I mean it seriously. Who's going to take the place of the men who go to the Front? The women, of course! It'll be all right, Mother, Eva will help you. Eh, what's the matter, Eva, sitting there pale and not saying a word?'

'Nothing, Father. It's the heat and the crowds . . .'

'Father,' interrupted Heinz, 'won't there be a chance for me? How long do you think the war will last?'

Old Hackendahl laughed. 'You young rascal! Six weeks – at the most till Christmas – and then you'll be thirteen. No, we'll be cele-brating Christmas at home as usual. With modern weapons . . .'

Thus the jolly scene continued. But old Hackendahl failed to notice that he alone spoke, and that the others were strangely silent.

Erich, his head bent, sat at the table. Yes, he was home again with everything forgiven and forgotten, and the money paid back. Tomor-row he would see his headmaster and enquire about his school report and leaving examination, and then become a soldier. Now as of old he was sitting in the midst of his family and one hour of it had been enough to depress him, the faces so familiar and so boring, his mother's eternal complaining, the way old Hackendahl used his knife, Otto who never smelled of anything but the stables – oh, it was all like a chain dragging on his leg.

While working at the lawyer's he had been quite unable to understand how he, Erich, had made himself a common thief in order to obtain wine and women. Now that he was at home again he understood only too well: he had done it to get away from this stuffy petit-bourgeois atmosphere. Was the war which Father was talking about so vulgarly and foolishly ('We'll give them a good hiding, those red-trousered Frenchies!'), was it the same war he had spoken about to the lawyer? No, this sort of thing, this home, these people, couldn't be defended – they were not Germany, they had to be destroyed.

Eva, who at other times was so ready with her tongue, was sitting pale and silent at the table, playing with her fork. The food nearly choked her. She heard other people talking far off. They were so far away, but at nine o'clock she had to be at the corner of the Grosse and Kleine Frankfurter Strasse, though her father would never allow her to go out after supper.

But when she tried to think of an excuse, everything became a blur. She couldn't gather her thoughts. The bronzed face with the small dark moustache and the evil black eyes prevented her. 'You whore!' he had called her. Nobody had spoken to her like that before, but if they had, she would merely have laughed in their face. Even if she hadn't been so very particular with men, she hadn't done that yet. But he treated her from the beginning as if she were one of those . . .

Her fate stood, unavoidable and inescapable, before her. She fleetingly remembered that Erich had given her 'her money' back just before supper, with an embarrassed murmur of apology. Now she had to recall how much she was worth: nearly 500 Reichsmarks and a lot of valuable jewellery. At the street corner where the gas lamp flickered in the summer evening Eugen would whistle and she must go to him. And Eugen will say, 'Empty your bags,' and she'll empty them. Then he'll say, 'Lie down!' – and she'll lie down.

But the third child – how was it with Otto? He was the only one of the seven sitting round the supper table who, at a time when life was so uncertain, knew what his lot would be in the next few days. Tomorrow he would report, receive his uniform, be sent off . . .

He climbs the stairs, presses twice on the bell – and then – then?

And Gustav, the little one, he'll already be asleep – and things will be all the worse for that. All alone, without interruption, she and Otto will confront each other. She will ask about his promise, the papers, the engagement, little Gustav . . .

His brain worked slowly. He remembered that the papers lay in good order in his father's desk, a file for each child. Straight away in the morning, before he went to the barracks, Father would unlock the desk and give him what he required: his military pass, his birth and baptism certificates. Did he need them too?

He couldn't get his head round the question: what documents did he need? Which for the military and which for the pastor? But anyway he had no time for the pastor: as soon as he had the documents he must go to the barracks. A pastor needs hours – the bridal coach, organ, speeches and marriage witnesses. And they hadn't even got their rings!

He looked up, helpless. He looked into the faces of his siblings and parents, and moved his lips. With a feeling almost of redemption, he thought to himself: I'll tell them, we still haven't got the rings! And you can't get married without a ring, can you?

'What are you talking about, Otto?' exclaimed Bubi excitedly. 'I think he's talking to the man in the moon.'

All laughed and Father said: 'Otto's already somewhere else. He's already reciting the regimental orders of the day, or war bulletins – aren't you, Otto?'

Otto murmured something, and the others immediately forgot him, as they habitually did. No, he thought, I can't possibly ask Father for my papers this evening, and if it were possible there'd be no point, because you can't get married at night, and there's no time early in the morning . . .

Old Father Hackendahl, Iron Gustav, sat comfortably at his re-united family's dining room table, with the feeling that everything turned out well and all had returned home, just as they should have done.

However, he was mistaken. He only felt so comfortable because he knew nothing about his children. They all felt they'd left home. All felt the weight of family pressure. All couldn't wait to leave. But Hackendahl noticed nothing, and was therefore flabbergasted that the family wanted to disperse straight after saying grace.

'But, children,' he said, admonishingly, 'I thought we'd all sit a bit cosily together. Bubi will fetch some cans of beer and a few cigarettes, and we'll chat on for a bit.'

But Sophie had to go to the hospital immediately, and Otto to the horse with the nose wound, which also had an inflamed leg that needed attention. Erich had to go to the Schloss to see what was going on, and Eva wanted to go with him part of the way. She thought her headache would clear in the evening air.

So only Bubi remained, and he naturally had to go to bed. His energetic protestation gave welcome excuse for exaggerated indulgence in military orders. Bubi was thoroughly worked over according to all the rules in the book, and when that was over and he lay howling in bed, Hackendahl discovered that his other children had meanwhile vanished.

Only Mother sat comfortably in the basket-chair by the window, looked out over the declining evening, and muttered contentedly: 'That was another lovely supper, Father. But the gammon was a bit singed. Did you notice, Father? And it was too fat as well. I always tell Eva she should buy gammon from Hoffmann, but she never listens.'

Father Hackendahl went into the stable, where he could at least chat with Otto for a while.

§ VI

But Otto isn't in the stable. He's gone over the two courtyards, and is now going up the many steps to the fifth floor – steps which he always saw as a challenge. He may be weak and without will, but that doesn't mean he's a coward. He climbed the steps and didn't stay at home. He didn't deal with the horse with the nose wound and the swollen leg. That he left to old Rabause.

Once Otto was up on the fifth floor he gave a great sigh, but he didn't hesitate. He pressed twice on the doorbell of Gertrud Gudde, seamstress. He had to wait quite a while before Tutti in a woollen nightgown came to the door, awakened from her sleep.

'You, Otto?' she cried, surprised. 'So late?'

And it turned out that she knew nothing. She had been indoors the whole day and her clients had not put in an appearance or sent word.

'It's the mobilization,' said Otto, looking at her timidly. 'I have to go back at once. Father doesn't know I'm out.'

'But what does it mean – mobilization?' she enquired anxiously. 'Does it mean war?'

'No, oh no. But it means I have to go to the barracks tomorrow.'

'Have you to serve again? But why, if there's no war? There isn't a war, is there?'

'No, Tutti.'

'Then why have you to go to the barracks?'

'Perhaps' – he tried to explain what he himself did not under-stand – 'perhaps the others will be frightened when they see how many soldiers we have.'

'And that's why you have to go to the barracks?'

'Perhaps – I don't know. Mobilization means I must serve again.'

'For how long?'

'I don't know that either.'

Silence, a long silence. He sat with eyes cast down, ashamed of lying to her when everyone had been saying there would be war. But he only ever said to her that mobilization isn't the same as war. Per-haps it was the last time they would sit together like this . . .

'What does your father say?'

'He behaves as if he were still in the army.'

'He says there will be a war?'

Otto nodded.

Long silence.

Her hand stole over the table to his, which he would have with-drawn but was too late. First it resisted, then it surrendered to the little hand with the seamstress's hardened fingertips.

'Otto, look at me . . .'

Once again the hand wants to retreat, and once again gives way.

'Otto!' pleaded Tutti.

'I'm too ashamed,' he whispered.

'But why, Otto? Are you afraid of the army?'

A shake of the head.

'Then why are you ashamed, Otto?'

He said nothing but again tried to free his hand and said: 'I think I must go.'

She came quickly round the table, sat on his lap and whispered: 'Come, tell me why you are ashamed.'

But he only had one idiotic thought in his head. 'I ought to go,' he repeated and tried to get away. 'Or else Father will grumble.'

She put her arm round his neck. 'But you can tell me why you feel ashamed, Ottchen,' she whispered. 'I don't have any shame with you.'

'Tutti . . . Oh, I'm useless. Father . . .'

'Yes, say it . . . say it, Otto!'

'I haven't got the papers.'

'What papers?'

'My papers! I'm too scared – Father would never allow it.'

A long, long silence. She lay so quietly on his chest, small, weak, fragile . . . as if she were asleep. But she wasn't. Her eyes were wide open, eyes which had a soft but glowing quality. She tried to meet his eyes, shy and pale . . .

Suddenly he stood up. He held her on his arm. Carrying her like a child, he walked around the room, forgetting her, forgetting himself, everything . . .

He was murmuring to himself, and whispered something like, 'Yes, you. You think you are something. But that your horse is lame I noticed and not you, and that you've cheated in business. But that's not all. You want to be everywhere, not just in the house and stable, but in Erich, in Heinz and Mother. You want to know what every coach driver thinks, and that must be what you think. When I was small I built myself a little watermill and worked it off the mains. You flattened it with your foot and said it was rubbish and used up too much valuable water. I never forgot that . . . You and your children . . . But your children don't want you and I want you least of all.

You think you've got hold of me more firmly than the others but you haven't, not a bit of me. I do what you want, just so as not to be shouted at . . .'

'Otto, what are you saying?'

'Yes, my sweet, my darling, you my happiness, I have you, you belong to me. But I never get you alone; he's always here, even when we sleep together.'

'Otto!'

'But if we have a war and I have to go to the Front, then I'll pray that I lose an arm or a leg so that I needn't work any more in his accursed stable, never out of his sight; so that I can go elsewhere, never see him, forget him . . .'

'Otto, he's your father!'

'My father? No, he's Iron Gustav as they call him, and he's so proud of it. But no one ought to be proud of being made of iron, for then you're neither human nor a father. I don't want to be just his son any longer, I want to be a person in my own right. As other people are.' For a moment he bore himself erectly – then his shoulders drooped. 'But nothing'll come of it, nothing ever does . . . I did think, if war came, that I'd have courage enough to speak to him. But no!'

'Otto, you mustn't worry about the marriage! I didn't speak about it for my own sake. We've always been happy together, you know that.'

'Yes, yes . . .'

'There's plenty of time. We'll get married when you come back.'

'If I come back . . .'

§ VII

It was morning, seven o'clock in the morning, and a weekday. But in the yard all the vehicles – four-wheelers and hansoms, first- and second-class cabs – stood side by side, no horses between the shafts, as if out of commission. The drivers, in their Sunday best, were running here and there or bringing the horses from the stables. By the pump stood old Hackendahl scrutinizing every beast to make sure that it had been properly groomed; now and then he had a hoof smeared and a snaffle tightened. The horses, restive without their customary harnesses, were as excited as the men; they tossed up their heads, looked across at the empty cabs and neighed.

'Hoffmann!' roared Hackendahl. 'Give Liese's mane a thorough combing again. Give her a parting, my lad, and she'll look smarter on the spot.'

'Yes, Herr Hackendahl, so that a Frenchie falls for her.'

'Or she picks up lice in Russia. They crawl up and down the parting and sing, "Oh, Nicky, Oh, Nicky, you taste very sweet!"'

'Silence!' thundered Hackendahl. But he too was excited and pleased; it was a great day for him. 'Rabause, are all the horses here?'

'Yes, Herr Hackendahl, thirty-two. Eleven mares, twenty geldings and the castrated stallion.'

'They won't take the stallion, anyhow,' said Hackendahl.

'They won't take a good many of them, Governor,' replied Rabause consolingly. 'Our horses are too light for the army.'

'I'd like to keep about twenty. Even in wartime there'll have to be cabs.'

'And where will the drivers come from, Governor? We've only got eleven men left; the rest have gone soldiering.'

'We'll take on lads as drivers.'

'There won't be any lads left soon, Governor. They're all volunteering.'

'Well, women must drive when the men are gone . . .'

'Governor, Governor, you have to be joking,' cried Rabause, bursting with laughter. 'I can just imagine it, your wife with a topper on and the reins in her hand. No, I'd really like to see that!'

'Off we go!' shouted Hackendahl in his stentorian voice. 'Quick march! Come on, Bubi,' he shouted up to the window. 'If you want to come with us, now's the time!'

Heinz disappeared from the window. Mother waved from above, at once tearful and proud. Never had there been such a sight: the day and night horses all leaving together, a hundred and twenty-eight shoes clattering on the cobblestones, tails switching, heads tossing . . . Yes, it was a proud sight, and it was also the last time the Hackendahl premises were to look prosperous.

'Why isn't Eva looking?' asked Hackendahl somewhat peevishly. 'The girl won't see something like this every day.'

'Oh, her! She's in her room again.'

'What's the matter with her, Bubi? She's quite changed.'

'I know that I don't know,' said the schoolboy, citing the classics. 'But I've an idea she's sweet on someone and perhaps he's had to join up.'

'Eva? Nonsense! I'm bound to have known!'

'You, Father?'

'Why ever not? What do you mean?'

'Oh, nothing, Father.'

For a while the two walked silently side by side. Down the Frankfurter Allee the horses clattered and people in the street stood still, pleased at the sight. That's something worth seeing, eh? Horses on their way to the war.

Under his arm Hackendahl carried a file of papers and the order to appear before the requisitioning authorities. With a measured dignity he strode along beside his troop, hurrying ahead at the crossings to see that the side streets were free, beckoning and admonishing. 'Franz, don't lose that grey.' 'Keep up with us, Hoffmann!' Bubi was even more occupied. He stopped at every advertisement pillar. He read the decrees. He rushed after Hackendahl. 'Father, a state of war has been declared.' 'Father, the Kaiser says there are no parties for him now, only Germans. Aren't the Reds any longer Reds?'

'We shall have to see how they vote in the Reichstag. The Kaiser's too soft-hearted. He always thinks everyone is as decent as he is.'

'Hey, Father, the population is warned to look out for spies. So how does one recognize spies, Father?'

'We'll soon see. Just keep your eyes open, Bubi! A traitor quickly gives himself away through his bad conscience. He can't look straight.'

'Come, Father, let's see who's coming. Perhaps they're trying to spy out how many horses are here. That's possible, isn't it?'

But then he forgot about it. 'Father! Father!'

'Now what, Bubi? I've got to look after the horses.'

'Have you read about the golden motor cars, Father? The Russians are supposed to have three golden motor cars in Russia, and we are supposed to stop them.'

'They won't get across the frontier,' said Hackendahl with satisfaction. 'War's been declared on the Russians. The frontiers are closed.'

'But supposing they cross over to the French? We haven't declared war on the French yet. Why haven't we, Father? The French are our sworn enemies.'

'Everything in its turn. Just take it easy. The turn of the French will come and, what's more, the English. They want to take away our navy and our colonies; they're so jealous, that lot . . .'

The throng was becoming denser and denser. At first they had seen here and there a solitary butcher's or greengrocer's pony led by its owner to the requisitioning, but now they met troops of horses – the breweries were bringing along their heavy Flemish beasts, the riding schools their light Prussian ones. Lordly, bewhiskered coachmen led Hanoverian coach horses not all the best people thought a car quite the thing in 1914 – and, amid noise and bustle, acquaintances were hailing one another; cabmen greeted their colleagues; butchers whose horses are the most spirited (according to legend they get ox blood to drink every day) were already making their arrangements. 'If they take yours, I'll drive your meat. If they take mine, you drive for me.' (They had no notion how little meat there would be to drive very shortly.)

Hackendahl too saw many acquaintances – the small fry who had only one or two cabs in use, an undertaker whom he helped out with black horses when business was brisk, the furniture chap across the road whose ponies so quickly became footsore.

'G'day, George. Things humming, eh?'

'Lot of old crocks.'

'Oh, they'll send us all back with them. What are they to do with us? They've got their horses.'

'Have you heard? They say the French have bombed Stuttgart.'

'I've got to join up tomorrow – my business will go phut.'

'What d'you think they'll pay for the horses? They ought to give us a bit extra to make up for the loss of earnings.'

'You ought to be ashamed of yourself, you old profiteer. There won't be any earnings in this war.'

'And how's my mother to live?'

Yes, Hackendahl had a lot to do, he had to mind his horses and greet his friends. Highly respected in his district and in his business, he was a man to whom people listened. And they agreed with him when he said: 'We'd better make a job of it and rap the English over the knuckles too. What's Tirpitz got a fleet for?'

They turned off the main road. Between the last tenements, in a big open space, at other times used for a small weekly market, posts had been erected with halter rings. Here were the military, the soldiers in overalls and the officers in full dress and – Look there! What's that? What's that supposed to be? D'you know the uniform?

'Well, I never! What are they?'

'What's the uniform?'

Hackendahl nodded, as an old non-commissioned officer, as one who knew: 'Field-grey!'

'Field-grey!' The words flew from mouth to mouth. It was something new, this field-grey. Yes, in this war they wouldn't be wearing the familiar brightly coloured uniforms, they would be wearing field-grey . . .

'But why? What a pity! Nothing to look at in that.'

'Stop jawing, man. D'you want our lads to be used as targets?'

'Kaiser Bill will have discussed that with Moltke all right.'

'And the Frenchies don't wear red trousers any more. That's a pity, because I always thought you could make a red waistcoat out of your first prisoner.'

The requisition had started. Names were being called.

'Now let's see him trot . . . Gallop . . . That's all right. Legs are sound. Hi, lift up that leg; isn't the hoof split?' The veterinary surgeon looked at the horse's mouth, examined its teeth. 'Eight years old.'

'I bought it as a six-year-old, sir.'

'Eight!'

'Service Corps, wheeler, section two,' barked an officer.

A clerk made an entry, and a soldier took the reins from the owner. 'No, man, we keep the headstall. Didn't you read the official notice? "With halter." '

The owner held an order to pay. 'Three hundred and fifty marks. Look, Gustav, three hundred and fifty for my chestnut. That's not bad. That's reasonable.'

'Just right,' said Gustav. 'Not too much and not too little. Just right – like everything in the army.'

Now it was his turn. Horse after horse was led forward . . . Hackendahl did not lead them himself. That wasn't necessary. He had his own men for that. He himself was a big man and he was aware of it. He was not only giving the Fatherland his sons, he was giving his horses, his property. And it pleased him to make a sacrifice in these times. He stood by the group of officers, Heinz behind him. Bubi could not have beamed more happily at the officers than did his father. Ah, here was the old curt tone, the bark or the drawl, and decisions made in a split second. No interminable women's gossip. No come along tomorrow if you can't come today.

An officer's monocle flashed. 'Why are you hanging about, my man? What have you to listen to? You're behaving suspiciously.'

'Those are my horses,' explained Hackendahl.

'Yours? Oh, all right. As you were! What was the work?'

'Drawing cabs, Herr Oberleutnant.'

'Cabs? We'll be finding them something else to draw, ha, ha! But they're in good condition – understand horses, eh?'

'Sergeant-major in the Pasewalk Cuirassiers, Herr Oberleutnant.'

'Army man, understands horses, can see it. Bit light, bit on the small side, but in condition.'

Yes, the Hackendahl horses were in condition – anyone could see that. One after another was accepted. Hackendahl felt quite proud.

'Father, they're taking them all,' whispered Heinz excitedly. 'How are we to drive the cabs?'

'Don't bother about that now. The main thing is the army gets what it wants.'

'What's the matter with this grey, Sergeant-major?' asked the officer. 'Young, but no spirit. Something wrong with the bones?'

'No, sir. Her wind was broken five weeks ago. Frightened by a car. She's not been the same since. My best horse.'

'Car? Bad business! I mean . . . Oh, well, a horse is more elegant. Quite unserviceable, your grey.'

Yes, the grey was unserviceable. They also rejected the castrated stallion and after a while three other horses. 'Nice, but too old.'

'Yes, sir!'

Hackendahl received his bank draft, one for a very great amount. Much money, and the horses which worked for the business from which they lived all turned into money. It was a lot, yet little – a high, five-figure number. But it was his life's work, what he had built up, what he'd really worked for – a number written on a sheet of paper.

He looked at the sheet and thought how he had tended the horses day after day, and how before deciding on each sale he ran hither and thither ten or twenty times doing the negotiations. And he remembered how he had had to keep on at the drivers to ensure that they didn't break a horse's wind, or had stood behind an advertisement pillar to see for himself that the beasts were fed and watered on their stands. All this had taken the place of the army in his life and given it meaning. Now there was a void . . .

'Hoffmann, find your way home alone with the horses. I'm going a little further with Heinz.'

'Yes, Herr Hackendahl.'

'Harness up when you get home. There aren't many cabs nowadays, and we must see that we earn a bit.'

'The old grey too, Herr Hackendahl?'

'Yes, the grey too. You can take him yourself, Hoffmann.'

'Will do, Herr Hackendahl.'

'Come, Bubi, we'll go on a bit. I feel like it.'

'Yes, Father.'

'That soldier shouldn't hold that brown horse so short on the reins – its mouth is a bit sensitive.'

But it didn't make any difference. They weren't his horses any more. They belonged to the Fatherland.

§ VIII

They went a little way farther along the Frankfurter Allee. The houses became more infrequent. Then came gardens and small fields – and then the first really big cornfield lay before them – rye.

'Look, Bubi, rye, corn – half harvested, but not finished. It's ripe, all right. The war's interrupted them. I wonder who will harvest it.'

He looked over the wide fields; all was quiet and abandoned. No one was to be seen at work. People could only be seen walking and going about their business on the streets.

'It will happen, Bubi, just as I said earlier today to Rabause. Women will have to do men's work.'

'Mother too?'

'Of course, Mother too.'

'Oh, Father . . .'

'What's wrong with Mother? If she has to, she'll be able to. I must see that I register as a volunteer this afternoon.'

'But aren't you too old, Father? And you have trouble with your heart.'

'There's nothing wrong with my heart!'

'Yes there is, Father, sometimes you go quite blue.'

'Well, I'm going to register and they'll take me. You'll see!'

'But . . .'

'They'll take me! And now you hold your tongue, Bubi.'

'Then they'll take me too, Father!'

'You hold your tongue, Bubi!'

For a while they continued, silent. They turned onto a pathway and came upon a raised railway embankment.

'Where does the railway go, Father?'

'To Strausberg, Bubi. Then further to the east, till Posen or to Russia . . .'

'There's a train, Father!'

'Yes, I can see it too.'

Behind two puffing engines, from the direction of Berlin, came a train with numerous cattle trucks with open doors. Horses' heads looked out of the trucks, and soldiers in field-grey uniforms stood in the doorways. On the open trucks were artillery cannon. Bubi was jubilant. This was the first train going to the war they had ever seen, and father and son were equally excited.

'Father, Father! They're going to war. They're going against the Russians! Bravo!' shouted Bubi. 'Hit 'em where it hurts!'

The soldiers waved back, laughing. The father cried 'bravo' too and waved. Carriage after carriage . . .

'Forty-one, forty-two . . .' counted Bubi. And then: 'Father, what's that – that black thing with a chimney? It looks funny. Does it shoot too?'

'That's a field kitchen, Heinz. They're called goulash cannon too,' explained the father. 'They only fire food, not shells.'

'Forty-four, forty-five . . .' counted Heinz enthusiastically. 'Father, there are forty-seven wagons, not counting the coal tender . . .'

'Bubi!' whispered Hackendahl.

'Yes, Father?'

'Not so loud! Bubi, look over there, to the right of the bush . . . but not so that you're noticed, unobtrusively . . . Do you see the man in the willow clump?'

'Yes.'

'Look away. Now he's looking towards us. Pretend to do your shoelace up. What's that man doing all alone in that clump? It looks as though he's hiding.'

Bubi adjusted his shoelace, squinting as he did so.

'Father, he just put something white in his pocket. Looked like a piece of paper. Do you think he wrote down the train number?'

'What do you mean, wrote down the train number?' growled Hackendahl.

'Soldiers, horses, artillery? Could it be a spy, Father?'

'Quiet, Bubi, not so loud! He's looking this way again. Why does he always look at us? We're nothing to do with him . . .'

'He's got a bad conscience, Father. It's a spy!'

'We've got to consider it in cold blood. What can he be looking for in this lonely spot? If we hadn't turned up by accident . . .'

'Father! Father! Now he's whistling . . . perhaps there are others here?'

'Everything is possible.'

'Come, Father. We'll go to him and ask him what he's looking for here. And if he refuses to have anything to do with us, we'll arrest him.'

'But we can't just capture him. He'd merely run away.'

'I can run faster.'

'But you can't capture him on your own – and I can't keep up, because of my heart.'

'As I said – it is your heart!'

'Be quiet! He's noticed that we're looking at him. He's leaving. Let's go after him.'

'Let's go, Father!'

'But slowly, Bubi. Don't lose your head. It must look as though we're going for a walk. He mustn't get suspicious.'

'He's going towards the main road.'

'Naturally, he wants to get lost among the people . . .'

'But we'll catch him, Father.'

'Did you see, he turned towards us again! He's already worried.'

Father and son were equally on fire – youth and age ablaze! They followed the suspect, and did so unsuspiciously so that they would have given themselves away to the most innocent. They pointed to a lark in the blue sky with outstretched arms, while not letting the man out of their sight for a moment. If he went slowly, they stopped altogether. Bubi picked a flower. Father hummed 'Gloria, Victoria'. Then they continued, and the man, who turned round to look at them, ran faster . . .

'He's losing us, Father!'

'I can still keep up!'

But Hackendahl was already puffing. It wasn't just his heart, and it wasn't just the heat. It was the excitement: a spy! The main road was very close, and full of people.

'We can tell a bicyclist,' Hackendahl consoled himself. 'A bicyclist is bound to overtake him.'

The running man had almost reached the main road. But he didn't run any farther, he stopped one or two men and spoke to them animatedly.

'Would they be his accomplices?' asked Bubi.

'We'll soon see,' groaned the breathless Hackendahl, now a blue shade of red.

The men, the wanted man in the middle, stared silently at the two of them.

'There they are!' cried the man from the willow clump, unnecessarily loudly.

Hackendahl stepped onto the road, and the men crowded closely round him and his son with threatening faces.

'Gentlemen!' said Hackendahl. 'This is a—'

'Listen here,' said a pale-faced young man, 'what have you just been doing on the railway line?'

'That man there,' shouted Hackendahl and pointed with his finger, 'hid himself in a bush and made notes on a military train!'

'Me?!' shouted the other man. 'What cheek! He's turning everything upside down. I heard exactly how your young brat counted the wagons – you wretched spy.'

'You're the spy!' shouted Hackendahl and went redder. 'My boy saw exactly how you put something in your pocket.'

'And you?' said the other. 'Who behaved as if he was picking flowers? Do you look like flower-pickers? You're already quite red from your bad conscience.'

The other men had heard these increasing accusations with bewilderment, and looked uncertainly from one to another, exchanging questioning looks.

'Perhaps they're both spies,' asked one, 'and simply don't know of each other.'

'So why did you hide yourself in a bush?' said a serious man with a beard to the pale one. 'It does sound very suspicious.'

'To answer a call of nature,' explained the pale one.

'What was the white thing he put in his pocket?' shouted Hackendahl.

'Loo paper!' shouted the other man. 'I always carry it with me – for all eventualities.'

And he showed some.

'And why did your youngster count wagons?' asked the serious man with a beard. 'That sounds very suspicious!'

'For nothing,' said Hackendahl angrily. 'Youngsters always do that.'

'That's no explanation,' countered the other. 'Come with me and we're sure to find a police constable in the Frankfurter Allee.'

'But,' shouted Hackendahl, 'I've got my ID. I've got my papers!' And he hit his pocket. 'I was here for the horse inspection. I'm the hackney carriage man Hackendahl.'

'Let me see!' The bearded man looked through the papers. 'That's all in order – forgive me, please, Herr Hackendahl.'

'But, but, he's—'

'Thank you very much, but I have my papers too and am going to the inspection. I am the teacher Krüger.'

Some laughed, others mumbled earnestly.

'Apologies to you too, teacher Krüger. So neither of you were spies. Shake hands.'

'Herr Hackendahl, I'm very sorry.'

'Herr Krüger, you only did your duty.'

'Let's go back together.'

And they did. All were satisfied, and even a little elated. Only Heinz dragged his feet unhappily behind. It really upset him that it was not a spy after all.

§ IX

When Hackendahl arrived home he found awaiting him a slip of paper with the message: 'We leave today at two o'clock from the Anhalter Station. Otto.'

Extremely agitated, his wife was laying the table herself, a thing she hadn't done for years – she wanted them to be ready in time. Eva was busy in the kitchen.

As they were all sitting down to table, in came Erich who had spent the entire morning calling at one barracks after another, where he had waited for hours on end and been everywhere rejected: we can't deal with any more men. Come again in two or three months' time.

'Good, and in the meantime you'll be able to pass your final examination,' said Hackendahl.

But Erich did not want ever to see the school again. The weeks at the lawyer's had changed him. He felt he'd grown up. It seemed impossible for him to sit on a school bench again. 'Somebody told me that they're organizing a reserve battalion at the cadet academy in Lichterfelde. I'll try there tomorrow morning.'

'Don't be in such a hurry, Erich,' begged the mother. 'Perhaps the war will be over in three months and something might happen to Otto.' This sentence was a little confused but everyone understood. Erich busily hummed a popular song.

'You shouldn't think of such things, Mother,' expostulated Hackendahl. 'If a soldier was to think like that he couldn't fight.'

'I was leaning out of the window this morning at ten o'clock,' she wailed, 'and when the horses came back, only five out of our thirty-two beauties and the grey's head drooping so miserably again, I couldn't help thinking – that's how all the horses will look when they return. And what about my sons, too?'

There was a moment's embarrassed silence. Then Hackendahl rapped on the table with his knife. 'Be quiet, Mother! If you get into a state like this we won't take you to the station.'

'I'm not in a state,' she cried, wiping her eyes. 'I just couldn't help thinking of it when the horses came back. But I promise I won't cry at the station. Take me with you, Gustav!' And, with a touching attempt to smile, she looked at the others.

'All right, Mother. But we have to hurry now. Anhalter Station – that means France.'

But at the last minute it turned out that Eva didn't want to go; with tears in her eyes she said she really couldn't, she had a raging headache. She felt ill.

'Won't do!' said Hackendahl. 'You'll kindly go to the station when your brother is leaving for the Front. On such an occasion one can't have headaches or be ill.'

Weeping, Eva assured him that she really couldn't go; she'd fall down in the street . . . But, just as her mother shouldn't have gone to the station because of her tears, Eva had to go despite them.

'Just you stop that, girl!' Hackendahl, remembering Bubi's remark, had a sudden suspicion. 'Perhaps there's some fellow, eh? You've been behaving in a very strange manner lately. Wait till we get back and we'll have a word or two.'

Out of humour, the harassed family marched off and Eva saw Eugen waiting at the street corner where she was to meet him; she could do nothing but make a despairing gesture. He seemed to threaten her, and was then lost to sight.

She remembered that the flat was now only under the care of the maid. And Eva would credit Eugen with doing anything – anything! Even breaking into her parents' flat. At best she would like to have gone back, but what good would that have done? If he were really in the flat, not even her presence would have held him back from stealing. She had no power over him at all, but he had complete power over her.

Meanwhile, time had passed so quickly that they were on Alexanderplatz. They had to go, otherwise they'd miss the train. Erich light-heartedly suggested to his father that they take a motor taxi, and was rudely shouted at for doing so. And when Mother suggested a cab, that was also rejected as too expensive. Fortunately a horse-drawn omnibus came by, with enough room. Jolting and shaking, it got under way.

The town was as full of bustle as on the first day of mobilization. Cars stopped in the street, boys threw bundles of newspapers among the crowds, and passengers boarding omnibuses brought the news that war had been declared on France, and German troops had crossed the Belgian frontier . . . A momentary hesitation and shock. Belgium? Why Belgium? But this was no time for consideration – people were already starting to sing: 'Victoriously we will conquer France.' And amid approving laughter old people hummed:

> *Who's hiding in the undergrowth?*
> *Bonaparte, I take my oath.*
> *What right's he to hang about?*
> *Come on, comrades, chase him out.*

The bus could make no headway through the crowds so the Hackendahls descended and pushed forward in a column. The station! They had to get to the station.

'Pardon me, sir, if I kicked you but my son's going to the Front.'

'A pleasure, my dear sir.'

Thank God, the station at last! Only another minute . . .

Through the hall, up the stairs. Crowds on crowds. A brass band somewhere. One minute past two. 'The train should have left, but as long as the band isn't playing "Muss i denn" it's not too late,' panted Hackendahl.

So large was the crowd that they went through the barriers without taking platform tickets; the collector shouted after them but Hackendahl yelled 'France! Paris!' and laughed. Many joined in.

How long the train was! Men dressed in field-grey were looking out of the windows; their spiked helmets had field-grey covers with the regimental number in red. How serious were all their faces! Many women, pale and serious too, were on the platform, with flowers, yes, but flowers in trembling hands. And innumerable children, their faces also serious, some of the smaller ones weeping . . .

Military music played, but faces remained serious, talk was quiet.

'Do write, Father!'

'I'll send you a picture postcard from Paris.' A pitiful little joke saved up for the last moment. A faint smile in reply.

'And keep well.'

'You too – and the children.'

'Don't worry about the children – I'll look after them.'

'Where's Otto?' They hurried along the train. Suddenly it had become very important to see the unimportant Otto, to shake him by the hand, to tell him to look after himself.

'Look, there's Gudde, the dressmaker. You know her, Father, she altered my black dress. – With a child! – How long has she had a child? Why, she's a hunchback. – It must be a neighbour's child.'

'Who are you seeing off, Fräulein Gudde? What's your name, sonnie?'

'Good afternoon, Frau Hackendahl. There's Otto – I mean Herr Hackendahl.'

They rushed forward – Fräulein Gudde was forgotten. Till the train departed, the despised Otto was the central figure.

'Good luck, Otto!'

'Write sometimes, Otto!'

'I've brought you something to eat, Ottchen.'

'And if there's trouble, Otto, think of your father. It'd be a proud day if you got the Iron Cross.'

'Have you heard if there are to be any Iron Crosses in this war?'

Otto was standing at the compartment window, his face greyer than his uniform. He spoke mechanically, he shook hands, he put the parcel of food on the seat where her parcel was . . . And his eyes were forever seeking hers, the only person he loved with all the tenacity of a faint heart and who loved him with a strength that forgave all. Glowing and tender, she looked at him without reproach and without claim, standing by the pillar holding the boy's hand. 'Don't cry, Gustäving. Papa's coming back.'

Otto could read from her lips the words he could not hear. 'Coming back.'

No, he might not come back, but that prospect, strangely, did not alarm him. He was going to war, to battle, to hand-to-hand fighting, wounds and lingering death, but these did not alarm him. I shan't be a coward there, he thought. And yet I'm too cowardly to tell Father about . . .

He'd like to understand why, but is unable to. He looked at them helplessly, under his compartment window, the old familiar faces, and then he looked quickly over to the pillar, to that dearest, unique face . . . No, he can't understand.

'Otto, why, you've got flowers,' called out Bubi. 'Who gave you them? A girlfriend, eh?'

Everyone laughed at the idea that Otto, the shy Otto, could have a girlfriend. And Otto too screwed up his face into a miserable smile.

'Where is she, then?' Laughing, they all looked round for Otto's girl. 'The one in the blue dress? Looks smart but she might be too smart for you. She'd take the very butter off your bread.'

Again Otto smiled miserably.

'The Gudde woman's still there,' whispered Frau Hackendahl. 'Who does she belong to, Otto? Have you seen her?'

'Who?'

'Fräulein Gudde, our dressmaker. You know!'

'Yes . . . I . . . That's to say I . . .'

They all looked at him. He turned red. But they were not suspicious.

'Didn't you see who she's with?'

'No . . . no. I saw nobody.'

And now the band began to play 'Muss i denn', the train gave a jerk and started, handkerchiefs came out, hands were shaken a last time.

The solitary figure beside the pillar pulled out no handkerchief, neither did she wave. She was standing there as if for ever, patiently waiting till he returned. His eyes filled with tears.

'Don't cry, Otto,' said Father Hackendahl. 'You'll be back soon.' And very loudly, for the train was moving off fast now: 'You've always been a good son.'

Bubi ran alongside Otto's carriage the longest, right to the end of the platform. He saw the train disappear, all the handkerchiefs waving, a bend, the round, red disk on the last wagon – and away!

Heinz returned to his family.

'Now, be quick!' said Frau Hackendahl. 'I must see that I can still catch Gudde. It's interesting to see who exactly she is and who she saw off.'

Gertrud Gudde, however, had already disappeared, with her Gustäving.

§ X

The head of the surgery department stood, tired, in his consulting room and washed his hands, as he always did when he was exhausted. Out of pure habit, he scrubbed his nails with a hard little brush, washed them with disinfectant, rinsed and dried his hands.

He lit a cigarette, inhaled deeply, went to the window and looked, deep in thought, seeing nothing, at the hospital garden. Tired and exhausted, he'd been on his feet for eleven hours, and still couldn't see the end of it . . .

But, he thought, this is just the beginning. Just the beginning . . . he thought slowly, and without being very upset or despairing. This is just the beginning . . .

Four days' mobilization had cost him three-quarters of his doctors. They'd gone. 'Good luck!' they said, and went. Three-quarters of the doctors gone, not to speak of the nursing staff, and more would be required. So this was just the beginning . . .

He put his cigarette in an ashtray. He'd only taken one draw. Without thinking, he went back to the basin and began for the thousandth time the ritual washing and scrubbing of his hands. He didn't know he was doing it. Sometimes a colleague pointed it out to him, or a surgical nurse said: 'Herr Professor, you're washing yourself again. You were at the basin only two minutes ago.'

But now no one was there who could remind him. Carefully, he brushed his nails . . .

'Good luck!' they'd said, and went. But how could one have luck with barely a quarter of the normal number of doctors? It would have to be done badly, eyes closed, neglecting the worst faults . . .

It would cost lives, he thought sadly. As long as he had practised his profession, and stood around so many sickbeds, he'd never lost the sense that people's lives were at stake, not medical cases: mothers whose children at home were crying, and fathers on whose lives depended the fortune and welfare of little communities.

It's going to cost lives, he thought. But nothing will be as cheap as human life in the immediate future. And it will not only be the sick, the exhausted and the old who will die. The young will have to go too, the young and the healthy. The strength of the people will be systematically reduced, day by day, week by week, perhaps for months . . . And here I stand complaining that I'm half an hour late for a burst appendix!

He looked around and listened. Once again he stood at the basin and washed his hands. His cigarette burned in the ashtray, but that didn't bring him to consciousness. Gradually he became aware that someone might have knocked on the door, and when he said 'Come in', the door really did open and a nurse entered, rather embarrassed.

'Well, sister, what's happened?' he asked distractedly and dried his hands on the towel. 'I'm about to go on a round. Or is it a new patient?'

The nurse shook her head and looked at him. She had strange eyes, a little shy, yet defiant. She also had a pleasant face, young but bright. She probably hadn't had an easy life.

'I've a personal request, Herr Professor,' said the nurse quietly.

'If that's the case, you'd better go to your superior, sister. You're aware that you are under her.'

'I've already been to her,' said the nurse quietly again, 'but she refused me. And then I thought, Herr Professor . . .'

'No, sister, no,' said the doctor emphatically. 'First, I never get mixed up in the affairs of the nursing staff. Second, I really have so much on my plate.'

He looked at the nurse as if in conclusion, sighed, rolled up his sleeves and went to the basin.

'Herr Professor had just finished washing when I came in,' said the little nurse bravely. (His obsession was naturally known through-out the hospital.)

'Thank you, sister,' said the professor. 'You can tell the operation nurse – you know, Sister Lilli – that I'll be beginning again in ten minutes.'

And he let the water run over his hands.

'Yes, Herr Professor.' She looked at him hesitantly, with a worried look. 'Herr Professor, forgive me for bringing it up again . . . Earlier today they decided who can go to the Front . . . And I – I'm not allowed.'

The senior doctor gestured angrily. 'Not everyone can go!' he exclaimed. 'There's work here too, a lot of work, and necessary work.'

'But, Herr Professor! I must go. Tell the staff nurse that I can. You only have to say the word, Herr Professor . . .'

The senior doctor turned around, looked furiously at the young nurse and shouted angrily, 'For this nonsense you disturb my few free minutes! You should be ashamed, sister! If it's adventures with young men you want, you don't have to be a nurse! You can do that at every street corner. But that would probably be too boring for you – a whole lot of old women . . . Oh, leave me in peace, sister!'

But if the senior doctor expected the nurse meekly to withdraw after this strong and decisive put-down, he was mistaken. Sister Sophie stood her ground, without flinching or hesitation. Perhaps she had even lost some of the shyness from her expression, which was stronger and more defiant. The doctor observed this not with-out interest.

'It's not because of young men that I want to go,' she said deter-minedly. 'The staff nurse has just moved me down to the old people precisely for that reason, because I'm not suited to the male wards. I don't like men . . .'

'Sister,' said the professor quietly, 'you shouldn't give me lectures on your preferences. I'm not interested. Just go to your ward.'

'Yes, Herr Professor,' she replied with unyielding determination. 'But, Herr Professor, I've got to get out of here, and you've got to help me . . .'

'In heaven's name, sister!'

'Herr Professor, I've never been able to stand other people. I've never been fond of anyone – neither my parents nor my siblings. Nor the patients here either . . .'

'Wonderful, sister,' said the doctor sarcastically. 'Excellent!'

'No, I've never been able to like anyone, and no one has been able to like me either. I've always thought I was completely useless . . . And now suddenly – please, Herr Professor, listen to me a moment longer – suddenly war is here. I don't understand politics, Herr Professor. I don't know the how or the why. But I suddenly started thinking that I could perhaps be of use after all, and do some good and not be in the world for nothing.'

She looked at him for a moment.

'Perhaps the Herr Professor doesn't understand what I mean. I don't myself. But I think the others, the women, my sister and so on – they think they'll one day have children, and a man they are fond of. But I've never had anything like that, Herr Professor! I've never been able to imagine why I was in the world. My father—'

She broke off. Then: 'Herr Professor, don't think that I think of holding young soldiers' heads all the time, and giving them water . . . No, I think of marching, and doing work which disgusts me from morning till evening, to destruction and further. And then, Herr Professor, perhaps I'll feel that I'm not in this world in vain.' And then, almost sobbing: 'It's better to have been a bit more than a nothing in one's life . . .'

For a while silence reigned between them. The doctor slowly dried his hands, went towards the nurse, lifted her head with its sobbing face, looked her in the eyes and said softly: 'Sister, do you think that's why a great people goes to war, so that – what is your name?'

'Sophie Hackendahl.'

'– so that Sophie Hackendahl no longer feels superfluous in life?'

'How do I know?!' she shouted, almost out of control, impatiently freeing her head from his hand. 'But what I do know is that I am now twenty-one years old and have never for a moment felt that I'm of any use!'

'Well,' said the doctor thoughtfully, 'perhaps this war has also come so that people once again feel that they are of some use. Perhaps.' He looked at the nurse. 'I'll see what I can do with your senior nurse. I gather you are not exactly in her good books. But now I know that, on this at least, you are of precisely the same opinion.'

The doctor smiled. Sophie too smiled weakly, nodded her head in thanks, and left.

The senior doctor resumed his place at the basin.

§ XI

Eva, the other Hackendahl sister, had hurried her parents and siblings along to get home as soon as possible. Now she sat, empty and exhausted, in her room. No, there was no sign of Eugen. No desk had been broken into, the crazy little parlourmaid Doris had not been attacked or raped. Everything was exactly as it should be.

And that was the worst of it! That Eugen hadn't done anything yet, that was the worst of it. That he could still do everything and that the threat was still there, that one still had to wait – that was the worst of it!

Eva sat listening through the open window to her father talking with Rabause in the stable, and thought: yes, Father has nothing to complain of. He has his business, his stable and cabs. But I . . .

She heard her mother talking eagerly to Doris in the kitchen; Mother had nothing to complain of, either. Otto, whose lot had been the worst of all, had left, and he was now a respected, an honoured man, one who had something to do in life. And Sophie too had a job. She might carry it out grudgingly – that was just like her – but she had her job. And Heinz had his school and Erich was always up to something new, something different. But what had she herself got? A mere existence, shabby and common – Eugen waiting at the street corner, whistling on his fingers – for her. She belonged to him now. That was her job.

When the day before yesterday he had forced her to drink and she saw he would not relent, that he meant to have her at all costs and immediately – not because he wanted her but merely to make it clear she belonged to him in that way also, and had nothing left of her own – then an idea had occurred to her, a last hope which might tide her over the next terrible hour. She had asked: 'Eugen, won't you have to join up too?' (Because she had seen the war as liberation, just like her sister. Eugen would have to go, and when he returned – if he ever did! But people like him shouldn't ever return. Otherwise, what would be the point of war?)

He had looked at her oddly and sneered. 'You'd like that, wouldn't you, sweetie?'

'Of course not, Eugen. But all the young men have to go . . .'

'You see, my sweet, they won't have me. I'm exempted. My Fatherland loves me too much.'

'Exempted? But all the young men . . .'

'You needn't worry, Evchen, I shan't leave you.'

'But . . .'

'Yes, you'd like me to go to the Front, wouldn't you? Nothin' doing! Let the other mugs get shot to bits if they want.'

'But if you don't report, you're a deserter. And then . . .'

'You're slow on the uptake, what? I'm not a deserter, I tell you – I'm indispensable. My Fatherland don't want me taking part in the war. You still don't savvy? Well, you fool, I've lost my civil rights, ain't got them.'

'How do you mean?' She hadn't understood at all.

'Yes, dearest, when they put me in jug they pinched my civil rights for three years. An' now I'm not allowed to wear my Kaiser's uniform and you're pretty down about it, from what I can see.' He leaned across the table, grinning. Remembering him made her shudder. Not that she was particularly sensitive about such things, but that someone could be proud of his own disgrace!

He must have read her thoughts, because all at once he became angry and threatening. 'Ashamed, are you? Ashamed of your Eugen, eh? Get on your back, and I'll show you what I mean by shame – civil rights and all.' And he grinned again.

Then . . . it happened.

She sat quite still. Father was still talking in the stable. One heard the pails clatter. Mother was still in the kitchen. Bubi was whistling.

Suddenly she remembered Fräulein Gudde as she had been standing on the platform, a little crippled creature holding a healthy child by the hand, and shuddered at the thought that she too might have a child, by a fellow who was outwardly sound but inwardly corrupt . . . the little cripple had something from life that she would never have, because for Eva it was all over.

Taking a length of material from a drawer, she wrapped it up in paper and shouted out to Heinz: 'If Mother asks, tell her I've gone out for an hour.'

'Tell her yourself,' shouted Bubi, with maximum fraternal politesse. 'I'm not your message boy.' But she didn't want to tell her mother herself that she was going to the dressmaker, because her mother would immediately think she was going for *that* reason. But that wasn't why she was going. She was going for herself.

Is she walking there? No, she's almost running. And she's running as fast down the street as is becoming for a young girl in a long dress in 1914. In the street she kept on looking round to see if Eugen were following her; he was a nightmare, an ever-present danger. But she reached the quiet little side street unmolested. She crossed the yard and climbed the steps.

Fräulein Gudde answered the door at once. Her eyes were red and she looked almost hostile. The child was holding onto her skirts. He couldn't be more than two.

'Excuse me, Fräulein Gudde,' said Eva, somewhat put out by the unfriendly glance, 'I saw you just now at the station and that reminded me I had this material. It's a summer fabric and if I don't have it made up now it will lie about for another year.' She gave a feeble giggle, quite disconcerted.

'No, I'm sorry, Fräulein, no! I can't accept this work. No!' The negation, so bitterly repeated, increased Eva's confusion.

'But, Fräulein Gudde, what's the matter? You've always worked for us.'

'I saw at once,' said Fräulein Gudde passionately, 'that you had guessed. But he's my child, our child. You can't interfere there, you Hackendahls. No. My child! If Otto wasn't good enough for you . . .'

'Otto!' cried Eva, dumbfounded.

'Don't pretend you don't know. You ought to be ashamed of yourself. Yes, Otto, my Otto, not yours, not the Otto you turned him into, you Hackendahls, you and your father! Iron Gustav! So I should think!' And with a sudden change of mood: 'He's just gone to the Front and I'm worried about him already. But when he comes back

I'll see that he frees himself of everything Hackendahl. Then I'll bless the war, bless, bless . . .' She let her head fall against the door frame and wept in a heartbreaking manner.

Eva had listened wide-eyed to this outburst; now she timidly reached out a hand to the weeping woman. 'Fräulein Gudde, please, please don't. Think of the child!' For the little boy was standing there, trying to embrace his mother. 'Mummy, dear Mummy, don't.'

'Yes, yes, it's over, Gustäving. Mummy's laughing. She's laughing again, Gustäving. Fräulein Hackendahl, now you know what you wanted to know and you can go home. What letters you'll all be writing to him now! Not even at the Front will he be left in peace.'

'Nobody suspects Otto, believe me, Fräulein Gudde. We wouldn't have thought him capable of such a thing.'

'No, you never thought him capable of anything.'

'And nobody will hear about it from me. You shall have the child all to yourself. I understand, I do indeed, I understand how you hate everything belonging to the Hackendahls. I'm a Hackendahl myself and – I'm just as unhappy as Otto.' Now it was Eva's turn to weep, but she soon recovered. 'You see,' she said to the silent woman, 'I've no little one – and mustn't have, ever. That's my fate. That's why I came, because I saw you with such a fine, handsome child. I've always wanted to have children and so I couldn't help being envious when I saw you. You must understand that.'

Gertrud Gudde looked at her for a moment. Then she said: 'Come in, Fräulein Hackendahl.' Holding the child's hand, she led the way. 'Give me the material, Fräulein.'

And Eva handed it to her and the dressmaker fetched fashion books and made suggestions and asked: 'Would you like it this way?' and said: 'I shouldn't have leg-of-mutton sleeves, Fräulein Hackendahl, I'd have quite a small puff.'

And Eva gave the right answers, just as she would have done with any other dressmaker, and even began to be a little interested. The blue material with its white dots was really pretty and would make up quite well.

But suddenly the other said: 'One moment!' and went into the adjoining room, to return carrying something very carefully. 'Look at this crucifix he carved. Isn't it beautiful?' And without waiting for a reply: 'I could have sold it ten times over, but I wouldn't part with it. All the other things I took to the shop. They don't pay badly and the proprietor says he has it in him to become a proper artist, he only needs training and materials. But nothing will come of it,' she added with her former hostility, gently putting the crucifix down. 'He has to groom horses and clean out stables.'

Eva looked helplessly at Fräulein Gudde.

'Of course I've never talked to him as I'm talking to you. I always said: "Do what your father says, Otto." I realize that he's weak and that he'd only be unhappy if I encouraged him to quarrel with his family.'

'Perhaps he'll come back a different man, stronger,' said Eva carefully. 'You can't be for ever on your own here with the child, and if Otto's so gifted . . . Father has enough money.'

'Oh yes, I can be. I can quite well stay here alone with my child and wait for him. Then I'll have the child to myself and him too, even if it's only for a short time. As for money – I don't want a penny of your money. You people think money gives happiness, but all it's done is to make all of you unhappy.' She was looking angrily at Eva again. But seeing how pale and tired the girl looked she softened at once. 'No, I won't scold any more. You say you're unhappy like Otto. But you don't know how unhappy Otto is.'

'Nor do you know how unhappy I am,' replied Eva. She took herself in hand, however. 'When can I come to be fitted? Or would you prefer me not to come again? I won't say a word at home.'

'You can come every day – if you wish to see Gustäving.'

'And,' continued Eva, 'it's possible Mother may send for you or come herself. She's very inquisitive. You mustn't give yourself away in that case – Mother won't ever be connecting you with Otto. You can say Gustäving is a relative's child.'

'I tell a lie about Gustäving? Never! I'll tell her that he's my child. She can't ask me who the father is.'

'I'll go now, then,' said Eva, with a last glance at the little boy playing at the other end of the room.

Gertrud Gudde noticed the glance. 'Give him a kiss,' she said. 'I'm quite happy with you now.'

But Eva merely made a gesture of rejection, whispered, 'No, no' and went like a hunted woman across the passageway to the door, without saying goodbye. She opened the door, and only when she was on the threshold, said. 'Perhaps I'll come again tomorrow.'

'Good,' said Gudde and nodded her head.

'I was wondering,' said Eva, bending down to see the name on the bell, 'what your first name is. I see – Gertrud. I'm Eva.'

'He calls me Tutti . . .' said Gudde quietly.

'Goodbye, Tutti,' waved Eva.

'Goodbye, Eva,' said Gudde.

Then Eva went – back to the street.

§ XII

Gustav Hackendahl had had an exciting day, a great day, a proud day. That morning there had been the imposing exodus of his thirty-two horses, and the curious faces of people turning round at the clatter of hoofs on the road. Then there had been the muster itself and the officer who had praised his animals. One could even look back at the somewhat unexpectedly unsuccessful spying adventure with a little pride. And in the afternoon he had been one of the very first to send a son to fight for the Fatherland. In a few days a second son would be wearing uniform, too . . . Yes, it had been a proud day: there were not many men today in Berlin who had given as much to the Fatherland as he had. But then he had come home – to home and stables, forever his pride, and it felt so strange, deserted, empty . . .

For quite a while he stood in the stable holding a conversation with Rabause or, more exactly, describing in detail his recent experiences. Rabause naturally had a lot to do; now that only five of the thirty-two horses were back the whole stables had to be rearranged, and the old man was running here and there, toiling furiously with meaning looks at his employer, who did once or twice lend him a hand. But Hackendahl found it irksome. It was, he realized suddenly, a very long time since he had done any sustained manual work. Now he would have to join in occasionally. He'd have to learn how to do it again. It would probably even do him good. Would it really be necessary, though? With only five horses there was hardly work enough for one ostler. And Rabause had been thinking along similar lines. 'In the winter the stables will be too cold for just five horses, Governor,' he said. 'We'll have to build a partition.'

Hackendahl grunted. He was an enemy to all building – it ran away with so much money. 'By winter the war will be well over and then I'll get my horses back from the military.'

'We'd better not be so sure that the war will be over by the winter, Governor,' contradicted Rabause. 'In 1870 it went through the winter and we had only one foe then.'

'Don't talk nonsense, Rabause,' said Hackendahl angrily. 'What do you know about war?' And he left the stables abruptly; the prospect of working for months with no more than five horses was extremely mortifying. This isn't a hackney cab business any longer, he thought. Why, it's not much more than a day and a night cab. I might just as well clap on my top hat and wait on the stands myself.

Irresolutely he walked up and down the yard. If only the cabs would return! Then he'd have something to do. But he at once remembered that only five were left, that he could polish off the accounts with his eyes closed, and there were no night cabs to get ready . . .

There he stood, a man who had never doubted himself and did not do so now, but who felt very empty all of a sudden. Had he in fact lived only in the lives of other people, and not they in him, as he had always thought? He didn't know. He hadn't thought about it. He only knew that suddenly life had gone sour. Look at the children! Up till now they had been his; he had brought them up and made them familiar with the virtues of punctuality, hard work and obedience; he had bawled at them or been nice according to mood or circumstances. But now they had gone; they could manage without him. There was still Heinz, but Heinz wasn't easy to order about. Heinz was very independent – he never talked about what he did at school, for instance.

And, of course, there was Eva . . . Why, he had told her that very day that he was going to have a serious talk with her. Just as well he hadn't forgotten. Hackendahl hurried upstairs, he had found something to do. But a disappointment awaited him – Eva wasn't at home. That was another thing he'd have to talk to her about. He wasn't going to have this continual running off the premises. Children had to say where they were going and why – that was only right . . . And now he stood there once more at a loss.

'What are you doing, Bubi?'

'My Latin scriptum, Father.'

Hackendahl looked in a puzzled way at the copybook. 'Can't you write better than that? That's a terrible scrawl.'

'Pooh, Father, our Latin coach scrawls much worse; he can't read his own writing. We have to help him.'

'Never mind, Bubi, you yourself must write neatly.'

'Yes, Father.'

And that was that. Nothing more to be said. Hackendahl cast another glance at what Heinz was now doing – the writing didn't seem to have improved much since he had spoken. It was no use arguing with the boy, however.

Hackendahl went into the kitchen.

His wife sat there drinking coffee.

Hackendahl sniffed. Not malt coffee but bean coffee, which he had forbidden except on special occasions, forbidden a hundred times, and he now forbade it for the hundred-and-first time, breathing fire and fury – he wouldn't have it, he didn't find money lying on the ground . . . And for the hundred-and-first time Frau Hackendahl had at least half a dozen valid reasons for her transgression. Otto had had to go away that afternoon; the heat had given her a headache; hurrying to the station had upset her; she had only had five beans in with the malt coffee; and so on and so on.

Somewhat refreshed by his outburst, Hackendahl went to his room. On the desk lay a file containing papers relating to the requisition, and it occurred to him that among them was an army warrant for a considerable sum. He looked at his watch; there was still time to go to the bank. The file under his arm, he marched off.

It looked rather empty behind the counter, but the clerk who usually served him was there and greeted him with his customary quiet politeness. 'Well, Herr Hackendahl, have you come to fetch a little money?' And in a whisper: 'It has just come through. Banknotes no longer redeemable against gold.'

'What d'you mean?' asked Hackendahl, annoyed. He was always annoyed if he did not understand something at once.

'There won't be any more gold in exchange for banknotes. Gold is withdrawn from circulation.'

'Well, it's sure to be for the best,' said Hackendahl. 'We must do what the government wants. I've had to deliver up my horses, too.' And he pushed the warrant over the counter.

The clerk looked at it. 'Pretty nice sum,' he said appreciatively. 'But the horses were pretty nice too, eh? On current account, Herr Hackendahl? For the present – yes, of course – I understand. Perhaps you'll be buying some stocks and shares later. I believe good shares will be getting cheap, people are selling.'

'I'll think it over,' said Hackendahl, adding very suddenly: 'Perhaps I might buy a few taxicabs instead . . .' Not that he really intended this – the idea had just occurred to him – but it would be interesting to hear what the bank chap thought about it.

And the man, of course, was enthusiastic. 'Excellent idea, Herr Hackendahl!' he said. 'There's no doubt you move with the times. Horses are done for.'

'If horses were done for, the army wouldn't be paying so much for 'em, young man,' said Hackendahl dryly. 'By the way, why haven't you joined up yet?'

'At present I'm being retained by the bank,' replied the young man importantly. 'Indispensable!' This last word he pronounced in a very insufferable manner, or so Hackendahl felt, who stumped out of the bank with a surly 'Good luck to you!' The bumptious and disgusting ass!

On the advertisement pillars they were already sticking up the announcement that banknotes could no longer be exchanged for gold. What did he care? He'd never thought in his life of taking his notes to the Reichsbank for that purpose, nor did he intend to do so in the future. Why worry? Money was money, whether in paper or gold . . .

In the Kleine Frankfurter Strasse it occurred to Hackendahl that in the neighbourhood there was a tavern frequented by horse-dealers – he'd look in and see if anybody was there, and find out whether there were any horses for sale. A few more in the stable would come in very handy.

The place was crowded, and he received a great welcome.

'They caught you on the hop this morning, Gustav! Nag after nag! But yours were all fine ones!'

'And it'll cost you a pretty penny to buy some fresh ones. You'll have to add more than a bit, you know, Gustav.'

'Are there any horses going, then?'

'Not today. In two or three weeks perhaps. I think I can collect some in East Prussia.'

'I'm going to Holland . . .'

'The Danes also have some nice little beasts.'

'There'll be horses on hand again, but heaven knows what they'll cost!'

'Don't talk rubbish. Gustav can afford to pay.'

'If they aren't too dear for me . . .'

'Listen to Gustav! How can they be too dear? You've got your stable and your cabs, so you've got to have horses too. How can they be too dear in that case? You've got to have them.'

'Or shut up shop.'

'Gustav shut up shop! You make me smile. He'll be hiring cabs out when I'm pushing up the daisies. He's made of iron, is Gustav. Ain't that so, Gustav?'

It did one good to be surrounded with so much recognition, so much approval. These men realized what he had achieved. To turn his father-in-law's bankrupt business into the paragon of stables had been no small attainment. Much work, thought and worry had gone into it; not so easy, coping with thirty drivers who were fond of their drop! At home they took it all for granted. Here they understood.

'And do you remember, Gustav, how old Kublank wanted to force the chestnut mare on you? The one he doped with arsenic? But you weren't having any.'

Stories of horses long dead, of horse-dealers no longer in business – ancient stories. But it was heart-warming. Hackendahl stayed sitting much longer than he had wanted to. But what was there to do at home?

They all ate their evening meal over their beer – cold meatballs or hot sausages with potato salad. And they even went on after. One of them knew a special beer bar nearby. There they sat round a large table, confronting a small stage with a mixture of curiosity, expectancy and naivety. On it a chanteuse sang shrilly, a miserable conjuror made miserable rabbits disappear, and to finish did card tricks which the horse-dealers could do better. Then a dancer threw up her white lacy layered dress and ran round and round showing her underclothes. The men applauded enthusiastically.

And then came a supplement – the owner was up to date. On the stage stood two girls, one of them with weapon and helmet – a simple soldier. The other had a sword and monocle, distinguishing her as an officer. The soldier was supposed to drill, but didn't want to. The officer shook her sword, made explosive sounds, even lost her monocle – but the soldier didn't move. She refused to drill.

That was all. It quickly turned out that the soldier thought she knew enough. She wanted to go to Paris! To Paris! The officer was delighted with this thought. She caught hold of her soldier, and the two waltzed the Victory Waltz to Paris. Patriotic flags were waved from the wings, Bengal lights glowed. The piano thundered out the national anthem, and the audience stood and sang. All were enthusiastic and in earnest.

Only as he went home did Hackendahl realize that his reaction was not one of total enthusiasm. One could see from the two girls that their rifle drill had not been a success. Girls didn't understand such things.

Anyway, such things shouldn't be attempted. Victory Waltzes to Paris – that made it look as though you need merely dance there, as if there were no need to fight – as if all the military work done in peacetime were superfluous. No, you couldn't do it like that!

Hackendahl promised himself never to enter this public house again. He also didn't want to be seen very soon again by the dealers. They should now do some work for a change and find some horses. A man of self-esteem doesn't drink more than he can take.

He went to his coach yard. Normally he would begin by going into the stable. Only a stable lamp was lit. Rabause was not there. It was clear that it wasn't worth paying stable security for five horses.

Hackendahl entered the grey's stall. The animal stood there, tired, head hanging low. It had enough hay in its rack, but it had a few stalks of straw in its mouth from its bedding, and had forgotten to eat them. So it stood there, rejected, stalks of straw protruding from its mouth, looking miserable. It hadn't got over the race. It had overdone it. Hackendahl thought to himself that the grey would never again recover.

But he didn't need to eat straw, or hay either. Hackendahl had something better for his grey. When earlier in the cabaret they finished with a cup of coffee, the waiter had put a bowl of sugar on the table. The horse-dealers had naturally all reached for the bowl, including Hackendahl. They emptied it, not for their coffee, but for their horses. In public houses where horse-dealers regularly assemble bowls of sugar are not put on the table. Individual sugar lumps are handed out – sugar bowls are emptied too quickly.

Hackendahl offered the sugar to his grey, who turned its sad blue eyes towards its master in the yellowing light. It snuffled his hand and the sugar with its lips – and sank its head again.

'Don't you want it?' said Hackendahl, suddenly annoyed. 'Well, leave it alone then!'

But he no longer wanted to share the sugar among the other horses. Angrily, he left the stable. He went upstairs, wondering in what way he normally went up at night – whether loudly or softly. But he couldn't decide. In any case he'd no need to be particularly quiet: he hadn't drunk more than he could stand.

At the top he stood still for a moment, thoughtful. Of course he must make his usual evening round; he didn't want anyone to think that he'd been drinking.

Opening the door into the boys' bedroom, he was surprised to find how dark it was. Then he recalled that he was doing his round much later than usual, which was why it was so extremely dark. It was night. What could the time be?

Cautiously, on tiptoe, he groped his way into the room and passed his hand over the top of the bed. He felt it once again; yes, he was right, the bed was empty. He stood lost in thought. It wasn't right. It was all wrong. The bed shouldn't be unoccupied. A son should be asleep in it. And he considered what he ought to do now. Ought he to reprove the boy? But how could he reprove a boy who wasn't there? Ought he then to scold the others? Of course he ought to! They should have kept their eyes open. It was always the same – let him be out even for a moment and everything went wrong.

He groped for the second bed. That bed, too, was empty.

Over his distressed features spread a smile – just as well that he had had a look round. Now he had caught two absentees. If the third son was also out – well, he'd show them what order meant in his house!

But the third boy was there, quietly sleeping in his bed. Feeling about in the dark, his father seized a lock of hair and pulled it. 'Bubi!'

There was a sigh.

'Bubi!'

'I'm asleep . . .'

'Bubi, where are the others?'

'What others?'

'Otto.'

Heinz sat up, gazing sleepily at the dark figure. 'Otto?'

'Yes. Stop repeating the name!'

'Father, you went with Otto yourself to the station.'

'I went with Otto?'

'Yes, when he joined up.'

Hackendahl became embarrassed. 'I mean Erich.'

'Erich?' asked Bubi, to gain time.

'Yes, Erich. Where's Erich?'

'Erich?'

'Yes, Erich. Where's Erich I want to know.'

By now Heinz had begun to understand and at once set about concealing Erich's absence. 'Erich – he's been helping Mother settle with the cabmen. You weren't here. Where have you been, Father?'

'I went to the bank,' said Hackendahl peevishly. 'But Erich . . .'

'The banks close at five, Father. Where did you go afterwards? Do tell me! Were you outside the Schloss?'

'I was making enquiries about new horses. We must have some. But Erich . . .'

'New horses? Oh, that's fine, Father.'

'There are no horses to be had in Berlin at present. But they'll be here soon. Then we'll get some.'

'Splendid! Father?'

'Yes?'

'Lie down here for a bit! You won't disturb Mother then. She's been asleep for a long time.'

'It won't disturb your mother. She never hears me coming to bed. But I won't take Erich's. Besides, where is he?'

'He was helping Mother with the cabs. Wait, Father, I'll help you off with your boots, then we can talk. I love talking in bed.'

'I won't take Erich's.'

'Otto's bed is also free, Father, and it's more comfortable than Erich's. Wait, Father, I'll hang your jacket here. We needn't switch on the light; nobody'll notice anything . . .'

'Notice what?'

'Hoffmann says they don't want to take out the cabs tomorrow, but the luggage vans. There'll be a lot doing for them, he thinks.'

'Rubbish! Luggage vans! Who's going to go away now?'

'But they're all coming back from the holiday resorts. They're clearing out and want to get home quickly, because nobody thought there'd be a war. There are hundreds at the stations with trunks – and no carriages to be had, Hoffmann says.'

'Oh, Hoffmann!' Hackendahl pulled the blanket over him. 'I must think about it. Carting luggage means wearing out the horses.'

'Father!'

'Yes?'

'You must have had a strenuous time with the horse-dealers.'

'Why strenuous? All business is strenuous. And there were no horses.'

'No, I was only thinking of the drink. You carry it magnificently, Father, but it's just as well Mother doesn't know.'

'Doesn't know what?'

'Well, that you'd had one over the eight.'

'Me? Not at all. It just seems like that to you because of the darkness. I was in the stables till now.'

'And whose bed are you lying in, Father?' giggled Heinz.

'Whose bed? Don't be silly! As if I don't know!'

'Well, tell me then. In Otto's or Erich's?'

'Bubi, Otto's gone to the Front. You said so yourself.'

'Well?'

'Then this must be Erich's bed.'

Heinz shook with laughter, hiding his face in the pillows. But his father's voice reached him. 'Bubi!'

'Yes, Father?'

'I didn't look at the girls. Help me out of bed. I must go and see whether they're at home.'

'The girls, Father?'

'Yes, help me out of bed, I feel a bit giddy.'

'But Sophie lives at the hospital, Father. For some time now.'

'Yes, that's a fine thing, that! But I won't have it. Five children – and not one of them at home.'

'I'm here, Father.'

'But where's Eva?'

'She's been in bed a long while.'

'I want to make sure.'

'Let me go – you'd only wake her up. Then she'd tell Mother.' Slipping out of bed, Heinz went into the adjoining room.

Hackendahl propped himself up on the pillows. I should have gone myself, he reflected. You can't rely on Bubi either.

Bubi came back. 'Eva's asleep, Father.'

'That's the real truth, eh?'

'Eva's sleeping, really and truly. She's lying on her side and snoring.'

'Well, that's all right. Then we'll go to sleep too. Goodnight, Bubi.'

'Goodnight, Father. Sleep well.'

§ XIII

Conversation in the dark.

'What I wanted to ask was why didn't you come when you got the wink?'

'Father was there!'

'So your father counts more than me?'

'And I had to say goodbye to Otto – he was going to the Front.'

'So your brother also counts more than me?'

'What else could I do, Eugen? Don't go on at me so. You upset me.'

'Well, you let me tell you something now, my girl, about bein' upset and all that. When I whistle, if you don't come from now on in

spite of your father and your mother and the whole blooming shoot,
there's going to be trouble. Got me?'

'Yes, Eugen.'

'There'll be a bloody row.'

'Yes, Eugen.'

'Yes, Eugen. Always "Yes, Eugen!" Got any idea what I'm like
when I cut up rough?'

'Yes, Eugen.'

'And you'll do whatever I tell you?'

'Yes, Eugen.'

'An' I'm more to you than your father and brother?'

'Oh! . . . Yes, Eugen.'

'That upset you, didn't it? Say it again.'

'Yes, Eugen.'

'I'll upset you a bit more. You're dossing here tonight.'

'Oh, Eugen, Father . . .'

'Father! Father! Who's Father?'

'Oh!'

'Come on, out with it, immediately: Father's mud. Say that or I
don't know what I'll do.'

'Father's mud.'

'That's right. Tonight you're staying with me.'

'Yes, Eugen.'

'And when your old man chucks you out tomorrow you'll turn up
here.'

'Yes, Eugen.'

'You want to come to your Eugen, don't you?'

'Yes, Eugen.'

'You like me better than father or mother?'

'Yes, Eugen.'

'See, you're eating out of me hand already. I c'd take on six like
you. You'll come to like it in time, you see if you don't. An' you'll
even like me too. D'you like me, Evchen?'

'Yes, Eugen.'

'Silly bitch! Get up, put your duds on and buzz off to your old
man. Quick, d'you hear? You get on my nerves. You hopping it
or not?'

'Yes, Eugen.'

'Well, maybe you'd better stay.'

'Yes, Eugen.'

'But you'd rather clear out?'

'As you like, Eugen.'

'All right, then hop it, idiot. But when I whistle . . .'

'Yes, Eugen, then I'll come.'

§ XIV

The young man in field-grey uniform ran up the steps in great bounds, two at a time. Without thinking, he rang the bell several times, and then twice more when no one immediately opened. Fleetingly he looked at the nameplates, many of them – big but plain, black on white enamel: 'Justizrat Dr Meier – lawyer and notary. Consulting hours from 10–1, 3–6. Member of the Reichstag.'

His finger approached the bell again – then the door opened.

'Why in such a hurry?' asked the person who opened the door in a deep voice. 'Herr Justizrat is not yet available. Oh, it's you, Erich. Come in. I'll tell him right away.'

'I'll tell him myself!' shouted Erich and ran straight into the deputies' room.

The heavily built, swarthy man was reading a newspaper. 'I don't want to be disturbed just now,' he said, but already recognized the disturber of the peace. 'Oh, Erich! Erich in uniform! You've managed that very quickly! I hear the whole army is overrun with volunteers. Where have you ended up?'

'In a reserve battalion in Lichterfelde. Three thousand registered and they took a hundred and fifty!'

'Including you. Excellent. I always said: you'll manage to get whatever you really want. And so you wanted to show your uniform to us Red comrades. You look good! Smart – the height of Prussianism.'

'I didn't come because I wanted to show myself in uniform! I'm not so stupid, Herr Doctor.'

'Perhaps, Erich, it is not so stupid after all? It must be a fine feeling for many to wear such a uniform. After all, you're defending us. You even want to die for us!'

'Of course, I too am pleased to be a soldier. But really not because of the uniform!'

'And the Prussian atmosphere – you like it? Screaming orders used to be like a red rag to a bull for you! Or is there no more screaming?'

'Yes, there is,' admitted Erich. 'It's horrible. Sometimes I can hardly control myself. And the screaming's not the worst, but the mocking and the bullying if someone can't do what he's supposed to! Some who've never done gymnastics really cannot do things . . . So they come under the hammer every day for hours on end.'

The politician looked attentively at Erich's excited face. 'Now, my dear Erich,' he said. 'I hope you can hold your tongue, Prussian-style. The war code is very strict, and rebellion is punished by death. I did once tell you you were really a rebel,' he added. 'You will always rage against any compulsion, to the point of your own destruction.'

'But now I can hold my tongue, Herr Doctor,' shouted Erich proudly. 'You can do anything when it's worthwhile. I think all the time: for a quarter of a year we'll do training, then we get to the Front and can fight!'

'Perhaps you'd rather come out, Erich. England's declared war on us now. Did you know already?'

'England as well?' exclaimed the young man, upset. 'But why? Our cousins of the same blood, and the Kaiser's a close relative. Why on earth?'

'Because we've infringed Belgian neutrality. That's what they say. And we really have.'

'But,' exclaimed the young man, 'England's broken hundreds of agreements in its history! It never respected the law when it was a question of the rights of its own people. And now it's a question of our rights.'

'They speak of Christianity and mean cotton!' quoted the Reichstag deputy, with a sinister smile. 'They say Belgian neutrality and mean our fleet and our colonies.'

'But England owns almost a fifth of the world. What do our few colonies weigh against that?'

'A rich man is never rich enough. We're going to have a hard time, Erich. Get it clear in your mind that almost the whole world hates Germany.'

'But why? We only want to live in peace . . .'

'Because we're divided. Because they can never understand us. They always want to, but Germany, my boy, cannot be understood. You must love it or hate it.'

'Yes,' said the young man, 'now I know why I came here . . . I was right after all, Herr Reichstag Deputy, Herr Social Democrat! You love Germany too – because you also voted for the war credits, all of you, one after another.'

'Yes,' admitted the parliamentarian, almost embarrassed. 'We approved the war. The Reich Chancellor's speech was lamentable. He told us the truth, but not the whole truth. Much remained obscure . . .'

'And you voted Yes!'

'Austria's position is ambiguous. The Kaiser speaks of a Nibelung oath, but those we came to the aid of haven't yet declared war on Russia. The gentlemen in Vienna want to pursue their punitive little war against Serbia, and we've got to take on the rest of the world for them.'

'And yet you said Yes!'

'Yes, because we love Germany, Erich. Endless mistakes have been made by the Kaiser, by this philosophizing Chancellor – by everyone. But you can't leave a child in the lurch because of mistakes – or its mother . . . We voted Yes. We couldn't do otherwise. The whole people said Yes, Erich. And we didn't want to be different. Let's just hope against hope that our rulers will be different in war from what they were in peace . . .'

'Everything will be different,' said Erich.

The parliamentarian looked doubtful.

'You'll be doing square-bashing on the barrack parade ground, as ever, Erich. And behaviour in government offices won't change. Now the *will* and the *faith* of the people are *one*, and they'll stick together. If they don't use this moment, if they don't take up their positions without stupid arrogance at the Front – if they let this opportunity pass unused as well, then, Erich, a terrible time will come. Then everything will come apart, and their time will be over.

Today everyone believes in Germany, everybody loves Germany. But if they lose this belief, this love – what then? Perhaps never again.'

'We will not lose them,' said Erich. 'They can make us do square-bashing, they may be arrogant. But they don't count. There are only a few of them. When I hear them shouting on the parade ground, I always think it's my father. It's his way of shouting, his expressions. I hated it so much, it was so unbearable to me, that I often shook at the sound of his voice.'

He paused for a moment, and then said quietly: 'Now I sometimes think he can't be any different. He's become like that. Deep down he loves us – in his own way.'

The parliamentarian shook his head a little. 'That's an excuse we can't accept, Erich. Like that, you could excuse every injustice and nastiness. However, I observe you've undergone a remarkable transformation, my son. Something certainly is changing in the Germans. The most rigid party functionary is changing. And it isn't just ultra-patriotism. Long may it remain, Erich. And may you not miss the moment. Perhaps it will never come again.'

§ XV

The Upper Third was in turmoil. Five minutes ago the bell had rung for lessons after the Long Interval but no master had yet arrived, which happened frequently in the period just after the outbreak of war. More than half the staff had been called up and the school was compelled to carry on with the aid of a few overworked assistant teachers unfit for service; the boys revelled in an unaccustomed freedom. The war, the victorious advances in Belgium and France, the military successes encouraged them to kick over the traces. They felt themselves members of an all-conquering nation: they were the sons and brothers of heroes. When flags were displayed, when church bells rang for the fall of Liège or Antwerp, that was also their glory, their success, their victory.

The pale, bespectacled assistant teacher from the adjoining classroom popped his head through the door and said imploringly: 'Boys, boys!'

'Be quiet a moment! He wants something!'

'My brother wrote that in one cellar they found so many barrels of wine . . .'

'Boys!'

'Do be quiet.'

'They simply knocked the bottoms out . . .'

'Silence, I tell you! Silence!' The teacher was purple with rage.

'Are *you* taking us, Herr Professor?'

'No, but I should like to take the class next door and with the noise you are making that's quite impossible.'

'Nobody is making any noise here.'

'Who's making a noise? I'm not. You, Hans?'

'You're the only one making a noise here, Herr Professor.'

'You ought to be ashamed! You call yourselves Germans? A German lad does what he is told. Only those who have learned to obey can command.'

But the unfortunate man had struck the wrong note – they turned spiteful.

'You've no right to give us orders.'

'Why aren't you at the Front?'

'At the Front you can order people about as much as you like.'

'If you're unfit for active service you've got no say.'

The assistant teacher turned very pale. 'To be ashamed,' he murmured. 'It's horrible . . .'

He took a few steps towards the dais, thought better of it, turned quickly round and left the room.

For a moment there was an awkward silence – and they felt a little ashamed after all.

Then a voice shouted: 'The German says Auf Wiedersehen and not Adieu.' Laughter. 'Gott strafe England,' shouted another. More laughter. 'And all teaching swine!' Thunderous applause. Two or three then started the song at that time on everybody's lips, the song of revenge:

> *What do we care for Russian or French?*
> *Bullet for bullet and blow for blow.*

And more and more joined in till they came to the refrain, when all took it up, the boys marking time with the lids of their desks.

We have one foe alone – England!

'Silence, please!' It was a quiet but very distinct voice from the dais.

In front stood their teacher, who had entered unnoticed during the singing – an elderly man with a high, bulging brow and a mane of red hair streaked with grey. His blue eyes flashed. Professor Degener, teacher of Latin and Greek, a pot-bellied little man, poorly dressed. 'Go to your places!'

Shamefaced, they pushed themselves through the benches, cursing under their breath. 'Make room, stupid.'

'Stupid yourself – just don't go to sleep.'

'You'll be for it!'

'Oh lummy! If I get jankers, they'll throw the book at me.'

'Degener's in a rage!'

'The class has behaved atrociously,' said the teacher amid a deep silence. 'Not only is it un-German to reproach someone else with a physical defect' – he spoke German as if he were translating from his beloved Latin – 'but it is regarded as disgraceful by all the nations of the world, even by the English. Indeed, it is disgraceful anywhere. Herr Tulieb is suffering from an affliction of the lungs and ought to be in a nursing home. But he is instructing you instead, because at present there is a shortage of teachers. One can die for one's country in other ways than on the field of honour. Shame on you!'

He stood over them like a flame. They sat below. Some hung their heads, others looked glumly out of the window. A few, however, looked straight at the angry teacher.

'Three of you,' said Professor Degener, 'the three who regard themselves as the most guilty, will now repair to the next room and apologize to Herr Tulieb in front of his class. They will request him to forgive them. Understand, boys, this is to be no mere form of words but an expression of your guilt and repentance. Your repentance!' He looked round the class. 'I shall leave you for five minutes.

During that time the class will decide upon the punishment to be self-imposed for its disgraceful behaviour.'

'That's one to the jaw!' came a whisper.

'Five minutes!' repeated the teacher, running his eye over his flock before hurrying out of the room, his little thin legs supporting his egg-like pot belly.

'One up for the old beast!' someone said.

'Choose your words, man,' said another, hitting the first boy on his biceps. 'Degener's quite right. Who's going to apologize?'

They looked at one another, embarrassed.

'Well, me to begin with,' said Hoffmann. 'Then – how about you, Hackendahl?'

'I don't mind. But I won't do the talking.'

'I'll go too,' said Porzig.

'No, not you, Porzig, you'll have to confer here about our self-punishment. But think of something that's going to satisfy Redhead – it'll have to be pretty stiff. You'd better be the third, Lindemann.'

They hurried away and knocked. 'Come in,' croaked Tulieb. Then he recognized them. 'Leave this room at once,' he cried.

The other class looked in delighted malice at the three penitents.

'Hoffmann and Hackendahl in Canossa!' shouted someone quite loud. 'Fetch some snow. It'll make kneeling cooler.'

'Sir, we've come . . .'

'Will you do what I tell you here, at least? Get out of this room! I don't wish to see you.' Herr Tulieb was not a magnanimous victor.

'We behaved like swine,' said Hoffmann hoarsely. 'We beg you to forgive us.'

'Forgive you? That's easily said. You disparaged my honour.'

'Do forgive us, Herr Tulieb,' cried Heinz. 'From now onwards we'll behave decently.'

'Will you?' Herr Tulieb smiled. 'I want this class to look at you lads and take an example from the melancholy results of disobedience . . . You're not going to be let off as easily as this, however. Has Professor Degener punished you?'

'No.'

'Naturally – he has left it to me. I can see in your faces that you're the three ringleaders . . . You're to write out three hundred times the line *Sunt pueri pueri, pueri puerilia tractant.* Translate, you!'

'Children will be children and do childish things,' said Heinz.

'Children, yes! That's how I regard you. Now go!'

Silent and furious, the three boys stood in the corridor.

'I could see you hesitating, Hackendahl,' whispered Lindemann. 'You were absolutely furious.'

'I certainly was! But I thought how as a soldier you had to let yourself be shouted at without pulling a face. I only wobbled a little.'

'*Merde,* we have to copy out the sentence 300 times and we never said a word!'

'It was mainly Lange, the wretched swine.'

'Well, there's nothing to be done now. Do you want to hear what the others have hatched out meanwhile?'

It was not too alarming: the class had decided to spend the next four Sundays helping with the harvest on the municipal estates, since labour was scarce and the harvest very much behind.

'Moderate!' declared Hoffmann. 'Will Redhead consider it enough?'

'And you? How did you get on with Old Four-Eyes?'

'Oh, don't let's talk about it . . .'

And indeed they had no time to do so, for Professor Degener now returned. 'Is it all settled? Good! No, thank you, I don't want any particulars. I'm quite sure you've arranged everything properly. Now, before taking out our Caesars, we have something to do. Stand up!'

They stood.

'Attention! The class is informed that two old boys, both of whom had been in the top form, have made the supreme sacrifice: Günther Schwarz, private in the 3rd Foot Guards, and Herbert Simmichen, volunteer serving with the 3rd Battery of the 15th Field Artillery. *Dulce et decorum est pro patria mori . . .*'

A moment's silence.

'Sit down! I will read you the reports of their Commanding Officers about the death of your classmates . . .'

§ XVI

'There's still a ring missing. Where's yours, Evchen?'

'I haven't got one, Father.'

'Of course you have – one with a brown stone. Isn't that so, Mother? Evchen had a ring?'

Frau Hackendahl sat tearfully at the round table whereon her husband had placed all the gold in the house – his beloved large watch with its heavy chain, her small enamelled one with a gold brooch for pinning it to the breast, a gold pencil case, a pair of large cufflinks – the value doubtful – a gold cross and thin chain which Sophie had been given on her confirmation, wedding rings that age had worn smooth and thin, a gold brooch and false pearl hanging from it, together with seven ten-mark and five twenty-mark gold pieces.

Everywhere, on walls and on advertisement pillars, was placarded the appeal: Gold I gave for Iron. Bring your gold to the Gold-Purchase Centres. The newspapers wrote daily about it. Gentlemen were much admired who were already wearing the thin iron chain that had replaced the gold one in their waistcoats.

'Not a bit of gold is to remain in the house,' said Hackendahl. 'We must give up the lot. Isn't there anything else? Mother, didn't you have some little things or other in the ears once – not earrings, more like buttons? I seem to remember them.'

'Oh, dear,' wailed the old woman, 'those tiny things – please leave me those. There's no harm in keeping something to remember one's youth by. They weigh next to nothing. A trifle like that won't make or break the government.'

'Oh no, you don't!' decided Hackendahl. 'We're supposed to give all our gold to the government and we will. I don't understand you, Mother. You had to give up Erich and Otto and now you're crying over a couple of gold thingummies.'

'But I also cry about Erich and Otto. When I hear the postman on the stairs I always begin to cry . . .'

'I know, Mother,' he said soothingly. 'It's not easy, but it must be done so that we win. And we get iron in exchange, Mother! Why otherwise am I called Iron Gustav? Iron suits us much better than gold.'

'I'll get them.' And she went into the bedroom.

Hackendahl looked round. Eva had gone too. No, he hadn't for-gotten Eva. He looked at the heap of gold – no, her ring wasn't there. Everything had to be given up. To keep back the article most treasured was no sacrifice at all.

He listened. The place was quiet. But it always was whenever Heinz was at school. He was the only one who brought a bit of life into the house. Eva used to go about singing, but she didn't now. Still as the grave. And he'd have to go to her room soon and fetch the ring.

Hackendahl sat down in his wife's chair and looked at the golden heap. For a man in his position he was sacrificing a great deal. But it was not enough. There was a ring missing. Though only a trifle was withheld it rendered the sacrifice to no avail. It was just as in the army – partial order was no order. A spot on a button, a speck on the heel of a brilliantly polished boot – and there was no order.

That's why you were here – on the planet, in Germany, in the coach yard, in this house – to see that in this place, for which the Hackendahls were responsible, everything was in order. Then you felt good and had a good conscience about yourself and before your Kaiser and the Almighty. You just mustn't give in, yield to no excep-tions, be cast-iron. Iron!

Lost in his thoughts, Hackendahl pushed the gold coins to and fro, building little towers and afterwards arranging them in some-thing like a cross. Yes, Otto had already been awarded the Iron Cross. Who would have thought the boy had it in him? But it must have been an accident, though he was certainly no weakling. It had been a good day, being able to tell people: my son's been awarded the Iron Cross. He had gone with the news everywhere, not forgetting the taverns, where of late he had spent a good deal of time, as one did now that Rabause saw to everything and one had nothing much to do. Hackendahl's whole life had been one of intense activity – who would have thought that a war, a great war, would force him to become acquainted with boredom and inaction?

Hackendahl sat there frowning and played with his gold coins. He was absolutely sure that neither Mother nor Eva had given up their valuables to him, which he would have to find and chase. But he sat there and could not decide! Was it because he feared a confrontation with his daughter? That ring with the brown stone – she must have been given it by her young man.

He sighed heavily and pushed the gold into a heap again. He looked searchingly around the room, still unable to decide. Finally he called out, endeavouring to give his voice the old commanding ring: 'Mother, where are you? I'm waiting.'

'I can't find the earrings,' she called back. 'And I forget where I put them. It's years since . . .'

'Hurry up,' he urged. 'I want to be at the Purchase Centre by twelve. They close at one.'

'I'm looking. I won't be a moment, Father.'

In that moment he could have gone to Eva. He already had the doorknob in his hand when he heard Rabause shouting in the yard. Hackendahl went to the window. 'What is it, Rabause?' he asked. 'Who's there?'

'It's someone from Eggebrecht's. But I said you had no time, you wanted to hand in your gold.'

'What is it?'

'Herr Eggebrecht returned this morning with horses from Poland. But you would have to go there at once or they'll be gone, like last time.'

'I'm coming,' cried Hackendahl in his old voice. Horses! For many, many months he had been looking out for some, unsuccessfully. 'Mother, don't bother about the gold now – or go there yourself if you want to. You know, the Reichsbank, Unter den Linden. I'm off – Eggebrecht has brought horses from Poland.'

'Father! Father! You must tell me how much money you want for the gold and how many iron watch chains. Shall I take one for myself as well?'

'Do what you like. I've no time now or the horses will go. I must have horses! Where's my chequebook? Evchen, I'm glad you've come before I went. Eggebrecht has got some horses and I must go at once or they'll be sold again. You'll add your ring to the other things, you promise, don't you? I have to fly now.' And he hurried downstairs.

§ XVII

'Listen, Evchen!' said Frau Hackendahl, almost laughing. 'Father's
running downstairs like a youngster. As soon as he hears something
about horses . . .'

'Horses come first with him.'

'Let him buy all the horses he wants even if business is doing
badly. You know, people are saying horse cabs are finished but it's no
life for Father without them – he was starting to drink. Well, that'll
come to a stop when he gets some more horses.'

'Yes, so long as he has something to order about – horses, drivers,
children – it's all the same to him.'

'Father was always like that, Evchen, even in Pasewalk when he
was quite young. On leave, why, he was so unbearable, never still a
moment, out of one room, in the other, all day long, measuring with
a ruler where the bedroom rugs ought to be put. And our canary –
but you wouldn't remember him – Father would weigh out Hänschen's
seeds on the letter scales. He used to go to the post office specially.'

'I don't know how you stood it, Mother.'

'Whatever do you mean, Evchen? How queer you are! Father's
always been very good – you wait till you meet other men. You
always do nothing but complain because he's a bit of a disciplinarian.
But you shouldn't complain about that – you've no reason to. You
know you do as you like! But where's your ring?'

'I won't give it up, Mother.'

'And there's no need to, either. Luckily Father's gone off to Eggebrecht's and I'm to take the gold. But I won't do it myself – it's too
far for my poor varicose veins. You go and tell me what it's like so
that I can tell Father I've been. But you'll have to hurry, though, and
come back quickly.'

'Yes, but Mother, I might just as well go to the bureau in the
Frankfurter Strasse. Surely it's all the same.'

'No, don't do that. The Reichsbank is the most important and
Father won't have less. If the rubber stamps on the receipts don't
show that we've—'

'Then I'll go to the Reichsbank.'

'Well, get ready and go at once. And listen, I've said you needn't give up your ring, I quite understand what that means to a girl but you ought to tell me more, Evchen. I can see quite well what's going on. So you take care he marries you before anything happens. Father wouldn't regard that as a joking matter.'

'Oh . . .'

'I know daughters would rather tell anyone other than their own mothers. But you'll come and tell me all about it one of these days. Well, I'm not giving up my earrings either; they weigh nothing and Father won't notice . . . And now look, promise me solemnly never to tell your father – I'm taking back three of the big gold coins and three of the small ones.'

'Mother!'

'That's not underhand, Evchen. I don't want them for myself – I want to put them by. They're always talking about sacrifices but nobody knows what's in store for us. Bread is already rationed. Sacrifice only holds good for us small people – nobody hears a word about what the bigger fry are doing. But you can guess. They won't make the Kaiser have a bread card or ask whether he's given up all the gold and silver plate in the Schloss . . . No, you're right, child. Well, you'd better go now. And when you come back don't run straight into Father, will you?'

§ XVIII

There was a great clatter of hoofs in the cobbled yard and Frau Hackendahl poked her head out of the window, which she ought not to have done because Eva had not yet come back from the Reichsbank. But Hackendahl was thinking neither about gold nor the Reichsbank at that moment.

'We've got our horses, Mother,' he cried. 'Now the business will buck up!'

His wife stared. She had seen many a horse in that courtyard and whenever she went into town with Father he made her look at horse flesh. She therefore understood something about it. 'Aren't they very small?'

'Small!' Hackendahl was terribly annoyed. 'Small! They're not smaller than you are. Come on, Rabause, help me get them into the stables. We've work to do now. Small! She thinks that in wartime we harness elephants to the cabs . . .' He swallowed hard. 'I'm not coming in for supper,' he shouted in another burst of anger. 'You can eat by yourselves. I've work to do.'

'Seventeen of them,' said Rabause. 'Well, we can put twenty cabs into service again and give the grey and the bay a rest – they couldn't have stood it much longer.'

'You're right,' agreed Hackendahl. 'That's what I thought. And the woman says they're small!'

'Not quite as big as our old ones, perhaps,' hazarded Rabause.

'Not quite as big!' protested Hackendahl. 'Don't talk nonsense, Rabause. Proper ponies – that's what they are. Russian horses, Polish horses – that's the name for 'em. Small! Of course they're small! They've got to be or else we wouldn't have 'em – the army would have taken them.'

'That's right,' said Rabause. 'Ponies I've seen this kind before, Governor, at the Circus . . .'

'Circus! What a thing to say, Rabause! Circus – that's as bad as my wife. This isn't a circus here.'

'I know, Governor. I only mentioned it.'

'All right, I just thought you were harping on the same string as my wife. Rabause, it seems to me we shall have to alter the harness. It won't fit these . . . ponies. I'll have the saddler round at once. And we'll have the blacksmith to alter the shaft irons.'

'It'll cost a heap of money, Governor, and then when peace comes and we get proper horses again . . .'

'But it isn't peace now, Rabause, it's war, and I'm adapting myself to new conditions. I've been waiting and waiting for peace but I'm not waiting any longer. As far as I'm concerned there's a war on, and I want to have something to do besides merely waiting. No, I'm glad that I've work to do again. And you're glad too, aren't you, Rabause? It wasn't a life with only five broken-down nags.'

'Yes, you bet I'm glad. We'll be able to feed this sort of horse however much oats are rationed.'

'That's a fact, Rabause. And if oats get scarce they'll manage with just hay. Eggebrecht says that in Russia they get nothing but straw. Not that I'd do that, though. Work calls for food.'

'They'll be cheap that way and if only they were as cheap to buy, since they're so small, Governor . . .'

'Small! Now you're talking just like my wife! I don't understand you, Rabause. How could they be cheap when there aren't any horses to be had? It's impossible for them to be cheap. You just think a moment . . .'

'No, they can't be cheap, Governor, I can see that.'

'They're dear! So dear I nearly turned tail and came away without buying. But I changed my mind. If I didn't buy them someone else would.'

'You're right there.'

'Between you and me, Rabause, but don't tell my wife, I had to pay Eggebrecht more for those seventeen than I received for my twenty-seven good horses.'

'Herr Hackendahl!'

'Don't let's talk about it. Remember, you know nothing. But I shan't think about the cost when my twenty cabs roll out of the yard again. I'll just be glad. I'll be thinking – now people are going to stare! Twenty cabs! And they'll say: "Yes, old Gustav's made of iron. You can't get him down, any more than you can get Hindenburg down. He's made of iron." And that'll cheer me up . . .'

THREE

The Evil Days

§ 1

In the night Gertrud Gudde, the dressmaker, was suddenly awakened by the winter wind, merciless towards all those who were insufficiently nourished and inadequately warmed. She shuddered, then snuggled down closer into her bed.

But immediately she started up again and struck a light. Had she not been awakened by a cry from Gustäving? Jumping out into the icy cold, she went across to him. He was sleeping quietly, lying on his side, one bony shoulder – blue with the cold – peeping out of his shirt. Gently she covered him up. The child's nose was too sharp; his little arms were as thin as sticks, looking as if there was hardly an ounce of flesh on them. She sighed. With a feeling of impotent resignation she once again tucked the blanket round the little body and returned to the warmth of her own bed.

Trying to go to sleep again, for it was only two o'clock in the morning, she lay listening to the howl of the wind as it shook the windows – she might be living not on the fifth floor of a tenement in the great stone city of Berlin but far out on the plains where houses are exposed to the full fury of the storm. Vividly she remembered how the blustering wind would shake her parents' house on Hiddensee, and how as children they would be in bed listening to the sound of the waves breaking on the shore, and how they could never forget that their father was out in his boat catching the herring off Arkona or flounders in the shallow waters. She remembered how they would whisper together about the all-absorbing little happenings in their lives, of the geese they tended or the amber they found; never a word was spoken of the father away fishing. A deep-rooted superstition forbade that. Nevertheless they thought of him all the time, and this seemed to give the storm a personal quality, as though it were an enemy who must not be informed where he was.

The way had been long from that poor fisherman's house to the crowded tenement in the East End of Berlin; from the timid child to the dressmaker who, hardly knowing fear, was utterly resigned to all that God sent her. An immense transformation. And yet, lying awake at two o'clock in the morning and listening to the wind, Gertrud Gudde experienced once again something of that early superstitious fear. She wished to go to sleep, not to think or to tell her fear to the storm. But sleep would not visit a heart so sorrowful, and the gloom of the cold night was within as well as without her.

The wind outside her window, was it not the same that was now blowing over France? Did not the storm rage there also? As in the old days, so now – a man of hers was out in the darkness and cold; not her father this time but her lover, the father of her child.

As it was, is now, and ever shall be! She buried her head in the pillows; she did not want to think. Thought meant anxiety – Otto hadn't written for a fortnight. And she called to mind the times when a fishing boat was late, and wife and children – the whole village – waited for news of it. Boats could on occasion be driven from their course as far as Finland and a long time must elapse before word arrived. And often the villagers hoped and waited for those who had long been dead. Otto hadn't written for a fortnight. And here she recollected that it was not Gustäving's voice that had woken her. Another voice had called . . .

In her sleep she had picked up a newspaper. Anxiously she had scanned it, page by page, and on every page she had seen only the innumerable black-bordered notices which, headed by the cross of the fallen, filled all the press – Killed in Action. Suddenly she realized that she had really been seeking the announcement – In loving memory of Otto Hackendahl, who made the supreme sacrifice . . . Terror-stricken she told herself: I couldn't be looking for that. Otto is alive. He has just written that he's been promoted to corporal . . . I won't look at the names.

But she read the names all the quicker. It was as if she were hungry for the name Otto Hackendahl – to find relief at last, a final decision after the endless, anxious wait lasting now already two years. The heavy black print of the papers confused her. The black crosses of the fallen seemed to jostle against one another. The wind howled outside the window . . . The boat is on the high seas, her father is on the high seas, and mother and children are alone in the house . . .

What did the fisherfolk on Hiddensee believe? If a drowning man called to his wife, that cry would travel all the way to her and reach her even in the deepest sleep. To the living woman the dying man said: till we meet again.

And now a cry had penetrated to a woman asleep, a cry had awakened her. At first she had thought it must come from the child. But it had come from him.

And weep she could not. This fear had been too long with her. Nor did it help to know that it was the same for all other women. None who did not dream night after night of a man fallen, a husband, a brother, a son. It could not be otherwise, she told herself. What was in the mind all day came out in dreams at night. No special significance attached therefore to such dreams. She had experienced something similar a hundred times, yet she had always heard from him afterwards.

Nothing availed her, though. And she knew that nothing would. It was the same for her as for all other women, sisters, mothers. This endless suspense must be borne until the postman once again delivered a letter from the trenches. Then, after a minute of relief, there would return those five hundred, five thousand, fifty thousand anxious minutes, the long torment.

No, there was no help – she bore it as did other women. She cried aloud that it was unendurable and must end one way or the other, but there came no end and she continued to endure, continued because she had a child to care for and the acquisition of the barest necessities of life imposed ever-increasing duties on her; endured because she had letters to write to the Front, letters which must never seem lacking in courage; endured because only unceasing work enabled her to send him parcels . . .

Each day confronted her first thing in the morning with a peremptory 'You Must!' – unable for one moment to relax or give way to her sorrow.

Eventually Gertrud Gudde did go to sleep again, just as she did in the end with her worries almost every night. Twice more she was awoken by her dreams, and stared into the night with her usual anxiety, listening to the storm. The first time she had lain awkwardly, putting her weaker breast under painful pressure, and had then dreamed her most horrible dream, which she sometimes did, until it had suddenly become clear to her what the widely trumpeted expression 'Suspected dead in a mass grave' actually meant.

She had lain with Otto under the others – alive under the dead, and had tried to crawl out . . . But how could people torture one another! And how could anyone with a heart say such a thing! She stared breathlessly into the dark and tried to push such horrible images out of her head.

However, her third dream had almost been happy. She had sat next to Otto in a wood, green with spring, and he had taken a long flute from the pocket of his field-grey coat and said, I've carved this – now I will play you something.

He had begun to play when birds hopped out from every finger hole of the instrument. And they remained sitting on the flute and began to twitter and sing in time to his playing. It sounded unbelievably beautiful. She leaned ever closer to him, and in the end embraced him. Then he said: 'But you mustn't hold me too close. You know very well, don't you, Tutti, that I'm dead and only dust and ashes?'

And she did know, but only held him harder. And he disappeared in her arms, like a light mist passing from a wood in springtime. Far away, she could still hear his flute and the twittering and singing of the birds.

Then she was awoken. Outside the widows, the storm was abating somewhat. The alarm clock showed half past four – time to get up.

§ 11

Freezing, Gertrud Gudde stood in an icy room looking longingly at the stove; if she lit it now she would have to freeze the rest of the day. No more briquettes were obtainable till the following week – she had used up too many already.

Taking a newspaper, she crumpled it into a ball and thrust it in the stove. It did her good to see the flames produce their illusion of warmth. Then, when there was nothing but black paper left, she washed, slipped on her clothes and went to Gustäving's bed. The child was sound asleep now but before she returned hunger would wake him. Taking a loaf of bread from the cupboard, she cut a slice with much thought as to its size; though it was so small it was still too large. This she tied with a piece of string to the bedrail.

She smiled to think how pleased Gustäving would be with his gift. He was like his father; he would eat the bread with deliberation, chewing it thoroughly, although it was not the palatable and nutritious bread of peacetime but was made from potato flour, and some even maintained that sawdust and sand were to be found in it also. No need to believe that, however – war bread was bad enough as it was.

Locking the cupboard, she pocketed the key. Gustäving was very young but hunger made the smallest children ingenious. One morning not so long ago, he had got the cupboard open somehow. Terrible days had followed. She was used to being hungry herself but – deny her child the commonest necessities of life? 'I can't let him go hungry for four days,' she had pleaded at the Rationing Bureau. 'He would starve to death.'

'They've all got some tale or other,' the clerk had replied, shrugging his shoulders. 'This one's cards have been burnt, someone else has had them stolen, another's lost them, and now your child's eaten up all your bread. You should look after him better. No, you won't get any more here.'

In the end her sister-in-law Eva had come to her aid.

She shook the cupboard door gently once more: the cupboard was closed. Once again she looked at Gustäving. He was asleep. She switched off the light and went onto the landing. It had just turned five o'clock, high time to start.

The stairway was dark, but footsteps were soon descending, and heavier feet were coming up. A door opened on the first floor, a man came out, and Gertrud saw him kiss his wife goodbye in the twilight of the corridor. Then he felt his way downstairs next to her and suddenly grabbed her and whispered, 'Well, my sweetie? Out of bed already, too?'

She pushed her hands against his chest. She knew it was the fore-man from the munitions factory. He was incorrigible! He'd been a perfectly decent man, but he'd been spoiled by the war, which had emptied Berlin of men. There were enough women now to run after every pair of trousers. So he thought every woman fair game.

'Leave me alone, Herr Tiede!' she shouted, fiercely defending herself against him in the dark. 'I'm only the cripple from the fifth floor.'

'Gudde? That's something different.' And, pressing her hard, he whispered: 'Be nice to me, little one! You're just what I want. I'll give you half a pound of butter if you're a good girl. Word of honour!'

She succeeded in freeing herself from him, and ran across both courtyards as if being hunted. She breathed again when she reached the street. By the light of a gas lamp she inspected the coat he had torn. Thank goodness, it wasn't so bad and could be repaired so that it would hardly be noticed.

She hurried to a butcher's shop in a small side street, but she was a bit late there, despite her rush and early rising. There was already quite a queue outside the door.

'That makes nineteen,' said the woman in front.

'Then I'll doubtless get something after all,' said Gertrud hopefully.

'No one knows how many pigs he has been allotted. But they haven't forbidden us to hope yet.' The woman's voice was incredibly bitter. Gertrud Gudde – it was not only the icy wind that made her shudder – thrust her hands into her coat pockets and stood on tiptoe. In this way one's feet didn't freeze so much. And she would have to wait a long time because the shop didn't open before eight.

For a while she stood there, freezing. The tiredness she'd just managed to overcome came back. But it didn't bring sleep, only depressing, dark thoughts. She was wondering what she would get – whether a nice piece of the head or only a few bones; it was all a matter of luck, and mostly she had little or no luck. People were prejudiced against a hunchback. But, miserably inadequate though it might be, one had to take what one could get of this unrationed meat – bones and offal that the butcher could not otherwise use. Anyhow, it gave a flavour to the swedes.

'What's the time?' enquired the woman in front.

'Twenty-five to six,' replied Gertrud Gudde.

'And my feet are like ice already. I shan't be able to stick it till eight o'clock. Keep an eye on my place, will you? I'm number eighteen.'

Gertrud agreed, and the other negotiated also with the woman in front. It was heartbreaking to lose a place after getting up so early and freezing for so long, and one had to make certain of one's neighbours in the queue. The woman, who was wearing clogs, ran clattering up and down the street, sometimes stopping to beat her arms against her body. But nobody joked about it. 'If you only have the strength to keep it up, you get quite warm in time,' said someone thoughtfully. No one else spoke.

The woman came back. 'There,' she said, in quite a different tone, 'now I can stand it a little longer. Do you want to go? I'll keep your place.'

But Gertrud Gudde, although she was freezing, shook her head. 'No, thank you,' she said in a low voice; she was shy of exposing her deformity. All, it is true, were poor and downtrodden, but there are always some who, however poor, look down on those still poorer. Besides which she was really afraid of losing her place – so many were now waiting behind her. The butcher wouldn't have enough bones for all that number. And only six o'clock! She prayed that a policeman might pass at eight o'clock and shepherd the people into the shop, a few at a time. Otherwise there would be a free fight when the door opened and she would be pushed aside.

Two of those behind were talking loudly about a new decree concerning leave from the Front. 'It's a fact,' said one; 'for every gold coin you hand over your husband gets a day's extra leave.'

'They wouldn't do that,' said the other. 'Only the rich would benefit. In the trenches, at least, everyone's equal.'

'The rich, eh?' said the first voice bitterly. 'The profiteers and hoarders, you mean. Every decent person handed over his gold long ago, when they first asked for it. Dirty dogs! The decent people have been fooled again, and there are plenty who're hanging onto their gold, you bet. They'll get their husbands home for ten days or a fortnight, p'r'aps three weeks . . . and in the meantime one of ours may be killed.'

'They wouldn't do that,' said the other, a little doubtfully now. 'That wouldn't be just.'

'Just!' shouted the first woman angrily. 'Don't talk such rubbish. Justice? Where d'you find any justice? Hand over your gold and you can go to bed with your husband; no gold and you can go to blazes.'

'People talk so much,' said the other hesitantly.

'Justice?' shouted the other woman, who couldn't stop herself. 'They've just put a piece of paper through my door. I don't generally read such things – it's all rubbish. Says we should break our chains. People who print such things should do it first, to show us how! If they'd broken their own chains they wouldn't have to slip notes secretly through the doors, would they?'

A few people laughed.

'Aren't I right?' asked the woman, a bit more friendly. 'It's all rubbish! But I've read the note. "Menu" was written on it. That means something to eat. "Imperial Headquarters" was written on top, "Homburg vor der Höhe" – since when is Homburg vor der Höhe at the Front? I always thought it was a German town.'

'You don't understand,' said another woman. 'You're too stupid. An emperor like Willem is unique, but your Emil or what's his name, there are thousands of them . . .'

'No, you don't understand,' said the first woman, but quite resigned, 'because you don't know my Emil. If you did know, you wouldn't say that there are thousands like him. No, he's unique too . . .'

They continued to talk like that. They went on about Emil and Willem and the menu with seven courses and all in French. And they understood this French quite well. They went on talking, they got excited and then serious again – but nothing changed; it was the same old story – but at least time passed.

Gertrud Gudde listened but the sense of what they said did not reach her. Cold was creeping up her limbs. By itself the wintry weather would not have frozen her so much – she was thinking about this business of leave. Otto had been over two years at the Front without having any. I don't write about it in my letters, she thought, and he doesn't mention it in his, but every soldier on the Western Front has had at least a couple of leaves in the last two years. All except Otto . . . And she began to brood as she had so often brooded before. Why didn't he come? He knew what it was like at home. Although she had never written about the food shortage, now and then some man on leave would ring at her door and hand in a parcel – a little dripping, two pounds of bacon, some sugar, lentils once . . .

'Why doesn't Otto get his leave?' she would ask them.

They shrugged and looked at her, embarrassed. 'I don't know,' they said, 'perhaps he doesn't want any.'

They looked at her so oddly that she never cared to ask further questions. Perhaps they were thinking: if I had a woman like you I wouldn't come home either.

At first she had thought Otto was a poor soldier and got no leave for that reason. But when she heard about his Iron Cross and that he had been made a corporal – well, perhaps he really didn't want leave.

The women talked on and on. It chilled the blood, this conversation. The world became utterly without hope or joy. And when they did laugh they screwed up their faces into a mirthless grin. She forced herself, she willed herself, to think about other things. She thought of the child, of Gustäving when he would plead: 'Tell it again, Mother, the story of the baker's shop.'

And she would tell him about the baker's shop, though it was no fairy tale. She told him how three years ago she had been able to go into a shop, point and say: eight rolls, four brioches with sugar icing, two loaves of bread . . .

'But he didn't give you two loaves of bread, did he, Mummy?'

'Yes, and he thanked me for buying so much.'

The child sat there, his eyes shining. His mother had to mime the bringing-home of the bread and show how she had cut it up into slices, so many for Papa, so many for Mummy, so many for Gustäving.

'Show me again! Oh, Mother, I could never eat all that up.' And then eagerly: 'Yes, I could. Just try and see. I'll get it down. Let's try. Just once, please, Mummy, please!'

And then, as a finale, the endless begging for a little piece of bread, just a tiny slice, half a slice, a crust only . . .

You were chilled if you listened to people's talk; you were chilled by your own thoughts. Start where you would, the end was the same.

But there was no need to brood any longer – the woman in front said excitedly: 'He's pulling up the shutters already. I hope no one treads my clogs off. Last time I lost fifteen places through it. Be careful, please, young woman!'

And then the rush – no policeman about anywhere, of course. They usually made a wide detour whenever they saw a queue like this, if for no other reason than to avoid hearing what the women said. Gertrud Gudde was swept off her feet, carried away, crushed against the door . . . For a moment she thought her arm must break. Then she was in the shop – by good luck pushed right in front against the counter.

'Well, and how much, young woman?' asked the fat butcher.

'As much as you'll give me.'

At once a portion of pig's head was pushed over the counter and, wide-eyed, she gazed at the white skin and crimson meat – a lump of pig's cheek, nearly two pounds of fat and meat. With bent head, her bag clasped to her bosom, she pushed her way through others who had not yet got anything and might perhaps have to go away empty-handed – the poor creatures.

She smiled happily. Early rising, the cold, the long wait, her despair, all were forgotten. A chunk of pig's cheek, almost two pounds of meat and fat!

She rushed upstairs. But at the door of the flat her heart gave a jump. Happiness fled. She laid a hand on the shoulder of the woman crouching there. 'What is it, Eva?'

Eva lifted a tear-stained face. 'Father has turned me out, Tutti,' she whispered. 'Will you take me in?'

'Gladly,' said Gertrud Gudde, and unlocked the door.

§ III

The stimulation Hackendahl had received from his new horses had long died away. They had brought nothing but constant worry concerning their drivers – the fellows at present on the box knew nothing about horses, couldn't drive, were not familiar with the Berlin streets and seemed quite indifferent whether they picked up fares or no, their main concern being to receive the guaranteed wage regularly. These fellows, either very old or very young, nearly drove Hackendahl mad.

To the worry with the cabmen was added the worry about fodder. So long as he had a supply of oats in the loft it was easy to say that the horses were small Russian ponies and if need be could live on straw, but when fodder became really scarce, when the supplies allotted were always insufficient and horses were rationed like men, then he had to admit that maybe they could actually live on straw but not, when it came to the point, do any work. If they had to work, then they had also to feed. And they were forced to work, for living had become dearer and money even tighter.

Yes, money had become tight in the Hackendahl household. Much of the father's liquid cash had gone to Eggebrecht for the ponies; the rest he had subscribed to the War Loans and it was now tied up. Had he used his intelligence at the time he would not have frozen so much of his savings in that way. But Gustav Hackendahl felt it was up to him to subscribe a large sum. And this was done. 'We don't need the money, Mother. The cabs will always bring in enough to live on.'

But the cabs didn't. They brought in practically nothing, and on many a pay day Hackendahl had trouble in scraping the money together for the men's wages. Money had never been so tight. A household minus two sons and a daughter should have been cheaper to run than a household in which they all sat down to table together. But no – living grew more and more expensive.

For one thing there were the countless parcels which Mother was everlastingly sending to the Front. The delicacies they contained were bought from hoarders and therefore dear. And though neither Otto nor Sophie wrote for money, Erich made up for them; the lad eternally needed something new – a smart cap, special boots, corduroy riding breeches. But at least he was already a second lieutenant with a cushy job at the Lille base, so that Mother didn't need to weep over him continually.

No, money didn't stay around, it leaked away. All the same, you continued to help. The main thing was that something remained to rattle in the cash till. Then you could manage all right.

And then one evening an official letter arrived announcing a second requisition of horses. It demanded that every animal be produced, including any bought since the last requisition and all discarded military horses acquired by purchase.

'It makes me laugh,' remarked Hackendahl. 'I can understand them calling up the men again. But the horses! Well, let 'em – they must have a lot of time on their hands.'

'They're calling up men whom they registered as totally unfit only a year ago,' said Frau Hackendahl. 'Father, supposing they take our animals . . .'

'If it must be it must,' said Hackendahl firmly. But he hastened to reassure her. 'They certainly won't take the ponies. As for my other five, they've not improved with the feed they're getting.'

'Starvation didn't improve the men either, but they've taken them now.'

'We shall see, Mother. Don't start getting upset already. You'll see, I'll come back with as many horses as I left with.'

An exodus of a different sort from that in the early days of August 1914! Back then he had proceeded with gravity, briefcase under his arm, alongside his own transport. He had looked at people's faces, and their admiring recognition had made him proud. Bubi was alongside him, and it was still unclear exactly with whom they were supposed to be at war. And there was warning of spies.

Hackendahl carried the official order in his jacket pocket, and led the first four beasts in person, while Rabause followed with another four. As to the passers-by, their sullen, hopeless faces were not cheering to look at. If they did notice the horses it was only to reflect that they ought rather to be going to the horse butcher, so that people could get a little unrationed meat.

But Bubi was at school, and that was a mercy. No one had gone hunting for spies. People now wanted the world to know how the food blockade was killing off innocent women and children. However, the world didn't want to know!

It was the old mustering place with the wooden barriers, but quite another procedure this time. No lengthy inspection of the horses. Just a glance. 'Good – the next!' Hardly a mouth was looked into or a leg examined. 'Good – the next!'

Hackendahl began to feel anxious. Leaving Rabause to trot out the horses, he approached the requisitioning committee almost furtively, and was at once snapped at. 'What are you hanging about for, man? Get back to your horses! No one is allowed to eavesdrop round here,' shouted a grey-faced captain wearing an Iron Cross of the First Class. Probably he was one of those who had been seriously wounded at the Front but who wanted to get back again and therefore hated and despised the entire civilian regime at home. His counterpart was the veterinary surgeon, a fat man with a rosy face, who cracked jokes at which no one laughed but himself.

'These your horses? Or are they performing fleas? Well, let's get down to it! Horses are horses – we're not going to measure them for the life-guards.'

With an expression of unspeakable disgust the grey-faced captain listened to this clowning. 'That one – and this!' he pointed. 'The next!'

'What?' Hackendahl asked the clerk. 'Nineteen?'

'Yes, the grey and the two bay ponies are rejected,' said the clerk indifferently. 'Here's your warrant.'

'But,' said the disconcerted Hackendahl, 'how am I to live? I have a cab business. With only three horses . . .' He looked at the paper without seeing what was written on it. Spots were dancing before his eyes.

'There's a war on,' said the clerk, with a spice of malice.

'You're not to hang about here. I've told you that before,' barked the captain. 'What's wrong?'

'Only three left out of twenty-two horses,' said Hackendahl, clinging to the one point he understood. 'I have a cab business.' He looked at the captain as if that grey-faced man ought to grasp the situation.

'There's a war on,' said the captain coldly. 'Tens of thousands of fathers have had to sacrifice their sons – and you're kicking about your horses!' He looked at Hackendahl again and then said, more amiably: 'Well, go away now. You an ex-serviceman, complaining!'

Hackendahl clicked his heels and went. That appeal could still produce the desired effect. Rabause followed with the three horses. Never had the grey looked so depressed.

Not till he returned home did Hackendahl discover how much the military authorities were allowing him for his horses – a hundred and fifty marks apiece. But he had paid Eggebrecht five hundred, yes, six hundred marks even. These are peacetime prices, he thought, staring at the warrant. In peacetime this would be called confiscation of property; in war we just have to sacrifice it.

For a long time he sat down and thought about it. It couldn't be changed – no, not any more. He wanted to kick himself. He really had become like iron.

Pulling himself together, he went down and paid off the cabmen. 'You can knock off for good,' he said. 'This business is finished.'

No flinching, no sign of weakness. There had been one such sign on the mustering ground – the blow was so sudden. But now no one should hear him complain any more, not even those at home. He would take life as it came.

'Listen, Rabause,' he said. 'From now onwards I'll drive one cab and you the other. We'll always rest one of the horses – one's always sure to be ill out of the three.'

Rabause looked at him. 'Yes, Governor,' he said. 'I will. We'd better take the money home. There'll hardly be any cabs left in Berlin after this inspection.'

And his boss said, 'You were absolutely right back then. The stable was too big. But I don't want to build anything new. I must see that I sell this whole show. Then we'll set ourselves up somewhere quite small. That would be good too, wouldn't it, Rabause?'

'Don't I know it, boss!' said Rabause. 'When the children were still little – what a time that was!'

'Indeed,' agreed Hackendahl. 'Perhaps we can do it like that again.' Perhaps . . .

§ IV

Gustav Hackendahl had returned to his former occupation. In a driver's blue greatcoat and shiny top hat he took his place on the cab ranks.

The other cabmen, when they first saw him behind his melancholy grey, called out: 'Well, Gustav, doing another chap out of a job? You want to get rich quick, you do!' And among themselves they said: 'No one drives well enough for him. Well, what's it matter? He'll soon have enough in this weather with only swedes in his belly.'

By and by, however, when they saw him out in all weathers, not declining the meanest fare, and it got about that he was working with only two cabs, they said: 'And he used to be at the top of the tree. But you have to say this for him – he's not chucking up. Old Gustav's really iron.'

Hackendahl let them talk. He accepted this changeover from prosperity to daily worry as equably as he endured bad weather. If a fare wanted to go all the way to Reinickendorf he merely said: 'Yes, we'll do it, sir, but please don't get impatient.' And he let the grey trot with an occasional walk as rest – the fare might complain as much as he liked but Gustav showed no impatience.

'If you was a horse, sir, you wouldn't hurry on the feed you'd get nowadays. Thank yer stars you haven't got to tote the cab along with the grey inside it, sir. It might have happened like that.'

The fare would laugh. And a laughing fare is a satisfied one. Gustav Hackendahl too was not dissatisfied – he took everything as it came, resigned to his setback in life and resolved to become a driver again. When he had risen in the world he had taken care to speak good German so as not to shame his family, but now he began to speak like a true Berlin cabby – fares liked to hear it. Everything had to be done the right way. He still insisted on this, at home with wife and children and in the stable. In big things one can adapt oneself, be amenable; in small things – one must keep to the rules.

So he sat on his box and saw without being seen. No townsman notices a driver. The cabby waiting for a fare is as much a part of Berlin as an advertisement pillar or the gas lamps. And thus it came about that Hackendahl sat on high and saw Eva approaching. She should have had better eyes than most people for a driver, her father being one, but her head was lowered and she did not see him. She wasn't even looking at the dark-complexioned young man talking so eagerly with her.

Moping . . . like the grey, thought Hackendahl. She's been hit all right.

'Gee-up,' he said to his beast, clucking his tongue, and the cab slowly followed the pair. Sometimes Hackendahl saw the young chap from behind, and sometimes from the side; the grey was in full agreement about not hurrying. Hackendahl had been standing at the Alexanderplatz and now he was going towards the Schlesische Station. Well, we'll soon know, he thought.

Outwardly the young fellow did not look too bad, that had to be admitted. He was togged up to the nines and, as far as could be seen, his face too was not so bad. But on the whole Hackendahl disliked him. In the first place why was a chap with sound limbs walking about Berlin without a uniform? And, secondly, he had such a fat backside . . .

The two were walking quite sedately along the Lange Strasse. A lousy neighbourhood for a courting couple, thought Hackendahl. But the chap's lousy too.

What talking there was the young fellow did, Evchen hardly saying a word, but he too didn't speak much as he slouched along at her side. They haven't much that's new to say to one another, that's clear, decided Hackendahl. Once the young man touched Evchen's upper arm, maybe in affection, but from her start Hackendahl guessed it to be something else.

You wait! he thought.

They were now passing the not unfamiliar signs: boarding house or hotel so-and-so, rooms from 1.50 marks upwards, also by the hour. Hackendahl could not understand why they should go the whole length of the Lange Strasse merely to enter the kind of sordid den which could have been found equally well at the beginning. For this is what the couple did. The place into which they disappeared was called the Oriental Hotel.

All right – Hackendahl was in no hurry. He put on the brake, changed the For Hire sign to Engaged, climbed down from the box and buckled on the grey's nosebag in which, together with a lot of poor chopped straw, was a little good maize from that Romania which had very recently declared war on Germany. Taking a rug from the cab, he hung it over his arm. If you have to bring a lady something she has forgotten then you must have that something to bring her. Any fool knew that!

'Well, Gertie,' said Hackendahl winking at the landlady. 'In what room are the two young people?'

'Young people? What do you mean? No young people are staying here.'

'Don't tell me that sort of yarn. The young people I brought in my cab!' And as the woman still hesitated, for even in wartime the police would spasmodically remember the laws against procuring, Hackendahl explained: 'The girl left this in my cab,' indicating the rug which was not clearly visible in the gloomy entrance hall.

'Give it to me,' said the old woman. 'I'll give it her myself later on.'

'Nothin' doin'! No, I must give it her myself, or later I'd be told you ain't ever seen me and my name's Nitwit.' And, calmly pushing the old woman aside, Hackendahl stepped in and inspected the doors . . .

'Not there – here!' she hissed furiously. 'Knock first, at least, you old fool.'

Hackendahl, however, had opened the door and gone in, casting a fleeting glance at the couple, but taking his time. With deliberation he locked the door, tried the handle and called out: 'You keep quiet, Gertie, I'm in now.'

Then he turned round. 'Well, Evchen?' His tone displayed no trace of anger.

Wide-eyed she looked at him. She stood by the foot of the bed; her coat was hung over a chair. She gave one glance at the fellow standing near the wall and then looked back at her father.

Hackendahl sat down leisurely in one of the red plush chairs, put the rug over his knees and smoothed it out. 'Nice chairs,' he remarked after a pause, 'but should be treated better.'

No reply.

'Well, Evchen, if you don't want to begin I'll have to. Or have you anything to say?'

'Oh, Father.' Her voice was low. Then it became a little firmer. 'Talking won't help.'

'Don't say that, Evchen, don't say that. Talking does help. Talking it over always does.'

An impatient movement.

'If one doesn't want to talk about a thing, Evchen, then there's

something rotten about it. I don't have to come into a brothel to
know that.'

'Listen, old gentleman,' came the young fellow's impertinent
voice – just the voice one would expect from such a rump, thought
Hackendahl. 'You come here and spread yerself—'

'Shut up, my lad,' said Hackendahl without raising his voice or
looking at him. 'I'm talking to my daughter, so you keep your mouth
shut. Listen, Evchen! You're right, what's there to talk about?
Bygones are bygones. But it just so happens that my cab is below and
you can come home with me right away. I'll drive you there in tip-top
style, gratis and for nothing.'

The girl had not stirred, but it seemed to Hackendahl that she
flung the swiftest of glances at the man.

'You mustn't look at that chap, Evchen. Don't think of him any
more. You shouldn't have anything to do with a man who takes a
decent girl into a place like this, in broad daylight, too. You are a decent
girl, Evchen, all my children are decent. All of them, you know that.'

He would have liked the fellow in the corner to have got saucy
now, so that he could sock him one. But trust the fat-arsed pimp he
was to know when to avoid trouble – he didn't as much as open his
lips. And Evchen, his favourite daughter Evchen – she stood there
without a word.

'Well, come on, girl,' he said persuasively. 'Put your coat on and
come.'

She shook her head. 'It's too late, Father.'

'Too late!' He tried to laugh. 'Don't talk like that, Evchen. How
old are you, eh? You're twenty! There's no such thing as too late at
your age.'

'It's impossible, Father. I can't. He . . .' – she made a movement
with her head – 'he can send me to jail. I've stolen . . .'

Old Hackendahl turned very red, then slowly pale. He was on the
point of going up to the young man – but he remained in his chair.

After a while he spoke, a little heavily. 'All right, Evchen, you stole,
then. I'd never have thought that any child of mine would ever say
that to me and see me sit still. But times have changed. It really is war.
I can't understand it, Evchen, I can't at all. Times must really have
changed and me with them . . .' He looked at her helplessly. Then he

began again. 'All right, then, I'm sitting here and you're there and you're a thief. In that case we won't go home, we'll go to the police station . . . I'll stand by you, Evchen. And you tell them of your own free will what this fellow knows about you. And then – well, you'll have to go to prison for a time . . .'

It was almost too much for him, then he pulled himself together and said: 'I wouldn't have thought I could ever speak like this. But I'm not trying to excuse you when I say that even a decent person can go to prison – once. A decent person can make a mistake – once. Or have bad luck. That fellow there' – he pointed – 'he's your bad luck. You can become decent again, Evchen.'

All this time she had been watching his mouth. Now she spoke. 'And when all that lies behind me, Father, prison and all the rest, what's going to happen then?'

'You'll come back to us then, Evchen. It's not our Eva who moons about not saying a word – and you used to sing so beautifully! No, my girl, everything will be the same as it was.'

'Never,' she said, shaking her head. 'It's too late. I've sunk too deep.'

'Don't go on saying it's too late, Evchen. You're not twenty-one yet.'

'And then – at home again . . . I know you, Father; you couldn't ever forgive or forget. You would always look at me askance even in twenty years' time.'

'You mustn't say that, Evchen. I've forgotten about Erich . . .'

'You see, Father! You think of Erich at once. You think, if the son's a thief why not the daughter too? You see, you can't forget anything.'

'What are you talking about, Eva?' cried Hackendahl. 'You know nothin' about me. Wasn't I nice to you just now? Did I throw your trouble in your face?'

'But you are throwing it in my face now. No, Father. What would I do at home? Potter about the flat, make the beds and do the cooking. No, I couldn't do that again. All that's over and done with. It'd be nothing but a stopgap.'

'Think, Evchen! Decent work is always good.'

'And look what I've become through your decent work! Do you

think Eugen would have got me so easily if I hadn't got like this through being at home with you? Decent work indeed – it was always duty, obedience and punctuality – but it was all wrong, Father.'

'No, no, girl! Don't say that. I worked honestly . . .'

'And where has it landed you? You're now sitting on the box just as you did twenty years ago. But the horse you had in front of you then was better. And you don't know what's coming either. This isn't the end yet, by any means.'

'No, Evchen, that's true. You're right there. To have a daughter who tells me to my face that she'd rather be in a brothel with her bully than stay at home with her father and mother – I'd never have believed it.'

He was on his feet – he had been standing for quite a while. Now he folded the rug over his arm and smoothed it out. 'But, Evchen,' he said, 'to ask me to play the pander to this pimp of yours, you can't expect me to do that either. It's better you go with him altogether. Fetch your things and then—' without meaning to, he suddenly bellowed: 'and then clear out. Clear out!'

He looked furiously at the startled girl, went to the door and, unlocking it, glanced back a last time. The chap stood well within reach of his fist, but it was all one to him now.

'Take care you don't repent this, Evchen,' he said.

§ V

Hardly had the old man shut the door when Eugen opened his mouth, of course. Hackendahl had summed him up correctly – he was cruel with the weak but cowardly and cunning with the strong. 'I don't know what your old man's thinking about! It takes two to live together – someone to go to besides someone who goes.'

She said nothing.

'You!' he cried threateningly. 'Didn't you hear me?'

'Oh yes.'

'Then answer. Did you think of comin' to me by any chance?'

'Father thought that.'

'So Father thought that, did he? What right has your father to order me about, eh?' He shook her.

'Eugen, don't! I can't help what Father said. I told him what I thought of him, I told him I didn't want to go back.'

'Well, what is it you want?' he shouted furiously, shaking her again. 'D'you want to come to me?'

'I want what you want, Eugen.'

'Told him what you thought of him, eh?' Again that furious shaking. 'But not a word about me not bein' your pimp. You never thought of that, eh?'

'No, Eugen.'

'And have I been your pimp?'

'No, Eugen.'

'Why didn't you tell him, then?'

Silence. Renewed shaking. 'I'm askin' you! Out with it!'

'I don't know, Eugen . . .'

'You'd like me to be your pimp, eh?'

'No! Oh, no!'

'But you said you wanted what I wanted. An' now I want you to go on the street for me, y'understand?'

'No!' she begged. 'Don't ask me that, please, Eugen. Anything you want, but not that.'

'So you'll do whatever I want! But that's just what you won't do! An' you've got no brains for anythin' else. When I picked you up I thought, fine, you'll do some very smart things with help. But no, no blinkin' good at all – you're just a dumb middle-class girl and you ain't goin' to change.' He looked at her furiously. 'There he sat, your old man!' he shouted again. 'He's a cheeky sod. "Move in with me," he says. Not bloody likely. I'll get a place for you but not with me. No thank you! I don't want your whining mug always hanging round me! Frau Pauli!' he suddenly shouted.

'I won't do it, Eugen. You can do what you like. I won't do that.'

'Lor, Herr Bast,' said Frau Pauli. 'What a row you're kickin' up today. The room next door's engaged – what'll the people think? An' especially you, Herr Bast, who's always such a gentleman! I suppose it's the cabby who upset you.'

'Cabby! That was her father! And, jus' imagine, Frau Pauli, she let her old man call me a pimp and never said a word.'

'That's not right of you, miss. You must know Herr Bast is a real gentleman.'

'Her? What does she know?' said Eugen Bast contemptuously. 'Hanging around like a sick cow, that's all she knows. But I'll show her! If she thinks I'm a pimp, she c'n have it like that for all I care. Has old Pirzlau a room free?'

'Wait a mo, Herr Bast. Jus' let me think. There's Fräulein Koko and Mimi and that Lemke – yes, there's a room free, I think. But, Herr Bast, you know Frau Pirzlau's strict. Her girls must be registered and have a police permit – and go every week to the doctor . . .'

'Well, what of it, Frau Pauli? Don't you think our Eva will? Our Eva'll do all that, and Frau Pirzlau won't have any trouble with her about that, will she, Evchen?'

'I won't do it, Eugen. I'd rather drown myself.'

'Don't say that, miss. That's a sin,' said Frau Pauli.

Eugen took the old woman by the shoulders. 'Get out, Frau Pauli,' he said, pushing her from the room. 'We'll fix this up between ourselves, all this about drowning. No, I won't make a row, I'll be as soft as soap. I'm like that, I don't beat girls, do I, Evchen?'

The woman had gone and they were alone. No, there was no row – only sobbing and tears – and tears meant nothing in such a house. No other sound.

Eva felt as if she were oppressed by a nightmare from which she ought to wake up and yet could not – a bad dream, ever darker, ever more desolate – the place across the road, the negotiations with Frau Pirzlau, the other girls who treated it as a joke and were put in a good humour by the new arrival, whom they laughingly rigged out.

And then, standing at the corner of the Lange and the Andreas Strasse. Standing there in torment, knowing that his eyes were on her. It had started to snow and the men were in a great hurry. They were all in a hurry as they passed the woman who was so ridiculously got up in a feather boa dyed green and a large hat trimmed with feathers . . .

Then the shrill pimp's whistle from the doorway – the signal to accost some man who seemed all right to Eugen. And his sudden appearance, his blows because she hadn't accosted the man after all. And his blows when she did accost someone but unsuccessfully. And her feeble attempt to run away, whereupon he fetches her back, almost breaking her arm . . .

And how in the end she succeeded and took a man to her room, with the other girls poking their heads round the doors and nodding encouragement. And how repulsive life was. Everything, yes, everything one had ever learned about cleanliness and purity a lie. And how she must go back to her corner right away . . .

And how in the evening she was involved in a quarrel with another girl who claimed that corner as her own, and how Eugen thrashed the other girl this time . . . with people hurrying by indifferently – life going on and nothing really changed . . . And how the other girl came back with her fellow – it was dark by now – and Eugen getting into a quarrel with him. And how she wandered away slowly, away round the corner . . . And, once she was safely round the corner, she ran. Ran on and on, into the town.

She had to make haste – he might be following. In her conspicuous finery she passed a hundred policemen and fifteen of the special branch but none noticed her, for she had a goal to reach . . .

She entered the dark Tiergarten and, to start off with, threw the hat and feather boa behind a bush. Quieter now, she went hurrying down the Bendlerstrasse until she arrived at the Königin-Augusta-Ufer. This was her goal.

She sat down on a wet seat under a leafless chestnut. What an impression a successful song can make! She had come all this way when it was only five minutes' walk from the Lange Strasse to the River Spree. But the whole afternoon that song had haunted her. 'In the Landwehr Canal there floats a corpse . . .'

The words had not seemed to her at all ghastly or horrible, but rather ordinary. In the Landwehr Canal there floats a corpse. It often happened and people were singing about it, laughingly. Not horrible – only needing a little courage . . .

That was why she had hurried so. This was the Landwehr Canal they had made the song about.

She sat there for a long time. At last she stood up – it was not so easy now. Already she was conscious of reluctance. And her reluctance increased as she went down the dark passage to the river, where she could hear a chill splashing, as if rats swam there. Yet surely a corpse ought to be indifferent to rats. Nevertheless she descended more and more hesitantly. But, however hesitant her progress, at last she came to the bottom step.

She was standing on a small brick platform. The water was high, almost lapping her feet. She bent down. She couldn't see the water, only the reflections from the lights on the bridge. Now is the moment to fall in, she thought.

But she did not let herself fall. Frightened, she drew back from the darkness which gurgled below her feet, and stood there, waiting.

People were passing over the bridge but nobody saw her, nobody shouted 'Help, help! She wants to drown herself', which would have given her strength to make the leap she was frightened of. To make the leap with the expectation of being saved.

And when, after a long wait, she tested the water with her foot and felt the icy cold seep into her shoe, all was decided. She could not.

Slowly she went back up the steps. Previously she had hurried, had been almost happy, for she was parting from life – life was over. But that dream was ended. Now she was returning, broken. Nothing had changed, life flowed on without end. Slowly she walked through the dark Tiergarten, through the dark town. Only at the approach of dawn dared she go into the more familiar places. He would be asleep now . . . And at last she had slunk to Gertrud Gudde, of whom he knew nothing. There, perhaps, she would be allowed to stay in safety. She was allowed. 'Gladly,' Gertrud Gudde had said, returning from the butcher's.

§ VI

While Gertrud Gudde talked to Eva, undressed the half-frozen woman and laid her in her still almost warm bed, and while Eva Hackendahl's despair dissolved into uncontrollable tears, and while both women discussed how they were going to live together, police registration, moving things and ration cards – while all that was going on, Corporal Hackendahl lay in a shell hole between the French and German lines. The shell hole was quite close to the French – not more than thirty metres away – but thank heavens it was so deep that the enemy couldn't see him. The German trenches were about a hundred and twenty metres distant, and that was bad, because he wanted to return to the German lines, and couldn't do so before nightfall.

Otto Hackendahl, if it were a consolation, had the consolation that he was not alone – a second man lay there, a Lieutenant von Ramin. They had met here for the first time. The lieutenant was attached to a company which had assisted Otto's regiment in an attack; this attack had been repulsed and only by crawling into the nearest shell hole had the lieutenant and Otto been able to avoid being taken prisoner. And then an infernal barrage had broken loose, thus making a return to their own positions impossible. Day broke . . .

A bitterly cold day, the sky obscured by low-hanging clouds. Thank God, thought Otto. Not aeroplane weather, anyway.

Lying there, he could see only the sky and the pit they were in. It was not advisable to look over the edge – they fired pretty smartly from both trenches. Now and again he heard a word of command from the French side, and sometimes someone laughed. It's easy for them to laugh, thought Otto. I feel damned cold. And I'll be colder still by the evening.

To distract himself he listened to the firing, which had re-awakened with dawn. Slowly the artillery got into its stride. There was a loud report. Our mortars starting! Sometimes only the field guns were to be heard, but for the moment they weren't working in his direction. Let's hope we'll leave the French in peace for a bit today. We're properly in the trap, the officer and I . . .

He looked towards the lieutenant, who lay curled up at the bottom of the crater, reading old letters. Sensing Otto's gaze he lifted his head and asked: 'Well, Corporal, what are you thinking of?' He had a cheerful, open face and Otto liked his way of speaking.

'I'm thinking, Herr Lieutenant, it would be a good thing if the trench over there didn't get peppered today.'

'I don't believe there'll be much happening,' said the lieutenant. 'Both sides got their bellyful last night. Are you damned cold, too?' he enquired with great feeling.

'Terrible! My boots are absolutely rotten. I haven't had my feet dry for weeks.'

'My boots are sound, but my feet are like ice just the same,' said the lieutenant. 'Got anything to drink, Corporal?'

'Yes, Herr Lieutenant, my flask's half full of cherry brandy. But I thought we'd better save it for later on – we won't be getting away before night. And a stimulant will come in handy then.'

'Before night! You saw how bright the moon was – and then these damned Verey lights. I'm not so sure we shall get away tonight at all.'

'It looks like snow,' said Otto hopefully.

'Snow!' The lieutenant was contemptuous. 'It's been looking like snow for days. But who can say when it's really going to snow in a damned winter like this one. No, no, Corporal, you save up your cherry brandy for later. Don't worry about me, I've got some schnapps.'

'Yes, Herr Lieutenant, that'll warm you.'

Otto, listening to the shelling, tried to guess the calibres, the trajectories, the position of the guns. Nothing calmed you so much when you felt nervous or anxious. You forced yourself to concentrate and thereby almost forgot the anxiety about yourself. Now and then he heard conversation in the French trenches; they seemed to be quite cheerful in spite of the recent attack.

'Swine!' said Lieutenant von Ramin suddenly, quite loud. 'Did you hear that, Corporal? One of them's got some hot coffee. What damned beastliness to tell us about it too.'

'We usually make our coffee about this time,' said Otto.

'Yes,' said the lieutenant, almost laughing. 'When you're in the trenches you curse 'em and wait only for the moment to get out. And now we're both heartily longing for a damp, louse-ridden dugout.'

'You never know when you're well off,' agreed Otto, 'till you're worse off.'

'True. But I'd rather put it this way – however badly off you are you can always be worse off. How long have you been in it, Corporal?'

'From the beginning. The very first day, Herr Lieutenant.'

'You were lucky, then. You went through the first enthusiasm, the advance. I came straight from school into the trenches. All the bloody mud in bloody Champagne. You ever been there, Corporal?'

'Yes, at Dormoise Valley, Herr Lieutenant.'

'Why, man, we were there too. So you can guess how a boy felt, chock-full of enthusiasm and high-falutin ideas, straight from his school desk into mud and filth and lice. And the men so irritable and depressed . . .'

'Yes, there were days when you could have killed anyone just for coughing.'

'Coughing?' said the lieutenant grimly. 'Just because he was alive! Yes, that was a time. And things are no better now, let me say.'

'But the Herr Lieutenant still looks cheerful.'

'Yes, I look like it,' said the lieutenant indifferently. 'I want to ask you something, Corporal. Last autumn, in September or October, my regiment went into action over twenty times in the same small sector. We called that hell-hole the "Rotting Appendix". It was really horrible and stank to high heaven. It was the remains of an old trench in one of our abandoned positions, no longer of the least use, but those above happened to have it on their plans. It didn't even have proper dugouts, it wasn't deep enough. Almost every day it got shot to bits but we had to go into it day after day, and it cost us hundreds of men – in the end it was given up for good and it made no difference. But if that was the case, why all those sacrifices?'

Hackendahl blinked. 'If the Herr Lieutenant starts asking questions . . .' he said slowly. 'You do what is ordered. It's no good thinking too much. That only makes life more difficult.'

'No, no!' said the lieutenant hastily. 'Look here, Corporal – what's your name, by the way? Hackendahl? Well, look here, Hackendahl, you'll have had a different sort of upbringing from me, but it all comes to the same thing everywhere – have you ever known anyone you could really love and admire? Think it over. A really great man whom you knew personally or had heard of, and who didn't think of himself or was vain? You see, you don't know one either. People like that are said to have lived once upon a time but not now. Everything we believe in, everything we worship, is now dead, in the past, no longer exists . . .'

The lieutenant looked towards Hackendahl. He no longer saw him, and he said: 'But when you're young you must have something to love and admire, something that's worth sacrificing yourself for. When you're young you don't want to live by bread alone. You want something more – something quite different.'

He fell silent again. Hackendahl looked attentively at the cheerful face. He had admired the lieutenant's casual manner; now he saw that he too had his troubles, and indeed not such very different troubles.

'When the war came, when Germany was in danger and we all stood together, then we thought we had this something. How enthusiastic we were, how happily we went into the trenches – we had something worth dying for. And then – quite suddenly – everything became grey, gloomy, depressed . . . just as in that small trench for which sacrifice upon sacrifice was made in vain. In vain! We didn't want to make vain sacrifices. If there's sense and reason in the whole there must be sense and reason in the parts. Don't you think so?'

'I don't understand much about it,' said Otto. 'I was happy because I had a job. Before that I had none.'

'You see, just like me! But the job must have some sense, mustn't it?'

'I don't know, Herr Lieutenant. I never thought about it. But I could imagine – when we're under fire, for instance, and the telephone wire's broken – the officer saying that a message must be delivered in the rear and I'd take the envelope containing the message and see that it arrived safely without knowing whether the message was really important or not.'

'Yes,' said the lieutenant after a while, 'that wasn't stupid, Corporal. You could see it that way too.'

He was silent for a long time. To the east and west the guns now rumbled incessantly. But where the two men were it was still quiet – hardly did a bullet whistle over them or a machine-gun begin to rattle. Then it went quite quiet again.

'And yet,' continued the lieutenant, speaking rather doubtfully, 'to be only a blind messenger! We had hoped for something more.'

He grew animated. 'And a messenger to whom? We know where we stand here – but what about those at home? Have you been on leave? But of course you must have been, if you were here from the beginning. Do you remember the embarrassed, eager faces? How they always wanted you to talk about the war? And how puzzled they became when you couldn't speak about anything except mud and cold and hunger? They wanted to hear about heroic deeds. Yes, heroic deeds! And think of their embarrassment when they saw how you hated going back to the Front. How frightened they were in case the beloved son or brother might turn out to be a coward. And how they tried to give you fresh courage. Corporal, the people at home have no idea what's at stake.'

'And what is, if I might ask, Herr Lieutenant?'

'Why, we are. We, the younger people! Because we're the real Germany. So as to find a reason for living, so as to have a life worthy of being lived! That's what's at stake, Corporal. You and me!'

The lieutenant fell silent. His teeth chattered – it was very cold. And one dared not make the slightest movement in that damned crater or else the French would hear and at once throw hand grenades into it.

'Corporal!'

'Yes?'

'It's horribly cold.'

'Yes, sir.'

The lieutenant looked at his watch. 'Anyway, it's past eleven. Six more hours – and then it'll be dark and we can go back. We can stick it till then.'

'Of course.'

They no longer spoke of the moon or Verey lights. They must get back that night. Must.

The lieutenant broke a slab of chocolate in two and handed half to Otto. 'There, that's chocolate I got on leave. They gave it to me as a parting gift of the greatest value. I find they make rather too much fuss at home about their turnips. Well, we won't worry! I've just been on leave and I haven't quite got used again to the life here. When were you last on leave?'

'I haven't had any leave yet.'

'What do you mean – no leave? Not from this position, I suppose. If you've been at the Front since the beginning of the war you must have had two or three leaves already.'

'No, I haven't had any leave at all.'

'But, man, that's impossible.' The lieutenant sat up so abruptly that Hackendahl had to push him down and say warningly: 'Be careful, Herr Lieutenant.'

'Oh, yes . . . But it's impossible. More than two years at the Front and always on the Western Front too! That right?'

Otto nodded.

'Well, it's impossible. There must be something wrong somewhere.' He looked at Otto. 'No. Iron Cross and two stripes – nothing wrong there.'

'No, nothing. The opportunity didn't present itself.'

The lieutenant pondered. 'Wait. What's your name?'

'Hackendahl.'

'Oh, yes – Hackendahl. That's why your name seemed so familiar. I've heard of you. They say . . .' He broke off and looked at Otto, almost embarrassed. Otto returned the glance with a faint smile.

'I can guess what they say,' he said. 'There's a chap in the Fifth who doesn't want any leave – he must be cracked. That's what they say.'

The lieutenant looked relieved. 'That's so. But you really don't look as mad as that, Corporal.'

'I'm not mad at all. I'll go on leave one day but it hasn't got to that yet.'

'What do you mean, to that yet? But perhaps I'm enquiring about your private affairs.'

'They're private but they can be discussed. After all the Herr Lieutenant has spoken to me about his private affairs too, in a manner of speaking . . .'

'Well, fire away, Hackendahl! I'm curious to know what could make a man forgo his leave for two years.'

'Nothing wonderful, Herr Lieutenant. In spite of what they say. It's only that – well, when I was at home I was a weak kind of fellow, without courage or a will of my own. However, I've now realized that I'm not that sort of fellow after all.'

'I should say not!'

'But someone made me so, a certain person who broke my spirit from the very beginning. And as a result I did something dirty, Herr Lieutenant. I have a girl, and we have a child who is now more than four years old. I'd sworn to Gertrud a dozen times that I'd marry her – the last time was before I went to the Front. But I didn't marry her and only because I daren't own up about it to my father and ask him for my papers.'

'Oh,' said the lieutenant, 'so it was your father who broke your spirit. And now you daren't face the girl, eh?'

'Herr Lieutenant, Gertrud's never said a word to me. It's my father I daren't face.'

'But, Hackendahl, you can't be afraid of your father still – a man like you who has proved himself a hundred times in action. You're quite different now from what you were two years ago. Is your father really such a tyrant?'

'Not at all, Herr Lieutenant. Fundamentally he's a good man, but anyone who isn't like him or doesn't do and think in his way he treats as an enemy and really hates. He imagines he's doing heaven a service by making life hell for him. And he regarded me – his son – in the same sort of way, as if I were a kind of enemy, and a bad one.'

'I know people like that,' said the lieutenant eagerly. He'd been moved by the corporal's story. Memories came back to him – he heard the droning sound of the grown-ups' Bible-reading when he was a child. 'I knew that kind of thing too,' he had called out, and then began to relate: 'Last time I went on leave I stayed with an uncle, a landowner. Not much hunger there, they provide for themselves. They don't need ration cards – they're called self-supporting. You must have heard of it.'

Hackendahl nodded.

'Yes, and when I left they asked me to take a packet of food to another uncle, his brother, who was a retired president of a provincial court of justice and lived in a town. "You'll manage it all right," laughed my uncle. I didn't quite know what he was referring to unless he meant the size of the parcel, which I had to lug about the train and not lose sight of.' The lieutenant stopped for a moment; he was thinking how annoyed he had been about all the bother it had caused him, yet glad at realizing the happiness such a parcel could bring. 'Yes, so I took the parcel to the other uncle. I hadn't seen him for a long time and was startled to see how greatly he had changed. His face was shrunken and hardly bigger than a child's. It looked dreadful. And then his neck, his pitiful neck, with the skin hanging down in flaps! You must know, Hackendahl, that my uncle was one of those people with a Prussian sense of duty; he had got it into his head that he had to live on his ration cards and in consequence he was almost starving to death. "The government knows what it's doing," he said, "and if it has worked out that one can live on one's rations then it can be done." '

Lieutenant von Ramin saw himself sitting with his uncle, who fittingly entertained his young guest, pouring him a glass of wine – magnificent wine – for wine could be had without cards and the uncle was a rich man. But on a wooden platter by the side of the glass lay a slice of bread, such a thin little slice that one could almost see the grain of the wood through it. And on the bread was a bit of fat, a very meagre portion of egg and a miserable salted fish . . .

'Eat, my boy,' the uncle said. 'I hope you like it.' And his voice trembled. 'I've already eaten.'

'And I had thought,' said Lieutenant von Ramin, 'that my parcel of food would be regarded as a godsend! But now I understood what my uncle in the country had meant when he said – "You'll manage it all right." For I didn't manage it. "Do you want to corrupt a German judge into breaking the law?" shouted my rich uncle. "Get out of my house! How could I sleep at night if I myself broke the law? I have sentenced tens of thousands of thieves and cheats in my life and I should have sentenced them all unjustly if I myself was unjustly privileged." And all the time he kept looking hungrily at the parcel. He must have suffered terribly, poor old man.'

'One can understand him, though,' said Otto. 'He was ashamed of weakening.'

'You say that,' said the lieutenant angrily. 'My mother said the same – he was a great man, he had died for an ideal! Because he did die, shortly afterwards, from a chill. No strength left. But he wasn't a great man, Hackendahl, any more than your father is. It isn't great to starve to death for one's Fatherland. How did it benefit his country? He died for a false god, an idol, the sort of thing that savages worship. Something wooden, lifeless.'

Hackendahl was silent.

'You see, Hackendahl, at first one is deeply moved to learn that so-and-so has died for an ideal, literally died, when he could have lived comfortably. But death isn't enough; you must die for something living, and the Prussian sense of duty is dead and has been a long time. It was born in a period more than a hundred years ago when people lived in the bitterest poverty and with nothing to guide them – they had to have some such standard of conduct. But all that was finished with long before the war. No, the old idols are done for. If this war is to have any meaning then something new and living must come out of it.'

Hackendahl said nothing.

'I say it is good that Uncle Eduard died. And you ought not to be afraid to go on leave and see your father. Man, it's you who are living and he who is dead.'

'I don't know,' said Otto Hackendahl in a low voice, 'whether the Herr Lieutenant sees things correctly – a man is still a child to his father and mother. And I should prefer it to be done decently, without a quarrel. He's my father and not to be blamed for what he is.'

'So you're afraid after all, Hackendahl,' said the lieutenant impatiently.

'Of course I'm afraid. That's why I don't go on leave.'

'You brood too much, man. You keep on imagining how you'll enter your father's room and what you'll say . . . But you know, Hackendahl, that when you're waiting for zero hour you imagine a hundred horrors, and every now and then you look at the time and then at the sky to see whether the Verey lights are going up – and to put it plainly you're in the hell of a funk. But when the moment comes you go over the top with a yell and you've forgotten all your terrors.'

'But there are some who don't, Herr Lieutenant.'

'Well, you're not one of them – you get stage fright, that's all.

And now I'll tell you something, Corporal. If we get back safe and sound from this blasted ice house I shall officially order you to go on leave, d'you understand?'

Otto smiled, but it was a cheerful smile. And when the lieutenant saw this, he too felt cheerful. For a long time they remained silent, freezing.

Twice the lieutenant said: 'Oh damn! Oh damn!' and yet again: 'Damn! Damn!'

'What are you damning, Herr Lieutenant?'

'Not being able to smoke.'

'Yes, that's really damnable. But the wind's in the direction of the French – they'd smell it.'

'And send us a couple of hand grenades.'

'That's so, Herr Lieutenant.'

Towards four o'clock the sky cleared, which made things worse, since the planes now came over – at this stage of the war the French dominated the air, flying low over the trenches, with machine-guns rattling or, higher up, signalling to their artillery with Verey lights.

Lieutenant von Ramin and Otto Hackendahl threw themselves flat on their bellies and hid their faces. Towards evening the gunfire broke out again and they heard the crash of shells coming closer. In the French trenches the machine-guns started and those from the other side replied.

'Will it never get dark?' they groaned.

Gradually it grew quieter; they could feel rain on their necks. Cautiously they began to stir; impossible for their stiffened limbs ever to be supple again.

'Damned cold!' said the lieutenant.

'We must manage it tonight somehow.'

'Yes, tonight! But it's raining.'

'It won't rain for long.'

More and more waiting, hour after hour. It never became really dark. The moon wasn't visible but there was a pale glow in the sky.

'Let's wait another hour,' suggested the lieutenant, his teeth chattering.

'I've still a mouthful of cherry brandy left, Herr Lieutenant.'

'Yes, pass it over! No, don't bother. No. Really no. Don't forget you promised to go on leave if we get out of here safe and sound!'

Otto did not reply.

'Say yes,' urged the lieutenant. 'I've a feeling it will bring us luck.'

'All right, then, Herr Lieutenant.'

It grew no darker, nor did the sector quieten down again. There was constant shooting, a scream, the rattle of a machine-gun.

'We're not across yet, my boy,' said the lieutenant grimly.

'I'm only afraid they may shoot us from our own trench,' said Hackendahl.

'You see – you're not indifferent, either, to the kind of heroic death you die.'

Midnight – and, if anything, rather lighter. The lieutenant was in a state of agonizing indecision, his teeth chattering from the cold and possibly from excitement also. It was easier for Hackendahl – he had merely to await orders.

Suddenly from the French trenches came a burst of laughter, immediately stifled, but—

'Now's the time, Herr Lieutenant!' whispered Hackendahl.

'Come on,' the other almost shouted.

They crawled out of the shell hole. The French parapet seemed so near that they could almost have touched it, the German trench so far as to be out of sight.

'Crawl!' gasped the lieutenant.

They had made their plans beforehand. They were to crawl within a certain distance of the German trench and then call out to the sentry. But the lieutenant was carried away by excitement. After thirty or forty metres he rose to his feet.

'Run! They can't see us now,' he yelled.

They ran, the lieutenant in front. Hackendahl thought he heard a shout – then came the report of a Verey pistol and a light rose above them, blinding and growing brighter . . .

'Lie down, Herr Lieutenant,' begged Hackendahl.

'Run!' shouted the lieutenant, and ran.

Behind them shots cracked, the parapet of the German trench was clearly visible, more Verey lights rose . . .

'Don't shoot!' yelled the lieutenant. 'Germans! Comrades!'

The French were shooting.

The lieutenant stood still. 'I've stopped one, though. Run on, man.'

Hackendahl dragged him along. He let himself fall over the parapet onto the shoulders of his comrades.

An hour later, when the firing had died down, stretcher-bearers carried Lieutenant von Ramin away.

'That was a bit of luck,' said he, smiling at Otto. 'A clean hole through the biceps. Won't even take me home. I'll be back in three weeks.' And in a whisper: 'You remember what you promised, Hackendahl, about the leave?'

'But the Herr Lieutenant hasn't come out unhurt.'

'Are you going to quibble with your sacred word? No nonsense, now! Report for leave at once!'

'At your command, Herr Lieutenant!'

§ VII

It did after all take some time before Otto Hackendahl got his leave. Outwardly, he didn't change much. Perhaps he put on his gas mask a bit earlier than usual when the shout went up: 'Gas attack!' Perhaps the day, with its shooting and minor skirmishes, seemed longer. But he did his duty as usual. His section was in the trenches. There was always something to do.

At night he slept deep and without dreams. He didn't think any more about the future conflict with his father. All that seemed to lie very far back. Ever since he'd spoken about his cowardice to Lieutenant von Ramin, so that another person – not just Tutti – knew about it, this cowardice seemed not to exist. Strange contradiction!

Then the time was up. His company commander shook him by the hand. 'Come back in a good state, Hackendahl,' he said. 'Don't let them get at you with their silly ideas back there. They say it's pretty nasty.'

'Yes, Captain.'

A couple of comrades accompanied him for a bit out of the

trenches. He was given letters to deliver personally, with greetings and parcels.

'Have a good time, Hackendahl,' they said. 'Who knows how we'll meet up again. We're due for another attack.'

He went on alone. The day had not yet dawned. The road was full of ammunition convoys returning from the Front, and out-of-service field kitchens and ambulances.

Once a lightly built, large vehicle went by – a staff car. Indistinctly he saw faces inside, and gained an impression of mirrors, crimson, silk and immaculate uniforms.

Later he diverted from the road. The day was gradually dawning. He had time. In farms that lay scattered under trees, life was stirring here and there. A light shone in a stable. He heard cows mooing for their food. Buckets clattered   good!

He walked as he had no longer walked for two years – slowly, comfortably, safely. He looked at the winter corn in the fields. It was emerald-green and glowed in the rising sun. It would be a clear day, today. A bad day for those in the trenches, he thought – good flying weather. He was happy and sad – happy that there were still animals and growing corn, and not just earth mangled by grenades and rats. And he felt a bit guiltily sad about the comrades he'd left in the trenches.

From far away he already heard the thunder of guns and was uneasy. The farms and the winter corn no longer made him happy. He began to go faster.

He looked at his watch. There was still plenty of time before his train left for Lille.

He went even faster. He forced himself to stop by a wild-rose bush. Winter had taken its leaves, but thick, bright red rosehips hung from its branches. They shone in the sun, wet with rain. I've got time, he said to himself, impatiently. I can take my time appreciating the beauty of these rosehips . . .

Suddenly he realized that he was terribly homesick, that he longed for Tutti, for her face and for her soft, dove-like eyes. He no longer knew what Gustäving looked like. He would now be twice as old as when he'd left for the Front. There had been big changes as far as his parents were concerned. Father again drove a cab by himself. He couldn't imagine his father on a coach box. He would like to see Father again.

Yes, he suddenly felt homesick – homesick for all and sundry. For Rabause and for the broken old nag, and he saw his own wood-carving knives before him.

He was homesick, and now, well behind the Front, he was worried that something could happen to him before he got home. He looked at the time. He had an hour before his train left, and hardly a quarter of an hour left to walk.

All the same, he began to run. He ran ever faster. He saw the station. Not a train was to be seen. Nevertheless he ran faster. Like most men, he'd often been frightened at the thought of a bullet in the balls, but had long got over it. Now the fear came again. They mustn't get him. Not now, especially not now when he was going home!

He was only calm again when he was sitting in the train, which was crowded with others on leave, who were going home like him, or those going to Lille for a few days. Those going home on leave were almost all very quiet: all the noisier were the others. They recommended pubs and girls to each other, cracked dirty jokes and were determined – after the spectral life in the trenches – to fill their few hours of leave with as much 'real life' as possible (life in this case mostly meaning alcohol).

In Lille he had more time. His train left at noon. He stood hesitating and undecided in front of the station. He could have visited Erich who, according to reports from their mother, was in some kind of office here performing useful and important work. But he couldn't decide to do so.

Instead he decided to have a look at the town, and slowly made his way. He was soon caught up in the hurly-burly. With astonishment he saw the shop windows filled with luxury goods, and the flashy officers with monocles and clinking spurs who went past him, little riding whips hanging from a leather loop round their wrists. Orderlies ran self-importantly about with briefcases; their spotless trousers had ironed creases, and the sun was reflected in the shine of their shoes.

Suddenly he was aware of what he looked like in his battledress, only cleaned in emergency, whose material had lost its colour and was worn, and in his clumsy, badly polished shoes, still with mud on them from the trenches.

The officers hurried past him. They neither paid him any attention nor even saw him. Enormous cars glided by on the road, with impressive staff flags stuck on their radiators. In an empty car sat a huge Russian greyhound, bored and arrogant. Two nurses passed him with pink, satisfied faces.

Otto Hackendahl did an about-turn and went back towards the station. All he wanted to do was to sit somewhere in peace and drink a glass of beer. A fat, dark-looking civilian with sad eyes asked him for directions. Irritated, he replied that he also didn't know his way around here, and was pleased when he reached the station again.

He sat down, sad and angry, at a wooden table, between others on leave waiting for their trains home and who looked like him. A man lifted up his head when he heard him order his beer angrily from the waiter, and asked: 'Well, Comrade, have you seen the town? Busy place, isn't it?'

The man put his yawning head back on the table and said: 'Now you see for the first time what stupid pigs we are! These fellow animals! These pot bellies! But you're in the right, aren't you, Comrade Porker?'

Otto didn't answer. He almost choked with misery. He cursed himself, Lieutenant Ramin, and his leave. If I hadn't walked away from my regiment, he kept on thinking, I would never have seen this rubbish.

And he wondered whether he shouldn't turn round.

§ VIII

'Good morning, Erich,' said the Reichstag deputy.

Erich was sitting at a dressing table manicuring his nails. He was wearing riding breeches (expensive corduroy from Bendix, a hundred and fifty marks), glittering patent-leather riding boots and a shantung shirt.

'You, Herr Doctor!' he exclaimed, taken aback. 'I should never have expected you in Lille.'

'In an official capacity, my boy,' said the Reichstag deputy reassuringly. 'Members of all parties have been invited to view the Front by GHQ. That won't compromise you!'

'Herr Doctor!' exclaimed Erich, still embarrassed.

'Now, now, no false shame! Everybody should try to get on in the world.' He looked at Erich benevolently – the lad had now slipped on his tunic. The epaulettes shone. 'I see that I have to congratulate you on your promotion to lieutenant. You're making your way!'

'The day before yesterday,' said Erich. 'I ought to have been promoted long ago. But you can understand, Herr Doctor, that Father's profession . . .'

'The goal seemed to you worthwhile, however, and so you've achieved it.' The deputy's voice was amused but his expression remained benevolent. 'You've put your ideals in cold storage and in their place wear silk shirts.'

Erich blushed again. 'All the officers wear silk underclothes,' he said defiantly.

'In the trenches?'

'I'm on the staff,' insisted Erich and fell silent.

'Well, well,' said the deputy, 'we don't want to quarrel, Erich. I understand perfectly that you've changed your views. I myself am not in the trenches and I've not the slightest intention of going there, either. I sympathize fully with anyone who wants to get out of . . .'

'I don't want to get out of it, Herr Doctor,' said Erich angrily. 'I've been detailed elsewhere.'

'Of course you have. You do your duty here just as you did it there. I don't suppose otherwise.' The deputy's voice was still suave. 'As I said, we won't quarrel either about words or ideas – we've all learned a thing or two in the last few years. But upon my word, Erich, things have turned out damnably different from what we thought in August 1914. You remember?'

'I'll go back to the trenches,' said Erich furiously, 'when they all go. But I'm not being shot to bits while the toffs here swim in champagne.'

'You prefer to swim with them, I suppose?'

'Herr Doctor!' Erich almost shouted.

'You're not going to throw me out, my boy, are you? What's the use of showing off before me, Erich? Be sensible and listen to reason. You're not a fool – you ought to tell yourself that if a member of the Reichstag personally calls on the unimportant Lieutenant X he doesn't do so merely to exchange a little repartee.'

'I'm no shirker!'

'All right, then, you're not. Are you satisfied now? Not yet? Well, Erich, are we going to talk or shall I go?' He did not wait for a reply however. 'I don't know whether you've followed the debates in the Reichstag, Erich? In the last vote on war credits thirty one of us voted against them, almost one third of my party group. Don't get alarmed – I don't belong to that section or else I wouldn't be here at the special invitation of GHQ. My party group will probably soon split into a Radical wing against the war and a majority in favour of it.'

Erich looked intently at him. The unpleasantness of a moment ago was forgotten.

'Of course we aren't really in favour of war either, Erich. If we were really in favour of it two years ago, we've learned much since, Erich. We don't have to come to your nice little base at Lille to know that the nation is no longer united. There's only general discontent now . . . in the interior. It looks bad in the cities, Erich. There have been riots already.'

'I heard about them.'

'Of course you heard about them – things like that can't remain hidden.' The deputy chuckled knowingly. 'But I say over and over again to my colleagues who vote No – discontent in the interior means nothing so long as the military still rule . . . So let's go on granting them their credits, let them carry on their war . . .'

Erich looked nervously at the door and windows.

'Yes, the morale at the Front,' ruminated the deputy, looking at Erich and falling silent. Then he spoke in a louder voice. 'This trip to the Front, my dear Erich, has been a very odd affair. We didn't catch a single glimpse of it. Once they showed us a trench – the dugouts were of concrete and I could have sworn that the duckboards had been scrubbed that same morning. One felt reluctant to step on the clean wood . . . Yes, that was the trench they showed us.'

He looked at Erich but Erich was still silent.

'It's as clear as daylight,' said the deputy with sudden determination, 'that this government will be overthrown as soon as the Front caves in. It has too many enemies both within and without. One only needs to wait. To wait and prepare. And when it gets to that point, then – then we're there. We shall be the only alternative. Because the workers, the proletariat, in fact the whole nation, will trust us.'

'You want to take over the government after a lost war?' Erich cried. 'You're counting on a lost war to win power? You must—' He broke off and stared.

'Be mad, what?' added the deputy. 'But we're not mad, we're far-sighted. The war at the Front will be lost. Erich, you must know that if you see what's going on here. This is surely not how one wins wars!'

'And yet you approve of the war credits,' said Erich obstinately.

'Because we want to win that other war, the world war. Don't you understand, Erich? The other war which has raged since the world began, the war for the poor and wretched, the workers, the proletariat, for all those in chains. That is the war we want to win.'

'I used to believe in such things once, but haven't done so for ages. Everyone's responsible for himself. It really doesn't look like the redemption of the proletariat, Herr Doctor!'

'Yes, it does, Erich! That is if you don't just see what's before your eyes, but look from a distance. Eternal peace can only be won when mankind loses faith in military war. This present war *has* to be terrible; it must demand many worse victims. Erich, the Front is about to experience terrible things! In England they're building fighting machines – hidden under the name of tanks – steel monsters without wheels which go over all barbed wire, all trenches . . . Our military doesn't believe in them, but you'll find out.'

'And it's a defeated people like that you want to govern?'

'Erich, we won't be the only ones to lose. Everyone will be defeated. Victims are required if much is to be achieved. The continuation of the war, for which the military needs us, will smash the belief in the military for ever. Then it'll be our turn.'

'Defeated victors!'

'But everyone will be defeated victors. Do you think we'll parley with the military? We'll call together the workers of the world! Do you think the French worker won't understand us when we say to him, "No More War"? Then comes the liberation of the workers of all the nations, our kingdom, Erich. You too believed in it once and you still believe in it – despite this, and this.' He touched the silver epaulette, the tunic.

'It would be fine,' said Erich dreamily.

'Fine? Believe me, Erich, this peace will happen in quite a different way from what people expect. They'll rush from the trenches Germans and French and English – they'll look in each other's faces and they won't understand why they were shooting each other.'

'It would be fine,' said Erich once more. 'And what could I do to help, Herr Doctor?'

'You should . . .' whispered the Doctor, and this time it was he who looked at the door and the windows. 'You should . . .'

§ IX

Towards morning the mood of those working in the packing hall of the munitions factory became still more sulky and irritable.

The charge-hand felt it plainly. If only nothing happens, he thought, putting his hands in his pockets and placing himself in front of a poster inviting people to subscribe to the sixth War Loan – he was firmly resolved to do nothing himself that would lead to an outbreak.

The women, mostly dressed in ugly overalls which robbed them of all feminine charm, sat in rows at long wooden tables packing the sticks of powder which a machine had cut from an endless band. If their work made it necessary to pass some such remark as 'Move the case nearer' or 'Hurry up', this was said quietly; nevertheless it sounded as if they hated one another.

Eva Hackendahl stood at her machine. She pressed a lever. Knives were lowered, cutting off a dark grey stick of powder. Hands stretched out for the stick and she released the lever, which automatically returned into position; then once again she laid her hand on it, to press it down.

This she had done since eight o'clock the previous evening. Deadly fatigue oppressed her – everything, even her own self, nauseated her. Fatigue lay like a ring bearing down on her head, not letting go for a moment. She sensed it even right inside her mouth where it left a stuffy taste, and it gave her a saggy feeling in her knees. Nothing but a lever that rose to meet her hand like something living, the grey ribbon of powder, the hands reaching between the knives . . .

She sighed. Only half an hour to the end of the night shift, yet this half-hour seemed unending. She thought of her bed, her nice warm bed, sleep and oblivion. Tutti she knew was already queuing up before some butcher's or baker's, but the bed which she herself used in the daytime and Tutti at night would have been made ready for her. She had to press the lever for one half-hour longer and then she could go home, to sleep.

But the time seemed endless – the last quarter of an hour was always the worst.

She remembered her schooldays (she depressed the lever) and the last few minutes before the bell rang (she released the lever) when often something would happen (the lever rose and lay under her hand) to spoil all her free afternoon. And even if nothing happened (she depressed the lever and the knives sank) those last minutes were always insurmountable (the lever was released and the women's hands appeared). Nothing was changed. Everything had stayed the same. She had experienced much. (The hands had now taken the sticks; the lever rose.) She was still going to school. She depressed the lever, the knives sank and, as in her childhood, so now the last deadly minutes must be endured in all their horror.

As in school! It was for this you went on living, suffered evil, learned to be patient, assumed responsibilities – just to go to school again, for ever. The marks Life gave you were bad. You were never moved up. You stayed at the same desk world without end.

Eva Hackendahl looked over the rows of women workers. She saw necks sticking out of grey blouses, necks bent over the table – weary, overburdened necks – and she knew that all these women, almost all of them, had a more difficult life than she, whom Tutti relieved of practically all housework. These women went on the night shift only because they had families to care for. No sooner had they returned from the factory than they had to wash and dress their children, make breakfast and send them off to school. Then they would rush to the food shops; their knees trembling with fatigue, they had to queue up, or fetch a bag of coal perhaps. During the day they snatched three, four, or if they were lucky five hours' sleep. They often remained in their clothes for days – what was the good of undressing for an hour or two?

And in a spare moment, before hurrying off to the endless night shift, they would tear a page out of the children's exercise books. For he is always in their minds; he is still thought of as the breadwinner, although they have replaced him. He has become the symbol of the good times of peace, when there was work but also an end to work, when one knew what hunger was but could eat one's fill too.

'Dear Max,' they wrote on the thin blue lines, trying to write as well and as clearly as they had done at school 'Dear Max, The children and me are still all right and I hope the same of you. This week we had an extra half-pound of groats on the ration cards and I get the heavy worker's allowance, so we manage quite well.' (The 'quite well' underlined three times.) 'So you need not save up your sugar. We make ends meet quite well.' (Again underlined.) 'It would be nice if you could come home for good. Can't you end the war soon? Please excuse this joke, I know we have to carry on . . .' That is how they wrote, without complaint, amid quarrelling children and the everlasting cry for bread. They wrote as they worked, as they looked after children and fetched food: naturally, without a fuss. They wrote so that father knew, after all, that we were all still well and alive. Life – that was what it was about. Life was sacred. They must preserve it for themselves, for their children. They didn't think about it. They acted.

'Carry on' – a slogan hammered into every brain. 'Carry on' – that meant to remain alive. Why? To what end? Was life worth it with the children almost starving? No good thinking about it – one had to go on living however difficult.

The lever rose, was depressed, was released, rose. At the

beginning Eva had dreamed every night about this lever and its knives, and the hands between these knives . . . She dreamed of hands bleeding, of amputated fingers, and would wake with a scream . . . It was nothing out of the way – it happened to all these women. Their men were at the Front; they saw more than strange hands covered with blood; they saw their own husbands mutilated.

Eva Hackendahl was indeed better off than the others, at least in theory, for Tutti had taken over nearly all of her daily chores. Eva had no children to look after, no husband at the Front to worry about. She knew she was better off, though she in fact wasn't. Once, and not very long ago, she stood on a small, stony, slippery ledge. Not far beneath her, invisible, the water sucked and splashed. She didn't do it. And yet – although Eugen was so base and repulsive, the conflict between her weakness and his brutality had somehow given meaning to a life which was now quite empty.

The charge-hand pushed the cap off his forehead and turned away from the poster. It was five minutes to seven – once more, against all expectations, the shift had gone off well.

And at that very moment he heard the scream. A piercing scream. He leaped to the control – one movement and he had uncoupled the transmission belts. The drone of the machines grew deeper, then stopped altogether.

In this silence the shrieks were louder.

'She did it intentionally. She saw I had my hand in the machine.'

Trembling and deathly pale, Eva Hackendahl stood there, the accused. Without a word in self-defence she was looking at the hand held out to her, a hand dripping with blood.

'She did it on purpose,' cried the injured woman – a little creature with a birdlike face. 'I was looking at her because I was a bit behind and she looked at me. And that was the moment she let the knives come down . . .'

'That's true,' cried another woman.

'Don't talk nonsense,' contradicted a third. 'You were asleep.'

'I wasn't asleep, I was a bit behind.' Suddenly she started to weep. 'Why did you do it? I've never done anything to you. Oh, my hand – I can't work now! See, I can't move my finger.'

'Show it me,' said the charge hand. 'Don't make that noise! It's nothing, only a scratch. You won't even get sick leave for that.'

'No sick leave?' she began.

'Blood!' shrieked a woman far gone in pregnancy. 'Blood! Get out of my way, I want to see it.'

The bell which was the signal for the shift to knock off had died away, unheard.

The tumult increased. Other charge-hands arrived, and an engineer.

'Silence! Keep the women quiet!'

Eva Hackendahl stood beside her machine. She was the only one who had not uttered a word. She was thinking: they say I did it on purpose. Did I? I don't know. Perhaps I did do it on purpose? I don't know . . . You can't always worry about something that is perhaps never going to be . . . These fatal last minutes at school when anything might happen. . . Perhaps Eugen will find me one day and all the suffering here will have been for nothing . . .

'Go home! What are you standing there for? You're suspended. Such a thing shouldn't have happened.'

'I didn't do it on purpose.'

'Who said so? Her? Oh, her! But you should pay more attention. Well, you'd better work as a packer in future. Ten pfennigs less an hour but you should have been more careful. We'll see later on . . . perhaps in Hall Five. But it'll get about, of course.'

'Perhaps I did do it on purpose.'

'Don't talk rubbish! Now don't you start too. Go home and have a good sleep. On purpose? What nonsense!'

§ X

The way home was harder and sadder than ever. Why go home, lie in bed and gather new strength if you get no pleasure out of it? Eva Hackendahl walked ever more slowly. It was already almost daylight, the lamps were out, grey figures stood in front of the shops. Other people were next to her and behind her – but they noticed no one, just as no one took notice of them. A woman in trousers would have been unprecedented in Berlin only two years ago. Times had changed. A well-dressed woman is a sight worth seeing nowadays, at least in this part of town.

In front of Eva Hackendahl was a heavily laden soldier in field-grey, someone on leave going the same way as she. Otto Hackendahl walked slowly, looking about him. When he left Berlin two years ago, the streets had been gay with flags and full of cheerful people; girls wore bright dresses, there were flowers and garlands, cigars and chocolates. And now he was back in a grey, desolate city, and the feet that shuffled over the early-morning pavements were already tired. Faces were grey and desolate too, and shoulders drooped despondently. Not a single laugh had he heard. Yesterday he was disgusted by the false luxury in the rear. Now he saw the crumbling, ruined town of the hinterland – and the bleakness gripped him and drew him in.

In the trenches, when they had spoken of the scarcity at home, many had said: 'They shouldn't make such a fuss about it. We go hungry for twenty-four hours when we're under fire. They exaggerate.'

But Otto saw at once that everything was much worse, a hundred times worse than they in the trenches had believed. It wasn't only hunger – seeing these hopeless faces one realized how dreadful was the complete joylessness, the lack of everything that really made life worth living, which was hope.

Now he could see their doorway. He hadn't written to her about his leave; he had deprived her of the pleasures of anticipation, and he became anxious. What will she be like? he thought. Will she have changed much? Aren't I already much too late, now that I've changed so much? How will I find her?

A woman in trousers overtook him, glancing indifferently at the bearded face of the soldier on leave. Not till she came to the next doorway did Eva Hackendahl realize that she had looked on the face of her brother Otto – a face with purpose in it, the eyes frank and manly.

Leaning against the wall, she tried to think out what her brother's return would mean for her. Odd that her first thought should be to wonder if Otto, tired from his journey, might want to lie down on the only bed, the bed standing beside the child's cot. Or would she be allowed to have it herself – at least for this morning?

As if that were important! Nevertheless she couldn't help wondering how they were going to manage during the next few days with only one room and a kitchen, and only one bed, too. How much leave did a soldier get – a week or a fortnight?

He was now entering their doorway. Quickly she hid herself and he passed into the rear courtyard. She followed, watching him. Then our former life would begin again. This echoed in her mind. But what was that old life? Suddenly she understood how provisional it was, infinitely transient, a life lived at a day's notice. One day the war would be over and there would be no more arms factories. One day her brother would come home and want the place for himself – but then what would happen to her?

He had started to walk upstairs. Terrible depression overcame her. But what did I really imagine? she pondered. Did I think it could go on for ever, night shift and shared bed, for a lifetime, a whole lifetime? Of course, it's all rubbish – I did it on purpose. She ought to have taken her paw away quicker, the silly bitch. I suppose I hoped they'd chuck me out. Well, if I must I must – there's no way out once it's written that you're to go to the bad.

Otto was now outside his flat. What he carried with him was nothing. He ran like a youngster, came out of the courtyard. Eva, as he touched the bell push, passed behind him and went a floor higher. She wasn't going to stand there beside her brother; nor would she open the door for him, although she had the key in her pocket. She had thought of this place as her home, but that was another piece of rubbish – it was his, alone – she had no home, that was the position.

She sat down on the stairs – homeless. She would see what happened, she had time! When you purposely injure someone's hand in your machine you can still deceive others and yourself about it. But when heaven sends your brother home that same morning, to drive you out of your bed and your sleep – your sole prospect of blessed oblivion – then it means you are inevitably destined for the mire.

But if that is the situation – which it is – you don't make a fuss about it. You settle down on the last step before the door to the attic and wait for what comes next. Mud will find mud. There's no hurry!

§ XI

Otto had watched the working woman in trousers in astonishment. What does she want up there? There's only the attic. But he forgets that immediately, because in reply to his ringing, a voice calls through the door: 'Mummy's not here!'

'Where is Mummy then, Gustäving?' asked the father, putting his ear to the door and trying to realize that this was his son, now no longer two, but four years old.

'Fetching coal,' said the shrill little voice within. 'Who are you? What do you want?'

'To see you, Gustäving.'

'Who are you? How do you know my name? What's yours?'

Otto Hackendahl pondered for a moment. He would have liked to say 'I'm your father', but somehow he could not. A door divided them – and he had to wait.

'Where does Mummy fetch coal, Gustäving?' he asked. 'Still from Tiedemann's?'

'From Tiedemann's?' questioned the voice. And a great light must have flashed on the child's mind, for suddenly hands were drumming against the door: 'Open it! I know who you are – you're my papa. Open the door, please – Mummy's always saying that you're coming soon. I want to see you, Papa.'

'Yes, Gustäving. But be quiet. I'm your papa, yes. Listen, Gustäving, I haven't got a key so we'll have to wait till Mummy comes. You won't recognize me, you know, Gustäving.'

'Yes, I will. You're my papa.'

'Because I've got a long, long yellow beard.'

'I don't believe it – my papa hasn't a beard.'

'I grew it at the Front, Gustäving.'

'Open the door, Papa! I want to see it!'

'But I've got no key, Gustäving. We must wait till Mummy comes.'

A brief silence for thought.

The girl on the stairs above was also thinking. Yes, that's home and homecoming. But there's nothing like that for me. And why not? I'm much prettier and at any rate as intelligent as Tutti. And nobody was more of a milksop than Otto. But they get it and I get nothing. And Erich has got on, too, and Sophie's been made a sister and has a Red Cross Medal. Only I . . .

Below it went on and on: 'I know, Papa, go down into the courtyard. Stand there and I'll look out of the window. Then I'll see whether you're my papa or not.'

'But you'll fall out, Gustäving!'

'No, I won't. Go on, Papa!'

'Wait a bit. Mummy may be coming any moment now.'

'Oh, do go, Papa. Go on.'

'You won't recognize me in my beard.'

'Yes, I will, I'll recognize you! Not recognize my own papa!'

'And you promise not to open the window?'

'Of course, Papa, I promise. I'll look through the glass. Hurry up!'

'But it'll take some time to get downstairs.'

'As if I didn't know, Papa! Five floors. Are you always so slow, Papa?'

'I'm going, Gustäving.'

'Well, hurry up then!'

Otto Hackendahl, bag and baggage, went downstairs.

The courtyard was narrow, not much more than an airshaft with, to make it worse, a criss-cross of washing lines overhead. He had to push his way among dustbins and, since the view of himself promised not to be very good, he climbed upon them, pulled off his field cap and waved it. He could see nothing himself, but roared lustily: 'Hurrah! Hurrah! Hurrah!'

Women looked out of their windows.

'A screw loose, eh?'

'Pretending to be loony, so he won't have to go back to the Front.'

But Otto Hackendahl had already climbed down from the bins and was running upstairs again to find that a miracle had happened – the door stood wide open and in the doorway was a boy, a very thin child with a large head . . .

'Gustäving! You see I am your papa! Who opened the door? Gustäving, are you pleased, too?'

'I said at once you were my papa. Your beard's not as long as you said. Have you brought me something to eat? I'm very, very hungry.'

The door, which had been opened after so much action, closed again behind them. They no longer puzzled their heads over what had happened. The girl above sat for a while, her shoulders shaking. She felt the same as she had not long before, standing on the little wet platform. Eventually she stood up and went slowly down the steps. Downstairs she met her sister-in-law, Gertrud Gudde.

The little cripple stood panting beside a bag of coal, only half a hundredweight, but much too heavy for such a fragile creature. Her hair hung down in wisps and the soft eyes looked anxious. But they lit up at once when they saw Eva. 'Oh, Eva, how kind you are, waiting for me. I was so afraid of all those stairs.'

Eva had originally intended to pass Tutti without a word, but now she stopped. What do I care about Tutti? I've got my own troubles to bear. Unprotesting, she shouldered the sack and carried it upstairs, all the while thinking that, without the mishap in the factory and her brother's return, she would long ago have been lying comfortably asleep in bed. She had never yet thought of helping her sister-in-law with the housework. Had she done so, how often might she not have seen this radiant gratitude?

They arrived at the flat. Gertrud, so that Eva need not put down the sack, had the key ready. But Eva barred the way.

'Here's your coal, Tutti,' she said with a strange expression on her face. 'Tidy yourself up a bit, you look all of a mess.'

Gertrud stared at her – Eva was so odd. Tidy herself up on the landing? No one had cared for years what she looked like. Under Eva's gaze she became quite confused, put a hand to her hair and tucked in a stray lock . . .

Suddenly she heard something – listened – trembled. In the flat she heard her child laugh, and a man's voice . . .

She looked at Eva.

'Yes,' said Eva in a changed voice. 'Yes, there you are! Tidy yourself quickly, Otto's home!' Leaning over the coal bag, she thought: you ugly old hunchback, you've got all the luck. What about me? I ought to hate you.

But she tidied Gertrud's hair and smoothed out with trembling hands the collar and neck of her dress. 'Yes, Tutti. Yes. Yes . . . Otto's there . . . and perfectly well.'

Two arms went round her neck. 'Oh, I'm so happy . . . My heart, my heart!' And, quickly releasing herself, Gertrud said: 'Do I look awful, Evchen?'

'You look wonderful.' (Hunchback!) 'You look splendid.' (Hunchback!) 'You've got a nice colour in your cheeks.' (Hunchback!) 'Now go in to him!'

And she, Eva, opened the door and pushed Tutti in. She, Eva – pretty Eva, Father's favourite – stood in her ugly overalls beside the sack of coal and listened to the cry of joy within . . . and the deep, warm voice saying, 'Yes, my good one, my sweetie, my beauty – here I am with you . . .'

Eva dragged the sack of coal into the dark corridor before she gently closed the door and left. She climbed slowly down the steps. Her tears flowed, and she kept on thinking, 'Why her? Why not me?'

She crossed the courtyards, went out of the house and came out onto the street.

§ XII

The fact that Otto Hackendahl went to look for his father already on the afternoon of the first day of the holiday was not only because he wanted to get his talk with him over as quickly as possible, but also because Tutti and Otto had waited for Eva with mounting alarm; but she had not come.

'I'll see her at my parents', no doubt,' said Otto. 'Where else could she have gone to?'

Indeed, where else could she have gone? Tutti remembered one morning when she helped to undress a half-frozen Eva, when one of her legs was drenched through up to her calf, but she hadn't said a word.

Otto went along the Frankfurter Allee, the old, familiar way known to him from a thousand walks. In his mind's eye he already saw the wooden fence and the sign: 'Conveyances for Hire. Gustav Hackendahl.'

As in a dream, where everything is the same and yet different, so

Otto next stood before this fence and read on the signboard: 'Hay and Forage Merchant. Hans Bartenfeld.'

Like a man who is lost he gazed up and down the street along which he had walked so often. And when he looked closer he saw that the board was new. It was a very recent alteration, then, which explained why he hadn't yet heard about it. Father would have carried out the sale secretly, holding it to be entirely his own concern – 'a man's affair' – and Mother wouldn't have been told till the last moment.

It was the same old yard but there were different curtains on the first-floor windows and another woman's face, not Mother's, looked out at him. Otto's heart contracted painfully. The son who had gone abroad, who had marched into war – the weak-willed son – had changed, become harder, more resolute. And with every day he had shed something of the home, had ceased gradually to be a son. Now that with his own eyes he saw how, both symbolically and actually, the old home existed no longer, the last link in the chain that had bound him snapped, and he was free.

He asked the woman at the window where the Hackendahls had moved to. She, in true Berlin manner, met this question by asking if he were one of the sons. Then Otto asked how long they had been gone and learned that they lived in the Wexstrasse. And was he the elder or the younger one?

Otto said thank you and left. He no longer saw either the woman or the courtyard. Nor did he turn towards the wooden fence, though he couldn't help thinking about how often, on Father's orders, armed with bucket and brush, he'd had to scrub away the slogans of the local youths, from 'I'm an idiot' to 'Teacher Stark's got false teeth'.

He went on. At last, it was all over. Earlier he obeyed Father's orders. Now he had his own voice in his own breast, the voice that gave orders about grenade craters and which told the strange Lieutenant von Ramin what had tortured him for so long . . .

Otto Hackendahl went along the Frankfurter Allee, and considered how he could most quickly get to Wexstrasse. It occurred to him that in this completely unfamiliar area of Berlin (like a completely different town, in fact), there was the circle line station of

Wilmersdorf-Friedenau. Wexstrasse must be near it. That's how he would get there fastest.

He hurried away, crossed the Alexanderplatz, went to the Suburban Railway and got in a train. Tack-tack-tack went the dilapidated carriages, grumbling and groaning. The winter wind blew through the broken panes. Their window straps had been cut off, the netting of the luggage racks was torn – but the carriages still did their duty, though not without protest. They were taking him to the destination for which he had prepared himself during two years on the Western Front – this destination was the Wilmersdorf-Friedenau Station for the moment.

The Wexstrasse was easy to find, everybody knew it. But he did not like the place. In the grey light of the early winter evening the street seemed to him narrow and cheerless. The Frankfurter Allee had been spacious and airy – here one could hardly breathe. Oh Father! Otto stopped dead. He had seen something familiar, a link with the past. By the kerb stood a cab without a driver. But Otto had no need to see the driver – he knew the horse. It was the grey, dismally hanging her head and seeming to study the pavement.

Otto ruffled her mane and rubbed her nose but the grey did not move her ears, nor sniff at the caressing hand – hardly bothered even to lift up her dull, half-extinguished eyes to her master's son.

How often have I groomed you! thought Otto. Do you remember how ticklish you used to be under the belly and how you always kicked out at me? I could never be careful enough. It wasn't your wickedness but just exuberance. In those days I was the one kept under and you were full of life. But now . . . No, I'm still not the exuberant type, but I still lift my eyes from the road and see the edge of the sky, rather farther than one can reach . . . So he chattered on, interspersed with, Horsey, where's Father? Horsey, what's happened to Father? Horsey!

No, it was naturally impossible that Father would ever drive this, his most miserable beast. True, Mother had written that business was bad, many reductions had to be made, and that Father was driving once again . . . However, the coachman sitting safely in the bar over there would be some kind of supplementary driver needing to pass the one and a half hours till going-home time.

Otto entered the tavern.

It was about half past four in the afternoon and the gas lamps in the street were beginning to light up. But inside they were sparing with their illumination; a solitary bulb burned dimly over the counter, just sufficient light for the landlord to see how much he was pouring into his glasses. In the corners were a few dim figures.

Otto sat down near the door and called out to the landlord: 'A bitter, please.'

For a moment there was silence. Then a hoarse voice said: 'Man, it's quite clear that the war can't be won. They asked for U-boats and now they've got them and still the Americans keep sending over soldiers and arms, no end to them.'

'Excuse me . . .'

'You hold on a moment, I'm speaking. Great offensive on the Western Front they said – and they're still in the same old place. Decision in the East they said – well, it's now been decided in the East, and what's it come to? You any less hungry?'

'Let me have a say, Franz!'

'Forget it for a moment. I'll just say one word. I'll say: international social democracy! Oh, yes, you'll think, the big bosses . . . Big bosses indeed, and the stories they've told us. But a light eventually goes on even with the most stupid, and when it goes on it goes red . . .'

'You'll get your mug punched – there's a soldier here.'

'Well, and what about it? What d'you mean, soldier? He thinks just as I do. When you're down, everyone turns on you – that's life.' But the speaker said no more, for the soldier stood up, took his beer glass in his hand and went obliquely across the tavern towards the speaker's table.

The speaker puffed himself up and was already half ducking himself under the table, calling the others almost pathetically as witnesses. 'But what did I say then? I didn't say anything. I just said that we'd succeed in the East.'

However, while he was still speaking, Otto passed his table. Beer glass in hand, he went to a table behind by the wall, put his glass down and said, 'Good evening, Father. It's me – Otto!'

The old man slowly raised his large, round, staring eyes from the dregs of his beer, which he had sat contemplating. With a sudden movement he held out his hand.

'You, Otto? That's good. Sit down, sit down! D'you find me by accident?'

'I saw the grey, Father, so I looked in.'

'Oh, the grey, the grey! There's less an' less to her every day, no feed an' no guts. I can't get her past the horse butcher's – she always tries to walk in.' The old man laughed, a dismal sound.

'And how are things otherwise, Father? How is the stable doing?'

'The stable? Haven't got a stable now. I've got a bay horse as well, but it's worn out, too. Not much doin' in my line, Otto.'

'Are you on your own, Father? Where's old Rabause?'

'What do I want him for now? With two horses? Even if the war finished I wouldn't have any work for you either. You're lucky to have your war.' Again he laughed, grimly.

Otto sat beside him, next to the beaten man. The blue coat hung loosely on the once robust figure; the formerly solid-looking face was flabby. Otto could recollect his father as a respected visitor to the bars in the Alexanderplatz, but here nobody looked at him, nobody listened to what he had to say – he was only an old cabman nodding over his glass of beer. A stricken man – and I'm going to strike him still harder, thought Otto.

'You've moved, Father?' he asked.

'Yes, I've moved. How d'you like the house?'

'I haven't been there yet, Father.'

'No? I suppose you were on your way. Where's your things?'

'I haven't got them with me. This time I'm staying elsewhere.'

'So you're stayin' elsewhere. All right, then.' Old Hackendahl gave his son a penetrating glance. All at once he was very wide awake and suspicious.

'The house, you know,' he said abruptly in his best German, '. . . I exchanged the yard for it. I don't need a yard with only two horses. And now I've a five-storey apartment house and the horses are in a workshop five steps up. But that doesn't worry them.'

'Father, just a moment! I've wanted to tell you this for a long time, even before the war . . .'

'There's plenty of time. Perhaps it can wait till after the war, anyway. As I say, my place in the Wexstrasse . . .'

'I'm living at Gertrud Gudde's, Father. You know, she used to be our dressmaker at the old place.'

'Gudde? Don't know her.' The old man was pretending to misunderstand. 'There are so many people in the new place. An apartment house, I said to myself, that's an investment! Always brings in money – if only people pay. Bit heavily mortgaged, though.'

'Father, I've known Gertrud Gudde for a long time. We've a son who's already four years old. We called him Gustav after you. And we want to get married.'

'Gudde? Isn't she the little hunchback who did our dressmaking? Always at the sewing machine – I thought it wouldn't do her any good. She's a bundle of misery as it is and with all that legwork . . .' The old man looked at Otto angrily.

'The child's quite healthy,' said Otto resolutely. 'Father, it's no use your talking like that. For a long time I was too cowardly to speak to you about it, but now it's different.'

'Gudde!' said the old man as if he hadn't heard. 'Now I remember – Mother let it out one day. Your sister Eva, who's become a whore, lives there. It seems to be a good place of accommodation. So the child's four, you say? Well, unwed you can go to bed.'

Otto had turned white but he controlled himself. 'Father, why do you say that?' he said indignantly. 'You're hurting yourself most.'

'And what's that to do with you?' cried the old man angrily. 'Marry your Gudde and brat if you want to. Called after me – as if I'd be taken in by such nonsense! Hurting myself! Well, Eva's a tart and I get from Sophie a letter once a month – "I'm quite well, the Senior Staff Surgeon tells me I'm capable, the Chaplain tells me I'm even more capable" and so on, all about herself, never a word askin' how Mother's doing. Erich – he only writes when he needs money. And after two years here's Otto on leave and he's actually got time to speak to his father about his marriage. Well, my boy, I'm made of iron. Even if I'm drivin' a cab again I still say there's something rotten about all my children. P'r'aps not Heinz, but it's too early to tell yet.'

'Father,' said Otto, 'you don't know Gertrud Gudde at all. She's capable, too, and hard-working. She's made a man of me.'

'She's made you the sort of fellow who smacks his father one an' then says: "Cheer up, Charlie – tomorrow you'll be in clover!" So you're going to marry, eh?'

'Yes,' said Otto firmly. 'I only came to fetch my papers. It's no use talking, Father. I can't leave Gertrud in the lurch just to please you.'

'I see – you only came because of your papers. And I, like a fool, was actually pleased when I saw you. Afterwards, of course, I could see you had something up your sleeve.'

'But what can you have against our marriage, Father?'

'Nothing at all – nothing. And now, my boy' – he dived into his pockets – 'here are the keys. You go home an' open my desk. Your papers are inside.'

'It won't do, Father,' said Otto resolutely. 'Give me a real objection – not merely that you don't like it.'

'You want me to say something, eh? Here are the keys – take 'em! And if you think I'm going to say I agree to your marriage, Otto, then let me tell you – never! Not even to save you from death and damnation. I'm of iron in that. "Yes, Father," it's easy enough for you to say that! Like one of those dolls you press in the tummy. And if you press yours it only ever said "Father" because you were hungry and I had to feed you.'

'Just tell me, Father, what you really object to in this marriage. I'm twenty-seven . . .'

'I don't object at all. What I say is, if you go to bed with a woman I'm not particular, I don't take offence; all I say is, get on with it if it gives you pleasure. But to wait till your child's four years old before you've got the pluck to tell your father about it and then only in a pub because he'll keep quiet in front of people – well! But Gustav doesn't keep quiet, he's made of iron . . .'

'Yes, you really are, Father. From the neck upwards.'

'Made of iron is Gustav! Calls a milksop a milksop an' a coward a coward. And he's not sitting at the same table as a coward, that's certain. I was glad to see you swaying towards me through the tavern, but now I'm taking my beer glass and I'll sit at another table.' He looked at his son bitterly, picked up his glass and rose. But he did not go at once. 'You've got the keys,' he said. 'At eight o'clock I'll have finished with the horses and you'll be gone by then. And if you want to visit your mother I'm out most of the day.'

'But, Father, what does it all mean? Please be sensible . . .' asked Otto once again.

'Sensible? Am I sensible? Are you? Neither of us knows that! But how you can ask me to be sensible? That I can't understand. If I'm not sensible, so be it, but I still remain iron all the same. I remain iron, and you're a milksop, and that's why I drink my beer alone . . .'

And with that Iron Gustav left. He did so with his glass of beer in his hand, but he didn't go through the whole tavern, only to the next-door table. There he sat, his back to Otto, and shouted: 'Landlord, gimme another, since it tastes so horrible.'

Otto sat there for a time, brooding. Now and then he looked at his father's back, and at the keys. But finally he remembered Gertrud waiting anxiously, and picked them up. Rising, he looked for a moment rather uncertainly at his father and then said: 'Goodnight, Father.'

'Goodnight,' said Hackendahl indifferently.

Otto waited but the old man merely picked up his glass and drank. So Otto went.

§ XIII

The tree had been transplanted from the nursery and flourished in fresh earth. It grew new branches and was stronger. The transplant had done it good. True, some roots had been torn off – it still pained Otto to think of his angry, incomprehensibly stubborn father, or his mother who, in a crowded, noisy house, longed to be back in the big, clean coaching yard.

Yes, these roots and been torn up, and such memories were painful. However, by and large, the tree flourished. For lack of light, it had not done so in the shadow of its father tree. Now it grew apace. Tutti was often surprised to see with what assurance this formerly weak man now went through life. He has become quite changed, she thought almost happily.

For she was happy – almost. Only occasionally did anxieties and doubts arise in her mind. Once she had the courage to say to him in the darkness before sleep: 'I used to be able to help you and make things easier. But what can I do now?'

He knew she was thinking of her deformed body and her little, sharp-featured face. After a moment he took her hand. 'In the trenches, whenever we spoke about home I thought of you.'

She said nothing in reply, but her heart beat quicker. And she felt a sensation of happiness pass right through her.

'When you think of home you don't ask what it is or what it gives – home is home,' he added.

She had felt like begging him to say no more – this happiness was too much. Or of saying: go on. Why are you silent? Go on speaking – I have never been so happy.

But she, as he, was silent. That moment might vanish, its emotion never.

One day Heinz visited the two of them – or rather the three, for Gustäving was inseparable from his father. During Otto's two years of absence Heinz had shot up unbelievably; his limbs were overlong, a crooked nose jutted out of a pale face and he spoke in a ridiculously deep bass.

'Well, Defender of the Fatherland,' he growled, 'Corporal and holder of the Iron Cross Second Class, when are you getting the First Class?'

'Probably never,' smiled Otto.

'Disgusting! I don't count at school now. Two brothers and neither of them with the Iron Cross First Class! Just don't take it badly, Otto. I was only joking. So you're my nephew Gustav, eh?' And to hide embarrassment he laid his hand in a fatherly way on the child's head and from his enormous height regarded him as though he were some sort of ant.

'Too pale and thin,' he decided. 'Yes, yes, beloved brother, war kills the strong and spares the weak. I'm saying that quite impersonally, you understand?'

Otto nodded with pleasure.

'So at school we decided to despise war. We rejected it root and branch, because it gave the wrong options. What do you think? What's your opinion?'

'Weak in the head,' replied Otto gently.

'Why? What do you mean "Weak in the head"? Our decision is naturally only valid when we've won this war. That's obvious. We'll see it through.' And he went on patronizingly: 'And how are the works on the Western Front? Air not too healthy, eh? I can well believe it.'

'Middling,' said Otto, grinning. 'We're only waiting for you to help us.'

'What rubbish! The war'll be over this winter. Definitely! You can take it from me – I had it from someone who's in touch with Hindenburg's staff. Vigorous old boy, what?'

'Listen,' said Otto, having acknowledged that Hindenburg was indeed a vigorous old boy and moreover understood his business, 'listen. Have you seen or heard anything of Eva at home?'

'Eva?' The lad's face clouded; he became reticent. 'No. Nothing.'

'Do you know anything about her? Don't look down your nose, Heinz – we're a bit worried. It might help if you told us what you know.'

'I only know she had a terrible row with Father. Mother told me – I know nothing otherwise. Wait – I saw her in the street once with a swell. Proper swell. Of course I didn't acknowledge her.'

'When was that?'

But it emerged that this had been when Eva had still been living with her parents. 'And I don't want to hear anything more about her. When she went Mother found a whole pile of pawn tickets for articles she had popped on the sly. Tablecloths, sheets – Mother still cries her eyes out when she thinks about it. I consider that's low, Otto.'

'I, too, Heinz, believe me. All the same we can't leave her in the lurch. That chap you saw, he'll be to blame. Eva was seduced, and that's the truth.'

'Seduced!' Heinz turned crimson and threw a glance at his sister-in-law. 'Does it mean anything, that word? Some of us at school have been reading a book by Wegener called *We Young Men*, enormously frank but utterly clean. Well, we've made a resolution to remain clean ourselves. You understand, Otto! Before marriage – nothing! That's the only clean thing.' At this point his eye fell on Gustäving and he turned a still-deeper crimson. 'Well, you know what I mean, as a principle. Naturally there are always exceptions.' He was silent for a while. 'Otto, let me tell you I'm sometimes afraid we are a decadent family.'

'A what?' asked Otto, amazed.

'Well, decadent . . . You don't know what I mean? If a family . . . Well, it's difficult to explain . . . But you know what happened with Erich. And now with Eva. Sophie's also a bit queer. And sometimes I can hardly sleep for thinking of what's going on in myself.' In a low voice: 'You'll hardly believe it, Otto, but sometimes I downright hate Father.'

'And that's decadent?'

'Well, it's just an example. If the family disintegrates, well, the family is the pillar of the State and if nobody achieves anything worthwhile, if everybody's rotten . . . What do you think?'

'I don't know if we're rotten or not. Perhaps the times in which we lived were rotten too, and infected us. Can't something that's healthy also be infected by a rotten environment? I at least became quite healthy again at the Front.'

'Absolutely. I can see it immediately. It's made you look terrific. Well, we won't lose hope, Otto. It's done me a lot of good, this talk with you. But I must be off now. You've no idea how hard I have to work. Simply colossal. You can't imagine it. Auf Wiedersehen, sister-in-law. Good luck, Otto. I don't know whether I'll see you before you go.'

'Don't forget your parcel, Heinz,' Gertrud reminded him.

'Parcel?' Heinz slapped his forehead. 'What a fabulous fool I am. Simply phenomenal. That's why I came round, because of the parcel. Mother sent it because she couldn't be present at the wedding. By the way, my hearty congratulations. I also was prevented from coming as you may have noticed – school, you understand.'

'Many thanks,' said Otto, while Tutti opened the parcel. 'It was only at a register office – over in five minutes.'

'I understand. What's your attitude towards the Church, Otto? We at school . . .'

But he got no further, for Tutti had unpacked six silver table-spoons, six forks, six knives, six teaspoons, a couple of tablecloths, some sheets and pillowcases . . . 'But it's too much,' she cried. 'Your mother is robbing herself.'

'That stuff?' Heinz snorted. 'We don't need it – there are only three of us now, and Father rarely comes home for meals. Mother's keeping the other half of each dozen for herself.'

'We can't take them,' said Tutti, but her eyes shone. 'You tell him, Otto.'

'What's he to tell me?' growled Heinz. 'He should say "Thank you". It makes Mother happy to be able to give you a wedding present at least. She would have come to see you long ago, only the distance, you know, and her legs . . . And then Father . . .' He looked at both of them questioningly. Then he thought aloud: 'I won't permit criticism of my creator. Only say: if I were a father I would do it differently. Wouldn't you, Otto?'

'There,' said Otto and threw his laughing little boy into the air. 'That's what I'd do.'

'Well,' said Bubi. 'It wouldn't be very easy for Father to do that with me. Well, cheerio. I'll come back, Gertrud, but perhaps not for a while. You know – school!' And with a dignified nod he went. But almost immediately his head appeared in the doorway again. 'One more question, Otto. Blade or cut-throat?'

'What?'

'I'm always quarrelling with Father about shaving. Well, safety razor or otherwise? Father of course swears by the cut-throat.'

'But you don't need to shave yet, Heinz.'

'Have you no idea? A beard like King Barbarossa!'

'Let it grow.'

'All right – safety razor! I'll tell Father from you. Many thanks.'

And this time Heinz – so justifiably called Bubi – disappeared for good.

§ XIV

As happy as this visit by the youngest Hackendahl had been, it had
not thrown any light on the whereabouts of Eva. During the next
few days Otto, acting on Gertrud's suggestion, made many calls. He
even dared to visit Police Headquarters at Alexanderplatz towards
which he had the good Berliner's attitude of respect mingled with
fear. But he learned nothing, they had too many Eugens on record,
and Eva Hackendahl was – thank God – absolutely unknown to
them. And waiting about in the Andreasstrasse and the Lange Strasse
proved just as unsuccessful. In the end Otto overcame himself so far
as to go to the last address Gertrud knew of – the Oriental Hotel. But
there he was met by Frau Pauli, who was not disposed to give any
information about her clients. She knew neither a Herr Eugen nor a
Fräulein Eva. No, she was sorry, but the gentleman must have made
a mistake – some confusion in identity perhaps. There were so many
hotels in Berlin, the Adlon for instance, the Kaiserhof, Esplanade,
Bristol perhaps his friends had put up at one of these. And she practically laughed in his face.

A little crushed, Otto reported failure. Tutti was now of the opinion that he had done enough. 'For you to have gone there at all,
Otto! For you to speak with such a woman! No, drop it now. Tomorrow we'll take the train to Strausberg again. They say the villages
haven't yet been stripped around Strausberg.'

However, if Tutti thought the villages beyond Strausberg were still
unscathed, she was mistaken. Or else the people out there were particularly hard-hearted. All day she and Otto wandered about in an
icy wind; unwearyingly they picked out the remotest, most isolated
farms, those lying on the worst, the most impassable roads. But
when they knocked at the door, when they asked for a drop of milk,
a few eggs, even a few potatoes; when on behalf of their child at
home they humbled themselves (and this with difficulty); when they
had offered double or treble the usual price – all they got was a rude
refusal. The door was slammed, and if they did not leave at once
they heard the people inside talking about 'everlasting begging' and

'hungry rabble'. And yet they had been very moderate; not a word about butter or bacon, the things missed most.

Otto walked on gloomily, without a word. Maybe he was thinking of the hard life in the trenches, of this farm for which he had fought, suffered, been in mortal danger – only to be called a beggar. Maybe he was thinking of Gustäving, who had such thin arms and a belly swollen with eating gruel.

He saw these farmsteads with other children running about in them, children with well-nourished bodies. He saw the rolls in their hands as he went through the village. It was school break and the children stood outside eating. This made him so angry, so desperate. And this was supposed to be a *nation*! Hundreds of deep rifts tore it apart and divided it. There were so many differences – the nobility, the middle class and the workers, and there were conservatives and Socialists, poor and rich, and soldiers at the Front and in the rear, and supporting troops. And now, in addition to all the others, were the ration card-holders and the self-supporters.

In the mouths of ration card-holders the expression 'self-supporter' had become one of abuse. Self-supporters were people who had any amount of food – fats and bread and potatoes. They ate and ate. They killed pigs, slaughtered calves and lambs, baked good bread from pure flour – and let the others starve. Yes, they let women starve, and children. With a curt refusal they banged their doors and called those a hungry rabble who were hungry only because of what was withheld from them. It was a cursed time. It was more decent in the trenches, God damn it. If you didn't have a good comrade there, you'd better get one otherwise you'd soon go to the dogs.

True, some had excuses. 'We can't give to everybody. There's been ten here today already.' Otto could understand this. But he had been to forty or fifty places and had received only refusals. Not an egg, not a drop of milk – and the hungry child at home waiting for what they would bring.

Gertrud saw her husband become more and more downcast. She herself felt as bitter as he did, and her worry about the boy was certainly not less than his, but she thought: people are like that. The rich never help the poor. These were laws of nature for her which had to be accepted. Otto, however, was losing faith in the world, its rules, himself even.

In the trains, returning home, he would sit silently beside those who had been successful. Their sacks of potatoes, their heavy suitcases, their mysteriously bulging knapsacks, filled the large fourth-class carriage. Smoking a stinking tobacco blended with cherry or blackberry leaves, he would listen to their talk.

If he caught the name of some village he would remark that same evening: 'We'll go there tomorrow.'

'Oh, Otto, again? It's no use, we're spending all our money on fares.'

But he was determined. 'We'll have good luck sooner or later, depend on it, Tutti. We'll go tomorrow.'

They went and were indeed lucky this time, getting twenty eggs, a loaf of bread, half a pound of butter. Otto laughed as they set out for the station. 'You see, they're not all the same, after all. You just mustn't lose faith!'

This time he sat next to her on the return journey. As far as he was concerned, others could have the world – his happiness knew no bounds. It was fine, thought his more practical wife, to be bringing the boy eggs and butter but was it worth it when she lost a whole day's work? This food was only a drop in the ocean. In such things, however, a man was like a child. Well, at all events they had got bread, butter and eggs.

But they were mistaken . . .

At Alexanderplatz, as people tried to leave the platform, police engaged in a large-scale search for hoarded food confronted them. They were letting nobody through; every suitcase had to be opened, every bag undone – all foodstuffs were confiscated.

How dark and threatening grew the faces! The police themselves did not like the business. They too had children who went hungry and they understood how the people felt; they said no more than was essential, they heard nothing that they need not hear. A cursed business.

'You're stealing from our kids to fatten your own, you bloody fat pigs, you!' a woman screamed.

But the police heard nothing.

Gertrud clung to her husband's arm – how grim he looked! Just as though he would commit a murder. For the sake of twenty eggs and a bit of butter. Desperately she patted his hand. 'Please, Otto, please – don't make me unhappy.'

He glanced at her. 'We'll walk straight on. I want to see whether they'll stop a man from the Front . . .' And they did.

'Please open the cardboard box. What have you got in it?'

Otto walked on, pretending he did not hear.

'Now be reasonable, Corporal.'

'You should be ashamed of yourselves!'

'Orders are orders, you know that.'

'If I'm not to have them, you shan't, you hounds,' shouted a woman – and egg after egg smashed on the platform.

'Come, Tutti,' said Otto, 'give him the bread. And here's a parcel of eggs and butter, Sergeant. Good evening.'

Silently they went home. In a low voice they told Gustäving: 'Nothing!'

For a long time they sat in semi-darkness in the cold flat, both hungry, both discouraged.

'Otto?' she said timidly.

'Yes, Tutti?'

'Shall we try again tomorrow?'

He was surprised and remained silent. He knew very well how she hated these trips and only went with him most unwillingly. And now?

'But why now, Tutti?'

'Because I have the feeling you want to go again now. And because I will only ever do what you want.'

'Good, we'll go.'

He said nothing else.

But both felt this was happiness. There was nothing better. A union forged by common sorrow in a time when almost everything else was falling apart.

§ XV

So next day they set out again and this time luck really smiled on them. At a farm from which they had already been sent away the woman suddenly noticed Otto's regimental number.

'Good God, you belong to our boy's regiment. Ingemar Schultz – there are so many Schultzes, that's why we called him Ingemar. Do you know him?'

Otto did. They were asked in, and as honoured guests they sat down to table, while Otto related what he knew of Ingemar Schultz, which was not much, because Ingemar belonged to another com pany. To the ears of the parents, however, the few words came as a divine revelation. For the corporal had seen Ingemar only nine days previously and had spoken with him.

So he and his wife got all they wanted – just as much as they could carry, even a whole side of bacon. And at the door the mother called after them her most cherished wish. 'In spring we're applying for Ingemar to come home for the sowing. You'll put in a good word for him, won't you?'

'That's not quite right,' said Otto, as they turned away, 'to be bribed to do something underhand.'

'Oh, you're a proper Berliner,' cried the delighted Tutti. 'Always grousing about something. We people from the Hiddensee don't complain . . .'

'I'm from Pasewalk and Pasewalkers don't complain either,' he answered, and they both laughed.

And now they had to fear the police control. But that night no one looked at their parcels – hate and despair were being sown in the hearts of people at some other railway station. They didn't feel safe, however, till their fabulous wealth was stored in the kitchen; in vain Gustäving tried with his 'One . . . two . . . seven' to count the eggs. Full of excitement, he watched his mother frying them in real bacon fat, and potatoes to go with it – potatoes fried in fat, not in coffee grounds. And from this cooking arose a glorious unknown smell, a fragrance which outvied the loveliest scents of flowers. It gave Gustäving the patience to wait till the food was ready.

'Do you like it, Otto? Do you, Gustäving? Don't bolt it, son. This is a great treat. Just this once. From now on Mummy will have to be terribly economical again, to make all the good things last. Oh, Otto, something decent to eat again . . . Those ghastly swedes!'

Half an hour later Gustäving started to vomit. In agonizing pain his stomach rejected the good, the nourishing food.

'Nothing agrees with him now,' wailed Tutti in despair. 'At last we've something that will do him good and he can't retain it. Oh, Otto, our child is half starved, and I've really given him everything I can.'

'We made a mistake, Tutti. It was much too rich to start with. It couldn't possibly agree with him. We shall have to go slowly with the boy. Anyhow, we'll take him to the doctor tomorrow.'

The three of them then set out. For a long time they sat in the overcrowded waiting room. Every chair was occupied and people leaned against the walls – grey-faced, tired, hopeless people. Mostly women. And almost all with their children.

This was not the waiting room of some fashionable practitioner in the West End – this was a panel doctor in East Berlin. Those who sat there were not turning over the pages of magazines; it was more like a large family assembly. Everyone talked with everyone else; all had the same worries . . .

'If only he would prescribe something for my child. The boy's fainted twice.'

'He prescribes all right – it's all the same to him. Everything's the same to him.'

'Don't say that! The man has a heart of gold. "You ought to go to hospital and have a real rest," he told me.'

'And did you go?'

'How could I, with five kids at home?'

'You see, what did I say! What help is his heart of gold to you, then?'

'Prescriptions are not enough,' began another woman. 'He prescribed milk for our Granny but it wasn't granted. He's got superiors over him.'

'An old creature like that! Why should she get milk when the young are starving?'

'You don't know what you're talking about. Our Granny gets an old-age pension of twenty-eight marks a month. That's a great help with the housekeeping. We'd like her to live to be a hundred.'

From another corner came a whisper, '. . . and if you can get a smoked herrin', take the skin an' the tail an' the head and all that's left over, chop it very fine and fry your potatoes in it. That makes 'em tasty. You've no idea how much fat there is in the skin.'

'I'll remember that. We only ever licked the skin. But roasting potatoes with it is better . . .'

'And you can cook swedes with the skin on – tastes delicious.'

'Just don't mention swedes! My mother-in-law made a swede pudding on Sunday, with raspberry juice. I vomited the whole lot up. The very smell of swedes makes me retch. . .'

'Are you pregnant or something?'

'For God's sake, please don't say that! I've already got four. No, it's because swedes just don't agree with me.'

'Each to his own! Without swedes we'd all have starved long ago.'

All was quiet again.

Then a woman said thoughtfully, 'They cleaned out a baker's yesterday morning in the Landsberger Allee . . .'

'That can't be true – I live in the Landsberger . . .'

'Yes, it is. I saw it with my own eyes.'

'How'd it happen?'

'Well, usual way. A woman said: "What, that bit of bread's supposed to weigh 930 grams? No, you weigh it, mister!" He didn't want to and suddenly they all shouted: "He gives short weight" – and so he had to weigh it.'

'Go on. Was it short?'

'Yes, thirty grams. And he apologized and gave her an extra slice, over a hundred grams. Well, I'd have taken it, I'm not too proud, but . . .'

'So it was you who made the fuss?'

'Me? Who's talking about me? I saw it, I said.'

'Go on, tell us, young woman. It's nobody's business who it was. There are no spies here – only poor people like yourself.'

'I should hope not. Well, listen, when he tried to apologize he made a mess of it, he's the bossy sort, won't admit he's in the wrong.

So they all turned on him and said what they thought of him. And, what with the excitement, a few of them reached over the counter for their bread.'

'Go on! Do tell me quickly – I'm the next!'

'Well, the baker like the old fool he is, when he saw them doing that he rushes into his back parlour where he's got the telephone and phones for the police. That's where he made his mistake! Two or three at once went behind the counter and turned the key so he couldn't get out. And then he got what for. The loaves were swept off the shelves and thrown to us and in less than three minutes the shop was cleared, no bread, no customers.'

A deep, an almost devotional, silence.

'Can't you hear – next!' called the doctor impatiently behind the door.

A woman rose reluctantly and disappeared into the surgery.

'I wish I'd been there,' said another, sighing. 'But no such luck for the likes of us.'

'Well, and what about me?' asked the narrator. 'I was there and I'm no better off than you.'

'How much bread did you get?'

'No decent person should ask such a question,' said a red-faced woman severely. 'That sounds like a spy.'

All fell silent and sank into themselves a little, thinking about what they'd just been told. Tutti thought about it, too. She wondered if, had she been in the shop, she would have taken a loaf as well. And with a shock she said to herself, yes, she would have taken one – she would have stolen! She would preferred to have paid – it wasn't the money that mattered to her, it was the food. And if she couldn't get it any other way, she would steal too. Without a bad conscience! Or perhaps with a bad conscience? It didn't matter. She would have stolen.

Otto's thoughts were similar. Here we are, like a ring surrounding Germany – but is it still Germany that we're defending? Everything's completely changed. These are no longer the same people who cheered in 1914.

Or is it their real face that now clearly shows itself? Hadn't Lieutenant Ramin said as much in the shell crater – that we no longer had faith? No ideas? It wasn't bread that this woman had taken – Otto understood that. Hunger always hurts, but it hurts a mother much more if she watches her children starving. That's a primal feeling, before which all barriers fall . . . No, it wasn't the bread . . . But it was this: that Otto, wherever he had been this fortnight, and also in the days before in the trenches – had never actually heard what the war was actually about – exactly what were they defending?

Germany? This wasn't Germany! No enemy could starve a people more or make them more miserable. You couldn't rob these people of the slightest hope – they've got none left. What, then, was he defending? The All-Highest War-Lord, the Kaiser? Yes, recently he had been at the Front, quite near anyway, not more than a hundred kilometres. And he had the exhausted and bleeding troops paraded before him, and been very gracious . . .

Oh God, that wasn't the thing anyway! The Kaiser was a great personage – no doubt he too was probably the victim of his own limitations. He knew nothing, nothing whatever, about his people. But they, the people – what about them? What were they fighting for? Why were they suffering in this way? Why were things so bad? There has to be a reason! A whole people can't simply go under and go to ruin, for some other people to appear, flourish and be happy for a while, and then also go to ruin. That was impossible. It couldn't happen. Even he could see that. If that were the case, it would be a thousand times better not to fight or defend yourself at all, but walk away with a hand grenade!

There *must* be a reason. Suffering all this for nothing is impossible. And if Lieutenant Ramin, I and my comrades don't yet know the reason, that doesn't mean that there isn't one. If the face of pre-war prosperity has been transformed into a grotesque visage of hunger, then behind it there is perhaps another face . . .

Somewhere there are people who know, said Otto to himself. It must be so. And if no one now knows, and if I never find out myself what I'm actually fighting for, my boy will find out in the end . . .

And he looked at the four-year-old Gustäving and said to him – but only he knew what he meant by it – 'Things will be better for you, Gustäving.'

Then the doctor opened the door: 'Next!'

§ XVI

He was a rotund little man with a weary, lined face. 'Hurry up,' he said. 'What is it – the boy? Of course, it would be. And you don't look too flourishing yourself, young woman. Insurance card? That's all right. No, I don't need to examine the child. It's malnutrition. Do you know, my dear soldier, I'm not supposed to use that word, mal-nutrition; at least, I've had it conveyed to me that I shouldn't make use of it with my patients. But I do – and why? Not because I want to sabotage the measures taken by the government. On the contrary. But I use it because I'm utterly tired of beating about the bush . . .' He was writing, rubber-stamping, writing.

'Half a litre of milk per day, 30 grams of extra butter, say 150 grams of wheaten bread. But you won't get all I prescribe, so I'll put down 200 grams . . . Yesterday,' he continued writing and rubber-stamping without stop, 'I had 180 patients. This morning by ten o'clock I'd over thirty . . . that's just in consultation hours . . . Then there are visits . . . And I'm always writing . . . I don't treat sick people any more! I'm a machine, that's all, a machine which applies for extra food and writes prescriptions . . . And I was once assistant to Robert Koch! But that won't mean anything to you – you have your own troubles.'

More writing and rubber-stamping. 'Vomits, you say? But that's very sensible of the boy. If a man gets too much of a thing he rejects it. Excellent! Why should he have to digest the whole lot? He'd only die of it. Bacon and poached eggs, potatoes fried in fat, and a little tummy brought up on gruel – no wonder he vomits! Have you any idea, soldier, how the world is going to vomit over this war?' The doctor gave a start. 'Excuse me, I shouldn't have said that. I oughtn't to say many of the things I do but I talk on and on – out of sheer exhaustion. Last night I got just one and a half hours' sleep, and not proper sleep at that. The last of my sons is at the Front. Three have been killed already. Well, that won't interest you; it hardly interests me now . . . Here are your prescriptions. Take them away, and wait outside with the boy. I'd like a few words with your wife.'

'But I have no Health Insurance card for her,' said Otto.

'Health Insurance card? I'm not asking for Insurance cards. I've got so many that I could paper my flat with them. No, I want to talk with the young woman about women's affairs, which you men don't understand. So out you go, soldier!' He ushered Otto out of the room.

The interview was rather a long one. Once more, he was in the waiting room among all the women, only able to keep the child quiet with difficulty. Then Tutti appeared – at last.

She took his arm affectionately, she seemed very happy.

'What did he say, Tutti?'

'Oh, nothing special. That I should take care of myself and go into hospital for a couple of weeks. Only to have a rest, nothing serious, you know.'

'And what else?'

'What do you mean?'

'He wouldn't have sent me out just for that.'

'Oh, Lord, Otto, he examined me – my chest and back, and he probably thought it would be embarrassing for me in front of you – because of my back. And it would have been embarrassing too, Otto. You can understand that, can't you?'

'And nothing else?'

She laughed. 'What else could there be, Otto? No, nothing else, really.'

'You're sure?'

'But Otto!'

'Then it's all right.'

He had the feeling, however, that she had not told him everything. It was a quite certain feeling. The thought came to him to return to the doctor again behind her back. But he let it be. Tutti would tell him the truth in the end. She'd never lied to him.

And he was right. He learned the truth in the end – she didn't lie to him.

§ XVII

They had gone much too early to the station, unnecessarily so, he thought. But Gertrud had been so urgent. 'You can't wait to get rid of me, Tutti?'

Her only reply had been a smile. Often in recent days, instead of answers she gave a lovely smile, gentle, as if she were lit up from inside, as if her happiness were inexpressible.

The boy had been left at home. Unaware that his father was going away, he was happy with a chunk of bread.

The station hall was badly lit. The train looked comfortless – the soldiers who were returning to the Front looked comfortless too. Hardly speaking, they stood among their families, who kept their eyes fixed on the departing men and nodded eagerly whenever they said a word. Father was going to the Front again; perhaps it was the last time they would see him . . .

Crushing misery descended on Otto – he too was going to the Front. During the first days, the memories of the trenches had haunted him painfully, but then daily life had followed – Tutti, the child, the arguments with his father, the search for Eva, the expeditions for food. It had been two weeks, for eleven days of which he had hardly thought of the Front.

In a flash, standing by the unheated, grimy train, it all came back to him – he saw the entrance to the dugout, the earth steps which, although reinforced with boards, were nevertheless deep in mud. He could smell the air, musty and yet cold as ice, the rotten straw of the beds, the stale smell of spirits, the bad tobacco; and the utter joylessness of the life to which he was returning overwhelmed him. The fortnight at home, filled with cares though it had been, was a blissful dream compared with that.

'We shouldn't have come so early,' he said. 'This damned train!'

'Now you're already on your way, Otto,' she said tenderly, 'but you should be here with me.'

He looked at her. 'You know, Tutti, it's difficult . . .' he said slowly and was ashamed.

'Do you remember when you left last time?'

'Yes,' he nodded, happy to be distracted from his thoughts. 'The whole family came – Father, Mother, brothers and sisters. You stood at the back by a pillar. I wasn't supposed to know you, you or Gustäving . . .'

'Today we're by ourselves, Otto. It's better this time, isn't it?'

He shook his head. 'No, worse – because you know what's in store for you.'

'Last time I didn't believe I should ever see you again,' she said, looking at him steadfastly.

'I, too – and this time . . .'

'This time I know for certain you'll come back.'

His eyes seemed to implore her for a moment he was again the old irresolute Otto.

And she helped him. 'Yes, Otto,' she nodded. 'You can be sure of it. You'll come back.'

'Nobody can say that. Once you've been out there and know what it's like . . .'

'Never mind about that – you'll come back, Otto.' She looked at the station clock. Another five minutes. She took his hand. 'I want to tell you something, something I concealed . . .'

'Yes?' he asked softly.

'I kept it so you should take it with you to the Front. Otto, I believe we're going to have another child.'

'Tutti!'

'Yes. Oh, I'm so happy!'

'Tutti, why didn't you tell me this before? I'd have . . . I could have . . .'

'And you'll come back, Otto, now you know this. Almost nine months to go yet. The war'll be over by then. When the child comes you'll be with me for ever.'

'Get in! Take your seats!' shouted the porters.

'Oh, Tutti, Tutti, why didn't you tell me before? Why only at the last moment? Oh, I'd like to . . .'

'Get in! Hurry up!'

'You'll come back, Otto. Otto dear, dear Otto, you've made me so happy.'

'Oh, Tutti, I must talk to you . . . Do you mind if I have the window, comrade? Thanks! – Tutti, take care of yourself. Will you get enough to eat? A woman expecting a child . . .'

'I'm to go every month to the doctor's. He'll look after me all right.'

'I'll send everything I can from the Front. Sometimes we capture marvellous English tinned food . . .'

'You out there, me here – we'll only think of the baby and that'll bring you back, Otto.'

The whistle!

The train started to move, parting their clasped hands. She tried to run alongside, her lips forming the word 'Happy!' again and again.

'I must come back!' he said, and shut the window. 'I'll come back. Because she needs me! Happy – yes, happy! Yes, I'll come back.'

§ XVIII

At noon the next day Corporal Otto Hackendahl was wounded by a shell splinter on his way into the trenches held by his company and died a few hours later, after much suffering. He died in that same dugout the vision of which had appeared to him at the railway station. If his eye perceived anything during his last moments it was the squelching muddy steps leading into the dugout; the last breath he drew was from the close yet icy-cold air inside, stinking of spirits and bad tobacco. He died on the rotting straw of his bed.

Otto Hackendahl had nothing for his comrades, who had looked after him, to give to his wife. The splinter from the shell had hit him in the abdomen. He could only cry out and groan. Even the two strong morphine injections the medical officer had given him one after another did not deaden the pain. By then, he was hardly any longer a conscious being. This existence, with its warm sympathy for women and children, and its clumsy questions as to why and what – it had all passed him by even when he was alive.

The company commander, informing his parents (Otto's recent marriage was not known to him), wrote that Otto Hackendahl had died an honourable death, in action. It would be a consolation to his parents that he had not suffered – death was instantaneous.

'They say that about them all!' sobbed old Frau Hackendahl.

And old Gustav Hackendahl, Iron Gustav, asked very gently: 'Mother, what else can they say? That he suffered terribly? Why not believe them – now he can't suffer any more.'

Gertrud Hackendahl learned only relatively late of her husband's death. After her initial inability to believe it, and a prolonged, raging pain, all her efforts were devoted to obtaining news of Otto's last hours. She simply couldn't believe that he had left her no word, no message . . .

In the end, she learned the following: men on leave from his regiment some twelve or fifteen of them – knew already by the time they'd reached their assembly point that the trenches had been under heavy fire for days. That night there had been numerous attacks resulting in heavy casualties. The regiment had suffered terrible losses.

People marched to their positions as quickly as they could. They did so to the ever-increasing thunder roll of the guns – and came back silent, morose, but very quickly. All were busy with their own thoughts.

Then, when they had nearly reached their destination, they discovered that the trench leading to their position had been completely blasted away. It had been almost flattened and lay open to enemy fire.

They waited for hours in a half-destroyed dugout for the firing to die down. They were undecided, discussed whether they should risk it, and went on waiting.

None of them now thought of home any more. They thought only of the trenches, about their exhausted, battered and worn-out comrades there, and about the attack that must follow this preparatory artillery onslaught. And that they would fail.

After yet another fruitless discussion, Otto Hackendahl suddenly said: 'It can't be helped. They're waiting for us. We must go on.'

He ran in front of the others. All reached the trenches unwounded. Only then, almost at the entrance of his dugout, was he hit.

This was all that Gertrud Hackendahl discovered. But it was enough. The words, 'It can't be helped. We must go on' seemed to her to sum up the whole of Otto Hackendahl as a man: patient acceptance of a grievous fate, but with courage.

She tried to live her life, and bring up her children – Gustav and Otto Hackendahl (born eight months and nineteen days after his father's death) – in difficult times in the spirit of these last words of Otto Hackendahl.

It can't be helped. We must go on . . .

There was something in these words, but there was something, too, in little Gertrud Hackendahl, née Gudde, born on the island of Hiddensee. There was something in her, too.

FOUR

Peace Breaks Out

§ 1

When Heinz, now seventeen, and now still called 'Bubi' only by his mother, got up from the midday meal to go out, old Hackendahl raised his head. Sitting there in the kitchen, he had been to all appearances asleep – the local newspaper lay on the floor next to him.

'Where are you going?'

Heinz reflected. That he wanted to walk the streets a bit, and see what was actually going on; he daren't tell his father.

The paternal hand lay heavy on the youngest and sole remaining child at home. All the more readily therefore did the lad seek refuge in dissimulation.

'To Rappold's,' he answered, after thinking briefly. 'Swotting up some maths. Trigonometrical equations – parallelepiped . . .'

The father looked at his son suspiciously. 'Where are your books?'

'Don't need 'em – Rappold's got them all.'

'Exercise book?'

'In my pocket.' Heinz showed the shiny black cover. Had his father had the slightest suspicion that this exercise book contained not mathematics but verse, the conversation would have taken a very different turn. As it was the old man merely growled, 'Don't go into the town. They're shooting there.'

'I shouldn't dream of it. Got to swot maths. Why are they shooting?'

'How do I know? Probably because they've got used to it, and they can't shoot at the English and French any longer. No doubt they want to blow to smithereens what little scrap of business we've got left.'

'A few days' rest won't do the grey any harm, Father,' said Heinz consolingly.

'The grey? She's only fit for sausages.' The old man looked gloomy. Then he added deprecatingly – as if ashamed of thinking about himself in the general collapse: 'Do you suppose my War Loans are still worth anything?'

Heinz looked uncertainly at his father. Hackendahl had never spoken to his children about his financial affairs but Heinz knew from his mother that twenty-five thousand marks in War Loans, the heavily mortgaged house in the Wexstrasse, the grey and the cab were all that was left of his father's fortune. The old man must really be worried to death, thought the son with a momentary uprush of pity – driving his cab day in, day out just to bring home a few marks. Yet everything Heinz required at school was always provided and the fees were paid without the least grumble.

'Your War Loans are as safe as houses, Father. Guaranteed by the German Empire.'

The father had his dark moments. He didn't smile. 'But the Kaiser's abdicated. He's crossed the Dutch frontier.'

Heinz grinned in contempt. 'Did you ever expect anything different from "Lehmann"? He's cut no ice with us at school for a long time. D'you think he was a guarantee for your money? He's not the German Reich!'

'Have you read the armistice conditions? The French want to come as far as the Rhine. There's shooting in town. Soon there may no longer be a German Reich!'

The son patted his fearful father paternally on the shoulder. 'It'll happen, you can be sure of it. Now it's our turn!'

'You!?'

'Of course! Isn't everything finished now. Who's supposed to build it up again? You old people?'

'You mean, you?!'

'Who else?'

'Get on with your homework,' the old man suddenly shouted. 'You must be crazy. You! – when we didn't win? Scum!'

'I'll ask Hölscher about War Loans,' said Heinz, unmoved. 'His father's employed by the Deutsche Bank.'

'You ought to be doing your lessons, your homework. I can look after my own concerns,' growled the father threateningly.

'Well, shall I ask Hölscher or not?'

Hackendahl growled – uncertain what to say.

'Besides, Erich may come home any day now – our lieutenant, the shining light of the family. Not forgetting the pious Sophie.'

'You're to be back at six!'

'Might be a bit later, Father,' explained Heinz. 'The parallelepiped is damned tricky!'

'At six, you hear!'

'As I told you, tricky! See you later, Father. Don't eat all the bread if I'm a little late.'

And having thus prepared the way for an unpunctual return, Heinz ran down the dark stairs and across the courtyard.

§ II

He had, of course, not the faintest intention of going to Rappold's to study, and seeing Hölscher about the War Loans did not appear urgent either. For a moment he looked down the Wexstrasse, which on this November day seemed particularly gloomy and cheerless, with people queued up in front of the food shops, and somewhere among them his mother no doubt. Nothing had changed, and yet: 'They're shooting in the town.' The words rang in the ears of the seventeen-year-old lad. One ought to have a look.

However, as was his habit, he took the turning to the right, then went straight on for two blocks before turning to the left and crossing the road – to halt in front of the stationer's shop kept by the Widow Quaas.

Heinz put his hand in his pocket; yes, he still had the mark wheedled out of his mother that morning, which would enable him to purchase two steel nibs (price five pfennigs) or five sheets of blotting paper (also five pfennigs). No great purchase, perhaps, but it did serve to keep up appearances.

The bell gave a feeble tinkle – how pleasant and familiar was the sound! The interior of the shop might be dusty, empty and cold, but to Heinz it was one of the most agreeable places in the world. The widow was a shrivelled little woman, depressed and helpless-looking, with the sunken eyes of those who have been through starvation and war; but the sight of her to Heinz was incredibly pleasing. 'Two Bremen-Change nibs,' he said as loudly as possible. 'Er, the very pointed kind – you know, Frau Quaas.'

'Heinz! Herr Hackendahl! I've asked you not to come so often,' said the widow helplessly.

'But I really need the nibs, Frau Quaas,' Heinz assured her in a respectful and yet over-loud voice. 'I must immediately make a fair copy of an essay on bird flight in the dramas of Euripides. I haven't come because of Irma.'

'Herr Hackendahl, you're only seventeen and Irma is barely fifteen.'

'Two Bremen-Change, EF, very pointed, Frau Quaas. We're not talking about Irma, that's not interesting.'

'What are you burbling about to me, Heinz? What's up?'

'Hello, Irma. Two Bremen nibs, sharp points!'

'Stop that nonsense! You've got more nibs than we have here in the shop. What's up?'

'They say there's shooting going on.'

'Ripping! We going to see it?'

'Well, we'll have to take the train or the fun'll be over before we get there.'

'Mother, can you let me have half a mark? You can deduct it from my pocket money on Saturday.'

'Irma, under no circumstances will I allow you to . . . There's shooting! Herr Hackendahl, you ought to be ashamed of yourself . . .'

'Plan: capital A, Frau Quaas: in the first place, they won't shoot. Second: capital B: if they do shoot, we don't go in. Alpha: where they shoot. Beta: If they don't shoot. Third: capital C: do I have the fare – Alpha: for myself, Beta: for Irma . . .'

'Herr Hackendahl, I beg you, don't start to speak so terribly to me again! It makes me quite giddy. Irma can't possibly . . .'

'Can't? I can give you on the spot three to seven good reasons, Frau Quaas, why she can. Firstly, as a question of free will; that is, even if we suppose it to be more a spontaneity than an act of volition . . .'

'Herr Hackendahl, please be quiet. You're always coming into my shop . . .'

'Stop annoying Mother, Heinz. Since she's given me permission to go . . .'

'I haven't, no, I'm not permitting it, Irmchen. Oh God, if something happened to you! At least put on your winter coat – no, you can't, the moth holes aren't mended yet. And put on a scarf . . .'

'Bye-bye, Mother, give me a kiss. Don't be so worried about – Heinz. I can look after him.'

'Animal! Unruly slave! – Please, Frau Quaas, I'd like to have my nibs. I don't want you to say I only come to your shop to see Irma.'

'Of course you do and of course I say so! And it'll bring some misfortune . . .'

'What sort of misfortune? Yes, what sort, Frau Quaas? There you are! You can't tell me. But you turn red – the older generation's depraved notions! We rise superior, isn't that so, Irma?'

'Show-off! Don't get annoyed, Mummy. You ought to know Heinz by now. All those grand words of his go to his head.'

'And yours too,' quavered the widow.

The fourteen-year-old Irma looked at her small, worried mother. 'What are you worrying about, Mummy? As if we hadn't any sense! I've got eyes in my head, I know what men are up to!'

'Excuse me, Irma, I know you want to lay down the law about men, but I'd like to point out that according to an unconfirmed rumour there's shooting going on in town,' said Heinz.

'Off we go, then. Bye-bye, Mother. If I'm late I'll tap on the window.'

'Oh, Irma! Herr Hackendahl!'

But the pair were already outside.

§ III

'Dawdle-walk or fast walk?' Irma had asked, and been told, 'Fast, but sedate.'

Taking two or three at a time, they rushed breathlessly up the station steps and jumped into a moving train.

'The wretch didn't even shout "Stand back!" '

'Perhaps for a moment he had other worries, O breathless one,' replied Heinz, himself huffing and puffing.

They sat opposite each other, true offspring of the four years of scarcity and hunger. Pretty tough, utterly miserable, but in general completely reliable in important things.

They were dressed so badly as can only be possible when a suit of decent material is simply impossible to find. Heinz wore a suit assembled from the best items in his brothers' wardrobes and much too short at the wrists and ankles, besides being a good deal patched. Irma, under a thin, shabby coat, wore a faded dress, a patch here and there indicating the original colours; the skirt barely reached her knees. Her cotton stockings had been darned repeatedly. But what looked most wretched of all were their shoes, which they themselves had repaired again and again with strips of leather stitched or glued on chaotically, and the soles were of wood – the clatter they made with them could be deafening . . . As it was at this moment, without any consideration for their only fellow passenger – their feet were very cold, the train was not heated, the windows were broken.

'Damned cold,' said Irma. 'Who's he?'

'Only a wretched tradesman with nothing to sell. He'll be wondering if he can't sell the holes in the cheese. Hey, you, fellow human!'

The sleepy man gave a violent start. Then he said threateningly: 'If you see someone having a nap and you wake him up, then you're a dirty dog and deserve to have your block knocked off.'

'One-nil to him, darling,' cheered Irma.

'I only wanted to know if the train's going right through to the Potsdamer Station,' protested Heinz.

'Why shouldn't it?'

'Because there's shooting in town.'

'Oh? Well, if they're shootin' you'll soon find out, and if the train don't get there you'll find that out, too,' said the man, leaning back in his corner.

'A philosopher of the gutter,' remarked Heinz, far from quietly, 'see telephone directory under mystic.' He yawned. 'D'you notice, Irma, that the train's gaping with emptiness?'

'Well, what do you think, if there's shooting! You're pretty bright today, Heinz. Didn't have enough lunch, what?'

Heinz slapped his belly. 'No,' he said. 'Not for years. Hunger Everlasting.'

'And they kept on telling us we should have as much to eat as we liked when peace came. Baloney! A fine youth they've given us.'

'Peace! This isn't peace. You've heard . . .'

'. . . that there's shooting in town, yes. Perhaps you'll now tell me why it is they're shooting.'

'No idea. But if it's a real revolution maybe the army won't join them . . .'

'What's a real revolution?'

'No idea. You had the French one at school – guillotine – king, emperor, minister – off with their heads!'

'But the Kaiser's gone.'

'Well, have a look at the East.'

'Alexanderplatz?'

'No, stupid – Russia, Lenin!'

'And who's our Lenin?'

'No idea. Maybe Liebknecht . . .'

'D'you like him?'

'Don't be silly! Know nothing about him. Except they locked him up for running down the war.'

'Have they let him out?'

'Couldn't say. But I suppose that's the essence of revolutions – those who are out get locked up, and those who are in come out.'

'Potsdamer Station! You see, the train got here all right. But, Heinz, suppose you've spent all that good money on fares and there's nothing doing?'

'Don't waffle, daughter of Quaasin. Act first, questions later. Come!'

Side by side they went through the almost empty, very dirty suburban station – alert, thirsting for life, half frozen, shabbily dressed and, whether as a result of the war soap or their own lack of interest, not very well washed. Both looked sickly, yellowish, with coarsened skins; their noses were bony and they had dark rings round their eyes. But each had the same direct, clear and disillusioned gaze.

They had been starved of almost everything and so retained an insatiable appetite for all that surrounded them – beauty, ugliness, the high, the low. In them was embodied the indestructibility of life.

They went towards the Potsdamer Platz next to each other, keeping step without wanting to – without even thinking of going arm in arm, without a hint of tenderness.

Cold, but full of light! Models of irrepressible life.

§ IV

'There!' said Heinz, stopping abruptly.

Out of the Dessauer Strasse came a big lorry camouflaged with dabs of paint and packed with sailors in their blue uniforms and wide trousers, with bared chests and the ribbons on their bonnets fluttering in the wind. They were armed with rifles and revolvers and in the lorry stood a machine-gun ready for action; overhead waved a red flag. They were singing but their song was drowned in the general tumult. Heinz could see their lips moving in unison, and their eyes, clear and cold.

A thrill ran down his spine. Excitedly he nudged Irma. 'Can you see?'

She nodded. 'First-rate.'

Behind the lorry marched an endless procession. Many of the marchers were wearing field-grey and those who were not looked nonetheless grey. They shuffled onwards, men and women, soldiers, workers, a man in a frock coat. One young fellow had his arm round a woman carrying a child. In the middle an errand boy pushed his handcart along. On they shuffled, out of step; some singing, some gazing fixedly into the distance.

But above them flags streamed in the wind, huge red draperies looted from some shop or other, small flags hastily nailed to broomsticks, long sheets tied to poles. Placards swayed overhead, some of roughly daubed cardboard, others carefully lettered and spanning the procession. These demanded 'Peace!' 'Freedom!' 'Bread!' 'Out of the Workshops!' 'General Strike!' 'Down with Militarism!' 'Bread! Bread!! Bread!!!'

Thus they marched towards the Potsdamer Platz, calling out to the people gazing from the pavements: 'Come on, Liebknecht is speaking.' Some joined the procession eagerly, others with hesitation, and there were people who pretended not to have heard or turned away embarrassed.

'Shall we go, Heinz?' asked Irma.

'Yes, but keep to the pavement. It seems a bit tame. Let's see if we can get up to the front, with the sailors, and the music.'

'Great!' agreed Irma, and they hurried along the procession, up towards the front.

But suddenly they were blocked. On the pavement in the opposite direction came two or three soldiers – NCOs – carrying cardboard boxes and no doubt going from one railway station to another, only passing through Berlin. They kept close together, without looking at the sailors in the lorry, as if with a bad conscience.

From the head of the procession a young man now detached himself – a smart young man in riding breeches and expensive tunic, an officer for certain, but without badge or medal and distinguished solely by a red armlet. And when Heinz saw this young man's pale, rather handsome, rather impudent face going towards the three NCOs, he seized Irma's arm and whispered excitedly: 'There, that's Erich!'

'Who? Where? Erich? Who's Erich?'

'My brother – and we thought the chap was still in France.'

Irma and Heinz and a good many others pushed towards the little group of soldiers before whom Erich had stopped. Two sailors jumped down from the moving lorry, flourishing revolvers – their wide trousers flapped as they advanced a little unsteadily towards the now ever-growing group of soldiers. Eagerly the people made room for them, casting admiring glances at the heroes of the revolution.

Erich Hackendahl, the young man in smart field-grey, touched the foremost NCO on his shoulder strap. 'That would be better off, eh, comrade?' he said in an undertone. 'All that stuff! It's finished with now.'

The NCO looked uncertainly at the young man, realizing he was, or had been, an officer. 'We're leaving by train right away,' he muttered, struggling to get the words out. 'From the Anhalter Station. All the same, I'd like to take it home – I earned it in action, comrade, and honestly.' But he mistook the young man, who was not as nice and handsome as he looked.

Without hesitation Erich Hackendahl seized both shoulder straps and tugged at them with such force that the seams gave way and the man staggered back. 'This rubbish is finished with,' he shouted. 'No more superiors! No more distinctions! No more militarism!' And after every 'No more', he gave the man a hard new blow.

To one side, having for some time extracted themselves from the fight as passive onlookers, stood Heinz and Irma.

'Perhaps it's inevitable?' said Heinz grimly. 'If all are equal . . . ? He looks miserable. And that it has to be Erich!'

'Can't you say something to him?' urged Irma. 'He's your brother, after all.'

'I'll try,' said Heinz, and took a step or two towards the fight.

And with that the incident was at an end. Some started running to catch up with the demonstration, others fled into the side streets, their faces expressionless. On the ground lay one of the NCOs. Over him bent another, and the third stood with lowered head, wiping the blood from his face.

'Erich!' shouted Heinz. His brother was walking on, between the two sailors.

Erich wheeled round and stared. First, his face expressed rejection, showing he hadn't recognized him. Then it went dark red, and he knew it was his brother, that it really was his brother at this very moment.

'You, Bubi?' he asked slowly. 'What are you doing here?'

'And what are you, for that matter? Those poor devils from the trenches! So they have to come home to get what they missed at the Front?'

'Your little brother, eh, Hackendahl?' said one of the sailors jeeringly. 'Hasn't seen any blood yet, what? Come with us, young 'un, and you'll soon learn.' Laughing, he held out his hand to Heinz.

'I'm against converting people with pistol butts. And I detest force.'

'That's what I used to say when my father gave me a hiding.' The sailor laughed. Those who won't listen to reason get their knuckles rapped.' And he looked mockingly at the three soldiers who were moving off – without their shoulder straps.

'Well, what about it, Hackendahl?' asked the other sailor. 'Schloss or Reichstag? Give us the truth!'

'Reichstag,' said Erich. 'Liebknecht's speaking there.'

'No kidding, or you'll be sorry for it, my lad,' threatened the sailor.

'Reichstag,' said Erich firmly.

'All right, let's go,' shouted the other sailor, and both jumped on the footboard of a passing car, said something to the driver and sped after the procession. Reluctantly Heinz had to admit that he had never seen such carefree men.

Erich seemed relieved. 'They'll get a surprise,' he grinned. 'Liebknecht's speaking at the Schloss.'

'And you're sending them to the Reichstag?'

'Of course – Liebknecht is more or less a rival firm – and people basically couldn't care less who they hear.'

'What are you then?' demanded Heinz. Irma stood right next to him, her eyes moving sharply from one brother to the other.

'My dear boy, I can't possibly explain here in the street the present rather confused political situation,' said Erich with all the superiority of an elder brother. 'In any event it would be better if you went home now and did your school work. After all, there's bound to be an occasional shot or two. Your parents will be worried about you.'

'Excellent, my Red brother!' said Heinz, who easily resumed his rough schoolboy tone when handing out a fraternal warning. 'But the old chief's been sitting for a long time with his squaw in his wigwam. When can I tell him that my Red brother has found his way back to the warpath?'

Erich had gone very red. The Red brother really had gone red.

'Stop this nonsense, Bubi,' he said abruptly. 'It's best if you say nothing – I've no time. I'll be coming back soon, perhaps very soon.'

'Not near me!' countered Heinz. 'A lie has never sullied my tongue.'

'At least you needn't tell Father my story. He wouldn't understand it.'

'Me neither.'

'Now listen, Bubi . . .' And Erich suddenly smiled, his friendly old self again. 'Your girlfriend? Won't you introduce me?'

'Irma Quaas,' said Irma immediately.

'Erich Hackendahl! Pleased to meet you. Look, Bubi. I've absolutely no time now. I've got to go to the Reichstag . . . one of us has got to speak there . . .'

'One of you . . .'

'. . . to the people. You should come and listen too, now that you're here. Then, perhaps at about seven o'clock, we can have a good talk. Come to the Reichstag – I've a room there.' He said it casually, but it was easy to see how proud he was of that room. 'I'll explain everything there. Here's a pass, to get in . . .' He gave Heinz a stamped piece of paper.

'So you've been here in Berlin quite a while already,' said Heinz suspiciously.

'Not really – not long! So, see you in the Reichstag around seven! I must go and sort out my things.'

Erich laughed. To Heinz it sounded arrogant. Then Erich ran for a tram, climbed aboard, waved once more and was gone.

§ V

Both stared after him, as if struck dumb. Then Irma took a deep breath and said: 'False coinage – no value for me.'

Upset, Heinz took her by the shoulders and shook her. 'What are you talking about, paper-shop baby! False coinage? Do you mean my brotherly love?'

'So say I! What beautifully dishonest eyes the fellow has! How he stared at me when he finally deigned to look at me! He thinks he merely has to look, and all girls will immediately want a child from him.'

'Irma! Behave properly! Think of your grey-haired mother who firmly hopes that you still believe in the stork! But you're right. He is dishonest, and has got worse since he was at the Front.'

'He's definitely never been at the Front!'

'Well, in the rear then.'

'I'm inclined to believe that more. Heinz, he only wanted to get away from you. If we ask for him in the Reichstag, no one will know a thing.'

'I don't actually believe that. He was extremely troubled about Father. He really had to work at us a little as far as reports to Father were concerned.'

'Show me the piece of paper he gave you!'

They both inspected it. The smudged, typewritten text, reproduced in multiple carbon copies, announced that the owner had the right to enter the Reichstag building. Signed: 'People's Representative, on the orders of . . .' with an unreadable scrawl. But the stamp read: 'Workers' and Soldiers' Council, Berlin.'

'Looks genuine,' concluded Irma. 'We can try.'

'I tell you, he's under pressure because of Father. And what shall we do until seven?'

'Let's listen to the speech. I would like to understand what is going on.'

'Me too – so, to the Reichstag!'

The square in front of the Reichstag was black with people and fresh processions were continually arriving, to wait patiently beneath their fluttering red flags till they were moved to and fro by the stewards, and were eventually seamlessly absorbed into the crowd, silent, grey, but determined.

But there was no need for Irma and Heinz to wait. With all the agility and cunning of the Berlin child they pushed on through the demonstrators, using their elbows freely, complaining of being trodden on, calling frequently to a lost mother whose hat they always saw in front, slipping laughingly under a steward's arm and landing breathless, their clothes rumpled, at the foot of Bismarck's monument – both in very good spirits. Somewhere in the distance they could hear a voice shouting.

A moment later they were on the monument itself, several metres above the crowd, Irma sitting on the globe representing the world, while Heinz was balanced on the shoulder of a bronze female. And, as always when somebody climbs up something, those left below were not displeased, but nodded approvingly.

'Smart lad!'

'The girl's no fool either.'

'Don't catch cold in your seat, lassie, you're sitting on the North Pole!'

'Look here, young feller, don't stand on the lady's breast – that ain't done.'

And then the query: 'You up there, who's speaking? Liebknecht?'

'Scheidemann, I think,' said Heinz at random.

But it wasn't Scheidemann. It was a rather plump, dark man who stood there on the steps of the Reichstag and shouted over the heads of the crowd. People stood quietly, listening or not listening – just as they always stood, thought Heinz.

If one had to have an example of the changes that had taken place recently it was enough, so Heinz discovered, to observe the gentleman who was speaking from the steps leading up to the Reichstag. He – it was not Scheidemann, by the way – was wearing striped trousers, and he held a bowler hat with which he occasionally gestured or emphasized a phrase. Formerly it was only men in uniform who made speeches to the public; the Kaiser had never been seen in civilian dress and even a man so unmilitary as the philosophic Chancellor von Bethmann-Hollweg would on most occasions wear uniform.

Trifling though it was, this difference struck even an inexperienced schoolboy like Heinz. For uniforms were not entirely absent – four steps below the orator there was a line of soldiers in field-grey with rifles and steel helmets, and plenty of hand grenades slung from their belts – a barrier between the speaker and his audience, those people whose victory he was at that moment celebrating.

From where Heinz and Irma were now standing, they could easily understand what the speaker was now shouting. He was speaking of the people's victory, of the victory of socialism: 'Let us not sully the honourable cause of the people!'

The voice stopped. A rattling noise had become audible, and grew louder and louder. The crowd began to stir; cries were heard in the distance. The cries came nearer. Heads swayed, just as when the wind ripples over a field of corn.

The rattling continued. There were shouts now. 'They're firing on us.'

'Machine-guns!'

'It's the Liebknecht lot!'

'Spartacists!'

'Murderers!'

And still louder: 'Run! Save yourselves! We will not allow ourselves to be mown down. Help! Help!'

The orator had stopped. He looked towards the rattling guns, gesticulated, and stood between the entrance pillars.

The soldiers were reaching for their hand grenades . . .

'They're shooting,' whispered Irma, very pale. 'Help me down quickly, Heinz. Heinz!'

'I can't see anything,' he said, peering towards the edge of the rapidly thinning demonstration. He could see people running, and the grey hood of a car.

'Hurry up! I don't want to be killed.' Irma let herself slide into his arms so suddenly that he lost his balance and, half slipping, half falling, they found themselves down below, in a crowd which was dissolving in wild confusion.

'Come along, come along! Do run, Heinz! Take hold of me!'

Everybody was running, running for their lives, men, women and children – some in silence, some shouting, some weeping. Many fell, of whom some were dragged to their feet and others trampled; no attention was paid to their shrieks.

The firing seemed to have grown louder . . .

Panic had seized everybody. People were running away from the speaker, from the banners which had fallen to the ground, from the torn placards with the inscriptions: 'Peace!' 'Liberty!' 'Bread!'

And Heinz and Irma ran with them down street after street. They were young, had long legs, and could run fast. They did so side by side, hand in hand. They had already left a long time ago, and were running through the streets, through quite different other streets.

'Can you keep on running?'

'Come on, run!'

And then they became aware that they were quite alone, racing now down a wide street in the middle of which was a strip of green grass. They were on this.

Suddenly they heard shots, in front, near at hand and coming nearer. The whole district seemed up in arms.

Heinz tried to think what to do – they were running straight into the firing. He saw an open doorway. 'Come in here!' he shouted and they ran hand in hand into safety, into its protection.

For some time they stood silent, wiping the sweat from their faces with trembling fingers and listening to the firing, which kept on breaking out again both in the distance and nearby. Once they thought they heard the wicked tack-tack of a machine-gun . . .

Gradually they regained their breath and their hearts beat more normally. Here in the safety of the doorway, alone with one another, they felt the goodness, the pleasure of life. Guns continued to rattle . . .

'Well, Irma,' said Heinz and tried to lift her head. Then he saw she was weeping quietly into a handkerchief. 'We're wonderfully brave, running away like that!'

'Be quiet,' she cried furiously, 'You coward, you!'

'Irma!' He was dumbfounded by this outbreak of the feminine in his friend, for she had been the one to suggest running away. 'Neither of us was exactly a hero!'

'Will you be quiet?' she shouted, stamping her foot; she had entirely lost control of herself. She was trembling in every limb and the half-jesting, half-consoling note in his voice was unbearable. When, jokingly, he now attempted to pull her handkerchief away, she hit out, and the blow landed full in his face.

'Good heavens, Irma,' he exclaimed. 'What's come over you? Have you gone mad?'

He was deeply offended and crossed to the other side of the doorway. There was an angry furrow between his brows and Irma wept harder than ever.

'Well, you little beauties,' came a mocking voice from the street. 'What are you hiding here for? Come out of it, both of you.' In the entrance stood a sailor, a little dark man with a bold, ill-natured face. He had a pistol in his hand.

'And hurry up,' he called out roughly when the two hesitated. 'Hands up, my lad. You were shooting just now, you swine.'

'I wasn't – I've nothing to shoot with,' said Heinz defiantly and went up to him. 'Have a look!'

'Not so much of your lip,' said the sailor threateningly. And with experienced hands he swiftly made sure that there was nothing concealed on Heinz. 'Your turn now, my girl,' he said but in a different tone. 'He slipped you the pistol, of course, the dirty dog. The bloody Socialist!'

Very pale, but both endeavouring to hide their fear, they stood before the furious little man.

'He hasn't got a pistol, truly,' said Irma. 'We went to the meeting at the Reichstag . . .'

'Oh,' drawled the sailor sarcastically, 'you heroes were with Scheidemann, were you? And you've run all the way here!'

'They fired on us,' burst out Heinz.

'Yes, a car makes a bit of a noise and twenty thousand people bolt like a lot of rabbits! We laughed ourselves sick!' And he looked contemptuously at the pair, who turned crimson.

'But there is shooting going on,' insisted Heinz. 'You've got a pistol yourself.'

'What, that little bit of popping! That's only because you Socialists are in a rage at your grand meeting being broken up. You'll soon see how quickly I restore order.' He looked at Irma. 'You come with me, kid! What do you want with this louse who messes his trousers? With us you'll get plenty to eat and see life . . .'

'Thanks,' said Irma, 'you'd better go by yourself. I don't want to get shot.'

'Who's talking of getting shot? I've put in four years at the war and I'm not dead yet. You'll see, kid, nothing happens to me.' He crossed the road to the strip of grass. 'Off the streets!' he yelled. 'Close your windows! Close your windows!' And, raising his pistol, he fired. They heard the crash of falling glass.

Then he turned to them again. 'Well, kid, what about it? You see, nothing happened.'

'No, thanks,' Irma called out.

'Then stay with your bloody Socialist,' he shouted back, unconcerned.

In his wide, flapping trousers he walked away down the street, scanning the houses right and left, sometimes shooting, sometimes shot at, but always calling out in a careless voice: 'Off the streets! Shut your windows!'

So he vanished.

§ VI

'He's certainly no coward!' said Heinz, and said so calmly rather than reproachfully.

'Well, I shouldn't like you to be like that,' said Irma nevertheless.

'That's just it. He certainly has courage – but is it the right kind of courage? Perhaps there are several kinds. In which case there would also be several kinds of cowardice.'

'Oh, do stop!' exclaimed Irma. 'That's all nonsense. I know quite well that if you have to be courageous you will be. And the same with me too.'

'There you are!' cried Heinz, delighted. 'So you think so too, eh? Though we undoubtedly ran like hares, and from a car backfiring!'

'Perhaps that wasn't true. He may have said it just to annoy us.'

'I don't think so. Besides, I saw the car.'

'If you'd only told me, then!'

'But you just fell straight into my arms from the North Pole.'

'You really are annoying me today!'

'And you hit me!'

'You know I didn't do it on purpose.'

'Yes, you did!'

'No!'

'Yes, you did. Definitely. Fist to Nose. On purpose!'

'You're being really mean!'

'No, I'm not!'

'You've made it up.'

'I've always been averse to lying.'

'Rubbish!'

'It's true.'

'Now, you're admitting you lied.'

'Rather be burnt at the stake – *eppur si muove!*'

'Idiot!'

'Thanks . . .'

Then they were silent, overheated, but cheered up too.

Then, after a while: 'Heinz!'

'No!'

'But Heinz!!'

'Again, no!'

'I only want to ask if the street is quiet again. We can hardly stay here till night-time!'

'No'.

'What no? Go or stay?'

'Both.'

'Fool.'

'Thanks.'

Again, long silence, then: 'Heinz!'

'Yes, but according to my birth certificate it's Heinrich.'

'Heinrich . . .'

'No, for God's sake!'

'Oh, Heinrich, Heinrich!'

'What's wrong? Are you crazy?'

'Yes, Heinz! Look at me!'

'So?'

'What am I doing?' She stamped with her foot. 'Oh, God, don't be such a complete fool.'

'Me the fool . . . ? Oh, Quaasin's daughter! Have you got toothache?'

'Heinz, come here! Closer! Look at me – no, don't look at me, shut your eyes! Shut your eyes, you fool! Tightly! You're not to cheat!'

'I've got my eyes shut.'

'Tight?'

'Word of honour! What's up? What's the stupid idea?'

Something damp and warm touched his chin . . .

'Damn!' He opened his eyes. 'What was that? Did you lick me?'

Trembling but resolute, she gazed at him. 'I kissed you,' she said solemnly.

He looked at her hard, wiped his chin with his hand and said: 'Damn me if that isn't the revolution! A kiss.'

'Yes,' she nodded, 'our first kiss . . . because I love you.'

'I think you've gone mad. Have you forgotten that we've rejected smooching as unaesthetic? And that this so-called love is just Nature's cunning trick for preserving the species? What's the matter with you, Irma? This shooting must have affected your mind.'

'I don't care.' And she emphatically denied their recently shared opinions. 'I love you, and that's why I kissed you.'

'Well, Irma, tell me – did you like it? The kiss I mean.'

'No, it was ghastly. But when you love someone you kiss them. That's right, isn't it? Perhaps you have to get used to it.'

'Then I won't ever.'

'I was terribly afraid,' she confessed. 'Do look at me, Heinz. How do I look?'

'How should you look?'

'I mean, can you see any difference?'

'In you? Not a trace.'

'No marks? I'm not blushing, am I?'

'No, you look about as red as a lemon!'

'Then let's try again,' she decided relentlessly.

'For heaven's sake, Irma, stop this nonsense!' The boy was horribly embarrassed.

'Please, Heinz, just once. I promise you, only this once. Shut your eyes. Yes, I do feel ashamed, but I'm not ashamed with you . . . and bend down a little or else I'll get your chin again.'

'Irma!' he protested feebly.

And something soft as a petal touched his mouth . . . he would never have thought that the lips of his little friend could be so warm and tender. And her arms were round his neck, those arms he knew so well, arms more like sticks and yet smooth and soft now. In his ears the blood began to beat, a delicious, a magic rhythm . . . for the first time he heard that melody which, in all the long years to come, would never cease from haunting him.

Irma gave a little cough . . . 'I think they've stopped shooting, Heinz.'

'Yes, that's right. Can't hear anything.'

They were hopelessly embarrassed; they did not look at one another. Adam and Eve had eaten of the Tree of Knowledge and were ashamed – they knew that they were naked.

'We've got masses of time till seven.'

'Yes, what do you think? Shall we go and see Tutti?'

'Oh, how right that would be! We've just got time.'

They rushed back to the city centre alongside each other. Both so skinny, badly clothed, undernourished and not very clean. But in both shone the spark of life. It almost shone out of their very eyes.

§ VII

Eva Hackendahl had called upon Gertrud Hackendahl.

The little dressmaker was busy at her sewing machine, listening vaguely and with scant sympathy to her sister-in-law's account of recent events in Berlin. She did not relish these visits when Gustäving had to go out of the room and was not allowed to kiss his aunt. In the last two years Eva had become what, lacking will-power and courage, she was fated to become – a prostitute. That was a good reason for Tutti not liking her sister-in-law. A woman for whom love is holy will always complain about someone who makes a business out of it.

And yet Tutti Hackendahl received her sister-in-law, tolerated her, let Eva pour out her heart; she understood that every person in trouble must have a place of refuge from the desolation of everyday life . . . This the little cripple understood very well, for she herself was not without such a refuge.

She looked at the chest of drawers where, arranged on a lace cover, stood relics of Otto – some photographs, the wallet containing her letters (it had been sent back from the Front; the stains on it had long ago turned black), all the examples she could obtain of his carving, and the box that held his knives, files, small saw and the piece of limewood in which the Christ figure had been roughed out – the work he was last engaged on. Nearby were Otto's school reports, a copybook or two and a thumbed geography book. These had been presented by Heinz.

Sometimes she would show the relics to Gustäving, six years old now – the other child, Otto's posthumous boy, was still too young. And she would tell him of a courageous, unselfish man, an artist in wood-carving . . . And when it was already dark, she would tell the child that the last words of his father were: 'Whatever happens, we must go forward!' Then she holds the little boy for a long time quietly in her arms and prays to God that the seeds of such things might be in him too. Enough to eat, she thinks sometimes, I can't give him, but I can give him faith . . . She didn't know exactly what sort of faith it was; it just seemed to her to be simple good faith, with heroes and hero-worship.

She might perhaps have been in some danger of exalting a man into a god, of transforming their love into a mere sentimental dreaming, had she not been obliged to live so close to earth, conscious of all its hardships; there were two children to provide for, she had to queue up at the food shops for hours and, although she came home tired out, she must see to the cooking, tidy the flat, do the washing and, in addition to all this, earn the daily bread. A war widow's pension was so small that she had to sit ten or twelve hours at the sewing machine to obtain the barest necessities.

Thus she never had more than five hours' sleep, and sometimes less. 'You won't be able to stand it much longer,' the kindly old panel doctor would say, shaking his head. 'You must go into hospital – I've told you that a hundred times.'

'I'll survive until my little ones are grown up, Doctor.' She smiled. 'Then I'll definitely take a rest.'

The doctor looked at her thoughtfully. He's not at all sure that this woman won't find rest long before she wants to take it. However, he mistrusts his medical judgement. As far as that's concerned, at least half of his patients would have long since starved to death. But they still come back, these women, almost without sleep, overburdened, theoretically dead – and they go on living.

And the flame of life in these weak, crippled bodies – it seems almost as if it burns stronger, not weaker. Two children and a dream: that seems to be sufficient for life, whatever the circumstances.

§ VIII

And the sewing machine whirred on. Bending over her work, she was now listening to Eva's account of the revolution, which was important, of course, only in its relation to 'him'. 'Him' still meant Eugen Bast.

Eva had never loved a man; her first and only experience had been Eugen Bast, and him she had from the beginning feared and hated with all the strength of a weak nature. If one had to take love into account, then Eva Hackendahl was virginal. She had never loved a man, never looked at one with desire. She only knew men from one aspect, and Eugen Bast and certain diseases had made sure that this aspect was utterly disgusting to her.

Sitting there with her sister-in-law she would talk unendingly. She had heard this. She had heard that. And she would twist everything first one way, then another. She was inexhaustible – for Eugen Bast as a theme was inexhaustible indeed.

Eva was still quite pretty but her features had grown sharp and her voice had taken on a whining note. 'Yes, and they say they'll let everybody out of jail tomorrow, everyone, not only the political prisoners . . .'

Gertrud's expression was negative. That wasn't what Otto had died for – so that the Eugen Basts of this world could be free once more to run around the streets . . .

'Now the thing is, Gertrud, he's not in Berlin at all but in Brandenburg, in the penitentiary there. Perhaps they won't let them out in Brandenburg. What do you think, Gertrud?'

'If they're intelligent they'll keep them in,' said Gertrud sharply, 'or else they'll have all the trouble of catching them again.'

'Perhaps there hasn't been a revolution in Brandenburg,' Eva went on. 'Brandenburg's only a small town. I've been there twice – I had a permit to visit him. Convicts are only allowed visitors twice a year and he's been in just a year now.'

Gertrud looked severe and unsympathetic; she was horrified to hear her sister-in-law speaking of such things – the utterly shameless way she was talking about prisons and thieves! She let her sewing machine rattle loudly.

'But I've always had ill luck,' continued Eva plaintively, 'and so they'll probably have a revolution in Brandenburg too and Eugen'll come out. And I always thought I'd have two more years of peace from him. Oh, what am I to do, Gertrud, what am I to do?' There was real fear in her voice.

Tutti stopped her machining for a moment, turned to her sister-in-law and said: 'You must leave Berlin. You've saved a bit; you can live somewhere else. As far as I know the chap, from what I've heard of him, I think he will have been so busy with this jolly revolution in Berlin that he definitely won't come after you.'

'But when my money's gone and I have to come back again he'll get hold of me. And then it'll be worse than ever. I told you how it was after I worked those few weeks in the munitions factory. I couldn't stand it again.'

She sat there utterly dispirited, thinking once again of that time when Otto had returned from the Front and there had been that accident in the munitions factory; she hadn't known what to do and had gone back to Eugen Bast. Yes, she had gone straight back to him just as a dog does which has been inhumanly thrashed by its master and runs away, only to return to the blows and the hunger . . .

And she had experienced all there was of inhumanity, of blows and hunger. He had thrashed her unmercifully and had taken her at once to a bawd, this time not in the Lange Strasse where the takings were very poor but to the Augsburger Strasse in the West End. Day and night she was forced to walk the streets – none of the other girls had to work as hard – but she could never earn enough for him. He took every penny, not leaving her a farthing for food, clothes or rent.

'Let the police give you board and lodging,' he laughed. 'You can kick the bucket for all I care.'

Indeed he went so far with his beatings and threats and exploitation that even the hardened 'proprietress' and the other girls took pity on her and in the end everything was arranged behind his back. But there was always the terrible fear that he would somehow nose it out. Oh, that frightful moment when he discovered that she possessed a silk dress! An evening dress with a low neck, which she had to have because gentlemen often wanted to take a girl into a restaurant or wine bar. He hadn't taken the dress away from her – that was not how he did things – no, he gave her a pair of scissors and made her cut it to pieces herself . . . cut up her one pretty frock till even the pieces were of no use to anyone.

And another time he had made her write to the Health Board of the city of Berlin registering herself as a prostitute – he dictating every word – Yours very truly, Eva Hackendahl. On a postcard!

Oh, how she had hated, and still hated, him – all the time feeling more and more strongly however that he was her destiny and that she could never find within herself the strength to oppose him. How she envied the other girls with their carefree lives. They could buy what they wanted, they could stay in bed when they were tired, they weren't compelled to cower before a cat-like tread and the brutal question: 'Well, idiot, how much dough have you earned for your Eugen? Don't stand like that or I'll sock you one!'

And then heaven or the judge had taken pity on her and sent the ingenious Bast once again to Brandenburg and three years' penal servitude – an eternity of freedom for Eva or at least a breathing space to be happy in, if one could salvage a shop-soiled remnant of happiness from a ruined life . . . At the end of the three years she would flee with her savings, perhaps to Austria or some remote spot, where she could buy a shop, a tobacconist's or better still a linen draper's business. She had quite good taste in that sort of thing . . .

And now, already, after only one year, there had come this peace, allowing Eugen Bast to come back to her again. She nearly groaned out loud. It was no use lying to him. He'd see through her immediately. And if that didn't happen right away, he would gossip with that woman and the other girls. He'd come and fetch her. She'd counted on the three years, and casually talked about her plans. Now he would take her money and her clothes, and would punish and torture her for every word she'd uttered . . .

She really did groan out loud, and her sister-in-law stopped the machine and said, 'What's wrong with you? Are you really so afraid of him?'

She nodded. 'They're bound to let him out. Then it will all begin again!'

Gertrud Hackendahl had known for a long time that Eva could

not be helped. So she merely said, with a sigh: 'What idiots can they be who let those sorts of prisoners out? They belong in there themselves.' And her thin, narrow-lipped mouth twitched. 'But just wait till the army comes back from the Front!'

'Do you think so?' asked Eva nervously. 'Do you think the soldiers would put Eugen back again?' For one moment a rather bleak hope lit up her face, but was immediately extinguished. 'No, no,' she said with a sigh. 'Such luck is not for me. The soldiers can't do anything. They've nothing more to say, now that they're defeated and we've lost the war . . .'

'What did you say?' asked Gertrud Hackendahl, and stood up from her machine. And she asked in such a way that it was suddenly deadly quiet in the little kitchen.

Eva just stared at her sister-in-law.

Gertrud stood in front of her – a small, crippled figure, with her hands on her heart, as if she were feeling pain. With eyes wide open, she stared at Eva.

'What was that you said?' she asked again softly. 'Germany is defeated? Germany has lost the war?'

'Everybody's saying . . .' began Eva innocently.

'You shut your mouth,' came the interruption. 'Don't ever again speak like that here! Aren't you ashamed? Have you no feeling of honour? You are Otto's sister.' Her eyes strayed briefly to the chest of drawers, but immediately came back to her sister-in-law, and looked at her, ablaze. 'You know how he died and why he fought – and you dare to say defeated and lost!'

'But Gertrud, please. Of course I didn't mean Otto . . .'

'So what did he die for, if we are defeated? Where have we been defeated? Tell me a single battle we've lost? Tell me! Devil take you – the shame of it! We've won. We've fought against the whole world and won. Not a single enemy soldier stands on German soil, and you say we're defeated! So where are we defeated? Where?'

She stood there furious. She had spoken ever faster and ever angrier. Never in her life had she been so angry. Gustäving had heard his mother's voice and now stood in the doorway, looking from his mother to his aunt, his hands making a fist.

'Don't do anything to Mummy!' he shouted.

But his mother didn't even notice him, and shouted: 'It's quite right that they're releasing prisoners. Everyone can see then what sort of a revolution it is!'

She stood there, shocked, looking at her sister-in-law. Then she realized whom she'd been saying all that to. It was pointless – Eva understood nothing. There was nothing to her. Otto had once been – almost – like her, but there'd been something in him which his father hadn't destroyed: he had the capacity to love. Eva had nothing to her.

'Just don't say that in my kitchen again,' said Gertrud finally. 'Gustäving, go into the living room and look after your little brother.'

She sat down at her sewing machine again.

After a pause Eva said, in a weak voice, 'I don't care what people say. Just as long as Eugen doesn't come out.'

Gertrud didn't answer but sat and sewed. She'd just got her first sewing job from a private client. She was altering a field-grey army greatcoat to become a lady's coat. She'd never thought of it before, but she suddenly realized that, up to then, there had been no such work. There had never been enough army greatcoats, and now what's in her hands is superfluous and would become a coat for a lady!

She sewed more and more hesitantly. Then she stopped entirely and stared at the coat.

Suddenly she realized, because of the work she was doing, that the war was finally over, that what Otto had fought for was no more . . . That people say the war is lost, and what that meant, and what it meant for her. Especially for her!

She sobbed and sobbed.

§ IX

'Gertrud!' interrupted Eva. 'Someone's ringing at the door. Didn't you hear? Shall I open it?'

'No, leave it. I'll go.'

The doorbell rang again.

'Gertrud! Gertrud! Oh – one moment!' Deep concern was to be

heard in Eva's voice. 'Supposing it's Eugen? Please let me go into the living room. I won't touch the children – of course not!'

'Do you really think,' said Gertrud, 'that I'd let that fellow into my house? Never! But go into the living room anyway. But, yes, leave the children alone.'

It was a completely different, an enlivened Gertrud Hackendahl who let Heinz into the kitchen with his girlfriend, Irma. Now she was the real Tutti, who never forgot that Heinz was the only Hackendahl who had congratulated her on her marriage and had been completely in agreement with her choosing Otto. She liked Heinz so much because he often visited them, just to chat, and because he spent hours with the children, because he liked bringing his young girlfriend to see them.

Despite his immaturity and his boasting, she saw in him something of her dead husband – an utter decency and a stolid, stubborn reliability.

'Heinz! Irma! That you should be here on such a day! Come in!' Then softly, 'Eva's here too.'

'Eva?' asked Heinz Hackendahl nervously.

He thought briefly and looked at Irma. He hadn't seen Eva since she left their parents' house.

'Well, I don't know . . . shouldn't we just leave?'

'For my sake?' asked Irma. 'Don't be so stupid, Heinz!'

'Come right in, Heinz,' agreed Gertrud. 'She's quite – at peace . . .'

'Hello, Eva,' said Heinz, and then, a little embarrassed, 'Long time no see. Old folk now! And now you're making a revolution too? Fantastic!'

But he turned back again to Tutti immediately. 'I must show you something. I've invested a few groschen in – the first steps towards an archive of the history of the revolution.'

He pulled a newspaper out of his pocket, unfolded it so that everyone could see the headlines and proudly asked: 'Great, isn't it?'

'*The Red Flag* – Organ of the Spartacists,' they read.

'First number, fresh from the barrel!' grinned Heinz. 'Tops, isn't it?'

'*Red Flag*,' said Tutti, frowning. 'I always thought the national colours made a good flag, Heinz.'

'Of course! What do you think we're talking about? You haven't got it, Tutti. Look carefully. This is just the usual old scandal gazette. The brothers have just printed it off and renamed it. If I think of Father getting the *Red Flag* through his letter box this evening instead of his favourite *Local Gazette* . . .' Heinz grinned again.

'And that's supposed to be funny?' asked Tutti sadly. 'I don't understand you, Heinz! They're simply pinching people's newspapers – stealing in other words.'

'That's revolution for you, Tutti.'

'Then be off with your revolution! For some it's letting prisoners out of jail, and you say it's stealing newspapers – and that's supposed to be revolution? I say it's a swindle!'

'I told you straight away,' Irma joined in, 'don't buy it. In the street-fighting there were also red flags, and then, when we left the meeting because we thought there'd be shooting – there were more red flags.'

'You seem to have been through quite a bit?!'

'Yes, I'll tell you in a moment . . . but first of all you must see something.'

Heinz couldn't help it. Despite his failure with the newspaper, he showed them his Reichstag pass, and told them what they intended to do and had already done.

Tutti's lips pressed hard together when she heard of the chaotic street-fighting.

'Non-commissioned soldiers, did you say, Heinz? Non-commissioned soldiers?'

'Yes. Of course I was a fool to have told you that, Tutti. It merely upsets you.'

'And your brother took part? Didn't he even consider that Otto . . . ?'

'I could never stand Erich,' said Eva. 'He was always Father's favourite, but—'

'No, Father's favourite was actually you.'

'No, Bubi. Father was just in love with me, but he really liked Erich. He could get anything out of him with his laughter.'

'He's certainly a cunning devil,' admitted Heinz.

'A dandy!' cried Irma, 'a regular matinée idol!'

'Heinz,' asked Tutti, 'show me that pass once again, will you?'

She took it and looked. 'Workers' and Soldiers' Council,' she whispered. 'But no soldiers are back from the Front yet!'

She held up the pass and looked at Heinz. 'Heinz, if you'll listen to me, you'll put the pass, with the newspaper, straight into the oven.'

'So we shouldn't go into the Reichstag? But what's going on there is extremely interesting, Tutti. I'm definitely not going there because of Erich. I couldn't care less what he does. But I know nothing about the revolution. You really have to know about that. What are the Spartacists? Why does my beloved brother Erich steal audiences from Liebknecht? Liebknecht is a Social Democrat, too, I believe? You've got to know something about all that, you know!'

'But why must you know more about it, Heinz?' asked Tutti, upset. 'You already know the revolution is bad, simply from how it feels . . . and don't feelings show you what's right?'

'Yes, perhaps – for sure. But that isn't enough. You've got a head on your shoulders too. You've got to *know* as well.'

'And you think you'll get anything out of Erich?' asked Eva mischievously. 'So idiotic! He merely wants to schmooze around, so you don't tell Father.'

Heinz kept his mouth shut tight. He knew very well that Eva could never stand Erich; and he didn't actually like him either . . . but Eva's way of doing things was not right – pure hostility, to find everything bad just because Erich was involved.

'Look, Tutti,' he said, and completely ignored Eva. 'I'm sorry to begin it all again, even if it does hurt you. About the street-fighting, I mean. I know you are shocked. But there were many hundreds of people on the streets, and war-wounded as well. You saw that too, didn't you, Irma?'

Irma nodded.

'And if no one had done anything, and if the old soldiers believe the street-fighting must stop, there must be more to it than just bloody-mindedness. I mean there must be a meaning to it somewhere.'

'Bloody-mindedness is always the same,' insisted Tutti. 'I can't understand why you're trying to make sense out of it. Injustice always remains injustice.'

'I'm not saying,' began Heinz again, very stubbornly, 'that injustice is justice. I only want to understand, Tutti, why—'

'I never want to understand such things,' said Tutti bitterly. 'I don't even want to know about them.'

'Yes, you do, Tutti. You do!' countered Heinz. 'You've committed an injustice yourself and discovered that it was quite just.'

She stared at him uncomprehending. 'I what?'

'You took butter and eggs where you could, and said it's right!'

'That's completely different!' she almost shouted. 'How can you say such a thing, Heinz? Should I have left my children to starve?'

'Of course it's completely different, Tutti,' he said quietly. 'I don't want to hurt you. What's the same is the others who are starving even more, and the judges who judge them as unjust.'

'Fancy comparing a pound of butter (and I never took more than a half) with street-fighting!'

'Just ignore the tearing-off of shoulder straps. It's just a symbol of people not wanting bosses any more. Everyone should be equal, or something like that.' He got confused, but soon found the thread again. 'Just think how it is with the Hackendahls – father and children. Wasn't it true of Otto, Tutti?'

'What do you mean, Otto? You shouldn't even mention Otto, if you talk about shoulder straps!'

'I'm talking about Father, about Father and Otto! Didn't Otto hate Father and didn't he in the end rebel against him? And what might Father have thought about that, Tutti? Didn't Otto tear off Father's shoulder straps too?'

For a moment it was deadly quiet in the kitchen. Heinz stood tall and pale over his little sister-in-law.

Her eyes were closed. She was finding it hard to think.

Then she begged him: 'Get out, please. All of you get out of my kitchen. No, I'm not angry with you, Bubi. You may even be right. Perhaps what you say is true, but I don't want to know . . . I don't want to hear about it ever again . . . You've really hurt me, Bubi. I only know that Otto was good, and if he hurt his father, it was because he had to, but he didn't want to . . .'

'Come along, Heinz,' said Irma. 'You're only tormenting her.'

'Yes, Heinz, go to the Reichstag. Go everywhere, listen, and whatever you like. You'll only find bad things.'

He stretched out his hand hesitantly. 'Goodbye, Tutti!'

She smiled weakly. 'Oh, Bubi, you dear boy! How you're going to get your fingers burnt! You've such a soft heart. What you said hurt you just as much as it did me. All you Hackendahls are soft – the children I mean.'

'Goodbye, Tutti.'

'Goodbye, Bubi! Try not to hurt yourself too much . . .'

§ X

Once down in the street, Irma asked, 'But we're going to the Reichstag, aren't we?'

'You can depend on it,' said Heinz.

'And when do we go home?'

'When it's time.'

'And what will your father say?'

'I don't even think about it!'

Of course he did think about it, but suddenly he didn't care what his father would say. For very many years his father's words had sounded like thunder, or the word of God, in his ears. Now he had become deaf to them, just as soldiers no longer heard their officers' orders, and workers no longer listened to their employers.

Everything seemed chaotic and increasingly confusing – Tutti and the newspaper, the torn-off shoulder straps, Otto's rebellion against Father, brother Erich with his office in the Reichstag, and the kidnapped Liebknecht-followers – and the sailor. All confusion! Nevertheless there was a light in everything, a ghostly but increasingly palpable light. There was a sense that some meaning must lie behind all the confusion. Perhaps it was only the feeling of being young, of wanting to live, and not be led by bunglers and become their scapegoats – of wanting to lead his very own life, with all the possibilities of victory and defeat.

'You say nothing,' said Irma, worried by her friend's silence. 'I suppose you are thinking.'

'Exactly!'

'So what about? About your brother?'

'That too. What do you think, Irma, did I talk a lot of rubbish at Tutti's?'

'Half-half.'

'No, tell me really!'

'You were perhaps right, but you shouldn't have contradicted Tutti, of all people, if you're angry with all the Hackendahls.'

'But I didn't mention that.'

'Of course you did – only that!'

'Oh, no . . .' He grew quite angry. So that's what it looked like to others – to stupid women, for instance – if he spoke to the point. 'Oh, you women,' he consoled himself.

'Thanks a lot! I'm not a woman – I'm your girlfriend!'

'Well, true . . .'

'And if you let your brother Erich have a bit of your anger with the Hackendahls, that would really please me. There's the Reichstag!'

Yes, there it was. Gloomy and dark, with no crowds swarming round it now, it lay wrapped in the mists of a November evening. Only a very few street lamps were lit. Somewhat uneasily Heinz and Irma mounted the steps to the main entrance, where they were stopped by a soldier, a proper wartime soldier with rifle, steel helmet and hand grenades. The man however wore an armlet with something stamped on it and Heinz assumed that this was identical with what was stamped on Erich's permit, but here he was mistaken. Folding up the slip of paper, the soldier returned it. 'No longer valid,' he said.

'But why? I got it only this afternoon.'

'And this afternoon we smoked the comrades out of here. Workers' and Soldiers' Councils have no standing now. We're Noske's people.'

'But my brother . . .'

'It's quite likely,' said the soldier indifferently, 'that they're still in the Schloss. But they won't be staying there much longer either; we'll see to that, even if we have to blow up the whole damned place.' And he turned away into the entrance. Rather depressed, the two went back down the steps.

'What are we to do now? Shall we go to the Schloss?'

'That's no use. The pass is for the Reichstag.'

'But it's not valid.'

'It'll be even less valid in the Schloss – that's logic, isn't it?'

Undecided, they prowled round the dark building. They tried a second door but were turned back again.

At the third door, however, they were luckier. The news that the Workers' and Soldiers' Councils had been thrown out seemed not to have reached the sentry at the back of the building. 'See that corridor? Go along there and you'll find a porter. Not that he'll know much either; nobody does at the moment. But you can try.'

They found the porter in his lodge – a dignified, white-haired old gentleman who seemed utterly confused by the excitement and uproar of the last few days. 'Yes, indeed, Herr Hackendahl has a room here. Of course!' Helplessly he looked at his telephone switchboard, and at the indicator on the wall, showing names and room numbers. He gave a disconsolate shake of the head. 'No, none of my gentlemen is called Hackendahl. But my gentlemen aren't coming here now. I beg your pardon, Herr Ebert still comes and so does Herr Noske, Herr Breitscheid, Herr Scheidemann . . .' He seemed to want to continue the list of those who still came there.

'But I'm looking for Herr Hackendahl. He's got a room here.' (Heinz however was not so sure of this now.)

'Then come along,' said the old man, going ahead of them. Their youth seemed to inspire him with confidence. 'I oughtn't to leave my post,' he confessed, 'it's against regulations . . . I should really hand you over to a messenger. But all our messengers have run away.'

This was strange but they were to come across even stranger things in the outwardly dignified gold-domed building, so often passed with such feelings of awe and respect . . . A door opened and from the room came a burst of laughter. A crowd of men sat there in a blue fug of drifting tobacco smoke; all were laughing and all were in shirtsleeves.

In their ugly, worn-out shoes Irma and Heinz strode over thick plush carpets. Halfway up some stairs lay a soldier in field-grey, snoring with open mouth, his head on a knapsack. They stepped over him and came to an open window looking into the grey November night. Peeping from it stood two machine-guns on long, thin feet, menacing the scarcely visible buildings opposite; they stood there forsaken. Not a soul was in sight.

They went up a staircase. Above, some laughing soldiers were clustered. They were watching a man on a ladder who was disfiguring with black paint a gold-framed portrait of the Kaiser.

Again and again their guide stopped to make enquiries, sometimes of men in dark uniforms like his – in which case the talk went slowly and amiably, with much shaking of heads. Sometimes, however, he timidly questioned soldiers or people who were not officials and was glad then to get his information and move on.

They were now in a far busier part of the great building. Everywhere men were running about, most of them soldiers in active service uniforms, and they could hear telephones ringing and the click of typewriters behind doors. Suddenly they were in a large, marble-flagged corridor, walking between pillars. Here tall doorways led to a huge, dimly lit hall. 'That is the chamber of session,' explained their guide.

This corridor too was full of soldiers, some sprawling on the benches, others strolling up and down smoking cigarettes and many still wearing their steel helmets. And they had actually brought a field gun there, a monstrosity on wheels camouflaged with daubs of green, brown and yellow paint. This was trained on a door.

And supposing this door opened and supposing there should be people outside, a big crowd, a mass meeting for instance, and by some accident this meeting was listening to the wrong speaker, then the cannon's mouth would vomit death and destruction on the unsuspecting persons below. By some accident! So much had happened by accident that afternoon.

Heinz Hackendahl closed his eyes. But he opened them immediately, for Irma had nudged him and was whispering, very excited: 'Look at that officer!'

This officer, standing there unchallenged with his brown, determined face, smoking a cigarette among the soldiers, observing everything acutely and occasionally giving an order in an undertone – this seemed the most extraordinary sight of all on that confusing day to those two young people. Had they not already both witnessed how the three unfortunate sergeants, on account of a pair of shoulder straps . . .

'So the old traditions haven't completely disappeared,' said Heinz quietly.

Irma pressed his hand excitedly. 'I'm so glad, Heinz!' she whispered.

He didn't even ask why she was glad, he understood immediately.

A little later their guide returned. 'Now I know where Herr Hackendahl is,' he said, hurt. 'Upstairs on the second floor. Herr Hackendahl's responsible for security in Berlin. You should have told me straight away, then I would have found him quicker!'

'Security? What security?'

Erich appeared ever more puzzling to Heinz.

'Oh, you know, against attacks, looting. You must know about that if you're his brother?' And the old man suddenly looked at him suspiciously.

'I really didn't know that, although I'm definitely his brother,' said Heinz. 'So show us where we should go. And many thanks for your trouble!'

§ XI

The carefully written notice on the door, 'Dr Bienenstich – Secretariat', had been clumsily crossed out in pencil. The fresh notice consisted of a piece of ordinary cardboard on which was scribbled 'Committee of Security' in blue. It could not be said that this was very informative either, but it was the place to which the porter, after many enquiries, had directed them. Heinz knocked and looked at Irma. She nodded. He knocked again. A voice shouted, 'Come in,' and they went in.

Erich was standing by the window talking with a swarthy and rather stout gentleman. He only looked briefly at his two visitors, shouted 'One moment!', and continued to talk quickly, in a low voice, with the swarthy man.

Irma and Heinz looked at each other. Then she nodded and Heinz said in a whisper: 'Of course! That's him!' There was no doubt about it – they had seen this gentleman before, this swarthy gentleman in a dark coat, with the elegant striped trousers. In fact, he had been the speaker at the meeting which had been so violently interrupted. Heinz was dying to know who it was. It wasn't Ebert. Ebert was smaller. And it wasn't Liebknecht, either, who was not fat . . . He searched his memory, but as a true war child, to whom only the military seemed important, he hadn't been interested in the civilian deputies, who were suddenly now important after all.

The swarthy gentleman said, 'Well, Erich, leave everything till tomorrow. I, for my part, must get at least five hours' sleep tonight – and it would do you good too. And by the way, we're putting off your visit.'

Erich smiled, but this annoyed Heinz. It was a smile that seemed to say how completely unimportant his visitors were.

But now the stout man looked at Heinz, and stretched a fat, very white, floppy hand towards him. Heinz had to take it and shake it.

'So you're our clever Erich's brother?' Heinz was asked.

'You could also say that Erich was Heinz Hackendahl's brother,' he answered provocatively.

The swarthy gentleman smiled in agreement. 'You're right,' he said. 'You don't always want to be a clever man's brother. And what are *you*? Student? At school?'

Heinz had to admit that he was still at school.

'And what's the atmosphere like with you, at your school?'

Heinz said the atmosphere differed.

'Of course!' The fat man understood straight away. 'Depending on what's just happened. Quite right too!'

Heinz thought the fat gentleman could be a little more sparing with his praise. He always had a deep antipathy to the praise of his teachers.

'And how do you feel?' he was asked.

'I heard you speaking this afternoon,' he said excitedly. 'My girlfriend and I had to run for it pretty quick.'

To his surprise this sally didn't seem to cause any wound at all. On the contrary, it produced hearty and quite sincere laughter.

'Yes, that was a regrettable incident!' said the fat man, laughing. 'But with not entirely unpleasant consequences, what, Erich, my son?'

Laughing, Erich admitted that the consequences had not been entirely unpleasant. No, certainly not!

Heinz became angrier and angrier. 'I saw women and children being badly trampled,' he said heatedly, in response to the odd, self-satisfied laughter.

The fat man immediately grew serious. 'I know, I know. It all happened a bit fast, and the others were . . . Well, I don't think such little bureaucratic mistakes will occur again soon.'

He nodded to Erich in a friendly way, repeated: 'Sleep, sleep, Erich, my son', stretched out his hand to Heinz, nodded towards Irma and went quietly out of the room, visibly preoccupied by the 'little bureaucratic mistakes'.

'Who was that, Erich?' asked Heinz, somewhat rudely, for the door had hardly closed.

'Sit down. Cigarette? You don't smoke yet, Bubi? They'll let you start soon, surely. When are you taking your school leaving certificate?'

'I asked you who that man was.'

'Don't you know? Why, you heard him speak. By the way, what did you think of it – the speech, I mean?'

'Splendid,' grinned Heinz. 'Except the backfiring. And who's the speaker?'

'A future minister.'

'Oh, Erich!' Heinz shouted, laughing. 'You still like to keep things quiet and swank about them, I see. Didn't I describe him correctly, Irma?'

Irma nodded.

'Well, so he's a minister! Oh, let's leave it, Erich. You needn't tell me his name. If he really is a minister, I'll get to know anyway. And you're his secretary, I presume, on the way to being head of a department, eh? Or higher up even?'

But Erich was not in the least annoyed; on the contrary, he smiled quite complacently. 'What did you mean by backfiring?' he asked in rather too innocent a way.

'Dear, dear, so you don't know. The death-threatening car, of course, that broke up your meeting.'

'Excuse me, the meeting was fired on by machine-guns.'

'Pardon me, Irma and I were sitting on top of Bismarck – it was a car with a grey hood.'

The brothers looked at each other.

'Did you by any chance do a bunk from the meeting too?'

Heinz turned red. 'One has to hunt with the hounds.'

'And run with the hares,' laughed Erich heartily. The more furious his brother became the more he laughed. 'Bubi, Bubi,' he said, 'you're still damned young, you know.' His little victory made him inclined to talk. 'Can't you exert your undeniably vast mental powers and see that in the end it's completely immaterial whether it was a machine-gun that fired or a car that backfired?'

'No,' said Heinz perplexed. 'I can't. You'll have to explain.'

'Is it immaterial,' cried Irma, 'whether people are killed or not?'

'I said in the end, little lady,' drawled Erich, incredibly superior. 'In the end!'

'I'm not a lady!'

'Then let's hope you'll become one.' Erich turned to Heinz. 'Listen, it's quite simple. I'll explain things . . . We have an agreement with the Liebknecht people not to disturb each other's meetings. A kind of armistice, so to speak. Comrade Liebknecht speaks from the Schloss, we from the Reichstag. Now if our meeting's been fired on we've got the right to complain of a breach of agreement and smoke out a Workers' and Soldiers' Council which has been found treacherous and unreliable.'

'But there was no actual firing.'

'Ass! We say there was – and that's sufficient.' Erich looked at his brother triumphantly. 'Don't you see it's enough if you can assert with some probability that a right's been infringed?' He winked an eye as beautiful and fine as a cat's. 'Why should we have to investigate whether it was a machine-gun or a motor car?' He bent over and whispered, 'What's wrong with producing a car or a gun yourself if it's going to help?' He straightened up. 'The W. and S. Council here in the Reichstag was really very disturbing. Was disturbing, my dear Bubi. Was – since this afternoon.'

Heinz stared at his brother. He had read about the tricks of diplo-macy, about treason, spying and knavery, but such things were always abstract, remote, historic. That they should take place today, in front of his very eyes and by his own brother's contrivance . . .

'Oh, Erich,' he said, and broke off. Even swearing did no good here. What would be the point of calling him a pig. He was proud of being one!

'And those sailors who wanted to listen to Liebknecht, you lied to them too?' asked Irma.

'The end justifies the means, little Fräulein.'

'Why employ such means?'

'Why tear off shoulder straps?' cried Heinz, upset. Then, reluc-tantly, he said, 'Supposing Father heard about this?'

'Please, stay still.' Erich was quite unmoved. 'No, sit down. It's precisely for Father that I'm explaining this to you and permitting your fraternal cheek.'

'I'll never believe you,' murmured Heinz.

Erich didn't hear him, because he didn't want to. 'Why do we resort to such means? Because we want power, alone and on our own!'

'But who exactly is that "we"?' cried Heinz desperately. 'Here's one speaker and there's another and both are waving red flags and they're all in revolt. You talk about a troublesome Workers' Council! Well, what's it all about? Do you understand it? No, it's a general collapse – utter chaos.'

'Not a bit, it's all quite simple. You'll understand the whole thing in three minutes. We – that is the great Social Democratic Party, the only party with the commitment and ability to win and hold power –'

'Because you're in it, I suppose?'

'Let's leave out the point-scoring. There are also the Independ-ents, the so-called Independents,' Erich continued. 'Those are members of the party who voted against war credits. One part of them tends towards the Liebknecht group, another wants to join us.'

'And the Liebknecht people?'

'Indeed, the Liebknecht people – they're the problem! Liebknecht

is now very popular . . . he's always written against the war. He's
been in prison. He wants to destroy everything. That's very popular
these days! But no one knows how many people are behind him. His
Spartacus group is only small. You remember Spartacus, Bubi?'

'Of course. Thracian prisoner of war. Began a slave and soldiers'
revolt against Rome, won, and gained a huge following.'

'Well, I believe in names,' said Erich. 'Spartacus . . . do you know
what happened to the Spartacists?'

'Yes, I do. In the end they were completely destroyed. Spartacus
fell with most of his followers. Thousands were crucified.'

'Absolutely,' said Erich reflectively. 'We don't do crucifying any
more these days . . .'

The silence in the room was oppressive.

Erich looked up and chuckled when he saw the serious, angry
faces of his two visitors.

'You look so grim. You don't belong to the Spartacists, do you? I
promise you, you would be backing the wrong horse. It's we who
will form the government!'

'I haven't backed any horse at all,' cried Heinz, furious. 'This isn't
a matter of horse racing.'

'No, of course not. One uses such stupid expressions. I
apologize.'

'I don't only believe in names, but also in expressions – in expressions which reveal those who use them,' said Heinz scornfully.

'My dear young fellow!' The older, superior, big brother was talking. 'Why such aggression? Of course I'm happy to be fighting on
the side of those with the best prospects! Is that wrong?'

'And what do you want to do when you're in government?'

'We'll build a democracy on the Western model,' explained
Erich.

'Yes, of course. That's the form you want it to take. I mean, what
do you want to achieve when you are in power?'

'Achieve? What do you mean?' Now it was Erich's turn to be confused. 'When we're in power, haven't we achieved our goal? What
else do you mean?'

'Oh, Erich. Don't be so stupid! What do you want to do with your

power? You must have plans, intentions, a programme. Just obtaining power—'

'Yes, my dear Bubi. Thank you for your flattering opinion, but for
a government programme you really must wait until our future
president announces it.'

'Don't talk rubbish! You're not an idiot. You must have intentions.
We've lost the war. What agreements, for example, do you want to
make with our enemies?'

'We'll think of something. Once we're a democracy, we'll be able
to speak to the French and the English. Naturally we'll have to pay
something, and more than the French had to in 1871. But two democratic governments will be able to come to a peaceful agreement.'

'Have you read the armistice conditions?' Heinz broke in, furious.

'But why are you so upset? *We* didn't make them! Don't forget,
armistice conditions are made between generals.'

'You mean dictated to them!'

'By the military. We civilians come along afterwards – and we
have President Wilson.'

'So as far as end of the war and peace conditions are concerned,
you simply say: it will all get settled?'

'Absolutely right! Or have you other suggestions?'

'And the people? I don't know if you've yet noticed that they are
almost starving? That thousands are dying of flu every day? They call
it starvation flu. What do you intend to do for the people?'

'My dear Bubi, please don't shout at me. You know very well that
the Social Democratic Party has something like a programme. It is
pretty long, and I cannot possibly recite it to you. If I remember
right, it contains something about an eight-hour day, the socializa-
tion of factories, and tariff reform . . .'

'And you want to achieve that?'

'Of course. Definitely. Gradually, in good time, it will all be
achieved.'

'In that case,' and Bubi almost shouted, 'you haven't a clue! You
simply want to be in power!'

'Of course we do,' shouted Erich back. 'Power! If we only have
power, everything else will follow. First, power!' And he stood there,
triumphant, beaming . . . And gave a violent start. There was a loud

rattle like a hailstorm on a roof, a horrible whizzing sound, glass crashing, voices shouting.

'Take cover!' cried Erich. 'Under the table! They're firing on the Reichstag.'

In a moment all three were on their hands and knees, crawling under the big oak table – not a second too soon, for the panes in their room were shattered and the fragments fell with a clatter. Something struck the frame of the door and they held their breath – but the stream of bullets had passed on.

§ XII

'We should have put the light out,' said Erich peevishly. 'Now they'll keep on peppering the room.'

Irma laughed, a rather unnatural laugh. It had been a bit too much of a shock. 'Now, Mr Hackendahl, do you mind whether it's a broken exhaust or a machine-gun?' she asked bitterly.

'We're well under cover,' said Erich cheeringly. 'They can't do anything.' Having been in the trenches a few weeks he was much the calmest of the three and not at all scared.

'Are those your friends, the sailors, who are shooting?' asked Heinz, trying to speak naturally.

'Don't think so. It's coming from the right. Someone told me that officers loyal to the Kaiser had barricaded themselves in the Architekten-Haus, so perhaps they've got a machine-gun on the roof. Well, our chaps will soon deal with little jokes like that . . . Listen, they're starting already!'

In the Reichstag scattered shots rang out. Then a machine-gun rattled and the first one replied to it. There was more crashing of glass and a whistle was heard.

'Let's hope it quietens down soon,' yawned Erich. 'I must admit I'd like to be in bed early.'

'We have to go home too,' Irma reminded Heinz.

'Yes, that's true,' said Erich casually. 'I hadn't forgotten about taking you home. I've got a car – a service car, of course. Now don't think—'

'I understand all right,' grunted Heinz. 'Just a service car. Private car soon, what?'

'Possibly,' yawned Erich. 'Father all right? I could say how d'you do to him then.'

'Made of iron, Erich, as you know. People have told him so often he's "Iron Gustav" that he really believes it now. But he's vastly changed, all the same.'

'Changed? In what way? More approachable?'

The machine-gun on the Architekten-Haus had not yet been silenced, and was spraying the front of the Reichstag once more. Nearer and nearer came the crash of broken glass until it reached their windows. Irma gave a cry.

'Don't worry, little Fräulein, we're in the blind corner,' Erich reassured her.

The firing withdrew elsewhere.

'No,' said Heinz thoughtfully. Sitting under the table, as if they had become children again, encouraged him to talk. 'Father hasn't become less severe, actually. I should say more obstinate and dogmatic if anything, especially now he's driving again.'

'Driving?' cried Erich indignantly. 'What nonsense! Why's he doing that?'

'To earn money, Erich.'

'Earn money? What's he got the other drivers for?'

'But, don't you know?' Heinz was gaping with surprise. Then he began to understand things a little.

'Know what? Come on, tell me. I suppose everything's in a frightful muddle at home and it's time I came and looked after you all.'

'Splendid! And don't forget to bring some money, Erich. Put money in your purse, the need is urgent.' Heinz did not hide the sneer. He now understood why his brother had been so friendly.

'Money?' Erich, preoccupied with what he had heard, paid no attention to the sarcasm. 'Money? Don't talk nonsense, Bubi. Father's a prosperous man. I always put him down for a quarter of a million marks at least.'

'All right – ask him yourself about his quarter of a million then.'

'But the money can't be all gone.'

'I don't know.'

'Bubi, what's wrong at home? What's happened? God, I should have known that he didn't understand anything about money matters. I ought to have looked into it sooner. Tell me, what's left?'

'A cab, the broken-down old grey, an apartment house so heavily mortgaged that the rents don't cover the interest . . .'

'But the capital? The capital!'

'I believe Father's got twenty or twenty-five thousand marks in War Loans – if he's still got it.'

'It's impossible. Where's the money gone to?'

'I dunno. Very likely Father never had any more. He used to earn a good deal.'

'You'll have to tell me all about it.' Erich was now really disturbed. 'Come with me for a bit and tell me as we go along. And please come too, Fräulein. All's clear now, they're only shooting a little among themselves. Now don't refuse, Bubi. You'll do me the favour, won't you? I must really know how things stand. Frankly, I had counted on getting something from Father. I'm just furnishing my place – you must come and have a look at it. And I'll introduce you to my lady friend. Wait till you see! You don't need to hesitate, Fräulein; she's a very nice little Frenchwoman – doesn't bite . . . Twenty thousand marks in War Loans! It's incredible.'

Yes, Erich was really disturbed. He still had to telephone, give orders. The car was due to draw up on the shadowy side of the Reichstag building, along the Spree. Then it turned out that all was not well with their passes. You apparently had to have passes for all possible parties. There were difficulties with the ones they had.

Hardly had they sat in the car – incidentally very new and apparently a private vehicle – but Erich started up again: 'Well, Heinz, I'm counting on you to tell me the truth. Mother once told me in a letter that Otto had married just before he was killed. Some kind of crippled needlewoman. I dimly recall seeing her once at home. Did she perhaps pump father? Cripples are often damned avaricious.'

'They're not the only ones,' answered Heinz mischievously.

§ XIII

The car with the Hackendahl brothers passed through a Berlin dark and almost deserted, except for the occasional sound of firing that died away almost immediately, however. They were approaching the West End, the exclusive, almost feudal, West End.

At about the same time, another car was setting out for the west of the city, the smart west, for Zehlendorf, Schlachtensee and Dahlem. It was also a car in which sat a child of old Hackendahl, of Iron Gustav. Sat? No, stood!

There were numerous obstacles to be overcome before the smart, almost new car reached its destination, although it held the future secretary of one who would soon be a minister – time after time it was stopped, searched for weapons and its occupants made to produce their papers. Heinz had frequently to interrupt the urgently desired account of old Hackendahl's finances . . .

The second vehicle, a battered grey lorry, did not trouble to hide its weapons – on the contrary. At back and front stood machine-guns ready to fire. And all its occupants – some in field-grey, others in civilian clothes – were heavily armed, except one. But no sentry stepped out of the shadows and signalled with his lantern, confiscated the arms or asked for papers. Unmolested, the big lorry rattled towards the West, a red flag waving above it. Among wild-looking men stood a pale and trembling woman – Eva Hackendahl.

After a hurried and awkward parting from her brother and his girlfriend, Eva Hackendahl had gone home feeling almost happy. The little argument, of which she had understood little, had cheered her up.

It really isn't so easy with little Gertrud, she had thought. She'd almost thrown him out! Out with you! That was what she'd said to him. I always seem get on best with her – much better than with that wretch who thinks he's so clever.

This thought of being above everyone else shortened her long walk to Augsburger Strasse. She was almost happy when she entered her room. But, opening the door of her room, all happiness was ended for her in that same moment. The light was burning; on her bed, fully dressed, a sports cap on his head, a cigarette between his lips, lay Eugen, with his dirty shoes on her pretty lace counterpane.

'Well, Evchen, been workin'? Good girl! Where's the customer?'

'Eugen,' she whispered, 'you back again?'

'Come on, let the customer in,' he replied. 'Don't keep the gentleman waiting. Or perhaps you haven't been workin'?'

'I was just visiting a relative, Eugen. Just for a few minutes.'

'Relative, eh? You've still got relatives? Haven't I drilled into your head that I'm your family and no one else? Come here!'

Terribly afraid, she approached him slowly.

'Hurry up. Or have I got to hurry you?'

She was now standing beside the bed. Terror stricken, she looked into eyes bright with fury and malice.

'Kneel down!'

She did so.

'Ashtray!'

'Oh Eugen, please! Please don't. You'll burn my hand again. I can't stand it. I shall scream.'

'Oh, will you? So you'll scream when I tell you not to, eh? Ashtray!'

Trembling, she held out her hand.

'Eugen, dear dearest Eugen, please don't! I've been saving up money for you, I've opened a savings account, really I have. I've worked so hard. I've saved up four hundred and sixty-eight marks for you. Please, Eugen!'

'Indeed,' he said. 'So you've saved something for your Eugen? That true?'

'Oh, it is true, really. I can prove it.'

'Prove it, then, you fool.'

She jumped up, ran to the wardrobe and looked for the savings book hidden in her linen. Gone! She searched feverishly. Where could she have put it? The other girls – no, they wouldn't do a thing like that . . . Very pale, she turned to look at him.

'Well?'

'It isn't there, Eugen. Did you—'

'What's that?'

'Eugen. Please, Eugen.'

'Come here!'

'Oh, I . . .'

'Come here!'

She went as she had always done. She knelt when he ordered her to, she did what he wanted, she endured all he inflicted.

He watched her get herself ready.

'Put a coat on! No, not a swell one like that. Where's your old brown one? Given it away? What d'you mean givin' away my belongings? All right, you wait! What money have you got? Hand it over! That all? What else you got? A watch? Lor! and a wristwatch too! See what happens when the old man's away! Shove everythin' in your handbag – you won't be coming back here.'

Silently she went downstairs with him. He whistled for a taxi. After some time they stopped in a dark street, where he dismissed the taxi.

They stood there alone. Gripping her by the arm, he brought her face close. 'I'm taking you to my friends. They want some fun now and then too, you understand? You won't mind that, will you – you cold bitch?'

'No.'

'Good! An' they're all out of Brandenburg, like me – pretty smart chaps. Don't you make a fool of me, you halfwit.'

'No, Eugen.'

'That's all, except – keep your trap shut! You're not there to talk. In you go now, you fool!' And he pushed her into a dark hallway so suddenly that she almost fell.

§ XIV

For Heinz the night had become increasingly unreal and dreamlike. There had been the long, cold trip in the car and an Erich at last convinced that this time he had completely miscalculated and had nothing whatever to expect from his father, a conviction which at once changed him from a comparatively polite and interested brother into an inconsiderate and bored stranger. 'Not a very bright idea,' he said with a yawn, 'dragging you out so late, all the way to

Dahlem. How are you going to get back? My chauffeur needs a bit of sleep.'

And then the car had turned into a gravel drive and they stepped from the misty November night, still occasionally disturbed by shots, into a large, brightly lit hall where beech logs burned in a large fireplace.

'You live here?' demanded the astonished Heinz.

'Here I have set up my humble abode,' grinned Erich, all of a sudden a different man again, cheerful and light-hearted. Indeed, he slapped his brother on the back with such goodwill that Heinz almost fell over, and Erich (indulging in a sarcasm quite foreign to his nature, for it was at his own expense), cried out: 'And see how well Father could have invested the millions he hasn't got, with me! He couldn't have got such high interest elsewhere.' Laughing loudly, he flung himself into a chair near the fire. 'Well, Heinz, what about some schnapps? And a liqueur for you, my dear young lady. Oh, nonsense! Once doesn't count, as the girl said, and then got triplets.' He seemed slightly drunk – no doubt with the drunkenness of a man who had never possessed anything and was now exulting in his new sense of ownership.

Almost immediately, however, he was on his feet addressing a man in field-grey uniform, who was pouring out the drinks. 'Listen, Radtke, tell Madame I'm as hungry as a hunter and would like my meal soon. And lay two more places.'

'Yes, Herr Lieutenant, sir.'

(Irma and Bubi exchanged a lightning-quick glance. So here, in this quiet house, he was a lieutenant. But outside all were equal, even if you had to force equality into them!)

'Listen, Radtke. Everything been quiet down here?'

'Haven't seen or heard anything, Herr Lieutenant.'

'See that the chauffeur and the watchman have their food at once, Radtke, and then all three of you can keep watch in turns. And have the weapons in readiness.'

'Yes, Herr Lieutenant.'

Radtke went, and the future ministerial secretary threw himself back into the chair. 'Last night some of the villas round here were looted,' he explained. 'That's what they call rounding-up hoarders, but it's all done by criminals and deserters who haven't failed to notice that the police are a little disorganized at the moment.'

'It wouldn't do at all if it happened here, would it, Erich?' laughed Heinz. 'Seeing that you're responsible for the public security of Berlin.'

'Me? Don't talk rot. Oh, you mean because of my room in the Reichstag? Well, they had to smuggle me in somehow, you know. Otherwise anybody might come in and ask for a room.' He laughed. And – was it because of the schnapps? – his visitors also considered him witty and joined in the laughter.

Erich jumped up again. 'Come along, children. Before we eat I'll show you my little dwelling. It's going to be wonderful. To call it mine is a bit of an exaggeration perhaps – only the bills belong to me at present. But we'll fix that up all right even without Father; up to now we've always fixed up everything.'

With the pride of the possessor he led the way and they had to see everything; nothing was omitted, neither the broom closet nor the lion in green pottery of the Ming period. Only once did his brow cloud and that was when, from a window on the first floor, they saw a big lorry tear past. In it were machine-guns and the vague figures of armed men.

Ought he to phone the police? No, better not burn his fingers. As long as the lightning struck somewhere else . . . 'And now look at this room – simple, modest, austere, masculine (just like me). In short, Roman. Roman, Bubi. Did you do them at school? Or was that one of your failures?'

The lorry did not go much farther, however. Two or three minutes later it slowed down and two men jumped out. With catlike agility they climbed the telephone poles. 'Well, they won't be able to phone now, anyway!'

The wrought-iron gates were burst open by simply driving the lorry against them. The front door, of course, was locked and heavily bolted, but a trifle like that need detain no one.

'That's right, Ed! Hand grenade on the door handle and then out with the pin. That's the way! Won't take a minute. Eugen, sock your wench one. Give the bitch something to scream for. Crash, bang! Yes, it's open. Open and in we go. Now for a good time, chums.

"Merry is the robber's life, faria, faria, fa!" Why, here we have the entire family. Good evening, Herr Baron, Herr Count. Have the honour to conduct a little search by order of the Chancellor of the Reich, Herr Ebert. Or it may be Prince Max still – we're not so particular. Now please don't bother about the telephone, Herr Count. The post office is so slow. The girls on the exchange like their sleep . . .'

'Well, ladies and gentlemen, let's get a little order into things. The ladies are requested to visit the coal cellar together. Don't scream, you old bitch! Think of my nerves! What made you so fat, then, if it wasn't hoarding butter while our children were starving? Ed, go with the ladies and see they find the coal cellar. Max, you go with them, too. Max, you watch Ed; Ed, you watch Max. I don't want either of you in the wine cellar yet. That'll have to wait till the business end is settled. Off you go!'

'Listen, Eugen, that squalling bitch of yours had better be locked up somewhere for the present. Work first and pleasure afterwards! But come back at once – we want to have a few words with this gentleman about his secret safe and so on. We'll get it out of him all right . . .'

'You don't think so, eh, Herr Baron? Oh, you've no idea how smart our Eugen is. You'll be glad if you've got enough money at home to put us in a good humour. Ever felt what it's like having the barrel of a pistol right on your tonsils and another one up your backside? And then they press both the triggers at the same time – and there's a click in your guts and the two bullets say: nice day, ain't it? Well, you'll soon be finding out about it. Our Eugen can think of funnier things than that – he's our vest-pocket variety turn . . .'

'Ah, here you are, Eugen! I was just praising you up to the Count. You'll be pleased to meet each other. Go ahead, my dear Count! Feel free – do whatever you want. It makes no difference to me. I used to be scared witless, too, but now it's your turn!'

'Now listen, you others. Go over the whole house with a toothcomb, don't miss a room and don't hurry. But leave anything that takes up space – we only want the little things, the valuables, gentlemen. Gold I gave for iron! You'll find out whether they did or not. And now, Herr Baron, may I ask you to join our little meeting? Please don't put yourself out – I know the way all right. You wouldn't have thought, would you, that the electrician who came this morning was me? You see, we've met already . . . Eugen, give the gentleman a little support in the back with your revolver. He seems to find walking difficult . . .'

'But who is it, Erich? Where on earth did you dig him up?'

'Allow me, Tinette – this is my brother, Heinz and Fräulein – ahem! Yes, my child, here you see in person one of the results of the blockade.'

'It's not possible! Lord, what expressions! How they keep staring! Well, do come here. What's your name? Heinz? Oh . . . Henri! I understand. Henri, let me see you – so you're so to speak my brother-in-law?' Antoinette Hullin, from the city of Lille, couldn't stop laughing. For Heinz, quite apart from his impossible suit, was standing there looking unbelievably foolish and young. And stared at this girl – at this woman with widely staring eyes. He had never seen a woman like this before; he could not have believed that such existed. He knew only the sallow, exhausted women of wartime; or their daughters, hardly developed and already faded, with poor complexions, wrinkled skins. Here, however, was a face pink and white, smiling lips (such lips!), gleaming teeth (such teeth!), and hair shining as though set with stars . . . To look at her low-cut dress was to become giddy . . . And this was a human being, someone like oneself, not artificial, not a work of art, but living, just like oneself – and laughing . . .

'Erich, how he stares! Haven't you ever seen a pretty woman before? Come closer, Henri, and kiss my hand. That's what they do at home – don't they here? No, not like that, Henri. *Fi donc*, you mustn't drag the lady's hand up to your mouth. No, bend down. Lower! Yes, bend your neck, no harm in that. A man's even allowed to kneel before a beautiful woman, isn't that so, Erich?'

'And this is a friend of Heinz. Fräulein . . . er . . .'

'Quaas is my name.'

'Kaas! But that's an impossible name! Oh, Erich, now I understand why you insisted on me coming to Berlin with you – if that's what they call a girlfriend here. Yes, we're coming, Radtke. No, Erich, tonight Henri must sit by me and I'll feed him. The poor boy!

He has certainly never eaten his fill in his life. What would you like, Henri? Some soup? Oh, don't have soup; it only fills you up . . . wait till the meat comes.'

'It's really charming, Tinette, the way you're looking after Heinz. You're positively spoiling him.'

'But I never saw such a lad – he's impossible. Oh, Henri, you haven't even got cuffs on. Henri, a gentleman always wears cuffs. And your fingernails!'

Heinz turned crimson. 'I'm not a gentleman. I'm only a schoolboy. And I've got no cuffs – my father's only a cab driver.' He had to say it. It was letting Erich down, but just because of Erich he had to.

'What is your father, Henri? Say it again! Cab driver? But your father is also Erich's father, isn't he?'

'Of course.'

'Oh, Erich, Erich!' She burst out laughing. 'What a boaster you are, Erich. I always knew you were. But I didn't know you were quite such a boaster.'

'Allow me, Tinette . . .'

'Erich, don't interrupt! He told me his father had a stable, a racing stable I thought, and an immense fortune . . . I kept on wondering why we didn't visit this legendary father. Oh dear, I grew so uneasy. You're not good enough, Tinette, I told myself; you were a dancer once in a cheap cabaret. You're not fine enough for the – cab driver.' Another peal of melodious laughter.

'Tinette, Tinette! Please stop that idiotic laughing. Let me tell you, Tinette—'

'He wants to go on bragging again. Oh! Cab driver!'

'Tinette, do listen! Heinz will confirm I only learned half an hour ago that my father was absolutely broke. Go on, Heinz.'

'That's true. Erich thought—'

'And the stable? The racing stable? Oh, Erich!'

'Pardon me, Tinette, it was you who imagined the racing stable. All I said was a stable. And when I left for the war Father had thirty horses. Isn't that so, Heinz?'

'That's right.'

'Thirty horses! Thirty carriage horses! But Henri is sweet. Henri says at once: "My father's a cab driver." As if one loved a man because

of his father! Erich, you silly, stop pulling faces. I have to laugh –
who's going to pay your bills now?'

She glanced round the dining room, brilliant with crystal and silver, looked at her guests and, her eyes sparkling, threw her arms, her
beautiful bare arms, round Erich's neck. 'My poor Erich – my poor,
ambitious boy! Does it worry you so much that your father is so
poor? You'll see, I'll turn away your creditors, they shan't bother you
a bit. I'll so enchant them with my smile that you won't hear the
word bill mentioned.' With her head against Erich's, bewitchingly
roguish, she looked across at Heinz – no, Henri . . .

'And you shall become something big, my Erich. Yes, you shall
indeed, something absolutely great. When you go past, people will
take off their hats and soldiers will present arms: "Here comes
Erich." We'll see that you become something terrific, a minister or
higher than that even – we won't let anyone notice that you're only
a silly boy.'

She soothed and lulled him, all the while looking at Heinz with
that distracting light in her eyes, as though the younger brother were
some tradesman to be tricked out of his money so that the elder
brother should live in peace.

Irma, to be sure, contemptuously scraped her fork on her plate,
considering such women ghastly, but she was quite alone in this
opinion. So much alone, in fact, that no one else was even thinking
about Irma.

The man – Ed, Max or George, what did it matter? – clumsily rose to
his feet, saying: 'Well, then, I'll send in the next one,' reeled towards
the door, knocked against a chair and fell down. 'Now then, now
then, who's barging about here?' he muttered. 'D'you chaps always
barge into people?' And fell asleep, dead drunk.

Eva lay motionless, listening to the riot in the house, the cursing
and the drunken cries. During a momentary lull she heard the
women weeping and wailing in the cellar where they had been
imprisoned; the drunken man snored loudly and a floorboard
creaked. Mechanically she pulled her skirt over her knees . . . She lay
there like that for a long time, hardly thinking of anything, just feeling, feeling that it was finally time to go.

Getting up slowly, she looked round and noticed her coat and hat, which she put on. To go out of the door she had to step over the drunk – this she did without hesitating; then she turned and looked at him and something like intelligence appeared on her ravaged, swollen face. Bending down, she deftly searched his pockets – she knew how to do that all right – she had been through the pockets of drunken men before now. The first thing she found was a heavy gold watch, but this she let slide back again. Her caution was stronger than her greed for money. But she kept the revolver from the other pocket. She did not know how to use it or whether indeed the thing was loaded, but she took it nonetheless, she who had left behind the gold watch. Desire for revenge was stronger in her than greed.

On the landing she leaned over to look down into the hall. All the lights were on, but only one man was there and he sat on the carpet beside a low table bearing a box of cigars and some bottles. No, it wasn't Eugen.

The pistol still in her hand, she went down the wide stairway, and although the carpets were thick the stairs creaked a little; the man below turned his head and with a drunken, trembling hand picked up the weapon at his side. Then he recognized her . . .

'Oh, so it's you . . . I thought . . . We'll be skipping later, the boys are just having a shuteye. Bit too much for us, jug yesterday and a binge today. But we'll slip off in a moment.' He looked at her again. 'What d'you want with that rod, eh? Put it down; nobody'll hurt a pretty girl like you. Come to me, for a change.'

But she went on, across the small vestibule and through the shattered door, into the open. In front stood the abandoned lorry, its lights out; the barrel of one machine-gun was seemingly aimed at her.

'Anyone there?' she called out.

But nobody answered. No one. There had been a lot of noise, they had burst open a door with a hand grenade, the women in the cellar were crying for help – but nobody came. Bad times! There had been war and people had grown so selfish that they could only think of how they might fill their own bellies and scrape through. Now that revolution had broken out they talked peace and sat at home, glad when disaster avoided their door and knocked at another's. There was no courage to spare for a neighbour. Each for himself.

She could go out into the night and escape; there was nobody to prevent her. But she had done this too often – fleeing to her sister-in-law, to the canal – and always returning in the end to him . . .

So she went back into the house.

By now the man in the hall was asleep. Treading softly, she went into room after room, observing the havoc that had been wrought, the curtains torn down, the drunken men who, after befouling everything, were now snoring like beasts. Yes, men were beasts, all of them – beasts.

She went up to the first floor – in vain. She climbed into the attic – no one there.

Descending again, she walked quicker, with beating heart. She must find him. Arriving at the cellars, she could hear the cries of the women, and she stopped. She now heard a voice, an evil mocking voice, his voice.

She trembled. She had known quite well, known for a certainty, that he would be the only one of them not to get drunk. No, he would remain sober – he never drank. He was so wicked that he did not even need to forget himself and his sins for a while.

Slowly, cautiously, silently, she crept towards the half-open door and peeped into the room, a laundry room or some such place . . .

Oh, she knew her Eugen! He didn't drink, but he had taken one of the women from the coal cellar, a girl, almost a child . . . She lay as if lifeless in his arms, white and with her eyes shut, while his evilly false voice never ceased. 'See, my sweet, I'm not doing you any harm – I'm your Eugen, your darling Eugen . . . say "Eugen" . . . jus' say "Eugen" once an' I swear I'll let you go. Come on, say it!'

'Eugen.'

'There, see how well you learned that. An' you'll say it a hundred times yet. Now tell me something more, my sweet, tell your Eugen, whisper it – have you already . . . come on, tell me.' And with his sudden transition into rage: 'But don't lie! Don't dare lie to me – I'd know at once.'

To the girl at the door, Eva Hackendahl, it was as if she herself lay in those arms hearing again for the first time that evil and so persuasive voice, the voice at the beginning of her dark road . . . And a nameless fear gripped her – for herself, for the other girl, for life, for her own life, the meaning of all life, she knew not what. 'Eugen!' she screamed.

The man started and jumped to his feet at once, letting the girl fall. He sprang at Eva – and she fired. Fired straight into the dark and sinister face looming before her. A stream of fire, a deafening crash . . .

She had dropped the revolver, she was running away – no glance back – running upstairs, through the hall, out of the house – stumbling against the lorry, falling over. But she got up at once and ran, ran farther and farther into the night.

And now she knew what she had done and that she would never again hear that false voice or look into those bright, evil eyes. All was over.

'I'm clearing! You tagging on or not, Heinz?' asked Irma. She spoke slangily on purpose. She was angry and irritable and in no mood to play the fine lady like the pink doll opposite.

But no one took any notice. Heinz had suddenly turned quarrelsome, perhaps a result of the drinks. 'And you call yourself a Socialist!' he said to his brother mockingly. 'Surrounded by soft armchairs and fat cigars.'

'And fat women,' murmured Irma, but no one took any notice.

'But if I ask you what you actually want to do for the workers, you've got no answer.'

'My dear young thing,' drawled Erich in an infinitely superior voice, 'I might inform you that my personal relations concern you not one whit. But even the brain of a schoolboy has enough logic to understand that I can do something for the workers, even if I'm not starving to death myself. Yes,' he said, enthused by his own words, because he had also drunk heavily.

'Bubi, come along!' implored Irma. 'We have to go home.'

'Yes, I can do something for the others much better if I first do something for myself. I must first create an effective home for myself, and such surroundings as these' – and he looked pleasantly about him – 'are exactly what I need.'

'According to your theory, then, millionaires make the best Socialists.'

'Oh, Henri, Henri, you're heavenly,' laughed Tinette, flinging herself on the sofa. 'Pure Parsifal – from the fairy tale.'

'There's something in what you say,' admitted Erich with a grin. 'Maybe a certain freedom from care is needed to act in a really social manner. If you've got to keep on thinking how to fill your own belly you can't think about others, that's as clear as soup.'

'Allow me . . .'

'Heinz, I'm going now.'

'No, you allow me,' broke in Erich. 'Naturally I presuppose that the prosperous man really does know how the poor feel, that he himself has been poor, that is.'

'And you think you know that?'

'Please don't forget, Bubi, that my father's a simple cabby.'

'Oh, you've got wise to that, have you? You see its use now, eh? What a swine you are, Erich! I can see you running around telling the workers your father is a cabman. Hadn't I better give you Father's address so the workers can convince themselves you're not lying? Otherwise you hardly need his address. I now already know that you won't be seeing Father in the next hundred years, unless, that is, you still need his War Loans.'

'The two angry brothers, Henri and Erich! Now it's your turn, Erich.'

'Bubi, please! Dear Heinz.'

'You're showing off a good deal, my boy, but I don't mind. Yes, my son. I admit it – I'm an out-and-out egoist. I learned my lesson in the war, in the trenches.'

'Three days.'

'Three weeks. Longer at any rate than you. And I say that a man who doesn't think of himself is a fool, and deserves nothing better than a bullet through his head.'

'You make me sick.'

'You'll change in time, my boy, and start thinking of yourself. I was an idealist myself once.'

'When you took the money from Father's desk, I suppose?'

'Get out, will you? Get out of my house!'

Crimson with fury, they faced each other.

Irma pulled Bubi's sleeve. 'Please, Heinz, do come now.'

But Tinette sprang from her couch, ran to the brothers and, standing between them, put an arm round each unwilling neck. Both made some attempt to release themselves, but with no great vigour.

'You silly boys! You're not out of the Bible – your names aren't Cain and Abel, are they? Make it up on the spot! I never heard such nonsense; no one quarrels about things like that. Men quarrel over a woman, and then they can even kill one another – but Henri doesn't want to take your Tinette from you, Erich. He's got a girlfriend of his own . . . Where is she, by the way? She's run off at the wrong moment, just when you ought to kiss her, Henri. That's just all ideas, rubbish! Erich, you're nothing but a gigantic egoist, and Henri, you are a sinister idealist. What more is there? Nothing.' And she looked, laughingly, at them both.

I must go, thought Heinz. Irma's sure to be waiting outside. I can't behave like this. But here was Tinette's arm round his neck and even though everything she said was insincere – or could it be genuine? – her arm was round his neck!

'And now we'll drink a loving cup together and all go to bed. You'll sleep in the spare room, of course, Henri, and tomorrow morning we'll all have breakfast together. I'll get up terribly early because of you, Henri. Your little friend's very silly to have run away, but don't you worry, I'll make a woman out of her yet. Do bring her as often as you like, and you yourself must come even more often. We'll always be pleased, won't we, Erich? And we'll see that he becomes a wonderful idealist and you become the great egoist, Erich.'

'If you'd only give us our drinks!' growled Erich. 'I'm already such an egoist that even in your arms I have to think of that.'

§ XV

The man, the old man, the iron man had woken in the night.

Was it the grey that had woken him?

He sat up in bed, listening to the sounds of the house – the inhabitants of this crowded human hive slept through many different sounds. He didn't want to hear these sounds. He'd just been sleeping himself. Now he wanted to avoid the sleep of others . . . Hadn't the grey woken him?

Hadn't it been the halter rattling? Hadn't a hoof been pawing the stable floor, to attract the master's attention? Hackendahl listened. Directly beneath him stood the grey in what had formerly been a joiner's workshop, five stone steps above the small courtyard; the bench was there still, leaning on end against the wall, and whenever the grey flicked away the flies her tail would brush over it. But there were no flies in November, surely.

For a moment, Iron Gustav considered what had been agreed about his taking over the carpentry bench. Did it belong to him now, or the inheritors of Strunk, the dead master cabinetmaker? The court-yard children of this house in Wexstrasse, number so-and-so, these starving, snivelling little children used to sing a rude song about him.

But Hackendahl didn't want to think about cabinetmaker Strunk. He wanted to think about his grey. The one which had woken him up. Already four weeks before they moved in, Strunk had hanged himself in this very flat, using the gas pipe on the little landing. He'd bent it over with a bootjack – you could see it was the same one. The same gas lamp, the same flat, the same workshop, the same tene-ment block, the same boss, the same going-bust, the same drinking, the same gas pipe . . .

Yes, I spend too much time on the drink. When I still had money, I didn't go often, but now . . . !

Oh, it's horrible how thoughts run into each other. The night's there for sleeping, like mother does, not for thinking. If only the wretched grey hadn't woken me. But now: one, two, three – and now you've got me!

The whole disaster began with the grey, with that race. Everything went wrong from that moment. And this wretched animal that lost him his best clients, was still there, rattling its chain, stamping its hoof, as if asking for something – but there was nothing it could ask for!

Who indeed could?

Otto? . . . Otto was dead. He left a widow with two children. He got his way, despite his father. No demands could come from him – rather the opposite!

Hadn't the grey always got her feed, more of it and better, too, than she deserved? Then shut up! Give me a bit of peace, you damned brute.

And Eva? She'd been a good girl once, a pretty girl. But she couldn't keep away from the men. Hadn't he warned her? Didn't I sit in her den myself and try and persuade her, without being nasty to the men? Away with you, girl! You can't be any man's daughter if you're every father's favourite. It's not my fault! Off with you!

Erich? Erich was a smart lieutenant in corduroy velvet breeches that cost a hundred and fifty marks, but he hadn't time to write to his parents. Well, nothing to be done there. Full stop.

And Sophie – Staff Sister and very busy. 'In the field hospital we have a wounded man without parents or relations. You would be doing a real service if you sent this lonely soldier a parcel, together with a few kind words . . .'

Oh, you cold bitch! It's never dawned on you that there are lonely parents without any kind words from their children. Well, Mother's sure to have sent that parcel and the kind words as well – and that's all you wanted, isn't it? Go in peace! Notice to quit follows.

And Heinz – Bubi? Old Hackendahl had given up pretending that it was the grey that had awakened him. Oh no! The poor beast was only too glad to get some rest. No, he had woken because it was three in the morning and his dear son hadn't yet come home. He had to admit that he'd recently thought more highly of Bubi. Bubi wasn't clever like Erich, but wasn't a failure like Otto. If someone talks about maths in the afternoon and is to be back at six – that is, lies, and lies to his own father – then a son like that isn't a son at all. No, that put a finish to him too. Decency is decency, lies are lies – and iron is iron too.

Old Hackendahl sat for a bit longer in the dark. He thought neither of the grey, nor of Strunk. He made sure that all was right as rain. Yes, it all came out in the wash. They'd all got what they wanted – and this was the end! Today they put rubbish through his letter box – the *Rote Fahne* instead of the *Berlin Lokal-Anzeiger*. If you take the *Lokal-Anzeiger*, you don't want to see the *Rote Fahne*. You don't want chalk instead of cheese. For a while you let yourself be cheated – not that you didn't know about it – but once you made up your mind it must stop, it stopped. A man was a man – there was no need to be a father as well.

Suddenly he turned on the light and Frau Hackendahl started up. 'What is it, Father?'

'I'll tell you, Mother. I was thinkin' about the grey . . .'

'Is Heinz home? I didn't hear him come in.'

'No, he isn't. Tomorrow I'll take the grey to the butcher's. With horse meat the price it is I ought to get something for her, she looks a sight in front of the cab, and I don't want to see any more of her, what with one thing and another.'

'And when you sell her you can ask them to give you five pounds from the best part of the leg; they can manage that quite easily. A bit of meat for a change would do you and Heinz both good.'

'You needn't tell me what would do Heinz good. Not that I care much now, anyway. I'll see about buying a bay or a chestnut – no more grey horses – I've been sick of 'em for a long time.'

'That's a good idea, Father. Driving will be a pleasure again.'

'A pleasure? Well, p'r'aps. One's not jus' simply a father, one's human also.'

'What d'you mean by that, Father?'

'Oh, never mind, we'll talk about it later . . . And then I've thought of something else, Mother. I'll go to Bayer, you know, the perfume shop chap who took the first mortgage on this house, an' I'll say to him: take the whole blasted lot as it stands. I don't want nothin' and you don't want nothin'. Then that'll be done with.'

'I don't know, Father. That leaves us with nothing at all.'

'And what do we get out of the house now? Only worry about gettin' in the rents and payin' the interest. No, I want to live without worry for a time.'

'Well, you do as you think best, Father. I never interfere with your money matters, you know that . . . And we still have our War Loans.'

'No, Mother, that's jus' what I want to say to Bayer as well – he c'n have what's left of the War Loans after I've bought my horse, in return for letting us both – the horse as well, that's understood – live here rent-free for life . . . then I'll be rid of that worry, too.'

'But we shan't have anything left except the little you earn with the cab.'

'Yes, we won't have anything left, an' that's what I want.'

Very perturbed, the old woman sat up in bed, glanced at her husband and said: 'Well, you must do as you like, Father. But you realize that Heinz hasn't yet taken his examination and there's a long time to go after that. It can't be done on the few coppers the cab brings in. And Erich will be coming home soon, without a job, and we can't say what will happen about Sophie either.'

'No, we can't, Mother, you're right there. We can't say what's happening to our children.'

There was a long silence, on her part anxious, on his almost defiant. Then he began to speak again. 'Mother, have you seen that rubbish newspaper they've stuck through the door?'

'Is that why you're so angry, Father?'

'I'm not angry, Mother. Have you read that our Kaiser, who we swore allegiance to, has scarpered to Holland? Just imagine, his soldiers fought four years for him and his people starved for as long, and now – when things go wrong – off he goes! Wilhelm the Runaway that's what they call him. Pullman Wilhelm!'

'So, Father? So? Do you want to leave everything – your children, your money – like Wilhelm?'

'No, Mother. Quieten down! I'm not going to do a bunk yet!' His big hand reached over into the other bed and comfortingly held hers. 'I'm an iron man, you know that. I'll stay with my cab. But, Mother, I don't want to hurt you, but I think it's our children who've done a bunk from us. To think of parents only when you want somethin' – no, that's not good enough. I'm tired of it.'

'But, Father, it's always been like that. When the young birds are fledged they leave the nest and don't worry about their parents. You can't expect anything different, can you, Father?'

'You can't compare human beings with animals, you know that. I was taught that a child should love, respect an' admire its parents. I dunno, Mother, I s'pose it's my fault, but not one of my children loves me.'

'Don't say that, Father. Heinz . . .'

'There you are, Mother! Only one of your five occurs to you and

he won't grow up any different . . . No, it's nothing to do with parents or children, and not the soldiers either. They did their duty – and
their chief of staff just scarpered. It's the times we're living in. And
if it is that, there's nothing we can do about it. We've just got to look
after ourselves, that's all. I'd like to have a bit of fun again, have a
proper horse in front an' go through the Tiergarten now and again
with a good fare and see the crocuses comin' up, yeller 'n' blue 'n'
white. And not keep on having to think: today you've got to give
Erich a talking-to. And Heinz ain't come home at the right time
either.'

'Oh, is it because Heinz isn't home?'

'How can it be, Mother? I've explained it all once. First it's one
thing, then another, an' now it's too much. No good crying over spilt
milk. Tell me, where d'you keep the odds and ends?'

'The odds and ends? What d'you mean, Father?'

'Why, the children's, of course.'

'The children's? Oh, they're in the linen press, at the bottom. But,
Father . . .'

She fell silent and, with anxiety in her eyes, watched the old man
get out of bed and go to the press, which he started to empty of
everything that had accumulated from the children – their school
reports, copybooks, textbooks; a cap of Erich's; the earliest baby
shoes belonging to the first child, Sophie; a half-used paintbox, some
photographs of classes at school. Not until her husband opened the
stove door and began to cram in all the paper and other things
did she speak and say softly: 'Oh, Father.'

He looked at her from under his bushy brows with his big
round eyes and said, 'Don't you fret, Mother – that's how things are.'
And he set fire to the heap of paper, made sure that it had caught and
then closed the stove.

Getting back into bed, he took her hand. 'I'd like you,' he said, 'to
call me Gustav again. As names go, it's a decent sort of name and in
future I want to live as Gustav. I've made a proper mess of being
Father.'

'Oh, Father.'

'Gustav!'

'I meant Gustav . . .'

'And I don't mind telling you, what with going to the pub and my risky life – driving or not driving, just as it takes me, Mother that must stop. For a start, because we can't afford it, because we're now poor folk again. And anyway, it's no fun any more either. No, we two oldies on our own, we want to live a bit of the sweet life, like we did when we started out. Even better, because now we know there'll be no more children to walk all over us.'

'Oh, Father, why did you take it so badly that Heinz didn't come home tonight?'

'For a start, I'm not "Father" but Gustav. But I'll have to tell you that a thousand times during the coming weeks. And I'll do it. I'm like iron in such things. And what do you mean by "taking it so badly"? If the grey doesn't pull any more, then off she goes to the knacker man, and when a child no longer wants to be a child, he'll have to stay away. I'm like iron about that too.'

'Oh, Father . . .'

'It's Gustav now.'

FIVE

Tinette

§ I

At any other time Heinz would have been astonished at his father's saying nothing whatever about his absence all night or his irregular mode of life, but stranger and more important happenings than this were nowadays ignored by Heinz Hackendahl, living in an enchanted world of his own. There was still fighting going on in Berlin (although the Independent Socialists and the governing Social Democrats had united and even formed a government with ministers and state secretaries), and looting in the city and the suburbs; iron shutters outside the shops offered little protection against the latest method of house-breaking with hand grenades.

Heinz saw it all on his various routes into town. And he heard and read about the dispute with regard to the calling of a National Assembly – the Workers' Councils were mostly against it while the Soldiers' Councils on the whole were in favour. And suddenly all the old parties were there – the Democrats, the National Liberals, the Centre and the Conservatives – telling all their supporters to back the new government, which then lifted the state of siege, ended press censorship, amnestied all political crimes, promised freedom of religion and opinion and introduced the eight-hour day. It went on to commit itself to fighting the housing shortage and even to support the unemployed, and promised the protection of property and person, and guaranteed sufficient food for the people.

Murder, theft and want were widespread and the food queues lengthened day by day – Heinz could not be unaware of all this but he was bewitched and the things that would have interested him passionately a week ago were hardly noticed now. So that when his father asked: 'When are you takin' your exam?' he barely looked up.

'I don't know, Father – probably at Easter.' The truth was that he had quite simply stopped going to school.

'Then do something about it – find out. I'm prepared to support you till Easter – after that, no.'

A little more attentive now, Heinz looked at his father. 'Then it's all off with the university?'.

The old man flushed. When he spoke it was not at all domineeringly. 'I bought the black horse with the last of my money. You seen him?' Heinz nodded.

'Fine little pony,' said the old man with more warmth, 'cheers me up. An' with what I still had left I've rid your mother and me of rent for the rest of our lives an' got rid of the house too – all gone!'

'The War Loans, too?'

The old man nodded, watching his son expectantly. Heinz however had smiled, thinking of his brother. But why mention Erich? Father had his own worries and so had Erich; he, Heinz, earlier called Bubi, had the greatest worry of them all. But that was a man's private affair. 'I'll speak with Professor Degener,' he said. 'Perhaps I can take the exam earlier. Then you'll be rid of me sooner.' Took his hat and left.

His father watched him go. Then he said to his wife in the kitchen: 'I was right after all, Mother. Heinz won't be any diff'rent from the rest. But I'm glad about the black horse. Black's a lot better than grey . . . grey's always getting dirty, but black's black.'

§ II

Heinz Hackendahl stood in the street, undecided, his hands in the pocket of his very shabby greatcoat. He could go to the station, or he could go to his friend Irma. He could also do what he told his father he would, and ask Professor Degener about his chance of graduating.

Heinz would have liked to go to the station, but not to his friend Irma, whom he hadn't seen since that fateful evening. However, going to the station would have been unpleasant, and the path to his faithful friend pleasant. But a cunning fox always finds a way out, so Heinz did neither and went to Professor Degener.

The professor was sitting at his desk. Giving Heinz a thin, blue-veined hand, he looked at him with his bright blue eyes and asked whether he would like a cigarette. 'We all have tea together later.'

Heinz declined the cigarette and, without wondering what was meant by 'all', hurriedly mumbled something about illness, absence from school and his examination.

Professor Degener made a vague gesture. 'We're all ill nowadays. We all attend school irregularly. You know quite well what you need for the examination. The written part will be in February. I'd advise you to show up in class now and again – if only on account of my colleagues, you know.' These remarks were shot forth somewhat contemptuously, as if such matters had no importance, as indeed they had not for Heinz. Splendid! That was settled, then. And, the invitation to tea forgotten, he rose and thanked the professor who, with some hesitation, held out his hand, saying: 'Oh, what I wanted to ask you was – have you seen any of your schoolfellows recently?'

'No.'

'If you'd care to wait a moment you'll be seeing quite a number of them. We have a kind of tea session here every day.'

Heinz, however, really had no time to spare . . . He didn't know which way to turn. 'Of course! By the way, have you heard about what's going on in Cologne – the Workers' and Soldiers' Councils?'

An incredible situation had occurred in Cologne. The town had been completely overwhelmed within three days, flooded with lawless soldiers fleeing in waves from the western part of the Rhine region. All were bristling with weapons, and lacking food and drink. A minority took the ascendant and wanted rapine and plunder. Then this Workers' and Soldiers' Council sprang up, formed human chains, disarmed people, gave them food and drink, helped them.

'All free and gratis, if you will, Hackendahl. Because when everything's finished . . .'

Heinz Hackendahl was silent. He'd forgotten he was in a hurry. But he was anyway not all there. He was like a traveller waiting between two trains. He had time, but no time to do anything with it. In his thoughts he was already travelling elsewhere.

The professor looked at him and said, raising his voice: 'If blood is infected, the healthy corpuscles attack the invaders. A battle follows. If the invaders are stronger, the person dies. But if the healthy corpuscles prevail, the person is restored to health.'

He reflected and thought: 'I could imagine that such a battle was now taking place in Germany. It all depends on each of the healthy corpuscles . . .'

The teacher fell silent. Then, after a while, Heinz Hackendahl began to talk about the officer in the corridor of the Reichstag – that man who gave orders in the middle of chaos, untouched by the chaos.

Professor Degener nodded. 'You see, he's an example of one. No, I don't know his name. Someone unknown. You can imagine how the machinations of the profiteers disgust him. But that's why he's for order. He may not be able to do more than guarantee that his people get regular meals – but that doesn't discourage him. He knows that order and cleanliness are good, and disorder and shady dealing bad. He's not put off, if others go to the bad . . .'

'But what's going to happen to it all?' asked Heinz.

'We don't know yet. Only no defeat. Your Reichstag officer and the people in Cologne – they're fighting for something they don't even know. It's sometimes good for people, Hackendahl, when they can only look a short way ahead . . . Perhaps that officer would despair if he knew how much longer the road is till somewhere is reached. Instead, he looks to the short term, and takes care to see that they have enough to eat and that their footwear is in order. He has nothing to do with disorder.'

Heinz Hackendahl went a little red. Everything Professor Degener had said could be directly applied to himself . . . It was undeniable that great disorder had come into his own life . . . and the extent of that disorder was measureless . . . But it was out of the question that the professor could have any idea of such a thing.

Professor Degener seemed not to notice his pupil's confusion. He chuckled and said, 'Your classmates will be coming along presently, Hackendahl – some who have gathered round me. We, too, aren't going very regularly to school. I sometimes feel really nervous on entering the classroom. I feel my colleagues look with disfavour on me – that I deserve punishment and should be in detention . . .' The professor chuckled, and Heinz Hackendahl felt the same ardent love for this man, who had remained as young as the youngest of his pupils, as had overcome him before.

'But I have to admit that it's not because we dislike order. However, I'm no more than adviser to your comrades,' exclaimed the professor; 'I'm not actually suited to the affairs we have in hand.' His smile was at once melancholy and somewhat sly. 'We're collecting arms, my dear Hackendahl,' he went on. 'Imagine – instead of harassing my boys with the second aorist I keep them on the run looking for arms. The task's not excessively difficult but it's far from unimportant. Some of the troops coming back home simply lean their guns – do you call them guns, by the way? – against the nearest wall or give them to anyone who asks for them. They've had enough of guns. Then there are the goods depots with wagons filled with machine-guns, trench mortars and field guns – the men are in a hurry to get home, one can understand that – and so the wagons are left there for anybody to open, whether he's for or against order.'

Heinz nodded. It was strange how you couldn't help coming under this man's influence, let him lecture on the garments worn by the women of Ancient Greece or on guns . . .

'That is,' said the professor, suddenly quite cheerful, 'our ambition doesn't reach as far as field guns and trench mortars; up till now our biggest achievement has been a few heavy machine-guns. I often try to find out from your comrades how heavy they are – I don't want them to injure themselves – but they won't divulge it. I suppose you've no idea, Hackendahl, of the approximate weight? I'm really worried at times.'

But Hackendahl had, alas, no idea. Moreover he was convinced that the professor wasn't worried in the slightest but was merely laughing at him – perhaps because this pupil had no share in these things.

'It's not altogether without danger, you know, Hackendahl. People have such strange prejudices . . . If a man in any sort of uniform whatever goes about with a gun, that's all right. But a pupil, a schoolboy, a youngster, let alone the parents!' The professor sighed audibly, then pulled himself together. 'But that's immaterial. The main thing is for the boys to get the better of our chaos and this they are now doing by collecting arms as frequently and as cheaply as possible.'

'And why do you collect arms, Herr Professor?'

The teacher's eyes flashed, but he spoke quite calmly. 'You've rather lost touch with us, haven't you, Hackendahl? Perhaps very different matters occupy you.'

Heinz flushed, confused and indignant.

'But there is no shame in being in chaos. There is only shame in remaining so, in disorder.'

What a terrible teacher stood before him! Heinz Hackendahl was shocked and wanted to leave. But he wanted to defend himself and stayed.

'It's odd,' went on the professor, 'but until now not one boy asked me that question. Perhaps they've told themselves that the fewer weapons there are in unknown hands the less the danger for the community. Or maybe they haven't thought about it at all . . .'

'But you, Herr Professor . . .'

'Yes, my son, I also see only the famous short term. I tell myself that all the troops now returning are still not the front line. The Front is still out there, Hackendahl. Don't forget that – the Front that's stood for four years against the whole world, the unknown Front, which we in the rear only get to see in individual parts. Now it's coming back to us in closed ranks, and we know nothing about it. Perhaps it needs weapons?'

'What for? The war's over isn't it?'

He felt he was speaking with his brother's voice. He didn't want to say what he had, but said it all the same.

'We've now got an armistice. An armistice still isn't peace.'

'We'll never fight again,' cried Heinz. 'The war must end! We must finally have peace.'

'An imposed peace? A peace for slaves?'

'But we just can't go on!'

'What do you know of what we can do?' The professor's blue eyes were flashing like a true Prussian. He was angry. 'Have you ever in your life gone to the limits of what you can do? And you want to speak about, speak *for*, us?'

Heinz thought of that villa in Zehlendorf, and his brother with his clever but unscrupulous talk. Luxury. Wine in crystal glasses, and the beautiful, unbelievably beautiful woman with glittering hair,

every schoolboy's earthly dream, and every man's . . . And she put
her cool white arms around his brother's shoulders, and talked of
idealists and egoists. And already all this meant nothing. Because all
of us want to hold the earth's dream in our arms, dream it, possess
it – 'Stay a while, you are so beautiful'! And we might want to run
around on cold November nights dragging heavy weapons about.
But that house is shining bright, with warmth and style. No, that's
not it! Not that!

It's the sweetness of a voice, the as yet unknown lightness of
being, magic and seduction . . .

What had the professor given him for homework? It is not a
shame to get into chaos, it is only a shame to stay in it.

The bell rang outside.

'Your comrades,' said the professor quite peaceably. 'Your comrades. You stay here, Hackendahl, where you belong.'

§ III

They entered, some in a hurry, some leisurely, others pale and a few
glowing with the cold, but all excited and happy.

'Hello, Hackendahl.'

'Evening, Professor.'

'Would you believe it? Heinz has found his way here!'

'Behold, Timotheus!'

'That's fine!'

Heinz shook his hands. He felt as if he were in a dream. The
familiar faces – not seen for a week, ten days, a fortnight – had
become strange, or was it he who had become strange? Some of the
lads hurried into the kitchen to make the tea – Professor Degener, of
course, was a bachelor – others reported that they were on the scent
of such-and-such weapons, and had collected this and that.

'What about hand grenades, Herr Professor? D'you understand
anything about 'em? How do you know if they're ready for use?'

'Ready for use, you oaf! I'll tell you all right!'

'Herr Professor, in the Artilleriestrasse you can buy revolvers . . .'

'So you can at the Schlesische Station.'

'Everywhere, you ass!'

'Let me finish – five to fifteen marks each, Brownings, Mausers, army revolvers, Verey-light pistols . . . I find pistols especially dangerous because anyone can hide them in their pocket. Other weapons can be seen.'

The professor sighed. 'How much do you want, you young rascals? It's costing me my entire fortune.'

'Perhaps five hundred marks to start with.'

'Five hundred marks! The bank clerks already look at me as if I were bankrupt. But all right, Hoffmann, drop in tomorrow morning at eleven.'

'Herr Professor, I've made the acquaintance of a roof sniper. He wants to retire – it's got a little too hot for him. A light machine-gun, fifty to a hundred marks. What about it?'

'Certainly, Bertuleit. Roof sniper – the devil! Tomorrow morning at eleven.'

It was a strange world, an enchanted world, a world gone mad. Heinz Hackendahl listened with astonishment and a certain indignation at being excluded from these activities. Moreover, he had the feeling that Degener was watching him unobtrusively and his wrath increased. What was the sense of it all? A mere game. Why didn't they worry about food for the starving instead? And he thought of the weary queues of women outside the food shops, of women who had struggled for the lives of their children four years and more – and now, when peace was at hand, these people were thinking about machine-guns.

Peace for slaves? There was an old saying – 'rather slavery than death'! Oh, no, no, oh, God! Erich must have reversed this – 'rather dead than slavery'. He didn't want a slave peace . . . But what are we supposed to do? Collect weapons? But we've no longer the hands who want even to hold such weapons. We can fight no longer! Mad, obsessive thoughts! Madness, disorder – rather do nothing than do something wrong. Rather do something wrong than do nothing at all?

And now a shrill voice was heard, naturally the voice of dear Porzig, who had just entered the room. 'Herr Professor, I would like to point out that a room exists in the Reichstag with the following

nameplate: Erich Hackendahl. I happen to have been in the Reichstag today and had a look at what's going on there. He's got a brand
new cardboard nameplate!'

For a moment there was a deathly silence. Everyone looked at
Heinz Hackendahl. He moved and tried to laugh scornfully, but he
angrily felt that he'd gone blood-red. However, his blushes faded in
extreme bitterness. Hatred rose up in him. As fast as lightning, it
occurred forcibly to him: yes, that's what they were like – these idealists! He who is not with me is against me. They suspect anyone who
doesn't collect weapons like they do. And just because Erich's got a
room there, they suspect him. Erich can really achieve something
there, something useful, something decent. That's what he's called.
Is he not in Security? Oh, that's all nonsense! I know he's not doing
anything decent at all. He's cold-heartedly ambitious, a pleasure
seeker . . . But what's it got to do with me? Why does he suspect me?
If Porzig shouts like that, doesn't it mean that I'm also suspect?

Then the professor spoke into the silence. 'I don't understand
what you want, Porzig? Our schoolfriend's name is Heinz Hackendahl, not Erich!'

Immediately all the faces, which had looked so strangely at Heinz,
changed. They were friendly. Conversation continued, Hoffmann
slapped Heinz on the shoulder and said, 'What an idiot Porzig is!'

Kunze muttered merrily, 'Am I my brother's keeper?'

Finally Porzig appeared, drew himself up self-importantly next
to Heinz, and explained long-windedly, though rather embarrassed,
in the following words: 'Don't misunderstand me, Hackendahl,
will you? You must understand that we're all playing dangerously
with fire here and must be terribly careful. Is that clear? These
people here are not all lawyers, but my old dad's a regional councillor, and I know my Criminal Code! Of course, Professor Degener
is a mere child . . . Well, you understand all right! All in order,
Hackendahl?'

And Heinz assured him that all was in order. But he didn't have
the feeling it was; he sat a while a little worried, laughing among all
the camaraderie and trust, repeatedly thinking: it's not at all true
what Degener said. That was Erich, and I'm Heinz. But we're both
Hackendahls and have an iron father. That's why we're too soft. And

even if everyone looks at me in such a friendly way and behaves as if
I belong to them . . . I don't, and will not. I only want one thing – to
be at the railway station as quickly as possible and go to Dahlem!
That's what I want, and I'm just bored with all this hunting for
weapons.

After a while, he stood up and said goodbye to everyone. Only
when he stood in front of Degener did he suddenly feel guilty about
him, and he said what he in no way had wanted to: 'I won't forget all
that with the chaos, Herr Professor!'

The professor unwillingly shook his lion's head with the red beard
and said: '*Kalos kathagos* – student Hackendahl – you still know that:
only what is good is beautiful, isn't that so?'

And that was the most puzzling and wonderful thing about this
Professor Degener. Because he couldn't possibly have heard of
Tinette, yet his last words sounded exactly as though he had just
written her a testimonial.

§ IV

Heinz had hardly rung the bell when the maid was at the door, saying reproachfully: 'Madame has already asked for you four times.'
And hardly had he taken off his overcoat and glanced in the mirror –
his damned tie would drag into a knot of course – when Tinette
entered the hall. 'But, Henri, where have you been all this time? You
were supposed to come at three. And now it's four! I thought you
reliable and Erich unreliable – now it looks as if it's the other way
round after all.'

Heinz was furious – she hadn't said a word about three o'clock.
But what was the use of contradicting her? And the maid hadn't
gone away yet; she ought to know better than to stand and stare at
him as if he were some strange animal from India or Baluchistan.
She should be ashamed of herself!

Tinette crossed her hands behind her back, looked closely into his
angry face and laughed softly. 'What a face you're pulling, Henri.
Exactly the same as when you were outside the door; I watched you
for five minutes. Didn't you want to come? Why are you so angry?

Look at me, Henri – you're just like Erich when he's in a rage. Neither of you will look at me then. But I – I keep my best smiles for people.' And she laughed again. That horrible maid was still there, too, holding his shabby overcoat. Tinette was terrible. She kept nothing to herself, whoever was present. Yes, she was utterly shameless. She hadn't the least idea of shame, like Nature; and like Nature she was just as unconstrained.

'Madame, shall I take the coat to the gentleman?'

'Yes, Erna, do. You don't mind, Henri, I hope? To tell the truth there is a gentleman here who's interested in it.'

Heinz made an angry gesture. He watched the maid go away. 'What is she going to do with my coat?'

'Silly Henri, silly, silly Henri! Does Erna embarrass you? All she thinks is – here's the young gentleman who has fallen in love with Madame. You have fallen in love with me, haven't you?'

'No! No! No!' he shouted furiously.

She laughed. 'You see! But there's no harm in it, you can love me, Henri. You don't want anything, you're a German, so you don't want to take me from Erich. I'm your German Gretchen – no, not Gretchen. Gretchen had a child.' She laughed.

Shameless! As shameless as Nature! She threw him into chaos and stopped at nothing. She stopped at nothing. But suppose she were not shameless, suppose she were simply coarse? What then? And as if she had guessed his thoughts she suddenly released his shoulders. 'All right, go, Henri. You want to leave me alone, too. I'm alone all day . . . So go, if you want to.'

Acting, of course! But where was his coat? Should he go without it? Was she so upset by this little disagreement with her seventeen-year-old brother-in-law that she wanted to let him go out in the miserable damp without a coat? Just acting! But there was the merest chance that she didn't really mean it. Or did she?

All of a sudden her hand was quite close to his mouth . . . She was looking so strangely at him . . . Yes, there was a faint chance that she did like him – not with the passion so tormenting and wonderful that he felt for her, but a genuine liking perhaps . . . And his lips fastened on her hand, breathing its fragrance, his mouth devouring the soft flesh . . . insatiable.

'Oh,' she said, her eyes quite serious now. 'You're learning, Henri! It wouldn't do for Erich to see this.'

And then they joined the gentleman to whom the overcoat had been taken, a very dapper man with a pointed blond beard, who turned out to be a tailor called in by Madame; and he, in accordance with Madame's instructions, had brought a suit with him. 'For you can't go about like that any longer, Henri.'

The new suit was, strangely, a perfect fit.

'Madame has certainly the French eye for style.'

But the real suits were yet to come, made to measure, of course, and from English materials . . . Together with a winter overcoat, an ulster.

Pale and without a word Heinz stood there and raised his arms as requested, so that the gentleman in the cutaway coat could take his measurements . . . This is the depth of ignominy, he thought, to let myself be clothed by Erich's mistress, with Erich's money.

But it was only the beginning of ignominy.

And more tormenting even than this dishonour was the sense of his own cowardice in not daring to quarrel with Tinette in front of the tailor. Or he could quite simply have refused to be measured by the man. Instead, he submissively made his choice between wide or narrow lapels, between single or double-breasted . . . After which the tailor took his leave. He really did have a pearl in his tie, and he really did kiss the lady's hand, but only shook his, promising delivery as soon as possible.

For a moment the two of them looked at him going without saying a word. Then Tinette in her sweetest voice said that Henri should pick up his suit and come with her. They were sure to find a suitable shirt in Erich's room . . .

Whereupon Heinz suddenly shouted that he wouldn't dream of it, and she as suddenly screamed that she didn't want some scrubby, dowdy-looking fellow near her. And there was an outcry about my money and his money and her money and about personal tidiness and idealism and materialism and daintiness, and about the justifiable right of beautiful women to be accompanied by young, well-dressed gentlemen . . . It seemed as if the quarrel would never come to an end, but end it did when Tinette called out in a voice of intense surprise: 'Henri, oh dear! I believe my shoe's come undone! Do help me!' And, looking helplessly at him, she put a foot clad in grey suede on a chair.

In the midst of all the shouting, he suddenly broke off and stared, stunned, at her little foot. She looked at him helplessly and he took it in his hand. However, the strap wouldn't reach, and he couldn't get the hole over the button. The foot, which seemed more naked than naked in its thin, blue-grey silk stocking, was so close to him! Its shoe was styled so that he could just see the beginnings of her toes. He liked that . . . A fragrance came from this foot, a fragrance of perfume and leather, which came also from her and from all women, from eternity . . .

And he brought the foot to his mouth, and thought, as he heard her laughing softly over him, what profound shame, and he kissed it and kissed it . . .

He heard her still laughing softly and went on kissing . . . And he thought, I mustn't, and went on kissing. And he thought, she's just making you do what she wants you to, and he carried on kissing. . .

And the wave rose higher and higher.

Suddenly he thought: if I don't stop now I'll be lost for ever. And she is not worth that. For a fraction he thought of freedom, and tore his mouth from her foot, looked not at her but at the door, and stormed out of the room and out of the house, without either coat or hat.

But even in the street, he thought he could hear her laughter . .

§ V

And of course he returned, he always returned. Sometimes he stormed in, full of reproaches. At other times, covered with embarrassment, he hovered round her like some reprieved criminal, accepting gratefully every kind word she threw to him. He was quarrelsome or tender, and occasionally was overcome by a mood to tell her everything in his mind; once he sat there for many hours reading to her from his favourite poets. On another occasion he helped her to arrange some underclothing in a wardrobe, and the sight of these utterly unfamiliar garments, with their delicate tints and texture, so confused him that he could hardly talk.

Of course he dreamed about her. At first he couldn't get to sleep. The memory of a part of her leg, which she had carelessly allowed him to see, and of the soft swelling of her breast, which he, behind her as she sat, had seen half reluctantly, all confused, tortured and disturbed him. But these visions, once he had fallen asleep, would lose their reality and he was led by dreams into a world where everything seemed to hide behind its first aspect a second, an evil, one. The wounds and deformities of trees became obscene; from the flower arose the pistil, intent on fertilization; the outstretched finger of a sign post seemed to point at his loins.

This he hated – without being religious he felt it sinful. To be obsessed thus by his brother's mistress humiliated him. I don't love her like that, he repeated to himself a hundred times. I don't want to steal her from Erich. I'm not a thief ... And rage overcame him when he realized more and more often, and ever more clearly, how much his body was cheating him, inflicting greater and greater defeats. I won't think of Tinette in that way, he decided. It's loathsome; it degrades both of us. And he resisted. He fought himself.

Then, in the midst of his struggles, he quite suddenly gave up all resistance – he surrendered.

He would perhaps be sitting with Tinette and Erich, with the enigmatic Erich who seemed to regard his brother's daily visits as a matter of course; though even more enigmatic was the woman herself – he could never make out why she always wanted him around – him, who wasn't particularly clever, who wasn't particularly good-looking, and who was unkempt and badly dressed. And out of the corner of his eye he would watch Erich sitting there with his whisky and retailing the latest news ... On one occasion it became too much for him and he rose, busying himself with the fire; then, straightening up, he stood behind her looking down into her low-cut blouse, watching with an insolent despair the rise and fall of her breasts and staring across at his brother challengingly. I'm not ashamed, his eyes said. On the contrary! I look and look and look!

Or he made one of his rare appearances at school. There sat the other boys looking frightfully honourable and boring while the

voice of Schneider, the senior master, jarred the ear. It smelled of
schoolroom dust, the great unwashed, ink and paper. And deliberately he set about visualizing Tinette as he had seen her the evening
before, Tinette kneeling in front of a chest, Tinette with her skirt so
tight over her hips that he could see the line of her slender thighs and
between them that mysterious triangle, the eternal object of all
dreams . . .

Full of contempt, he looked at his schoolfellows. There they sat,
leading their stupid lives, thinking of homework and examinations
and collecting firearms – childish pursuits. He, however, was a man
and went every day to a beautiful woman. His life was a life of vice,
of secrets, of transgressions; all they ever did was to scribble in their
exercise books. Schneider said: 'Good, Porzig!' and Porzig was
happy. Such children were they, such a man he.

Another time, in the midst of a conversation with his brother and
Tinette, he had run out of the hall and crept up to her bedroom,
where he had knelt by her turned-down bed and buried his face in
her pyjamas . . . inhaling a subtle fragrance, the very fragrance it
seemed of the primeval mysteries of life – seduction and sin, source
and action, life's eternal secret, and inexhaustible wellspring.

This, however, happened not at the beginning but later, when he
had fallen still deeper under her spell, for he became more and more
her plaything, her minion, her slave. He gave way, at first, open-eyed,
then closed his eyes and threw himself into the abyss. He was masculine (though not yet a man) and she feminine (and very much a
woman). It did not lie in his nature to quarrel day after day about the
same things; they wearied him and when he had repeated his point
of view five times he was loath to utter it a sixth. Her willingness to
argue, however, remained unimpaired. She could start again every
day, and say the same thing. Every day? Every hour, every minute.
Nor would she yield an inch. So often did she tell him to manicure
his nails that in the end he began to cut and clean his nails, and scrape
off the dead skin – do all those little things which had up till then
seemed so boring, so unnecessary, and such a waste of time.

And finally even took pleasure in it. He gave way not only for the
sake of peace and so as not to hear over and over again the same nonsense, but also because it was such pleasure to sit with her, half an

hour – an hour – she manicuring her nails, he manicuring his. And they talked – there was something almost comradely about it – she giving advice, taking his hand in hers, cutting a nail more expertly, speaking of these matters with extreme seriousness. Gradually he came to understand how important all this can be to certain women and that a fastidious woman finds it almost impossible to care for an unfastidious man or even to bear him near her.

Therefore, when she asked with a laugh: 'Well, Henri, silly boy, wasn't I right about your nails? Don't you look smarter now?' he laughingly admitted that she had been right, and that he was now smart – dead smart. He gave way, no longer tested if she really was right, whether or not manicured nails were really necessary for him. He was now sitting next to her. In that case, she must be right!

And when she repeated for the thirtieth time that he must put on the new suit, that he must go and be fitted, that no man who valued himself could go around looking as he did, that it was impossible for a woman to be seen with him and that there was nobody else with whom she could go for a walk – then he finally gave way here also.

'But only that suit he left,' said Heinz.

She was agreeable.

But it turned out that the suit didn't fit; it bulged at the back. She placed Heinz between two mirrors and pointed it out till he could see for himself . . . No, it was impossible. He couldn't go about like that. He would have to visit the tailor.

And since he was going to the tailor anyhow, he might just as well try on his overcoat – it was wintertime now. All right, the Germans didn't call it winter, then! But for her it was, and in any case she couldn't go out with him unless he wore an overcoat. They were going to go out together, weren't they? For long walks? Well then—

'But it's impossible, Tinette. I can never pay for it.'

'Don't be silly, Henri! The tailor won't send in the bill for six months – you may be a rich man by then.'

'But, Tinette, that's quite impossible.'

'Why should it be? Look at Erich! He'll be rich in a year's time. Surely you can do what your brother can.'

'But you're quite wrong, Tinette. I believe Erich is fearfully worried about money.'

'Erich? Worried about money?' She was thunderstruck. Such an idea had never occurred to her.

'He counted on Father being a rich man, you know.'

She laughed, laughed in his face. 'Oh, Henri, you unworldly creature, you! Things have changed since then. Erich's rolling in money, I tell you, rolling in it! Only a few days ago he bought this villa, paid for it, paid ready cash – I don't remember how much. It was a fat gentleman who got the money. And you – you won't even let your brother give you a couple of suits?'

He looked suspiciously at her, convinced that she lied. 'But where would Erich have got so much money? He must have borrowed it then.'

'Oh, you mustn't say that. Erich's really smart. He's got some kind of contract . . .'

'Contract? For what?' It seemed less and less credible. Erich, only twenty-one, fresh from the army, in the Reichstag security service, and then no longer in it – and suddenly a wealthy contractor! 'What kind of contract?'

'It's true. And I consider it only right his friends should do something for him. He's very useful to them.'

'But, Tinette, do listen . . . What can he contract for? He's got nothing.'

'Well, he buys things. They've commissioned him to supply some regiment or other. They say he's so capable. A friend of his was here recently and said that Erich has produced a surprising amount of butter in spite of the blockade – Danish butter. Or was it Russian? I've forgotten. In any case . . .'

'So my dear Erich's become a profiteer. I think it's . . .'

'Oh, do be quiet, Henri! For a fortnight you've made my life a misery with those suits.'

'I? The other way round, you mean.'

'First you say you don't know how you're going to pay for them, then I tell you that Erich's giving them to you. I discussed it with him a long time ago.'

Again something quite fresh. So Erich knew about it. But she was lying, he was certain she was lying . . .

'Then you say Erich hasn't the money for such presents. I tell you he has, he earns a lot of money. And so you call him a profiteer. Yes, my dear boy, you're demanding that Erich earns his money in a way you approve of.'

'I demand nothing,' he burst out. 'I don't want to hear anything more about it. I—'

'Very well then, that's settled at last. And please remember that it's settled. You've no idea how sick I am of that shiny suit of yours. Come along, I've got you some shirts and underclothing.'

Heinz fled. He ran out of the house, desperate, furious.

Will she never understand anything, he thought. I can say 'No' a hundred times, I can shout it into her ears, all it means to her is 'Yes'. I won't stand it any more. I won't come here again, and if I ever do, I swear never to wear this wretched suit. She ordered underwear for me. But I'll never . . . I'm going to stay at home. I must study anyway, otherwise I'll mess up the exams too. (What else he'd messed up he didn't say, but he had a pretty clear feeling that just about everything was a mess.)

No, I'll go regularly to school for at least a week and swot terrifically. I'll show her!

And he imagined what she would see . . . How at first she would be surprised, then worried that he no longer came at all and stayed away without saying a word.

She'll just have to miss me. Even if she doesn't love me, she's used to me. She can't be on her own . . . And to break it all up because of a couple of stupid suits! She understands, she must understand, that it's impossible.

§ VI

At home, his parents had a visitor. But visitor wasn't exactly the right word; a daughter had returned home. After four years of absence Sophie was back from her field hospital on the Eastern Front – a senior nurse now, sitting there in her blue-grey uniform, a Red Cross badge on her fully rounded breast and with some order or decoration

pinned a little to one side of it – Sophie, Heinz's sister, eldest daughter of the Hackendahl family, completely familiar and yet completely
transformed!

The Sophie of former days had been a sharp-nosed, rather
ill-humoured creature, thin and pale. The senior nurse was fat, with
a flabby face, as if appearing up from the miasma of the sickroom.
After saying something she would shut her mouth and compress her
lips as though tasting something.

My, she's certainly become revolting, thought Heinz, a sort of
cross between a nun and amateur whore. And she's learned how to
be bossy all right.

Without getting up, she had extended a plump hand to him. 'So
you're Bubi. I suppose you have to be called Heinz now. Well, well. I
need hardly tell you that you've grown very tall. Yes . . . yes. And at
school? Are you getting on there? Are you at the top?'

'Thanks,' said Heinz dryly and sat down. An absolutely unbearable female! She was behaving as if he were some very small boy and
she an affectionate maiden aunt. It was funny, but why was he especially chosen to have exclusively unbearable siblings? (That they
found him equally unbearable didn't occur to him.)

Sophie continued: 'And everything's all right at home? Yes, I can
see of course that your circumstances are reduced somewhat. Well,
we've all had to make our sacrifices, in our purses or our persons.
Poor Otto also fell. Yes, yes.' She shut her mouth tightly. It was as if
she were closing Otto's coffin lid.

'An' what'll you do now, Sophie?' asked old Hackendahl. 'You c'n
see for yourself that we haven't enough grub for you too. Bubi's
already got his notice to quit at Easter.' He laughed.

Heinz thought his father had changed tremendously of late. Not
that he had fallen farther than the general decline. It was rather as if
recent times had brought him to himself with a jolt. He seemed to
be secretly amused at everything, making fun both of the world and
his children.

'No,' answered Senior Sister Sophie slowly, 'I don't think I shall
become a burden to you. The Senior Staff Surgeon, Herr Schwenke,
has offered me a post as theatre sister. There's only too much to do
at home, unfortunately – instead of uniting in the hour of trouble

we assist our enemies by killing one another. Sad! Yes, yes.' She lowered her pale eyelids. All she said was undeniably true, but she said it in a manner which Heinz considered loathsome.

'There are also other plans for me . . . Well, we shall see, there's no hurry. But it's very unlikely that I shall ever be a burden on you.' Her lips closed.

'That's fine, my girl,' said Hackendahl. 'I c'n quite see you've feathered your nest all right. Well, you've bin a lot smarter than your poor ole dad. He's only a common cabby again.'

She evaded commenting on this. 'I haven't been in Berlin for a long time,' she said, 'and perhaps I may be mistaken but you used not to speak in such a . . . a local way, did you, Father?'

'You notice everythin', girl,' grinned Hackendahl. 'No. When I had a proper business I did me best to speak refined like but now, as a common cabby . . . it don't pay. See?'

'I see. Yes, yes. I understand, Father.' The nun lowered her eyelids. 'Previously you used to play the part of – what did they call you? – of Iron Gustav! And now it's the jolly Berliner. Original, Father! Really very original.'

'Played a part? No, there you're mistaken, Sophie. It's other folks who're acting here an' I know why. You can't frighten me. I've always bin Iron Gustav an' I'll stick to it. As for my way of talkin' it fits in better with our reduced circumstances.'

'Yes, yes,' said Sophie. 'I understand entirely, Father.' And then, possibly to change the subject: 'And what is Evchen doing? Where is she? You never mentioned her in your letters, Mother.'

Frau Hackendahl started and looked anxiously at her husband. Eva's name was never spoken before him. But although he scowled he nevertheless replied equably: 'Eva? We had nothing good to say about her. She's become a whore, that's what she's become.'

Silence reigned. Sophie, a study in white under her nurse's hood, had not winced but was sitting very still, her hands in her lap. 'Pardon me, Father,' she said at last. 'Just one more question. Are you merely dissatisfied with her mode of life or is she really what the word implies?'

'Of course, a real whore, with what goes with it – permit and pimp.' Only the way he spoke showed Heinz how difficult it was for his father to speak thus about his former favourite. 'It has nothing to do with disapproving or approving her mode of life. That's not the issue. It's just a fact.'

'And now we won't say another word about it,' said Frau Hackendahl, unusually firm. 'You're only upsetting Father, Sophie.'

'I'm not upset,' said Hackendahl heatedly. 'Everybody must do according to their lights.'

Again silence. The four members of the family dared not look at each other.

'Yes, yes,' said Sophie, lost in thought. 'And Erich? How's Erich?'

'You'll have to ask Heinz. He's there every day.' And Hackendahl got up.

Unexpected, this – Heinz was not aware that his father knew about those visits. Of course he had told Mother one or two things about Erich but it was news that she had passed them on.

Hackendahl clapped on his top hat and, after being helped by Heinz into his driver's coat, took the whip from the corner by the cupboard. 'I want to exercise meself and me horse,' he said. 'So long, Sophie. Bin a great pleasure. Good luck! An' before you start on anythin' new don't forget to ask yourself what you'll get out of it. Bye-bye, girl! Bye-bye, Mother! Heinz, you might fetch your mother a sack of coal sometime – if it ain't too much trouble, that is.'

And old Hackendahl went. He hadn't changed – the only difference was that, instead of bellowing at his family, he now relied on sarcasm.

Sophie too had observed this. 'I don't know, Mother,' she said, having waited for the outer door to bang. 'Father has changed a good deal. It almost sounds as if he's angry with us children. I've certainly done nothing to him. After all, I have achieved something – it's not impossible I may be appointed Matron.'

'That's all very well,' said her mother, 'but a child ought to think now and again of the parents. During the last two years you've written only three times.'

'Of course, if you take that amiss . . .'

'I don't know – Father never speaks about it. But we can't say our children show any interest in their parents.'

'I don't understand you, Mother. I had to look after hundreds – thousands – of wounded. At times we were fifteen hours on end at the operating table . . . You simply can't write letters afterwards.'

'Surely you had a free hour now and again in two years!'

'That's when I slept. I had to sleep, Mother, to keep myself fit. The wounded came first. I knew from your letters you were all well . . .'

Sophie, of course, ended by convincing her mother. Silently Heinz sat, admiring his sister's skill in pumping their mother about the family affairs. There was little doubt that Sophie had had intentions similar to Erich's, but now that she knew there was nothing to be got at home she wouldn't be making a nuisance of herself by too frequent visits.

When she left she asked Heinz to accompany her for a bit. (The streets were so unsettled. Not even a nurse was safe from molestation!) But this was only a pretext; of that Heinz was quite convinced – Sophie didn't at all look as if men could frighten her nowadays. No, he in his turn was to be pumped. And this proved the case. What did he know about Erich? She was now much less guarded and showed her interest quite frankly.

'Yes, Erich is clever, he'll get along all right . . . Splendid! Twenty-one and he's got his finger in the pie already. Yes, yes. He knows one has to earn money. Very sensible. Very clever. What did you say his address was? . . . Yes, I'll definitely look him up soon – a connection like that's worth using. I've got certain plans of my own, perhaps I can interest him in them.'

Heinz returned home in the best of spirits. He'd tell Erich about it that evening and prepare him for Sophie's visit. Erich would be extremely amused.

§ VII

So he went back into the house. But he wasn't yet so dishonest as to persuade himself that he did so to bring his brother news of Sophie. No, he struggled with himself, resisted but in the end gave up.

When Erich smirkingly said to him, as he was showing off the splendour of his new clothes, 'Well, Bubi, for the extreme idealist you are, you look damn materialistic!' he would have liked to beat him up out of anger and humiliation.

However, man, the most adaptable creature on the planet, accomodates itself to everything, especially if no one notices anything special about his new appearance.

Heinz began to wear his splendid new clothes.

'Well,' said his mother, 'Erich's doing something for you at least even if he can't find his way to us.'

And old Hackendahl exercised that grim new humour of his. 'S'posing it gets awkward for you to see me in the street you don't need ter look away or hide yerself. I won't be recognizing you.'

No, none of them found anything special about it. Heinz's reputation among his school classmates even rose considerably. It was rumoured – and no one knew who started it – that he had a rich girl-friend. And they were all so young that, despite emergencies and weapon collections, their young hearts got completely carried away with the idea of consorting with a beautiful and wealthy woman.

But naturally, it was inevitably and indeed enviously discovered that an inner voice remained in him which repeatedly reminded him that shame was shame . . . One thing was very soon made clear to Heinz, however – these new suits were not going to be used for walks. Once, and once only, did he and Tinette go out into the wintry Grunewald; and after five minutes she insisted on going back immediately. 'Call this a wood? Brooms! Ugly bristly brooms stuck upside down in the ground, that's what the trees are! Ground that immediately fills your shoes with sand and pine needles.' And she enthused about some park or another to the west, with its soft, abundant foliage and yellow pebble pathways.

'But it's winter there now, too, Tinette!'

'Winter? What are you talking about, Henri! It's never really winter there – I mean among the people! You're all winter people here, miserable, cold. But we're always happy, always like spring.'

'Always happy – that's not possible, Tinette.'

'Not possible – oh, you should see . . .' She paused, then it burst out of her: 'If the French hadn't only got as far as the Rhine; if only they'd come as far as here! We would at least have had people whom

we could laugh with. Here, you feel completely alone. I've never frozen so much in my whole life as during these last few months here.'

'And Germany has to have the French, so that you can laugh with
some lieutenant? Poor Germany!'

'Why should I care? If I'd known who you really were, I would
never have come here. But I came upon Erich – and thought you
others would be a bit like he is. But not at all, not at all.'

'Well, Tinette, if it's so terrible here, you can of course always
return to your own country. Erich isn't in a position to tie you down.'
Heinz felt personally hurt.

'That's the point. Oh, Henri, how stupid you are! Do you think I
can go back? I wouldn't stay here for another hour, Erich could earn
a hundred times as much. But of course I can't go back, definitely
not for the time being . . .'

And she told him that over there, at home, they despised women
who had gone with Germans.

'I would never get another job. I could starve. They would
stone me.'

And me. Me? He had wanted to ask. Do I mean nothing to you?
But why ask? Didn't he already know the shameful, humiliating
answer? He was nothing but a toy, a pastime, the companion of long,
grey, lonely hours – someone one immediately and totally forgot as
soon as something more amusing came along.

(And perhaps one was a little bit more, after all. Someone one
could torture, and try out one's power on – a servant, a slave, a
bonded serf. Yes, bonded, the shame one no longer felt, the shared
shame – inflicted and suffered – that bound them together!) From
then on they went in every day to town, at first only in the daytime
because Erich came home in the evening; then in the evening also,
because Erich was working till late at night. This Erich, so self-
indulgent and charming, had an extraordinary toughness when it
came to making money. This weakling could become strong when it
was a question of cash.

What were his thoughts on seeing his brother and Tinette always
together? It could not remain hidden, nor did they make a secret of
it. The servants knew, and Tinette would ring Erich at his office to
ask for the car, so that she might go shopping with Henri.

What did he think?

Ah, the amiable fellow was inscrutable; he was much more difficult to understand than Tinette. Although Heinz had no desire to
think about his brother at all, he was constantly forced to do this.
What was going on in Erich's mind? He had never really been a caring brother. He worked all right and did little deals, but such deals
are themselves also work, and Erich noticed how his girlfriend and
Heinz spent the money he himself made like water.

'You're both enjoying yourselves, I hope? You're not bored, are
you? Here, Heinz.' And he would push a wad of notes into his brother's hand – an incredible sum. 'No nonsense, Bubi. It's impossible to
go around without a penny in your pocket; Tinette told me you
walked from Dahlem to the Wexstrasse. What nonsense! Take a taxi.
I may be self-centred, but I can appreciate the kind way you're looking after Tinette.'

He smiled – was it in scorn or friendliness? Or was he merely
tired? Perhaps he was glad to know Tinette was safe with his brother;
she had to have some companion, and another man – any other
man – would have been a greater danger than this seventeen-year-old
schoolboy.

Or was everything quite different, much more difficult and complicated? Some even lower motive?

Oh, it was impossible to discover! Heinz had thought women
very difficult to understand and certainly he understood very little
about Tinette, but concerning his own brother he was completely
ignorant . . .

§ VIII

So, instead of walks, they went out shopping; it was surprising how
much shopping a woman like Tinette had to do and what a long
time she spent on it. Shopping Heinz had always considered a tiresome domestic duty – Mother would set out with a shopping bag
and queue up for hours to buy a packet of dismal spaghetti. Tinette
and he, however, always went by car, gliding past long queues of

women before the food shops, drab, silent women with pinched faces. On his knee rested a fold of her dress; the movement of the car caused their arms to come in contact; she opened her mouth to speak – oh, how beautifully shaped were her teeth!

They went to the dressmaker and milliner. Three weeks after the revolution there had returned to certain elegant streets some very elegant shops with extremely French names – ladies who called themselves Madame So-and-so and Mademoiselle This-and-that de Paris, and who sold the most magnificent and ever more and more abbreviated French creations. In their establishments Heinz would sit on some stool or in an easy chair, privileged to watch Tinette trying on hats and dresses. Girls, surprisingly painted, walked with long, proud legs to and fro; they carried dresses, they fetched dresses; under their closely fitting skirts their little buttocks swayed with delightful nonchalance. At Tinette's side there always stood a somewhat older but still very good-looking lady and the two talked together with never-diminishing excitement and rapidity.

They took the hat, tried it on, looked in the mirror, in two mirrors, in five mirrors, put the hat contemptuously aside on the table, took up another, tried that on, returned to the first one, pushed it a bit to the right, a bit lower down the side, straightened the feathers, put them back again . . . and the older lady would turn almost passionately to Heinz, begging Monsieur to say how the hat suited Madame – but his genuine, his real, his sincere opinion!

And while Heinz was struggling to pass careful judgement they stood watching his lips as though the God of Fashion (if one existed) spoke from them. But the moment he stopped they turned away and forgot him entirely, removed the hat, put on another, and seemed no nearer a conclusion.

In any case he never understood exactly why, in the end, some hat was bought . . . Why that particular one? Why must it be altered, returned, sent to be altered again, exchanged? It was a mystery.

At the dressmaker's he had other torments. In the beginning Tinette had disappeared into a cubicle but on the third or fourth occasion she omitted to do so . . . Ever slimmer and more seductive, he saw her emerging from her garments till she stood there in long silk stockings, knickers and something over the breasts. She raised her arms and the dress glided on. Then she changed again, revealing herself afresh . . .

A hundred times he vowed not to look. Leaning forward, a cigarette in his hand, he would stare at the lights reflected from his spotless shoes – but in the end he had to look. There she stood, more alluring than if she had been naked. He shut his eyes – yet looked again; sweet torment ever repeated.

Soon the girls in these shops greeted him with a familiar, an almost sisterly smile – as if he belonged there. At times one of them would sit on the arm of his chair and assure him that Madame looked dazzling again today; she had an adorable figure. The bosom perhaps a trifle too full – but men liked that, didn't they? Smiles . . . and they glided off, with a gentle sway of the buttocks.

Heinz racked his brains wondering what these girls thought about him; whether they took him for Tinette's lover or brother, whether they were out to torment him or whether they knew him for what he really was – a dependant, a slave who no longer needed to be in chains, because much stronger, invisible ties held him . . . Ties that bound him ever tighter and sent him ever more swiftly into the abyss.

Back home again, it was there she was least desirous of being left alone. She wanted to talk about a thousand things she had noticed and of which he had seen nothing; she took him up to her dressing room, she changed in front of him. Sometimes her maid was present, sometimes not . . . She laughed, prattled away – he had only to throw in a 'Yes' or a 'No', while he sat half mad with longing, feeling like some hunger-crazed animal which sees food but also the fatal trap containing it . . . He trembled, despising himself and her but himself more – and yet he would not have missed a single hour of that torment.

Once, when he could bear it no longer, almost groaning with pain he exclaimed: 'Oh, Tinette, please! Please, Tinette!'

She turned to him.

'Oh, you're not suffering, are you, my friend?' She smiled. 'You're like my own brother, aren't you?'

She went up to him. He fell on his knees before her and pressed kisses on the strip of flesh between garter and knicker.

She laughed and ruffled his hair. 'Oh dear, Henri,' she said lightly, 'you must get used to it. A soldier can only prove his valour under fire, you know that!'

With a laugh she freed herself and returned to the dressing table, where she went on talking as if it had all gone out of her mind immediately.

Ever deeper and ever more swiftly downwards.

He thought only of her. He dreamed only of her. Yet he did not wish to possess her. A slave is without possessions. His ignominy, his disgrace – those are his possessions and pleasure.

He continued on his way. At times he was even proud – proud of being able to discover this world. He never for a moment considered whether this world was worth discovering.

He entered the villa, and went into the bedroom. Tinette lay in bed, perhaps still asleep. Under his gaze, she slowly awoke. She stretched, yawned, and from the warmth of the bed came her hand, which he could kiss. Or else she stretched her leg from under the covers, and said that she had cramp and he must give her a massage.

Brother, as much as sister, the prisoner of instinct, slave of lust, in love with suffering – Eva Hackendahl and Heinz Hackendahl alike. Ever deeper downwards.

§ IX

While the year 1918 ended in bloody street-fighting, the year 1919 began even more bloodily and with more militant strikes. On his way to Dahlem, Heinz was searched twenty times for weapons, on the one hand by the Civil Guards, on the other by the Military Guards – the so-called Noskitos (under General Noske) – and then by the Spartacists and, on the next corner, by the Independents. Meanwhile, the barbed-wire entanglements of trench warfare were to be found in the streets of Berlin, and everywhere there were notices: 'Halt! Anyone proceeding further will be shot!'

Meanwhile, cannon were being fired at Police Headquarters, the Berlin Schloss and the Imperial stables, the sailors were settling a wage rise – while at the same fighting for a National Assembly or a

Soviet state, and also negotiated for better armistice conditions – and the Spartacists were promising the workers a six-hour day, and Lieb-knecht and Rosa Luxemburg were being shot. Simultaneously, hunger grew, murders increased and the troops returned from the Front dispersed themselves and joined the masses. Uniform upon uniform returned, and only a few groups remained armed, at the wish of the government, or with its permission, or else in defiance of it. At this time, the general death rate in Berlin 'only' tripled, but death from pneumonia increased eighteen times.

And while all this was going on Heinz Hackendahl, under Tinette's guidance, was becoming acquainted with Berlin nightlife. That winter very many bars had opened and every week saw new ones added to their number; all were very much alike, living on pimping and prostitution; their customers drank heavily and in a hurry, as if someone stood behind them to snatch the glass from their lips.

Here then was Heinz Hackendahl, seventeen-year-old schoolboy, in a wine bar. The dress of the lady with him was not more open than the dresses of those other ladies parading their seductive whispers from table to table; neither was it less so. The jazz band (it had to have if possible at least one black deserter from the army of Occupation on the Rhine) was clamorous. And then they all sang in English . . . And Heinz could feel the champagne going to his head; he talked faster and faster while Tinette was splitting her sides with laughter . . . Yes, he was released at last, laughing at himself as he told her how timid he had been at first and how he had not even dared to look at her. But now he was sitting next to her, a champagne glass in his hand . . .

The music stopped. Swiftly, noisily, the iron shutters rolled down. In a shaking voice the manager asked the ladies and gentlemen to be quiet a moment. A small crowd of unemployed had collected out-side . . . The police would be coming any moment.

But before anyone could speak or even set down a glass, the lights went out . . . Darkness . . . The ends of cigarettes glowed, a woman laughed shrilly, a man burst out with 'Sickening rubbish!'

Then there was silence, for through the shutters penetrated a buzzing sound, malignant as from a furious swarm of bees, a hum that rose and fell – and now and then they thought they could distinguish voices . . .

Suddenly all understood that this was no casual meeting of unemployed in the square outside, but a demonstration against that particular bar. They had heard the shouts of 'Down with the profiteers!'

Suddenly the street door burst open, glass splintered.

'Not a visitor here – my word of honour!' screamed the manager.

Then the lights flashed on. Obviously one of the waiters was in league with the crowd outside; however large the tips there was always a traitor. Three or four soldiers in field grey were standing in the entrance, looking at the frightened faces.

'Come out, the lot of you,' said one of them grinning maliciously. 'We want to say goodnight to you.'

The guests sat as if thunderstruck. 'This is scandalous!' called out one, and broke off when he met the soldier's eye. 'Well, hurry up, or shall I give you a hand?' cried the soldier still more threateningly. And he pointed to his belt, where hand grenades hung.

A guest rose. 'I've come from the trenches,' he declared. 'I hold the Iron Cross. I demand that you inform the people outside.'

'Go and tell them yourself, my boy!' replied the man in field-grey, giving the other a push so that he reeled to the door, where a second field-grey with another push assisted him into the street. One heard a dull roar, shouts, a scream . . .

'I won't go out,' yelled someone. 'I'm not going to let them beat me to death. There must be an exit at the back.'

'Come on with you!' The soldier reached out – the guest hit back. There was a short scuffle, then he too was thrown outside and once more the riot in the street became audible.

'Man, be sensible,' implored someone. 'I'll give you a hundred marks if you'll let us go to the lavatory or the courtyard.'

'Three hundred from me!'

'A thousand!'

'Offer him five hundred, Bubi. I have some money with me,' whispered Tinette. 'Offer a thousand.'

'A thousand!'

'Oh, no, we'd only become rich then. But we want no money from profiteers . . . Our kids are starving and you dirty dogs swill champagne!'

'Come on, come on,' cried the field-greys, who were increasing in number. Others were coming in from the street, civilians too; angry faces, pale, lined faces, rough faces. They dragged the chairs from underneath the guests, they pushed men and women towards the entrance.

'Clear up the joint from the back. Watch the doors! Don't let anyone go to the lavatory. Don't let yourself be diddled by the women.'

'My things! My fur coat!' screamed a woman, defending herself vigorously.

'Fetch them tomorrow, love. I doubt if your fur will survive unscathed.'

A gentleman got on a chair. 'It's madness to let ourselves be pushed out one by one – it'll only be ten times worse for each. I suggest we all go out in single file, close together, a gentleman and then a lady, and so on. Come on . . . I'll go in front. Come along, Ella, keep close . . . And get through as quickly as you can. Oskar, behind Ella!'

'Here, wait, you've been to the Front, comrade,' said the field-grey. 'Why are you swilling champagne with profiteers? Here, wait a bit!'

'Didn't we swill in the trenches?' cried the man angrily. 'Didn't you go to a pub sometimes and have one? This is my pub!'

'Wait – I'll let you out through the yard, comrade!'

'No, thanks. I'll share what the others get. Now, all behind one another! Come on, Ella.' And he made for the entrance, the others following. Through the open door came the bellowing of the impatient crowd.

'Come on, Tinette, we mustn't be the last.'

Tinette was very pale, but not from fright. 'Fetch my coat!' she commanded. 'Nonsense! I won't go in the street half naked.'

They were outside.

'Another chap with a tart,' jeered someone.

The dimly lit square roared with a thousand throats, screaming, threatening, laughing, mocking . . . a mass of dark faces, many women there . . .

'Hurry up, Tinette. Keep close behind me. For heaven's sake don't let go of my coat.'

A man with arms raised to protect himself rushed into the narrow passage left by the crowd and Heinz hurried after, he too protecting his face with his arms and keeping his head well down. He could feel Tinette clinging to him.

On either side people struck and screamed at him. 'Profiteer! Traitor! Shirker! Pimp! Tart's lapdog!' A woman spat on him. Blind to everything, hardly feeling the blows in his excitement, he pressed forward, anxious only not to lose touch with the powerfully built man in front who was forging ahead through the crowd like a battering ram, clearing a passage with his broad shoulders, brushing aside those who tried to stop him, but never answering or hitting back – irresistibly forging ahead.

In all that turmoil, amid people who spat and struck at him, Heinz was comforted to feel Tinette's grip on his back, sometimes firm, sometimes weak, but always there; he was not able to look round or to say anything. Once he cried out. A woman had stabbed him in the cheek, possibly with a knitting needle, getting past his arm. A swift, burning pain, followed by the soothing trickle of blood . . .

Would it never end? It was only a small open space which at other times one could cross in two minutes; yet it felt as if he had been there hours. On and on, ever deeper into the crowd whose blows and abuse had lost nothing of their force. Somebody tripped him and he might have fallen but for the grip on his back.

Suddenly it was all over – one last weak cuff . . . He saw the big man in front of him turn and make for the pale-faced lad who had struck out. Here stood only spectators attracted by the noise. The square was behind them. They were in a street.

'You strike me, eh, you dirty scamp?' shouted the big man, infuriated by the humiliation he had undergone. 'Come on, I'll give it to you.' And he went for the retreating lad, while those around muttered.

'Come on, come on,' urged Tinette. 'Let's get away from here. I've had enough of it.'

Side by side they hurried on in the middle of the road, faces – inquisitive, malicious, frightened – looking at them. They turned a corner and Heinz took Tinette's arm. 'Shall we get a car?' he panted. 'You weren't hurt, were you, Tinette?'

She pushed his arm away. 'Don't touch me!' she almost screamed. 'You're one of these – these Germans!'

'Tinette, they're half starved and poor, they don't know what they're doing. And after all perhaps it wasn't quite right of us to go into such places at a time like this. These people have had to endure terrible suffering. Naturally they're envious.' He spoke incoherently, excitedly. Although they had beaten him up and cursed him, he felt they were justified. He was on their side, because he understood them. Still in his confusion, because he said to himself that he was confused, he felt he was perhaps worse than them. 'What do you think, Tinette?'

'Yes, that's what you're all like,' she said bitterly. 'Just because you're gloomy and drab and dull you hate brightness, gaiety and laughter. You'd like to make the whole world as gloomy and drab as yourselves. You kill anything that's cheerful.'

We used to be cheerful, he thought. It isn't true what she says. Our gaiety disappeared in these last terrible years. Or weren't we ever gay?

'You Germans,' she went on feverishly, 'all you love is Death. You're always talking about it, about dying; one must know how to die, you keep on saying. You fools, anybody can die. One must learn how to live! Yes, one must understand life. Oh, when I think of the lovely happy life there is in my own country! I haven't been able to laugh since I came here.'

'That's not true, Tinette,' he cried. 'Look how often you've cheered us up with your laughter!'

She wasn't listening. 'That's the reason why you started this war, because you hate laughter, you hate life. You wanted the whole world to be as boring and serious as you are yourselves. But you lost the war!'

She looked at him with flashing eyes – they were standing in the glare of a wine bar – looked at him as if he were her enemy, one loving death and hating life. Then she saw the cut on his cheek.

'Oh, so you got something? Look, a souvenir from one of your sisters! And you say they don't know what they're doing. I'd soon teach them what I think of the way you go on here. And you can be certain we will teach you too.'

'Come on, Tinette,' he implored. 'Come home . . . Erich will be anxious.'

'Home?' she said. 'Do you think I'm going to be put off by that? Never!' Looking round she saw the wine bar. 'Bar Napoli. We'll go in here! I'll go in bars every evening – just because!'

'Do come home,' he begged. 'What can we do there? It's only boring now the mood's gone. It's not because I'm afraid . . .'

'Are you coming or not? I'll go by myself then.'

'Please, Tinette . . .'

'Are you coming?'

'Be reasonable, Tinette. There's no sense . . .'

'Then I'll go alone. But if you abandon me tonight, Henri, you need not come again, you understand?'

'No. No. I can't . . .'

'Go ahead! Stay with your soldiers. Be one yourself. Be dirty again and unkempt – then you'll be one of them.'

'Tinette!'

But she had disappeared through the door.

Mechanically he took out his handkerchief and began to wipe the blood from his cheek, looking hesitatingly at the wine bar. Suddenly he noticed he was without hat and coat. It was cold, a January frost. He'd have to fetch his coat . . .

Turning round, he retraced his steps. Though they had left it barely a quarter of an hour before, the little square was already deserted and the bar lay in darkness. In front of the splintered door stood a policeman talking to a civilian.

'Your things?' asked the policeman. 'Oh, were you in there then? Bit young for such places, aren't you?' Civilian and policeman both looked at Heinz in disapproval.

'I only want my things,' he said stubbornly. 'If it can be managed.'

'There's nobody in the place now, they've all gone home. Did you get much of a hiding?'

'Enough to go on with.'

'Give me a few marks,' the civilian suggested, 'and I'll take you in and get you your things. I'm a waiter here. Have you the cloakroom ticket?'

'I have,' said Heinz, following the man.

'There's also a lady's hat on this number,' said the waiter. 'Must be some mistake.'

'No, that's right,' declared Heinz, giving the man his money. He had taken only Tinette's coat from the peg when the trouble started. 'Don't worry. I'll take it to the lady.'

'Where is she then?' asked the waiter suspiciously.

'Where should she be? In a bar.'

'In a bar? What, already?' The waiter was indignant. 'Well, that's a bit thick, you know. It's not surprising if people lose their tempers.'

Heinz, however, did not care what the waiter thought and he was equally indifferent to the policeman calling after him. Balancing Tinette's little hat on the tips of his fingers he returned to the Napoli Bar, gave up his coat at the cloakroom, handed in the hat too and approached Tinette, perched on a stool. He sat down beside her.

'I've just fetched your hat,' he said.

She turned round and faced him. Her mouth smiled but her eyes remained hard. They weren't so much serious as angry, as she said, 'So you've come back! I knew you would, Henri. You shouldn't give up until your side is totally defeated, should you? Come on, let's drink to the defeated, to their total defeat!' He clinked glasses with her, without saying a word, but he clinked.

§ X

Heinz went towards his destruction with open eyes, proceeding from defeat to defeat with a kind of stupid determination. Deaf to all warnings – from without and within – he shamelessly clung ever more strongly to Tinette, regardless of her abuse of him, and without paying any attention to the mounting mockery of his brother.

One evening Erich came home unusually early, bringing with him a girl in a black, high-necked dress. Her complexion was pale and unhealthy-looking and her dark hair was smoothly parted in the centre.

All four had dinner together – little conversation but much drinking. Something was afoot. Something was being prepared which Heinz didn't know about, about which the three others seemed to be in agreement. Again and again Erich rose to give the servants directions which he subsequently reported to his guest in a low voice . . . 'No, no upper light at all . . . Perhaps it would be better to have only the fire.' Or: 'The violinist has just arrived; he'll sit in the gallery. No, he needs no light, he's blind.'

Or: 'Some more roast beef, my dear Fräulein?'

'No thanks, I eat hardly anything . . . before.'

'I'm sorry. I wasn't thinking.'

Heinz heard all this, considered it fleetingly, and thought about it no longer. He sat there in a pitiable condition. Tinette had ignored him all afternoon. For hours on end he had been alone in the study, had picked up a book, glanced at it, then put it down . . . Going into the hall he had listened, and two or three times he had knocked on her door but each time she had sent him away.

He then did what he had never done before – he went to Erich's cocktail cabinet and drank in quick succession several brandies. He didn't do it for the taste, but to get senseless. During the dreary hours of that afternoon his chronic state of living in unfulfilled desire became unbearable. It can't go on like this, he said to himself over and over again. Rather an end with terror than terror without end.

At last he went to the telephone and ordered a taxi, and was about to leave when Tinette barred his way.

'You can't go now, Henri. I need you.'

'It hasn't looked like it all afternoon.'

'You've been drinking! How disgusting! Minna, give the taxi man a tip. Herr Henri's not going.'

'I am – you stay here!'

'You're not – send the taxi away at once.'

'Well, I'm off. Goodbye, Tinette.'

Suddenly she laughed. 'Au revoir, you bad boy. But come back this evening, won't you? I have a surprise for you.'

She had run after him and put her arms round his neck. And – what she had never done before – she kissed him on the lips. 'Be off, you bad boy. But come back, won't you, Henri?' He had almost not gone; had she again asked him to stay he would have done so but she turned away immediately.

And so he had got into the taxi, still conscious of the blissful sensation of those arms seeking to retain him, of those lips on his mouth. It was as though she had clanked the chain on seeing her slave about to escape – that chain that seemed to truss his feet together, so that he would never be able to escape from her. It was shameful to be kissed like that; she had stirred up his senses to revolt against his brain. And yet . . .

The taxi stopped. Heinz slowly got out. Although it was dusk no light burned within the little shop; only with difficulty could he distinguish the dusty paper flags commemorating victories long since forgotten. The pile of boxes with letters from the Front was still upright. As always, the shop bell seemed to tinkle for ever and, as always, nobody came even then until he had twice shouted out 'Hello!' And when at last Frau Quaas did come, he could hardly see her in the darkness.

It was so odd to stand there again, at the home of his first girl-friend, after all that had happened to him, all that he'd experienced, and from where he now came. Many lights were now shining in the Dahlem villa, all radiantly bright. But he stood there in obscurity. Why had he come? What did he expect from the young girl who understood nothing? Help . . . ? But he knew that help could only come from within, never from outside.

Then he was gripped by the memory of that kiss at the city gate. It came to him as if from far away – a memory of purity, youth, her moist mouth. Not all the fires were burnt out, the trees still had their leaves. Was that why he was here?

'Frau Quaas,' he said doubtfully, 'I would like two nibs, Bremen-Change, EF, very pointed. My name is Heinz Hackendahl.'

The woman did not move or make any attempt to reply or serve him.

'Well, Frau Quaas,' said Heinz, a little embarrassed. 'Won't you give me my nibs?'

No reply.

'I would like to speak to Irma. I'm Heinz Hackendahl. You know!'

Suddenly, there in the dark, he felt quite uncertain whether she'd even understood that.

'Leave my shop,' said Frau Quaas suddenly. She spoke in her old plaintive voice and yet resolutely. 'Please leave my shop at once.'

He was taken aback. 'But, Frau Quaas . . . I only want to have a few words with Irma.'

'You're to leave my shop,' she insisted. 'I can call the police if you continue to molest me, you know that. I don't want you in my shop. You're wicked.'

Heinz groped for a chair. He knew where it ought to stand, for Frau Quaas needed it to take down the cardboard box with coloured paper for the children. And find the chair he did. But in every other respect things had changed . . . 'I'm sitting down, Frau Quaas,' he said. 'I shan't go until I've spoken with Irma.'

'Then you must go on sitting,' she called out sarcastically – for such a timid woman she seemed unusually courageous. Then the door slammed and he was sitting alone.

Well, what was the good of staying? There was nothing to be done there. And what had he wanted to do, anyway? Exchange a few words with Irma? See his childhood friend and convince himself that she had no hold on him, that he had to return to the other woman, the beautiful, the evil one? Sunken garden of childhood – for ever sunken – you can still hear the rustling of its leaves in your ear, and feel on your cheeks the warmth of its sun, which will never again set with such purity and strength.

No, it was useless waiting there any longer. Irma was certainly not at home, he sensed it. And yet he remained. However brightly the Dahlem villa was lit, however attractive the beautiful woman was, he stayed where he was. He sat in the cold, dark, dusty shop.

It was as if a hand slowly turned the pages of his youth, an impoverished youth, without ideals, full of hunger for everything with which body and soul can be nourished. And to every page he spoke the words: 'Stay a while – you are so beautiful.'

Nothing stays. There was an impatient hoot from the taxi outside. We are not put into this world to look back. We've got to be on our way, to our destination, or upwards – or down. What we can't do is stay put. Heinz got up, said a few words to the impatient chauffeur, handed him some money, then went back into the shop.

Frau Quaas was back in her shop and standing on a chair with a lit match in her hand to light the gas lamp. As soon as Heinz entered, she dropped the match, which glowed for a moment on the ground, then went out. Frau Quaas, still standing on the chair, moaned: 'Oh, please, please go away! This is torture . . . Please go.'

'Me torturing you . . .' he said uncertainly. Then quickly after: 'Where's Irma? I just want to say a few words to her.'

'She's not here, she's staying with relatives. It's true, Heinz, really.'

'Please tell me where Irma is, Frau Quaas. I must speak to her.'

'You can't. She's in the country near Hamburg . . . No, I'm not giving you her address. You nearly killed her once and—'

'Nearly killed her,' he repeated. The words seemed to him meaningless.

He stood, Frau Quaas still above him on her chair – it was almost completely dark now. From time to time she struck a match mechanically and dropped it before she could light the gas.

'Sneer if you dare!' she cried indignantly. 'You must have known my daughter was in love with you. You kissed each other, didn't you? She almost died when you didn't come all this long time.'

'Frau Quaas . . .' he begged.

She wouldn't listen. 'That night when it all started she came home at four o'clock in the morning, she'd walked all the way from Dahlem. When I got her to bed she was shaking so and her teeth chattering I thought she'd caught a chill and I got her a hot-water bottle. But she said: "It isn't that, Mother, he loves someone else, and that's the end of me!" ' On her chair the old woman was weeping.

'I'm very sorry. I didn't know, Frau Quaas, that Irma took it so seriously. '

She stopped weeping. 'No, of course you didn't know, Herr Hackendahl! You never thought about it at all. You kissed Irma, she told me so herself, but then someone else came on the scene and you forgot her at once. Was she serious? You couldn't care less! You're only interested in what's serious to you. Just as I said – you're a bad lot!'

'Good evening, Frau Quaas,' said Heinz Hackendahl. 'If you write to Irma, tell her I'm very sorry.'

For a moment he hesitated, his hand on the door latch. Then he said it after all. 'I'm not wicked, Frau Quaas, only weak – for the present at any rate.'

Before she could reply he had gone.

§ XI

And yet here he was back again in the villa, in the dining room, eating roast beef with fresh vegetables. However, the pale girl with the black Madonna coiffure did not eat roast beef, because she never ate 'before', whatever that meant. Hardly a word was being spoken. Sometimes a spoon clinked against a plate – otherwise there was silence.

We're like conspirators, he thought. But what are we conspiring about? He looked at Tinette. She was twirling her wine glass so that the wine danced round inside it, and she was watching this with a soft, enigmatic smile. Then he glanced over at the strange Fräulein. Her face, he noticed, was thickly powdered and the painted lips shone like blood; he felt as if he were sitting opposite a woman who had risen from her grave.

'I went to Irma's this afternoon, Tinette,' he said loudly, to break the spell.

'Yes, Henri,' she replied absent-mindedly. 'It's all right.'

Then there was silence again.

Erich returned from one of his mysterious errands, the embodiment of brotherly love. From the hall strange sounds were heard, sometimes shrill, sometimes soft, and Heinz almost jumped out of his chair. Then he remembered that this must be the violinist tuning his instrument . . .

In what was almost a whisper his brother reported that the servants had left. 'They have leave of absence till tomorrow. Minna will clear the table when we've finished, then she'll go too.'

'Good,' said Tinette. 'We're ready. Do you want anything more?'

Erich looked over the dishes as if he were considering what he would like. Suddenly he made a gesture. 'Thanks, no more . . . May I show you to your room, my dear Fräulein?'

That girl, thought Heinz, walks like a queen. No, rather as you walk in a dream, when the body loses all weight and you feel you can fly. She walks like that.

Tinette and Heinz were alone.

'What's the meaning of all this?' he asked almost belligerently, in an attempt, and a vain one, to exorcize the spell which bound him.

'Yes, we must seem very mysterious,' said Tinette and laughed. Then she got up and led the way into the hall.

A big, flaming, very bright fire burned in the fireplace. At quite a distance from it stood three chairs – the table in front of the fireplace had been taken away – and the huge Persian carpet in its soft colouring was like a summer field.

'Sit down, Henri,' said Tinette, pointing to one of the chairs.

He sat down.

She stood beside him. Again he saw that enigmatic smile which seemed to dwell in the expression of her eyes. Her fingers closed round his wrist, felt for his pulse.

'Is your heart beating too?' she whispered. 'Feel how mine beats!'

She guided his hand to her breast, which was warm and sweet; remote and mysterious was the beating of that other heart . . . He shut his eyes. There was that song again, the magic song of his own blood, with which the whole world seemed to be joining in.

'I'm going now, Madame,' said Minna.

Heinz opened his eyes. The maid was standing by the door, her face expressionless.

'All right, Minna,' said Tinette. She kept his hand on her breast; the mysterious smile still dwelled in her eyes. 'Don't forget to lock the front door. Goodnight, Minna.'

'Goodnight, Madame.'

Minna had gone. Tinette put his hand gently on the arm of the chair. 'Where's Erich?' she whispered.

Going to the middle chair, she sat down, leaning forward and fixing her eyes on the flames. Now and then a piece of wood fell with a thud into the grate and the flames leaped up in brightness, casting radiance on a face which seemed to shine from within – the most beautiful face in the world.

I shall never love any woman like this again, thought Heinz. And in this moment I love her more than ever.

Erich was back. He glanced at his brother and Tinette, both gazing into the fire from chairs widely separated, and he smiled. 'She's coming.'

'Splendid, my friend,' replied Tinette, without looking up.

Heinz turned round. 'I wish you'd explain,' he said crossly, 'the meaning of all this. Who's coming? Why have the servants been sent away? Why all this secrecy?'

'Didn't Tinette tell you?' Erich was pretending to be surprised. But good liar that he was, his lying was still sometimes clumsy.

Heinz noticed immediately. 'Go on, pretend!' he said ungraciously.

'I consider it very charming of Tinette,' replied Erich, imperturbably courteous, 'to want to give you so pleasant a surprise. But it's nothing mysterious, Bubi. I can tell you all about it. My dear boy' – he bent down close to Heinz and whispered as though he didn't want even Tinette to hear – 'my dear boy, you're to have a wonderful experience. The young lady you saw just now is the most beautiful, gifted and celebrated dancer in Berlin. And she's going to dance just for the three of us . . . She dances Chopin, Bubi!'

Heinz looked flabbergasted. Was that all? Then why this secrecy? Dancing to him meant nothing more than the kind of trotting up and down which he had seen in nightclubs recently. 'All right, Erich,' he said. 'Charming of you! Now I understand why she wanted no more roast beef.'

Erich made a furious gesture.

Heinz sat back in his chair and looked with a superior, challenging gaze at his brother, who now no longer appeared friendly but very angry.

'You still don't understand,' said Erich. 'She doesn't just dance like that . . . But—' He broke off and again looked at Heinz secretively.

'But?' he asked provocatively, feeling that, despite everything, his brother had still not told him all, and really was keeping a secret.

'But, well, she dances . . .' began Erich hesitantly.

'It's time!' a voice suddenly called from Tinette's chair.

'It's time!'

Tinette was lying back in the soft hollow of her chair, her mouth half opened and her eyes tight shut. It looked as though she were asleep – as if she were talking in her sleep.

'Time!' she called a third time, almost singing, but what it was time for, that she didn't say.

'Yes, it really is,' said Erich. 'Excuse me, Bubi, but you'll see for yourself now. Perhaps Tinette too will—' He did not finish the sentence but sat down in the chair on the other side of hers, out of sight. It was quite still in the large hall, though occasionally a log in the fireplace crackled, sending up very red sparks.

Heinz, though annoyed, nevertheless found himself sharing the expectancy shown by the others. To dance, all well and good. But neither Erich nor Tinette would make such secretive preparations for a bit of dancing. Servants were to leave the house, and Tinette would also . . . Erich had said.

He was just about to speak when he heard the violinist (the blind violinist) playing . . . but just listened. Clear and silvery the sounds – Heinz, as if he had been called, now turned his head. She was coming down the stairs, the stranger, the woman with a regal air who had made him see for the first time that the upright posture of man is divine and distinguishes him from all other creatures . . .

With heavenly rhythmic limbs she descended – and she was naked, utterly naked. He shut his eyes. Was it a dream? No, she was naked . . . of course she had to be naked . . . for one who can walk thus, moving so harmoniously, all garments are a clog and hindrance.

Down the stairs she came like a white flame – beautiful, silent, noiseless – passed close to Heinz and stood in front of the fire. Upstairs the violin began to call, to allure . . . With bent head she stood as though listening to her own heart, motionless as if, like Heinz, she heard the call of the violin not from without but within.

What was happening? Had she stirred? At what sound? She swayed, her hands moved, her arms glittered through the air – and all was over . . . The white flame leaped and yielded; a flurry of wind seemed to blow her down and away. But again she was there, whiter and more regal than before. Then – miraculous! – with feet together, immobile, she yet seemed to free herself from the earth, to rise, ethereal . . . What was that?

Why has she stopped? She stands there, listening, while the violin sings on. She is tranquil and is waiting. Light dances over her body, caresses her hips, lifts a nipple out of the darkness and is swift to brighten the arm she now raises, beckoning, luring . . .

Heinz turned his head. Whom did she beckon? Whom did she lure?

Tinette – Tinette had risen from her chair. Slowly, as if asleep, she was taking off her clothes, one after the other, and letting them glide to the floor. Down slipped her skirt, to lie round her feet like a husk shed by a silver fruit. Slim and white she stood . . .

I must shut my eyes, he thought. I can't bear it. I don't ever want to see her like that, I'd never be able to forget it.

However, he continued to stare at her, watched her standing – a silver, dreamlike figure, actually descended from the clouds, the anxiously guarded Venus of his boyhood dreams.

What enticement, invitation, in the violin now! The world was saluting her, Life calling. What we had dreamed came true and was beyond all our dreams.

The two women swayed nearer, stretched out their hands – but, as if something had come in between, one glided away while the other sought to reach her. Again they approached. Gentle was the violin, the soft crackling of the fire . . . And now they were held in each other's arms.

Embracing thus, each seemed to be searching the other's face, the other's eyes – for what? And both were smiling as Tinette had been smiling all evening . . . a smile ancient and sad, knowing the transitory nature of all things, the futility of desire.

Didn't they know how they were smiling? Far too close they were, body against body, breast on breast . . . closer, closer . . . They no longer held each other in their arms. They were pressing against each other . . . No, I don't want to see that! We've all had our childhood paradises, but we had to come out of them, because mankind doesn't live in paradise, and doesn't want to. Man wants to work with other people!

But if we no longer live in paradise, do we have to stoop so low as a result? No, I don't want to see it. No! Go away! I disliked you from the beginning – you with Madonna-like hair – I knew you were evil. I won't have you clasping her like that, pursuing her with your mouth. Erich, she belongs to you. You tell her she shouldn't. You tell her – I can't.'

In this moment Erich turned his head, just as if Heinz had actually addressed him. 'Well, Bubi, how d'you like it? Did we exaggerate?' And he looked at his brother triumphantly and with scorn.

Heinz rose. He wanted to reply – no, he wanted to go away – and yet he could not take his eyes off this woman who now came slowly, very slowly, towards him.

'I want to go. I must go . . . I . . .'

'Bubi,' she said, laying her hand on his shoulder. And under that soft touch he gave way as if a fist had struck him, and he knelt down, while her hand played very gently in his hair. Pressing his face against her body, he groaned with desire and despair. He sensed the smell of life and of life's transience . . .

And he hears a laugh.

Does a violin laugh like that? Can a violin mock a man like that?

The lights went on – all the lights had been turned on to reveal him, the seventeen-year-old Heinz Hackendahl, kneeling before a French whore and kissing her naked body as though it were the holy tabernacle itself. And in the door stood his brother and the wretched dance woman, laughing at him, mocking him, mocking his pain, his innocence, and his whole life.

'Splendid, Tinette,' cried Erich 'Have you vexed him? Now have him kiss your feet. Oh, I'd love see him licking your feet.'

Tinette, pushed away suddenly, gave a little shriek and fell. Heinz sprang at his brother and the pair, furiously struggling, crashed to the ground, Heinz aiming blow after blow at that dissolute, impertinent face. And felt, as he did so, that only a brother can be struck like that, because of what is in truth detested in oneself – one's own softness, weakness, cowardice. It was a real fight. He wanted to beat his whole past with his fists, to beat himself clean again, just as silver is beaten clean. He hardly noticed the women dragging and clawing at him . . . Only when his passion had spent itself did he get up – to go without heeding anything, without looking back.

In the lobby he slowly put on his coat, the beautiful tailored coat he had bought with his brother's money. He adjusted his tie, put on his hat. His pale face with its staring eyes looked back at him from the mirror. He tried to smile but didn't succeed.

His hand felt for the switch. The light went out and with it his face in the mirror. Then he unfastened the security chain, opened the door and stepped out into the frost-cold, frost-hard January night.

He took a few steps, but when he reached the street he remained standing. He looked back once more at the house. There it was, lit up here and there, a stately building of fine aspect, of a certain unostentatious wealth.

That's where he'd been a guest, for many weeks. Weeks of torture! A guest? He'd been a prisoner there! And he knew with total certainty that he would never go back there again. No matter where his life might lead him, he would hardly be likely to enter the villas of the rich again, for the purposes of bloated and lecherous pleasure. The escape had come from within him. The prisoner had freed himself. From the sick cravings of his master, the slave had made the tools that had broken his own chains.

He looked at the villa once more and went. Went free.

§ XII

The collecting of firearms was over – this task Professor Degener could no longer allot to the returned wanderer.

'That's finished, Hackendahl,' he said with a thin smile. 'You would have missed it. You were quite far away, weren't you? All arms must now be delivered up to the government. Unauthorized possession is punishable with imprisonment up to five years or a fine not exceeding a hundred thousand marks. And of course I do not possess a hundred thousand marks.'

'You delivered up the arms to the government?'

The professor smiled again and gazed at his slender hands. 'There are no more weapons, Hackendahl,' he said gently. 'I hear from your comrades that there are no more in the whole of Berlin; doubtless they have been handed over in accordance with the law. No, I think it would be quite a good thing if, after your sojourn in a far country, you occupied yourself with your exam. The written part begins in a fortnight.'

Heinz made an exasperated movement. 'I'd like to have a real task, Herr Professor. Something to absorb me. I feel so empty . . .'

'Well, well, that's always the case on returning. Work is uncongenial – that is how they put it. In any case, simple hard work would be worth the sweat of a Hackendahl. I hear not very favourable rumours in certain circles about a certain pupil.'

'Do understand me, Herr Professor,' urged Heinz. 'I'd like to have a real aim in life. Something I can devote myself to completely.'

Professor Degener nodded. 'Certainly. Fine! Fine! By all means. But the point is, I know of nothing of that kind. Your schoolfellows asked the same thing when the arms-collecting came to an end. I was only able to tell them to wait and be patient.'

'But . . .' began Heinz Hackendahl.

'Quite right,' his teacher interrupted. 'But youth has no patience for waiting. It wants to reap before it has sown. Very well – but your first task, Hackendahl, is to take honours in your final.'

'But I can't do anything with it,' said Heinz despairingly. 'My father has no money to let me go on studying.'

'Idiot!' said the professor fondly. 'You're to take honours for your own sake, not in order to be able to study – you should also be able to study with very average honours – but to demonstrate to yourself that you can achieve something. Tell me, my dear pupil, exactly what have you achieved in your life?'

'Nothing,' said Heinz miserably.

'Once again, idiot,' mocked the professor. 'Lose five places, master Hackendahl! With your education you were still unable to achieve anything in life at all. But now you've got to pass your Abitur. That is your first task in life, master Hackendahl. And you're going to do it for me most excellently! I—'

'I—'

'Silence! Which of you students are so pursued by the Furies that you dare interrupt the flow of your teacher's words! I promise you that, notwithstanding your achievements in the dead languages, I myself will fail you in Latin and Greek should you not be well grounded in other subjects.' He laughed scornfully. 'You'll be flunked ignominiously, Hackendahl.'

Faced by so much determination, Heinz began to feel hot under the collar. He was at that moment vividly conscious of certain problems – problems which had also not remained hidden from his teachers. 'If I fail,' he said with a certain defiance, 'I'm done for. My father can't afford to send me to school for another year.'

'All the more necessary for you to make a special effort,' said the professor dryly. 'Surely you don't mean to founder in the first squall – always supposing this is the first . . .'

Professor Degener was silent. He had always been a man to call a spade a spade, and he would have deemed it unworthy to spare out of sentimentality the wounded feelings of this extremely undisciplined lad. These wounded feelings hardly resulted from a very noble battle – you only had to see the poor lad's sickly pale face and frightened eyes. Professor Degener displayed all his sympathy for youthful stupidity, but he was without a trace of sentimentality.

Nevertheless he did not press him too far, but continued encouragingly: 'Task number one, then – your examination! And to judge from what you tell me, task number two seems already indicated, which is to do something for your parents. You're strong and healthy, you've had a good education – my dear boy, you will quite naturally and without any fuss get a job for the first time in your life and learn how difficult it is to earn the money which your father has provided for you every day for seventeen years.'

Heinz Hackendahl was silent. He had come as a penitent, dreaming of performing great deeds in atonement. He had thought of his fatherland in danger, had dreamed of sacrifices, of heroism . . . And now he was told: take your examination and earn a living. He was terribly disillusioned.

'You don't like the tasks I set you?' asked the professor. 'My dear Hackendahl, I see bad times ahead – even worse than those we have been through. Each one of us will find it difficult to establish order and cleanliness in his own little locality. I'm afraid no one will be free from obligations, but will most probably lack the strength to fulfil

them. I know very little of your personal circumstances, Hackendahl, but I should say there was quite a number of problems, even in
the more restricted family circle, for an enterprising young man to
solve.'

The teacher stopped talking and waited. But Heinz wanted to go
on. He had big ideas in mind.

'Hackendahl, be honest with yourself! I can read in your face that
you know of plenty to be done. But these tasks are too small for you.
You talk of Germany – but isn't it possible that you are not quite big
enough for that – just at present? And then, dear fellow, just think.
How can the body be healthy if its cells are sick? Make your cells
healthy first, then we'll see . . .' He stretched out his hand to him
over the table.

'I expect to see you from now on daily in school, and actively taking part in your lessons. Then we'll speak again, Hackendahl, after
you've passed your exams. After you've passed your exams, is that
understood?'

§ XIII

And thus it was that Heinz Hackendahl returned to school. For a
while, he had travelled widely and lived in an unhealthy, feverish
atmosphere. However, he had eventually found the strength to escape
the swamp, and now returned to school with his fellow pupils.

In the beginning he found it hard, just as he found the meagre
food of Wexstrasse hard, after the luxurious fare in Dahlem. However, just as his body adjusted itself in a few days, his mind soon got
used to performing the tasks given him, instead of trying to antici-
pate the wishes of an almost sadistic woman. Sometimes – in the
breaks, sitting with the others on the benches, when they clattered
the lids of their desks up and down, used their favourite, exaggerated, odd school jargon, and were generally quite rough, with slangy
language and fisticuffs – he was overcome with the memory of how,
as a young man about town, he had sat in a French fashion house,
perched on a bar stool, and watched a beautiful woman doing her
make-up.

Then, with other eyes, he suddenly saw the immature, pale, ill-shaven, spotty faces, and listened with disgust to their dirty jokes, and smelled with equal horror the general atmosphere of hunger and unwashed bodies. Is it really worth it, he asked himself. Life could be so much easier.

But then, just at that moment, Professor Degener would enter the classroom, and he would recall the expression – although you fall in the mud, you don't have to remain lying in it. Or else he experienced a shudder at the thought of that easier life. Then he accused his enemy, Porzig, of once again cruelly leaving him behind with his history tables instead of helping him with them. 'And, you miserable wretch, if you go on like this, you'll find that you and the whole class will be put to shame and flunk your Abitur. Then you'll be despised by everyone, and be ripe for the public noose and a grim squint up at the gallows!'

'However thick the rope, there is always some hope!' Porzig whispered, with a shifty look, the opening lines of a Frank Wedekind poem from a popular anthology.

'Of course that doesn't mean that all ropes break,' chimed in a couple of secret Norns.

Then, altogether in a choir, stamping their feet, and clattering their desk lids: 'Other way round – most ropes stay sound.'

'Have you gone mad, class?' shouted Professor Degener, entering the room like a flaming firebrand. 'The whole First Year will go to church behind the Sixth Year – because you are more childish than those little milksops. Hackendahl, what are you grinning at? Only an idiot grins; a real person laughs. Everyone sit down! Häberlein, try and explain to us why Plato . . .'

Yes, Heinz Hackendahl had come home. Once again he was wearing his old school uniform – worn smooth, much repaired and much too small. Once again he was wearing ugly field-grey army undergarments and badly cut shirts. He completely neglected his manicure set, although he still cut and scrubbed his fingernails more often than in 'olden times'.

He had feared that his comrades at school would make satirical remarks about his backwards metamorphosis from iridescent butterfly to colourless larva. However, with the amazing sensitivity of adolescent lads – the most tactless of social groups – no one said a word about it. He once again belonged to them totally. He was one of them. They seemed completely to have forgotten that he hadn't participated in what had been one of their most important activities – collecting weapons. He took part in their heated disagreements as if he had never been away, and was listened to, and laughed and sworn at, like all the others.

They had many, daily and very heated disagreements, in almost every break. The National Assembly had met in Weimar. It had made Fritz Ebert President of the Reich, and chosen black, red and gold as the colours of the new German republic. But these were comparative trivialities, much as one could argue over them.

For them, the main question was: how would the war end? What would the peace look like? That was the question that stirred them. Many different things were said in the National Assembly, but very little was spoken about peace. Of course, it was said that Germany would never accept an enforced peace. There was also one deputy who announced that any hand would wither who signed a 'slave' peace . . .

But even the rare strong language which came out of Weimar was also heard with suspicion by the youngsters. They had learned the Latin phrase '*Principiis obsta*', which in German means 'Resistance from the start'. And they considered that, right from the beginning, no resistance had been offered. They considered that the government constantly protested, but, despite such protests, always did what it had just said was impossible. The youngsters heard the 'No' loud and clear, but were totally sceptical, as were the whole people. 'We don't trust them at all,' they said. 'We've been lied to by those above us far too much in the last four years.'

The lads talked about all these things in the school breaks, and on the way to and from the dormitories. They talked about it in their school jargon, spicing their sentences with Latinisms, and were not shy of using expressions like 'colossal' or 'right as rain'. They had rough voices and often curly hair on their chins. If the war had continued, they would have gone to the Front. Now they were just youngsters, pupils, but their interest in what was going on was none the less.

Ten years earlier a generation had immersed itself in Hof-
mannsthal's poetry, made fun of Eulenburg's *Rosenlieder*, and generally
got hot under the collar over the question – airships or aeroplanes.
But all within bounds. All very moderate. That was an overfed, aes-
thetic generation who tended to flirt with the idea of beauty and
suicide. (The very word 'suicide' was a bit too much for them; they
called it *Freitod* – 'free death'.)

The new generation, brought up in the critical hunger years, was
of stronger metal. It proved the truth of the saying that the fruits of
poor soil are healthier than those of rich soil. This new generation,
which had only experienced the war at home, always felt it had been
deprived of something in life. It was not content to be deprived any
longer. It followed all events with alert senses and ever-wakeful
mistrust.

Heinz Hackendahl joined them. He had returned to his comrades, to his generation. (Erich, although only four years older, was
definitely from the pre-war generation.) Already after a very short
while, Heinz found it miraculous that he had devoted time every day
to the care of his fingernails. It was not long before he felt the strong
aversion of youth to the painted women of the Tauentzienstrasse.
His heart hardly missed a beat when he thought of Tinette. On the
other hand, he sometimes thought for a long time about Irma.

§ XIV

Professor Degener had also shown acute insight into such matters,
when he had asked Heinz Hackendahl to be patient, in that he would
soon hardly be without tasks to perform. He was right: there was at
that time no lack of things to do. Heinz Hackendahl took on his
share.

One morning, towards the end of February – it so happened that
there was no school that day, probably because of another strike, or
a protest – Heinz was awakened by a prolonged ringing at the door.
In any case, he was still in bed. His father was away driving the horse
cab and his mother was queuing up outside some food shop, once
again making her swollen legs worse. Diving into his trousers, he put

his coat on over his nightshirt and shuffled through the icy flat in his slippers. A woman stood outside and he had to look closer before he recognized her as his sister Eva – the once so pretty, fresh and rather provocative Eva. 'You, Eva? Come in.'

She, too, hadn't recognized him at first, not so much because he had changed as because she herself seemed very excited and rather drunk. She was leaning against the wall. Her face, which had grown fat, trembled; her discoloured eyelids twitched. 'Where's Mother?' she demanded. 'I must speak to her at once.'

'Mother is out shopping. Do come in, Eva.' He led her into their parents' bedroom – the only place where there was the slightest degree of warmth. She sat down on the bed and looked round . . . 'Where's Mother?' she repeated anxiously. 'I must speak to her at once.'

'Mother has gone shopping,' he explained again. 'Can I do anything, Eva?'

She seemed not to hear him. She was certainly drunk but her drunkenness was as nothing compared to her agitation; she was so excited that you wouldn't notice any more that she was drunk. 'What shall I do? What shall I do?' she murmured to herself.

For a moment she laid her head on the pillow and closed her eyes, as if about to fall asleep from utter exhaustion; but she started up again, rose from the bed and, paying no attention to Heinz, wandered about the room, stood in front of the chest of drawers as if she was on her own, and pulled open the upper drawer. She took out some of the papers there, held them in her hand and scrutinized them as if trying to guess what they could possible mean.

'Eva!' shouted Heinz from the oven. 'Eva!'

She wheeled round. 'You, Bubi? What is it? I wanted to speak with Mother . . .'

'Mother's gone shopping, Eva,' he said for the third time. He approached her, gently took the papers out of her hand, put them back and said: 'Do tell me what you want? Perhaps I could help.'

'What shall I do?' she asked again, despairingly. Her gaze was fixed on him but there was no change in her expression nor, in spite of her misery, did any tears show in her burning eyes. 'I must go away.'

'Where to, Eva?'

'Away from Berlin.'

'Why must you go?'

Into her gaze came something like terror. 'Why?' she whispered and fell silent.

'Come, Eva,' he said gently, taking her by the hand and leading her back to the bed. 'Come, lie down. Wait, I'll take off your shoes. You're cold as ice. There – now cover yourself up with the blanket. Is that better?' But though she let him attend to her she made no reply.

He took her hand again. 'And now tell me why you must leave Berlin.'

She didn't answer, but a different expression came into her eyes. She looked around her like a child. 'What's this?' she asked. 'Am I in Mother's bed?'

He shook his head.

'In Father's?'

He nodded.

She laughed, laughed abruptly and hysterically. It was just as if she were shaken by sobbing. 'There!' she said, pointing. 'I was born there. Twenty-three years ago. And now I'm lying in Father's bed. Won't Father be pleased to know that a whore's lying in his bed!'

Her laughter just as suddenly stopped and she opened her handbag, searching. A key, a powder box, some change slipped from the bed – she paid no attention. 'Read that!' she said, handing him a page torn from a copybook. On it was written in a child's clumsy hand: 'The Fir Tree. The fir tree grows in the wood. It is our German Christmas tree. No nation celebrates Christmas so beautifully as the Germans do. The fir tree . . .'

'Can you understand it?' she whispered, not taking her eyes from his face. 'No, no – the other side!'

He turned the sheet over. On the other side, disregarding the lines, was scribbled: 'You bitch, you shot me dead but I'll get you.'

Nothing else.

He looked at her.

'Can you understand that?' she whispered again, her lips trembling.

'No. Who wrote it?'

She looked at him. Finally, after a long pause, she whispered: 'He did.' She seemed afraid even to whisper.

'The man I heard about at Tutti's?'

She nodded.

'Well, what's it mean? You're not going to let yourself be frightened by that nonsense, are you, Eva?'

'It isn't nonsense.'

'Of course it's nonsense. It—' He broke off. He saw that she was struggling with a decision.

At last she murmured: 'But I did kill him. I fired right into his face. I was standing in front of him.'

'But, Eva, if you killed him he couldn't write to you. And if you haven't killed him it's nonsense for him to say he's dead. If you really did shoot at him you must have missed.'

'I shot him dead. I saw it go off in his face.'

'It's impossible, Eva . . .'

'Not with him – nothing is!'

He thought again. Then he sat down beside her on the bed, took her cold hands between his and said coaxingly: 'Tell me everything, Eva. Perhaps I can help you – I may be able to.'

'Nobody can.'

'Yes, perhaps I can.'

'You could, if you had the courage to kill me! Oh, Bubi, I've thought so often – if only someone had the courage! I'm too cowardly to do it myself. But I wouldn't be too cowardly for that. I promise you I wouldn't run away. I wouldn't even cry out.'

'Please, Eva, tell me just how it happened. You shot at him, you say. Why? One doesn't shoot a man just because he's bad. You're my sister. I know you. Such a thing must have been very difficult for you.'

She nodded, half listening. She'd gone back to her former thoughts.

'No,' she said. 'I'm not to die. I'm to die only through him – when he's tortured me enough. You know, Bubi,' she said feverishly, 'you know, it all happened some time ago, the shooting. And afterwards I didn't know what to do. I drank all the time. I'm drunk now. But even if I were dead drunk . . .' She was silent a moment. Deep in his own thoughts, lost in his own memories, Heinz unthinkingly stroked Eva's hand.

'So I thought I must find peace,' she continued. 'And because I've never found peace in life, I thought I must die. Then I heard they were planning something against the sailors, and that evening I crept into the Imperial stables. And I'd hardly got there when the Noske soldiers began to shoot. They shot at the Imperial stables with cannon, and they began to burn quite merrily. But when I heard all that – the shooting, and the cries of the dying, and how the flames leaped up – I went half mad for joy, because I thought that now I would die too. And I danced and sang in front of the soldiers, and helped them with their guns, and they said: "The little one is right." Because the other women had to be locked in the cellar. But no one knew why I was like that.'

She was silent. Then she said: 'And it did me no good, after all. Once again dying escaped me. When it got to the stage when everything was burning, and the crunch came – they just surrendered! And they dragged me out with them, no matter how much I pleaded. No, it's fated to be like that – either he dies through me or I through him. And the probability is that he'll be the one to do it.'

'Do what? You said you killed him.'

'Yes, right in his face. He fell as if he was made of lead.'

She considered for a while. 'Do you think, Bubi, that Mother will give me some money to go away with?'

He looked at her thoughtfully. It seemed to him as though she were more confused than a drunken person should be; had she crossed the borderline between sanity and madness? He didn't know, and he also didn't know anyone he could ask. He could only ask her. Cautiously he started to question her and gradually wormed out the story, from the theft at the Stores down to the bullet in a Dahlem villa hardly five minutes away from that other house.

And, as he listened to the account of how his sister had come more and more under the domination of an evil person, it seemed as if she were describing his own recent sufferings. 'What was I to do, Bubi?' she demanded passionately. 'I couldn't do anything at all – and sometimes the worse he behaved the more I somehow seemed to like it. But you can't possibly understand.'

Heinz, however, nodded. 'I can, Eva, I understand only too well. You're pleased when something within you is killed and you say to yourself: that's what I wanted. The sooner everything goes to blazes the better.'

'Yes, that's right,' she cried, and carried on spiritedly with her story.

However, when Eva had finished, and began to accuse herself, Eugen, her father, God and the world in general, Heinz had to consider what was best to do, what he himself could do, and the extent to which she could help him do it, and how much depended on her. Going away, running away – out of the question! They had no money, neither she, he, nor the parents – that was the first thing he had to emphasize. And nothing could be achieved by it anyway; even when she had thought Eugen dead she still hadn't been at peace but had wanted to die, too. She had taken to drink in the hope of forgetting. No, first of all the truth about the shooting in the villa must be ascertained.

'If you had really killed him, Eva, the police would have arrested you long ago, you mustn't forget that.'

Here, however, Heinz had made a false move; to Eva's fear of Eugen was now added fear of the police and of courts and of prisons – more than ever did she want to leave Berlin at once, and if she couldn't do that, then she wanted to change her address at least. She knew a dozen places where she could stay without registering.

With deep astonishment Heinz realized that Eva had as much fear of the police as if she were still the respectable daughter of a respectable citizen. He had been thinking of persuading her to give herself up so that, by paying off the old debt – the theft from the Stores – she need have no further fear of Bast's threats. But of this there was now no hope. Getting out of bed, Eva hurried into her shoes – she must move on the spot! Perhaps the police were looking for her already.

So the first thing Heinz had to do for his sister was something quite against the grain, a flit in a taxicab – hasty packing, hints big as bricks given to the other girls in between tots of spirits, whispered enquiries of the landlady about other landladies – a flit which the most stupid policeman could have tracked down without any difficulty. Heinz, however, was at least able to help with the packing,

watched by the girls, some insolent, some inquisitive; quite unblush-
ingly they discussed him with his sister and decided that he was still
rather young. He thought so too and went off to the laundry where,
with a great deal of trouble, he got them to hand over the washing,
wringing wet though it was. 'My sister has to leave town urgently.'
The laundress grinned; she knew quite well what sort of a sister his
was and that urgent departures in such cases were customarily made
in green police vans.

But at last they found themselves in the taxi, Heinz somewhat
irritated by all this slovenliness and haste; he would have preferred to
clear up matters rather than confuse them still further. Eva, however, smiled suddenly (the tots had had their effect), and declared
that she was glad to have left, because the old woman charged a
great deal too much for board and lodging . . . And besides, the
Tauentzienstrasse was not the right beat for her – only the youngest
and smartest got on there. North, in the Tieck- or Schlegelstrasse, it
would be easier. Didn't Heinz see she was getting wrinkles already?

And then she started to weep. How old she looked now! Besides,
with one foot in quod and the other in hospital a girl's life wasn't
worth living . . . But it was all Father's fault; if he hadn't shouted at
them so much she would never have taken up with Eugen.

Heinz listened gloomily. He was wondering whether the task
which had awoken him that morning was actually a task at all or
whether this whole business of Eva had not been settled a long time
ago, and for good.

§ XV

During the following weeks Heinz was perpetually asking himself
this question for, in spite of his endeavours, things became more and
more involved, although Eva seemed hardly to suffer under this;
confusion and disorder might have been her element.

Later, however, he ceased to worry himself with doubts. Professor Degener had once said that he had to create order in his own
small circle, to master the small tasks before the big ones. He tried to
do that. If he felt very depressed, he tried to imagine how there were

thousands of people in Germany who were engaged in slowly building up the war-damaged country, stone by stone, little by little, with
great patience. It all begins with the healthy cell, said Professor
Degener.

I clear things away, thought Heinz, and pursued his fruitless ways,
ignoring his sister's reprimands – even thinking with smiling superiority: all your resistance won't help you. I'll get you out of this mess
even against your will.

It was not so easy. After school he would go about trying to get at
the facts concerning the shooting, enquiries which had to be made
cautiously for he dared not go to the police – how could he be sure
that Eva was not implicated in other of Bast's crimes, as well as in
the jewellery theft? She'd never tell the whole truth.

At first it seemed very interesting to run round Berlin like a
detective in a thriller and track down what might turn out to be a
notorious criminal – certainly a blackmailer, robber with violence,
petty thief, gangster, *souteneur*, perhaps murderer – well, that was
sufficient, quite sufficient, thank you!

But it was not so interesting to wander night after night accosting
every street girl or letting oneself be accosted and then, after the
usual silly talk, to bring up the subject of a certain Eugen, 'Dark
Eugen' as he was called. There seemed to be quite a number of Dark
Eugens in the profession.

While he continued to live like that – always in a rush, getting
paler and paler, thinner and thinner – the world went on its way.
They began to sell off the merchant fleet, and there were big protest
meetings against the enforced peace. The National Assembly also
spoke, though more moderately, against the enforced peace. There
was uproar in the Ruhr and a general strike in Württemberg. The
first national congress of the unemployed met in Berlin, and the first
national budget was drawn up, involving fourteen million marks, of
which only half were missing. In Munich a Soviet republic was set
up, and the War Minister in Dresden was shot dead by the
war-wounded. But the First of May was declared a holiday, strictly
according to the Social Democratic Party programme, and an official Easter message was announced: 'Put an End to Self-Destruction!
Go to work!'

In addition, there was a general strike in Brunswick. In fact there was a tendency to strike almost everywhere.

While all this was taking place, when so many terrible things were happening, no one any more felt that something terrible was terrible.

Moreover, he had at the same time to prepare himself for his final examination, and pass it – which he did, just scraping through. And this was not what Professor Degener had expected of him. But he'd had a meeting with his favourite teacher. He reported to him. The professor had shaken his head and murmured: 'That's not exactly what I meant by creating order . . .' But he'd let him through all the same.

'What will you do now?' his schoolfellows asked.

'What do you want to be?' wailed his mother.

His father said nothing, but his look was explicit enough.

Heinz Hackendahl, however, had no time just then to occupy himself with such matters. First Eugen Bast had to be found – that nightmare, that bogey, that living corpse!

And found he was. Heinz came to see Eugen Bast face to face. Nor was this finding of him to prove difficult, requiring detective abilities. The way of it was this. One day, when Heinz was sitting in his sister's room, the landlady brought in a young lad. 'Isn't Eva in? The boy says he's got something for her.'

'Eva must be at Olga's. She's only just gone,' said Heinz and looked at the lad without, so far, any suspicion.

He was about thirteen years of age and watched Heinz with a timid yet sullen expression. Then he grinned. 'You her chap?'

'Yes.' Heinz held out his hand. 'Show me what you've got.'

The lad grinned again and shook his head. 'What'll you give?'

Heinz was far from wealthy at the moment – as a result of his search for Eugen Bast nearly all Erich's splendid suits had vanished in fares and tips – so he offered a mark.

A shake of the head.

'Two.'

'Nix.'

'Three marks.'

'Fork it out,' said the lad, taking a slip of paper from his trouser pocket. Heinz handed over the money and read what was written on the paper, which the other did not let out of his hand.

'A hundred marks,' was written there, 'or ashtray.' Nothing else.

What 'ashtray' signified he knew from Eva, but this was not the same handwriting as in the first note. 'Eugen hasn't written this,' he said. 'Well, anyone can say that!'

'I wrote it,' explained the lad. 'But Eugen told me what to write.'

'Why didn't he write it himself?'

Heinz seemed to have asked a silly question, for the lad grinned, evidently thinking himself very clever. 'Gimme a hundred marks an' I'll tip you why Eugen didn't write it.'

Heinz looked thoughtfully at him. A hundred marks were absolutely out of the question – he hadn't got them. But in any case one thing was certain. Eugen Bast was alive. 'Don't tell her you showed me that note,' said Heinz, snatching up his hat and coat.

'Not such a mug. She got any dough?'

'You must ask her yourself. I'm clearing out.' And Heinz went.

He had to wait a long time in a doorway opposite before the messenger shot out of the house like an arrow. Heinz tore after him. Had the lad suspected anything it would have been difficult to follow him; the chase went in the direction of the Oranienburger Tor, then down the Friedrichstrasse – Heinz on the other side of the street – past the station and across Unter den Linden.

There were many depressed-looking people about. No goods had yet appeared in the shops – Germany was still subject to the blockade. Yes, it had even been tightened up . . . But one thing was there in superabundance – poverty. Beggars lined the great thoroughfares, leaning against the walls, squatting on mats, hawking obscene postcards; nearly all of them were war-wounded or at least claimed to be such, if one went by the placards on their breasts. During the four long years of war, people had become accustomed to the sight of maimed men, otherwise anyone finding himself unprepared amid these horrors might well imagine himself in hell . . .

Armless and legless – trousers pushed up to show the thick purple or red scabs on the stumps – there they sat, the mutilated, those with faces terribly scarred and burnt, those with missing jaws – horror upon horror. The shell-shocked, groaning pitifully, shook heads or arms; with perfect regularity a man in field-grey knocked the back of his head twice a second against the wall – a hundred and twenty times a minute, seven thousand two hundred times an hour – and the back of his head was one enormous wound. People saw it. The police saw it. The government saw it.

Although the dollar was already worth fifteen marks, instead of four marks twenty before the war, the word 'inflation' was still widely unknown. People spoke of price increases. A pound of bread cost twenty-five instead of fourteen marks, butter three marks instead of one forty. However, apart from the rich, no one could buy as much food as he wanted, because all life's necessities were only available with coupons in very small quantities, so the price increases did not make themselves immediately felt. People would have been willing to spend more money, if only there had been more products to buy.

The government stuck to the fiction that a mark was a mark. The war-wounded received their small pension – but in fact they often received nothing at all because their reduction of income had first to be calculated. However, because the war-wounded also wanted to live and many could not work, they took to the streets. In groups of three, five, ten they went up and down the houses, sang in the court-yards, made music. Or else they sat at major crossroads, selling shoelaces and matches, or begged. The government and the police could only look on. They couldn't order people to starve in silence.

It seemed incomprehensible that they could all live by begging, that an impoverished nation preoccupied with its own troubles could every day provide money enough to make it worthwhile for each one to sit there. Of course, those were best off whose wounds were unique, that is to say, were the most horrible – and therefore had the most powerful effect on the passers-by.

And it was in front of such a uniquely wounded man that the lad had stopped. This man might have been young, but there was no means of saying; the whole face was an immense scar with terrible black edges running into each other like the frontier lines on a map. Of the lips there was hardly any trace; the nose looked as if burnt black; most horrible, however, were the shrivelled eyeballs without pupils.

The beggar, leaning against the wall of a house, kept his face to the passers-by and, as if that and his placard ('War-Blinded') were not enough, at regular intervals, without altering the pitch of his voice, or any accusation, he said over and over again the one word: 'Blind. Blind. Blind. Blind . . .'

And in this word 'Blind' there was something terrible, something more terrible than a lament – it was like the soulless ticking of a clock. The word seemed drowned in the street noises and yet people in a great hurry, in a very great hurry, stopped and put money into the hand held open against his chest.

Never a word of thanks did the man say nor was a sign given that he felt the money in his palm. Uninterruptedly he called: 'Blind. Blind. Blind. Blind.'

Even now, when his messenger stood beside him whispering, he went on as if this word 'Blind' were spoken without his being conscious of it, something automatic, like breathing or a beating heart. 'Blind.'

Heinz crossed the road and stopped in front of that terrible face. He took no notice of the lad looking at him in terror, but said in a low voice: 'Hackendahl.'

The scarred face, more ghastly than ever at close quarters, did not change; the burnt mouth continued its speech. 'Blind. Blind . . .' But the lad's face was distorted with pain. He was trying to run away but could not; the blind man's foot was pressed down on his foot. Inescapable, agonizing.

And on seeing this Heinz Hackendahl knew the man to be Eugen Bast, Eugen Bast as Eva had described him, the tormentor whose sole response was to punish the boy without enquiring whether betrayal had been intentional or not. Eugen Bast the destroyer of Eva, and her victim – Heinz now saw the result of that shot.

Emotion akin to hatred rose in him. 'Take your foot away,' he ordered, trembling with rage.

'Blind. Blind. Blind,' said the man, his foot remaining where it was.

'Take your foot away,' repeated Heinz. And, nothing happening, he placed his own foot on the beggar's.

'Blind. Blind. Blind.'

Money rattled in the blind man's hand. People looked at the

terrible face, not at the foot. The coins were swiftly stowed away and
the hand was out again. 'Blind. Blind.' The foot remained where
it was.

It grew obvious that this man would never give way; he would
rather let his own foot be crushed. So Heinz withdrew his. Unmoved,
the beggar went on with his 'Blind . . . Blind', but a minute or two
later the lad was released. He looked ill with pain, yet he uttered no
sound, nor did he flee – and it seemed so easy to flee. It must be
some nameless, indefinable fear which bound this lad to his tormentor, a fear mixed with strange hankering, the fear to which Eva
had succumbed.

Heinz was young and inexperienced; he had no idea how to deal
with a man like this – he had thought the matter quite simple. He
would, once Eugen was discovered, threaten him with the police and
penal servitude; then the fellow must soon realize that it would pay
him to leave Eva in peace. But – here stood Eugen Bast and Bast had
immediately made it clear that he was not to be threatened. He
would always only behave as the evil in him told him to, even when
he harmed himself.

'Blind. Blind.' It went on and on . . .

What am I to do? thought Heinz in despair. Even if I fetched a
policeman . . . I used to think it would do Eva no harm to be in
prison a year or two. But as soon as she saw his face at the trial she'd
fall under his influence again and try to get him off by taking the
blame on herself . . . Eva was correct. Flight is her only hope. But in
that case she'll drink herself to death. Would Sophie give her money?
Sophie's sure to have some.

'Blind. Blind.' Coins rattled, the hand went into the pocket, was
held out again. 'Blind. Blind.'

Oh, once upon a time Heinz Hackendahl had thought that life
was quite simple. But, either life was much more difficult and dangerous than before, or he himself was useless. He was through with
Erich, just managed to scrape through his Abitur, and again done
nothing for Eva.

'Blind, Blind . . .'

Heinz gave a side glance at Eugen Bast. He would have liked to
clear off, throw the whole thing up; he had bitten off more than he

could chew. And yet something kept him there. He couldn't go away like that. It would mean losing all self-respect, all confidence in his own powers; he had the feeling that he would never get anywhere in life if he fled now without having carried out his task. He must do something.

While he was thus brooding and spurring himself to action the repetition of 'Blind . . . Blind' ceased as if a clock had stopped. What was happening? Did Eugen Bast always go away in the mornings between eleven and twelve, just as the rush of traffic and pedestrians started? For Eugen Bast was certainly leaving. He had placed his hand on the boy's arm and, without Heinz being able to notice any communications pass between them, the boy now led the blind man away – Heinz following – down the Friedrichstrasse. Although they were just in front they paid no attention to him – even the boy never once looked round – nor did they speak. Obviously it was their custom to leave at this time.

Suddenly it occurred to Heinz that he could at least give Eva the news, and he retraced his steps. Should he ever want Eugen Bast he could always find him, though there would be little need for that now. For he was able to tell Eva that Eugen Bast was no dead man, no haunting ghost, but a beggar whom she had blinded. No need to tell her how terrible he looked; the thing to emphasize was how helpless he had been rendered through his blindness and how easily she might avoid him. And he would assist her to move again, with more precautions this time, so that she could live in peace from his threats; it was ridiculous to be blackmailed by a blind man. Ashtray indeed! Even if he were in the same room she could laugh at that. All she had to do was to walk out.

Heinz was suddenly sure of victory; his task was accomplished. He did not consider how readily he had given up trailing a man whom he had sought for weeks, nor did he remember that in Eugen Bast's presence everything had appeared hopelessly insoluble. No – away from Eugen Bast all was well. He wandered up the Friedrichstrasse again. About to cross Unter den Linden, however, he bethought himself that this was an inconvenient time to call on Eva, being the hour when the girls, always late risers, began to gather in one another's rooms. It would be better to wait a while. Then he could speak with her alone . . .

So he went along Unter den Linden, through the Brandenburger Tor, into the Tiergarten. It was April. In spite of the devastation and neglect there was still some greenness to be seen in the park. Not all the turf had been trodden into slush. And though the flower beds were empty, Heinz in one corner discovered, half hidden under a bush, a few crocus blooms.

He knelt down beside them and saw that some were yellow, some blue and white, just as before the war. So there was something as it was before – these crocuses! People have changed, no one can be the same. But the flowers have remained. There was something comforting about this stupid thought – stupid, he thought, but comforting all the same. It was like the promise of the impossible – that people could also be the same as they were before. While looking at the crocuses Heinz thought briefly of Eva, and for longer of Irma. Had Irma – he tried to recollect – had Irma ever possessed a yellow or blue or white dress? Then he admitted that this was all nonsense, not worth the least thought, and that he only wanted to kill time to delay talking with Eva.

He sighed and stood up. He would have liked to take a flower with him, but it somehow didn't seem right. Not that he particularly respected the Tiergarten, which for many had long been the place for collecting firewood. No, he just didn't want to appear before Eva with a flower at that moment, which would have immediately made him think of Irma. So he went without a flower.

Thus it was that, entering Eva's room, he found someone had stolen a march on him.

There sat Eugen Bast on the chaise-longue, his fingers clutching the boy's arm as if he were about to march off at any moment. In no way did he give the impression of being as helpless as Heinz had imagined.

With a white face Eva looked up from the trunk she was packing, glanced at her brother, compressed her lips and went on with her work.

The blind man, hearing the door open, had turned his head to listen. Once again he seemed not to receive any information from others. 'Your brother, you whore!'

'Yes, Eugen,' said Eva – and by her tone Heinz knew he had lost what little influence he had.

'You got anythin' to tell your brother, whore?' said Eugen (and Heinz was frightened at the false amiability of that whisper).

She looked at her master with helpless anxiety.

'Eva,' said Heinz, took her by the chin and turned her white, forlorn face towards him so that she had to look at him. 'Come with me, Eva. Don't do what he wants. All he wants is wickedness, he's wicked; tell him to go. You can live anywhere. I promise I'll get the fare today to Leipzig or Cologne – wherever you like. Don't forget he's blind. He can't follow you.'

Eva did not stir. It was impossible to tell whether his words had had any effect.

The blind man on the sofa nodded. 'Brainy, your brother,' he said kindly. 'Brainy! Didn't get it from you, you tart! Chap's right, I'm blind – so clear out.' He sat there screwing up his helpless mouth, as though that were his laughter. Suddenly he shouted: 'Clear out, fool. I can't follow.'

Eva drew back from her brother. 'You're not to abuse Eugen,' she muttered. 'I'm going with him, Heinz. I'll stay with him.'

. 'Will you?' sneered Eugen Bast. 'Thank your brother for it, Evchen. He's brought us together again. Say "Thank you", stupid.'

'Thank you, Heinz.'

'Don't hang about then, get ready. Yes, brother-in-law, I was going to let her go. She's too much of a bloody fool, your sister. An' now that she's taken up shootin'! . . . I'd have milked her a bit every month, so as to keep her on the jump, jus' to ginger her up in her profession like . . .'

'Eva,' begged Heinz, 'please come. Go with me to the police – it won't be as bad as you think; the judges will realize that you couldn't help it, it was he who made you. A year or two in prison, with nobody there to torment you as he does, and then you'll be free, you can start afresh . . .'

There was no reply. As if she had heard nothing his sister went on packing. Eugen Bast spoke, however. 'Well, when you was standing next to me, brother-in-law, with your beetle-crushers on mine I thought to meself, well, what's wrong with having a girl to look after me, eh? The other blind men have got dogs. Well, I've got the sister of the young gentleman who's exercising himself on my plates o' meat. I bet that'll please the young feller when he sees his sister making herself useful . . .'

'You hear,' cried Heinz, 'you hear how wicked he is? Eva, he'll torture you to death!' At these words she shot a penetrating glance at him. What had she once said, in the beginning? Either he dies through me or I through him. Was that her hope?

'Young feller,' said Eugen Bast, 'don't talk such drivel! Me wicked? I'm the best-natured sod in the world. You find another chap who'd let himself be shot in the dial like me, with me blinkers gone – and not a hard word.' He passed a hand over his face, exploring his wound. 'The rest tell me I'm no longer a beauty an' I used to be quite the good-looker. Well, she made a proper job of it, so I shouldn't even see me lost looks, what, Evchen? That was yer sense of humour, what?' He laughed.

A moan from her. The blind man turned his head. 'Come here!'

She came, she stood before him, she gazed on the terrible face.

'Tell yer brother – am I handsome in your eyes or am I ugly?'

'Handsome,' she whispered.

'Still fond o' me? Still love me? Out with it!'

'Yes.'

'Tell him.'

'I still love you, Eugen.'

'Show yer brother – gimme a kiss!'

She bent over the blind man, and Heinz Hackendahl no longer saw them . . . He saw himself with Tinette, and Tinette looked good – but if what looked good was good, as the ancient Greeks said, she was as ugly as Eugen Bast. He saw his own enslavement, his own masochism. Once more he was humiliated, once more felt his own shame.

'Eva!' he begged.

With her lips touching the dark-grey scar, she looked at him – a quick look, almost a smile. A soul in torment. It will pass, her smile seemed to say. Pain passes just like pleasure. In the end, when it's all over, it doesn't matter what's happened to you. Pleasure or pain . . .

No! no! he thought. I don't . . .

Eugen Bast pushed her away. 'That's enough of acting,' he said. 'Get ready. And you, young feller, you c'n go straight to the police – we'll be here for quite a while. They c'n come an' fetch us if they like. But you take it from me that yer sister'll be in quod just as long as I am. I'll see to that, an' so will she. An' when she comes out, say in ten years' time, then she's goin' to have a life of it – what she's got now is heaven compared with it. You can depend on that, young feller.'

'Eva,' begged Heinz once more.

But she shook her head.

'And now hop it, young feller,' cried Eugen Bast in a very different voice. 'You're not wanted here. Every minute you stay here, I'll pinch your lady sister a bit harder . . . Eva, come here to me . . . Give us your arm . . . no, the thick part of your upper arm . . . So, young man; can you feel it, Eva . . . ?'

Heinz rushed out of the room. He fled, running faster and faster through the streets. He ran away from the terrible Tieckstrasse house, from the images it conjured up, from his own shame, his own disgrace.

Eventually he found a bench somewhere. He sat there for a long time, his face between his hands; it was still broad daylight. He let his tears run between his fingers – tears of pain, or sympathy – but above all tears of fury over his own helplessness, his cursed weakness . . .

I must be strong, he thought. If only I could change. I must change. Just to be sympathetic is only weak, cowardly. The world has to be changed – and for that you have to be strong!

Such thoughts went feverishly through his head. He imagined a future in which he was strong and capable of destroying Eugen Bast. Only gradually did he calm himself down. When he got up, a sympathetic soul had placed a groschen on the wooden bench beside him.

He looked at it for some time. Strange! On the same day he had seen Eugen Bast go begging, he himself was given money too.

He took the coin and threw it in a bush far away. No! No more gifts. By his own strength! Only by his own strength!

XVI

The National Assembly had repeatedly and uncompromisingly said 'No' to a dictated peace. There had been thousands of protest meetings throughout the Reich. The speakers had shouted their 'Nos' and the crowds had agreed with them.

Then a delegation was appointed to accept the enemy's peace conditions in Versailles.

But a simple delegation was not enough. The enemy demanded ministers, senior civil servants. So they were nominated and went to Versailles.

The people waited; perhaps things would not be as bad as they feared? Perhaps the enemy would show mercy?

With eighty members, accompanied by fifteen representatives of the German press, the German delegation arrived in Paris. They were almost treated as prisoners. No one was allowed access to them. They were allowed to go nowhere. Their base was a strongly guarded hotel. They made them wait eight days, like humble petitioners in a rich man's waiting room, until they were vouchsafed the terms whereby Germans confessed to being a convicted criminal and promised to be enslaved to the others for ever . . .

They left with a document of humiliation and made it public. Again the people shouted 'No'. Again there were protest demonstrations. They exchange views. The hand that signed this treaty should wither. They ring up Wilson, the American President. They ask experts, they beg, they appeal, and even threaten a little. 'Unacceptable,' they say and make counter-suggestions. The German Social Democratic Party unanimously declares itself against this dictated peace. But nothing changes. Opinions are exchanged in vain, the protests die away. Versailles is merciless: 'There will be no negotiations!'

Suddenly the National Assembly says 'Yes'. Those who just said 'No' now say 'Yes'. If the others don't give way, you must give way yourself. If the others insist Germany is guilty and denial achieves nothing, you can only plead guilty. Firmly united, the Social Democrats vote 'Yes'. Firmly united, the Centre Party says: accept . . .

They make a few qualifications a few exceptions . . .

But – 'No negotiations' . . . is repeated.

Then, on 23 January 1919, the National Assembly declared its agreement with the unconditional signing of the peace treaty, its members solemnly assuring each other that they acted equally patriotically whether they voted Yes or No . . .

Two German ministers signed the peace agreement in the Hall of Mirrors of the Palace of Versailles. They had been led like prisoners through barbed wire, watched by a silent and gloomy crowd. When they returned, loud curses were heard. Stones were thrown and empty bottles . . .

§ XVII

Heinz Hackendahl went along the Grosse Frankfurter Strasse carrying two cases. One was light, containing all that he possessed of clothes, linen and shoes; the other was heavier, if not actually heavy, and held his books and whatever else of spiritual treasure had been accumulated during his school years. It was 1 July, and hot. The peace treaty had been signed two days before.

Passing the fence where his father's premises used to be, Heinz stopped at the gate, put down his suitcases and, full of curiosity, peeped into the yard. It seemed to have changed hands again. The great stable had been divided into garages, taxis stood in the yard and a driver was washing down his car.

Heinz nodded. He was not depressed by these changes, even though they meant the end of all his father had been; old ways had to go if the new were to come. There was nothing to be depressed about in that. On the contrary it offered a consolation. Disgrace and shame passed away too. You can get up from the dirt into which you have fallen.

A car entering honked furiously – Heinz picked up his suitcases and walked on, turning into a side street, into a second one, crossing a couple of courtyards and climbing up five flights of stairs.

The nameplate – Gertrud Hackendahl, Dressmaker – was still on the door. For a moment he hesitated. It had been barely nine months since he was last here. But it seems an infinitely long time when he considers everything he'd experienced since that evening – Erich and Revolution, Tinette and Irma, Abitur and Eva . . .

For a moment he hesitated. But then he pressed the bell firmly.

Gertrud Hackendahl opened the door: 'You, Bubi?'

'Yes, me, Tutti – but before I come in with my cases, I want to ask you if you will have me? Do you understand? I want to live with you. I've got a little job at the bank. Perhaps I can help you a bit with the lad . . . ?'

He'd said what he'd planned to say. But it now seemed weak and false. So he added: 'And perhaps you can help me a little too, Tutti? We've got peace now . . . Perhaps you can help me. I think you are the only strong person in the family . . .'

She looked at him, then she shouted and didn't hide her pleasure: 'Come right in, Bubi! – Of course you can help me – with the lad!'

And in he went.

SIX

The Old Cabby

§ I

Old Gustav Hackendahl – we mustn't forget that there also existed a young Gustav Hackendahl, Otto's eldest son, the old man hadn't even seen him – old Hackendahl was finding it more and more difficult to make one horse support two persons, namely himself and his wife. Formerly, before the war, one could even bring children up on the earnings of a single cab if only one chose the right stands and had a horse that inspired confidence.

But who thought of taking a cab nowadays? Couples did in the summer, and drunks at all seasons of the year, while there was also a certain demand at election time, when one could take old and ill people with a sensible dislike of motor cars to the polling station. But what did it amount to? There was nothing else doing nowadays – a horse couldn't even keep itself, much less two old people. Gustav Hackendahl had contracted the habit, as he rattled homewards through the Kaiserallee, of stopping at Niemeyer's, the grain merchants, so as to make sure of his fodder – the horse came first – and he thought it was the end of the world on the day he was forced to give six hundred marks for a hundredweight of oats that hadn't cost more than six before the war. But he had been paying six thousand now for some time and the world still went on, in accordance with the saying: the older the madder. With this difference that Hackendahl had long stopped buying oats by the hundredweight. 'They can say what they like at Niemeyer's, Mother, I'll go on getting my twelve pounds of oats a day! The horse gets ten of 'em and that always leaves two over for the Sunday. I look ahead now.'

But even looking ahead didn't help. Often Hackendahl had to drive past Niemeyer's with his head averted, because he had no money, not a single person having stepped into his cab all day. Then he would stand beside his horse in the former joiner's workshop and make up some feed out of a little hay and straw, while thinking of the old times when oats had been brought down from the loft by the hundredweight – his own oats from his own land – and how fodder master Rabause (whatever had happened to him?) would go through the stable with a full tub of fodder.

'Good times, old boy, good times! Only realize now how good they were. No, I haven't got anythin' for you. You can push your muzzle against me – it's no good.'

Very well, in his old age Iron Gustav learned to cope with any situation. But it was no pleasure any more. Despite all efforts, things didn't go forward but resolutely backwards. What difference did it make if he took on a job or two for Niemeyer, delivering oats, hay and straw? No difference at all. Talk about a joke! – that is if you preferred a joke to tears – there was plenty of bread and plenty of butter now, oh yes, but the four-pound loaf cost twenty thousand marks and you had to put down a hundred and fifty thousand for a pound of butter! Such were the fellows who now ran the regiment. First nothing to eat; then no earnings with which to buy anything. That's what they were like. Somehow they got everything wrong.

Standing beside his horse, Hackendahl would rack his brains, wondering how he could manage to earn a little more money. He moved the dead butt of his cigar from one corner of his mouth to the other. His wife's appearance was a real mess. The clothes hung off the woman as if a beanpole had been dressed as a scarecrow. Mother simply must put a little flesh on her bones. This starvation was a misery. During the war there had been a certain equality in starvation; everyone had gone hungry, or at least it looked like it. Starvation had been regulated by law and by coupon – one had, so to speak, been able to accommodate hunger to circumstances. But now people were starving in an utterly haphazard way. The shops had plenty of goods, for those who could buy them, but people went past the sumptuous windows without even looking, or if they did it was only to ask themselves what they had done to have to starve. Was their guilt greater than that of the gluttons? But such questions didn't help much, and poor people queuing up with flat-wagons on hire didn't help at all. People slaved away for a half a day, and when it came to being paid, they were told: 'It's not exactly convenient today. Come back on Friday when Maxe brings his pay packet home.' The hell with it! If any money was there on Friday, it was only a few farthings, worth only a crumb.

Sometimes his wife said, 'Go to the children, Gustav. Sophie and Erich are bound to be doing well. They won't let their old parents starve, I'm sure.'

But no, in this matter Gustav was of iron. Rather than go to his children he'd prefer the workhouse. Things had got to the point where he could grin about himself, about his children, about the whole world. He, the former sergeant-major of the Pasewalk Cuirassiers, had brought up five well-fed children. But the five children, all of them better educated than their father, couldn't feed the two parents. That was what he was grinning about.

'Well, it's the way of the world, Mother. An' it's no good me changing it. Sometimes I see Erich rushing past the Zoo in his car. But he don't see me! And he's quite right. What's the good? Here's me in my old moth-eaten coat and there's him in a nifty sealskin what d'you call 'em – well, it don't go together and God didn't mean it to. No, Mother, you be glad that they've left us in peace. We ain't dead of hunger yet and we'll manage somehow. And Heinz still comes . . .'

Yes, Heinz still came. He came regularly once a week to supper, because his father was at home then, and he brought his own food, which was the proper thing to do when visiting nowadays. And what he brought was so ample that it left enough over to provide his parents with their lunch on the following day. Which must be accounted to his credit, seeing that he himself was far from prosperous. With sorrow his mother saw that he was still wearing the same overcoat in which he had left home four years ago.

But, in reply to her questions, he would laugh and say: 'I'm getting on all right, Mother, don't you worry. We old people can manage. The main thing is to look after the children.'

'Fancy you concerning yourself about the Gudde's brats, Heinz!' (To Frau Hackendahl Otto's wife was always the Gudde, even though she had to some extent forgiven her, once just by sending her some cutlery.)

'They're marvellous kids, Mother. You let them alone. Life wouldn't be any good without them. With them there, you know why you do all the work.'

'Shush! Your father!'

But here things had improved a lot. One could now venture a word or two about the grandchildren; in fact old Hackendahl would sometimes mention them himself, even though in a far from friendly way.

'Ain't one o' them really got a hump, Heinz? You're kiddin'. Even if the hump's not visible, it's there inside 'em – I'll eat my hat if it ain't.'

'Then eat it, Father!' smiled Heinz, and went on talking about it, no matter how much Mother signalled him to stop. It wasn't easy to upset Heinz these days, twenty-two years of age as he was, but calm and collected, and as set in his ways as an old man.

'No, I can't tell you, Father, what's going to happen to our currency. I'm only a bank clerk, you know. Probably the mark will go on falling and the dollar rising, especially now that the French want to occupy the Rhineland.'

The old people said nothing.

'And what am I going to feed my horse on?' asked the father after a while.

Heinz reflected. He knew that it was not so much a question of feeding the horse as of feeding two other beings. 'I'll tell you next time, Father,' he said at last. 'Perhaps I'll find something.'

But the next time he came his father was out, which was just as well since he hadn't found anything in spite of all his endeavours. But – to make up for that – his father had. His mother was very worried and stressed. 'You'll see, Heinz, it'll only end up with Father going on the drink again, just as he did when Otto was killed.'

But Heinz had confidence. 'Father's quite right! You'll see, Mother, he'll earn something, and he's suited to the work. And don't worry about the drink. Father's far too proud ever to become a drinker.'

§ II

On a good day in these bad times, Father Hackendahl found a travelling customer, with long legs and teeth like a horse, at the Zoo
Station. The man, who immediately planted his feet on the front seat
of the cab, while leaning back on the back seat, demanded to be
taken round town by Iron Gustav. 'What did you say? Two hours,
ending up at the Schlesische Station at twelve!'

It was a dream fare, a boon – a real blessing, an Englishman – no,
as it turned out an American, who wanted have a look at Berlin as he
passed through. Under Hackendahl's guidance, he took a thorough
look; in other words he tried Berlin's beer, wine and schnapps very
thoroughly. And if at first he entered a local bar like a quiet American, with a 'Just a moment, please', the more he approached the
centre of town and the eastern part, the more its sociability embraced
him, and Father Hackendahl had to accompany him no matter what
kind of place he entered.

He was a great fellow, with a face as white as snow, completely
unaffected by alcohol, with long, flaming-red hair. Over there, in his
alcohol-dry home country, he must have developed a manic partiality
for bottles. He couldn't be without them even for short stretches in the
cab. He put them in his coat pockets, he piled them up on the front
seat, and he surveyed them with bleary-eyed but good-humoured
looks, shaking them tenderly. And when they glugged, drinking from
the bottle, he laughed.

It was a lucky fare, but a difficult one. It was lucky that at least the
old nag didn't have a taste for alcohol. (They once tried to quench his
thirst with cognac, but he refused.)

By some miracle Hackendahl really was in time for the twelve
o'clock train from the Schlesische Station. But the American insisted
that 'my friend Gustav' went up to the platform. So they were both
carried up the station stairs, each by two porters, in a state of height-
ened and enhanced jollification.

The pain of parting came with the arrival of the train. They
embraced each other, and a porter picked up Hackendahl's bowler
from under the train. Another porter held his whip, while the two

other porters propped up the parting friends. America invited Gustav Hackendahl to go with him a bit of the way, till Warsaw. And if it hadn't been for another porter, who kept on reminding him of the old nag, he would perhaps have done so. As a parting present, the American received a bottle of Mampes bitter schnapps from Hackendahl's coat pocket, as did each of the porters – which they then had to give back, because the compartment looked much too cheerless and lonely without them.

In turn, the American emptied out all his German cash, and Gustav even got a genuine American ten-dollar note. After the station master had made a to-do about the to-do, he was so tipsy himself that he gave the signal to depart two minutes late. Then the train got under way, with a large pair of brown shoes hanging out of a first-class compartment, went round a curve as it left the station and disappeared – towards the border, Warsaw, Moscow and certainly numerous glasses of schnapps.

Meanwhile, the porters carried poor Iron Gustav down to his cab, put him in the corner, wrapped him warm with blankets, hung the old nag's nosebag round its neck, and kept a watchful eye on the carriage the whole afternoon. Because the Schlesische Station was then a real vulture land, and vultures notice every corpse, especially if it has an American ten-dollar note in its pocket.

It was in this state that Gustav Hackendahl awoke, after undisturbed sleep, with a well-rested, if slightly numb, head. Yes, it had been a real inflation fare, he thought on his way home, a fare normally only paid to the wretched autocars. But of course it was only an exception, and would remain one, and ten dollars would not last three hungry mugs for ever. No, from that alone Gustav could not feel so happy. He shoved his cigar (genuine American) from one end of his mouth to the other and wondered and brooded over why he actually felt so happy.

He remembered he had had an idea, and sometimes his brain flashed far away from it, but he didn't get any further. When his brain so registered, he noted that it had to do with the fact that he was Iron Gustav. However, that was pure nonsense, because everything had to do with the fact that he was Iron Gustav. Without him everything would stop – as far as he was concerned anyway. If I'm

dead, everybody's dead, he thought comfortingly, for it was a very
pleasant feeling.

The old nag trotted on happily – down Lange Strasse, Warschauer
Bridge, across Alexanderplatz, through the Königstrasse to the
Schloss. Gustav had actually wanted to go home via Unter den Linden
and the Tiergarten, but in the end he pulled on the left-hand rein and
went 'the back way'. He went zigzag hither and thither, round corners and back round corners. And the more corners Gustav
negotiated, the clearer his head became, and when he stopped in
front of the cellar bar in Mittelstrasse, he remembered what a splendid idea he had had in the middle of his intoxication, and nodded
fondly and familiarly at the sign outside.

The sign bore the inscription 'Rude Gustav's', and the history of
the wine bar was this. The average Berliner, as is well known, is a
highly sensitive creature and one very easily offended yet, at a certain
stage of intoxication, this self-same Berliner is extremely fond of
rudeness and is then simply dying to have his sensibilities trampled
on. Down Rude Gustav's narrow staircase would stumble not only
unimportant people such as clerks and tradesmen but the leading
representatives of industry and intellectual life – merely in order to
be treated rudely in the cellar. It was extraordinary what a happy
sigh rose from some chief councillor of the Board of Finance when
Rude Gustav in his red waistcoat greeted him with the words, 'Well,
old sleepyhead, it seems you've gone and put your face in your pants
and your backside in your face again today, what?'

In addition to the greatest crudeness, this bar boasted wooden
tables, and everything informal – the gents was called the Knights'
Castle and the ladies Dripstone Cave, which aroused the imagina-
tions of the men and reduced the women to giggles. In addition,
every half-hour there was a guided tour through the chamber of
horrors where you could admire the enema syringe used by Conrad
the Hard to scatter his enemies at the Battle of Popocatapetl. You
could also see a genuine crocodile tear, Abbess Fringilla's chamber
pot, not to mention the Nuremberg funnel for pouring knowledge
into children's heads, and a lock (horse hair) from the head of Karl
the Bald. Then there were the seven lanterns (kitchen lamps) of the
seven foolish virgins, and – in accord with the times – the curse on

the hand that signed the Versailles Treaty. Not to mention the dirty jokes the men took the opportunity to crack at the sauciest remarks. Because it's fun to let the mask of decency drop for a bit and to speak to other men's wives as if they were your own . . .

Such, then, was the bar into which Iron Gustav stumbled on that happy afternoon. And once again he was lucky. Because he even met the landlord and owner – Rude Gustav himself – although the place was actually a night bar for drunks.

The two Gustavs, Rude Gustav and Iron Gustav, sat down at a table together. Iron Gustav talked of his American and quietly waved his ten-dollar note. Rude Gustav had the afternoon melancholy of innkeepers, and at once began complaining about the cut throat competition in rudeness. Inflation, like a good hen laying eggs, had deposited all over town rival haunts proud of their rudeness, and every mediocre boor seemed to feel himself competent to insult customers.

All this was grist to Hackendahl's mill. From a normal cab driver, he changed himself into Iron Gustav (of whom Rude Gustav said that he had heard), and in a very short time the two Gustavs were shaking hands in agreement. Iron Gustav was to sit at the large round table by the entrance all evening and part of the night, with a glass of beer and a brandy before him – the real cabby with his long coat, shiny hat and whip. The part he was to play was that of the embittered, old-fashioned driver, rude to those who arrived in cars, and thus encouraging them to drink to entertain them. In a word he had to supplement with authentic Berlin humour their somewhat crippled capacity for enjoyment.

And in exchange Gustav Hackendahl was to have free drinks (but in moderation) and two hearty meals, one when he came and the other when he left. As for what was spent by the guests at his table, here he was to have ten per cent of the bill, as agreed upon between the Iron and the Rude Gustavs and confirmed by handshake.

Ten, even five, years ago Gustav Hackendahl would have laughed in contempt had someone asked him to play the buffoon in a wine bar – now it was he who offered. There had been the war; that army which had been his pride existed no longer; the empire that was his mainstay had broken down miserably; none of his five children had done anything to be particularly proud of. He himself might have thrown in the sponge or have grown harder. He did something else. He laughed. It was a disease of the times. Before the war people had been told (and they believed it) that mankind was good, helpful, noble, full of faith, painstaking, dutiful (and ought to be so). Now they said: mankind is bad, murderous, lying, swinish, lazy, ignoble – and this too was believed. They were even proud of it. It cheered them up – cheered them up, to be sure, in a crapulous way, grinning as though they had swallowed vinegar, an-end-of-the-world cheerfulness (and for the older generation the world actually had come to an end).

Therefore Hackendahl didn't regard himself as the hired buffoon of others; no, he wanted to poke his fun at them, he wanted to tickle their drunkenness so that when the vulgarity came out, he would be able to think: it wasn't only me who had the bad luck. They're none of them any better than my own children, they're all baked in the same oven, soft on one side, burnt on the other and doughy in between.

That's how he'd thought it out when his fantasy had been fired by the Irish-American's drink. And even if he later forgot most of what happened, Iron Gustav never did think of himself as a professional joker. Yes, he could afford to grin when he looked around, for things went much better than expected. The table of the 'Original Berlin Cabby' was rarely unoccupied and Iron Gustav, after he had trained his black horse, achieved a kind of fame in Berlin nightlife, for it turned out that those who got intoxicated at his table invariably wanted him to drive them on to the next place, Rude Gustav's being rather a port of call than a destination. Since he was supposed to be a cabman he had better drive as well. But the landlord did not at all relish the round table being without its chief attraction for an hour at a time perhaps, when even half an hour counted a lot in a place that had little more than six worthwhile hours in twenty-four.

Hackendahl, however, had another idea. He trained the black horse so that when he called 'Gee-up!', instead of advancing, it backed in the shafts, crab-fashion, and forced the vehicle against the kerb. And the more the driver shouted and cracked his whip the more unmanageable did the black horse become – until it at last lay down in the road. Then there was nothing for the guests but to get out and look for some other means of conveyance, which they always did with the greatest of good humour. Indeed, it was rare that Hackendahl was not handsomely compensated for the fare he had thus missed; so everybody was satisfied – landlord, customers, cabman – and it is to be presumed that the horse (now called Blücher) also enjoyed the fun.

Heinz had been quite right to comfort his mother. The business at least brought money into the house; after only a short time, Mother's clothes began to look less ill-fitting.

And yet Heinz had been wrong. For Iron Gustav, there were dangers. He had been a man of perhaps restricted vision but with an ideal according to which he had shaped his life, in obedience to the dictates of honesty, work and duty. Now, however, he became every day more of a cynic, one who did nothing but scoff. To be sure, he did not neglect his obligations. There was his wife at home – her wants had to be attended to – and let the atmosphere in the wine cellar be as lively as it liked, every half-hour he went out and saw that the horse was properly covered, fed and watered as it should be.

But all this he did more out of habit than from a sense of duty. He hadn't a single thing to do. His world was shattered – bit by bit, till nothing remained. Ten years before, he would have been horrified by a life of such cynicism and empty bars. He couldn't have led that life. He would have been incapable of entertaining his guests. Now he could do so.

It was precisely that which he and others called iron. His insistence, for example, that he could still drive a horse cab, despite the fact that everyone knew that the era of the horse cab had gone for ever. But that wasn't iron, that was just old. Had he been younger, he would have been sitting behind the wheel of a motor taxi long ago. What seemed iron was that he didn't chase after his children any more, or want to see his grandchildren . . . But that too wasn't iron, but his age. A younger person gets up after a fall and tries once more, but Gustav Hackendahl never wanted to love anyone again – Eva gone! Erich gone! Never again!

No, all that cannot be called iron.

And yet there was something indestructible – a life force. He never winced, he never complained, he lay on his bed as he'd made it, but also as others had made it. Naturally – without giving it a thought. With a powerful endurance, a matter-of-fact endurance. He had no realization of his sufferings and would have turned purple with rage, roaring the place down, had he been told he was of iron only in his endurance . . .

But there came an evening when even this virtue seemed about to forsake him, when endurance itself seemed impossible, and when everything in him seemed empty.

§ III

It was not an evening out of the ordinary for the people of Germany – but it was also a particularly bad evening for them, who had become used to such bad days and evenings over the last years. It was the evening of that day when passive resistance had been decided on in the Ruhr. The Cuno government had proclaimed a Day of National Mourning and had called upon the German people to prepare for sacrifices, and to renounce luxury and high living. But, doubting the effect of this appeal, they had ordered all places of public entertainment to be closed at ten o'clock at night.

Not for a long time had the centre of Berlin been so crowded as on that evening; people seemed possessed by the devil of contradiction. Having been ordered to go home by ten o'clock they made a point of going out at precisely that hour. That was a result of the period that had just passed. They mistrusted every government, and every order. They had completely lost all trust in anything. The police had to bear the brunt. No sooner had they chased the people out of one place than they crowded into the next. This the police emptied and in the meantime the first place was full again. Behind closed shutters, behind locked doors, sat those who were rejoicing at this chance of snapping their fingers at the government and the police.

But meanwhile, French and Belgian battalions were marching on the Ruhr. They took possession of the drinking places, the mines and the factories, and they occupied the banks, having confiscated the money. They also confiscated – in the middle of the coldest winter – coal deliveries to hungry, freezing Germany, and they imprisoned anyone who didn't carry out their orders. Into a densely populated part of the country they brought extreme misery and the worst death. At the end of the battle for the Ruhr, a hundred and thirty-two people had paid with their lives, and countless had lost their freedom; a hundred and fifty thousand people had been expelled from their homeland, and the damage to the German economy was estimated to be four milliard gold marks.

However, Berlin celebrates – but mourns when it wants to, not when ordered to. The worse things get, the more we'll celebrate; when things are really bad we shan't be able to celebrate at all – we'll be dead.

At Rude Gustav's they were at first uncertain whether to shut down or not, but by ten o'clock the place was more than half full and in those days of devaluation a landlord was not inclined to eject patrons simply because they wanted a drink at all costs. So the windows were darkened and a couple of lads sent out to do their best to fill the bar by the back door, through the courtyard.

Gustav Hackendahl sat alone at his round table; it was too early for him to play his part yet. At this hour most of those present were couples; he could see them sitting in dark corners where possible, or at least separated from the next couple by a vacant table. A dead cigar in the corner of his mouth, Gustav was sleepily discussing the evening's prospects with his namesake and what would happen to a landlord and what to a cabman should the place be raided, and whether Marshal Retreat, the black horse Blücher, wouldn't be giving them away by standing outside.

By eleven o'clock the bar was crowded. Over and over again the door leading to the service rooms and the coal cellar opened to admit guests who, bewildered by the dark entry, looked surprised to have got there at last. Then he was slapped on the shoulder. 'All right, fatty, are you here too? Your friend Olga is already sitting back there by the pillar. What? I would never have known! It's your wife! Couldn't you have been a bit clearer and given a hint? Then I'd know straight away to be more careful. Well, it's too late now. Fancy our fatty as a philanderer! What do you think of that, my good lady?

Blows his own trumpet occasionally, says he has an important business meeting. But haven't I seen you before somewhere, my good lady? Weren't you sitting over there with the bald-headed fat man, kissing his pate? My, how wonderful love can be!'

So the old jokes were churned out, to the thankful laughter of the guests whose dim flame of matrimonial love was thereby a little fanned into life. Then, when the wine list was placed before them, the silence which could be heard . . . 'Spot of Rhine wine? Oh no, you don't, there's only champagne going tonight. D'you think I'm risking me licence and quod for the sake of a thimbleful? Stop being so mean; you don't behave like that with your girlfriend . . . Well, hurry up, man, the dollar won't wait.'

Suddenly a new batch of visitors was admitted and this time it was for Iron Gustav to receive them. 'Eh, chaps, shove the silver away. These nobs only eat with silver knives and you don't want to pay for a stomach operation to get 'em back again . . .' Settling himself in his chair – one hand round the stem of his glass, his whip in the other – with the shiny hat over his brows and his head sunk on his chest, he looked the genuine article, a cabby dozing off in the warmth of a bar.

And indeed he felt like dozing. As through a fog he heard the new arrivals, the waiters, the landlord talking. Then a rather unctuous voice called out: 'Champagne? Of course! Champagne!' Something was slapped down on the table. 'Money? What's it matter about money? Get rid of it! There's plenty more where this comes from. No end! You can just go on dipping into their pockets for ever – long live all suckers! Champagne!' Then the voice was lowered. 'You, landlord, get that old cabby away from our table. Why's he dossing here? He should sleep it off somewhere else. Anyway, I can't stand cabmen, I've taken a dislike to them.'

Old Hackendahl had by now realized whose voice this was, in spite of its having changed so, and for a moment he thought of stealing away; but he had never been a coward, and wasn't one now either. Pushing his hat back off his forehead and blinking in the light, he looked across the table at his son Erich who, all his intoxication suddenly leaving him, stared back at the old cabman with the grizzled beard, baggy, bloodshot eyes and stained blue greatcoat. He had turned pale. His tongue refused to speak, he wanted to jump up from the table. Yet he could not free himself from that unrelenting gaze. For his father continued to stare at his son with big round eyes, across the table on which the waiters in their red waistcoats and shirtsleeves were ranging bottles of champagne in the coolers. Nothing in his face showed he had recognized his son . . . had recognized in that puffy white face, with greying temples and thinning hair, the Erich of old, his hope and pride, the possessor of charm and ease, the quick-witted lad whom he had locked up in the cellar for throwing away four gold coins on women . . . Now the son was sitting between two women under the eyes of his father, one of them with a white arm over his shoulder; the father could see they were obviously local girls dragged up from another bar.

And all that was over in a moment – just a *moment*, in which the past went by. Nine years had flown by since they had seen each other, and now they met again. Time passed, life rolled on, an autumn wind tore the last bright leaves from the branches. Now it was all over, all wrinkled and dead. Yes, it had been just a moment in which both recognized that everything was irretrievably over. And the guests had hardly noticed that the jolly Erich Hackendahl had fallen silent.

And the old man was already in his role. 'Well, young feller, what's up, eh? What've you got against cabmen? P'r'aps you had to gather horse dung orf the street for Ma's allotment, what? And that's why you've got a grudge against the cabbies. Chuck it, man! These days you've got the stink of petrol from the cars instead. It's just the same. Only you don't notice it.'

There was no need for Erich to reply – his friends had burst out laughing and the girls from the Maxim Bar (who had, of course, heard about Iron Gustav) hastened to instruct their gentlemen concerning the real position of this odd character. The very fat dark gentleman, the only one of the company to be tolerably sober, merely smiled, however – as Erich's friend and patron he no doubt knew that the young man's antipathy to cabmen was no drunken whim. But it had escaped even the clever lawyer and experienced Reichstag deputy that Erich was startled by meeting his father. He also had no idea that father and son were now sitting opposite each other, and that, misunderstood by everyone, the battle between the two continued.

The champagne glasses had been filled to the brim, the waiters in accordance with the charming custom of inflation bars surreptitiously adding a couple of empty bottles to the dead ones, so as to swell the bill. The trick worked in ninety-five per cent of cases.

The glasses clinked together, and the girls laughed out loud as they lifted them to their lips as the thickset gentleman, in a dinner jacket and with a monocle and duelling scars on his bulldog face, had knocked with a champagne bottle on the side of the cooler. The flower of successful business Berlin began to commemorate the Occupation of the Ruhr, and the man in the dinner jacket spoke: 'Comrades! Respected Ladies! Esteemed cabmen! To what we are – Youth!'

They drank.

'To what we love – the sweet life and all that goes with it!' And he pinched the neck of the girl beside him, who gave a little scream.

They drank again.

'To what we want – that the wretched right-wing Cuno government recovers the Ruhr, so that it's ours again! And soon!'

They drank and laughed. Only the lawyer smiled weakly; he didn't much like such behaviour in public houses.

'And now,' said the gentleman with the monocle, sitting down, 'relate us some amusing episode from your life, respected charioteer. You're bound to have had a lot of experience.'

'I have,' agreed Hackendahl. 'Only, when I'm in company with educated chaps in monocles who plump money down on the table like the young 'un over there, so that all the waiters immediately sharpen their pencils an' get the bill ready – I don't know, out of sheer respect me tongue freezes an', poor ole fool, I go on rackin' me nut without ever findin' out how you folk earn the dough you do while I can't buy me ole woman the dripping for her bread.'

'Don't soak so much, old boozer.'

'When I see that,' said old Hackendahl, pointing to his son who was glancing at him uneasily, 'that's a young chap all right and I ask meself, how's he do it? Naturally he's got education but education don't earn you money nowadays. I ask meself, how do the likes of him do it? I should have been in quod long ago.'

Erich compressed his lips and tried to look threateningly at his father but shrank immediately from the old man's eye.

Some of those round the table protested. 'Dry up, old fellow. We're not here to drink their apple juice and be made fools of by you.'

'The old chap's jealous.'

'No, it's dense I am,' went on Hackendahl. 'I can't an' don't understand it. I'd like to be put wise.'

'You can't be,' said the man in the monocle. 'You've got to be born to it. The gentleman you're speaking about was born to it, that's all.'

'Well, I certainly wasn't or else I wouldn't be actin' the ole fool before you puppies.' Complacent laughter. 'But I'd like to get hold of it all the same.'

'What is it you want to get hold of?'

'Well, how you set about it, profiteering, I mean. People talk of nothing else but I don't grasp it. How d'you pull off a big deal now? I rack me bloody brains but what can I profiteer in? The young gentleman here – I ask him with all due respect – is he a profiteer p'r'aps?' And he pointed to his son.

All except Erich were amused. The girls beamed. In such dens of extortion to be a profiteer was a kind of honour. Money has no smell; that saying was to many their one and only article of faith.

'He a profiteer! Why, you can call him a king of profiteers,' said the man with the monocle. 'He could sell you and you wouldn't even notice it.'

'There you are then! But p'r'aps I'd get to know I'd been sold in time. Young feller,' he was addressing his son now, 'show a bit of kindness to an ole man an' tell me how you get yer money out of the mugs.'

'I . . .' began Erich defiantly. Then he reached out for his glass. 'I find this boring. Can't we go on somewhere else?'

'You can't get away now, young feller. Don't you hear the police whistles outside? What a comedown if you had to go to the police station! It don't matter about me, but then I'm only a common cabby.'

'Hackendahl,' said the man with the monocle, 'let's do the old man a favour and show him how you make money. As a matter of fact I've got something for you.' He reached into the inside pocket of his dinner jacket and brought out what was, for such a well-dressed gentleman, a rather soiled pocketbook. 'Now where was it?' he muttered, turning over the pages.

'Don't bother,' said Erich, annoyed. 'It's all too idiotic . . .'

'Please do be nice, my dear. Here's some real profiteering.'

'A little more caution in public,' advised the lawyer, Erich's patron.

'Do an ole man a favour,' begged Hackendahl. No less persuasively the gentleman with the monocle chimed in. 'And why not? Everybody's profiteering now. The cloakroom attendants deal in cocaine, mothers deal in their daughters, daughters deal in silk stockings on the sly in the big stores – everybody's in the game. And I really have something for you, Hackendahl. I can offer your four trucks Silesia at thirty-six.'

'Oh, not now, Bronte.'

'Silesia? What's that stand for?' asked old Hackendahl.

'Can't say. Potatoes, I think – there's no need to know what you deal in . . . Well, Hackendahl?'

'You don't have to know? Marvellous!' said the old man admiringly.

'Do leave me in peace,' said Erich furiously. 'I'm in no mood now.'

'Very well,' said Bronte and was about to put away his pocketbook when a small, lively-looking man at the table called out: 'Stop, Bronte! Four Silesias at thirty-six? I bid two at thirty.'

'You bid two Silesias at thirty, I offer two at thirty-six.'

'You offer two at thirty-six, I bid two at thirty and a half.'

'You bid two at thirty and a half, I offer two at thirty-five and a half.'

Across the table, the champagne bottles and the glasses they flung their mystic formulae to and fro, while all stared open-mouthed. At the nearby tables people turned round with a smile but their faces soon grew respectful, even grave. It was clear that business was being transacted – and business was a god.

'I'd like to advise against,' said the lawyer, smiling weakly. Then to Erich: 'Quite right, my son . . .'

'So that's how money is made?' marvelled old Hackendahl.

'You bid two trucks at thirty-two and a quarter,' shouted the man with the monocle. 'I offer two at thirty-four and a half.'

The girls goggled and then broke into a foolish laugh.

Old Hackendahl was the only one who comprehended that this jobbing went beyond mystic formulae and profits, and had to do with the staple food of the poor. Potatoes, to which if necessary you only need add a bit of salt, and which are still nourishing. Many a day, till he had become buffoon at Rude Gustav's, potatoes had been the only dish on the table at home and even then had been too dear. And, had it not been that the father was sitting there, Erich would have done the bargaining, Erich, his favourite once.

The two were still yelling at one another, the rest intent on the struggle; the protagonists were now separated only by a half – half of what, the devil alone knew.

Getting up, the old man threw a significant glance at his son and slowly went to the lavatory . . . There he waited. It was an ugly, stinking place. The only good thing about it was the clean water that ran lightly gurgling through the stand-ups. But that immediately became sewage water and filth. Everything clean in this life immediately becomes sewage and filth.

He stood and waited. Then the door opened. But it wasn't his son, it was someone else.

Yes, Erich hadn't changed. His hair was thinner, his face had become puffy – but otherwise there was no change. He had always been afraid to face his father. As a child he would slink off to bed and sham sleep when he had been up to mischief. The water gurgled and ran. The father waited.

Well, it was at least good to know that his son couldn't escape. This was the exit.

Finally old Hackendahl returned. Five tables away he could see his son's back – the lad had always cringed like that when he was afraid of a box on the ears . . . Tapping Erich's shoulder, he said: 'Well, young man, you had something to say to me, hadn't you? Or shall we talk about it here?'

The deal in margins seemed to have been concluded – all were laughing, talking, drinking. Nobody paid any attention to the pair, or hardly anybody.

Erich turned towards his father and the two looked into each other's eyes. Then Erich said quietly: 'It's useless, Father.'

The father looked into his son's eye without blinking. He saw it, as a whole blue but with brown and green flecks, and round it he saw a face a little like his own, ageing and getting puffy. His son's eye seemed so cold, so empty . . . there was nothing there, neither sadness, love, nor regret. For a moment the father's image came to the surface, but the son only had to turn his eye, to look at a champagne glass, or a prostitute, and the father's image was extinguished, as if it had never existed.

The father removed his hand from the son's shoulder. Walking backwards, keeping his gaze on his son (as if wanting his image to stay with him as long as possible), he went to the door. When the door closed, the son breathed a sigh of relief and grabbed a glass. Suddenly he had to laugh. Now it was all over! The old man would never pester him again . . . Erich, liberated, laughed and drank.

§ IV

Old Hackendahl had left the Rude Gustav bar. He'd experienced much with his children, but not yet this. That a son should say to his father's face, 'It's useless, Father' – that was completely new. Now it had got this far. They didn't creep like a coward in front of their father – that had been bad enough. No, now they said to his face that they didn't want him any more!

Old Hackendahl could well imagine that a son who had grown rich might be ashamed of an impoverished father; that was despicable but it was human. With Erich, however, it was not so much that he was ashamed. It was something far worse – his father was less to him than the wench with whom he was sitting or the waiter juggling with the empty champagne bottles under the table. With them he could talk but to his father he had nothing to say, nothing whatever.

That was inhuman, that was little better than patricide. A play like that had had a long run in the theatre. The father clearly remembered reading about it on the advertising pillars when he stopped at his cab stand. So the whole world had been reduced to a play – to nothing but a mean travesty! You had to laugh at the very misery of it.

Old Gustav, without noticing that the beast looked round at him very surprised, took the rug from his horse's back. Blücher wasn't used to his master driving away unaccompanied at that time of night. Where were the fares, then, for whom one had to go crabwise? The driver, however, clicked his tongue and the cab rolled on.

The streets were still full of people, even though the crowd had begun to thin out a little. The police patrols untiringly asked them to move on. But these people were true Berliners; they stopped before the sign of each night haunt and stared. The signs were unlit, the places closed, there was nothing to see, but they waited in the hope that something might happen.

And at last it did. Hackendahl was trying to cross the Friedrichstrasse. Seeing a gap in the throng of idlers, without thinking he said, 'Gee-up!' And Blücher, who knew his lesson well and thought it good fun, reared just enough to check the cab's momentum and then began to push backwards and sideways, like a crab.

Those standing nearby fled screaming; those farther away laughed and approached. Cars honked furiously. Hackendahl, cracking his whip, slapped the reins against Blücher's quarters. 'Go on, go on!' he shouted. 'What's the matter with you? Go on, I tell you.' But the black horse ignored these commands. He wanted to do his little trick. And when an obstinate horse starts backing, the driver on his box has a difficult job. He can put on the brake, he can use his whip; but if the horse insists on backing at all costs, he cannot prevent it.

At this point the ever-helpful Berliners joined in – with the idea of taking the animal by the head – whereupon Blücher, fully prepared for this, reared up and pushed backwards with all his might – after which he lay down right in the middle of the crossing. It was the hour when the traffic was at its worst. Promptly everything came to a standstill, inextricably tied up in knots.

'You foul beast,' shouted Hackendahl at his recumbent horse. 'You wait till I get you alone.'

But that was not to happen so easily. A couple of angry policemen were pushing through the crowd, and one had already produced a notebook.

'Your number's up now,' he said furiously. 'We've had our eye on you for some time but we didn't want to be hard on an old man. '

'You cat's meat,' exclaimed Hackendahl, punching his nag in the ribs. Blücher, however, despite police and crowd, made no effort to get up. 'I'll skin you alive!'

'What do you think you're doing, acting like this in the rush hour in the middle of the Friedrichstrasse? Eh? Who's going to straighten it all out? Come on, get your animal up. An old man like you, the oldest cabby in Berlin, playing the fool!'

A bit of popularity has its uses. The policeman was very young, couldn't have had much experience, and was rather strict. When he rushed onto the scene, seething with anger over the idiot who – on that evening of all evenings – had brought about such an unholy mess, he had been determined to drag the driver to the guardhouse and charge him with causing a public nuisance, endangering public transport, and God alone knows what else.

But the more he scolded the old man, who was patiently trying to deal with the horse, the more his anger diminished. He had of course already heard of Iron Gustav. Colleagues had pointed the man out and described how, before the war, he had had over a hundred cabs on the road and been quite rich, and how he was now on his last cab, as poor as a church mouse – almost a monument, a relic rescued from before the war, a reminder of the mutability of human affairs.

Thus it came about that the compassion which his son had not shown him was shown by the policeman, who was a real Berliner from Pankow, and the real Berliner is only outwardly bumptious and aggressive; inwardly he's quite different. Still cursing, the policeman had put his notebook back in his pocket and was now helping to push the cab – Blücher on his feet at last – and after they had shoved it a little way Blücher, changing his mind, not only let himself be pushed along but started to pull too, and the Berliners cheered.

'Listen,' said the policeman when the cab came to a stop in the side street. 'Don't do that again, you hear?'

'Someone must have confused the old nag,' said Gustav Hacken-dahl angrily.

'Not a bit! Everyone knows you taught the old horse those tricks. But that's enough of this, you understand. You're Iron Gustav, aren't you?'

'That's me, young man. But I don't feel like me name tonight.'

'Well, never mind,' said the policeman almost kindly. 'I've heard a lot about you . . .'

'Yes, people talk.'

'Not only from people, but from your grandsons. I live in the same house, except they're in the second courtyard and I'm in the first. But from my kitchen I look straight into their bedroom.'

'Well I never!' marvelled old Hackendahl.

'Yes. Other kids play at motor cars and chauffeurs, but your grandsons – you bet not! Always cabs. One of them the horse and the other the driver. First the big one in front and then the little one.'

'You don't say so!'

'Yes. I just thought I'd out with it because I know you don't go there at all, but it might please you to hear it, what with this business with the horse. But see that it doesn't happen again.' And the young policeman, having spoken the last words in a more official voice, strolled off. Hackendahl, however, when he and his cab came to a dark avenue in the Tiergarten, got down from his box, took the reins firmly in one hand and the whip in the other, and cried 'Gee-up!' And when the black horse, as he had been taught, began to move backwards, he thrashed him. And thrashed him again . . . For the animal had to learn that the days of walking backwards were at an end; from now on it would be – forward!

The joyrides were finally over; they had anyway only been a bit of a racket. The days around the big round wooden table in the cellar were also over. It had horrified him to be the joker again at that table, where his son had disowned him. The old man had learned his lesson, and his old nag had also quickly learned its lesson, too, you would hardly believe how much a few blows can sometimes help.

Then the two of them trotted wearily home together. And if Iron Gustav had not been so tired and exhausted, he would have been a bit surprised that he hardly felt either anger or pain over his lost son, only sometimes had the comforting thought: playing horse cabbies, why not? Ignore cars! Do cars need whips? The policeman never mentioned them. It would be a bit strange!

§ V

Erich had to drink a lot before he could feel free again. The bearded old man who sat at his table, as if resurrected from his grave, had always stayed in Erich's life, and now he knew for the first time to what extent. The old man didn't visit him, he'd avoided him – but he had been there, in the villa in Dahlem, and in the inner-city office, among his employees. The grown man – the swift, ruthless business operator – had feared the hand of the old cab driver. The grown-up son had feared his father like a small child.

Erich laughed, relieved, and had another drink.

'Well, Erich,' asked his friend the lawyer, 'what's the matter?'

'Nothing,' laughed Erich, drinking. 'Just pleased, that's all.'

The other man nodded. 'And what was the trouble with the cabman?'

Erich leaned over the table, gestured with his head towards the empty chair, and whispered, 'That was my father.'

The lawyer raised his dark bushy eyebrows in polite surprise. 'Interesting,' he said with a thin smile. 'And?'

'I beat him,' Erich blurted out. 'Usually it's the children who are beaten by the parents; this time it's . . .' He stopped. 'I'm speaking metaphorically, of course.'

'I understand,' said the friend. 'I understand completely, Erich. But you've done nothing out of the ordinary. There's an old proverb to the effect that a child treads on its mother's lap to begin with, and later on her heart . . . And fathers are very like mothers after all.'

Again the lawyer nodded. Through the haze of cigarette smoke in front of Erich's eyes and the haze of alcohol behind them, the terrifying spectacle of the nodding head and laughing face of his friend appeared to be approaching.

However, nothing at all terrifying happened, but the lawyer just said, 'Should you therefore unexpectedly experience some remorse, Erich, remember that you've only done what a hundred per cent of children do . . . Your health!' He raised his champagne glass in greeting. Erich returned his greeting, and both drank.

The night seemed to vanish in a whirl of intoxication, of girls, of laughter . . . Never before, felt Erich, had he been caught up in a vortex of pleasure so ecstatic. They all let themselves go, shrieking with laughter, riotously merry – oh, how they got going on that night of the Ruhr Occupation! They linked arms – there was no dance band in that pit of a cellar, so they made their own music. Swaying to and fro, they sat round the table roaring out the beautiful, the witty, the daring songs of that delightful period: 'We're boozing away Granny's cottage', 'Who rolled the cheese to the station?', 'Well, if you can't, let me!', 'Yes, we have no bananas'.

'What's he want, the rude fat landlord in the red waistcoat? Iron Gustav? No one's iron to us. We can just squeeze you with our bare fists. We're not to make a noise or the police will hear us? Let them! They should pay attention to us. We're above all the police, paternal police, official police whatever! We are the past, present and future members of the Reichstag of the united German people. I'm to shut up, Herr Doctor? Of course I'll shut up. I won't make things difficult for you. Of course we're not members of the Reichstag! Do I look like one? I haven't even got a tummy – or almost not! I'm a profiteer!' And Erich began to sing:

> *I'm a bit of a crook and my flag is the national*
> *colours, black, red, gold,*
> *And even if my goods go bad,*
> *Fifty per cent I make on all you've had.*

What's this? They had pulled him down from his chair; the waiter was standing beside him with a coffee; the man with the monocle held a hand over his mouth. 'Be sensible, Hackendahl. What's the matter with you? You haven't been drinking as much as all that.'

Yes, what was the matter with him? He wasn't in an alcoholic haze but a victory haze. He had shown himself, his father and the whole world that one had to be bad in order to succeed. Everything he had been told earlier about goodness and love was a lie. In this world you had to be bad – and this was the only world there was! The bad flourished, the good went to the wall. In that case the bad was actually good, and it was only the bigwigs and moneybags who taught the stupid people that they had to be good, the result being that people have for a long time had a very bad time on this earth!

In triumph he looked at his paternal friend. Then he suddenly took his hand away from his mouth and shouted. 'One must be bad – that's the secret!'

'Only being bad is not enough, either,' smiled the lawyer. 'The prisons are full of people who believed in such a precept. You've got to be clever, Erich, too.' And without turning round, he gestured with his head towards the back door. 'There, listen to the magic effect of your really rather horrible song.'

Erich looked. Policemen were now standing at the door through which his father had gone. Rude Gustav, rude no longer, pale and submissive, was bowing to them. What were the police doing here? Erich gradually began to think. They can't want me for anything at all . . . They'll never want anything from me. I'm too clever for them. Bad and bad again, just as he'd said . . .

'Drink your coffee,' said the lawyer, and Erich did. The others at their table were now standing a little apart, sometimes looking at the police and sometimes at Erich. 'His damned shouting's got us into this mess,' he heard Bronte remark.

'Looked at from one point of view,' whispered another, obviously referring to Erich's friend the lawyer, 'it's a bit odd for a member of the Reichstag to be found, on a day of mourning . . .'

'Of course! After all, we're private individuals . . .'

'Friends in need,' smiled the lawyer. 'All the same I should find it embarrassing to have to show my identity card to those uniformed gentlemen. Despite all the trouble we have taken, the police are still deeply reactionary . . . I could easily pop up in tomorrow's local newspaper.'

'I could kick myself,' said Erich. 'I've been a fool. I can't understand myself.'

'There are only three of them,' mused the lawyer. 'One to guard the door, another the lavatory, and one to examine cards and take the names. That can't be done quickly. Our turn will be at the end, so we have a chance.'

Erich thought about all that he'd said, but could no longer remember. Had he had a business disagreement with Bronte in front of the whole bar? Did I . . . ? he wanted to ask the lawyer. But he wasn't taking any notice of him.

'One could but try,' he murmured. 'Listen, Erich, can you perhaps remember if there is anything in your coat or on your hat – letters, tailor's label which would clearly identify you?'

'No, I don't think there is.'

'In that case we could try to get away, by sacrificing coats and hats.'

'There's nothing in mine but the tailor's label. I could drop him a hint tomorrow morning . . .'

'All right, let's try it. Now look at the bar, and tell me exactly what the police are doing.'

'Bronte is talking to the man at the entrance, and the one by the cloakroom's got hold of a drunk.'

'Splendid – splendid,' said the lawyer's soft, even voice. A key grated in its lock. 'Our table is right next to the door leading into the street. At ten o'clock the landlord simply turned the key and I've just unlocked it again. Please describe the position now. Pretend you're chatting.'

'There'll be a shutter in front of the door,' declared Erich. 'Everybody's occupied with their own troubles, they're paying no attention to us.'

'That's one of the possible snags,' admitted the lawyer, to all appearances sitting at ease while actually fiddling with something at the door behind Erich's back. A draught blew against their feet. 'The second possibility is that they've posted a man at the door. The third is we may be stopped in the street because we're without hats and coats on a cold night. The fourth is that Bronte or one of the others will give us away. But no, that's not likely, all they'll get is a fine and nobody wants to be on bad terms with a Reichstag member.'

'The first obstacle,' burst out Erich, 'doesn't exist. There's no shutter before the door. As for the second, I don't think we need

worry much there – a man on guard would have seen the light once
the door was ajar.'

'He could be facing the street! Well, let's try our luck. Remember
the cellar stairs, six or seven steps. And if we get separated, Erich,
don't worry about me. Everybody for himself and the devil take the
hindmost.'

They sat waiting for a favourable moment. Once Erich reached
out for his glass but his friend put his hand over it, saying: 'Better
not.' Then a little later he added: 'Now, Erich, I think! You go first.'
And, quite unflurried, he opened the door.

Erich sprang into the darkness and up the cellar steps. The street
was full of people; one or two faces turned towards him, but he saw
no policeman. Slowly the lawyer followed and took his arm. 'They
won't be after us for a bit,' he said. 'I locked the door on the outside.
And now we must quickly get a taxi. Our unseasonable attire is creating a sensation.'

§ VI

When they sat in the taxi, they both broke into roars of laughter.
They felt like schoolboys who had just taken their teachers for a
complete ride.

'No, no!' shouted the lawyer eventually. 'When we're back in control, I must have a serious word with Severing over the measures his
police are taking. To forget where police are supposed to go on the
street! Now I understand why our hostile brothers, the Communists,
are always cursing the police!'

Eric laughed, for a different reason. 'And to think,' said Erich gleefully, 'that I didn't pay for the champagne! They forgot all about the
bill in the excitement. Twenty or thirty bottles, too. God knows how
many. And the coffee.' He could not get over it, so pleased he was at
the unexpected bilking.

'Drinking coffee reminds me,' said the lawyer. 'I think we should
go to my place and have a drink and a chat in comfort. I have anyway
got more to discuss with you.'

'Nothing will come of that, Herr Doctor,' said Erich. 'I'm not in the mood for either coffee or a discussion. I want to go out, and quick! Nothing will stop me.'

'But I really don't want to repeat . . .' began the lawyer.

'Oh, don't talk a lot of nonsense,' interrupted Erich. 'You'll see how much fun we will still have' – and he began to laugh again. Having survived the two recent lots of danger so happily, he was overcome by a noisy, self-righteous euphoria. He was sure he was born under a lucky star, which would apply to all situations.

Meanwhile, the lawyer had conferred with the chauffeur and said, 'All right, Erich, if you absolutely must . . .'

'Of course I must,' shouted Erich. 'No sleep for me tonight! Definitely not now!'

'All right,' conceded the lawyer. 'The chauffeur reckons there are plenty of bars still open in the old West End. The bar owners there have particularly good relations with the police, you understand,' and he pretended to pay out money. Then he sighed, cheered up and resigned himself: 'We've got the right conditions here, my boy – just the right conditions . . .'

'In fact,' said Erich, laughing, 'such conditions suit you very well, Herr Doctor. In fact, you have a horror of making sacrifices, and find your present life quite pleasant!'

'You're not far off the mark,' admitted the lawyer with a contented sigh. 'Now, come up to my place, Erich, and we'll see if we can find something suitable.'

Together they went into the lawyer's flat, and Erich tried on coats and hats amidst much unwarranted laughter.

But not only coats were tried on for size – schnapps as well. And it must have been the schnapps that caused Erich to be somewhat unusually dressed as he descended the steps again with the lawyer. He wore a short but far too big fur-lined leather coat belonging to his friend, with a stiff black hat, which – because it was also much too big – he set right at the back of his head.

They then drove through the night streets, from the bright inner city out to the darker districts. It was already after twelve. The streets had emptied. The bars were dark. Only occasionally did the sound of music reach them – the beat of jazz. Behind closed shutters, Berlin danced and drank itself towards the abyss, nearer and nearer the ultimate hangover . . .

'Let's hope the chauffeur knows a good bar,' murmured Erich.

'If he doesn't, I do,' answered the lawyer. And once again they were silent, smoked, and neither of them could wait to see the faces of new girls across a table, or to have new drinks poured for them.

The taxi stopped outside a bar whose landlord must have had very good relations with the police, because all its windows were brightly lit, music sounded across the street, and when Erich put his hand on the door handle it was not locked.

'This one's fine,' he cried happily.

Bowler on the back of his head and coat wide open, he made his entry. Carefully, his head a little withdrawn (for who knew whom one might find in such a place?), the lawyer followed as quietly as he could.

The bar was quite full, very smoky and stank of drink. Confetti was strewn and coloured paper chains hung everywhere. It covered the carpet and made a rustling noise when trodden on.

'Nice, isn't it?' Erich, pausing, asked the lawyer.

A girl danced in the narrow space between the tables. She had a nice hairstyle and was very well made-up – and was completely naked. She danced to the sound of a violin – played with schmaltzy sentimentality by a gypsy violinist – with much lascivious bowing and scraping, and a falsely melancholic smile.

'Lovely body, hasn't she?' asked Erich. 'Still really young . . .'

He put his hand on the lawyer's shoulder and leaned against him, staring, just like the others, staring at what he'd seen a hundred times, that can be bought on every street corner – something thrown away in hopeless, rank indifference and disgust. As he did this, he thought: my God, four years ago, when I made little what's-her-name dance naked for me in Dahlem, I sent all the staff out of the house because I had no idea what I was doing! And now it happens in a public bar, and everyone accepts it as natural. We've come a long way. But it's not my business: I'm not a member of the Reichstag.

He looked at the lawyer.

But he didn't take any notice of Erich. He was doing business

with the flower seller, buying for an enormous sum a whole basket
of sweet violets and throwing the blooms at the naked dancing girl.
She felt flattered and smiled, but also looked worried because the
lawyer wasn't a very accurate thrower, and the dance the girl had
painfully learned from her handler and impresario was interrupted
when violets hit her in the face.

'Let me have a go,' said Erich and put his hand in the basket. 'I can
throw better.'

'They're my violets!' the lawyer shouted, unusually angry. 'Get
your paws out!'

Eventually, at the insistence of Erich and a good deal of money as
a present, the pretty young girl was brought to the gentlemen's
table. In private she was wrapped in a kimono (the strict landlord
only allowed her to go naked when on duty).

This beauty, however, proved to be something of a disappointment. She too openly showed her lack of interest in her two
chivalrous escorts, in favour of her lust for cash.

'Why do you idiots think I dance naked for you? For your sake?
You make me laugh! I've got five little brothers and sisters at home.'

'And your mother's sick, and your poor but dishonourable father
died on the field of honour . . .' mocked Erich, furious. 'We know all
that stuff! Can't you tell us a different story, sweetie?'

'But it's all true. You think it can't be true, because the tarts have
told it before. But it is true.'

'And don't forget the lieutenant who seduced you and wanted to
marry you, but who was killed in action before the wedding.'

'Leave it alone, Erich,' said the lawyer, now angry himself. 'Don't
be so aggressive. You're drinking too fast again.'

The girl looked quickly from one to the other with sharp eyes.

'I don't like to be cheated and taken for a ride!' shouted Erich.
'And when I even hear anything about five hungry brothers and
sisters . . .'

'But there are hungry children,' said the lawyer, calming things
down. 'Quite a number, in fact. I know because I've had to read statistics about it recently.'

'Fatty,' said the girl to the lawyer and snuggled up to him. 'Tell me
honestly – am I a very bad dancer?'

'Why do you want to know?'

'Because I want to. All the men never tell the truth because I'm naked. And Krukow, there, who learned me the dance . . .'

'Taught me, taught me, sweetie!'

'That's what I said, stupid! He said I dance like a tipsy cow.'

'Well, my child,' pronounced the lawyer, 'if you really want to know: you have a pretty figure and are young and naked. If you wore a dress, no man would turn a head to watch you dance.'

'Well, there you are,' cried the girl, very satisfied. 'That's what I always thought! There are people here who want to persuade me to become a dancer, and say that I should learn to be one, at their expense, as friends, of course. But I always thought: don't be a fool – they just want you to learn to go on the game, and nothing more. No, I'd rather jump around in my birthday suit, and as soon as I can earn decent money, simply work in a shop. I once worked for a butcher. Then I can marry a decent man, and give up this sort of life.'

'God damn . . .' began Erich, but thankfully never got as far as expressing what he felt about what he was getting for his money.

The bar was very keen on its naked ladies. The men, already the worse for wear from much drinking, wanted a bit of spice to liven them up. And the ladies didn't deny it them, because men with a bit of life in them are better spenders than sleepyheads. It all went quickly. The dancers had no more difficulty with their costumes, and the violinist had enough schmaltz.

'Isn't it strange?' said Erich half grudgingly. 'Although I know what a boring bit of fluff she is, as soon as she jumps around naked in front of everyone in the full glare of the lights, I find her really quite nice.'

'It's always been the same,' said the lawyer, yawning. 'What others find pretty, we find pretty too. And what others want, we want too. By the way, Erich, the whole evening I've wanted to ask if the name Eugen Bast signifies anything to you.'

'No, I don't think so,' said Erich uncertainly. 'But of course I do business with so many people . . .' A little anxiety crept into his voice. 'Is it someone I'm connected with who's got into a mess?'

'He's in a mess all right. And he'd like me to act in his defence. And he's connected with you.'

'Well, hurry up and tell me,' said Erich irritably. 'Eugen Bast? Not the faintest idea! Or was he the man from Italy with the silk? No, he was called Becker. By the way, I'm counting on you taking up my defence if anything should go wrong.'

'Erich, Erich! And you've always sworn that your deals are above board. When I made your acquaintance in 1914 I expected you to become something better than a speculator, you know.'

'Yes, indeed,' cried Erich, furious. 'You thought I would be taken in by your idiotic social democracy. Idiotic! Today you're as much of a Social Democrat as . . . as . . .'

'Let's say – as Kaiser Wilhelm,' said the lawyer. 'He also always had such a hopeless and unrequited love for the Social Democrats. Well, don't let's talk about it. We've both, alas, turned out different from what we thought. Everything seems easy when you're in opposition, but as soon as you're—'

'I want to know who Eugen Bast is.'

'Eugen Bast is a young man who has been in prison three or four times; at present he's on remand charged with robbery, housebreaking, blackmail, living on immoral earnings and a few other trifles.'

'Out of the question,' said Erich, relieved. 'I've certainly had nothing to do with the man. I earn my money less stupidly.'

'What's more, Eugen Bast is blind – which seems to be the only extenuating circumstance, otherwise he's a thorough rascal.'

'Blind! And the man mentioned me?'

'He was shot and blinded – by your sister.'

'Eva! I always knew she would still make difficulties for us all.'

'Eva, that's right. Eva Hackendahl. She's his mistress. She seems to have shot him in a fit of jealousy.'

'Damn and blast,' growled Erich furiously. 'I won't let myself be dragged into it. What do I care about Eva? I haven't seen her for years. I refuse to give evidence. I must say,' he said bitterly, 'you've got some fine clients.'

'Well, we all do our best, my dear Erich,' smiled the lawyer. 'Incidentally, you've only just asked me to conduct your defence.'

'Do me a favour, Herr Doctor. Decline this fellow's defence.'

The other shook his head. 'That would be unwise, Erich. The man has money, or his friends have, which amounts to the same thing, and he'd simply go to another lawyer. It's better to keep it in our own hands.'

'I want nothing to do with it.'

'You'll certainly be drawn in if it goes to another lawyer. This Bast has made your sister tell him all sorts of things. He knows, for instance, that you earn a good deal and he maintains you stole some money once. Excuse me, Erich, control yourself. I'm only repeating what Herr Bast has concocted. If stealing runs in the family, as he claims, then it's clear he didn't incite your sister to steal, isn't it? She might have led him astray.'

'I'll go abroad,' said Erich. 'I can live abroad for a time quite well. If you'll give me a hint now and then I can speculate in London on the fall of the mark . . . No, in Brussels! That's the place. I know Brussels. Brussels is the very spot for me. I'll give you a share of course.'

'Very kind, Erich. But how much a German parliamentarian can speculate on the reduction of the mark has to be taken into account . . . All the same, this Bast case requires thought. If it's played up in the courts, as Herr Bast seems to wish out of professional vanity, then it would be grist to the mills of our beloved press. All the penal reformers and do-gooders in the world will blubber over the poor, blind man and bring discredit on the name of Hackendahl.'

'Eva was quite a harmless sort of girl.'

'According to Herr Bast she goaded him into all his crimes by her insatiable thirst for pleasure, her immoderate love of dissipation . . .' The lawyer surveyed the heaving, chaotic, drunken bar.

'And there are other examples of hedonism in this family,' he said.

'Oh, stop these insults!' cried Erich, furious.

'You're right, Erich. What is certain, however, is that your sister admits all this. She did instigate him, she says. She did demand money from him. And she did shoot him for no reason whatsoever.'

'She admits all that?' said Erich, dumbfounded. 'Is she mad? That means—'

The lawyer nodded. 'Six to eight years' penal servitude.'

'And has she turned out like that?' Erich could not imagine Eva as a confirmed criminal – Eva as vamp. 'No, that can't be true.'

'Of course it isn't. She's lying right and left. She's under his thumb – you understand?'

'That's right,' said the father's favourite son. 'She's the true daughter of old Hackendahl. You saw the old man yourself this evening. He shouted and beat any sense of free will out of us. He's the one to blame! I want to have nothing to do with the affair. I'm going to Brussels.'

'I have to defend both him and your sister. And he wants the defence to blame everything on her.'

'But that rests with you,' said Erich, annoyed. 'If Eva's under his thumb she can hardly be held responsible.'

'Quite,' said the lawyer, smiling. 'And in that case Herr Eugen Bast would reveal everything he knows about your family and, above all, drag you into the proceedings.'

'So that if we want to have peace, Eva has to suffer?'

'Right, my son.'

'Nothing like a bit of blackmail?'

'You understand perfectly, Erich.'

'Perhaps Herr Bast wishes me to pay your fee into the bargain?'

'Herr Bast knows that we're friends and that you earn a good deal of money. As I said – an unmitigated scoundrel.' Smiling, the lawyer looked at Erich. Erich was silent, ill-tempered. He was reducing the carbon dioxide in his champagne with a straw, lit a cigarette and was silent.

'Well?' asked the lawyer.

'Oh, yes,' said Erich, starting. He didn't answer immediately but looked towards where the little naked girl was playing with a teddy bear. 'She looks really very nice,' he said eventually, upset.

'You're right,' said the lawyer. 'It's one of those seldom instances when something looks better naked than clothed. And what do you think of our case?'

'Oh, do just as you . . . you know, Herr Doctor.'

'So I may say it by quoting the name of a famous novel – *Arme Kleine Eva – Poor Little Eve*.'

'Everyone must help themselves.'

'Understood,' agreed the lawyer.

'And since she herself wishes it . . .'

'That's so, that's so.'

'Six years' penal servitude – it might change her perhaps.'

'Undoubtedly – for the worse.'

'Why do you sneer?' said Erich furiously. 'You've spoiled the whole evening for me. I was in a wonderful mood. What do I care about my sister and her Eugen? I want to get on. I don't want people here in Berlin nudging and winking behind my back. I don't want to be dragged into the gutter press. I'm not responsible for my sister!'

'Of course you're not,' agreed the lawyer politely. 'I seem to remember that old Jehovah once received a similar answer from Cain when he was looking for Abel.'

'But I did not kill my sister!' cried Erich angrily. 'Let her get ten years – twenty if she likes. It'll do her good and we'll be left in peace.'

'All right, all right,' said the lawyer. 'Now I'm much clearer about what I'm doing, and have got to know you much better, my dear Erich. In addition, I suggest,' he said as Erich was about to vent his anger again, 'that we change bars. I know one very nearby where I sometimes go to study.'

'Waiter! We want to pay, please.'

§ VII

By the time both of them stepped into the street it was snowing softly and close to freezing.

'No, no car,' said the lawyer. 'It's only a step away. The fresh air will do us good. We've both drunk too much.'

'I can still walk all right,' contradicted Erich.

The lawyer made no reply and the two walked next to each other, each wrapped in his dark, alcohol-inspired thoughts. An overground train only occasionally glided over the iron arches of the Bülowstrasse. Otherwise everything was quiet. Barely a light burned faintly in the windows of grey, dead houses.

Suddenly Erich stopped, seized the lawyer by his lapel, and asked him angrily: 'Why do you provoke me like this? Why do you force me over and over again to expose myself? I sometimes think you were never my friend . . . You've done this to me – do you still remember my room in Lille . . . You encouraged me to continuous humiliation! Why? I ask. Why? Why did you keep on at me till I told you to your face that – out of pure selfishness – I wanted my sister punished as much as possible? You already knew that! Is that friendship, or are you my enemy?'

He spoke increasingly quietly but ever more excitedly, and continued to hold the lawyer by his lapel as if he wanted to close with him. Now the lawyer removed his threatening hands, adjusted his own coat and said, peacefully, 'You really have drunk too much. Let's go on.'

Erich was furious and wanted to contradict him, but controlled himself, because the lawyer said, 'We're nearly there. It's a really nice bar. I don't know if you know that kind of bar. As I said, I sometimes go to them, often in fact. I too have my little amusements . . .' He smiled faintly. 'You've just reminded me of your room in Lille . . . Yes, I remember it all now. You were a fresh young lieutenant and wore silk shirts . . . God, what a long time ago that all was. Yes, it's a homosexual bar we're going to.'

'I'm not going into a homosexual bar!' said Erich, almost shouting. 'I'm not a homo.'

At first the lawyer made no answer. He was busy humming a song that was then all over Berlin – 'We, thank God, are different from the others'. He hummed it proudly and triumphantly.

'As far as you're concerned, my dear Erich,' he said, lowering his voice, 'you're on the one hand a sort of project of mine, and on the other a kind of hope. As hope, you must admit that I've several times cared for you like a father – that you owe your pleasant and fancy-free life in the first place to my efforts.'

The lawyer continued softly and smoothly in this vein. A raging anger rose in Erich, but something held him back from giving way to it; he wanted first to hear if the lawyer really imagined that he, Erich – no, it was impossible!

Worried, the lawyer now said: 'In your momentary irritation, you accused me of tempting you down this path, from which one might infer that it does not please you. But, my dear Erich, I have to say that up till now you have found this path very pleasant. Yes, it's only a little while ago that you were making currency speculations in Brussels, which very much looked as though you wanted to continue on such a notorious path.'

That lawyer! thought Erich, bitterly. That damned shyster – he twists everything into a hangman's noose!

'Well,' continued the lawyer, more quietly and concerned, 'I'm not saying no! People will say to me that a way can be found of initiating you into modern affairs. For the mark is going to fall, and fall very deeply, but one day it will stop falling. Such a day could be a gloomy day for you, my dear Erich, without me.'

The lawyer remained standing, gasping for breath. Snow hindered his progress and his vision. He took his spectacles from his nose, dried them carefully and said, proceeding slowly: 'But such a clever and egoistic man as you, Erich, will not doubt the fact that other people can also be egoistic. Me, for example. You'll have to pay your way; I've long expected you to admit that, and I don't doubt that you'll pay on the nail.'

'I've already told you,' answered Erich Hackendahl with a surly look, 'that I'll share the profits of this currency business with you . . . Otherwise . . .'

'You're an ass, Erich!' said the lawyer quietly. 'Even without you I earn more money than the comrades like. No, the bill . . . I've told you already where we're going . . .'

'I'm not a homo,' Erich repeated stubbornly.

'I've heard that it sometimes happens that one doesn't want to pay a bill,' said the lawyer, smiling. 'Nevertheless one pays it – unwillingly. Unwillingly.'

He smiled again and looked at Erich attentively through his round spectacles, then: 'I already said, you were a project. My project. When I made your acquaintance, if you remember, you had just levied a forced loan on your father and sister.'

'I won't listen to any more of this rubbish,' Erich almost shouted. 'I've paid it all back.'

'Yes, and with my money. As I say. You were on the edge, but a fire – which was then going out in me – seemed to burn in you, a self-belief, a belief in others, in goodness, or in whatever it was, and I loved you because of that fire.'

'So I was supposed to join the Social Democratic Party, was I?' Erich mocked angrily. 'You no longer believed in the party, but just exploited it, and I was supposed to be the dummy, was I?'

'I gave you every opportunity,' continued the lawyer relentlessly, 'to go over to, let's say, the light. But you insisted inexorably on the dark.'

'You forced me!'

'No, Erich. Who slunk from the trenches to the High Command?'

'And who in Lille taught me to do a bit of malingering?'

'Right! When I saw that no fire burned in you, but only a tendency to laziness, dirty business and dirty pleasure, I wanted to see how far you would go – if there was at least some part of you which was worth something, a little fragment unknown to you . . . a little hope.'

'Farewell, Herr Doctor!' said Erich, but the lawyer did not stir.

'I clawed my way up in the party,' said the lawyer reflectively, ignoring Erich. 'I went through the difficult years, when it was a crime to be a Social Democrat. We were heavily persecuted then, but that didn't put us off. Back then I still believed in the good in mankind, in a better future, in progress, in the slow progress of human society.'

'You've got a bit fat to be that much of an enthusiast,' mocked Erich maliciously.

'Oh, Erich, what an idiot you are! For the cunning chap you are, you really are too stupid. I've just been telling you about my getting fat, about losing my illusions so that I now only believe that mankind is bad. You were my last project, my last spark of belief. But unfortunately, my dear Erich, you've been a complete failure from the very first moment.'

The lawyer sighed. 'If a debtor,' he went on to say almost professionally, 'cannot pay cash, we go for his material assets, as we jurists say,' and was silent.

Erich looked at him, gloomily silent, his teeth biting into his lower lip. They were standing in front of a café, a rather dark café. It was the end of their journey. The lawyer went no further.

'You must admit,' the lawyer once again started to persuade
the silent Erich, 'that I've spared you for a long time – from my
importunities, I mean. There was always the remote possibility that
there was something, let's say, decent about you. It was a very
remote possibility. But since this evening . . . You must understand,
Erich. What difference can it make to you? You can do me a favour
for a change.'

Erich looked tensely at the lawyer's imploring, bloated face. Then
he said with venom: 'Your cheeks are wobbling, Herr Doctor! Are
you really so upset? Do you really think I would do that?'

The lawyer didn't seem to have heard anything, and said simply,
'I'll take your sister off your hands and that oaf Bast, and you'll be
left in peace for a long time. I'll make you into a rich man, Erich. It's
really only a trifle. Come on, Erich.'

And he clung onto him and wanted to pull him towards the café,
desperately stroking his hand. 'Erich, please . . . Just once! I've waited
so long . . .'

'Leave me alone,' shouted Erich, freeing himself. 'Don't touch
me. You want me to abuse myself in that way too!' He looked at
him, full of hate. 'I'll never do it, never.'

But that meant nothing to the other. He only saw his booty, the
booty which wanted to escape from him and for which he had
waited so long. 'Erich!' he shouted, and reached for his hand, gripped
it and held it tight, no matter that Erich pulled away as hard as he
could. Then the lawyer bent down and wanted to press his lips on
Erich's hand. Erich could already feel them.

For a moment he hesitated. Then he overcame his inhibitions and
hit the lawyer hard on his lowered head. The latter hesitated, tried to
stop himself, but then fell backwards onto the cobblestones in the
snow with a pathetic groan.

Why don't I go, thought Erich, and stared at the prostrate body. I
shouldn't have done that – I'm drunk. He can do me a frightful lot of
harm . . . Now it's too late . . . I'd better go.

And yet he stood there, staring at the figure on the ground.

The lawyer stirred, half sat up and looked around.

'Oh, Erich?' he asked. 'Did I fall? Give me a hand will you?'

Mechanically Erich stretched out an arm and helped him up.

The lawyer stood up, wiped snow from his coat, and put his hand to his eyes: 'I must have lost my spectacles. Will you look, Erich. They may not be broken.'

They were not broken. Erich found them and gave them back.

'And if you could get me a taxi, Erich? There's a rank just round the corner.'

The taxi, too, was found. Clumsily the lawyer got in and settled himself, while Erich stood hesitantly by the door. Ought he to go with him or not? He waited. But the lawyer said nothing. 'I'm very sorry, Herr Doctor,' said Erich in a low voice.

'Goodnight,' yawned the other. 'One really shouldn't drink such a lot. Fancy falling down in the street! Well, goodnight, Erich.'

'Goodnight, Herr Doctor.'

The taxi moved away into the night.

§ VIII

An unending stream of people passed through the prison in Berlin-Moabit. Ten years ago, going to prison was still a disgrace. Now, in 1923, people said, 'Can't be helped – tough luck!'

It had begun during the war. Almost everyone had procured butter by devious means, and potatoes on forage trips. Many didn't feel it was right, but the laws no longer seemed to fit the needs of daily life – most of them were drawn up before the war, after all. If a hungry, unemployed man stole, people considered it was not the same as when someone stole before the war, when no one needed to.

Honesty was also made more difficult, because dishonesty was so widespread. Black-market racketeers, born of the war and despised and hated during it, had almost become popular figures. The unhealthy-looking fat man with a briefcase in a big car was not so much despised as envied. The words 'black market' came to sound modern – and not just the words.

'Yes,' people said, 'is it just racketeers who deal in the black market? What about inflation? Stock Exchange racketeers must be to blame for that. Why doesn't the government simply put a ban on the Stock Exchange? It's all a racket! Those at the top are behind the inflation. They want to be rid of the War Loans, and swallow up our savings. And every week they cheat us of our wages!'

That's how people talked. Never in this period did they feel at one with their government, whether it was called the Scheidemann government, the Hermann Müller Cabinet, or Fehrenbach, Wirth, Bauer or Cuno. It was always 'those at the top', who had nothing to do with them. 'They just want to take their cut and do us down.' That's what people thought, and that's what they said.

A worker sweating in a factory could hardly suggest complicated theories about the Versailles Treaty, reparations, currency problems, the Occupation of the Ruhr, but he could understand only too well that his weekly wages, as high as the amount might sound, were only a fifth or a tenth of what he earned in peacetime. Well might people say: 'Yes, we lost the war and must pay for it' – but the worker says: 'Was it me? What about the racketeers, the war profiteers and the fat bosses?'

And anyway, what did it amount to – a bit of stealing, cheating, embezzling? It was an era of much more gruesome crimes, crimes the papers wrote about for weeks on end. Real crimes – murders, mass murder, people who slaughtered other people, made sausage-meat out of them and then sold the sausage . . .

At first it was still considered gruesome, but senses became blunted. In the end utterly shameless people came and even made a musical hit out of it. Soon they were singing it everywhere – in offices and in the streets – young girls and old pros outside the dance halls: 'Just wait a little longer, and Haarmann will be with you, with his little axe . . .'

Was it surprising that the prisons filled up! They were like machines. They stopped and started, creaked and cracked, while grinding through ten thousand souls: paragraph such-and-such, sentence so-and-so. Settled. Next! Whether you feel guilty or I find you guilty makes no difference. The law has been broken. That alone decides.

Moabit Prison. Hundreds of cells and every cell holding four times, even six times the normal number. Throngs of people. A confusion of languages. All ages, all classes, all professions. Visiting rooms which were never free from shouting, weeping, reproaches, quarrels . . . Minute clerks, advisers, detectives, examining magistrates, public prosecutors, their assistants. Senior public prosecutors and chief public prosecutors.

'Come on, come on, we haven't got much time for you – seven minutes! I've still got seventeen examinations and two sessions, so will you plead guilty or not? It's all the same to me. Then perhaps you'd better stay here a little longer and think it over.'

'Cell twenty-three, Hackendahl, visitor for Hackendahl. Is cell twenty-three, Hackendahl, allowed to have visitors? Who is it? The brother? Are you sure it's the brother? It's a bad case. Has cell twenty-three, Hackendahl, confessed yet? Any danger of obscuring the facts at issue? Enquire from the examining magistrate.'

'The examining magistrate begs to inform you of his recent death – he's got to get four hours' peaceful sleep sometime.'

'I understand, I understand. But how we're to get through it all I don't know. All right, here's the visitor's permit for cell twenty-three, Eva Hackendahl, brother's visit, let us say five minutes, nothing to be said about the case. Tell the warder that nothing is to be said about the case.'

'I must remind you that not a word is to be said about the matter which is the cause of your being here on remand. Not even a hint. The first word, and your permission for visits will be withdrawn.'

'I don't want any visitors. Who is it?'

'Come along, no nonsense. The permit's already been granted. Come on!'

'Who is it?'

'Your brother, I think . . .'

'Eva!'

'Heinz!'

Silence . . .

(Nothing is to be mentioned about the case.)

'How are things with you?'

'Better, thanks.'

The official raised his head. Was that an allusion?

'Can I do anything?'

'No, thanks. I have all I need.'

'And money, too, Eva? I would see if . . . I'm in a job now.'

'No, thanks. I need nothing.'

Silence. Both agonized over what they should talk about. No mention to be made of the case. And yet the case was the only topic they could talk about. How empty life had suddenly become! In this bare, shabby visitors' room, with a wooden barrier in the middle and an official looking wearily at the clock to see how the five minutes were progressing, all that existed was Eva's case. All other human relationships had vanished – they no longer existed, gone! Only the thing they were not allowed to talk about remained.

'I've been living at Tutti's for the last four years. Did you know?'

'Yes – no, I haven't heard. I've not been out of the house for a long time – months.'

The official lifted his head, looked sharply at them and tapped the desk with his pencil. He was not a fussy man but everything was possible; the prisoner's statement that she had not been out of the house for months might be a hint to the brother about building up an alibi.

Once more the conversation froze; brother and sister looked at each other. The once so familiar faces had grown strange. What was there to say between them?

'Tutti's boys are so big now. You knew that she had two boys? Otto is six and Gustav eleven; splendid little chaps. They always keep us cheerful.'

'I can well believe it.' Timidly she went on: 'How did you know?'

He understood her at once. 'I was asked to go to the police station – to make a statement.'

The official tapped admonishingly.

But she: 'Do our parents know?'

'Up to last Saturday they didn't. Shall I go there?'

'Yes, please. Tell them . . . tell them . . . no, don't say anything.'

Silence again. If only these interminable five minutes would end. I couldn't help her when she was at liberty. How can I help her in here?

'Would you like me to get you something to eat? Biscuits or fruit? Or would you like some cigarettes?'

'No, thanks. I need nothing.'

The official got up. 'Visiting time over.'

Very quickly: 'Goodbye, Eva, keep your end up.'

'Goodbye, Heinz.'

'Oh, God, Eva – fool that I am – have you a solicitor?'

'You must go now. Visiting time is over.'

'Yes, I have. Don't bother about anything. And don't come again. Never again!'

'You're to go now, do you hear?' said the official.

Eva, almost screaming: 'Tell our parents I'm dead, that I died long ago – nothing is left of their Eva.'

'Stop that! You never come out with anything till the very last moment. Listen, if you do that again when I've said "Time's up", I'll report you and you'll get no more visitors at all.'

'I didn't want any visitors. I've told you that already.'

'Then you should have shut up. But to start shouting when it's too late – you all do that. Oh, stop talking. Go back to your cell!'

§ IX

A prison is a complicated edifice made secure a dozen times over by walls, locks, bolts and bars; a complex mechanism with officials to keep an eye on the prisoners and with senior officials to keep an eye on the officials; not forgetting clocking-in apparatus, regular and surprise inspections, the censorship of letters and prisoners spying on prisoners . . . A net skilfully woven, mesh upon mesh, so that nothing can slip through. Moreover the women's wing lies isolated from the men's prison. Yet twenty-four hours had not elapsed since the arrest of Eugen Bast and Eva Hackendahl, before a prisoner carrying round food had slipped a note into Eva's hand, the first warning from the blind master to his slave: even in prison you're not free.

That first day she had walked up and down her cell from wall to wall, from door to window, passing between her fellow prisoners as if she did not see them. This was permissible – hers being a serious case, she commanded their respect. Continually the door was flung open: 'Hackendahl for examination.'

The others could wait for three days – no examining magistrate demanded them. She, however, was being asked for all the time.

A case has only to be *very* good or *very* bad . . . the stupid are easily

impressed. Eva impressed them: 'What can have been eating her?'
they asked. 'She doesn't look like one of those.'

'Idiot! It's just the ones who don't look like it who are the worst. I
once saw a poisoner who looked just like my grandmother . . .'

'No wonder, if your grandmother looked anything like you!'

Eva paced up and down. She accepted the respect of the others
just as she accepted prison itself. It was outside her, far away, meaningless. Inside she was still cooped up with Eugen Bast, slave to a
blind man. She had told Heinz the truth; it had been many, many
months since she had last been out of doors. Eugen Bast had kept
her like a prisoner. A professional blind beggar, he also accepted
chairs for re-caning. He did not do this work himself, of course –
that was her job – but it gave him a pretext to get into people's
flats and spy out the land for his friends. No one ever suspected the
poor blind man led by a small boy; yes, he was cunning, was
Eugen Bast.

Monotonous as life had become for Eva, it was not so terrible as
in the early years before she had got used to his sway, the years when
she still dreamed of freedom and escape, dreams for which she no
longer had the will. She had become dulled, she accepted everything. When he thrashed her she wept and said nothing; she cried for
as long as he pulled her hair (which she found particularly painful –
much more so than the beatings), but in the end he stopped both the
beatings and the hair-pulling.

It was just this apathy which infuriated him constantly. He was
not uninventive. Nobody could deny him a certain talent in the dis-
covery of new torments, but they had ceased to have an effect on
her – the dull bitch! Had she not been useful he would have thrown
her out long ago; Eugen Bast, though, was not so young as he once
was. Blind, he could not get around so easily. He had become fat,
comfort-loving; appreciative of order, cleanliness, good eating. And
these things she saw to, she who cost him no more than the food she
ate and who, in addition, was reliable – no chatterer; without a word
of protest, blinder than the blind, she refused not one task.

Eugen Bast himself could no longer take part in burglaries, or
force girls to walk the streets for him, but after his first rage he had
soon come to realize that the man behind the scenes fares very much

better than those who pick the chestnuts out of the fire. The blind man nosed out the likely cribs to crack and for this service he claimed a substantial part of the swag. Thus he became a fence and later one who financed his thieves. Eugen Bast had money, a banking account, and a safe holding the soundest foreign currencies.

He became a great man, did Eugen Bast. He became even greater. Once, when the boys had brought him a packet of letters instead of the expected securities, he stormed about the blunder and as a penalty reduced their share very considerably. Later he made Eva read these letters out to him. He lay on the bed and digested his meal, and made her kneel by the bed on a brush and read aloud. In that way he received all the pleasure he could wish.

Letters up till then had meant very little to Eugen; it was beyond his comprehension what one person could have to write to another on several sheets of paper. However, one gets as old as a cow and has still something to learn. Eugen Bast now understood that it was highly uplifting to listen like this to a She writing to a He on four pages.

She started every letter ecstatically, stupid with love and longing. But on the second page one came across piquant recollections, honeyed indelicacies – the lady knew how to get a gentleman going all right! Eugen Bast, who had never seen her, felt his own blood warmed by her active eroticism.

He made Eva read on until she fell off her brush. Smoking cigarettes, he lay thinking far into the night. It was uplifting reading, no doubt, but Eugen with his shrewd brain soon grasped that very much more could be made out of such letters . . .

They were very expensive English chairs that Eugen Bast had been given to mend, made with a particular brown cane, which he had to order especially for this commission. And it was a very careless householder who, thinking the blind are blind and wishing to give an advance for the purchase of the cane, had fetched out a banknote from a safe concealed by wallpaper. Though blind men cannot see, their hearing is all the better for it, and the gentleman would have been very surprised to know that Eugen Bast could describe the position of his small safe to within an inch or two. Judged by the chairs and safe, the man was well-to-do; he was also married, with children. And from the letters, which the boys had brought along instead of securities, it had been easy to guess that she too was prosperous and married.

It was a brilliant business for a blind man – something which ran itself. The boys took care of the letters, without any idea of how much they were worth (it was funny, but almost every third money box contained such a letter). Then Eva made the first gentle hints, and the poor blind beggar merely made the offers, just played the messenger: 'I've a packet here for Herr Lehmann – you know who I mean!'

Oh, how Eugen Bast now blossomed forth! He, by the way, hadn't called himself Bast for a long time; he was Walter Schmidt or Hermann Schultze, with excellent papers, a man blinded in the war, a man in receipt of a pension; everything in good order, police officer! Yes, he flourished. He wallowed in his own evil. He had plenty of time to think out his letters, his blackmailing letters, and how to torment these men and women, leaving them no peace, extorting money by means of their adulterous correspondence – a lot of money with his dark threats, pleas and lies.

He would never get another woman like Eva. Without question, without complaint, without resistance, she did what he commanded. She would never betray him. During all those years she had never freed herself from his spell for one moment, and now she was unable to discuss anything with another person, for he locked her in the flat when he went out; she had nothing to think of but him. He was indeed never out of her mind, any more than was that taunt, daily harped on for three years in every variation of reproach, complaint, sneer and threat, the taunt that she had made him blind and ugly, that she had to pay for it, that she could never pay for it . . .

But even the most cunning old lag can come a cropper. Let him calculate never so shrewdly and think he has taken every factor into consideration, yet, in the moment he is quite unsuspecting, life calculates differently and trips him up. And when Eugen Bast came a cropper it was quite by accident, without the police having the slightest notion who he was, without any of his rather numerous crimes being the cause of his downfall – he came a cropper in a completely unexpected way, from a change of lodgings. Life itself betrayed him.

And this change was not even his own. Mazeike the landlord at last won his case before the Tenant and Rent Agreement Office against the chronically non-paying Dörnbrack, upon which the Welfare Bureau allotted some sort of army hut to the Dörnbracks and their former flat became empty.

Eugen Bast knew nothing of all this. He did not know his landlord, nor the Dörnbracks, nor the new tenant, a certain Querkuleit. And yet it was Querkuleit who tripped him up.

Bast lived in one of those huge East End tenement buildings which seem to consist of thousands of flats; he found it convenient. In this overcrowded human beehive Bast was lost to sight, lived unnoticed. He was the blind beggar. People had seen him in the Friedrichstrasse; he had a young lad to guide him there and back, and was said to live with a woman but no one had seen her – possibly she looked uglier than he did. Finished and done with, labelled and put away – there were so many tragedies in that building. Children were born and beaten, women had their fights, one day one man was drunk, another ill the next day. It was one of the poorest blocks. It was no pleasant place (except from Eugen Bast's point of view); it was a house similar to many in that time of misery and the newly married Querkuleits would certainly have preferred a pleasanter one had there been any empty flats elsewhere. As it was Querkuleit, a young clerk in the Municipal Housing Bureau, had not missed the chance of the Dörnbracks' flat, for which he could not be blamed seeing that he was on the waiting list, had a little influence and no choice.

So these two young people settled down in the overcrowded tenement, in love with one another (even such things existed during this curious, nightmare year of 1923) and anxious to have a life of their own, which was difficult, for the house encroached on them; where Eugen Bast passed without making any comment, Frau Querkuleit would say: 'Well, my little chap, what are you howling for?' And in about three months young Querkuleit had involved himself in at least six feuds arising out of the lavatory, the dustbins, the wash-house, Frau Schmidt calling Frau Schultze a bitch, and himself mentioning to Frau Dobrin that there was always such a smell from the Müllers' flat. In short, the Querkuleits were innocent young people who thought one ought not to make other people's lives more difficult than they were already, seeing which the whole house set out to make life for the Querkuleits just as difficult as was possible.

But the Querkuleits were young. Things would have to go very hard indeed with them before they yielded.

Bitterly they fought for justice and decency in a world where injustice and cheating were victorious. Nor had they enough with their six feuds. Frau Querkuleit, who as a woman should have been the more practical of the two, said again and again: 'Listen, she's crying' – 'Do you hear? He's beating her' – 'Wake up, she's just fallen down. Now she's shouting!'

Querkuleit was always dead-tired in the evenings and fell into a sound sleep at once but his wife was rather a light sleeper and she soon became very worried by the noises in the flat below. Night after night she woke up to hear a woman weeping and moaning; once she heard a shriek and thought to distinguish the sound of blows. However, she never heard a man's voice, which had to be part of all the noise, and that was particularly strange. So she awakened her Querkuleit and he had to listen too. Happy herself, it was a flaw in her happiness to know that another woman was so wretched. At first Querkuleit grew impatient at being aroused from sound sleep to listen to a woman weeping – even a man fond of justice loves his sleep – but as time went on his fighting spirit awoke too.

No one, his wife pointed out, had ever heard a sound from the man, not a word, no curses, no shouts of his, only ever the woman. That was odd. It was not difficult to find out who lived in the flat below – a blind, disfigured man who went out begging and repaired cane chairs, a man to be pitied perhaps. Dumb? No, he wasn't dumb. Querkuleit had heard him speak a few words to the boy who guided him. Dumbness wasn't the explanation of his silence.

Another odd thing – by night only the woman was heard, by day only the man was seen. The Querkuleits watched. They questioned the neighbours. No, the woman was never to be seen. Nobody could describe her.

'It's mysterious,' said Frau Querkuleit.

'I must clear it up,' said Querkuleit.

Oh, what fancies one can spin in such tenements of a thousand destinies when one is still young and life is new! When one still believes one has a place to occupy in the world, when one is not yet reconciled to this universe of contradictions – when one still retains a hint of that mysterious darkness whence we come. Day after day the Querkuleits looked at the scarred and leathery mask of the blind man, and listened night after night to the weeping and moaning.

They were humble people; they knew that women were frequently beaten by their men, a thing they considered base and vulgar yet not inhuman – but there was something about the blind beggar which was inhuman. They discussed it a great deal but it remained nonetheless inhuman. And what was inhuman had to be changed . . . In the end Querkuleit went to the police station and spoke out his doubts.

The officer in charge shook his head, however. 'Let me tell you, young man, the police don't like making fools of themselves. A woman who's ill-treated at night but who makes no attempt to get in touch with the world outside – that's too much!'

'But . . .' Querkuleit turned red.

'Well?' said the police officer amicably. 'Perhaps he keeps her chained up all day! So that she can't even knock on the wall! No, no. You've too much imagination.' He looked at the card in the file. 'And anyway, they've been registered there for over three years. They may be living in sin, but it's a long time since we did anything about that.'

'But can't one . . .' began Querkuleit despairingly.

'Of course you can. And you will learn, young man. There's a good proverb: don't meddle with what doesn't concern you.'

'And it's a cowardly proverb,' said the indignant Querkuleit. 'If we're only to concern ourselves with our own troubles the world would be in a fine way.'

'Looks pretty fine now, what?' The police officer surveyed the young zealot benevolently. Then he became official. 'We regret to be unable to take action.' He gave another glance at the young man. 'Of course if you could report that the woman had asked for help . . .'

Very thoughtfully Querkuleit went home. To his wife he defended the police officer, but she was far from satisfied. 'Yes,' she said, 'the police have to see somebody lying dead before they do a thing. They make things easy for themselves.'

'Well, don't wake me up any more,' he said firmly. 'It's quite futile and I need my sleep. The quarrels at the housing office will soon be unbearable.'

But you're probably not called Querkuleit for nothing. It gave him no rest. He woke up by himself now in the middle of the night, lay still so that his wife didn't notice, sensed that she was awake too, and listened. Both listened to the crying in the night. It was difficult to get to sleep again, very difficult to accept that the world had to continue in such disorder. When young, it is difficult to leave abandoned projects behind . . .

He made no attempt to get in touch with the woman. With the wonderful, youthful notion that he was the leading star in the firmament, he felt that he must now act on his sole responsibility.

Finally, when it got too much for him, he went to the police station without saying anything to his wife and stated that for four or five days there had been knockings on the walls, with appeals for help. He chose a time when the officer in charge of the station was absent. But although the official who interviewed him was unsuspicious, he nearly tripped himself up. Why hadn't the woman called other neighbours? How did she know him? What reason did she give for the ill-treatment? Had she complained about unlawful restraint? Why hadn't she called out of the window for help? Almost every day a policeman went across that courtyard.

It is not so easy for an idealist to live in this world as he would wish. A stubborn attitude rescued Querkuleit from the bog of lies which threatened to engulf him. 'Very well, I was simply asked to fetch help. I've notified you – you do as you like.'

The police official made up his mind. Once more he drew attention to the unpleasant consequences a false charge might have but when Querkuleit remained unshaken he detailed a policeman to accompany the young man to the flat and have a look round.

Querkuleit and the policeman stood before the door. They rang and rang but nothing stirred within. Querkuleit suggested a locksmith.

The policeman shook his head. 'That's more than I can do.'

'But the woman's definitely in the flat.'

'Why doesn't she answer the door then?'

'That she doesn't answer is a sign . . .'

'In any case we've no right to break open the door.' He was an elderly officer with an iron-grey moustache, a man devoid of zeal, in fact rather apathetic, Querkuleit considered. However, the policeman pressed the bell once again, with no result, and then said what all say who want an easy life: 'We can't do any more about it.' And was on the point of going.

At that moment Eugen Bast set foot on the stairs. The blind man was groping for the banisters. As was his custom, he had sent away the boy at the bottom; he knew every step and wanted no spies in his flat.

The two heard him coming, heard the cautious tap-tap on the stairs. Even more distinctly they heard his hand shuffling along the banisters. Now they could see him, but he couldn't see them, and couldn't hear them either . . .

And seeing him thus, with his scarred, terrible face above a faded field-grey overcoat, blind, menacing, Querkuleit involuntarily placed his hand on the policeman's arm, meaning to warn him to keep silent. But the policeman had understood this.

The blind man did not see them, did not hear them, but he sensed their presence. His head was raised as if he were casting for their scent, as if he wanted to smell them out. 'Who's there?' he said.

Again the hand on the policeman's arm.

'There's someone!'

Silence.

'I'm only a poor blind beggar. Don't play your tricks with a blind man,' went on the false imploring voice.

Silence.

The speaker was now standing in the light of the window, his repulsive face turned full towards them, scarcely a metre away. The face with the open mouth was very near them. It seemed incredible that he could not see them – even though one knew he could not see, it nevertheless remained somehow incredible.

The policeman scrutinized the man. No, he didn't know him. But perhaps it was something in the sound of his voice – one who has much to do with liars instinctively perceives them; perhaps it was also an indefinable something in the man's whole bearing, something the policeman was hardly conscious of – but a blind beggar would have been helpless and afraid, while this one was tense and suspicious. Querkuleit, however, was now simply frightened of the terrible face close to him.

'Who's there? Tell me, boys! I know there's someone . . . What d'you want?'

And now the policeman proved to be not so old and dull as he seemed – he had an inspiration. Putting his hand into the pocket of his greatcoat he brought out something, holding it tightly so that it shouldn't clink.

Nevertheless the blind man had heard the friction of skin against greatcoat. He gripped his stick . . . In a surprisingly malignant voice he said: 'If yer don't say what yer want I'll bash yer.'

(Querkuleit understood now why he had never heard the man's voice in the night – even now, pale with fury, he spoke only in a whisper.)

The policeman let the handcuffs clink.

'Cops!' shouted Eugen Bast. 'Arrest me!'

And he aimed his stick at the policeman with such sureness that the point struck the man's belly and he fell to the ground screaming. Eugen Bast, however, glided down the stairs with a dreamlike swiftness – Querkuleit, for all that he could see, was not able to catch up with him. The policeman, in such pain that he could not get to his feet, did one useful thing – he blew his whistle. (He could act now; a man who responds thus to the clink of handcuffs is no disabled soldier with a good record but – well, that would soon be investigated.)

The shrilling of the police whistle brought the whole tenement out. 'Stop him!' shouted Querkuleit.

Suddenly the blind man met everywhere with obstacles. He tried to evade them, tried to beat them down, got confused, lost his bearings, stumbled, fell – and Querkuleit was upon him.

The blind man lay still, making no attempt to escape.

'What do you want?' he whined. 'A poor blind beggar. I've done nothin'. You frightened me.' But it was too late to play the innocent now.

The policeman had had enough; the man was a bit too determined and nasty to be a harmless beggar. He had seen the man's reaction at the sound of the handcuffs. The policeman knew what he knew, and the rest was only a matter of patient, careful investigation . . . For even the best false papers only last as long as their owner is not under suspicion. Clever Bast soon grasped that: admit what must be admitted, once it's been proved three times over, but deny everything else. Blame all, in any case, on that stupid bitch Eva, escape oneself, and not let go of her for a moment.

Thus the surreptitious message. No directions as to the evidence to be given, only the words: when I whistle you kneel.

She was pacing her cell. She had been away from it a lot, what with being questioned by the magistrate and her brother's visit, but she was thinking neither of the questions nor her brother nor her own fate; what worried her was – did he whistle while I was out of the cell?

So much was she his slave that it never occurred to her how immaterial it was whether he had whistled or not, since he couldn't observe the effect of his whistle. And that she was really free at last. No, such a thought could not enter her head now.

She was just having her meal when the summons came to her across the courtyard, through the window – the shrill whistle.

Putting the spoon back in the dish, she went into the corner and knelt down, paying no attention to what the others might think or say. She knelt down, redeemed, almost happy – she was again in the hand of her lord and master – his creature, his! Once again, she knelt.

§ X

It hadn't been easy for Heinz to go to his father. He found the burden he had to carry quite enough and, what's more, there was what he had to report about his sister. No, it wasn't easy.

Old Hackendahl sat at the table cutting a stick and listening in silence to Mother's complaints about his night work being at an end. Look at the money it had brought in! Just as soon as they were once more beginning to live free of worry, it was finished. 'But Father never tells me why he does something.'

'Tomfoolery,' was all the reply old Hackendahl made.

His wife took this personally and went on complaining in tears. Heinz however understood that his father was referring to his night work at Rude Gustav's. He became restless and would like to have spoken. Not for the first time, he thought that his mother complained a little too much and that his father showed rather more patience than he was given credit for. His mother had naturally forgotten how much she at first complained that his father would get used to drinking too much. His father had definitely not forgotten that, but didn't say a word to her about it. That was sensible of him, and patient.

Eventually his mother paused, and her son was able to report about Eva.

'I always knew that would happen,' wailed Frau Hackendahl. The old man looked at his son, nodded, but said nothing. After a while he rose, paced the room and finally said: 'Go and make some coffee, Mother.' Frau Hackendahl departed, slowly and crying, but she cried so easily and naturally that it was painful to see. She cried like that over every little mishap – over a burnt rice pudding, for example.

'How does she look?' asked his father, stopping in front of Heinz.

'She's changed a lot. She looks old and done for.'

'Is it the same fellow? Bast he was called, Eugen Bast.'

'Yes.'

'Then nothing can be done. I saw the chap once.'

'I also saw him once,' said Heinz. He closed his eyes, and the blind man, who had let her kiss his gruesome scars, stood in front of him again. Ghastly! 'Have you seen him since he was blind?'

'Blind? Is he blind now? That's God's punishment on him.'

'Eva fired and blinded him.'

'Eva? Then perhaps she can still be helped, after all.'

'No. Less now than ever. She hasn't the power to stand up to him.'

'You're right, yes. Will you keep an eye on her?'

'Certainly.'

'Good. And will I have to make a statement?'

'Yes.'

'But what am I to tell them?'

'Everything, just as it happened.'

'Just as it happened?' Iron Gustav laughed. 'That'd be difficult, Bubi. I dunno how it happened, I don't know why it's like that with my children. Why do you think it is, Bubi? Aren't you worried sometimes that you'll be the same?'

'No, Father, I'm not worried any more – not at all. I was worried once.'

'Well, there you are!'

'I sometimes think that it got like that for my brothers and sisters only because they are so much older than me. They had the impact of everything, not just the inflation, like me. I know so little about the war, and hardly anything of the peace. The peaceful time before the war was particularly bad, Father.'

'Oh, nonsense! Things were good in peacetime. It was a golden period.'

'But all that's not true, Father! It might have looked like gold, but it was merely gold plate. It wasn't genuine. It rubbed off as soon as it was used.'

'None of it rubbed off with me.'

Heinz could have contradicted him. He thought of his father's affluence, which had been 'rubbed' away. He thought of the children's love, something not to be had on command, which had also been rubbed away. And he thought of the iron in his father, which was getting softer and softer – ever diminishing, the more often he referred to it. But what would be the point?

'Well, I'll look in on Eva from time to time,' Heinz said.

His father was still deep in thought, and said: 'Back then, it was easier for an old man to manage things for himself – but not any more, no longer!'

He looked at what he had been carving and his eyes grew more animated. 'Any case, I do what I like these days, I don't bother about anythin' now, whether it's the law or me children or the pastor preachin' – I follow me own ideas . . . Heinz, what's this goin' to be?' And he held the stick up.

'I don't know, Father. A whip? But it's too small . . .'

'You wait another five minutes, my boy,' said Hackendahl in his old autocratic manner. 'I'll put a handle on it and a lash . . . Is it true that they like playing at being cab drivers?'

'Quite true,' said Heinz, suddenly understanding. 'Wouldn't you like to take the whip yourself, Father? They're really very nice kiddies.'

'What, you're ashamed to be seen carrying a child's whip? – I'll put two knots in it. I s'pose you'll be able to crack it.'

'I think you'd show them better, Father.'

'Rubbish! Once is enough. To have been taken in once is enough. And it happened to me four times. You're all right, Heinz. I don't count you . . .'

'They're nice little chaps, they really are. In your place I'd have a look at them.'

'But what did I say to you, about being taken in? There's no way that I'll do that.'

'It would really be the right thing to do, if you brought it to them, they'd enjoy it.'

'I've nothing to do with Gudde's children!'

'But her name's been the same as ours for a long time now, Father. She's called Hackendahl.'

'When she got the kids her name was Gudde.'

'I don't understand why you've suddenly gone all moral about her, Father. We're not the clergy.'

'Otto was a softie and she's a hunchback. No, I don't want to see the children. If I want to give my heart to anything, I go to my horses.'

'Otto was only like that with you . . .'

'So it's all my fault, eh?'

'He wasn't a softie out there at the Front. And for you to reproach a person for not having a straight back, that's not like you at all, Father.'

'All hunchbacks are false,' said the old man stubbornly.

'Nonsense, Father. You could just as well say that all red-haired people are no good.'

'They ain't. Judas had red hair. P'r'aps he was a hunchback too, only we don't know.'

'A person who can bring up a family alone in times like these . . .'

'Did you say alone? Then what are you doin' there?'

Heinz flushed crimson and this made him all the more angry, and his father was getting upset too.

'Not that I mean you have any dealin's of that sort with the Gudde . . .'

'Oh, do shut up, Father. You just don't want to see them.'

'You tell yer father to shut up?'

'If you don't want to see them you needn't make a whip for them.'

'Will you take it or won't you?' The old man held the whip out.

Heinz did not stir. 'Take it yourself. Look at the boys for yourself. Softie and Judas! So that's how you talk about your children!'

'The Gudde isn't my child.'

'G'night, Father.'

'G'night, Bubi. It's no good you being in a rage with me. I'm an old man an' I've always bin made of iron. No one can make me do what I don't want to.'

'G'night, Father.'

'G'night, Heinz . . . Heinz! I'll put the whip in the corner by the stove. When you've got over yer temper you can take it along sometime or other.'

'I'll not touch it. Never!'

'Blockhead! Never say never.'

'I wonder who's the blockhead here.'

'Why, you.'

'No, you, Father.'

'Who's not taking the whip, me or you?'

'Who doesn't want to take it there? You or me?'

Half angrily, half ironically, they faced one another. But it was not a deep anger – there was too much fondness between them for that.

Frau Hackendahl came in with the coffee. 'Why are you quarrelling again?' she asked plaintively. 'I've made such a nice cup of coffee – and now you're quarrelling.'

'No, we're not. But I must go now. Bye-bye, Mother.'

'Oh dear, and the nice coffee!'

'You and Father have it. I must be off.'

'How d'you know that I want coffee now? That's just what I don't want. I'll visit me horse in the stable. He won't tell me to shut up.'

'Oh, Bubi, how could you say that to your father!'

But Frau Hackendahl was already alone and the two disputants clumping down the stairs side by side. In the yard they stopped and looked at each other. Heinz began to grin, while his father's lips also twitched.

'Well, have you thought it over about the whip? Bring it down.'

Heinz laughed. 'That's what you want, Father! Always having your own way!'

'Well, and you?'

'I'll tell you what – if you bring down the whip I'll present it to the boys from their grandfather.'

Hackendahl swallowed as if something were sticking in his gullet. 'You wouldn't make an ole man traipse up and down like that, would you? No, you come up again and have the coffee. It'll please your mother.'

'You fetch the whip down, or it'll stay here.'

'All right, it stays here.'

'All right. G'night, Father.'

'G'night, Heinz.'

His son was already in the gateway when the old man called out: 'Bubi!'

'What is it now?'

'Wait! I'll throw it down to you from the window. That satisfy you?'

Heinz thought for a moment. 'Right!' he said. But as the father disappeared in the entrance hall he had to shout after him: 'Old blockhead!'

This time Hackendahl kept his answer back till he was looking down from the window. 'Here it is, you blockhead,' he cried. 'Take care it don't fall in the mud now it's nice and white.'

The son caught it. 'Well, so long, Father.'

'Well, so long, Bubi. An' I ain't a blockhead. I'm made of iron, that's the truth of it.'

'That's what you imagine but you're just simply a blockhead.'

'Like you, you mean? No, iron's what I am.'

And with that the old man slammed the window so as to have the last word.

§ XI

As always, when he had been at his parents', Heinz did not take the direct way to the station but made a detour past Frau Quaas's stationery shop, where he would stand for a while studying contemporary developments as seen in the window; at the moment popular songs on postcards, half sentimental and half indecent, were the rage. Into the shop itself, however, he did not venture – the Widow Quaas remained unmolested since that letter saying: 'I don't want to see you ever again. But for you to torment Mother too I think perfectly low-down. Your Irma.' Since then he had contented himself with standing in front of the shop and waiting about five minutes, no longer – for five minutes were long enough. Then he went. Sometimes he would think: it's silly of me to hang around here. I wouldn't be able to recognize Irma if I saw her. She was only a flapper in those days. But nonetheless he continued to go to the shop and even tried to imagine what Irma looked like now – a not unpleasant pastime when one had to stand about for five minutes.

Today he threw only a fleeting glance at the window. Since his last visit, only a new picture postcard series had been added – part sugar, part sour. The pictures were sweet, the text . . . contemporary smut. One rhyme Widow Quaas had not put in the window – it was a bit too crude for her.

Heinz turned round, looked up and down the empty street and started to play with the little whip. A fine whip, this of Father's. Swish! With a proper whiplash, too, and a nickel-silver handle through which the brass already dimly glimmered. Heinz hadn't held a whip for a long time, and soon he would have to demonstrate with it before his nephews – would he be able to crack it properly? He tried. The street was empty; besides, what did he care what people thought of him? But perhaps he did care a little, for his first attempt was indeed feeble – the crack might have been a dying sigh . . .

With a frown he looked at the window. No one was watching him, however; his failure had no witness. So this time he lashed out properly, a crack like a pistol shot.

And as if this had been a signal, a girl's head popped out of the shop door and an angry voice shouted: 'You seem to have gone quite mad! Will you go away at once? You probably imagine—'

'Irma!' Heinz was taken completely aback. 'Listen, Irma . . .'

'Oh, bother you! It's finished with us, you stupid boy. I wrote that in my letter.' And the shop door banged to, making the wretched bell tinkle madly. Then he heard the key turn in the lock.

With a bound he was at the door. But once a key has been turned it is too late to press down the latch.

'Irma!' cried Heinz imploringly to the glass panel entirely obscured by picture postcards. 'Irma, do open! I only want to explain to you.' This was the first time he had seen Irma for five years and already there was a fresh misunderstanding. 'Irma,' he implored, glaring at the rubbishy postcards.

A white hand pushed the cards aside. It hung up a notice – a printed notice, the sort of thing Frau Quaas kept in stock for customers – hung up the notice, pushed it straight and disappeared.

CLOSED TODAY

Because of a Family Celebration

Heinz stared. Stupidly. Till he suddenly grew conscious of his ridiculous position – he outside, she probably watching through some slit and laughing at the silly figure he cut. Turning about, he cracked the whip three times in challenge and marched off.

Thank heavens, he thought, that Father gave me the whip. If I hadn't had it! Well, you wait.

§ XII

A deep, eerie, almost alarming silence reigned in the kitchen of Gertrud Hackendahl, née Gudde. The eleven-year-old Gustav sat, almost motionless, under the light, reading his school book. Now and then he gave a quick glance at his mother, who sat at the table opposite him, sewing. His look returned immediately to his book, and he continued to read, concerned only not to draw his mother's attention.

And the six-year-old Otto was no different. How often – after he had reorganized his coloured building blocks on the floorboards in front of the hearth – had he been about to shout: 'Mother! Look at my puffer train!', or 'Mother, do billy goats have tails?' But even he, who so easily forgot things, swallowed his own words, looked at his mother, and was silent.

On other days, Gertrud Hackendahl would never have tolerated such worrying silence. Of course she was all in favour of accommodation; any handicapped person living with children has from the very beginning to see that disorder does not descend, otherwise their authority will be lost for ever. But there is a big difference between obeying and creeping. On other days, Gertrud would immediately have noticed the children's careful looks and unnatural quiet, and it would not have pleased her. Today, however . . .

Today, however, she wasn't thinking of the children at all. She sat there and sewed, a deep furrow between her eyebrows, her thin lips pressed hard together. She was completely alone. She had never again felt so lonely since the news of Otto's death reached her. No, now it was perhaps more painful, because she had been so horribly betrayed! Otto had never betrayed her. Otto was always open and honest, never deceitful.

She sewed away at her material as if her needle were red-hot. She tried to recall the pleasure she experienced when the postman had brought her the registered letter that morning, with the news that she had come into an inheritance – that she had become the owner of a house, and on the special island of Hiddensee. She would have her own house, her own boat, her own fields, her own stables, by the sea, where the air never stagnates as it does in this urban wasteland, and where every breath tastes strongly of salty expanse.

A dream expectation had been fulfilled, an accidental inheritance, from some old uncle whom she had hardly ever seen. 'In the absence of the Testator's last wishes, as the closest known heir . . .'

A dream had come true – and a mass of faces and of new dreams bombarded her: first, when should she go to look at it all? How she could organize things with the boat and the fishing nets. Whom would she rent the land to – naturally only until Gustav is old enough to deal with it all himself. How she would chat with the people. Oh, how she had longed for years to speak the local *Plattdeutsch*! She had never liked the Berlin dialect – even in her husband's mouth and in the mouths of her own children it had remained a foreign language to her. Otto will learn fast – Gustav will at first be thoroughly teased at school. These island children are a rough lot!

There were a thousand thoughts and considerations. What will the house look like? She is bound to have been in it, but she can't remember. She tries, and for one moment sees before her the darkness of a brick entrance hall, strewn with white sand, which crackles under her feet. There is a big built-in hearth with an open chimney above it, through which even at midday you could see the stars in the sky – a never-ending miracle of her childhood. But, it is her parents' house she is thinking of! There, in its dark casing, the wall clock is ticking, with painted flowers on its face. However, it was not her parents' house that she had inherited.

She looked at the kitchen clock, a hideous object with a stoneware face. Suddenly she could bear it no longer. Heinz must be told straight away about this inheritance. He must know about it before the children.

She took her coat, locked up the flat, gave the neighbour the key for the children and went on her way. It was a very long way for the fragile woman she was; it was also a difficult one. The paving stones were packed smooth with snow, and the house-owners were not very conscientious about their duty to clear the snow away. Still more important duties were neglected at this time. 'Oh well – best of luck!' says a Berliner laughing, if someone falls flat on his backside on the pavement.

She mustn't risk falling over. She's convinced that if she did, she would indeed at least break a leg. She walked apprehensively and carefully. Once, she looked with yearning at the electric tram, but a possible inheritance was not to make her light-headed. A return journey would cost half a day's wages – impossible.

She went with furrowed brow, preoccupied by her journey, but equally preoccupied by her visit to the bank. She didn't like to have Heinz called away from his work; she knew that would not go down well. In any case, she wanted to speak to Heinz, so she said, 'It's an urgent family matter.'

The doorman carefully folded the list, put it in a drawer, removed his pince-nez from his nose, cleaned it, put it back on, looked penetratingly at Gertrud, and said, 'Herr Hackendahl is not in the office.'

He then removed the list from the drawer he had just placed it in.

For a moment Gertrud was totally confused. She knew nothing but that Heinz spent his whole working day in this building in a certain room, busy with something called statistics. And now he was not there.

'Oh, if you please . . . !' she said to the doorman.

He raised his eyes from the list and looked at her through his pince-nez.

'Can I please wait here?'

'As far as I'm concerned,' he replied, and watched her sit in an armchair, looking towards the entrance, so that she could speak to Heinz as soon as he returned. The doorman had first to deal with three or four other visitors. With some he was very polite, whereas to a small messenger boy, who looked freezing cold, he was even more impolite than he had been to her.

Eventually he had time, so he looked over to her and shouted, 'You there!'

She gave a start, jumped up and went to him. 'Yes, please?'

'Have you time to wait?' he asked.

'Will it be very long?' she replied.

He appeared to be thinking hard and fast. Then he said, 'Until early the day after tomorrow!' And before she could say anything in return: 'Because Herr Hackendahl has just taken a three-day holiday.' And then, to destroy her completely: 'Shouldn't you have known that, if he lives with you?'

She was convinced that she had been messed about. He merely wanted to protect a relative from family matters, leaving the bank's working time unmolested. Or else there had been a mistake . . .

However, the doorman, who had shown her ample proof of his power and glory, suddenly became human when he saw how upset she was. He got out the holiday list and she saw with her own eyes that Heinz Hackendahl had already gone on holiday yesterday, was on holiday today, and would still be on holiday tomorrow – and Heinz hadn't mentioned it to her!

She had detached herself from the now very worried door-man and had gone home. She was in such a hurry. She was sure the explanation would be at home. But there was nothing there.

Later the children came. They had eaten, and told her what they had done, and although she only ever answered with 'Yes' and 'No' and 'Really', at first they didn't notice at all that their mother hadn't been there for them all day, until in the end she shouted angrily: 'For goodness sake be quiet and leave me in peace! Go away and do something!'

Now she was sitting undisturbed and could grumble again. The morning's great pleasure was over. Already when she had gone to Heinz, that pleasure was no longer unadulterated and complete. She had thought that she would have to leave her brother-in-law, her only friend.

But they were already apart; he was no longer her friend. She simply did not know it. She had thought they had everything in common; at least she had never hidden anything from him. But for him it had been different. He had deceived her. If she hadn't happened to have gone to the bank – perhaps such things had often happened and she simply hadn't noticed!

Thoughts of the inheritance returned – and suddenly she greeted it as a redemption. Yes, it meant separation from Heinz. And it was good that the separation came for such understandable reasons. Now she could never live with him again – once mistrust is awoken, it never sleeps again.

No, it was all over.

She tried to imagine life on her island farm – a life with children, animals, wind and water. But it would be so empty . . . She is so used to him, to someone bright, dependable, when he first came to her. Back then, in summer 1919, when he moved in with her, he was still like a hunted man, restless, without aim.

Then he became steadier. He found an aim: with her to feed the children from the most wretched, often worthless, income. Patient work, day by day, work without glory or thanks – work for work's sake, perhaps, for the sake of a future which neither he, she nor any-one else would know.

She couldn't remember that he ever lost courage, that he ever slowed down. She recalled no failures.

Oh, Heinz! She thought . . .

And suddenly she was overwhelmed by a thick, all-enveloping pall of sadness – that sadness that everyone experiences again and again, and that separates a person from the rest of us. Life runs irretrievably through our fingers, and what we once held onto is already gone.

Irretrievable.

'Mother's crying,' the children whisper, and little Otto is the brave one this time and is with her first. She holds the children and presses them to her. Life flows, runs away. You too will one day leave me and go away – irretrievable.

§ XIII

She didn't look up when he came in. Already outside in the corridor, he whistled contentedly to himself. The children threw themselves at him; she was pleased that she was busy with his meal and didn't have to speak to him. It was exactly the time when he was used to returning from the bank, exactly to the nearest five minutes. What a torment life sometimes is! All the courage to resist disappears; the worst is tolerated simply through weariness.

'Heinz, Mummy cried!' And 'Mummy, he brought us a whip!'

Children's sadness and children's joy, mixed together. But the sadness is already almost forgotten. They've got a whip. Mummy will surely be pleased? The older, Gustav, glanced at his mother.

'Mummy cried, Heinz!' he repeated emphatically. And now that he had done his duty, leaving grown-up tears to grown-up comfort, he devoted himself with his brother entirely to the investigation of the whip.

'What is it?' asked Heinz. 'Did you cry? What happened, Tutti?'

'Nothing. Really nothing. Go to the yard, Gustav. Little Otto, you can't play with the whip here. No, stay here!' She realized that it was better to have the children there. However, she then thought it cowardly to hide behind them, and said irritably: 'Oh, go out then! You'll break something up here. Just don't crack it at me!'

'Stop!' said Heinz to the children who wanted to go out. 'Where does the whip come from?'

'Impossible to say,' declared Otto.

'Let the children go – your meal's getting cold.'

'One moment, Tutti – you'll be pleased. So where did it come from? Try!'

'If you came from the bank . . .'

'Yes, if!'

'So. Didn't you come from the bank, Heinz?'

'If I tell you, it would be too easy.'

'Heinz, your meal's getting cold.'

'What sort of a whip is it then? Have another look at it, Gustav.'

'Yes, Heinz.'

'From a shop!'

'No, Otto, not from a shop. Look, Gustav.'

'I know, I know!'

'And I know too.'

'No you don't, Otto. Your soup—'

'So what do you know, Gustav?'

'It came from Grandfather.'

'Yes, indeed. That whip was made for you, especially for you, by the oldest cab driver in Berlin – Iron Gustav!'

'Will he come soon? I want to ride in a cab.'

'Always on to the next thing! Out with you, enjoy your whip! Afterwards, take some polish, Gustav, and polish up its handle a bit. Grandfather didn't have any more time. So now, out with you!'

'Will you give us a cloth to clean it with, Mummy?'

'Give it to them. Out you go! What is it, Tutti?'

'Nothing – nothing at all. Please eat now.'

'But I can see, something is wrong. Are you angry with me?'

'Please, just eat!'

'So you are angry with me. Why?'

'Please eat, Heinz!'

'Not until you tell me . . .'

'I'm not saying anything. You must eat! Are you deaf?'

'But what in heaven's name is wrong, Tutti?' he asked, completely mystified. He knew about women's whims from his colleagues at the bank – from Irma, and mostly from Tinette. And he should have known from experience that a woman in non-answering mode is more stubborn than a mule, and only makes all questions and pressure more useless.

But no, he declared decisively: 'I'm not eating a mouthful until you tell me what's going on, Tutti.'

She was enraged and said: 'Eat now, or shall I clear away?'

'Please, Tutti. Tell me what's happened.'

She looked at him, almost begging for help. It should never have come to this. She felt she'd done the wrong thing. If only he would eat! He must have his meal. He must spare her having to clear away.

But no, he spared her nothing, absolutely nothing. 'Please, clear away. I'm not hungry any more.'

And she did clear away, with death in her heart. He'd come home from work, or rather he had not come home from work, but without food, and then he hadn't eaten. It made her desperate. And all that time not a single word had been spoken about what she really wanted to accuse him of. They really had started an argument about nothing. What would have happened if she had talked about his lies?

Nevertheless, she did not clear his meal away completely, but kept it ready to hand. She hoped that he would still eat, despite everything; order means not going to bed without eating. There are still four hours to go before bedtime. He must eat within that time. She would like to feed him spoon by spoon like an unruly child!

That child fidgeted about in the kitchen, picking up this and that and putting it down again. He looked for letters in the little shoe cupboard – but there were none, because the one letter that was there she still had in her bag from her journey to the bank. Heinz was visibly undecided what to do. She felt she would give way at the first kind word. But he was as incapable as she was of uttering it.

In the end he disappeared into the front room, where he slept with the boys (she slept in the kitchen), and she heard the sound of water splashing. She settled down at the table with her sewing, deeply unhappy – even more so than in the morning when she discovered his deceit. Because now that she had seen him again, she was almost certain that everything was different. Hadn't he said that the whip came from Grandfather? So, that's where it came from. So she had only needed to ask him, why now from Grandfather and not from the bank? But she hadn't asked. And now it's all a mess.

He should have told me for sure before; her thinking was dogged and bitter. I don't want to have to interrogate him all the time! At the same time, she was sound enough in herself to feel that everything, including the interrogation, was a bit exaggerated.

During the next ten minutes, Heinz went numerous times past the kitchen, in a hurry, as if on fire. He went between the front room and the corridor. Outside, in the corridor, his voice was pronouncedly carefree. He was cleaning; in the front room and in the kitchen, he was silent. At one moment she nearly flared up, when he rummaged through her mending basket for a cloth, and – typical man – took away the one indispensable item – a patch for Gustav's trousers.

However, she controlled herself. If he doesn't eat, he can ruin the mending of Gustav's trousers too. She would have to find a new patch. Let him go on being like that!

She simply accepted everything like no other woman, and her silence was so striking that it was almost audible . . .

Heinz perhaps felt that too. Because he stopped walking up and down like a fireman, and for a while she heard him still whispering with the children, telling them to be quiet – 'Don't upset Mummy, the poor thing's not well' – and then she only heard the children whispering.

She didn't really trust the apparent peace. And, after a further quarter of an hour, when she looked for him, she established that young Heinz had gone, not just to the lavatory halfway up the stairs, but that he had completely gone, with hat and coat.

The children were playing with the whip. They had made it into a cab. One grasped the handle, the other the lash, and easily, at will, turned it into a horse and driver. Just as easily as Mummy and Heinz had changed from being the best of friends to being bitter enemies.

Because that's what they now were – Gertrud could see it no other way. The fact that he had deceived her about his holiday, and that he not only refused his meal, but even left the house without saying goodbye – and at a time when he never went out. No, that really crowned his behaviour! She would never speak to him again – and if he spoke to her, then she would give him a bit of her mind, and tell him exactly what she thought of him.

For the next three-quarters of an hour, she seemed to sew everything that she thought of him into Elfriede Fischer's dress. The sewing held, but every needle prick must eventually make itself felt a thousand times on the said Fräulein Fischer!

Then she had to give the children their supper, which took place – against all custom – almost in silence. Then Gustav put Otto to bed, and she heard the children chatting in the front room, with their grandfather as their favourite subject. Grandfather who had sent a whip and imagined it would make everything all right . . . Grandfather, whose stubbornness Heinz had inherited. Oh God, she would have to take much more care of the children to see that they did not inherit the same. Defiance is a curse! Stubbornness is too. Just as Heinz had always stubbornly said: 'I won't have any soup today' – just as in *Struwwelpeter* – unbearable. Horrible!

Then Gustav came back into the kitchen to read for another hour, as he did every evening before going to sleep. Just then, Tutti thought she heard Heinz on the staircase, and wanted to be alone with him on his return. So Gustav was sent off; he had of course forgotten to cut the little one's nails.

Gustav stubbornly insisted that tomorrow, not today, was the weekly nail-cutting day. But such persistent stubbornness made Gertrud very angry: 'Go and cut his nails at once! You must do as I say. Your stubbornness is horrible.'

However, it had not been Heinz on the staircase, so Gustav had to suffer the downpour from his mother's storm clouds for nothing. She immediately regretted this very much, but then comforted herself with the thought that it was enough if he learned to obey, even if he didn't understand the meaning of the order.

However, her ear-slapping mode prevailed. It was in Heinz's favour, because it brought her a small step closer to him. She took the letter about the inheritance out of her little handbag and put it visibly on the little shoe cupboard. That would be a starting point. If

he didn't take it up out of pure defiance, then she would consider
him lost – lost for ever.

Shortly before seven o'clock Heinz returned, all sweet innocence,
cheeks freshly reddened by the cold. He had a lively talk with his
nephew, first about the whip, then about the Occupation of the
Ruhr, which the English Law Courts had now also declared illegal.
As a result of that, the mark had become a little stronger.

And then, at table: 'I did a quick shop and bought what was available. We at the bank don't think the French will give way. So the
mark will fall again. There are also two hundredweight of briquettes
in the cellar.'

'Thanks,' said Tutti. 'We already had enough briquettes.'

And she would have liked to hit out again, first because what she
said was not the case, and second because, whatever she did, she
could only make the war situation worse. In these icy conditions, to
drag two hundredweight of briquettes from the coal merchants to
the cellar was an achievement indeed!

Heinz responded to this expression of thanks with a surprised
shrug of the shoulders, fetched a book from the front room (and in
doing so quite needlessly whispered for a long time with little Otto,
who should have been asleep long ago), sat down at the table and
began to read.

Unbroken silence reigned until half past seven, when Gustav
closed his book, said goodnight, and disappeared. Two minutes later
Gertrud got up, went to the little shoe cupboard, within sight –
incidentally – of the reading Heinz, made a provocative noise, as he
wouldn't look up, with the document from the Bergen court in Hiddensee, and then disappeared, leaving the letter behind – to go into
the adjoining room to see that that rascal Gustav was washing himself properly.

When she came back into the kitchen ten minutes later, she
looked first at her brother-in-law, then at the letter. He was reading
as before, and the letter was also lying where it had been.

She began her sewing with a feeling of total devastation. Two
hours lay before them before bedtime, but she was convinced that,
after so much accommodation on her part, she was no longer

capable of uttering a word. Were they to go to bed in a state of strife? And what about? About nothing. (She was now convinced that it had all been 'about nothing'.) And he had dragged two hundredweight of briquettes into the cellar! And he'd thought of coconut oil too. What misery!

Time went by in total silence. The reader's face was near her; occasionally she heard the sound of pages being turned. He wasn't just pretending to read; he really was reading. About every half-hour he got up and went into the corridor. It was just the same as ever; he never smoked in the kitchen. He went into the stairwell to smoke, so that she didn't have to sleep in a smoke-filled kitchen. That was actually thoughtful, but not today; it was just habit. She was almost convinced that, had he only thought of it, he would have smoked in the kitchen just to annoy her.

By the time it was past nine o'clock, she was feeling ever more anxious. Only twenty-five minutes to go! She had never gone to bed with such a burden, and she still had to talk things over with him. But he was completely pig-headed.

At ten minutes before half past nine, Heinz went out to the stairwell for the last time to smoke his habitual last cigarette. While he was outside, she controlled herself heroically. Once again, she gave way. She took the letter from the little shoe cupboard and put it in the middle of the table. Two minutes later she pushed the letter nearer his book, and a minute after that close up to his book. And if he had come back a little later, her spirit of sacrifice would have driven her to put it on the book itself.

But he had already come in. 'Well, goodnight, Tutti,' he said carelessly and took his book. He started when he saw the letter. (He really started, so he really hadn't seen it before. Incredible!) He read the sender's address, repeated 'Well, goodnight, Tutti', and went towards the door of the front room.

'Heinz!' she cried, like a drowning woman.

'What's wrong?' he asked, a bit grumpy.

'The letter!' and she pointed to it.

'Yes, so what?'

'Read it, Heinz. Please read it.'

He looked at her and suddenly, seeing her standing there, a bundle of misery, almost in tears – suddenly he began to laugh, to roar
with laughter.

'Tutti! Tutti!' he cried, laughing. 'Whatever is wrong with you
today? You make a thorough mess of me, you don't feed me, and
you don't utter a word – you're not going sick on me, are you?'

And when she saw him standing there like that – tall, laughing,
young and full of life – it suddenly hit her. She understood immediately why she had got so upset that morning over his 'deceit' – why
she had argued with him and sulked. She understood, and she felt
that she loved him – that the younger man had outlived, really outlived, the older one – that nothing more of Otto remained in her.

In the same moment that she was conscious of her love, she was
also conscious that he should never ever notice it. She saw herself as
if in a mirror – her head, which with age had become more pointed,
more bird-like, her hump . . . and she remembered that he was ten
years younger than her.

While all this went through her – a huge wave of happiness and
misery which totally overwhelmed her – she was still at the same
time his old sister-in-law Tutti, whom he knew. Then she pressed her
lips together again and said: 'You were absolutely right to laugh at
me, Heinz. I've been completely crazy today. It must have been the
excitement. First, excitement over the inheritance, and then my
being upset when you were not at the bank, but on holiday. Why
were you on holiday, by the way?'

However, while she was still speaking, she felt the wave inside
sinking and sinking, until it had gone. It had been – once again – a
moment, before her life declined, which had raised her up as if on a
high mountain, and enabled her to see, and for a fleeting moment to
feel, all the treasures of love, happiness, and sadness too. But as she
was more than halfway through her life, she easily sank back into her
petty, daily round of duty and renunciation.

The two of them sat there for a long time, talking with one
another, about Irma and about the only partially persuaded grandfather, about Eva, whom Heinz had gone on holiday to help, but
who didn't want help, and about his miserably botched attempt to
spare her the excitement over Eva. 'Because you're not in the best of

health, Tutti, and I sometimes worry when I hear you coughing at night.'

'I've always coughed, Heinz, and at home we used to say, "If you keep coughing, you'll keep living." '

'Yes, you and your "at home",' he said, 'but who here is going to make my bed? Oh, Tutti. I'm going to find it damn difficult to live in a furnished room again, and without our boys.'

'Well,' she said and could even smile, 'I don't think Irma would like to live in a furnished room, and your own boys are always better than "our boys".'

She saw him blush, and actually blush in a way that a young man in 1923 should not have to at such a remark. And she was almost happy when he stood up and said: 'Don't talk such rubbish, Tutti! With Irma, of all people! Don't forget: Closed for Family Mourning.'

'Liar! For Family Celebration!'

'Well, a celebration like that would be like mourning.'

§ XIV

During the fortnight which Erich Hackendahl needed to wind up his affairs in Berlin, he wondered over and over again whether or not to ring up his friend the lawyer. More and more nebulous and drunken did that night of national mourning over what had happened in the Ruhr now appear to him; one ought not to take such things too seriously. He himself had been drunk, the other had been drunk and, as is well known, drunkenness impairs the memory – one need not remember things too clearly. In any case his recollections of the evening were vague, very vague. Several times he had picked up the receiver, only to put it back when the exchange came on, or ask for another number. Despite a faulty memory, the relationship with his father had been violated. A friendship had been damaged. But he showed more decision about converting his property into money – that is, into stable currencies. With the villa in Zehlendorf he had luck; he sold it lock, stock and barrel to a foreigner who, having acquired a fortune on the London Stock Exchange, was thinking of buying up half Berlin. He had even more luck in that both he and this purchaser were of the opinion that the State, or more exactly the Exchequer, should be involved in the matter as little as possible. A bit of a wangle, of course. And so Erich became the possessor of a demand draft in Norwegian kroner on an Amsterdam firm, and the foreigner paid him pro forma a couple of million paper marks on a very backdated purchase agreement.

And his luck held in other things – the disposal of his firm, the collection of outstanding debts, the getting rid of his car. Erich, on the eve of his departure, could say: everything I possess is abroad.

He paced up and down his hotel room, delighted that he had been able to invest what was left of his wretched paper marks in a fur coat, a gold watch and a diamond ring. He was wondering whether the Customs would object to the fact that everything he possessed was brand new.

But what are one's connections for? Erich went to the telephone, asked for the lawyer's secret number, and half a minute later he heard the sound of the familiar soft, slightly ironic voice in his ear.

'Hello, Erich. Yes, I was thinking about ringing you – Yes, of course, we did have rather a lot. In those places they doctor the drinks too – Quite right, for days on end I thought I was poisoned – Yes, I can hardly remember . . . A dim idea that we went on somewhere . . . My doctor says methylated spirits would have that effect – And the champagne actually cost ten dollars! Crazy! Really? That's splendid – Indeed? Brussels? Why Brussels, by the way? Do you particularly want to go there? Not particularly? You have no particular connections there then? – Only from the war; yes, of course, I understand, I understand . . . Wait, Erich, you got half an hour to spare? I might have a suggestion to make. Magnificent! In your hotel? Splendid. Well then, I'll be in the bar in half an hour – So long, old chap. So sensible of you to ring me up.'

Smilingly Erich replaced the receiver . . . Everything OK now with the old fox; memory a bit off, fuddled with methylated – all right! Let him come, that was the main thing. You wouldn't be yourself, Herr Doctor, if you didn't want to earn a few pounds, dollars, Norwegian kroner.

And in the small but cosy hotel bar took place a memorable conversation. Never had the lawyer been so paternally benevolent or

Erich so tractable and filial. There they sat – a young and enterprising businessman, not badly off, on the eve of departure to try his
luck in the wide world, and the experienced politician ready to assist
his protégé a last time with advice and help. Oh yes, he was definitely
against Brussels; as a money market it was not in the first rank. The
great things took place in the city of Amsterdam, where gigantic battles were now being fought over the mark. 'And the mark, we're at
one there, is to be your main field of activity. I could regularly give
you tips by means of a very simple code which we can arrange
together.'

The waiter brought their sherry cobblers. 'The pegging of the
mark is to be your task, my dear Erich,' said the lawyer raising his
voice.

Both gentlemen smiled a little and thoughtfully stirred their drinks.

'No,' said the older man, 'have a look at Brussels by all means but
Amsterdam is the place for you, if only on account of the still very
strong hatred of the Germans in Brussels. In Amsterdam I could give
you a cordial introduction to my friend Roest the banker.'

This time the consumption of drinks was kept within very moderate limits, but the lawyer handed his young friend a little parcel to
take to Amsterdam – his share in the business. 'I am participating
with you to the extent of this sum; you can dispose of it in accordance with my advice.' And no small amount! The lawyer however
remained gentle and modest. 'Let me in on your deal when you
think fit . . . No, that's all right. An ordinary receipt. I have one prepared . . . A loan, that's the simplest way . . . Participation and share
in profits had better remain a verbal agreement. I trust you completely . . . How are you going to get across the frontier? Wait, let me
think.' He thought. 'Postpone your journey for a day. I think it can be
arranged for you to travel as a special courier for the Foreign Office.
You understand – diplomatic bag.'

Both smiled again.

'I would prefer, however, to send the receipt when I'm safely over
the frontier with the money,' said Erich, modest but firm.

'As you like, my dear Erich, as you like. You shall run no risk. I rely
entirely on you. Anyway, you'll be needing my information about
the mark. We're dependent on each other, isn't that so?'

This time both looked serious, both pondered, both finally nodded. Gravely.

The deputy then proceeded to expand on the prospects of the Ruhr uprising and the Cuno government. He was against the latter. 'It will fall: what can a government do nowadays against the Social Democrats, the strongest party? It must fall.'

'And the Ruhr uprising?'

'If you lose a war, you shouldn't make a fuss. The French demanded a lot, and we endorsed it. We should have given way on this too. The Ruhr uprising will fall as well.'

However, what will fall most will be the mark. What was the dollar that day? Forty-two thousand marks! And it was going to be quoted at forty-two millions, at forty-two milliards, till the bottom dropped out of it. The only thing that mattered now was to know when this stage was going to be reached so that the bears should cover. 'I'll wire you, Erich – you'll see!'

Three days later Erich travelled as special diplomatic courier to Brussels. It pleased him considerably that the Reich paid for his journey in pursuit of his further speculations. It was a drab February day when he arrived in Amsterdam; he disliked the town, thought it narrow, gloomy, overcrowded, noisy. The canals lay inert, stinking and foggy. And the offices of Roest the banker were three small, dirty rooms on a third floor. He had to go there several times before being received.

Herr Roest was a pale, tall, restless man with gold-rimmed spectacles. Failing to ask his visitor to take a seat, he paced up and down, continually wiping his face with a big coloured handkerchief.

'Who's he sent me?' he muttered. 'Nothing but scroungers. I've no vacancy in my office. There are only scroungers left in Germany. God, I suppose you know that the Belgian franc stayed firm? Like iron! And I'm a bear for a million.' Very depressed, Herr Roest looked at his visitor without seeing him and, wiping his face continually, expressed himself at length on the perfidy of the Belgian government which, while secretly supporting the franc, had led people to expect a fall in it. 'They're all criminals! A plague on them! And I'm a million down.' At last he remembered that his visitor had come with a letter of introduction. 'What d'you want?' he asked suspiciously. 'They all want something out of me. But who gives me anything?' Having decided to read the letter, he grew more amiable. 'So? You want to go to the Stock Exchange? Do a bit of foreign currency exchange? Then you're on the right track, I'll look after you like my own son, just like myself. But marks! Marks! What d'you want with marks? You'll burn your fingers; no one knows what'll become of the mark. Poincaré – he'll ruin it. What does he gain? Nothing at all. All very well if he did – but things are just like that anyway. Isn't that so? How much are you going to start off with?'

Erich Hackendahl muttered something about fifty thousand dollars but he wanted to think it over first – get his bearings. He didn't much like Herr Roest with his dirty, gnawed-at nails, his alternation of lament and aggression, his coloured handkerchief . . .

'Go, young man, go and ask round. Ask about Roest – you'll hear. And what'll you hear? God, I was caught short, caught short for one million Brussels.' He recovered himself and held out a damp and bony hand. 'You'll hear, you'll come back.' Lord, what a greenhorn to think that he could hang onto his money and make a fortune as well. He'll see!

Erich Hackendahl did see the city. He saw the city in turmoil. That is to say, he didn't see the city at all. He had intended to go to the Rijksmuseum and see the Rembrandts. The landlubber wanted to see the harbour and the overseas traffic – he saw nothing of it. He sat about in the lounges of the luxury hotels, in bars, in the cafés frequented by the stockjobbers; he went to the brokers' offices and sat with other clients staring feverishly at the glass panels which showed the quotations in illuminated figures, flashing off, flashing on again.

Wherever he went he heard only talk of gold currencies, bear selling, offer and bid, arbitrage, guilders, francs, dollars, pounds – he heard nothing else. It was possible that the Dutch people in general were leading a different kind of life – sometimes, going back to his hotel at four in the morning, he met fishermen on their way to the harbour, saw their tanned, leathery faces and remarkably light eyes – and for a moment it would occur to him that these people went to work, to real manual work, for a single guilder while nearby on the Stock Exchange tens of thousands, hundreds of thousands, millions of guilders were won (and lost) every day of their lives. But such moments grew rarer. It was not his business anyway.

He had been indignant with Roest for receiving him as though he were a beggar and a greenhorn, but he soon saw that he really was a greenhorn in this city riotous with millions. Roest in his three dirty little rooms had engagements to the extent of fifty million guilders in the money market.

Others, people whom formerly he wouldn't have cared to sit next to in a café – so unkempt they looked – were engaged in even larger transactions. He was glad to sit beside them now, indeed seeking them out, and listening reverently when, peevishly stirring their coffee, they said: 'I got a hunch. I dreamed of a black cat with white spots. I got a hunch the dollar will sag tomorrow.' And he saw these creatures get into their luxurious English or Italian cars and race off at a hundred kilometres an hour to Scheveningen or Spa . . .

Burning envy filled him. In Berlin, with well over half a million marks, he had considered himself a rich man; here he saw that that was nothing. There were people here – he spoke to them – who had lost twenty times that amount in half an hour, and who laughed about it. 'I shan't have to sell matches – I'll get it all back,' they boasted. And get it back they did.

Erich Hackendahl both envied and despised them. He envied them their nose for the market, their nerve – the reckless courage with which almost hourly they risked their whole existence, all their goods and chattels – he even envied them their frivolous feelings. But he despised them profoundly for their inability to do anything with the money they had gained, for their inability to clear out once they were really rich, to flee the excitements of the money market and lead the kind of life which he personally desired.

Vaguely it dawned on him that these people were different, that they were not in this game just to become rich, but for the sake of the game itself. Fundamentally they were gamblers – and like all gamblers they could never stop, not even to think – all they wanted was to go on gambling. He, however, wanted to become rich in order to live well. He wanted to buy beautiful things, to live with beautiful women, to travel. Throughout his youth he had breathed the air of a stable; he shuddered when he remembered it. One must never be poor again, he thought, one must never have to worry over money.

He started cautiously. He deposited certain amounts as margin with two or three brokers and began to give buying and selling orders. He felt very uncertain, always conscious that the ground on which he trod was insecure. The banker Roest (whom he also visited as a client) had summed him up correctly in the first five minutes. He would have preferred to keep his money intact; he wanted to gamble without any risk.

He would see, the nebbish! smiled Herr Roest to himself, and gave his customer careful and prudent advice. He knew that you first had to feed your birds before you could trap them in the net.

That spring the mark was remarkably firm, even recovering by fifty per cent. Erich, who believed he knew more about the fluctuations of the mark than anyone else, did no business at all. Throughout the whole of March and April the telegrams said the same thing: 'Dora's condition unchanged. Father.' This Cuno government continued unyieldingly to support the mark through all this; the bears either experienced miserable shipwreck or were simply stranded.

Erich, getting impatient, once or twice speculated on the franc, which, however, proved incalculable. He gained a couple of thousand francs, did not sell out and eventually lost fifteen thousand. By the middle of May he was further from his object than he had been at the beginning of February. On the whole he had lost money, and living expenses in Amsterdam were exorbitant. By now his life differed in no way from that of any other habitué of the Stock Exchange. He used his hotel room only for a couple of hours in the morning; the rest of the day he hung about banks and offices, listening to the brokers' jargon or waiting feverishly for the New York opening quotations (even if he was not involved). His nights were spent in cafés and bars – not having carried out his original intention of acquiring a permanent lady friend, he contented himself with the pleasures occasionally to be found in such places. He was now twenty-six years of age and had already noticed that women had lost much of their attractiveness for him – much more important was the best of food and wine, though not to excess. Rapidly he became fat and slothful.

At heart, however, he was more restless than ever, obsessed by the thought of money; he wanted to get back what he had lost and multiply it twenty times over. And on this idea he would brood for hours, sitting over his coffee, a dead cigar between his lips. He made a thousand plans but even when one of them appeared reasonably safe he shrank at the last moment from the risk. Poverty scared him. He had had a taste of that once – of what he considered poverty – with his parents. Never again! He must hold onto his money. And as a last resource there was always his friend in Berlin. But maybe this friend was no longer a friend, although he had entrusted him with so considerable a sum of money. It might be a trap.

Early in May, arriving at his hotel about five o'clock in the morning, he was informed that a gentleman had been waiting for him since the previous evening; from the night porter's expression it could be gathered that this gentleman was of no great importance. And in truth the visitor, who had to be shaken out of a deep sleep in an armchair, did not look very impressive; he was a young fellow, poorly dressed and badly nourished, like all those now inundating Amsterdam from Germany. He stated that he came from the gentleman's friend in Berlin and his message could be delivered only in private. Erich Hackendahl took the lad up to his room. Here, without further ado, the visitor slipped off his jacket and took out from its lining a slip of paper folded several times.

Erich took it reluctantly and unfolded it. It was a typewritten message to the effect that within three or four days the Reichsbank would withdraw its support from the mark and that Erich should be a bear with all he possessed. 'What I foretold is now about to come off.'

Erich gave the lad a ten-guilder note and promised him a further hundred if the message brought him luck. He should come and enquire in a week's time.

He did not sleep that night, brooding over what he should do. Might this not be the moment his friend had chosen for his revenge? Nothing on the exchange had pointed to any such collapse. During the last four weeks the mark had slowly fallen but it was still higher than at the end of January. Supposing he did as instructed and speculated for a fall with all he possessed – supposing his friend was deceiving him and the mark remained firm? He shuddered.

The expedient upon which he finally decided was characteristic of Erich. He himself would wait for a time but the money his friend had entrusted to him should be invested in conformity with the message. Roest urged him to desist. 'The Germans are standing firm in the Ruhr. The mark is like iron.' But Erich was also of iron, with his friend's money.

A fortnight later he was cursing himself. Support had been withdrawn and the mark had fallen; he had earned on his friend's money fifty thousand marks, but he could easily have earned half a million. The friend had been a genuine friend and he a suspicious fool. Of little consolation was the studied respect paid him by Herr Roest. The greenhorn had known more than the whole Stock Exchange in Amsterdam – if he'd given me a hint I'd have gone in with him – and we'd be in clover now, I can tell you!

And Herr Roest dried his sweating face on a silk handkerchief.

From that day onwards Erich's affairs became lively. Telegrams from Berlin announced a worsening of Dora's condition; Erich no longer mistrusted them or his friend, but rather his own timidity – it was now a question of estimating how quickly the mark would fall. And on that point also messages came from Berlin, telegrams or sometimes by hand.

Towards the end of July Erich was a millionaire. But a million was nothing – Roest was involved on the Stock Exchange to the extent of fifteen! In August, when the Cuno government fell and was replaced by a Cabinet under Dr Stresemann, when once again friendly tones were to be heard vis-à-vis France, when the dollar rose from one to ten million marks, Erich possessed over five millions in gold marks. But he had done it on his nerves, sleeping only with the help of drugs, avoiding all exercise, conversing unwillingly. He sat two hours over his lunch and could talk the jargon of the Stock Exchange to perfection; brokers greeted him respectfully, bankers asked in a friendly way for his opinion on the Norwegian currency. His hair was getting very thin . . .

But all this was only a beginning – the riot hadn't started yet. In

September passive resistance in the Ruhr was given up and within three weeks the dollar had risen from twenty to one hundred and sixty million marks. Erich no longer knew how much he was worth. The greater part of his fortune was involved in various commitments, with quotations fluctuating continually. Sometimes he pulled himself together and tried to work it out, but he got confused; the endless columns of figures exhausted him and he gave it up.

I'll stop now, he swore to himself. Only once more . . .

Erich Hackendahl had always been a bear; he had made his fortune on the collapse of the mark, on the collapse of the German currency. Never go back to Germany, he said often, and everyone agreed. But he knew that the mark must stop falling one day, and be stabilized somehow. Already there were rumours of a gold currency, even of one based on rye. Throughout the whole of October, while the mark plunged down into milliards, there was a noticeable uncertainty. When would it stop? Would it be possible to get out in time?

Erich was preoccupied with these questions. He had known beforehand when the mark was no longer to be supported and had been a coward about it. This time he would get his tip, and this time he would risk everything. Risk? No risk at all. The friend was a real friend. Every tip of his had come straight from the horse's mouth. Once only – just once – Erich wanted to be a bull, and then he would get out. He even intended to settle accounts honestly with his friend, who should have no cause for regret.

During the latter part of October, rumours and uncertainty about the mark increased. A Rentenbank had been established in Berlin. At what level would the mark be stabilized? Erich decided to send a messenger to his friend. He found a German waiter who, because he was homesick, wanted to go back to Germany (what a great idea!), paid him his travel money and sent him back to Berlin with a note.

On 1 November he received through a messenger the information that the mark would be stabilized at a dollar parity of 420 milliards, the dollar then standing at 130. One day . . . another day . . . and Erich still hesitated. Then, on the third day, the dollar being quoted at 420 milliards, he made his decision, cursing his cowardice and putting everything he possessed on at 420. The bear for the first time became a bull.

'God save you,' exclaimed Roest. 'You're in for it! I shall hear you bellowing tomorrow.'

Herr Roest was mistaken: 4 November came and went; the mark remained firm. Erich triumphed and trembled. On the 5th Herr Roest became doubtful. Was the greenhorn right after all? The fellow had been recommended from Berlin. Ought he himself to jump in now? There was still time . . . No, no, no, he wouldn't, he put no faith in the Germans. Despairingly he wiped his face.

On 6 November the mark was still like iron, standing at 420 milliards. Erich calculated his gains, his fortune. If he deducted half a million gold marks for his Berlin adviser, there remained about twenty-three million marks.

I've brought it off, he thought, and fell asleep.

But an hour or two later he was woken by the telephone. 'Where are you? Why are you sleeping?' exclaimed Herr Roest from the receiver. 'The mark's opened weak, the dollar has come in at 510, and the man's asleep! You're done for.'

Very quietly Erich put the receiver back. He did not get up. He stayed in bed; there was no strength in his limbs. I'm beaten, he told himself. He's taken me in.

Yet he could not believe it. All those months of merciless hell – and to what end? The loss of everything! It was impossible. He rang up a broker. The dollar was quoted at 590.

'Come and see, the mark's done for. What a currency! Enough to make you sick.'

But he didn't go, he didn't cut his losses. He lay in bed, trembling with fright. It was exactly the same fright as he had known in the trenches. If I'd gone with him into that café, he thought, I'd be well off now.

Yesterday, even twelve hours ago, he had believed that success was his – twenty-three millions! And he recalled how he had had to cringe, cheat, deny himself to scrape together the first twenty thousand. I'll never be able to do it again, he thought despairingly. And what then? For a man of his sort, who had become what he had become, it was impossible to return to nothingness, to poverty, to some petty job, for instance. Well?

Twice he put through a trunk call to Berlin and each time cancelled it.

Roest implored him to come and rescue all that could be rescued. Actually there was still something to save, even with the dollar quoted at 630 milliards. He could have retrieved part of his money.

He dressed and left the hotel. No, he didn't drive this time; he walked. He went to neither broker nor banker, he went to the Rijksmuseum. He wanted to see the Rembrandts.

But 7 November, almost exactly the fifth anniversary of the armistice, was not his lucky day – the museum was closed. I'll come again tomorrow, he thought. I would like to have seen the Rembrandts at least . . .

On his way back to the hotel he had an inspiration, and slapped his forehead. It was quite clear: the German government was behind this fall in German currency. It wanted to buy back its marks cheaply, so as to stabilize at 420. A colossal deal at the expense of the world's money markets!

He spoke like his father. 'I'm of iron. I'll hang on till the mark goes to 420. Iron!'

For six days, from 7 to 12 November, he held on, the dollar standing without fluctuations at 630 milliards; he still hoped for stabilization at 420, in accordance with his friend's message. The brokers, since his deposits still covered his losses, left him in peace. Only the banker Roest said: 'You've got to be as cast-iron as the mark is! You're lost.'

On 13 November the dollar was quoted at 840 milliards – exactly double what Hackendahl counted on. That day the brokers closed his accounts, collecting his margins to cover his losses. Hurrying from one to another, he begged them to wait only another day; he swore that the mark would be stabilized at 420.

They shrugged, they smiled. Roest said: 'They all like to win, these small fry, but not to lose . . . Herr Hackendahl, be a man. You've still got a fine car, a diamond ring, no family – I've been worse off in my time.'

Again and again Erich put through a call to Berlin – not till evening did he get his friend on the telephone. But by the sound of his voice he felt at once there was no hope.

Nice of Erich to ring him after all this time . . . How was he doing? Why had he been silent so long? What was he doing in Amsterdam? Ah, business going badly? Really? Business bad, eh? Worrying . . . for Erich! What was that? Written? By wire? He was joking, surely! Hopefully, Erich hadn't been taken in by some practical joker. But of course he was much too shrewd for that. No, not that tone, please, in spite of their friendship. Letters? Telegrams? One moment, please, Erich.

'The Managing Clerk speaking. Yes. Herr Justizrat has just asked me to take down your grievances in case the matter goes further. You allege you received letters and telegrams from Herr Justizrat? Herr Justizrat asks me to inform you that he has neither written nor telegraphed you at any time. His name must have been used, then. Oh, the letters weren't signed? But what makes you assume . . .'

Hopeless. Erich hung up. He thought of suicide the whole night, but no way of doing it seemed sure and painless enough. The two had to go together. And nothing there corresponded to Erich's wishes.

The dissolution of his Amsterdam household went much quicker than the Berlin one. He only had to sell his car. As much money as he might temporarily have possessed in Amsterdam, he hadn't owned anything but the car. So this time he had nothing to fear from Customs; even if he was still well kitted out, none of his things looked new any more.

With three suitcases, one gentleman's fur coat, a diamond ring and a gold watch, Erich Hackendahl departed from Amsterdam with a burning, heartfelt hatred for his former friend. It was 16 November 1923. The dollar stood at 2,520,000,000,000 against the mark. The question as to what rate of exchange the mark would be stabilized at was still unanswered.

The weather was grey, foggy, raw; very much as on the day of his arrival.

Not till he was sitting in the express to Cologne did it occur to him that he hadn't seen the Rembrandts after all. And he had the feeling that nothing would ever make up for this.

§ XV

About the time that Erich Hackendahl went back to his native Berlin, Heinz Hackendahl also returned there, from a shorter journey. He had taken his sister-in-law and her two boys to the island of Hiddensee, where Gertrud Hackendahl née Gudde had received a small inheritance – a little house, some land, a cowshed.

While Erich had been fighting great financial battles over real money, suffering defeat, Heinz had been fighting over paper millions. In spite of Tutti's untiring efforts it had become increasingly difficult to get bread for four mouths; unlike wartime, bread was waiting at the bakers' – one merely needed the money to buy it. When, in due course, a trip to Hiddensee went not unfavourably, with a clamp of potatoes, a cow in the byre and three pigs in the sty, the nourishment of the eternally hungry children seemed assured.

The evening before his departure Tutti and he had sat on a fishing boat on the beach; the boys, dead tired from rushing about in the unaccustomed sea air, had gone to bed long ago.

'Oh, this does you good,' said Tutti, shivering in the breeze.

'A bit chilly, though,' said Heinz.

'It's a clean wind and a clean chilliness,' cried Tutti, happy to be home again.

'That's true! You'll have to keep an eye on Gustav, though. His throat's very delicate.'

'You never get really ill here. Doctors don't grow rich on this island.'

'You must take care, Tutti,' said Heinz emphatically.

'Of course. My sole thought is for the children, Heinz.'

Of course she was right. It was stupid to remind her. She'd never thought of anything else but the children.

'If you'd have stayed in Berlin six months longer, Tutti, I'd have succeeded in getting Father to see the children.'

'It's not so important, Heinz.'

'Not for you or for them,' he admitted. 'But it might have been for him. Father is pretty unhappy.'

Both were silent. It had become almost dark, except that a misty glow lay over the waters and at short, regular intervals they saw the lightning flash of the lighthouse on Arcona and the more peaceful reddish beam from the Bahöft lighthouse. Both thought of the old man who had stayed brave on a bad day – very brave.

'You'll have a look at Eva now and then?' asked Gertrud Hackendahl.

'Of course. As often as possible.'

'I'll write to her. And send her a parcel when we do our slaughtering.'

'I'll enquire if that's permitted. The regulations . . .'

'We'll be killing shortly before Christmas, surely it's permissible at Christmas time.'

'I'm not so sure. You must remember it's a penitentiary. A penitentiary is the strictest form of punishment there is.'

Again they were silent.

After a while Gertrud said thoughtfully: 'Two years – when you're outside it doesn't seem so much. Inside it must be an eternity.'

'If it hadn't been for Father it would have been five or six years.'

'You know that I don't like him, Heinz, if only on account of Otto – I can never forget how he behaved to Otto. But the way he stood up in court when the others were putting the blame on Eva and she just agreeing to everything, the way he got up and said that his girl was good but weak, while the chap was utterly rotten . . . and when the solicitor attacked him . . .'

'Yes. And when he said to the lawyer: if the girl's really as bad as you make out, she wouldn't agree to everything you say; she's protecting that scoundrel and all he wants is to drag her in the mud.'

'After that they were more cautious with him.'

'Yes, it was Father who saw to it that they gave Bast the heavier sentence and not Eva.'

'Yes,' said Tutti. 'He got his eight years all right. Will she really be free of him when he comes out, I wonder?'

'Eight years!' exclaimed Heinz. 'Who can think as far ahead as that? In eight years it will be 1931. What will it be like?'

'Let's hope life will be a little better.'

'Yes. If only we had proper money again. You don't know how crazy it is at the bank. They're off their heads at the counters, off their heads in the stocks and shares, and the foreign currency is the craziest of the lot. As for the management, they're completely out of their minds.'

'There must be a change soon,' said Tutti consolingly. 'It can't go on like this.'

'Yes, and what then? Nobody will have any more money. Most people have lost everything.'

'You mean because of the banks?'

'Partly.'

'Oh, the banks will always have work to do, Heinz. And so will you. You're so efficient!'

He laughed lightly in the dark.

'Things are also easier for you, Heinz, aren't they, now you're rid of us?'

'Of course, only you know very well that . . .'

'Keep on the flat whatever happens. Whatever you do don't give up the flat. You need to move into a furnished room.'

'No, no,' he said. 'I'll keep the flat for your furniture.'

'The furniture is yours now, Heinz. No, I want you to have it. Then you have a flat and you have furniture.'

'But Irma doesn't want to, Tutti! She absolutely doesn't want to.'

'She'll give in eventually.'

'No, no. She's worried. She's really worried that I'll run away again.'

'What rubbish! You'll never run away from anyone! You didn't run away from me, either.'

'But I did once run away from her.'

'Oh, you were still a youngster then.'

'Not for Irma I wasn't.'

Again they were silent.

Then, suddenly standing up, Tutti said: 'It's really cold. Come, Heinz, let's walk along the beach a bit. And let me repeat: you mustn't give up the flat. With the flat, you're a real prospect, and Irma will see that too.'

§ XVI

Heinz was once again home in his flat. He walked about, put on the heating, opened the window and let in a bit of the dismal, damp air. He laid out the beds, and considered how he should arrange the furniture. The children's beds could go upstairs . . .

The children's things were no longer on the wall, and the cupboards and drawers were mostly empty. That's why there was such an echo when he walked about. It sounded empty. Everything had become empty, not just the drawers and the flat – his whole life.

The young ones would soon get used to the island, and for Tutti it was a real homecoming. But he would never get used to the empty flat. He thought about what it would be like, from now on, when he came home from the bank. No one would be waiting for him in the flat. He would have to do the heating, clear up, cook – and all just for himself.

He thought about how much it had helped him through the terrible years that lay behind him that he had had to care for someone, in fact for three people. That had helped him get over Tinette, and it had also made it easier for him to come unscathed through the terrible years of the inflation. From one day to the next, he had always had to do some caring; there had always been small objects in view – a new suit for Gustav, radiation treatment for Otto, the dentist for Tutti . . . Those had been his extra duties, beside the usual daily ones: paying the rent, bread, gas . . . In his early twenties he had already had to become father of a family. That had often been difficult. He couldn't go to cafés like other people, or dance in dance halls, or sit in cinemas. It had often been difficult, but always good.

How often his colleagues laughed over him! 'Hackendahl, you're a double idiot! Burden yourself with two brats! What's social welfare for?'

Yes, of course he was an idiot. For such people, Heinz Hackendahl was by and large an idiot. However, he would outlive them, with all their shallow pleasures, in all his stubborn idiocy. There was something in him and about him – he had a project.

'We will survive,' they said. 'How we do it doesn't matter.' But it certainly did matter, how they did it. You can't survive on dancing girls and cocaine, but you can survive with two children. Professor Degener, a widely unknown man, had given the right advice when he said: 'Small things first, Hackendahl! Organize your cells: without proper cells you can't have a healthy body.'

The man was right. Bravo! He should be consulted again. Perhaps he could think up a little election slogan for someone in a cold and empty flat, once more without a project. Heinz Hackendahl knows more about himself now than he did when he was seventeen. He knows that he is no great shakes. He is a manual worker, but one still confident that he can properly occupy his position. Only, he would just like to know what his position was. And a project? You don't want to have spent your time on earth creeping along with aches and pains, and then being fully satisfied. You can think about God and heaven however much you like, but you still believe you are more than a microbe. Or do you?

Heinz Hackendahl hit his bed angrily. His thinking was fired up. It seemed quite out of the question that his aim in life was to go to the bank and establish first-class statistics on the developments of exports in the electro-industry (with special regard to plants built by German workers abroad), and then creep home in the evenings to tidy up his digs. Definitely not.

Suddenly Heinz Hackendahl was in a hurry. He shut neither the oven door nor the window, and the beds were unmade. Instead, he put on his hat, pulled on his coat and stormed out of the house and through the town, not even thinking of driving. You can't cope with impatience by driving. You've got to walk it off.

The result was that he rushed into the shop of Widow Quaas in a state of greater impatience. 'My dear Quaasi, don't make a fuss! I must speak to Irma immediately.'

And already, even before the increasingly miserable widow could utter a sound, he jumped over the counter and into the front room.

'Irma, excuse me, but I'm in a terrible hurry . . . When are we getting married?'

'You seem to have gone clean mad, Heinz. I'll never marry you, never.'

'I tell you I'm in a hurry. Wait, I put the rings in my pocket. Where are they? I've been to the registrar's. Your mother gave me your papers. What about Wednesday?'

'I never . . .' began Frau Quaas, but her thin wail faded out unnoticed.

'Mental,' said Irma. 'Absolutely mental. How old are you, young man?'

'Please, Irma, get a move on. Stop showing off.'

'I beg your pardon? I'm not showing off!'

'Of course you are.'

'No.'

'Yes.'

'No.'

'And who started all the kissing?'

'I gave you a box on the ears then, and would gladly give you another.'

'Irma, please do.'

'What?'

'Please do. You want to hit me one, don't you? Go on then. But come along with me afterwards.'

'Where am I to go with you?'

'I'm telling you for the umpteenth time – to look at our flat.'

'So he's got a flat as well.'

'If you want to marry me I must have a flat. That's only logical.'

'I don't want to marry you.'

'Of course you do. Now don't go over it all again.'

'I won't.'

'You can't get out of it now. We've had the banns put up at the register office!'

'That's your business – cancelling it.'

'I don't want to cancel it.'

'But I do.'

'There, you see!'

'What do I see?'

'That we agree!'

'Are you crazy?'

'Well, of course!' he said and grinned. 'What else?'

'You think you can drop me in it. Me – never! I remember already telling you that when we were teenage friends. Now you're a man – never!'

'Irma! Irmchen! Irmgard! I suggested it to you myself – so please do.'

'Suggested what?'

'The box on the ears. You wanted to give me a box on the ears. So please do.'

'I shouldn't dream of it.'

'I can see you're suffering from a frustrated box on the ears. Please give it to me – for the past. Please, Irma.'

'I shouldn't think of it. And about the past you'd better be silent.'

'With pleasure – when you box my ears. Other people give each other a betrothal kiss but we're content with a betrothal slap. We've passed the stage of kissing.'

'Of slapping, too.'

'God, what a stubborn girl you are. So you won't let yourself be taken by surprise?'

'Not by you.'

'All right. Then I must give you time to think it over.' He snivelled significantly, pulled a chair for himself up to the table and sat down beside her.

'I beg your pardon,' she exclaimed indignantly. 'Are you making yourself at home here?'

'That was my idea. Until you've thought the matter over.'

'You're too – never mind, don't bother, Mother. Behave as if he wasn't here. It's too silly for words.'

'I didn't give him your papers, Irmchen, truly,' whimpered Frau Quaas. 'I've just had a look, they're still there. It's a lie.'

'Of course it's a lie. Don't get excited, Mother. He's just a common liar.'

No reaction from the accused.

'And about the rings, that was a lie, too. Of course he hasn't got them. Every word's a lie.'

Heinz said nothing.

Very disdainfully: 'And of course he hasn't a flat either – he's glad enough to be able to pay for a furnished room.'

'That's not right,' said Heinz coolly. 'The flat's really true. Oh

God!' He jumped up, startled. 'Now I've left the gas alight and the milk on it.'

He rushed to the door. Terror-stricken they looked at him, picturing the milk boiling over and stinking.

He turned back, pale but resolute. 'It's all the same to me,' he said gloomily. 'Let it burn, let the fire brigade come. I'm not leaving until I'm out of this awful suspense. I must have a definite answer at last.' He sat down beside her.

'I'll never marry you,' she shouted into his ears. 'Now you've got your definite answer.'

'Please, dear Heinz, your milk!' Frau Quaas was absolutely overwhelmed.

'I told you so,' he said, nodding his head. 'She hasn't decided yet. She must have time for reflection.'

'Please, Heinz, the milk.'

'Are you going, Heinz, or aren't you?' Irma's patience was at an end. Crimson with fury, she stood in front of him.

'If only you'd think it over quietly,' he begged. 'You're too excited now, Irma.'

'You're to go and see about your milk. You're upsetting Mother.'

'It's only half a litre,' he said apologetically. 'By the time I got there it would be burnt away, anyhow. I'd rather wait here.'

'You're to leave at once.'

'And then' – Heinz looked repentant – 'I find lying beastly. To tell the truth I've got no milk on the gas at all, Irma. And the gas isn't turned on either, but—'

Smack! That was his slap all right. Smack! Smack! Smack! Three more than he had bargained for.

'There! There! There! You miserable liar, to torment us like this. You do nothing but torment people.'

But he'd got her in his arms. 'Oh, Irma,' he said, 'thank heavens you've boxed my ears at last. That's been on your mind for five years.'

'Let me go,' she said faintly. 'You must let me go. I don't want to hit you again.'

'No, now you'd like to . . .'

She made desperate efforts to free herself. Then she exclaimed impatiently: 'Mother, there's somebody in the shop. Do have a look.'

And hardly had the door closed behind the confused old woman – who did not understand what was happening at all, who understood neither her shop nor her daughter nor money nor the milk on the gas nor the whole world – hardly were the two alone when Irma said: 'Listen, Heinz. I've let . . . that pass once. But never again, you understand. I never wish to experience such anxiety and misery again. You understand?'

'Yes.'

'Good – and now it shall be forgiven and forgotten for ever. You can kiss me, Heinz.'

SEVEN

Work and No Work

§ I

At the bank they had been using machines to count and bundle up the notes, and the clerks had had to work overtime at the same job of counting – there were virtuosi among them who could converse while doing this; their fingers counted for them and a machine in their heads added up to a hundred while they were saying: 'Damned cold today, isn't it? Well, yes, I was on the razzle last night. Pretty hot! Perhaps that's why I'm freezing now.' And all the time counting infallibly and bundling up the million-mark or milliard-mark notes. No cash box, no steel safe was large enough to hold these piles of money; there had been a great demand for laundry baskets, found eminently suitable for keeping money in, and which were also completely safe as a rule.

And then, all of a sudden, this madness was over – the Rentenmark had come. The floods drained away and, as is usual with floods, left behind mud and destruction. While plenty of notes of high denomination were circulating, people hadn't grasped how poverty-stricken they really were, not even the poor. The enormous figures, the vast issue of paper money had made it impossible to think clearly.

And then the banks started their great clean-up. Accounts were looked into, stocks valued and adjusted, and letters sent to clients. 'We beg to advise you that your account with us is closed because of its trifling nature. Your stocks and shares, etc., are at your disposal during office hours. Yours truly . . .'

Now began the invasion of the cheated, the expropriated, the bankrupt, of those who had, through hard work, acquired stocks and shares against old age, the rentiers, the small investors, the petty and the high officials, and it became evident that these people had been very far from businesslike. They hadn't gone in for foreign currency speculations or shady deals – they had simply waited and lost everything. For days on end the counters echoed with the laments and protests, the weeping and the cursing of the aged. The bank employees tried to cheer them up, but it is difficult to persuade a person who feels cheated to suffer in silence. In fact it is impossible.

'Listen,' an old gentleman would say, thumping his beautifully printed shares with their flourish of signatures. 'Here are shares. Shares for twenty thousand marks. And you say they're worth nothing?'

'You must take the dollar quotation into consideration, Herr Counsellor. The dollar finally stood at four thousand two hundred milliards of paper marks. And the shares are in paper marks. So they're not worth even a pfennig.'

'But when I gave the factory my money it was in gold currency. The Reichsbank exchanged my money every day according to the gold standard.'

'Yes, but that was before 1914, Herr Counsellor. Since then we've lost a war.'

'We? You, perhaps – not me! My sons . . . but that has nothing to do with it. The factory which received my money's still there, isn't it? I had a look at it only the other day. The chimneys were smoking.'

'Yes, but that was before the war, Herr Counsellor.'

'So the factory hasn't turned into paper!'

'You must understand, Herr Counsellor, the devaluation of the mark . . .'

'Oh, yes, I understand, just like my War Loans. You remember – the gratitude of the Fatherland is assured!'

'We lost the war . . .'

'Excellent – and the others have to pay for it. Good day! I'll never set foot in a bank again.'

And he left – and the unhappy employee, whose twentieth disgusted customer of the day this was, looked despairingly after him.

But even this came to an end when the tidying-up was over, and all was ready for new customers – who, however, did not come, despite all the preparations. Interest on their savings was to be, in view of the times, proportionately high, and the new shares issued by manufacturing companies promised the handsomest of gains. Yet still the customers came not. They wanted neither interest nor profit. They had no confidence. They stayed away.

It was in this way that it became common to refer to the enormous distension of the system. Inflation was like a medical distension of the market (a very good, indeed a precise comparison for something so noxious). The banks had distended with the system – and now were being dismantled! (This comparison was not quite so good. One didn't talk so much about dismantling before; it was called demolition. However, dismantling sounded better. Each period has the expressions and technical terms it deserves.) So, long live dismantling!

Inevitably the day arrived when Heinz Hackendahl was requested to see the staff manager. The staff manager's waiting room was crowded. Every three minutes his office door opened and his secretary's voice melodiously sang out: 'The next gentleman, please.' People were being dismissed as on a conveyor belt. Those waiting knew of course what was in store for them, but in most cases they did not take it tragically. Hitherto there had always been work. Hardly anybody had yet experienced real unemployment.

'I'd had enough of the joint long ago.'

'Fat lot I care! I can get a job tomorrow as foreign correspondent.'

'Let them see how they'll get on without me.'

'The next, please.'

But when Heinz Hackendahl entered the staff manager's office he saw a different spectacle – a bald, elderly clerk for whom the manager had poured out a glass of water.

'Do calm yourself, Herr Tümmel. With your abilities you'll get a post tomorrow.'

'What am I to do? What shall I do? No bank will take an old man like me. '

'Please, Herr Tümmel, please calm yourself! Eighty gentlemen are waiting outside. If I had to spend as much time with each of them . . .'

'I've worked here thirty-five years and now you're turning me out into the street.'

'But who's talking about the street, Herr Tümmel? A man as efficient as you! We're not responsible. It's the hard times. We didn't make them.'

'I've earned millions for the bank and now . . . But that's the capitalists all over.'

'I must ask you, Herr Tümmel, I must really ask you not to drag in politics. I've no time now. Please, Fräulein, take Herr Tümmel to his room. Well, Herr Hackendahl, you know what it's all about . . . Reductions in staff forced upon us . . . deep regret . . . your valuable services . . . when conditions are more favourable perhaps we could re-engage you . . .' The staff manager reeled it off like a robot, for the fiftieth time that morning. Then, with incontestable legality and preciseness: 'Notice to take effect on 1 July. It rests with you whether you leave your employment now, receiving your salary up to 30 June.'

'I can stay away from tomorrow, then?'

'Yes, of course. We're as accommodating as we can be. But old employees such as Herr Tümmel, they won't see that. He talks about his thirty-five years of service. But he forgets that for thirty-five years he also received his due from the bank. The man doesn't think of that. Please sign here that you've received your notice.'

'Will he get another post?'

'Good Lord, an old stick-in-the-mud like that? He couldn't adapt himself. Two years ago I wanted to change his room for one three doors away, similar in all respects, same size, same furniture – my God, didn't the man make a fuss! Said he was homesick. How can you be homesick for an office? No, Tümmel's finished. Ah, Fräulein Schneider! Got rid of him? Well, the next one, please. See you again – sorry, I mean good afternoon, Herr Hackendahl.'

Heinz went to his office. He had fully three months' holiday before him. That had never happened in his whole life. How happy Irma would be! They could travel, they had money. They could go to Hiddensee? To Tutti? It was wonderful. How good the new mark was!

As he went he saw an open office door. Behind it sat Herr Tümmel surrounded by sympathetic colleagues. With his head in his hands he repeatedly sobbed the words, 'I'll never get another job! Never, ever!'

Poor fellow: he really would never get another job. How bad it was to be old. Homesick for an office! How good it was still to be young! He would always have work – sometimes more than he wanted.

Heinz packed his office belongings and took leave of his colleagues. Then he went to the cashier and collected his salary for three months. Five hundred and forty gold marks! Never before had he carried on him so much money of his own – it encouraged to recklessness. On the way home he stopped for a long time in front of a shop displaying electrical appliances, muttering to himself, calculating.

At last he entered. Negotiations with the salesman were lengthy, strange words known to him before only in print were uttered; he purchased brown cords and green wires and a small board on which were mounted mysterious objects, all shockingly expensive.

He didn't have a clear conscience when he left the shop. Now that he had made the purchase, his worries began. What would Irma say? After all, they were not in a position to spend over fifty marks on a toy . . . That's no plaything, he imagined him saying reproachfully to Irma; it's a very serious matter!

Then he went home, extremely anxious to hear what Irma would say, or to be more exact a little scared. For the stormy weather which had gathered round them before their wedding had not deserted them in marriage – they quarrelled a good deal, if without ill-feeling. Irma, however, said nothing when he came in, for she wasn't there. Probably at her mother's. He had come home some hours earlier than usual and everything in the garden was lovely; nevertheless it would have been nicer, of course, to have told Irma at once. There was no need for her to be always at her mother's.

But when she did come he was in no hurry to talk. On the contrary, he snapped at her when she closed the door a little noisily. 'Be quiet, Irma – please! I believe I've got something. Oh, Lord, the clock's ticking much too loudly. Please, Irma, put the alarm under the pillow.'

'Well!' She stared perplexed at the queer apparatus and her husband with headphones over his ears, moving two green circles of wire towards one another. 'What's gone wrong? How is it you're already home? It's not four o'clock yet.'

'Radio,' he replied mysteriously. 'I just got . . . I believe it must have been Nauen . . . Or Paris . . . Irma, please sit down, don't run about like that. I can't hear a thing.'

She was still staring, agitated by doubts and anxiety. 'Are you ill, Heinz?' she exclaimed. 'Is that why you're not at the bank?'

'Dismissed,' he murmured. 'That's to say, three months' leave first. Oh, Irma, if you'd only sit down for a moment I'll tell you everything presently.'

'Dismissed!' With this word she did sit down. 'And you . . .' She was completely helpless.

'Not bad,' he muttered. 'Oh, God, must they run their damned tap at this moment? Just as I'd got . . . Irma! There!' His face was shining. Cautiously he took out one of the receivers from the headphones. 'Irma, do come. On tiptoe. Put that to your ear! You hear it? That's music, do you realize that? I believe they're playing Wagner. It may be coming from Nauen. Or even from England, I'm not sure yet. I'll get it clearer soon. You can hear it, can't you? Please, Irma, don't look so stupid. You know, wireless! You must have read about it. Music from the ether! They're transmitting it from Nauen, Paris, London, everywhere. Radio.' He spelled it very quietly while continuing to listen. His face was shining.

'Of course,' she said, much too loudly. 'I know that, man. Radium – what they radiate you with. But for God's sake, Heinz, what are you doing here with radium?'

'Radio! Radio! It's completely different from radium.'

'But why are you fiddling with this when you ought to be at the bank? Why have you been discharged? Why have they given you leave?'

'There, now it's gone again. Can't you be more careful? Well, I'll get it again . . . Listen, Irma, I've been given notice but only from 1 July. And I needn't go back. I've been given leave, think of it, Irma, three months' leave. And with full pay.' Beaming, he slapped his pocket. 'Think of it, Irma! Five hundred and forty marks . . . That is,' he added, 'I've bought this radio out of it. Fifty-three marks. A real wonder.'

'What?' she said indignantly. 'Over fifty marks for that stuff?'

'Well, it's a radio! Music through the air, through the walls.'

'Oh, rubbish! If you'd bought a decent gramophone and a few records! All this does is crackle in your ears. And you said Wagner. Well, it was the Waltz Dream by Strauss. Or is that by Lehár?'

'It was the Overture to *Tannhäuser*.'

'I heard it clearly.' She began to sing: 'And I have only kissed her on the shoulder.'

'That's from the *Fledermaus*!'

'Well, I've been saying Strauss all along. Not a bit like Wagner. And why have you been given notice?'

'Lack of work. They dismissed over a hundred men today. They call it economizing staff – another new invention. And I tell you, Irma, there was an elderly man from the Stocks and Shares. You should have heard him crying! Thinks he'll never get another job. Well, it must be pretty difficult in such a case, so old.'

'And you?'

'Me? I'll always get a job, I'm young. Those who can work properly are always in demand. Oh, Irma. Don't pull a face! No, we'll go and see Tutti to start off with . . . And then . . .'

'And then?'

'Everything will be all right, Irma. Cook, but don't make a noise. I'll see if I can tune this thing. It's wonderful – music out of thin air. Marconi! Oh, Irma! I'm really so terribly happy. A radio and a holiday!'

'And no job!'

'Can always get another.'

'That's true. You're nothing if not hard-working. And I'm terribly happy about Hiddensee too. Everything is going to be fine.'

§ II

The time of the rich foreigner was over. There were no more happy American drinkers for Father Hackendahl. Since the stability of the mark meant that life was no longer cheaper in Germany than in other countries, and since you could no longer buy a block of flats for a month's wages or acquire fur coats for a tip, Berlin had become a wasteland. Germany was left to itself by other countries. Let them get on with their eternal bickering between the Reich and the regions, between Bavaria and Prussia, and within the army. Let them go on arguing about compensation for the princely estates and which flags to wave – if only they pay the war reparations! Other than complete disarmament, this was the only question that still concerned countries outside Germany.

In the early morning when old Hackendahl would cruise down the dismal Kaiserallee towards the Zoo Underground Station, the only question occupying him was whether he would get a fare that day or no, for there were days on which he did not get a fare at all – gloomy days, black days – days when he waited from morning till night at the Zoo Station, seeing the taxis come and go, but hearing no porter call out: 'Hi, first-class taxi with horseshoes! Well, Gustav, what about it? D'you believe your old horse capable of a jaunt as far as Knie?'

To tell the truth the taxis were having a lean time too, and Hackendahl realized it. That was another change in him. He no longer despised chauffeurs; he talked with them, admitting that they were men like himself, with similar worries.

'You're all right,' he would say. 'Your thing don't eat if it don't work.'

'But the taxes, Gustav! Think of the taxes! Car tax, the licence – whether we're on the go or not.'

'I have ter pay for a licence too,' said Hackendahl.

'An' what of it? Five marks, that's all. But we . . .'

No, there was little reason to be envious, if only one could get a fare which was worthwhile; but that became harder and harder. For a while he managed by forwarding packages. Indeed, his cab was for a time a competitor of the Berlin Parcels Delivery. The office messengers would come along towards evening, shortly before the post office closed and the express trains left for the West.

'Well, Gustav, what about it? You give us a helping hand, too? For a glass of beer and a schnapps?'

'Righto. Do anythin'. But why must you chaps always come along at the last moment when everythin's got to be rushed?'

'Now, keep calm, Gustav. Your charger'll do it all right, he's got staying power. Off you go!'

At times some firm or other would so fill up the cab with parcels that the clerk would have to enthrone himself beside Gustav on the box – stacks of parcels which, to the fury of the postal clerks, were rushed to the post office in the last ten minutes. Sometimes there were consignments that had to be put on a train. 'We must make the express for Cologne, Gustav, or I'll be fired. Whip up Blücher.' Such fares ranked among the best that Hackendahl got at that time.

Not bad clients, these office chaps! Plenty of backchat, always ready for a joke and a laugh in spite of their own troubles, and not mean in settling up either.

Naturally, it was an inconceivably long time since Gustav Hackendahl, in first-class livery, had driven camouflaged ambulances and senior medics into the Charité Hospital. To have lived like that before, and even had one's little worries – that was almost a joke.

And then the time came when carrying parcels would have seemed the pleasantest thing in the world, if they hadn't gradually come to an end, the devil take it. Cruising along the streets, angling for a catch as he called it, Hackendahl would see one of his old acquaintances pushing a handcart with a few parcels or carrying his load quite easily under one arm.

'Well, Erwin, how's business? Never see you now. Don't you have anything now to be carried?'

'Carried? Stow it, Gustav. Carry, eh? Why, they can't even carry us now. The boss has given me notice for the first.'

Bad news, sad news; no news at all finally. He saw them no more, the friendly office messengers with their unbelievably white and wide dancing trousers, creases ironed razor-sharp. They had disappeared. It was as if they had never existed.

Old Gustav began to feel very ancient, as though he with his horse and cab belonged to a vanished past, having experienced and outlived all. Now and then it happened that the station porters sent strangers to him so that he should tell them what Berlin had looked like twenty or thirty years ago, where they had built the Kaiser-Wilhelm Church, as the Kurfürstendamm church was called, which also signified the Wild West, with its day trips to the smart

suburbs in smart carriages, and how his grey had once raced a motor
car . . .

'Yes,' he would say, 'it was all diff'rent then, everythin's changed.
Except me. 'Cause I'm of iron. That's why they call me Iron Gustav.'

But he had changed nonetheless. He hadn't stayed still; that
wasn't possible. He also swam with the tide; he was part of the
people. He could not avoid what his people experienced; he had to
live. And he was always thinking of Mother at home, waiting for him
so anxiously, so very anxiously. Waiting, or rather dozing, on his box
he often thought of his wife at home; if he was late she went to bed,
but she never fell asleep till he came in. Then she would raise her
head from the pillow and enquire anxiously:

'Well, Father?'

'Hello, Mother. All right?'

'Any luck, Father?'

'No, not today. Well, it'll be all the better tomorrow.'

'Oh, Father . . .'

It was so difficult to tell her that he had brought nothing home.
Without her he wouldn't have minded so much. As long as the horse
had its fodder, he would have been quite satisfied with bread and
bacon and a pot of coffee. But his wife was like a child. She thought
she'd starve to death if they didn't have one hot meal a day.

So, if he had had a good day for once, he kept back a part of his
money to be able to give her something next day. Thus he exerted
himself, tried to think of new fare opportunities, was restless, would
not let go. Perhaps it was even a good thing that Mother was always
there with her aches and pains. There were so many who simply
keeled over. For them, it was no longer worth it. Just don't bother –
it's all hopeless . . .

Old Hackendahl, however, went on persevering. He worried. If
there were no longer enough passengers or parcels, he would have
to make do with night work. Something had to be done; he must get
money for Mother somehow.

And once again day was put aside for night. It was dark now
when he drove to the West End, along gloomy, silent streets
where the clip-clop of Blücher's hoofs echoed hollow between the
dimly lit houses. It was so quiet, so dismally quiet . . . The cab went

at as slow a pace as the horse could manage, Hackendahl always on the lookout.

How times have changed, and us with them! Iron? Oh, yes – iron, in our behaviour, iron in our survival, iron in our will to live! Iron in our determination to bring Mother money home – the daily miserable five marks on a good day, but two marks fifty would also do.

The girls strolled along or stood at the corners alone, though sometimes they kept in twos and threes. They were not the expensive ladies who haunted the Tauentzienstrasse and Kurfürstendamm, the girls who were far above anything like a horse-drawn cab – these were the lesser lights, for a certainty no longer pretty, for a certainty no longer fresh; shop soiled, as the saying goes; girls lying in wait for the shy birds or bent on ambushing drunks whom the night air had sobered sufficiently to make them understand what a girl wanted, or waylaying the slightly sozzled upset by that same fresh air – yes, that was the prey hunted here.

And when the prey had been caught, then it was not at all a bad thing to have old Hackendahl's cab handy – good fun to drive behind a horse again; it pleased the gentleman in his present mood, and it was just as well for a girl if her gentleman could reach his destination quickly, for drunken people make very sudden decisions and another idea might occur to him at any moment.

But the old man on the box saw to it that there was no delay. He knew all the accommodation addresses in the district, the distinguished boarding houses with night bells, the places that let rooms by the hour. In addition, unlike a taxi driver, he wasn't afraid of having his vehicle stolen. He helped the girls out, rang the bell for them, supported their gentlemen upstairs – oh, the old cabby was a real sport! He knows Berlin by day and by night, knows how Berlin laughs and how it weeps – he's not squeamish, he's of iron . . .

'Don't worry, Gustav,' the girls would say when the gentleman positively refused to pay for the cab. (Why should he? He hadn't ordered one. And besides, what was he doing there at all?) 'Don't worry, Gustav, I'll settle up with you tomorrow.'

Yes, those were his night fares, that was the money he took home to his wife. But of such things he never spoke to her.

Had he hoped that they might be spared him? He was spared

nothing. He perhaps didn't like it; in fact he definitely didn't like it – putting drunken gentlemen to bed, and in what beds! But if he wanted to live, if he wanted to bring money home to Mother, he had no choice. He had to take what was offered – he had the choice between life and death. To die was open to him; at that time there prevailed in Berlin a certain joy in dying about which statistics were compiled. Suicide statistics. They showed that the very young and the very old were mainly affected.

But he did not want to die yet; above all he did not want his wife to die. So he had to make his living the best way he could, even if it were not a good living or a clean one – just a living.

No, he did not complain. He didn't complain at all. He was now in his mid-sixties, not yet really old. Like almost everyone of this time, he had the vague hope of outliving it. One day, things had to be different, had to be better. Life couldn't always be going downhill.

If anything worried him on his night drives through the sombre streets it was the thought of Eva. He would not like to meet her again, he on his box and she in the cab with a man. To have to drive Eva to some accommodation hotel would be the end of him. Father and daughter! As long as only he knew what sort of fares he took on nowadays, life was endurable – he alone could decide what rightly might be asked of himself. For someone else to know, however, and that someone a member of his own family, and precisely the one he had turned out of doors because of similar conduct – impossible! The thought of Eva worried him unceasingly and he would gladly have given up his night work on her account. But then there was his wife to think of . . .

The last time he had seen Eva was in the dock, when she hadn't once looked at her father but only at her Eugen Bast. This fellow alone, obliquely opposite her, she had continued to look at. Her sentence must be up by now but he had no wish to see her again, ever.

But there came an autumn night, an October night, when a gusty, furious east wind drove the rain in sheets through the desolate town. Hackendahl had put the cover over his black horse but it was of no use – the wind slapped it continually against the creature's flanks, and everything was dripping wet, so that there was nothing for it but to drive home, money or no money. Not a soul about.

He was already on his way back when he was hailed from a café. 'Hi, driver!'

A gentleman in a raincoat ran towards him, glad to have found a conveyance. 'Driver, here . . . I've got a lady with me who's had as much as she can carry. Well, we'll manage. Not too expensive, you know.'

'Righto! Six marks the night for you an' the lady an' you needn't clear out too early next mornin'. But hurry up, my horse ain't a champion swimmer an' he might drown.'

The gentleman brought a girl out of the café and put her into the cab.

'Come on, off we go!'

The father drove a daughter he did not recognize, who did not recognize him, to an accommodation hotel.

Life spares us sometimes, after all.

§ III

Three days previously old Hackendahl had been engaged by one of those servants who no longer exist – an old woman in a white starched apron and a cap with two white streamers down her back. On Thursday, punctually at ten o'clock in the morning, he was to wait outside No. 17, Neue Ansbacher, and drive her old mistress to a nursing home.

'Righto, Fräulein.'

'Don't forget. Ten o'clock!'

'Righto.'

The following day she got hold of him again – he hadn't forgotten, had he?

'All fixed up, Fräulein. Day after tomorrow. Ten o'clock in the morning. Seventeen, Neue Ansbacher.'

She was satisfied with his memory, yes. But was he a careful driver? He wouldn't run risks with cars, would he? Her mistress hated cars. She had never gone in one. For over twenty years she hadn't once been out of the flat. She was ninety-three.

'I'll take care of her, Fräulein. I'm getting on for seventy meself.'

'And I'm sixty-three.'

They smiled at one another, both very proud of the distance they had travelled in life.

'But at ninety-three she shouldn't be going out, when she ain't used to it. It's bound to upset her.'

'But she has to go to the clinic – an operation. The Herr Geheimrat insists on it, otherwise she'd never be well again.'

'Me, if I was as old as that I wouldn't let them cut me about, Fräulein. I'd leave things as they are.'

'But she wants it. She's made up her mind. She wants to live till she's a hundred and eleven – she says that's a nice age to live to. Even as a young girl she set her heart on it.'

'Well,' said Gustav, 'we old 'uns are another make from the tender young growths of today. They'd never be able to stand what we've bin through. We're of iron.'

And with that he drove away.

The next day, being again reminded, he said:

'I'm talkin' against me own int'rests but I advise a private ambulance. You know, Fräulein, at ninety-three a cab's goin' ter shake you up a bit, an' in an ambulance everythin's rubber and springs.'

'But she won't have one. The Herr Geheimrat has ordered an ambulance for eleven o'clock but, just like her, she's going an hour earlier in the cab. Secretly . . . She's very tickled at the thought of outwitting the Herr Geheimrat.'

'Must be a caution, your missis.'

'Indeed she is! What she wants, she wants, and what she doesn't want she won't do. An ambulance is a motor car and she won't have one. A car means petrol, she says, and petrol explodes if you light it. All cars will explode sooner or later, she says.'

'Well, well,' said Hackendahl, 'can't say I'd mind, though I haven't much hope of it.'

And the next day the old woman of ninety-three took her first drive for twenty-one years.

From the porch of 17, Neue Ansbacher emerged an enormous armchair, an upholsterer's triumph of bulge and curve, covered with a very faded velvet on which were seen embroidered birds – colibris and a great yellow and blue parrot. Two removal men were carrying the chair by means of straps while a third held the back. And behind him followed the house porter with rugs and pillows, and behind him in turn came the old servant who had a small travelling case in her hand – all these people looked half solemn, half amused.

In the chair was sitting a little old woman – such a tiny old woman, only a remnant of humanity – with hands no larger than a child's and scanty white hair beneath a smoothly fitting cap of jet beads. Her small face was covered with a network of lines and wrinkles, the mouth had fallen, but her eyes still looked alertly at the world.

They were looking at Gustav Hackendahl now. 'Yes, that's a real Berlin cabman,' said a very clear voice, contentedly. 'You did well, Malvine. What's your name, my dear man?'

'Gustav Hackendahl,' said Hackendahl, grinning all over his face and feeling like a young man again. 'But people call me Iron Gustav.'

'Iron Gustav! Do you hear that, Malvine? Yes, that comes from our old, our good, Berlin. But are you feeding your horse properly, my good fellow? He looks so thin.'

Iron Gustav preferred not to tell this old woman anything about his feeding difficulties, but he assured her that his horse got his daily twelve pounds of oats, only that his digestion was so bad because he had chewing problems: his teeth didn't bite together properly.

'Yes, his teeth! His teeth! And his digestion – with old age. Now earlier! Earlier!' But the old woman immediately quietened down again. 'All right, Malvine, give the horse its sugar then.'

And behold – everything had been anticipated – Malvine brought out the sugar from her apron pocket. 'Three lumps now and three lumps more when you've taken us safely there.' Then the old lady was piloted into the cab, in which she was firmly anchored with pillows and rugs, and Malvine got in.

'Start, driver! But go slowly. I want to have a look round, I can't bear the way they used to rush you.'

Away went the horse, walking slowly, and every time a car glided past the old lady cried out: 'Disgusting!' And, looking at the shops, she began to rummage in her memory. 'A confectioner used to live there. You must remember, cabman. Dietrich. Yes, Dietrich was the name.' She started back with a cry, however, when a big double-decker bus thundered past and it was quite a time before she enquired whether there were not any of the pleasant horse buses still in existence. Not now? Not a single one?

And soon she became confused, no longer recognizing the streets they were driving through. Wasn't Hackendahl going the wrong way? Here there used to be a promenade and water. 'The lakes can't have gone as well. I can still see the children splashing about.'

Ah, the children whom the old lady saw were probably long dead and their children in turn had stopped splashing about and were themselves being driven to hospitals. The cab drive to which she had looked forward with so much pleasure proved too much for her after the first ten minutes. Indoors she had been able to think that the old Berlin still lived. Now everything was changed – the streets, the buildings, the shops. Different people everywhere. And suddenly it must have dawned on her how old she was, how very old. Her world had long since passed away and she alone was left – terribly alone.

Closing her eyes she asked to be driven faster, so that she could be put to bed. A bed doesn't change as a town does; everywhere and at all times it is alike. And the old woman longed for hers. When the cab drew up at the clinic the bearers couldn't bring the stretcher quickly enough; driver, horse and sugar were utterly forgotten. Thus she vanished, the weeping Malvine behind her, and Gustav Hackendahl had to wait some time before a nurse came to fetch the rugs and pillows and other things.

'You're to go to the Matron's office for the fare, driver,' said the nurse.

Grumbling, old Hackendahl descended, took the bit off the black horse and put on the nosebag. Then he went to the office. The Matron was looking out of the window. She turned round, a stately, determined woman. His daughter Sophie.

'You, Sophie?' he said. 'That's funny . . . I have to drive a half-dead woman so as to see you again. Curious how things turn out between parents and children.'

'I saw you draw up outside, Father,' she said coolly. 'That's why I called you in. I could have sent the money out just as well. How's Mother?'

'Yes, it's you all right, Sophie. You haven't changed. Cold-hearted an'—'

'I didn't make myself, Father.'

'Is that meant for me?'

'Don't let's quarrel, Father. How's Mother?'

'How should she be in these times? The main thing is we have enough to eat.'

'Things not going too well? Yes, I can see that from your horse and cab. And by looking at you, Father, too.'

'No need to tell me that. I do me best. Gimme me fare, four marks fifty. I may be in a bad way but I don't have to stand an' listen to me daughter preachin'. I don't need you, but you needed me once.'

She considered him with her cold eyes. 'I needed you as every child needs its father, no more and no less. But we won't talk about that. Let bygones be bygones.'

'That's what you say. I still see you children as when you were little. But you don't want to know that. You want always to have been grown up.'

'I still remember being small; I dream of it sometimes. Not good dreams. I've only been satisfied since I stood on my own two feet. I'll never be completely satisfied. It's as if something was lacking, Father.'

'I was never unkind to you, Sophie. I did what I could.'

'Yes, and so did I,' said she. 'Well, Father, I'm Matron here and have a share in the place and do pretty well – if you like I'm in a position to do something for you and Mother . . .'

'I don't want yer money.'

'I wouldn't give you money. Money helps no one. But what about moving here with Mother? Downstairs there's quite a nice little flat and you could attend to the central heating and the boiler.'

'No, Sophie, I'm a cabby and a cabby I'll remain. I'm not becoming a porter in me old age.'

'Well, consider Mother a bit.'

'Mother's satisfied if I'm satisfied. I've always bin able to earn a crust of bread.'

Not in the least offended, Sophie looked at him thoughtfully. He, the father, was perhaps stubborn and embarrassed but she, the daughter, was quite cool, cold . . . Yet perhaps she was not so much at her ease as she seemed. Confronted by the old man in his stained and patched greatcoat, seeing his tanned and bearded face, something troubled her – not love, far from it – something more like duty or pride. If she no longer saw him, if she no longer knew of him, it wouldn't worry her. She could build up a private clinic, really up to date, a good place of work, a secure income and, above all, a meaning to her life – a world in which she would give the orders, to carers, to nurses, and to the sick – she, who had for so long been ordered about.

There he stood, the one who had ruled over her most sternly and most fatefully. Yes, perhaps it was not only the sense of responsibility which influenced her; was there not also – she herself realized it – the wish to order him about as he had ordered her, to have as a dependant the one on whom she had been dependent? No, she had not this intention of ordering him about, of letting him feel her power. Desire for revenge was not so strong as that, nor she so petty. It sufficed to know: he is dependent on me, he works for me. That would be sufficient. The trouble was, he wouldn't have it. She continued to look at him while all this went dimly through her mind, and at the same time she quickly made another plan.

The old man had become annoyed. He didn't like being looked at in this way, least of all by his own daughter. 'Come on,' he said, 'gimme the money. Four-fifty, I said.'

'Of course. Forgive me, I was only thinking . . .' She took the money from her desk and gave it him. 'Please sign the receipt. I need it for the patient.'

'What's the matter with her? Such an old woman! Will she pull through?'

'Who? Ah, the one you brought in. I don't know. I think it's cancer. No, she won't pull through. Hardly. And she's lived long enough, don't you think so?'

'Let's hope you won't be sayin' that of me, Sophie. I'll be seventy soon.'

'Of you? Why, then? Oh no, Father, you'll carry on for a long time yet. I think you'll live to be very, very old. One has to admit one thing – you've given us iron constitutions. Thoroughly sound.'

A pathetic twinge of happiness passed through the old man – the first appreciation he had had from this daughter.

'Listen, Father. I've had another idea.' He made a defensive gesture. He wanted nothing from her, but then he listened to her all the same. And she went on to explain that the nursing home with its eighty beds called for much cartage to and fro; patients' luggage had to be fetched and removed again; provisions, coal, wood must be brought in – there was always something.

'I'll never turn carter,' he said. 'I'm stayin' a cabby. I might just as well drive a car.'

But she did not give in. She'd talk it over with her doctors. 'With my doctors,' she said. 'The patients need fresh air and a car is not really good for them. They're then either in a draught or shut in. Yes, we ought to buy a small open carriage; it would pay us. We'd cover our outlay. We only receive wealthy patients and we would charge them for each separate drive and pay you a lump sum monthly. There'd be no charity in that, Father.'

'I work for myself,' he said stubbornly. 'Not for wages an' never have done.'

'Yes, you did, Father,' said she quickly. 'I remember before the war you drove people regularly at a monthly rate.'

'That was with me own cab. I've never driven someone else's for a wage. Except p'r'aps at Whitsun or an outing.'

She was shrewd enough not to press him. 'Well, you think it over. You needn't decide today. And I'll have to speak with my doctors first. In any case, you could keep on your cab as well – the work here wouldn't amount to so much.'

He went, he promised to consider it, but naturally no consideration was necessary. He didn't want to do business with his daughter. His feelings told him nothing can go right if parents are to depend on daughters, if daughters are to give advice to fathers. (He sensed aright: exactly what attracted her repelled him.)

In addition: he wanted nothing of it. Drive sick people around the streets? – out of the question! He's a cab driver, used to the regular sound of the taximeter, his destination, waiting at cab stops, and the gossip with other drivers and chauffeurs . . . He's Iron Gustav! Perhaps she wanted to put him into a uniform – she's quite capable of it.

He wouldn't even bother to discuss it with Mother. It wouldn't help. He must have known: if Sophie wanted something, Mother would be behind it. And precisely because he didn't tell Mother, she'd be in favour of it.

'The fact that you no longer ask me about such things, Father!' she complained. 'That I hadn't thought of you! But of course such a man couldn't give a damn about what his wife cooks for him, or how she manages with the money. Sometimes you give me nothing three days long – and then we should have had a regular income!'

He didn't answer, but Mother continued to speak and to complain. Whenever she saw him, whenever he gave her only two marks instead of five, whenever he wanted to take a rest, it was always the same: 'He could have had a regular income, but he refused! The older he gets the more stubborn he becomes. He just refuses everything. He never listened to me. He would rather not have mentioned it to me.'

So it constantly went, whether they were eating, or he wanted to sleep. He could still get angry, oh, yes – go over the top, lash out – but to what end? At nearly seventy you can't explode every hour, not even every day. And Mother was tough; she could go on complaining. Even when asleep her breathing sounded like a complaining groan . . . 'Regular income, regular income, regular income,' she seemed to snore.

It was nearly a month, however, before old Hackendahl gave way and went back to Matron Sophie.

'Mother keeps on about it. You shouldn't have gone to see her. It was a matter between us.'

But Sophie was very busy that morning, besides which everything had been arranged; it annoyed him greatly to see how sure she had been of his consent. He was given a note telling him to look at a carriage in such-and-such a place, a cart in another, and be measured for a new blue greatcoat, new boots. Everything had been thought of and in such a way that he could raise no objection. Even the tailor seemed to have received instructions. 'That's understood, of course,

Herr Hackendahl. Like your old coat – naturally! The Matron spoke to me about it.'

And the work started. It was winter, so that he could not very well grumble at having no patients to drive. Instead he had to deal with luggage and provisions, besides carting refuse and ashes in the evening. But when one morning they wanted him to take thirty urinals to a laboratory he demanded to see the matron. Matron, however, was in the operating theatre and couldn't be spared – naturally! Would he please hurry up, the tests were urgently required . . .

So he drove off, consoling himself with the reflection that ultimately it was all the same whether he took people's urine for a ride in bottles or in its natural containers.

It's all human, he said to himself.

§ IV

Happy though the days were on the island of Hiddensee, Heinz often felt restless at passing the time so without thought for tomorrow, buoying himself up with, 'I'll get a job all right, once I'm in Berlin.' He couldn't help a little anxiety. When he and Irma went back to Berlin on 1 July they wouldn't have more than about six weeks' money left. And what then – with a baby coming? Would he get a job? He'd never go on the dole. Well, they'd scrape through somehow. And the child?

Damn it all! It's a funny thing. If he sees the unemployed – who still exist even here on the island – standing around, he gets really worried about not being worried. 'Am I irresponsible,' he asked Tutti and Irma, 'for not bothering about a job? What are we going to do if I don't get one?'

'Oh, that's impossible,' exclaimed Tutti, who had worked all her life. 'Whoever wants work gets it. Those who don't find it just don't want it.'

Heinz Hackendahl actually thought the same, but he said: 'There are two million unemployed. They can't all be lazy.'

'Why not?' Tutti contradicted. 'They've been degraded by the war and inflation. Just look at the young layabouts with their flat caps over one ear and cigarettes in their mouths – they just don't want to work.'

'So you think I needn't worry?' he asked once again.

'Not at all,' she replied. 'Don't go and spoil your holiday. You'll get a job all right.'

Irma said nothing, she was often silent now. 'That's due to my condition,' she had told him.

That evening, as they went towards the winking light on the dunes, she suddenly squeezed his arm and said: 'Heinz, please don't let's get back as late as the end of June.'

'No? Are you afraid about the job after all, then?'

'Heavens no!' she said. 'I'm afraid on *his* account. No, not afraid. But everything ought to be ready.'

'Logical,' he said. 'So let's go in the middle of June.'

Silently they walked on.

He had said 'logical', but that was just a way of speaking. He found it strange, how women think. He could never work out what Irma was thinking about, how she came to her conclusions. She was convinced that he'd get a job, he felt that. She had no fear on account of money; not even in her dreams was there any question of the dole. But they had to leave early so that the baby should find everything in order. The baby who had yet to learn about order . . .

It was a funny thing. As something begins, it is easy to work out that it will so continue. What is good enough for the parents is far from being so for a baby.

'The first thing I must do,' explained Irma, 'is to get his layette ready. It would be splendid if you could earn a bit more in your new job. The layette's bound to cost a good fifty marks – would you be able to get that for your radio?'

There you are, you see! Dole and worry and more salary and having to sell a radio – it was closing in on him from all sides. And he was worried that he was not worried! Of course he was worried, naturally so – about what the future held. And between himself and dark fate, there was nothing, absolutely nothing but belief in himself, self-confidence. In Berlin dialect he would say to himself: Heinz, things are going to be all right.

§ V

And then everything went miraculously well. In Stralsund, Heinz bought some Berlin newspapers and, as the train carried him towards an impoverished, hungry city, he studied the advertisements.

'Here's something for me, Irma!' he exclaimed, pointing to a notice inserted by the banking house of Hoppe & Co. 'Required, young accountants, energetic and good-looking. Interviews from three to five in the afternoon.'

'Don't you fancy yourself!' she naturally retorted. 'Good-looking and energetic!'

'Hoppe & Co. Never heard of them,' he reflected. 'Well, we'll see . . . I won't accept just any old job.' His freedom from misgiving was in fact miraculous.

Shielded by this innocence, he entered the premises of Hoppe & Co. in the Krausenstrasse. When a man has been accustomed to palatial bank buildings he is no doubt justified in turning his nose up at a smoky, dirty-looking office, but on the other hand if he is out of a job . . .

'Vacancy?' asked the young fellow behind the grille. 'Vacancy? All filled long ago. Do you live in the past?'

'I'm from outside!' said Heinz, determined not to be imposed upon. 'At the sea resorts we get the *Berliner Zeitung* one day later.'

'Oh, you've been swimming in the sea?' grinned the fellow. 'And I was thinking you'd overdone things a bit, because you're not quite normal.'

They laughed at each other.

'Well, as far as being not quite normal is concerned, you're not doing such a bad job yourself!'

'You've got to! You've got to – especially in this place! I say, I seem to know you. Are you also from . . . ?'

'Of course. You bet. Export statistics.'

'My name's Menz. Erich Menz. Stocks.'

'Heinz Hackendahl.'

'Axed too, eh? Yes, everything's filled. Pity! I'd gladly have done something for an old colleague.'

'What do you do here, anyhow?' Heinz glanced at the five young fellows sitting behind the counter. They all looked rather bored.

'Do? We've nothing to do.'

'And you take on more people?'

'Oh, we'll be breaking out on the first of the month, we're moving to the Friedrichstrasse. Swell place. Pity that everything's filled. Day before yesterday we sent away a hundred applicants.' Suddenly he became animated. 'There's the old man coming in. Have a go at him. You never know.'

The old man, not more than thirty at the most, was a sandy-haired fellow elegantly dressed and with a rather dissipated look. He wore a monocle.

'Herr Doctor,' said Menz addressing him, 'excuse me, this is a colleague of mine, Herr Dahlhacke, from the same bank. He has just become disengaged. Terribly efficient. Excellent testimonials . . . If you think it could be managed, Herr Doctor.'

'Be managed what? I'm always being asked to manage it. I'd like to know what you manage in return for my good money. Well, let's hear what you, Herr Dahlhacke, can manage.'

Heinz waived for the moment a protest against his new name. 'I've learned all branches of banking. My testimonials . . .' He dived into his bosom.

Herr Hoppe motioned him to desist. 'I put no store on testimonials – they've all got 'em, ha, ha!' He laughed explosively into Hackendahl's startled face. 'You haven't got much presence of mind, Herr Dahlhacke,' he said, dissatisfied. 'Here a young man has to be energetic. He must be able to get rid of a client if necessary. He must be able to eject him.'

'We had a lot of that to do at my last bank in recent months, Herr Doctor.'

'Oh, well,' said Herr Hoppe. 'Are you married? Good, I like my employees to be married. I myself am a bachelor. Children? You're expecting? Splendid. I've never had a young man in the family way yet. Ha, ha, ha!' More spluttering into Heinz's face. 'Well, start on the first. Herr Tietz, Herr Dahlhacke is engaged from the first of the month, two hundred marks to begin with and every six months an increase of fifty up to a maximum of two hundred. Ha, ha, ha!'

Suddenly serious, he looked critically at his new employee. 'But kindly wear another tie, Dahlhacke. Too much red. Won't do. We're neutral here.' He disappeared into his sanctum.

'Seems a bit cracked,' said Hackendahl, full of sympathy.

'Don't you believe it! It's all eyewash. He's rather a sly dog.'

'But that's no real banker.'

'Why worry? Long as he pays. You be glad of two hundred marks! And net – no deductions.'

'Well, well,' said Heinz thoughtfully.

§ VI

It was really a very strange establishment, this into which Heinz Hackendahl had strayed, and it remained so even when the firm moved to imposing offices in the Friedrichstrasse. As to the madness of Herr Hoppe, the proprietor (for the Co. never put in an appearance), Heinz soon came to the same conclusion as his colleague Menz – Herr Hoppe was far from being mad. Herr Hoppe was a bright lad, a sly dog. But Heinz got no nearer to finding out what Herr Hoppe otherwise was. As before he could only reply in the negative – Herr Hoppe was no banker. And it needed little wit to discover this, for Herr Hoppe made no secret of the fact.

'You stallions of the banking world,' he would say when some employee bothered him about a book entry, 'you gelded accountants, for aught I care you can carry forward the debit into the credit as long as it all comes out in the wash. Ha, ha, ha!' Concluding splutter into some face or other.

Herr or rather Doctor Hoppe (it was uncertain whether he really had his doctorate but he set great store by the title) had acquired, it seemed, some small banking firm that had collapsed during the inflation; and now, when the big banks were anxiously looking out for clients, he too was getting ready to angle for them. Heinz Hackendahl learned that shortly before the removal to larger offices some thousands of persuasively fraternal letters had been dispatched urgently advising recipients to invest money with Hoppe & Co.

And their continued dispatch, together with determining who

was to receive them, seemed to be Herr Hoppe's most important task. Surrounded by dozens of directories he closeted himself in his holy of holies and far from him was any inclination to joke or splutter into laughter. The words he spoke to his employees as they rummaged through the directories were indeed sage.

'Gentlemen, always remember we seek to interest a virgin clientele, gentlefolk who so far have had nothing to do with banks, people who have lost confidence in savings banks, men for whom stocks, mining shares and bonds are unknown things – in short, the small man. The small man is starting to save again. He's just received a bang on the nut – and yet he's saving again. But how? In a cash box or a stocking! Idle money, at the mercy of thieves. And we want to introduce it to the capital market. Even the small man likes to make money. Eh, what?'

Herr Doctor Hoppe, as all agreed, was a queer fish but he took care that his suggestions were carried out.

'Who's been sending a letter to Herr Regierungsrat von Müller? You, Dahlhacke?' (In spite of all declarations he adhered to that form of name.) 'I must ask you most distinctly to comply with my wishes. Don't argue! A Regierungsrat, and a von Müller at that, has never been a small man; he may own stocks and shares, he may even be on some board of directors. Be more careful! Now if it had been a clergyman – clergymen are always good. And market gardeners aren't so bad.' He became thoughtful. 'Senior schoolmasters are excellent. Midwives – all right, Menz, you were going to make a joke – but midwives as a class are thrifty. That comes from their profession. By the way, is there a National Midwives' League? I've a feeling there is . . . if so, we ought to get hold of its membership list. I already thought of going for all the midwives at a blow . . . No, you're right, Krambach. Farmers are a waste of money.'

Such was the talk when the promotional letters were sent out. It was clear then that Herr Hoppe wanted the custom only of the inexperienced and unimportant, which needed signify nothing more however than that he thought it worthwhile catching the small fry ordinarily disdained by the big banks. Many a mickle makes a muckle. With regard to the promotional letters, though, Herr Hoppe did not like his employees taking personal interest in them.

They came from the printers set out in a fount deceptively similar to typescript and with very handsome headings. Herr Hoppe could not prevent employees who had to insert name and address at the top from reading them, but . . .

'Herr Menz! Herr Menz!'

'Yes, Herr Doctor?'

'May I point out politely but firmly that you're here to get letters ready for the post, not to pass the time reading them? I'm not paying fifty per cent more in overtime for the sake of evening classes. Please, gentlemen, this batch of a thousand has to be posted tonight.'

In spite of this supervision a few things leaked out, however. Herr Doctor hadn't got eyes in the back of his head; when his attention was distracted the young fellows simply pocketed a letter to read at home. Perhaps Herr Hoppe came to realize this or he may have understood that his employees had to cope with the clients at the counter; whatever the reason, he gradually became more informative.

'I could tell at once by the faces of you lads,' he said grandly, 'that you were taken aback when I promised the clients three per cent interest a month, yes, in some cases even four and five per cent. You immediately thought there must be something shady. Am I right, Dahlhacke?'

Embarrassed at thus being singled out, Heinz said: 'To tell the truth, Herr Doctor Hoppe, I don't understand . . .'

'Of course you don't understand, that's why I'm telling you, because you don't understand. But actually you ought to understand. You come from a big bank, you ought to know that sometimes, and not infrequently, a transaction crops up which yields fifty, a hundred, even two hundred per cent.'

'Rarely, almost never,' said Heinz.

'But it does occur, doesn't it? It can happen, Krambach, can't it? Speak, man!'

'Oh yes, naturally, in the course of thousands of transactions . . .'

'But it's not net profit; one has to set against it all the deals which yield nothing or even a loss,' objected Heinz Hackendahl.

'With the big banks, naturally,' said Herr Doctor Hoppe contemptuously. 'Ten good and ten thousand average transactions is what they have in a year and that's why they can't give more than

one or one and a half per cent interest. But when a man comes
along, a simple Dr Hoppe, who makes only one transaction but that
a very profitable one – what interest can he pay then, eh?'

They looked at him silently, expectantly, suspiciously.

'Lüneburg Heath!' continued Herr Hoppe. 'We struck lucky in
seven places on Lüneburg Heath.' He took a deep breath, then said
carelessly: 'I'm boring for oil in Lüneburg Heath and I've got it. But
we need capital – concessions, derricks, pipelines, refining plants,
roads, railways – so I apply to the thrifty for it, giving in return, as no
bank does, a generous share of the profits. I can do that because I
save the enormous petrol duty.'

'And our bank's engaged in nothing else?' asked Krambach.

'Nothing,' said Herr Hoppe firmly. 'One first-class investment
only – nothing else.'

'Do you know,' said Menz to Hackendahl later, as they went
home together, 'of course it can be as the old boy said. It's possible.
But it's also possible that it isn't. That's a possibility too. What I
noticed is that he never says what he really thinks, and the stupidest
thing he said was when he spoke about oil.'

'Yes,' said Heinz. 'If good business really is to be made with oil,
which could be true, I've already read about borings on the Lüneburg
Heath. Then he can naturally get money anywhere, and not for
thirty-six to fifty per cent, as he promises, but for ten to twenty per
cent. I don't know, but Herr Hoppe doesn't really look to me like
someone who would make a present to the little man of twenty or
thirty per cent royalties just for love.'

'That's correct! As long as he just uses the little man and strictly
rules out anyone with banking experience?'

'You're in deep water, my friend!'

They walked for a while silently side by side.

'Two hundred bucks are not pig's shit,' said Menz thoughtfully – 'and being on the dole is damned hard on the feet.'

He was silent. Heinz Hackendahl was as well.

'And all that amounts to nothing,' continued Menz. 'You can't run
to the police and the law with anything like that.'

'On the contrary,' said Heinz Hackendahl. 'The whole thing could
backfire, and involve charges of slander and professional damages.'

'Exactly! We know nothing.'

'But we're careful.'

'And when . . .'

'Then!'

'It's a deal!'

'Despite two hundred bucks!'

'And the dole.'

'Goes without saying.'

'It's only logic.'

'Well then!'

'Well then, indeed! Till tomorrow.'

'Goodnight.'

§ VII

They were both young, Hackendahl and Menz, like all the employ-ees of Hoppe & Co. – perhaps Herr Doctor Hoppe had good reason for engaging the young – and were therefore naturally pleased with an undertaking which went so smoothly; where others believed, they too were ready to believe, succumbing to faith, to success, to the general opinion. While things had only been preparing, with cir-culars going out and merely a trickle of money coming back, they had been critical, doubtful, unenthusiastic.

But there came a time when people thronged the counters, when no more circulars were sent out and yet the stream did not diminish; a time when Herr Doctor Hoppe no longer saw all his clients and the young men themselves had to do this – be persuasive, explanatory, paint rosy pictures. And what is repeated many times with zeal and conviction ends inevitably by creating its effect. Heinz Hackendahl had so frequently explained the point about the petrol duty, he had mentioned so many times the borings on Lüneburg Heath in seven, in ten, in fifteen places, he had shown so many photographs of the derricks and had given so many technical elucidations, had for so long talked people out of their doubts and converted them to faith in Herr Hoppe, that in the end he had talked away his own doubts too and was now numbered with the converted.

And what security was offered the investor! Any day anybody could call back his money without notice and yet be entitled to his three per cent monthly interest. But one who let his money stand for more than a month received four per cent, if for more than six months, five per cent. 'Here's your money and your interest – if you should feel disposed, visit us again.'

'Never let yourselves be offended, gentlemen,' Herr Hoppe begged his employees. 'Don't take suspicion amiss. People entrust us with their hard-earned money and they have a right to be suspicious. Always stay polite and obliging, and in cases of doubt side with the small investor rather than with the bank.'

It was really surprising how they came, how trusting they were, how much money they brought. Yes, they trusted neither the government, nor captains of industry, they suspected banks and savings institutions – but here they had confidence. They would stand hesitantly in the hall, looking at those in front of the counters and those behind. They would study the piles of banknotes stacked beside the cashiers. And when they asked for information they were irritable, suspicious. But suddenly they would say: 'All right, I'll put in a hundred marks.'

They came with the most trifling of sums, ten-mark notes, five-mark pieces, Rentengroschen; not the smallest deposit was to be refused – on that point Herr Hoppe was emphatic. The meanest client had to be treated as politely as the largest. It wasn't as though he came out of his office only when well-to-do clients were at the counter – no, Herr Hoppe paid equal if not more attention to workmen handing over ten marks out of their wages, talking with them, spluttering his 'Ha ha' into their faces.

Of course, the reason all these people were suspicious was that they had bad consciences. Banks and savings banks were offering their depositors ten and even twelve per cent interest, but here they were to receive thirty-six per cent, yes, up to sixty per cent interest a year, which was impossible in the ordinary way, so that there must be something wrong. Greed waged war with suspicion; greed won and they brought along their money. But on the way home suspicion returned. No doubt they sat up all night, remembering how they had been done out of their savings before, and how they had vowed never to trust anyone again; for on the following day they were back at the earliest possible moment, mumbling apologies for changing their minds or lying about a wife taken suddenly ill and their needing the money for an operation.

Whereupon they got their money, with interest for one day, amounting perhaps to a few pfennigs only. And they with their bad consciences were met by cheerful smiles. 'Certainly! It's your money after all. If you want to deposit it again, please come along.'

One shaggy-haired man in a green overcoat came every other day. The cashier in charge of his account was quite out of his head about it. 'Pays in a thousand marks, takes it out (interest to be calculated), pays it in, takes it out (interest to be calculated again).'

'Well, well,' said Herr Hoppe soothingly, 'he'll end by giving in, Krambach. And with a round sum like that he makes the calculation of the interest damned easy for you, ha ha!'

'But today he was back for the eleventh time,' complained Krambach. 'I hate the sight of him. And I just can't stand his smell at all. The fellow must live on garlic, Herr Doctor.'

'Garlic is said to be good for you,' said Herr Hoppe. 'Ask him why he takes it. A question like that gives people more confidence.'

But the green coat showed no increase in confidence, on the contrary. One day he paid in his thousand marks at nine o'clock in the morning and fetched them the same evening, demanding a day's interest.

'We're sorry, Herr Lemke,' said Krambach regretfully, 'but this time no interest is due. We're exceedingly sorry.'

'But I have a right to the interest,' cried Herr Lemke excitedly, smelling even more strongly of garlic. 'I entrusted you with my money.'

'But you must leave it with us, Herr Lemke, at least twenty-four hours, you see, your money hasn't done any work for us yet . . .'

'Work!' Herr Lemke's voice filled the hall, a thing that had to be prevented at all costs. 'My money work for *you*! You have to work for *me*. I was promised interest. I entrusted you with my money!'

'Are you dissatisfied?' gently enquired Herr Hoppe. 'What is it, Krambach?'

Krambach explained the case excitedly, interrupted even more excitedly by Herr Lemke.

'Give the gentleman his interest,' said Herr Hoppe.

'But the paying-in day is the same as the paying-out day,' protested Krambach. 'How am I to enter that?'

Herr Hoppe looked gravely at Krambach's chest, so gravely that Krambach began to think that, inadvertently, he was wearing a tie of the forbidden red.

'We wish to satisfy our clients, Herr Krambach,' said Herr Hoppe, adjusting his own tie, Krambach doing the same with his. 'Debit my private account with Herr Lemke's interest. Confidence is a tender plant.'

For a week Herr Lemke brought his thousand marks in the morning and fetched them in the evening plus interest. 'No decent joint would put up with this,' said Heinz Hackendahl to Erich Menz. 'It's a fraud!'

Then, one morning, came Herr Lemke, paler and shaggier than ever. With trembling but resolute hands he paid in ten thousand marks. And did not draw them out again. When he appeared next time he brought with him a fat, apple-cheeked woman who paid in three thousand marks.

Herr Lemke had changed from Saul into Paul; he had turned evangelist for Hoppe & Co. Sometimes he stood at the counter, a dirty slip of paper in his hand, having his interest worked out and checking the cashier's figures by his own calculations.

'Don't you want to withdraw your money?' his old enemy Krambach would jeer. 'Just to see it's still there?'

But Herr Lemke shook his head. 'You're all right,' he said, almost reluctantly. 'And as for your chief, he's a real sly dog.'

§ VIII

Heinz sometimes spoke with Irma about his reservations; in fact he often spoke about them with her. 'The place can't be above board, Irma,' exclaimed Heinz. 'A man who runs after clients like that for the sake of their deposits isn't straightforward.'

'None of your business. Be glad you've got a job.'

For even the young Hackendahls had lost some of their optimism. Unemployment was spreading like a plague, sweeping away whole trades with it, and Irma was no longer so certain that Heinz would get a post whatever happened. And then, in a few more weeks – the baby! And Irma was in favour of establishing order for the baby.

'But the whole show may crash, Irma. And I'd be involved. As an accomplice or something.'

'Don't be ridiculous. There are fourteen of you. Why should you be picked out?'

'Well, there's something wrong, Irma. We see the money paid in but no one has the faintest idea what happens to it. That is Herr Hoppe's business. I've tried to pump my colleagues.'

'You seem to be trying to lose your job,' she exclaimed, exasperated. 'Remember you'll soon be a father.'

'Irmchen, do stop criticizing. You yourself wouldn't want us to live by defrauding the poor.'

'Please stop that now! You're defrauding no one. You get your two hundred bucks, and go to work.'

'But . . .'

'Tell me, did they inform you at your last bank what they did with their clients' money? Don't be funny, Heinz. Everybody has to think of himself.'

'But . . .'

He had many buts, about only thinking of yourself as well. He considered it wasn't right. To him, if everyone merely thought of themselves, things were bound to go wrong. However, Heinz Hackendahl conceded that Irma was now too preoccupied with the baby to make a correct judgement. Heinz Hackendahl was soon to be a father, but he was still on his own.

He was following events in the banking house of Hoppe & Co. very anxiously, for in his heart it wouldn't have pleased him at all to obtain clear proof that the business was dishonest. He watched Herr Hoppe as if he himself were a detective and his employer a criminal, and established with relief that Hoppe hadn't changed any of his habits. He wore the same suits and smoked the same cigars. He

didn't smell of alcohol, and he didn't disappear at midday to an official Stock Exchange 'breakfast'. Punctually every morning at nine
o'clock – irksome example to all unpunctual employees – Herr
Hoppe appeared at his bank. No seductive feminine voice ever
enquired for him on the telephone.

No, Heinz Hackendahl found nothing out of the way, nothing
extravagant or villainous about the sandy-haired Doctor. Neither did
Erich Menz, to whom he would sometimes whisper his doubts.
Menz had begun to think they should let sleeping dogs lie. 'Be glad
you've got a cushy job. Being on the dole's no fun.'

But an inner voice gave Heinz no rest. It was a very tiresome
voice, and he would much rather it had been silent. Things would
have been easier. It was the same voice that had made him prevent
Tinette's seduction, and had forced him to visit Widow Quaas's stationery shop once more, until he'd made his peace with Irma. At a
time of egoism, godlessness and lack of conscience, it was the voice
of conscience itself, somewhat imperious in a lone young man – a
voice which told him neither to rest nor to indulge himself, without
first asking where his food came from.

Then came an afternoon when Herr Doctor Hoppe seemed quite
changed. Restlessly he wandered through the bank, not hearing the
questions addressed to him, vanishing hurriedly into his holy of
holies, dashing out again immediately for no apparent reason –
good-humoured, noisy, buttonholing everybody, spluttering his 'Ha
ha' into each face – then abruptly gloomy, taciturn, almost
bad-tempered. One might have thought he had had a drop too much,
but it wasn't that.

'Today I accept no deposits,' he shouted suddenly. 'Gentlemen,
decline all custom. No more money.'

The employees stared at each other, perplexed.

'But what are we to tell the clients?' whispered one.

'Never mind what you tell them,' shouted Dr Hoppe. 'I've had
enough of it. I don't want any more money. Tell them,' he said, suddenly calmer, 'that at the moment we have no profitable investment.
Perhaps tomorrow.' And he vanished into his office.

'Cracked!' whispered Erich Menz.

The doubtful Heinz shook his head. And, doing so, saw a man

come in through the revolving door. Heinz ducked and almost disappeared behind his desk.

The man spoke in an undertone with a clerk at the barrier, who looked hesitatingly towards the private office. Then the visitor whispered something soothing and the clerk let him through.

Heinz, as mentioned, had hidden himself. It wouldn't have been pleasant to be recognized by his brother Erich – Erich, fat and puffy but very elegant, almost too elegant in his top hat.

After a quarter of an hour Herr Hoppe came out, escorting his visitor to the door. This time Erich was carrying one of the bank's attaché cases.

And as he came back to the counter Herr Hoppe remarked cheerfully: 'I've received good news. Three more borings have struck lucky. Gentlemen, we accept deposits again!'

§ IX

From the moment Heinz Hackendahl saw his brother Erich in the main hall of the bank, leaving with an attaché case belonging to the boss, his suspicions almost crystallized into a certainty. Hoppe & Co. was a shady business! Erich was involved, and up till now he had only known Erich to be involved in businesses that were shady. The business must be shady if Erich was in it.

It wasn't a thing he could talk about to Menz – he didn't want Menz to know he had a brother like that; while with Irma, who certainly didn't think any better of Erich than he did, he didn't want to talk about it – the baby would be coming in barely a fortnight. He had to decide for himself and shoulder the responsibility. What am I to do? he thought. If I give up the job of my own accord I won't be entitled to the dole. Shall I go to the police? I haven't a shred of evidence. And Irma and I have nothing to fall back on – a hundred marks at the most. What on earth should I do? He thought again. Yes, I must give up the job. I won't have a hand in anything dirty. But Irma – Irma will reproach me. And with a child coming, and no job . . .

Such thoughts ran through his head, but didn't stay there. There

were future worries, too – but those of the present were more
urgent. Gloomy-faced he sat at his desk. Of course it was insane to
be paying thirty-six per cent interest! It must be a fraud. He'd been
blind not to have seen through it from the first. Everybody had been
taken in. They were so suspicious and greedy; their thirst for money,
their desire to win the lost war in their own case at least, to do a little
fleecing on their own account and let the others die like dogs, cried
to heaven. This Lemke was a perfect example. When Hoppe made
him a present of money by paying interest to which the man was not
entitled – that is, did the most bewildering thing a businessman
could do – then Lemke became trustful. Just when he was really
being cheated.

Yes, one must get out of this rotten joint! I've been a fool, thought
Heinz. I've sworn never to have anything to do with Erich again. And
he started looking in the newspapers for vacancies. How few there
were; only now did it come home to him how really very few there
were. And he always arrived too late. 'Sorry, filled long ago. You
must get up a bit earlier, young man.'

It was a miserable atmosphere that one took from such job applications. But it couldn't be helped – miserable or not, job or no job – it
was a dirty business, and he wouldn't put up with it.

Each morning as he took leave of Irma – now very heavy indeed –
to rush to the office, he cursed himself for his cowardice. He ought
not to go. He was a coward. The same thing had happened with
Erich and Tinette. No, he could never forget Erich; everything
brought him back to mind. In those days he had vowed a hundred
times never to return to her luxurious villa, and yet he had gone, as
he did now to the office every morning. He had been a coward for so
long, he had reached rock bottom – humiliation and ignominious
defeat. That couldn't happen again. He must give up the job . . . Yes,
if it weren't for Irma and the baby he'd have the courage to do so.
However, making plans about everything you would and would not
do, if and when, was merely a cowardly excuse. If only Herr Hoppe
would give him notice! Then he'd be entitled to the dole. (Yet
another 'if and when'.)

Heinz became irritable and taciturn. He answered enquiries
vaguely, sat openly chewing his pen when there was plenty to do,

said 'Herr Hoppe' instead of 'Herr Doctor Hoppe', and sported a tie with a good deal of red in it. It was all very childish, he knew, and he was being a horrible coward in thus throwing the decision as to his fate onto another person, but he did it nevertheless, persevering in it, shirking the issue. One must be practical, he consoled himself, be a realist. You are not to throw away dirty water till you've got some clean, that's proverbial.

And then it was all over much more quickly than he would have thought possible. Indeed someone else did take the decision out of Heinz Hackendahl's hands; for, as he was rushing off to the post office with some letters one day, a man entered the bank and, looking through the glass of the revolving door, saw Heinz going out. Both were pushing energetically; Heinz pushed Erich into the bank with no less determination than Erich pushed Heinz out, and while they did this the two glanced at each other through the glass. Heinz looked furious yet embarrassed; Erich seemed calmly to take in the situation – the letters in his brother's hand, the fact that he was without an overcoat . . .

Heinz came to a stop outside – impossible not to. In there, in the hall, he could see his brother watching him through the glass. Erich made no sign of recognition, showed no intention of speaking. For a moment the two enemy brothers stared at each other. Heinz thought of something quite superficial. He's got his top hat on again, the idiot – but he always was an idiot. As if he hadn't got anything worse against his brother than this idiocy! Then others pushed in between them and Erich vanished. Very slowly and thoughtfully, Heinz went to the post office with his express letters. Whatever happens I'll end it today, he said to himself. I'm a miserable cur, and a coward. I'll give notice, dole or no dole.

But he didn't give notice after all, because it was he who received it. Brother Erich had few scruples; it was enough for him to have seen Heinz there.

'Tell me,' said Herr Hoppe throatily, 'tell me – I hear your name is Hackendahl?'

'Yes, Herr Hoppe.'

'Why do you call yourself Dahlhacke? Tell me!'

'Never have called myself so,' said Heinz. 'You called me it.'

'Very odd! Why should I call you Dahlhacke if your name's Hackendahl? Perhaps you'll kindly explain that to me.'

'Evidently you misunderstood my name.'

'Oh, indeed. And obviously you didn't correct me because you
didn't want me to make enquiries about you, what?'

'And now you've made them – from Herr Hackendahl.'

'Do you know to whom you're speaking, young man? I'm your
boss . . . you wouldn't live without me.'

'I always thought it was my father . . .'

'Young man!'

'Hackendahl's my name.'

'Well,' said Herr Hoppe after a moment's thought, 'I've no more
use for you. With me every day's the end of the month. You're given
notice as from today, and dismissed; here is your month's salary.
Tiedtke, or whoever has time, will complete your papers. And now
clear out!'

'Good day, Herr Hoppe,' said Heinz, unbelievably relieved. It had
happened; he had survived. He was ready for anything. Erich was
good for one thing: he was an excellent cure for cowardice.

§ X

One evening two days later, Irma put aside her half-finished baby
trousers, sighed lightly, and said: 'I think it's time, Heinz.'

'Then let's go,' said Heinz. 'But will you still be able to walk?'

'Of course I will!' – and they walked in peace to the hospital.

'Go gently with the young mother,' said Irma. 'I must first be sure
that it really is time. What I've got is hardly more than strong stomach pains.'

She then told him once again the embarrassing story of her friend
who had herself driven to the hospital with the most terrible pains,
with husband, mother and chauffeur in a veritable panic, thinking
that it could happen in the car. Into the hospital they went, waited a
night, one day, a week, two weeks. Went home because it was nothing like time – and, hardly reaching home, gave birth.

'I'd die of shame! No. Let's wait another half an hour.'

For that half an hour, which lasted two hours of the night, they walked up and down in front of the hospital. Sometimes Irma held fast to the railings, sometimes to the lamp-post, sometimes to her husband. 'It's stupid that we've no experience, Heinz,' she complained. 'We could easily have stayed at home another hour.'

'The first time's the first time,' said Heinz sagely. 'You'll know all about it next time.'

'But I could have finished the baby's trousers, and then everything would have been proper.' Irma was in ignorance that not everything would have been proper even so, to wit, the main thing – his job. She didn't know yet that Heinz was unemployed. He hadn't told her that the last two days he had gone to the unemployment office instead of to the bank – astounding how many documents you had to produce proving you were unemployed, unemployed through no fault of your own and willing to accept work at any time since it wasn't the desire for a settled income which had made you prefer the dole to a decent salary.

Married women must have something like clairvoyance. 'Heinz,' asked Irma suddenly, 'is your job all right?'

'Of course,' he lied boldly. 'Why shouldn't it be?'

She looked at him with suspicion. 'You've seemed so cheerful the last few days.'

'Excuse me, but do you think I'd be happy if I was out of a job?'

'Heinz, don't do anything silly while I'm in hospital.'

'Lord, no. But I think we'd better go in now.'

'Give me five more minutes. I don't want to make a fool of myself.'

And she managed it so that she was rushed from the reception room without any of the usual formalities, and the last Heinz heard from her was: 'You see, Heinz, I didn't come too early.'

'Well, young man,' said the senior nurse in the reception room, 'couldn't you have come a bit earlier? Grudged the fares, I suppose, eh?'

However, Irma's way of doing things spared Heinz a sleepless night, for the various papers were not completed when a nurse entered: 'It's all over, young father. Congratulations.'

'Well, I never,' he said surprised. 'That's quick work. What is it?'

'The young mother will tell you herself tomorrow. Now you'd better make yourself scarce. It's already past midnight.'

However, although it was past midnight, Heinz did not go home. He found the weather just right for a long walk. Spring was approaching, which generally means particularly unpleasant weather. A biting wind soon brought snow, then rain, in his face. Nevertheless, a very relaxed Heinz reached the little stationery shop, and gave Widow Quaas a nearly lethal shock by drumming on the window pane.

Then, when she was sure he was not a thief, but merely her son-in-law, she received another shock when she learned that she was now a grandmother. She fiddled about, hands shaking, with her dressing gown, while he stood outside. He was supposed to go in, but did not want to.

'Oh, goodness me, you're such a sight, Heinz,' she complained. 'There's nothing wrong with Irma, is there? At least have a coffee! When did it happen?'

'After twelve, Quaasi,' said Heinz. 'And it nearly happened on the street!'

'Oh, my goodness! But do come in and have a coffee. You'll catch your death in that wind. Oh dear! I didn't even ask – boy or girl?'

'They don't know yet, mother-in-law,' shouted Heinz out of the dark, stormy night. 'They're waiting for the doctor. They'll know by midday tomorrow – no, today.'

And he ran off into the dark. For a long time he thought he could hear her moaning, but it must just have been the wind whistling in all the joints, cracks and keyholes of the buildings.

In Wexstrasse he didn't even need to go upstairs. A light was already on in the stable. His father, sitting by his horse, slowly turned his head towards his son as he came in and listened wordlessly to what he had to say.

He also asked: 'A boy?', but was told that his son did not yet know.

'What does it matter?' said his father. 'It won't have to go into the army any more – whether boy or a girl. It's all the same now! Are you pleased?'

'Of course!'

'Of course! Funny, when you consider how pleased I was with all of you. You can't possibly understand how stupid one felt.'

'That's probably why I'm so pleased now.'

'Naturally, because you think you'll be a completely different kind of father. Well, let's leave it at that. I don't want to annoy you. I only hope that your child doesn't hurt you as much as you hurt me. Then you can be happy.'

'Thank you, Father. Now I'll slip home and get a few hours' sleep. I've still got a lot to do today.'

'What have you got to do? Have you got to go back to your job, or can you take a holiday?'

'My job – oh, Father! I suppose I can tell you. Irma knows nothing. I no longer have a job. They threw me out three days ago.'

'Oh, no!' exclaimed the old man. 'It never rains but it pours. You must be under pressure. Will you have to go on the dole again?'

'I must see. I hope not.'

'Shall I ask Sophie? Perhaps she can help. She's important in the clinic. I think the whole thing even belongs to her.'

'No, better leave that, Father. I never did get back on good terms with Sophie.'

'You're right. Relations are bad enough without having business dealings with them. Will you come back later and tell Mother? I don't want to do it myself. I don't have the necessary happy touch!'

'I'll see, Father. Perhaps we'll leave it till tomorrow.' He hesitated. He didn't like to ask his father, but then did so anyway. 'Father, have you heard again from Erich?'

The old man turned his big head slowly towards him, and said slowly, 'From our Erich? Are you just asking or is something behind it?'

'He was probably the reason the bank suddenly gave me notice.' And he briefly told his father about his encounter with his brother.

'That's Erich,' nodded the old man. 'He's done that. Jus' like him. No, I know nothing about him at first hand but I've seen him twice at the Zoo Station.'

'So you know nothing either,' said Heinz, a bit disappointed.

'Let the ole man have his say. At the Zoo Station with a top hat an'' binoculars, an' attaché case, round about three o'clock. That convey anythin'?'

'He was wearing a top hat at our place and carrying an attaché case.'

'An' binoculars,' insisted Hackendahl meaningfully.

'I don't know.'

'A nod's as good as a wink to a blind horse,' said the old man a little scornfully. 'What sorter trains leave the Zoo Station about three o'clock in the afternoon?'

'I really don't know. There are so many.'

'I mean goods trains, not trains with binoculars and top hats. Don't you twig?'

'Oh, you mean—' exclaimed the son, really startled.

'Yes, that's what I mean. About three o'clock you c'n go from there on to Karlshorst, Hoppegarten and Strausberg. I used to take plenty of racin' chaps there once, an' bettin' chaps too.'

At first the light thus thrown on his brother's connection with the banking house of Hoppe & Co. blinded Heinz. Then everything became clear. Did they say crazy? Correct – in so far as an obsessive is crazy. Reckless, unscrupulous betting! Ten or twenty per cent interest obviously made no difference in that case. Those scoundrels – cheating the poor.

'You're right, Father, that's what it is,' he shouted and went to the door. 'I must just . . .'

'What must you just? It's only five o'clock.'

'But, Father, early tomorrow morning we've got to rescue what we can of people's savings. This Hoppe – a cunning chap like that naturally wouldn't go there himself, so as not to be seen. What a swine! Poor people's savings!'

'Yes, the savings of people who want their fifty per cent. You needn't waste much of yer sympathy on 'em.'

'But it's all a cheat and a fraud – petroleum on Lüneburg Heath!'

'Sit down, Heinz. Why you gettin' so worked up? They've sacked yer, an' you're out of it now.'

'But Father, there must be—'

'Well, what mus' there be? Justice an' law? An' administered by the pair of us, what? No, that's their business. What've we got police an' judges an' public prosecutors for, if it ain't to keep a lookout? Where do you come in?'

'No, Father. That's not right. You used not to think like that.'

The old man was silent for a little. Then he asked: 'You seem in a howling rage with Erich. You're not upset 'cause they kicked you out, are you?'

'I'm not . . .' began Heinz. He wanted to say 'angry with Erich'. But he didn't say it. Because it wasn't true. Because he was furious with Erich. Because he hated Erich. Not only because of what had happened, but also because he felt that Erich was evil. Yes, Erich loved what was evil, loved it for its own sake. There will never be any progress with people like Erich around. But . . .

'But, Father, I don't want to lay a charge just to get at Erich. Certainly not! I don't want revenge. I only want this fraud to stop.'

'All right, bring a charge, but give Erich a hint. We've had enough with Eva.'

'I can't do that, Father. If I warned Erich he'd warn the others. Then people's deposits would be utterly lost.'

'You c'n wait till the last moment. Then he won't have time.'

'Father, I can't. I oughtn't to.'

'Yes, you can. What's it matter? What used to be decent don't exist now. Why stop 'em, I often say. It won't change anythin', Heinz. Let him go, our Erich!'

'Things will change!'

'How? I don't see it happening. Things only get worse 'n' worse. An' I'm sick of it all, Bubi. The way she stood there in the dock – Eva, I mean – didn't look at me once but only at that pimp, an' I had to tell the judge about me own child, an' he asked me in front of everyone if she'd ever pinched anythin' before an' when had she started with men and whether she was much of a liar, an' I kept on thinkin' – there's me daughter and she won't look at me . . . Well, that's my contribution to the German nation . . . No, Heinz, we can't have it all over again, an' this time with Erich . . . No, my boy. We can't, neither me nor your mother.'

'Well, so long, Father,' said Heinz after a while. 'I'll do as you say. Even though it's certainly not right.'

'Lor, Heinz, if you can tell me what *is* right . . .'

No, it wasn't right, Heinz was convinced of it. He had been sitting in Alexanderplatz police headquarters, watching the unsympathetic and indecisive faces of its officials, on which he could read the suspicion that they were dealing with a dismissed and vengeful employee.

Berlin was in chaos. So many obvious, quite blatant crimes were committed. Officials were overworked and exhausted, and they were also frustrated because they were so often hindered from taking action against an obvious crime – for political or personal reasons, or connections. There were other banks than the tiny local Hoppe & Co.; there were big firms like Barmat, like Kutisker, as a result of which many an official had already been forced to leave banking.

No, they were not very willing to intervene merely on the hearsay of a dismissed employee. All right, they would look into the matter, make enquiries . . . They had his address.

'It'll be too late then,' said the young man. 'Is there anyone else I can see here?'

'You're in a terrible hurry,' they laughed. 'All right, come along.' And they put him into the waiting room of one of the big beasts, a much-feared bully boy. They gave the register clerk his file and then they left him. 'He'll soon get bored,' they said.

There Heinz Hackendahl sat and waited, thinking about his brother Erich, which made him so determined. And all of a sudden he knew that he hated him as he hated no other person on earth. His father, the old man whose children had not given him much happiness, wished to shield his son and that was understandable. But the son here in the police station was not understandable – indeed he did not understand himself. He was sitting there because of his brother, but once he had attained his object and they wished to proceed against Erich, then he intended to run to the telephone and warn him. (He had the telephone number in his pocket on a slip of paper.) He wanted to warn him, not because he thought his brother would mend his ways, but out of a frail pity, himself persuaded at heart that Erich would continue to do evil.

He had to make a decision. The issue was whether one had the courage to do damage to oneself, to act entirely after one's own heart. No one was asking him, no one would help him. It was entirely up to him. Oh, if only it had been someone unimportant, like Hoppe, for instance, and not precisely his own brother! And he recalled how quick and bright Erich had once been – how very much he had once admired and loved him.

Perhaps, he thought, only what has been extremely loved can be extremely hated. And he would once more have liked to evade a decision, and sneak away. There were excuses enough – Irma would be wondering where he had got to and . . . But then all hope of this was over; a door opened and Heinz was ushered into an office. (But he would keep quiet about Erich and telephone him afterwards.)

'Ah,' said the stout man, having read over the brief statement already on his desk. 'And now tell me about it again, in your own words.'

Heinz did so, repeating what had already been taken down, and no more.

'Is that all?'

Heinz nodded vigorously.

'Something's missing,' said the red-faced man. 'And you know very well that something's missing.'

Heinz behaved as if he did not understand.

'You're screening someone,' said the bully boy in a friendly way 'You want to protect someone.' He smiled. 'You see, when you've sat here as long as I have you can sniff things out. There's no magic about it. And in your case the missing link is how you came to pick on racing bets.'

'I just thought it likely,' said Heinz, embarrassed.

'Naturally, you just thought so!' said the stout man getting up. 'Good morning, my dear young man, and don't come here again. We haven't yet found out how to make omelettes without breaking eggs and you won't find out either. The world stinks like a big dung heap and if everybody tries to segregate his own little stench then we'll never get rid of the smell . . . We'll catch this Hoppe all right; I know who he is. A clerk who ran away with what was in the till. But what interests me is your own private pile of stench. However, as I said, we've enough on hand without you, and if you're satisfied with being a coward and not a man, good luck to you. After all it's your own affair.'

Each hard word stabbed Heinz to the heart. The red-faced man had sat down again and was reading his files, and seemed to be under the impression that his battered visitor was long departed.

'Detective Inspector!' said Heinz in a low voice.

'What is it? Haven't you gone?'

'Detective Inspector!'

The man so addressed looked in his files, read, and heard nothing.

'Detective Inspector!' said Heinz louder.

'What do you want? Haven't you gone yet? You're asking for trouble, my lad!'

'Detective Inspector!'

'All right. Fire away. But on target, otherwise it's not worth listening to you.'

And Heinz fired away . . .

'That's still no good!' said the Detective Inspector, when Heinz finished. 'A top hat, an attaché case and binoculars are not sufficient. All respect for your brotherly love, but that's no proof either.'

He grumbled and muttered to himself, then asked: 'You wanted to ring him up, didn't you? Wanted to warn him? Let me have his number!'

Heinz did so.

'Good!' said the Detective Inspector. 'Now you shall see what charming people we are here. You can use my telephone and ring up your brother, and you can tell him – well, tell him that in, say, half an hour the CID will be calling on his friend Hoppe, and if you like you can give him a hint about the bets – just as if you were standing in a nice quiet telephone booth.'

There is something odd about the human heart. Now it was offered him, and the police were allowing him to do so, Heinz wanted on no account to ring his brother. Indeed, he shrank back from the proffered telephone, afraid of hearing Erich's voice.

'Well, what's the matter, young man? Squeamish again? Or do you think I'm trying to take you in? Not at all. I'll be quite frank with you. My men are already at Hoppe's; and should there be a warning from your brother now – of course too late – then we'd have some evidence.'

Yes, things never changed – having taken one decision you were urged to another unavoidably; it looked as if he had, against his father's wish, hopelessly betrayed his brother. But that he himself should act as decoy, that his voice should bait the trap – no, a thousand times no. 'It seems a pretty dirty thing to do,' he said desperately.

'Dirty! I should say so,' growled the bully boy. 'So are all half-measures, you're right there. What's bad is bad and half-measures won't cure it. The best thing you can do now is to go home and get something to eat   you're looking quite green. No, you needn't phone – d'you think I needed you for that sort of joke? I only wanted to see what kind of chap you were. Well, goodbye. There's still hope of your becoming a man one of these days. Goodbye, I'm busy, I'm not a teacher!'

But perhaps he was after all – this bulldog.

§ XI

Yes, young Heinz Hackendahl had much on his plate at this time. But whatever he did, the growling voice of the fat man with the red face echoed in his ears. Not only could he not forget it, but it made him stronger.

And very soon the hour came when Heinz had to tell his young wife that all was up with the job at Hoppe & Co. – had to, for the newspaper headlines would have given it away in any case, announcing as they did that hundreds of small depositors had been cheated out of their savings. Petroleum and Totalisator. Clergymen Who Seek Exorbitant Interest. Hoppe's Evil Star. And so on. Therefore he had to tell her. And although he did not have to tell her about his part in the breakdown, he did so, because that voice was still ringing in his ear.

'I had to do it, Irma. Immediately I saw Erich, I had to.'

And, as is nearly always the case with women, she took the news quite differently from what he had expected. 'It will be all right somehow,' she said. 'Others were able to do it.'

No – no blame.

Father also took it differently than expected. Heinz visited him that evening, still sitting in the stable by his horse.

'Sophie wants to buy me another old nag. Mine doesn't look good enough for her,' said the old man. 'But, I don't know. I'm so used to him . . . So your business has really collapsed, has it?'

At this point, Heinz could have once again remained silent, saying nothing, because there had been nothing yet about Erich Hackendahl in the newspapers. So if Heinz did tell his father everything after all, he did so because he still heard that voice; what it had said about half-measures still seemed right.

'I see,' said the old man. 'So that's what you say. Well, I kind of half thought so myself. But you can't jump from your own skin into someone else's, even if we're all the same underneath.' But, as Heinz was still standing by the stable door, the old man added, shouting, 'You, Heinz, so you know nothing of Erich?'

'No, Father.'

'Well then, go away! But tell me immediately if you do hear something. Just no half-measures to save me from what I said back then. Half-measures are rubbish!'

Heinz went away thoughtfully and considered how curious it was that such different people as a detective inspector and an old cab driver could have the same opinion about half-measures.

But he had to go on. He had no time to stay still for long. There were visits to be made – to Irma and the baby, who was his own son, named in memory of a distant, half-forgotten brother called Otto, to the delight of his sister-in-law. But these hospital visits were soon over; after the statutory eight days, Irma returned to their little flat.

There the three of them lived, and began to set themselves up as three, and to settle down as three. It was sometimes not so easy. It was quite different from living as two. But you got used to it.

What you didn't get used to were the daily visits to the unemployment office, from which he always came away sad and tired, and often angry as well. In principle it was a very simple matter – millions of people had to do it every day. (Later it was twice a week.) You went to an office and showed your card. This card was then stamped as evidence that you had shown it, and you could leave. And once a week there was money. Really a very simple matter.

But it made you sad, tired and frequently angry . . .

Take the unemployment office itself. It was housed in a former villa, in a small street of villas – nothing distinguished, God forbid – a street inhabited by pensioners, retired teachers, confidential clerks – people who, perhaps just before the inflation, had been lucky enough to invest their life savings in a respectable villa with two hundred square metres of garden. So that those who lived near the unemployment office were clearly people of quite small means. And yet Heinz Hackendahl was told by the other unemployed that these residents had made application after application for the office to be removed; in their opinion the street was spoiled by it and the value of their property impaired – even the coffee tasted sour when they saw unemployed pass by. For all these reasons they felt the unemployment office might well honour some road inhabited by people with smaller means than theirs.

Naturally one never heard what the unemployment office itself thought about this but somehow there were always policemen to supervise the behaviour of the unemployed in this street. No shouting or singing! We've an eye on you . . .

The unemployed, of course, talked about it constantly. And they had plenty of time to do so, as they queued up and waited for their cards to be stamped. They talked about it more and more, with passion and bitterness. Passing those wretched front gardens which no one thought of profaning – so why the policemen? – they looked with real hatred at the plaster of Paris dwarfs, the glass balls, the pitiable gardening; if the residents disliked the unemployed, that dislike was reciprocated tenfold.

Another thing was the treatment at the unemployment office. Since it was obvious that those behind the counters there were employed only because others were unemployed – they lived off unemployment, the unemployed were their employers – they ought to have been a little politer, or so their true employers, the unemployed, thought; yes, they should treat their employers with consideration and respect.

But of such respect and consideration there was not a trace. On the contrary these people did everything to make life difficult for those who in truth employed them – they were always demanding new documents or poking into antecedents, all the time pretending to ameliorate what they called the lot of the unemployed. They pried into every unpleasantness. If someone had had a row with his foreman he was called insubordinate, and if another had gone sick and the consultant to the Health Insurance reported him as fit again, then he was a work-shy.

That was the sort of thing they gave you to understand, the smart gentlemen behind the counters, before they slammed the enquiry window and let the unemployed wait while they did themselves well on the lunch they had brought in greaseproof paper and Thermos flask. Those were the people who talked about 'work-shy'! They behaved as if the miserable sums they paid out were their own money. What airs they gave themselves! It was time they heard a thing or two.

And this they did. There was a row every day. But they were such a mean lot that if a chap told them the truth for once they had him thrown out by the porter or even sent for a policeman, which meant that the man was punished by getting no dole for two, maybe five, days – just because they didn't want to hear the truth.

Yes, the circumstances in which you stood and waited for your stamp, sometimes for hours on end, were enough to make you heart-sick and desperate. You felt utterly wretched when some man, foaming at the mouth, shouted that these bloodsuckers were stopping his dole, and at home his wife and children were dying of starvation. 'Yes, you behind the counter there, I mean you, pop-eyes, you've never heard your kids crying from hunger at night, you greedy-guts, and not a crumb to give them, not a penny to buy anything with!' And it was useless for your neighbour to whisper that as a matter of fact the chap had boozed his unemployment money on the day he was paid – sometimes it was true, sometimes it wasn't. But it was bad that people revealed themselves so blatantly and shamelessly to one another.

It was bad, too, if a neighbour pointed out when someone in front of them in the queue not only had his card stamped for today, but for yesterday and the day before. 'The person behind the counter has a party member's book, and in this case the person this side of the counter has one too, and if you want things to be different for you, you better get one of those little party books too. Then you'll see how the place lights up!'

Heinz had already heard such talk at his bank. But he didn't take any notice of it. In the unemployment office waiting room there was a big notice: 'Political talk strictly forbidden!' But the notice was completely useless, because everyone waiting there talked about politics. If they didn't talk about their own lives, they talked about politics.

God, how Heinz Hackendahl came to hate this dole queue place! Its unhappy neighbours could not hate it more. This dreary grey, these figures who seemed to grow ever more dreary – always the same figures, the angry and bitter ones, the skat players, and the envious, resentful ones. (To be envious of that! 'He's all right! He's only got one leg. He still gets a pension. I should be so lucky!') And colleagues who maintained a pathetic elegance and told new stories about the smart women they went out with the previous night . . . and other colleagues who suddenly gave up, whose suits look soiled more or less from one day to the next. Suddenly they used string instead of shoelaces and had holes in the sleeves of their jackets.

Spring gave way to summer. Sometimes the sky was radiantly blue and the sun shone. In the gardens of the little villas the lilac was fresh. The people, however, were old and grey. Their lives were spent on the dole. There was no summer for them. For them there was only one thing: the dole. It was like a sickness that had them in its grip – a sickness which killed every pleasure, deadened every desire, and which slowly, gradually took people over completely.

Very soon Heinz was coming home miserable, tired and hopeless, and was even envious of Irma, who was running the household, and for whom there was not only no unemployment, but who was busier than before because of little Otto.

Heinz sat down and watched Irma, knowing that he had nothing else to do all day.

After a while, she turned round to him two or three times and said: 'You give me the creeps staring at me, Heinz. Come, see if you can do the baby's washing.' And sometimes he did stand at the scrubbing board and began to rub. But even if he succeeded, it didn't bring him any pleasure, because to give pleasure work has to have meaning. To work merely to work – in a sense, to pass the time – is stupid.

For that reason he soon gave up doing it, or she took it out of his hands and said: 'Leave it, Heinz. I don't want to annoy you. Only, it can make you mad seeing you do something. It always looks as though you want to go to sleep. I know you, I know you, and I'm sorry for you too. But can't you do something? Can't you go and see your old friends? Or visit your old schoolteacher? You always wanted to do that.'

'Oh, did I?' asked Heinz. 'I don't now. It looks like rain. But perhaps I'll go . . .'

For a while he stayed at home, undecided. Then, after Irma gave him a little push, he left after all.

§ XII

By now he had not seen Professor Degener for a good many years. In fact, he should have been ashamed not to have had anything to do with his beloved teacher for so long. A long time ago, when he began his apprenticeship, he had still gone once or twice. But then he stopped. It was strange how two people who liked each other had suddenly so little to say. How all of a sudden it became clear how one was a philologist and the other a bank apprentice – two ridiculously different spheres, apparently with no connection.

However, now he was going to him. It was good to retrace his steps, see the old street name, and press the old doorbell. When times had been very bad, when he didn't know what to do, he had gone there many times. And now it was a bad time again.

The same old maid opened the door, looked at him searchingly, and said, 'Yes, I recognize you from the 1919 class, even if you haven't been here for a long time.'

'It's bad times, Fräulein,' said Heinz.

'The Herr Professor has changed a lot. He's lost his job since he had his accident. But don't mention it. It only upsets him. And even if he doesn't recognize you, he'll be pleased. No, go straight in. You won't disturb him.'

Professor Degener was sitting at his desk with his head in his hands. His once flaming-red hair had now become quite grey, and as he raised his head and looked at his visitor, the latter could see an ugly red scar above his once fine, clear forehead; something also seemed to be wrong with one of his eyes. The eyelid hung deep and motionless over the eye itself.

'Yes, Hackendahl. I remember you well,' said his old teacher. 'But I recall there being two Hackendahls – but, of course, you're the other one. The other one . . . never visited me.'

The old man chuckled. Some of his earlier humour was retained in these remarks, but only a very pale copy.

'You know, Hackendahl – take a seat! You must answer a question. You're older now and have made your way in life. I take it from the ring on your finger that you are married, and perhaps are now a father. You're nodding. You're feeding a family.'

'Unfortunately not, Herr Professor. I'm unemployed.'

The professor nodded in assent. 'Yes, I've heard about it. Many people are unemployed. It seems to be the latest occupation – and no easy one, either!'

'No,' said Heinz Hackendahl.

'Well, nevertheless,' continued the professor, 'you've made your way. You are something. Now tell me quite honestly, student Hackendahl, did what you learned with us help you at all? Has it helped you in your life? Does it still give you something?'

He looked at his former student with his single Prussian-blue eye, the other eyelid lightly trembling. He didn't want an answer yet, and continued to speak: 'You see, I remember you very well. You were sufficiently open-minded. You tasted the tang of the Homeric world, and Plato was also not just a name to you. Now tell me, student Hackendahl, is anything of what you learned with us still in you? Does it help you? Does it give you pleasure?'

Heinz Hackendahl had never thought about it. It was all so very long ago. Something strange and half forgotten only now slowly began to stir in him at the words of his teacher. However, the fact that he had first to think about it already provided an answer in itself. But it was an answer he was reluctant to give the old man.

'You see, Hackendahl,' the professor started up again. 'I sit here a lot and think. No, I'm no longer teaching, since . . . since a long time. I'm also unemployed, but of course I'm an old man. My job is behind me. But I always have to ask myself: have I really done my job? I've calculated that I've introduced well over a thousand students into the world of Classical Greece. But did I really do so? So that something remained in them?'

His chin was in his hand and his blue eye looked at Heinz Hackendahl as clearly and as alertly as ever.

'No one could have done it better than you!' exclaimed Heinz Hackendahl.

'Your teacher is not asking you for grades, student Hackendahl,' chuckled the old man. 'Just tell me what you took away from those classes. Do you still sometimes think of your Homer?'

'I live in such another world . . .'

'So . . . you too,' said the teacher, sad. 'He doesn't think of him, either. No matter how many I ask. You see, Hackendahl, when you get old, you begin to ask yourself: why have you actually lived? What have you achieved? So much out there cherished and valuable to us older people has collapsed, and every day yet more collapses . . . So I wanted to console myself, and said to myself: you have taught over a thousand young people. You have introduced them to a world of beauty, of manly heroes, of love and battle. But it has made no difference. That world meant nothing to any of you. It was a false consolation.'

The professor no longer looked at his old student. He looked down at his desk, onto the worn-out green tablecloth, on which the work of a thousand students had lain. He'd read them, marked them, improved them, criticized them, encouraged them, and praised and blamed them. But nothing had remained. It was as if a child had made marks in the sand: the dew obscured them, the wind blew the sand away, rain washed the marks away. Nothing remained. It had all been just a game.

Student Hackendahl looked at his old teacher and said: 'Herr Professor, we who are now unemployed, we often think as you do: why are we actually living? We aren't allowed to do anything. When I stand in the dole queue – that's somewhere, Herr Professor, where we have to go every day in order to prove that we really are not working. Because that is now our only duty: to do nothing. So when I'm among the others at the dole queue, it feels to me as if I'm always growing older immeasurably fast. It is so difficult to explain – as if I were still young, but ageing at an infinite rate. And between the two there is nothing – no achievement, no pleasure, only an incomprehensibly fast ageing process.'

'Just like me,' murmured Professor Degener. 'I didn't want to grow old either, and suddenly I was, and noticed I hadn't yet done anything.'

'In this situation, your time at school,' repeated Heinz Hackendahl, 'seems infinitely far away, as if it had never really been. However,' he said, and laid his hand gently over the thin, white, blue-veined hand of his teacher, 'if I don't think of the *Iliad* and no longer of *Antigone*, I have always thought about something that you once said to me. When things were going very badly for me, you once said: "You can fall into the mud, but you don't have to lie in it." And another time, when I was making big plans, you said: "Healthy cells first, otherwise the body can't be healthy." '

The professor shook his head, dissatisfied. 'Just expressions, Hackendahl. Anyone can tell you that. It's nothing. It has nothing to do with Classical Greece and my life's work.'

'Yes, of course, Herr Professor, one can perhaps hear such things everywhere. But they don't work everywhere. They don't help if just any person says them. But because you said them, they help me.'

The professor continued to be dissatisfied. 'Oh, Hackendahl, just because things were going badly for you then, and your heart was open, it worked. It was nothing to do with me. You can say "Honesty's the best policy" a hundred times and no one will listen. But if you say it precisely to someone planning something dishonest, it will work. No, it has nothing to do with me.'

And once again he leaned his head on his hand.

'You say you absolutely didn't help me, Herr Professor. But you did so nevertheless. If it didn't matter who our teacher was, if instead of you another could have taught us our Greek subjunctives, why did we still always come to you – always rely on you? Homer I might have forgotten for a while, but I never forgot Professor Degener. It was the same for many.'

'Almost no one comes any more,' said the professor. 'T' bell hardly ever rings.'

However, just as he said that, the doorbell rang and Hoffmann, one of Heinz Hackendahl's class comrades, entered. He was taller, larger and had some scars on his face, but was easy to recognize all the same.

They greeted one another, and Heinz Hackendahl said: 'Listen, Hoffmann. Herr Professor insists that he was just an ordinary teacher. And he still maintains that it made no difference if the trainee teacher – Lieblich, Liebreich or Liebling, or whatever he was called – or he took the class.'

'Oh, rubbish,' laughed Hoffmann in his deep bass voice. 'We'd better not say that. Do you remember how angry we made him, and had to go to his classroom to apologize? You insisted, Herr Professor!'

'You must have behaved very badly.'

'It was sheer cheek – really disgusting cheek!' said Hoffmann, assuming the old language of school without any difficulty. And the two of them quickly took up school talk, and the professor joined them after a while, turning his back on the present.

The elderly maid came in with tea and cakes. A little concerned, the teacher looked for a cigarette weak enough not to harm the young. He also greatly surprised student Hoffmann by now admitting to him, after years and years, that the teacher had known very well that the examinee Hoffmann had copied his exam paper from another's. 'But I didn't want to fail you, Hoffmann. It was the very lowest Abitur grade, with minimum demands. You would never have managed a normal exam. You were always a very lazy person, Hoffmann.'

All three of them were much amused, including the old teacher. He no longer worried over what he had actually achieved in life. That is in general a very tricky question, and now it was even trickier.

Later, Hoffmann and Hackendahl went home together. 'Wait a ____nt! I'll take you,' said Hoffmann. 'Where do you live, Hacken-

____' said Hackendahl. 'I've got time.'

____'ve masses,' said Hoffmann. 'I did my exams

exactly two and half years ago, but must wait another two and a half years for work. Or perhaps five.'

'So you're unemployed too?'

'Of course, what else? From what I gather of our class, all are unemployed. Yes, Hackendahl, my son, three or four years of study, and then nothing more.'

'I studied for three years, too.'

'But then you were able to find some work after all. We always prepared ourselves for life and its work, and just when we were ready for work, there was none. And what were you doing? Already married and a father? You managed it! I, however, on the other hand . . .'

'You could do that any day.'

'Don't be silly. How could I? I'll have you know,' said Hoffmann, shuffling his arms and legs about, 'this is the only decent suit I've got left. I only wear it on solemn occasions like a visit to Professor Degener, or for completely unsuccessful job applications. My other pair of trousers – well, my old woman says they are irreparable.'

'Just like us!' exclaimed Heinz Hackendahl. And he was undeniably almost happy that things were no different for the qualified academic.

'Only that you can go on the dole,' said Hoffmann. 'Our trouser bottoms have holes in them too, but of that we are proud. However, we don't consider it good form to go on the dole.'

'A pair of academics are on the dole with us,' explained Hackendahl.

'Ah, well,' said Hoffmann, 'they're pioneers. The day will soon come when the noble fathers will say: I'm not forking out any more for that lot.'

'You thought it would be a bit different, didn't you?'

'Thought what?'

'The whole kaboosh – life.'

'Of course, naturally . . . It's a shithouse.'

'Yes, a shithouse!'

'Of course, a shithouse!'

And for a few minutes they enjoyed saying shit to one another. It wasn't just a word for them, it really was – shit.

Later they talked about their old teacher, Professor Degener.

'What sort of a disaster was that?' asked Heinz Hackendahl. 'Do you know anything about it, Hoffmann?'

'Of course. Didn't you hear? A perfect story – fits well into the general shit.'

And Hoffmann told how Herr Professor Degener, a man who, after all, was against all demonstrative expression of his emotions, nevertheless – given the occasion – would hoist a black, white and red flag on his balcony. This balcony – as normal in the city – had a neighbouring balcony, whose owners were not for that flag, but preferred the red flag.

As the Reichstag was also in disagreement over the colours of the German flag, and a regime had been overthrown because of it, and Herr von Hindenburg personally intervened, but without success, because feelings were already too embittered – because, therefore, the whole German people were involved in fighting about a flag, the neighbouring balcony occupier didn't see why he shouldn't have his own such fight. He forcibly took the black, white and red flag from the professor's balcony onto his own, and destroyed it.

The professor, more of a quiet academic, but not without spirit, had thus far not considered flags very important, but the abuse of flags he considered very important. He therefore replaced the broken flag with a new one, and kept watch.

However, an old teacher is in no better position than his youngest student. He must be as punctually in school as he. When at midday the professor left school, he had to accept that not only had his flag disappeared, but that a red flag had now replaced it.

Professor Degener had had a humanistic education, and was therefore of the opinion that, even in the worst people, there was something good, which it was his duty to cultivate with kindness.

The professor gently folded up the alien flag, allowed himself the liberty of putting it back on the neighbouring balcony, and set off to buy himself another flag for himself. However, he had now got so excited that he bought a bigger and better flag than before – one that was not so easy to destroy.

By the time he returned, the red flag was once again waving over his threshold. But this time, the neighbour was also standing on his balcony looking angrily at the professor. The latter had thought little about him. Now he looked at him – a large, indeed massive man with dark eyes.

'I'm sorry,' said the professor gently, and started to undo the ribbons that tied the flag to his balcony rails.

'Leave the flag alone,' said the neighbour threateningly.

'Not at all!' answered the professor and went on untying. 'Your views are not my views, so it would be a lie—'

'Take your paws off!' ordered the other man. 'I'm not going to let this façade be defiled by your rag.'

'You will have to admit,' said the professor more directly, 'that a forced opinion can only be a slave opinion. Precisely if you love your flag—'

'Your rag makes me sick,' said the fat man. 'Wilhelm's own rag!' and he began to sing in a hoarse voice: 'O Tannenbaum, O Tannenbaum – send the Kaiser out of town.'

The professor had untied the flag, held it in his hand, and spoke more animatedly: 'It's dishonourable to make fun of someone who may be weak, but who was never bad. Please . . .'

'Leave your rag alone, little man,' said the fat man threateningly. I'll show you who the weak one is!'

Unflustered, the professor unfolded his own flag. The fat man reached from time to time across the partition wall and prevented the flag from being tied. Professor Degener stepped two steps further and tied it out of his range. The fat enemy took his own rolled flag and hit out with it at the other.

'Stop that!' said the professor and went to the end of his balcony.

'That flag stays away!' shouted the fat man threateningly, but it was only an empty threat: he was beyond reach.

Professor Degener, who (erroneously) believed that the battle of the flags had been solved through compromise, went on quietly tying his flag. (The gentlemen of the Reichstag had fallen into a similar error when they invented the black-white-red ensign.)

'Take your snot-rag away!' shouted the fat man, but the professor carried on quietly tying.

Now his enemy was boiling-mad. First he looked as though he was going to climb from one balcony to the other, but a glance down saved his life. So he took hold of a flowerpot and threw it.

'Stop such stupidity!' said the professor, turning round. He was not yet aware that a flowerpot is somewhat different from a snowball – that a cheeky schoolboy is less dangerous than an overheated member of a political party.

The second flowerpot hit him in the face as he turned, and broke. The professor let out a sound of pain, not so much because he was hurt, but out of pity for his fellow men. Then he fell backwards.

His enemy looked darkly towards the fallen man and murmured: 'That'll teach you to hang your filthy rag elsewhere!' and disappeared.

'Was he at least locked up?' asked Heinz bitterly.

'Of course not! The professor naturally didn't take him to court. No, he'd had enough and didn't want any more. He took retirement immediately. You can understand it well enough – if you lose the pleasure.'

'Yes, he's old, too. He got something out of life – but how about us?'

'Yes, us . . . have we lost the pleasure too? But we already had!'

'Yes, already. It's true.'

'Just think about it, Hackendahl. I'm now twenty-seven and getting a paunch and a bald head – and never earned a pfennig. But stop: I tell a lie! When I was seventeen and eighteen I earned five marks a week for coaching. But since then I've never had it so good.'

'But better times may come, Hoffmann.'

'Let's watch out for them – if we can't make them come any other way.'

'But how?'

'Yes, son, that is the question – how?'

§ XIII

Periods of deepest depression alternated with periods of exhilaration.

When Heinz felt depressed, attendance at the unemployment office became almost impossible. Going there he would meet the lucky ones who were on their way to work, briefcases containing sandwich boxes under their arms, and they would look at him vacantly, or perhaps find his coat very shabby. Then he would look bitterly at them. They were so much younger than he was. Every year saw a fresh crop of youngsters going to work, and a tormenting anxiety often seized him that he was getting old and would become unfit for a job, he who had only just started! Worn out – worn out by unemployment.

Then he would reach the unemployment office and take his place in the queue, one of the many and increasingly more numerous unemployed.

By now he knew certain of the regulars, feared the company of some and looked out for others. One, surely a very silly fellow, would say, beaming: 'Well, mate, here we are again. Well, never mind, the worst of it's over.' He said this week after week, month after month, always with the same kindly but rather foolish expression, not to be shaken in his hope.

Then there was another chap, called Marwede, beside whom Heinz didn't want to stand. 'Morning, mate. You know Pries, the little fellow who's been here a long time, used to be with the Transport people, you know him, don't you? Done himself in! Took Lysol. They took him to hospital but everything was already burnt out. Yes, mate, he's taken the plunge but we haven't yet . . .'

Marwede looked at Heinz Hackendahl. 'Painful to hear isn't it. But that's how it is! Suicide or crime – that's our way out. There's nothing else.'

'Things can pick up again,' said Heinz.

'How? Why should they? Tell me that. And even so they won't want us. There are so many younger. We've got out of the way of work – I had a go the other day. No good – after two hours I was taken ill.'

'You're undernourished.'

'I suppose you think we're like boilers – another shovel of coal or another slice of bread and dripping and your brain'll work again. No, your brain don't want to, it's fallen asleep, it wants to be left in peace. Suicide or crime, mate, no other prospect!'

'Well, you still have the dole for the moment,' said Heinz, unnecessarily angry.

'Yes, for the moment. You don't know, mate, how I sometimes feel in the morning. I lie there, I don't undress at night because you never know whether you'll feel like dressing again in the morning, and tell my buttons – suicide, crime, dole.'

'They must be funny buttons if they always end up in favour of the dole.'

'That's because I'm a coward. There's no need to sugar the pill. Man's a coward above everything else, a coward! You, me, all of us.'

'So don't squabble here about suicide and crime.'

'Rather say nothing! Suddenly such things happen. You know, every evening I have a Tauentzienstrasse bar on the watch. A fat man comes every evening with a huge thick wallet . . . And at about one o'clock he goes in the half-dark across the Wittenbergplatz . . .'

'Stop your drivel!' cried Hackendahl, furious. 'You're making it all up.'

'Don't get angry. You probably thought of something similar to be angry about. But of course you're as much of a coward as I am.'

'If you don't shut your mouth, Marwede!' – and Heinz Hackendahl threatened him with his fist.

After this sort of conversation Heinz arrived home utterly worn out. Then he would look at his son Otto who, curiously enough, cried very little. He had been lying in that small bed when his father first went on the dole; his father was still on the dole when he had made his first attempts to walk; by the time he had learned to chatter, his father was still on the dole. Perhaps in a little while the son would be able to accompany his father to the unemployment office and, later still, the two could have their cards stamped together, father and son.

Thus could one think sometimes, and then words as drastic as suicide or crime came to mind.

'You, Irma,' he would then say, 'aren't you fed up having an unemployed husband?'

'In a bad mood?' she asked. 'Don't worry. Good times will come back . . . Cheer up! Things will get better, you'll see. Things can change very quickly when you're hopeless and don't expect it.'

'Then it will have to be quick, say in about the next three

minutes . . . No, it won't happen, but what I want to know is if you haven't had enough.'

'Oh, no! A real Berliner doesn't lose heart anything like so easily. Go to Mother. She wanted to see if she could get some pickled herring for us. But hurry along!'

'Herring pickler!' he said, but went all the same.

But Heinz also knew days of exhilaration. The sky need not be blue – it could rain if it liked – but the heart beat differently, full of hope, full of energy. He jumped out of bed with both legs.

'I've got a feeling, Irma, that something will happen today. Something pleasant, of course. And don't keep any food for me, I'm going to see Sophie.'

'Good,' she said, 'and best of luck!'

On optimistic days like this, queuing for the dole was only unpleasant if it lasted long. Marwede was just a joke. 'So, still no murders? No suicides? My dear colleague, you'll be celebrating your golden jubilee here yet. You'll be an honorary unemployed, with the dole card round your neck!'

At which Marwede again exploded.

But no one minded. Hardly was the dole register over, everyone ran free. You were full of pep, altogether elated. In the newspaper offices you at once got the newspapers you wanted, saw immediately the advertisements at all promising. And your elation, self-confidence, hope carried you into strange offices, where you surveyed rival applicants with a grin, enchanted the staff managers and drew a smile from the grumpiest employer. You were able to do everything: not only book-keeping by double entry, Italian and American accounting (and first-rate, of course, at striking a balance), but also typewriting, shorthand, English and French correspondence. Decorate shop windows? Of course, nothing easier . . . On such days you hardly minded when they ended by saying: 'We'll let you know.' The confirmation never came. Or, 'All vacancies filled. Sorry, we could have done with someone like you. We'll make a note of your name.' And you hardly winced when you were told. 'What, *that* advertisement? We handed it in six weeks ago. Those chaps keep on inserting it simply to have a Situations Vacant advert in the paper. We're very sorry. Perhaps you could make a fuss there about it.'

No, you hurried on. If not here, then elsewhere; that was almost certain today. You had had that feeling on waking up.

And when after all you had been everywhere in vain – what did that prove? You went and saw Sophie.

'On the hunt again?' she would enquire coolly. 'Good that you're not losing courage. Of course you can use the duplicating machine. But clean it properly when you've finished. The last time you left the rollers dirty.'

Even this did not upset you, although the machine had been left spotless. But who knew how many others were duplicating their testimonials? The demand for such machines was enormous these days.

'Have you had your lunch?' Matron Sophie asked. 'Oh! Well, I don't believe you but I won't force you. Set to, then. You know what to do. Oh, and by the way, if you must smoke I'll leave some cigarettes here. Do take these, please. Yours smell so horrible – the office is unusable afterwards.'

She went. Was she really like that or had she only adopted that manner? A person who has to keep order in an establishment where there are a lot of females can't be gentle or amiable. Sophie, therefore, was not gentle or amiable. Never had been.

Despite being a little annoyed, Heinz got his duplicator working. However, its rhythm gradually overcame his mood. Since he wanted only tip-top copies to send out, the ink a deep black and not at all smeary, he had to take great care – the first impression, the look of an application, was so tremendously important. Actually he had very few testimonials – the bank's apprenticeship certificate and the leaving reference; for a young man in the middle twenties it was damned little. Looked as if the fellow had never worked.

However, Heinz Hackendahl had improved the document. In the first place, he had added his Abitur certificate. Later he had added, because it was also very good, his One-Year Voluntary Service certificate.

To have a back-up, his curriculum vitae would also be copied, though some required such documents to be handwritten. Others again had nothing but contempt for handwriting, and wouldn't even consider them.

He tried to imagine the position he might obtain on the basis of his application. No, he didn't expect much – a normal income, and the boss or department head need not be particularly amiable. And his colleagues? Well, colleagues here, colleagues there! He'd be able to live and let live. Nothing fantastic, just decent work, something with a bit of life: 'Hackendahl, please fix that for me quickly. Stay an hour longer today, otherwise the work won't get done.'

To think that there was once a time when you worried that a job didn't get done – when there was too much work! Nowadays, one stretched the work out, so that it provided for many. Short-term work was invented. (In the war heavy workers were invented. Destructive war was a better employer than the construction they called peace.)

Sometimes his stomach grumbled, and he thought of his sister, Sophie, the Matron. She had asked if he had had lunch, but he had said he didn't want any. Anyone else would have perhaps brought him some lunch, or at least a plate of something. This was, after all, a clinic – a place in which there was always something to eat.

However, Sophie was not like that. Thank you! Lunch is over. No one's forced to eat!

Now and then she looked in the office but not in connection with food – most probably to keep an eye on the duplicator. And make sure too that he wasn't smoking any of his evil-smelling cigarettes. Not that she referred to them. That matter had been settled – she had expressed her wishes and no more was required. What she said was: 'Can you spare me any of your time this evening, Bubi? Good! I've a little dispute with the financial authorities about the turnover tax. You could make out a statement from the accounts.' She nodded and went.

If Heinz had not been in such a good mood he would have been annoyed. That was typical of her. Well, hadn't she placed at her brother's disposal a duplicator free of charge, a complicated apparatus with rollers and wheels which, of course, had no more than a certain life and was brought nearer to its end every time it was used – all free of charge, as mentioned above, in spite of wear and tear and the consumption of ink? And in return the brother could well give three or four hours that evening to looking over the accounts. Was she mean? Perhaps only very careful. She wished to give nothing away. Nobody, after all, had ever given her anything, no, she was against giving things away.

At first Heinz had thought that at the conclusion of such a tax consultation she would press a sisterly five-mark coin into his hand, but he was determined to reject it. However, she said: 'Many thanks, Heinz. You know I'm not permitted to give you money when you receive unemployment relief and are prohibited from subsidiary employment.'

Funny! Earlier she had been sharp, sour and flat-breasted.

Sophie came in again, sat at the desk, took one of her cigarettes (without of course commenting on his having taken none) and smoked for him, so to speak. Then she began to talk. She had done so much for Father. She had given him a new rig-out and bought him a cart as well as a carriage; she was even willing to buy a new horse. 'But Father's so difficult. You're supposed to have some influence with him, according to Mother. Do speak to him, Heinz.'

'How is he difficult?'

'Well, for one thing he doesn't treat the patients politely enough . . . After all, they're sick people and mostly well-to-do, so one has to adapt oneself to their wishes, even if they are a bit liable to grumble. Well, you know, he really did recently snub the factory owner Otto, of the big accumulator factory, in the middle of the street, and told him to get out of his carriage.'

'Father's old.'

'He's always saying that he's of iron. Let him show it! Herr Otto is bound to be bad-tempered, but I always get on with him. And then about the money. Father maintains that I'm not paying him enough. He says he earns more with his cab. But he must take into consideration that I supply everything, the vehicles and his clothes; what is he after all but a coachman here? I've asked Mother how much they need a week to live on and that's what he gets. He's not meant to grow rich out of it.' She looked at her brother thoughtfully; the cigarette was finished. 'All right then, you'll speak to Father about it. He must realize that I could hire dozens, even hundreds, of people for a small weekly wage. And that it isn't pleasant for me when he tells all the patients that he's the oldest driver in Berlin and that the Matron is his daughter.'

Heinz industriously turned the handle of his machine and made no reply. And she didn't seem to expect any. She had said what she wanted to him, and now she was going.

Naturally, Heinz wouldn't talk about it with Father. If she wanted to start a fight with Father, she didn't need Heinz. Life was complicated enough without that.

When enough copies were ready, he sat down at the desk and started with the applications, in his conventional book-keeper's hand. He had actually wanted to do that at home, but as he still had to do Sophie's books in the evening, it wasn't worth going back. He hoped Irma wouldn't make anything of his absence.

And so he began with his impersonal, sweeping, accountant's hand-writing. 'Dear Sirs.' He had made a note of five or six advertisements which stipulated 'Applications to be made in own handwriting'. If he continued, and Sophie didn't interrupt him too much, he should be able to finish by the evening. Perhaps if he posted the letters on his way home he would have replies the day after tomorrow, and at this thought there came more flourish into his writing and a fluency into the extolling of his merits and qualifications, always a difficult business. If self-praise could easily be overdone, modesty on the other hand was equally foolish – applications written in that vein always sounded so empty. Something of the lively tempo of the morning came back to him; hope rose again. As he got up, he thought, today it's going to be all right! Now he thought, it will be all right the day after tomorrow – perhaps.

It had diminished since the morning, but hope was still there, and life is a hundred times easier even with only a little hope. This little makes a huge difference. Without it there is nothing but despair; with it life is bearable.

And so he sat and wrote. For every letter he took a fresh nib and blew on the paper, since a speck of dust could disturb the evenness of his penmanship; and he used a ruler. Before starting to write, he mentally set out in paragraphs all he had to say; a job application must not be too detailed, but it mustn't look too thin either. What creative joy was left him went into these applications for work. His was a mind not devoid of common sense and memory, and common sense could have told him that all these letters were useless. With two million unemployed the odds against him were tremendous. At the unemployment office they said that the single insertion of an advertisement often brought two or three thousand replies, among them offers to work for half, even a quarter of the standard wage, a mere pittance. So that the chances of success were exactly nothing, not worth the postage. Should he write: 'Dear Sirs, I am the first of May, Summer is on the way,' his letter would have infinitely better prospects of being considered.

As for memory, that could have told him he had already dispatched dozens, even hundreds, of such applications. And what had been the result? Memory replied without hesitation. Some hundreds of letters had remained unanswered; as regards about ten letters he had been notified that his application was being considered and he would receive further particulars later, particulars he never received of course; five or six times he had been invited for an interview. (Sorry, but the vacancy has been filled.)

Yet he still wrote, still hoped. Once upon a time they had gone on at the dole office about the right to work. But that hadn't been mentioned any more for a long time.

Now he had only the hope of work – spurts of hope. So he went on looking, writing and applying.

Until once again hope slowly left him and its place was taken by an endless despair which made him feel that it was almost impossible even to go to the unemployment office.

§ XIV

During this long period of unemployment fortune smiled twice upon Heinz – twice he found work. On the first occasion he was temporarily engaged at a bank, for the yearly balance; glorious to sit again in a real office and do the old familiar work! Not altogether familiar, though. New ideas had been introduced. The cloth-bound ledgers where the first page was traditionally inscribed, in many a flourish, with the words *Cum Deo* had been abolished. Book entries were made on index cards; the book-keeping machine had been introduced; there was no opportunity to mention God even in print.

All this was new to Hackendahl and it was new to have to ask younger people for advice and information; in the days of steady employment he had been one of the youngest. But even more surprising was to discover that he no longer seemed capable of concentrated labour and that it was difficult to sit for eight hours with work, and nothing but work, in front of him. The jobless days resulted in a painful restlessness in him. He was plagued by a desire to jump up and move about. The fact that one had to do the same thing for eight whole hours was so difficult to take in.

In the recent long months, it had always seemed that he could at any point have been doing something else. He had helped Irma with some work, and had suddenly said, 'Just a moment! I'm just going to get a few cigarettes!' and gone into the street.

By the time he was back, Irma had generally already finished, and he played for a bit with the little one. Then he got tired of that too, and went down to the street again to look at the newspapers on free display. Then he came back to the flat.

He was not at the time really conscious of how much his joblessness affected him. However, now, with the prospect of work again, he did feel it, and he wanted to jump up and down and run about all the time – and not in a particular place, or to do anything in particular. He just felt like running free.

Although he took care not to give way to this craving, once or twice he had to put up with a reprimand to the effect that he was going far too much to the lavatory and could never be found in his place. It became clear that, in spite of all the efforts he made, he would get no permanent situation at this bank.

The second spell of temporary employment was at a big textile mail order firm. For weeks on end hundreds of thousands of printed items were dispatched in a huge publicity campaign on the American model, to buoy up the ever flagging sales – the right sort of work for unemployed people, a dozen of whom sat together, men and women. They had to fold printed matter, insert enclosures, add an order card, write the addresses, put the letters in envelopes, and cart it all off in laundry baskets to the post. This meant one could move about freely and change one's work all the time, now doing a little folding, then unpacking bundles of publicity matter, now typing addresses, and then taking the baskets to the post three streets away; all this amid laughter and talk, for the feeling of having work and earning a few marks cheered up even the grumblers.

There were some petty jealousies, of course, trifling quarrels, discussions about a vanished ball of string; and Fräulein Pendel and Herr Lorenz were surprised kissing behind a door. 'Hello, hello, you're sly ones! I suppose you call that imprinted matter!' Followed by never-ending laughter . . .

Heinz, having gained the appreciation of his bosses, was put in some sort of command over his undisciplined fellow workers and told to adjust disagreements, see that there was no idleness, and have the work done to time.

'The entire northern territory including Hamburg by Saturday? Yes, we'll be able to do that, we'll get that done. Just let us have the directories as soon as possible; it's the addressing which delays things.'

For a while Heinz could allow himself, and was even encouraged, to hope that he would be taken on permanently, being industrious and responsible. But nothing came of it after all. 'We're sorry, Herr Hackendahl, you know how much we'd have liked to engage you, but our publicity campaign hasn't been as successful as we hoped. No, don't look so down in the month – as soon as we take on anybody we'll think of you. Then you'll definitely hear from us.' (He never did.)

That made two rays of light, but two rays of light don't make a dawn. What money they had the Hackendahls spent on the essentials, rent and food – not on even the smallest purchases. Yet some were necessary. Underwear wore out, and shoes got into such a state that the cobbler said: 'Well, young woman, what do you want me to do about 'em? The soles are gone and the uppers ruined but the shoelaces are still quite good. In your place I'd buy a pair of new shoes to go with 'em.'

Married couples did their sums, but it's well known that, however many sums you do, ten marks still remain ten marks, and doing sums doesn't increase them. Undeniably, support for the jobless was increased, but it still wasn't enough. Jobless support became unemployment insurance, dole offices became unemployment offices. 'And that won't be the end of it,' grumbled the eternally dissatisfied.

No, it wouldn't be enough, no matter how many sums were done. Slowly at first, then with increasing momentum, the home deteriorated. Shirts became frayed and overcoats thin; broken crockery was no longer replaced, the gasman was an anxiety, the inspector who read the electric meter a terror. They got behind with the rent. It started with a small balance left over, which was settled the next time. Then one day this balance was left unsettled and soon they were a whole month in arrears

The landlord's agent barely acknowledged them now and letters began to arrive from his office, polite at first and then sterner ones sent by registered post.

'There's nothing for it – we can't afford to live like this,' said Irma over and over again, putting out feelers. 'It's the rent that gets us down.'

'Well,' he said, 'we don't want to be hasty. Perhaps I'll find something soon.'

Four weeks later Irma repeated her remarks on the subject of the rent.

'Let the agent write if he wants to,' said Heinz, annoyed. 'He can go to hell. I don't care what he writes!'

But he did care. He suffered at not being able to fulfil his obligations, as the phrase so nicely goes, and took little consolation in the thought that others were not carrying out their obligations to him, by providing a chance to work.

He made one last effort and became a travelling salesman. Like many of his fellow sufferers, he ran around with a little suitcase. In it were an air pump and a tub of liquid floor wax, as well as a few brushes. And he proceeded to spray wax on the floor of every housewife who allowed him to, and made it beautifully smooth.

Oh, but only a few put up with it! And few of them wanted to go so far as to buy an apparatus. And of the few who did want to, even fewer had the money to pay for the thing. No, all this running about wasn't worth it.

'For goodness sake, leave it!' said Irma. 'You're wearing your shoes out quicker than you can possibly earn with the stuff.'

And he did leave it – with pleasure. He wasn't cut out to be a salesman. It went against his grain to try to sell something to a woman who didn't need it – who was certainly just as short of money as Irma. He often had a guilty conscience when he sold an apparatus.

'What do you think? Should we give up the flat?'

'I don't mind – if you think we ought to.'

'You know that the rent . . .'

'All right! I said yes!'

'It can't be helped, Heinz. It's also a sacrifice for Mother.'

Naturally it was a sacrifice for her. Frau Quaas, that small, fragile, anxious woman, received the family and its furniture, which took up a lot of space in her not very large sitting room, although most of it went into the garret.

'Now we'll be able to manage. We shall save the rent and it'll be much simpler when I'm cooking for Mother as well. She'll let us have something over for it and we can buy a few things at last.'

'First of all we must pay off the rent – I don't want any debts. Certainly not with people who behave as if you were a scoundrel because you can't get work.'

Yes, things became a trifle easier for the Hackendahls. Irma served in the shop and Frau Quaas helped with the housework, turn and turn about. They were rather on top of one another; mother and daughter and child sleeping in one room, Heinz banished to the kitchen . . . A topsy-turvy existence, of course – a marriage without wedlock, the simplest kiss embarrassed by the mother's presence; the women at work, the man sentenced to inactivity . . . a world upside down – but hardly more upside down than the world outside, the big world, the political world where – with much hue and cry – they were just initiating the Dawes Plan, whereby the debtor is lent money by the creditor, so that the former, without means, can better pay the latter.

Naturally there were some bright spots at times. Old Hackendahl would stop his carriage outside the shop, Otto would be placed in it and his father beside him, and then Blücher would trot off, with old Hackendahl cracking his whip for no other reason than that it amused the boy. They would drive three or four streets away, to keep Grandfather company to the nursing home.

Then father and son would alight and slowly walk back, stopping in front of every shop – they had plenty of time – Otto prattling, with his small hand trustfully in the large one. A nice sight and a harmless deception! The child was still ignorant that his father did not rank just below the Lord, but was unemployed, an outlaw, a pariah.

How much a pariah that same father was yet to learn when he next handed in his card to be stamped. The clerk scrutinized a piece of paper, and then Hackendahl's face.

'Herr Hackendahl? Will you please go to Room 357.'

Heinz Hackendahl went to Room 357. When he was told to do a thing in this place he did it. He was only one of thousands without a destiny of their own or an individuality; he had long ago given up taking matters here personally. But on this occasion he was being considered as a person, for once.

At the desk sat a scraggy, sallow man. What a funny head, thought Heinz. That really is what they call pear shaped . . .

'You are Heinz Hackendahl, your particulars are this and that, you have been unemployed for so long, living at such-and-such address. Is that so?'

'Yes, that's correct.' But what was not quite so correct was that, though a chair stood available, no chair was offered him. But it wasn't worthwhile getting upset about a trifle like that. Here one mustn't get upset by anything.

'What kind of a flat have you got?' asked Pear-head (naturally you take against such a head, when it asks in such a stupid way. Otherwise, you would just think it a joke).

Heinz thought he was being asked about his old one. No doubt the agent had complained about the arrears of rent. But those had been paid now and this he explained.

'So you were in debt for rent and now you've paid up. Where did you get the money from?'

That was the sort of questioning which made a man slowly angry. Heinz said that unfortunately he had no other income than his unemployment benefit and he had paid his rent with that.

'Fine. So previously the benefit wasn't sufficient for the rent and now it is. How's that?'

'Because we don't pay rent now. We're living at my mother-in-law's.'

'All right then. You're living at your mother-in-law's. Costs nothing. What do you do there?'

'Nothing.' (That, unfortunately, was the trouble.)

'Nothing at all?'

'No – what else am I supposed to do?'

'And suddenly you get so much money that you can pay your arrears? Did your mother-in-law give you the money?'

'No, she can barely make ends meet. It's only a small stationery shop.'

'So she has a stationery shop. Perhaps you help her sometimes?'

'No.'

'Think carefully before you reply. Do you work in the shop?'

'No.'

'And get remuneration for it?'

'No.'

'The remuneration needn't be given in cash; it can consist of free lodging and food, you know.'

'I pay my share of everything.'

'Nevertheless you can meet arrears of rent.'

'Yes, because a joint household is much cheaper than two separate ones.'

'And you're certain you don't assist in the shop?'

'Yes, I'm certain.'

'You know that working while on unemployment benefit is prohibited?'

'Certainly.'

'You know you aren't permitted to do any spare-time work whatever for remuneration?'

'I know that. I've never . . .'

'And that remuneration can of course be made in kind, as for instance the use of a flat?'

'I've never . . .'

'Are you acquainted with the penal clauses relating to unemployed assistance? Not only are you liable to deprivation of benefit but a charge may be preferred for fraud.'

'But I . . .'

'In accordance with the information before me you sold the informant on the fifth of this month about six o'clock in the afternoon three police registration forms for ten pfennigs; you were alone in the shop. The informant is ready to swear to his statement. Well?'

'This is ridiculous . . . It's too dirty for words. And you listen to accusations like that? You order me to come here . . .'

'When you've stopped using abusive language perhaps you'll give me a proper answer. Do you admit that the informant's statements are correct?'

'Tell me who the skunk is!'

'You don't even remember? Are you so frequently serving there?'

'I don't serve in the shop at all. There are two women there and they serve perhaps twenty customers a day. They can manage that between them.'

'So in spite of the sworn statement you deny working while on benefit?'

'Of course I do. It isn't working if I go into the shop for once. I'm not taking work away from anybody. No doubt my wife was standing at the gas stove stirring a saucepan and possibly she said: "Go and have a look at the shop!" How can that be working while on benefit?'

'The interpretation of working on benefit may be left to the magistrate. If it was as you say, why didn't *you* stir the saucepan and leave the shop to your wife?'

'Because cooking is a woman's work and . . .' He broke off.

'. . . And serving customers is man's work,' concluded the other. 'You see – our view entirely. So you left the cooking to the woman and did the man's work, that is, serving customers. You admit that.'

'I admit nothing at all. All I said was that I might have given my wife a hand once or twice.'

'All the same, these isolated instances occur so frequently that you are unable to recollect the incident in question!'

'Are these legal proceedings?' shouted Heinz. 'This is ridiculous.

Do you really think I want to lose the benefit and risk prison by sell-ing ten pfennigs' worth of goods?'

'First of all control yourself. You're shouting at me and that can-not be allowed. Take a seat and calm down.'

'Yes, you offer me a seat now when I'm too excited to sit down.'

'But why are you so excited? If you have a clear conscience there's no need to get excited at all. Well, what's the position?'

'I've told you already.'

'You deny having worked while on benefit but admit to serving in the shop. That is a contradiction.'

'It isn't. What I did wasn't work.'

'That is your opinion.'

'Yes, it is.'

'All right. You can go for the present.'

'Really? May I? Don't you want to arrest me on the spot?'

'You may go.'

'All right!'

His anger had already almost subsided as he left. He no longer understood himself. Those people were nothing but pedants. Some wretch showed them a job offer and they immediately took action. They puzzled things out and were accurate, but inhuman. He'd already heard of such things. Someone had helped his sister move house – illegal work. Someone had dug up a bit of land for his mother – illegal work. Every hint of human helpfulness was suspect. It was no use getting upset about it – they had nothing on him – but it was unpleasant all the same.

And it became still more unpleasant.

That he now always had to sit in the front room or the kitchen and no longer dared go into the shop for fear of coming under renewed suspicion was bad enough – and that he always felt like a prisoner under secret surveillance.

However, they tortured him further. They sent him from official to official. It transpired that his first interview had created an unfavourable impression. Pear-head had categorized him as 'refractory' – an undesirable quality. He should be flexible, not refrac-tory. He would have to kindly prove his innocence, because they were clearly holding proof of his guilt, with his conviction in their hands.

'Yes, my good sir,' said a softer-spoken older official. 'Even if everything had been as you said, it shouldn't have been. As main provider, you should have avoided suspicion. And you didn't avoid the appearance of working illegally.'

'I never thought helping my wife would look like illegal work. There are thousands of unemployed who cook and clean while their wives earn a few pfennigs.'

'You were in the shop – as salesman. That is different. Timing, Herr Hackendahl! You got the timing all wrong. If you're paid by public services, you must always remember to keep up public appearances.'

Those three ridiculous police registration forms in exchange for ten pfennigs: they had ended up making Heinz Hackendahl heartily sick. When called to such an office again, he could see his file lying there, gradually getting bigger and bigger. He would be going from one department to another. Perhaps he had already been to the police and the legal department, and his file was only not yet quite thick enough for a case against him being brought for fraud.

In the end, Heinz Hackendahl had the feeling that his case was even beginning to bore the officials – as if they were only pursuing it because the file was there and none of them had had the courage to write 'Case closed' on it.

No, all Heinz Hackendahl had learned was that he was nothing – a grain among millions. How the wheels took him was quite arbitrary. No one entirely survived such a mill. Some were only partially damaged, but some were totally ground down and fell like dust and ashes from the machine. They no longer existed.

Sometimes, when he thought about his three police registration forms, he feared that this would one day happen to him – that he too would be totally crushed. In the end, nothing seemed to have come of the forms; the case seemed to have run into the sand. However, if he had really done something wrong, if he really had taken a five-mark piece from Sister Sophie for searching through her books, it would have been over with him ground to dust and ashes!

He suffered for long under all the pressure and was deeply depressed. He didn't want to do anything, to put his hand to anything, neither to clean his shoes nor help the boy into his overcoat;

he wanted nothing. He was sentenced to a fate much harder than that of any criminal. A criminal could, indeed had to, work in prison. His hand shaped something even if it were merely a mat or a shopping bag. He, however, went about in the world with everything forbidden to him, a man who was not allowed to do a stroke of work. He had abilities and intelligence but he was forbidden to use these abilities; he might employ his intelligence only to brood with. Excluded from life, wait till you die. We'll give you just enough to keep you going – quite a long time yet – until you die. To wait, that's your occupation.

His mother-in-law, Irma, his own mother, his father – they all tried to cheer him up.

'Get along with you and don't be such a fool. On Sunday I'll take you and yer fam'ly for a drive into the country. The horse too 'll like to see a bit of green again and not only the green seats in the Kaiserplatz.'

'Yes, the seats – did you read, Father, that they're to be forbidden to the unemployed? An application's been made. They say we loll about on them and take up all the room.'

Nothing could be done with him – it had become an obsession, this question of unemployment.

§ XV

One evening towards ten o'clock Heinz was sitting in his shirt and trousers on the makeshift bed in the kitchen, watching his wife tidy up.

'Well, Irma,' he said, his eyes gleaming, perhaps because he had just yawned or maybe . . .

'Well, Heinz,' she answered vaguely. 'Tired?'

'Tired!' he retorted irritably. 'Tired from what?'

She glanced at him, then continued her tidying-up without a word. And this silence annoyed him at first. He was right, wasn't he? Why should he be tired? From hanging around in the streets?

Gradually his irritation passed, however. He watched her. She had such a brisk way of moving about. How lovely her arm looked, putting away the plate! Yes, she was part of him, part of him for ever.

'Irma, listen . . .' he said.

'Yes, Heinz?' Again that glance.

'Sit by me for a moment.'

'Presently.' And she went on with her work.

He looked on patiently for some time, and then said: 'Aren't you coming?'

'Oh, Heinz . . .'

'What do you mean by "Oh, Heinz"? Don't you want to sit with me any more?'

She turned round. She was holding a spoon. Later on he remembered clearly that she had a spoon in her hand when she said: 'We mustn't.'

'Mustn't we?' he asked slowly. 'Not even that any more?'

She shook her head, her lips pressed together. She was still looking at him.

'But . . .' he said after a while in a stricken voice, 'but . . . we have up to now.'

She did not look away. Probably she had forgotten that ridiculous spoon in her hand. Better than any word her gaze said that this was no whim but a resolution which had slowly matured within her.

'But . . .' He was struggling to think things over, to get them clear in his mind. 'We have up to now . . . it was quite all right.'

At last she spoke. 'I can't stand it any longer . . . I'm frightened to death every time, till I can be sure that . . . No, never again.'

'Never again,' repeated Heinz dully.

'Don't look at me like that, Heinz,' she said passionately. 'You know I'm fond of you and I love children more than anything – I can't pass a pram without looking in it, you know that. I'd like to have children more than anything in the world, lots of them.' She seemed to be looking at some bright, sunny house, a place of happiness enlivened by children. Then her eyes grew dim with pain. 'But children you can't feed,' she said, 'children where you have to run to the Welfare for their napkins . . . No. No. No.'

And this triple 'No' stiffened her; her decision no longer to be a wife must be irrevocable. She looked at him. 'I'm sorry too, Heinz,' she said. 'But I . . . I can't help it. I've not made these times . . .'

She seemed to wait for a reply, as though he could say something which would overcome all this despair, this stricken existence. Then she shook her head – it was not meant for him but for herself – said quickly 'Goodnight, Heinz' and left the kitchen. In her hand she still held the spoon.

EIGHT

The Journey to Paris

§ 1

First, old Hackendahl saw only curious black crowds swarming round the station at Wannsee. Flags fluttered – the new German and the French flags – and there were soldiers, music, and in addition a speaker now mounted the podium and spoke.

Gustav Hackendahl could see it all very clearly from his cab. He could also see a female in black riding habit on the bay horse. From the distance at least, the female figure did not look very special, but the bay did look good.

A nice little horse, thought Gustav – quite wasted on such a woman. He'd be something for my cab.

'What's goin' on?' he asked a taxi driver.

'Eh, you seem to live on the moon nowadays, Gustav. That's the woman what's ridden from Paris to visit us. Yes, on that horse – I wouldn't have cared to have been either the 'orse or that woman's backside, but luckily they've both survived, and now they're bein' made a fuss of.'

'What for?'

'Lumme, Gustav, they ought to get an electrician to look at your head. You've enough juice there to supply the whole of Berlin. They're makin' a fuss because she's ridden from Paris, that's why. All the way on horseback.'

'That all? All this fuss fer that? Why, me and me Blücher could do it any day. An' I'm nearly seventy! Just Berlin to Paris! We could manage that, too, couldn't we, Blücher?'

The taxi driver laughed. 'D'you hear that?' he said, turning to the other drivers. 'Gustav's goin' ter drive ter Paris, for a bit of fraternizing.'

'Yes, Gustav, why don't you?'

'But old Blücher will suffer all right, Gustav.'

'Cab's better than on horseback.'

'I'm 'earing Paris all the time. You do mean the Paris behind the Spandauer Krug, don't you, Gustav?'

'Still made of iron, is Gustav! They needn't cast a statue of you in Paris, they'll simply hoist you up on a pedestal as you stand, Gustav. You'll last.'

'I don't know what's got hold of you,' said Hackendahl surprised. 'What's in it anyhow? I c'n do it if I wanted. An' I've a good mind to, lemme tell you.' He returned thoughtfully to his cab, climbed onto the box, and saw from a distance how the meeting proceeded. An escort of riders had come to welcome the French horsewoman; now they surrounded her as clouds surround the sun, and the procession set forth, led by bands. Everyone cheered.

'I dunno,' thought Gustav, 'if they also have cabs in Paris. But if they do, it would be great to have fifty cabs altogether. It would be a change from those eternal cars which – whatever people say – look as though they're missing something at the front.'

And then three people hired him, and he had to follow the procession. He could hear them talking behind him. 'I take my hat off to her.' 'Quite an achievement.' 'Yes, the French, did you see them – their phizogs pure yellow, but stuck up like anyfink.'

And Hackendahl, as his black horse trotted along, thought: 'They might've bin talkin' about you, Gustav. Not that it'd be like the old times when I had a business – bit crazy p'r'aps – but it'd be a change from drivin' others about – forty years of it. Yes, it'd be a change . . . and if I get to France, I could visit Otto. I dunno – sometimes I still think he wasn't so daft after all, and he also knew something about horses.'

So his thoughts went, always with the procession. And, hearing the cheers and seeing the welcoming throngs at the Brandenburger Tor, he said to himself: 'Gustav, me bright lad, take a look at it! P'r'aps, who knows . . . ?'

§ II

Yet he would never have seen the lady from Paris had it not been for his daughter Sophie, who had so arranged matters that he had gone back to his cab. He looked at the visit from Paris from a cab driver's point of view, and began to think about it.

She would not have been the calculating, unlovable creature she was had she not felt it a drawback – and the feeling grew – that she, mistress of a prosperous nursing home, had as father a cab driver. This the patients learned, not through the nurses – for she could have stopped that with a word – but through her father himself. He couldn't spread the tale quickly enough that he was Iron Gustav, the oldest cab driver in Berlin, and that the Matron was his daughter.

'Only she used to be thin as a lath – it was durin' the war she blossomed out. As people say: one man's meat is another man's poison. Well, p'r'aps I shouldn't put it like that. You're a patient here an' our Sophie has ter live on yer illness.'

Sophie could not be certain whether this was merely an old man's loquacity or pure malice, as though he wanted to pay her back or humiliate her. Whenever such remarks came to her ears she would take him to task, upon which he replied cheerfully: 'But what of it, girl, what of it? I'm a cabby an' you've got on in the world – that's a fact, ain't it? Or are you ashamed to be the daughter of a cabby? I can tell 'em I had a business with thirty cabs when you was born, if yer like. Wait a mo . . . No, when you was born I hadn't got as many as that. But I can ask Mother so I c'n tell 'em the exact number.'

'You're not to talk with the patients at all. You're only to take them for a drive.'

'Here, hold on! The patients talk to me! But I'll do jus' what you want, Sophie, I'll keep me mouth shut when they start chattering.'

'You know what I mean! If you like, say that you're Iron Gustav, though I don't consider it in very good taste. But to tell everybody that the Frau Matron is your daughter . . .'

'I always say Fräulein Matron, Sophie. Or have you had a husband?'

And so the quarrel would go on, Sophie growing more and more furious and the old man remaining as cheerful as ever. Senile gossip, self-importance, malice . . .

Oh, how much she would have liked to get rid of him again! But it must come from his side. And she tried to do it by devious means. The patients were sent less frequently for a drive, while the carrying of coal, refuse and urinals – which he so much disliked – grew more common.

But if she was sly he was cunning; sometimes – a most unpleasant feeling – she felt that he saw through her entirely. Besides which, it grieved her frugal soul that the carriage and horse, bought out of her money, should not be fully utilized. So she made it a habit to be driven despite the fact that she would have much preferred to walk – she resembled those people in a restaurant who, having ordered food which they find they do not like, eat it because they have got to pay for it. In the same way she drove in the carriage from one shop to another, and these jaunts were pleasant neither for driver nor driven, since they were never quick enough for her, and the business of turning the carriage round was so cumbersome. People stared and said: 'Look, there's a carriage! Straight out of the Märkische Museum.' This made her boil with fury, so that it became certain there would be a flare-up sometime.

And it came, one morning when she had to go to the station. The carriage had been ordered for nine o'clock and old Hackendahl was punctual. But, as often happens in a big establishment when the head of it wants to get away, if only for a few hours, all sorts of things intervened at the last moment and it was twelve minutes past nine before she got into the carriage.

'Twelve minutes past nine, Sophie. I don't think we can make it. Better take the Underground!'

'Of course we'll make it. Just put the horse to it. You've got to make it. Away you go!'

'I don't think so.'

'The horse must get a move on. Please hurry up, Father.'

'All right, Sophie. But don't blame me if we don't make it.'

'If you don't, it'll be to spite me.'

'What are you sayin', Sophie? You're in a temper. Why should I try ter spite you? That's not me at all.'

And they moved off. And he really did drive like the real Blücher, keeping the horse to a steady trot. All went well at the crossings and he chose the quieter side streets; she had to admit he did everything possible to arrive on time.

After a while he turned round and said cheerfully: 'I believe we'll do it. Yes, takin' you out puts Blücher in a better humour than dragging a load of ashes an' refuse.'

'Drive on,' she exclaimed irritably.

'It's still at red,' he answered unruffled but started immediately the traffic light turned amber.

Sophie watched him, annoyed because she had grudged the Underground fare, and because he had been in the right, yet though it was really almost too late, nevertheless he cheerfully tried to get her to the station in time; annoyed with herself, with him, the cab, its rattling, and with the whole world. Annoyed, too, because she still wasn't rid of him.

They had reached the Potsdamer Platz, with only a little way to go now. They would definitely come at the right time.

'Yes, me an' Blücher!' beamed her father, turning round. In spite of herself she nodded.

On the traffic tower in the middle of the square appeared the amber light.

'Gee-up, Blücher,' urged old Hackendahl.

The black horse started forward, turned out of the Potsdamer Strasse into the square and trotted briskly amid the throng of cars and buses, cycles and lorries. In another moment they would be in the narrow street by the station.

The horse began to slow down, wanted to stop.

'Gee-up, Blücher, gee-up,' shouted Hackendahl. 'Get along, old boy.' And over his shoulder anxiously: 'Don't say he's goin' to . . .'

'Going to what?' Sophie exclaimed furiously.

But the black horse had already stopped, nearly causing a car to run into them. The chauffeur began to curse, a policeman ran towards them, a crowd formed – but the black horse stood tranquilly in the midst of all the turmoil and passed his water.

Old Hackendahl cursed, the motorists cursed, the policeman cursed. Somebody took the black horse by the bridle and tried to lead it to the kerb. But Blücher stood like iron, and pissed away.

For Sophie Hackendahl, a middle-aged spinster and Matron, it was like some terrible nightmare when one is standing quite naked among dozens of properly clothed people. There she sat, noticeable enough already in the only horse-drawn vehicle among so many cars, held up while the traffic drove on and the wretched creature passed its water. It seemed as if the splashing was never coming to an end, and when she glanced to one side she saw quite a stream . . . Around them were nothing except grinning, furious, jeering faces. And herself in her Matron's uniform the cynosure of all eyes! But, unlike a nightmare, she wasn't nailed to the spot. Oh, no, most decidedly she wasn't.

'Officer!' she called to the policeman, 'please help me to the pavement.'

'Certainly, Nurse. Come along. Bit unpleasant for a lady.'

'Where yer goin', Sophie?' shouted old Hackendahl. 'He'll have finished in a moment. It ain't his fault. Needs must . . .'

She saw the people laugh.

That evening all arrangements with her father were broken off – by her. She was sorry, but such an out-of-date vehicle, such an embarrassing situation – no, she couldn't expect her patients to put up with it.

'Nor you yerself. Nor yer cash box either,' said her father. 'Well, never mind, Sophie. You've bin wantin' to get rid of me a long time. D'yer think I couldn't see that? It was as plain as a pikestaff! Well, never mind, if I managed to bring you all up without help, I c'n feed yer mother without help. Only don't think you can fool me. Even if yer nursin' home gets as big as the Charité Hospital you'll remain a nasty mean bitch. G'night, Sophie.'

And from that time Hackendahl had turned cabman again. Not gladly, to be sure, but he was in the same position now as Blücher – needs must. And that was how he came to see the horsewoman at Wannsee Station.

§ III

Business was better than it had been in recent years. People suddenly had money again, unemployment decreased – the effect of the foreign loans now raining down after a long drought, bringing luxuriant growth which flourished in abundance. The only question was how long this moisture would last. It was like a greenhouse; it only needed a cold wind . . . The very fact, however, that people did not trust in their good luck helped the cab drivers. Everyone was in a hurry to spend his money, it burned a hole in the pocket, one gladly parted from it. There was something to spare for a binge. Old Hackendahl and his Blücher had work again, not overmuch but enough.

And it wasn't so bad, to be able to take things a little easy after all his work for the clinic. Hackendahl no longer felt the old urge to earn money at all costs. Maybe it was age but he often sat dozing nowadays on his box, thinking: If there ain't a fare today then there ain't. I've managed all right so far an' I don't see why I won't now. An' besides, if I want to . . .

With that his thoughts would stray towards Paris . . . Nothing tangible, no immediate intention, not even a plan – just a day-dream, the sort of thing a man imagines while telling himself: That wouldn't be a bad thing to do . . . And makes no attempt to do it.

Hackendahl had told his wife about the horsewoman who had ridden to Berlin and told her story, and he added, 'I wouldn't mind doin' that either.'

'You're mad!' Mother merely said.

'What's that? Mad? D'you mean I can't do what that Frenchie did?'

'At your age, Father? You must have a screw loose.'

He saw she hadn't the least idea he meant it seriously, and it was this utter disbelief which egged him on. They all think I'm cracked, he thought. I'd like to have a chance of showin' 'em.

However, there was a big distance between thought and deed. It was soon obvious to him that he couldn't simply mount his box and set forth. It would all have to be prepared beforehand and money provided for him and Blücher, and for Mother to live on when she was by herself.

One day in a side street he saw a barrow on which an unemployed man was exhibiting the model of a mine. Getting down, he had a look at it, watched the tiny lamps flash, the little trucks run, the miniature hammers fall – a very fine bit of work. One couldn't grudge buying a picture postcard of the thing.

'Well, how's business, young feller?' he asked.

'So-so. You scrape through. Brings in a bit more than the dole.'

I ought to do somethin' like that, he thought as he drove on. Sell picture postcards. The oldest cabby in Berlin. On his way to Paris an' back. People'd buy, it'd amuse 'em . . .

Thus bit by bit he approached his decision. But that didn't mean an actual decision by a long way. Something else had to happen before so old a man could make up his mind, some impulse from without to set him in motion, something particularly sad or cheerful or at all events extraordinary . . .

And this came . . .

'Mother,' he said, 'I dunno what you're doin' with the money. We used to do all right on five marks a day an' now all of a sudden it ain't enough.'

'Everything's dearer, Father. The butter . . . meat . . .' It was so long and tearful an explanation that Hackendahl gave up listening. What his wife said wasn't important; the main thing was to make the money do, and that didn't seem to be happening.

'Mother,' he said a week later, 'Heinz bin round?'

'No, Father. Why?'

'I dunno. There's a smell of tobacco hanging about.'

His wife thought for a bit, then it occurred to her that the gasman had smoked.

'Well, tell him not to, Mother,' remarked Hackendahl, 'otherwise he'll set our place on fire an' we'll be in the soup.'

But he soon forgot about it. He was hardly ever at home except to sleep, and that not for long; he spent ten or twelve hours on the box according to what business there was, besides sitting near his horse for an hour and a half, morning and evening, watching him eat, grooming and watering him. Very often his wife brought his supper into the stable, in the old workshop belonging to the man who had hanged himself – he no longer recalled his name – where he liked to be when the streets had quietened down and another day had passed. Then, after giving the horse a last drink of water, he would go straight to bed, very fatigued indeed. But with old people fatigue like that doesn't last – it's more a weariness of life than a desire to sleep; after he had slept two, three or four hours, he would wake up, lying quite still so as not to disturb his wife. He simply lay there as he had woken up – not the worst thing to do, just to lie there. One could think about many things besides the journey to Paris, which was more a matter to brood over in daylight; at night he thought of past events, of projects successful and unsuccessful, of the children, of horses he had once owned, of drivers who had worked for him, of old Rabause; of his time in the army, of officers and men. And he could still remember many things about the home village he moved from to Pasewalk. He would like to have seen that village again. He'd wondered whether it wouldn't be possible to go through it on the way to Paris, but decided it was hardly possible, as it was too far north.

It's a funny thing about a place in which you have lived for years – you know it as you do a suit worn for a long time; if there's something in the wrong pocket it worries and irks you till you change it round. And here was old Hackendahl in his bed, the old familiar bed, which the same woman had made for him, wide-awake as so often at this hour, but aware that tonight there was something, he himself didn't know what, that irked and worried him . . .

He wasn't thinking about the smell of tobacco for instance, or that his wife seemed suddenly unable to manage on her money – no, he wasn't suspicious – he was merely restless and that was odd . . . Hadn't someone coughed just then? Not coughed perhaps but cleared his throat, as you do in your sleep? It sounded exactly as if it were in the flat, say in the small room where Heinz used to sleep . . .

It could not possibly have been in his own flat, but without listening any longer or waiting to make sure, he gripped his wife's arm and shook her. 'You, there's someone in the flat.'

His wife moaned and then replied quickly: 'You're imagining things, Father! You're dreaming. Who can possibly have got in?'

'There's somebody here,' he repeated stubbornly. 'I know it. Who is it?'

'Father, you're dreaming. There's no one. How could there be? There's nothing to be got here.'

'In Heinz's bedroom – I know it as well as if I could see it. There's someone in Heinz's room.' He was groping for matches to light the candle.

'Father, Father, don't make us unhappy. Yes, I've given someone a shakedown, I told him he could, but I'll send him away tomorrow. Or I'll go now – let *me* go – I'll send him away at once, Father.'

She began to weep, wept bitterly, clutching him . . .

But Hackendahl was in no hurry to leave his bed now. 'Who've you got in Heinz's room, Mother, that I'm not to see or know anything about? Who can it be, Mother?'

'It's a lodger, I don't know what he does. So's to get a penny or two because I can't make the money reach. That's why, Father.'

'You're tellin' stories, Mother, I can hear that all right. As if I don't know when you're tellin' fibs! I knew it when you spoke about the gasman. That was a fairytale, but I didn't bother.'

'It's true, Father, it's only a lodger . . .'

'You wouldn't be tellin' me lies about a lodger, you ain't ever lied to me about money. It's always bin for your children. Underhand dealin's with them behind me back. I know who it is sleepin' there.'

'Father, don't go. Do me this one favour and don't go. Let him sleep, he needs sleep, he's quite done-up.'

'An' why's he done-up? Why's a swell like that have ter come crawlin' to his mother when he usually puts up in a fine hotel?'

'I don't know, Father. Let him sleep! I'll see to it that he goes. He'll have gone by tomorrow night – I promise you that, Father.'

'Why's he got to wait till night? What's he been up to?'

'How should I know, Father? I haven't asked him. He's my child and I'll not cast him out when he comes to me. Let him have his rest. I don't want to know what he's done. What he did to me, I've long forgotten.'

'This ain't a doss-house for crooks on the run. He was always a bad egg and he'll take you down too.'

'And suppose he does? I don't mind, Father.'

'He must go,' said the old man, rising and taking the candlestick. 'I'm not blamin' you, Mother, an' I'm not goin' ter blame him either, so don't worry. There was a time when I'd have raised hell about something like this but in those days I used ter think it's an ill bird what fouls his own nest. Now I think diff'rently. They fouled my nest all right, and my proud life in the army, too. Now I just laugh at such stuff and don't even look at it.'

Standing there before his wife's bed, candlestick in hand, old Hackendahl looked far from laughing, however. His fat face quivered, and his beard quivered too . . .

'Let him sleep, Father,' she begged. 'Don't hit him.'

'Don't be silly, Mother. Why should I hit a man thirty years old? That wouldn't help us now. No, you stay in bed.'

In his bare feet he crossed the passage and opened the bedroom door. Holding up the candle, he looked, he listened. Then he approached the bed . . .

There, sleeping on his side, lay the son who had been closest to his heart and perhaps still was, in spite of everything. Had his wife stuck to it that it was a stranger Hackendahl would probably not have recognized him. A puffy sallow face, dark bags under the eyes, a worried frown above them, a chin covered with ugly bristles – a stranger's face!

The father bent over the bed, throwing the light on those sleeping features, searching for the face of the youth he had loved, the one who had been so much more spirited than he, admired, alert, joyous. But now what he lit up was only something troubled and miserable, stubborn, insistently transient and death-bound. This man slept as if he were dead . . . His grace and high spirits had died, no doubt, long since . . .

The father straightened himself. He examined his son's clothes. No, these were not the clothes of one who could go into a smart hotel – a month or two more and they'd be worn out . . . Item by item he examined them, looking at the shoes, feeling the join between the upper and sole, going through the pockets – all rather mechanically.

The father sighed, then he picked up the candlestick and went out. His wife, sitting in bed, fixed her anxious eyes on him. 'You needn't worry, Mother,' said he. 'Still snorin'. Gimme your purse. Got any other money?'

He went through his own pockets; he scraped together all the cash in the flat, even down to the small change which every cabman likes to carry on him. Then he went back into the other bedroom.

The son still slept. Putting the money into one of the pockets, the father marched up to the bed, shook the sleeper's shoulder and barked out in his old military voice: 'Get up, Erich!'

In the twinkling of an eye the son awoke. One saw that the tone of command spoke to every limb; the flight of fifteen long years had not caused his body to forget that imperious voice. His eyes blinked and as the waking man saw the dark figure with the light and grasped who it was that stood before him, fear showed in his face. Fear and terror.

Thus the father at last saw the child's face beneath that older face. He recognized his son by his fear, his cowardly, grovelling fear, his fear of punishment when he had been up to no good and his father admonished him for it.

'Get dressed!' ordered the father.

The son obeyed. He did not hurry; the fear was wearing off. He had grown shameless and the shameless readily turn insolent when they realize that the other intends no harm.

Thus it was not long before the son opened his mouth. But what did the former loved one say? What did he say?

'Once you locked me in the cellar out of pure love, what, Father? And now you're turning me into the streets out of love too, eh? You can't get rid of me quickly enough, what?'

Everything had become coarser, language and expression, thought and manner.

'Yes, you fathers!' said the son with a contempt either real or assumed. 'Fine mess you've got us into. You could get children all right, but you couldn't make men out of them, because you yourselves were lacking.'

Every word a lie, every word cowardly and deceitful. The father's fist itched, but he had promised his wife not to strike the boy. And he had no desire to reply – the other would only twist every word one uttered.

But he did something, he blew out the light; and the son became silent. As soon as he could no longer see his father the old fear returned. Who knew what might happen now? He cursed under his breath. 'What tomfoolery's this?' he asked. But he made haste.

And it was just as if his father could see in the dark, for hardly had Erich put his hat on when a hand took him by the neck and pushed him into the passage. Erich offered no resistance. He could go now . . .

But he was propelled past the front door and in the direction of the bedroom. It was in vain to struggle. The hand on his neck was like a vice; at the least resistance it gripped the harder.

Mother had heard the noise. 'Father! Erich! What is it?'

'Say goodbye to your mother,' whispered Hackendahl in his son's ear. 'And thank her, you understand? Politely! Properly!'

Erich started to struggle but the old man's hand tightened and the voice in his ear said still more threateningly: 'Will you obey?'

Erich cleared his throat. 'I'm going now, Mother. Thanks . . . very much.'

'Erich,' she called. 'Erich, my boy. Why isn't there a light? Come and give me a kiss . . . Father, bring a light!'

Father, however, brought no light. Cloaked in the darkness he pushed his son, his hopelessly unsuccessful, wretched son, up to the mother's bed. 'Do what she wants!' he whispered. And again: 'If you don't, I swear I'll call the police!' He pushed his son down by the edge of the bed, and his son kissed his mother goodbye.

'Oh, Erich, look after yourself, do! Don't let them get you, see that they don't, Erich. Goodbye . . .'

She was crying. To the sound of her tears the son was taken out of the room, to the front door and out onto the stairs . . . There the hand released him and, before he had a chance to vent his spite in words, the door had closed between father and son.

§ IV

The next evening old Hackendahl saw in the paper that the police had recognized in the street a criminal, one who had betrayed his country. No name was mentioned; there was nothing to indicate that this traitor was Erich Hackendahl, but his father – saying not a word to anyone – knew in his heart that it was he.

For a few days he was worried that the police could come and ask after Erich, but all was quiet. Slowly rage and sorrow ebbed away. He was too old to be angry for long, so old that a vague grief hung about all he thought, said or did.

However, during all this time, as the excitement over his son died down and the greyness of everyday life resumed, he thought more and more about the journey to Paris. For many, many years now he had been driving about Berlin, and suddenly he was tired to death of it. These miserable little fares – eighty pfennigs or one mark twenty, or at the most three marks to the Schlesische Station! No more than a dog's cart worth, with a child's pram, he thought suddenly.

He wanted to drive into the country for a change, not always through the same cobbled streets; he wanted to see the fields he had worked in as a boy, see from the box how the men were at work with plough and harrow, sowing the seed, rolling the ground. Something like homesickness and wanderlust gripped him . . . He wanted to drive and drive further and further into the country. All the country-side is home to the country-born, the town never. Why go then to a certain village in the Pasewalk district when every village he drove through would somehow be native to him? In every village the people led their teams to the fields in the morning, rang the church bells at noon, stood before their cottages gossiping in the dusk. A girl clat-tered with her pails to the well. In the country it must be the same now as it used to be. Oh, how he would like to see it once more!

Yes, he was sick of the town. He wanted to leave it, get away from the too familiar. Before facing that which no mortal can avoid, he wanted to do something new, something never done before. He had brooded so much about this journey to Paris that it no longer appeared strange. Heavens, people never stopped travelling; all his life he had driven tourists to the station – why shouldn't he himself travel for once? What was there mad about that? It was quite simple. If he added up all the trips he had made in Berlin he must have driven the distance to Paris hundreds of times. Nothing out of the ordinary – as soon as you got used to the idea.

I'll just set out, he thought. It's nothing special. Why not? Let 'em say I'm mad. The madder they think me the better; everybody'll buy a picture postcard of a real loony.

So from a vague idea was slowly formed a fixed resolve. Meanwhile he continued to ply with the cab all that winter. And whenever he came across a shop selling maps or globes he had a look at them and was surprised to see how close the two cities were. Why, it's hardly any distance, he thought; I could cover it with me thumb. Dunno why they make such a fuss about it. Couldn't take more than a week surely.

And then there were the picture postcards; he'd have to enquire about those too. So he poked around till he discovered a small printer's, the sort he could enquire of . . .

'Picture postcards? Certainly! Thirty-five marks the thousand. With a minimum of five thousand, thirty-two marks. Caption? Yes, we can do that. What do you want? "Iron Gustav, the oldest cab driver in Berlin, drives from Berlin to Paris and back again." Bit long, but we'll do it for the same money. Are you Iron Gustav?'

'That's me.'

'And have you thought what you're doing at your age?'

'I ain't so old as all that. I'm not seventy yet. And what's in it, anyhow?'

'Maybe it's all right. Only – have you got a permit? And you must have a passport. You can't just cross the frontier as you like, not with a horse and cab. There's such a thing as Customs duty, you know.'

'Why, d'you think I'll have to pay duty?'

'And can you speak French? You'll have to speak French. I mean, if you're alone with a horse in a French village . . . What does it eat? Oats, of course, yes, but what is French for oats? Otherwise they'll give your nag pickled gherkins. Not that they don't taste good, eh?'

Old Hackendahl was so preoccupied with all these unforeseen problems that he did not perceive the other was mildly poking fun at him. 'Many thanks!' he said, and made to leave the shop.

'And what about the postcards?' cried the printer, realizing too late that he had scared away a client with his leg-pulling.

'I'll sleep on it,' said Hackendahl, going. He climbed onto the box and drove. He stopped at a relay and fed Blücher. He even found customers and drove them. Then he eventually came home, fed the horse, ate himself, and crept into bed – but he didn't sleep. All the time he was thinking and calculating.

Four months it'll take, he thought. That means I'll have to leave
Mother two hundred an' forty marks at least. Well, two hundred'll
do. An' fer me an' the horse I need another five hundred – lodgin's
and stablin' and food an' feed. An' then the duty. Blücher'll have to
have new harness. An' the cab mus' go to the smith an' wheelwright
or there'll be trouble. So all in all I need a thousand marks. A thousan' marks are ten thousan' picture postcards at ten pfennigs each.
On the other hand ten thousan' postcards'd cost p'r'aps three hundred marks. That means I want one thousan' three hundred marks,
which means I have to sell another three thousan' cards which'll cost
an extra hundred marks . . .

Thinking over things in this way for days on end, he neither slept
nor ate.

'What's the matter with you, Father?' asked his wife.

'Oh, nothin'! The spring I s'pose. Wakin' up me rheumatism . . .'

No, he did not breathe a word to her but he was beginning to realize he couldn't carry out his plan by himself. Impossible to raise five
hundred marks, let alone a thousand.

We'll see, he thought, we'll see. Jus' wait and see. It's quite
simple – only needs settin' about it in the right way.

After long deliberation he decided to ask the advice of a travel
agency.

§ V

Like everything connected to the journey to Paris, old Hackendahl
carefully considered which travel agency he should consult. He was
not in favour of the agencies at the railway stations. They only want to
sell tickets, he thought. An' if I ask 'em about me an' me cab they'll
just pull me leg. And he didn't want anything to do with the steamer
agencies, either, which had such pretty little ships in their display windows. (I should buy one of them for me grandson, Otto, to play with.)

In the end he chose one which was housed in the premises of a
big newspaper. He had a feeling, not altogether mistaken, that this
particular agency had something to do with the newspaper and that
newspapers knew a good deal about the world.

Thus it came about that Gustav Hackendahl one day entered this building, put his shiny hat on a peg, placed the whip nearby, and reviewed place and people. Then, after he had inspected everything, he advanced towards a young man who looked rather more alert than the other clerks – in no way deterred by the fact that the sign-board over his brilliantined head bore the words: 'Traveller's Cheques and Foreign Exchange'.

'Young feller, I don't want ter buy anythin', I'm only askin' for information. I want to trundle in me cab to Paris, for a joke you know, an' I want to find out how long it'd take an' what money an' papers I need an' whether I must learn French . . .' Hackendahl had managed to pack all his worries into one sentence. Then, rather short of breath, he gazed at the young fellow who in turn looked at the old man not without interest but also not without the genuine Berliner's fear of being made a fool of. So he answered the last part of the question first. 'Would you learn French if it were necessary?'

'O' course, young feller.'

'How old are you then?'

'Seventy this year. Has that got anythin' to do with my journey?'

'When you get older, languages become more difficult,' the young man explained.

'You think so? Well, young chap, don't you worry. What the little French babies c'n learn you bet I c'n learn too.'

The young man looked at Hackendahl. 'You really want to drive your cab to Paris? No leg-pull?'

'Listen, why would I pull your leg? You're a stranger to me. I wouldn't do that with strangers.'

'H'mmm,' said the young man thoughtfully. 'So you really want to go to Paris?'

'Yes, I do,' Gustav Hackendahl confirmed again and awaited patiently the result of this thought. But if he thought that the young man was thinking of travel money and passports, he was wrong. He was thinking of a cousin, at that moment leading a miserable life as a junior reporter two floors higher up. He, the clerk, didn't in the slightest believe in this Paris trip, of course, but he found the old cabby odd and amusing, and wondered if his cousin Grundeis

couldn't write him up; you know, Old Berlin, Real Berlin Humour –
the sort of thing people liked to read . . .

'Listen,' said the young man thoughtfully.

'Well?' asked Hackendahl hopefully.

'I know a man up on the newspaper. I'll send you to him; he
knows much more about such things than I do.'

Hackendahl grew suspicious. 'What's this got to do with a newspaper? I want to make a journey and you're a travel agency, ain't you?'

And the one Berliner understood immediately the doubts of the
other Berliner. 'If the man upstairs doesn't know,' he said reassuringly, 'you can always come back to me. But he'll know all right. He's
just the man you want. I'll ring through about you. Grundeis is the
name. Third floor, Room 317.'

'Yes, I always thought Grundeis was the right man for me,' said
old Hackendahl, and it was perhaps just this name that made him
move on, despite his mistrust, and wait quite patiently for the young
Grundeis in the editorial waiting room upstairs.

As for the young Grundeis – Grundeis the firebrand, the young
reporter – he had been an apprentice on the editorial floor for some
years, and whenever he contemplated the comfortable backsides of
his superiors, he had to admit that there was little prospect of his
moving up in the foreseeable future. There they sat, and however
much he ran, whenever he reached somewhere, there they already
were. However much he ran, there was no place for him, and he was
much too energetic to wait patiently till someone died. In fact it was
he himself who was slowly expiring – from frustrated ambition, for
whenever something really good broke he was left in the office and
nobody ever said, 'That's the man who wrote such-and-such a thing,'
but they just shamelessly introduced him: 'This is our young whippersnapper. Runs like Nurmi – a great runner. Does he write, you
ask? Yes, he does that too. I must once have seen something by him –
in the wastepaper basket.' Yes, ambition was killing him. Sometimes,
at night, he would scurry through the dark town imploring heaven
to let something happen right in front of him – it couldn't be too
extraordinary or too horrible. But nothing, not even the smallest
item of news, ever did. Then he was overcome by a feeling of

terrible apathy. The whole world might collapse but the place where he was standing would remain unaffected, he was sure of that.

So when his cousin rang up about the crazy cabman who wanted to drive to Paris, he said: 'What these old chaps think of! Going by cab's nothing. Now if he were using a scooter! Well, all right, send him up.' Inwardly, however, he felt some excitement. That could be something. That could be something really big – the chance of a lifetime! Article on Berlin Humour? Oh no! Nothing in that. What mattered was the chap himself. Anyone could produce crazy ideas but it was the man, not the idea, that mattered. The man had to believe in his craziness and not find it crazy at all and, what's more, be man enough to carry it through.

Grundeis, having had a look at the man, carried him off to an empty room and got his claws into him. First he got him to talk, and when the old man was completely squeezed out, and had said all he had to say for the third time, then Grundeis brought forth all the objections which occurred to him, dwelling on difficulties, picking the idea to pieces, in fact crying down everything. And was watching his victim.

Grundeis looked at the old man as a journalist. How would he photograph? Had he got it in him to become a popular character? Could he make a speech? Had he a ready sense of humour? How would he behave in a difficult situation, at a reception or banquet, or if an axle broke? Was his health good?

But most of all he was concerned to discover whether he had endurance, or was easily influenced by other people's opinion, if he was sound, and especially whether he was enamoured of his project.

And when old Hackendahl to the tenth objection merely replied stubbornly: 'That's what you think, young 'un, but it ain't so difficult; at that stage everything'll go like clockwork,' then he was convinced that he had found a man of the requisite tenacity – in other words Iron Gustav himself.

'Good,' he said. 'I'll think the matter over then. It's not quite so simple as you believe, Herr Hackendahl. Come again in a week's time. And the main thing at present is not to tell a soul.'

They looked at one another and both grinned. 'That chap in the

travel agency probably told you I'd a screw loose, eh?' said Hackendahl very pleased with himself.

'Yes, those young people who've seen nothing of the world like
we have!' smiled young Grundeis.

With that they parted on the best of terms, old Hackendahl sure
that his troubles were over. For Grundeis, however, trouble had just
begun. He had got hold of something good – he felt that in his
bones – and it might become something big. But there was a snag,
and a bad snag. Grundeis was only a junior, that is to say, a nobody.
And a nobody cannot pull off something sensational on his own,
however much he may consider it to be his. For that, Grundeis
needed the newspaper; not only its money but its connections, its
organization, its provincial correspondents, its Paris representatives . . . in fact the entire newspaper.

Those, however, who could set all this machinery in motion were
precisely his dear colleagues, that's to say the men in front, the envious brakes on others' ambitions. And once they came to hear about
the project they would either make a mess of it purposely or they
would handle the thing themselves and reward its discoverer with a
dry bone, such as the drive through Brandenburg. Grundeis, however, wanted the choice morsels – the start from Berlin, the frontier,
the reception in Paris and the return to Berlin . . . the whole story!

Unsuspecting Iron Gustav! If he wondered at all about Grundeis's
difficulties it was probably to picture him concerned with the passport and the postcards, or the housekeeping money for Mother and
the expenses for himself. Of the real extent and nature of Herr
Grundeis's difficulties old Hackendahl hadn't the slightest idea.

How can I get the stunt into my own hands? brooded Grundeis
day and night, and when he thought of passports and money, he
would say, like Father Hackendahl, 'That will all be all right, as soon
as I've got a grip on things.'

In this perplexity he thought of a man who was known in the
great newspaper building as 'The Pullet', the bird who laid the golden
eggs, a man highly respected and even more highly paid, who had no
other duty than to have ideas. He was the man of brain-waves – and
when editors and editors-in-chief were utterly desperate they would
run to him and moan: 'Nothing's happening and we've run dry. For

God's sake let us know what kind of an Easter number to bring out. What Carnival cover can you suggest for our popular weekly? We want something brilliant to arrest the falling sales of our magazines. What would people like best on the first page of the paper? – Have you anything that'll do for the housewife? – For little girls? – The young man? – Through our idiotic serial we've offended the professional honour of the barbers. What can we do to placate them? – Eva Lewa the film star has already been photographed front view, back view, from above, from below, undressed and with her clothes on. What can we do with her now?'

And in reply to all these questions The Pullet laid ideas and inspirations, usually on the spot, although sometimes there was a delay, and since the ideas were good and pleased the public, the eggs he laid were of real gold. If he cost money he also brought money in.

To this fat man lacking in all personal ambition the flaming redhead Grundeis now betook himself. He found him in the corner of a pub sitting dejectedly before a beer.

'Sit down, whippersnapper,' he said. 'And don't talk. I think I'm having an idea.'

Young Grundeis sat down, whispered an order for a glass of Pils and gazed respectfully at the great man, who now in any case didn't look like a happy man, for his face became ever more mournful. Gradually, he found ever more to moan about, shifted about in his chair, wiped his brow, groaned, threw what was left of his cigarette into his Pils, tried to fish it out again and then forgot it, because he was busy grabbing a little notepad out of his pocket .

Tall, remote and infinitely lonely, he looked at the young Grundeis, began to scribble, stopped, looked at him again, and put the notepad back in his pocket . . .

'I thought it was him,' he said, 'but it was nothing. I can't think of anything. I can never think of anything on Thursdays, and certainly not in a hole like this!' And he looked disapprovingly at the pub. 'Why do I always go where I can't think? Man is his own greatest mystery. Did you put the ash in my Pils, whippersnapper? What do you want? Fire away!'

Whereupon Grundeis told him about old Hackendahl's plan, and his own wish to have the story to himself.

'This stunt,' said The Pullet, and it sounded as if he had been thinking about it for the last ten years, 'will have to begin in a small way – just a paragraph. And let your cab start off on April the first or second so that if the public won't fall for it you can say it was only an April joke. But if they do, then you can follow it up and supposing they still like it you can splash it from Paris, front page, banner headlines, your own photo . . . And that's what you want, isn't it? – to see your own likeness in your own paper, where you feature so many pictures of honest and dishonest people.'

'So you think I should carry on? There's something in it?'

'Oaf! Do you think I'd waste my time sitting on addled eggs? Come on, pay my bill, and that'll teach you to ask my advice. I've had seven Pils and four cigars. Now we go to the director for some money.'

They returned to the newspaper building together, to Director Schulz. That was the man who had to endorse all money transactions, and he guarded his treasure like a hell-hound. Director Schulz was he who guarded the newspaper's wealth; the most wonderful ideas couldn't coax a smile out of him. 'But, gentlemen,' he would groan, 'that won't go down in the provinces. It'll cost us our circulation there. I wouldn't invest in that!' And if something else were suggested then he would shout: 'That won't suit my Berliners. I know my Berliners too well. And Hamburg won't want it either. Yes, giving money is easy, and earning it even easier, but keeping money is an art, gentlemen!'

The Pullet and Grundeis, then, went to this confirmed sceptic. By himself Grundeis would never have been admitted but The Pullet commanded great respect and so Grundeis slipped in with him.

'Dearest Director,' said The Pullet, 'this little red whippersnapper has had an idea . . . just the thing for the spring when it's getting warm and people cancel their subscriptions – it'll last the whole summer . . .'

'Don't talk,' said the director. 'I know you. Tell me what his idea costs.'

'A hundred thousand marks net,' said The Pullet calmly. Grundeis flushed; he had never counted on more than five thousand.

Director Schulz studied their faces suspiciously. 'A hundred thousand marks,' he said disapprovingly. 'Have you ever seen a hundred thousand marks cash down?'

'No, only on a cheque, dearest Director. Don't you remember the American film rights?'

'You're always digging up your petty successes. Eighty thousand will do just as well.' He scrutinized their faces again. 'I'm pretty well convinced that seventy will do the trick.'

'Say seventy-five, Director dearest, and I'll let you in on the thing.'

'I promise nothing. First I want to hear what it is and then I must ask the other Directors and then it has to go before the Board and after that to the editors in chief. What's the young man to do with it anyhow?'

'You've got to take him with the story – if it's not assigned to him then there's nothing doing.'

'Seventy thousand marks and still so young! Have you ever seen seventy thousand all together?'

'Yes, I have,' said Grundeis, 'and had it in my pocket too – during the inflation.'

A pale, thin smile appeared on the faces of the hardened pair. It was as if the sun had appeared for a moment in a snowy sky, or when a baby gives a first little smile when it is put on the breast after endless crying.

'Well, we can discuss it,' said Director Schulz. 'Sit down, gentlemen. Cigar? All right. Let's hope there's a love interest somewhere – there's a keen demand in that direction again.'

§ VI

The old year changed into the new and January became February but Gustav Hackendahl drove his cab as usual, sat beside his Blücher and watched him eating, brought his earnings home, sometimes a little, sometimes nothing – all just as usual – and said not a word. Had he wished he could have spoken of great schemes, now that all had been settled with the gentlemen in the newspaper office and he had even signed a contract – but he said nothing. At meals he would sit opposite his wife at the table with the oilcloth cover, chewing his food and watching – staring at her with his great big round eyes, which were more and more veined with red.

'Why do you look like that, Father?' she asked. 'What's on your mind? You're always looking like that now.'

'Nothin',' said Hackendahl peevishly. 'Jus' thinkin'.'

'But what d'you keep thinking about, Father? And at mealtimes, too. At mealtimes you should think about eating, otherwise the food won't agree with you.'

'I'm not thinkin' about anythin',' declared Hackendahl.

But he was. He was wondering all the time how to break the news to her about his journey to Paris, how to make it seem all right. Not that he was really afraid of being stopped – all his life he had done what he wanted – but he was afraid of never-ending laments and groans. He wouldn't find peace any more even to sleep.

So Hackendahl let things slide; they'd all know when the time came. And it would save him a lot of trouble if that time were as late as possible. Then they would have less time to chatter!

It was thus nearly March when Irma read a notice in the newspaper.

She read it with the greatest astonishment. Then she ran to her mother, read it aloud to her, and both marvelled. Only yesterday old Hackendahl had stopped his cab outside their shop and taken little Otto for a drive. And he hadn't said a word.

'It must be some mistake.' Irma was still staring at the newspaper. There it was, however, name and everything!

'Heinz is sure to know about it,' piped Frau Quaas. 'Men always stick together.'

'Heinz? He hasn't the slightest idea, I'm sure of that,' exclaimed Irma indignantly.

And now they disagreed over the question whether a man is truer to his father or to his wife, and as a result of this argument they rather lost the thread.

That evening as Heinz, coming home rather tired, sat down on his makeshift bed, Irma enquired somewhat aggressively: 'Tell me, don't you ever read the newspapers?'

'Why?' he asked, surprised at her tone.

'Didn't you see that?' asked Irma, pointing to a news item. It was merely an eight-line report, a typical Grundeis report – but it read:

OLDEST BERLIN CABBY DRIVES TO PARIS

> Gustav Hackendahl, at seventy years of age the oldest cabby in Berlin, will set out for Paris at the beginning of April. He will travel the whole way there and back in his hackney cab No. 7. From Paris we learn that the Cab Drivers' Guild is arranging a gala reception for the courageous Berliner, justifiably called 'Iron Gustav'.

'Well, if that isn't the limit,' said Heinz Hackendahl, staring at the newspaper as if he could not trust his eyes. 'It's impossible,' he muttered.

Irma looked at him critically, but however she looked at him, he definitely had no idea, so she had been right with regard to her mother. 'I thought you should know about it, Heinz!' she said cautiously.

Then lightning struck. 'You knew about it!' he shouted. 'Father had talked about it with you. Of course you knew – behind my back!' He was furious: 'And you call this a marriage!'

'If you please,' cried Irma, shocked. 'I had no idea. I thought that Father had . . . I mean, Mother thought . . .' But she preferred not to say what Mother thought. 'I wondered if it was an April fool's joke.'

'April fool!' he exclaimed. 'In these times! And in February. What are you thinking about?' He looked again at the paper. 'Perhaps,' he said more calmly, 'Father's fallen into the hands of one of those newspaper reporters. But it does sound a bit as if there's something in it. What shall we do, Irma?'

'Speak to your father,' she suggested.

'Yes, but suppose Father's made up his mind and these people are encouraging him? All they want is to make money,' he sighed. 'I don't grudge Father anything but it isn't the time for stunts like this.' And he cast a disapproving glance at the newspaper.

Irma was silent. An intelligent wife, where she is not of the same opinion as her husband and cannot persuade, keeps silent.

'Do have a word with your father,' she said once again.

'Yes, I'll do that,' said he, getting up.

He hurried and found his father in the stables.

Old Hackendahl glanced at his son, bent down again and diligently greased Blücher's hoofs. 'Well, Bubi,' he said finally, 'I c'n see all right what you've come about. Better hold yer tongue, though . . . Blücher's gettin' the sack – they said he couldn't last the journey. I'm havin' a new horse. It's a pity about Blücher, he was a good little beast. Quite diff'rent from the grey. You remember the grey, Bubi?'

Heinz was silent. So it was true! It wasn't just an April fool. His father really intended to drive to Paris.

Hackendahl, busy with Blücher's hooves, gave a sly look. 'Well, go on,' he said at last. 'An old man wants his fun – to be old's a melancholy business, Bubi – take it from me.'

'Those newspaper chaps'll diddle you, Father. They're not doing it for your sake.'

'No, no, Heinz, you needn't worry about that. I've a real contrac' with 'em.'

'A contract? What sort of contract?'

'Oh nothin'. On'y that I undertake ter make the journey ter Paris an' back in the cab, an' they defray all expenses an' gimme a new horse. I get five hundred marks for Mother, an' what I make on the sale o' picture postcards an' so on belongs ter me, an' no one but them's permitted ter write about me an' take photos. That ain't a bad contrac', is it?'

It was obvious to Heinz that his father was very satisfied with his contract. 'Father,' he pleaded, 'don't do it. Withdraw, say you're ill, say you don't feel equal to . . .'

'But why? Mother an' me'll be free o' trouble fer a bit. An' we c'n keep what I get for Blücher too . . .'

'But, Father, you won't be able to stand it. Think, at your age! Out in all kinds of weather!'

'Well I never,' grinned the old man. 'What thoughtful children I've got suddenly! Out in all kinds of weather. Funny you never tell me that when I do me rounds in Berlin.'

Heinz bit his lip. 'Don't go on with it, Father,' he begged again. 'You won't be able to stand it and you'll make a fool of yourself and the whole family . . .'

He stopped. The old man flung up his head so suddenly that even the black horse started.

'Whoa!' said Hackendahl. 'Steady now, Blücher, you needn't shy at every sort o' foolishness.' And to his son: 'What d'you mean by makin' a fool of meself? Can't I do as I like? Have I ever prevented you from makin' a fool o' yerself? I remember a time when you was always hauntin' a certain villa an' stayin' out whole nights. Did I stop you behavin' like a fool? So you leave me alone.'

He signalled angrily to his son. In his indignation he was once more the old Hackendahl of the barrack room and the thirty horses – neither age nor the times had broken him. 'Me make a fool of the fam'ly? I can think of some others – siblings of yours – who've made fools of the fam'ly in a very diff'rent way, draggin' its name in the mud. I know, Bubi, you're not to blame there, you're decent. But you didn't run to yer brother an' yer sister an' bark at them: "Stop makin' a fool o' yerself." You keep that for yer father.'

Gazing at his son, he shook his head.

'Don't stand around like that, Bubi. What's the point? Leave an old man to his pleasures. If people make fun of me, it shouldn't hurt you.'

'All right, Father,' said Heinz after a while.

'There you are, Bubi! I knew you're a reasonable chap. An' now do me a kindness fer once an' go an' make yer mother understand about this journey. She's guessed there's somethin' a foot but she dunno fer certain an' she'll listen to you. Be a good boy for once, Bubi, eh?'

§ VII

And February turned into March and April drew nearer; they had had time to get accustomed to the idea of the old man who wanted to make a long journey – incredible, but he betrayed not the least sign of excitement or hurry. Day by day he mounted his box in the search for a living and if he looked doubtful this was usually when his eye fell on the new horse, unaccountably called Grasmus. 'I dunno,' he would remark, 'he's quite a nice little beast an' willin', but two thousand kilometres! I dunno.' Checking the animal's legs, he would shake his head in concern.

In March, however, it suddenly looked as if it would all fizzle out; old Hackendahl fell ill, the first real illness of his life – influenza. For a long time he refused to believe that anything could be amiss with him but in the end he was forced to take to his bed with a high fever. 'Fancy this happenin' to me!' he groaned, his teeth chattering. 'Never bin ill before. An' now when I want ter travel fer the first time in me life! But I ain't giving in. Mother, give me a bit more tea! What more can I do? I'll do everything I have to – as long as I get to Paris!'

It was this illness which converted them to his plan. However ill he might be he still wanted to go to Paris . . .

'Heinz, you givin' the horse plenty o' exercise? Tell the butcher he c'n use him when he drives to the slaughterhouse. Grasmus mustn't get stiff joints. Oh, Lord, supposin' I won't be able to go to Paris after all!'

'You'll go to Paris, Father. Certainly you'll go to Paris,' said his wife, who had been so perturbed once at the very idea of the journey.

'You, young 'un,' grinned the old man, shivering and sweating, 'got the wind up, eh? Don't you worry! All me life what I've said I've said. Iron, that's me. Always have bin. Iron Gustav.'

'Perhaps we could publish a short notice,' said Grundeis wretchedly, 'about you being ill and making the journey a little later. What do you say?'

'No fear, there's no such word as "later" for an ole man! I'll start on the day appointed – you c'n depend on that.'

'But there are only three weeks to go,' moaned the unhappy Grundeis.

'Three weeks! That's all right; if I c'n get ill in a week I c'n get well in three, can't I? Fine thing if I couldn't! Don't cry for me, Mother. Don't cry and don't worry about me in Paris. You won't see me there.' And, quite satisfied, the old man laid his head on the pillow, smiled and fell asleep.

'He'll never make it,' groaned the red haired Grundeis.

'Father must succeed,' said his son Heinz, speaking from his heart. 'He must enjoy that pleasure.'

'I would have allowed him to go anyway,' sobbed the mother.

'He'll definitely make it,' said Irma. 'Nothing will stop him.'

Don't cry for me, Mother. Don't cry and don't worry, and you won't see me in Paris – and old Hackendahl chuckled in his sleep.

§ VIII

Outside the main entrance to the newspaper offices stood Cab No. 7, gaily decorated. A large notice on the back announced:

GUSTAV HACKENDAHL

THE OLDEST CABBY IN BERLIN

WILL DRIVE THIS CAB TO

BERLIN – PARIS – BERLIN

A band was playing. The inquisitive stopped, read the notice, laughed and went on. Grasmus, the chestnut, was trying to eat his garland, with only partial success. Of the driver himself there was no glimpse.

The driver was in the newspaper building and took his leave.

Director Schulz, shaking hands, wished him the best of luck. 'And remember how much . . .' He coughed. He had been about to say: 'how much we have invested in you', but, suddenly conscious of the festive gathering, he said instead: '. . . how much we expect of your strong constitution.'

'Nothin' wrong with that now,' said Hackendahl, unmoved. 'How about you an' a postcard, Herr Director? A groschen apiece.'

Trembling and pale, Grundeis was watching his protégé. What impression was he making? Oughtn't he to have trimmed his beard? Wasn't he overdoing the postcards? The old chap was setting out on his adventure carrying young Grundeis's good fortune and success; and of this he had no inkling whatever. He only thought of himself. There he was now, forcing a whole dozen postcards on the managing director, Klotzsche, and refusing to give him a discount. Yes, he was overdoing it. And what would it be like in Paris, too, with a foreign language and strange people? Oh, I wish I'd never let myself in for this, thought Grundeis.

But perhaps it wasn't so bad after all. They were all laughing, all looking in a friendly way at the old man in his blue greatcoat and white top hat. Perhaps the start-off should have been arranged on a much larger scale; there were not enough people waiting outside in the street – probably the others had taken it for an April fool joke. But The Pullet had been dead against laurels in advance. Grundeis, much more anxious than the central figure himself, perspired – turned pale, turned red.

Now he was being offered a bunch of flowers as well. (How would he behave?) It was the general director's secretary who was doing it – a very important personage! (He should have been warned. Oh, this ignorant fellow – impossible to warn him about everything that will happen to him on his journey.)

Gustav Hackendahl looked now at the flowers, now at their presenter. 'What should I do with 'em?' he asked. 'What do? My nag won't 'ave 'em. – You 'ave 'em!'

And now the flowers are with Grundeis.

Thank goodness. The first bit of jollification! Everyone is happy – the upper echelons chuckle, the lower echelons laugh. Excellent!

The Pullet approached, fatter and more cumbersome than ever. He shook Iron Gustav's hand, ceremoniously, as if offering his deepest sympathies. And what did the cunning dog ask – maybe in the hope of tripping him up?

'Parlez-vous français?' he asked.

And 'Yes!' answered Gustav Hackendahl, without turning a hair.

Roars of laughter.

Cheerfully the procession passed from room to room, accompanied by a splendid sale of postcards. The first expectant autograph hunter approached.

'What d'ye want, Frollein? What d'ye want? I, write me monicker? Whatever for? So you can write over it later that I've borrowed a hundred knackers off of you? Oh, no. Old Iron Gustav's not such a

fool! Here, Red-top, write your signature down here. You go better
with a young lady!'

Once again, things were good. No, he's really not stupid, old
Hackendahl – he knows what he's doing. He's not nervous, and
knows what's expected of him. No solemn ceremony, but a bit of
fun. People like to laugh and are grateful to anyone who makes
them laugh. Therefore, let's laugh . . .

'Wait a moment! Don't push, young man!' Grundeis was told. 'I'll
still get to Paris in time. My special train won't go without me. I
must just change some money . . .'

He emptied his pockets out, and the cashier had to count out
every groschen.

"That's good business. We've sold nearly five hundred cards. I'm
very pleased with you young people 'ere today. If I'd anything else to
do, I would give the job to you!'

He can't stop. He's in full bloom. A real Berlin card – born not in
Berlin, but in a village near Pasewalk – was having a ball.

§ IX

It was almost eleven o'clock when he mounted the box. Meanwhile,
Grasmus had completely destroyed the bunting. But there was no
time to rearrange it. The musicians were already cursing: 'Because
of your mucking around, our legs are freezing.'

A moment later the music burst forth triumphantly, the chestnut
gambolled, and Gustav, pulling off his top hat, saluted the laughing
faces crowded into the many windows of the newspaper building. In
the cab sat an honorary fare – no taximeter for him – one at whom
his colleagues gazed with benevolence and also envy.

Gustav Hackendahl turned round. 'Well, how'd it go off, Herr
Grundeis?'

'Splendid! Excellent for starters. I'll get you in the paper for sure.'

'Look at the people starin'! They're not starin' just because of the
music, but 'cos of me,' Hackendahl sighed. 'Sometimes life ain't at
all bad, Red-top.'

'I'd say so!'

'Actually I ought to get down at ev'ry turnin' an' sell a few post-cards. But it'd hold us up too much. Herr Grundeis, would it hurt you to hand out a few cards from the cab?'

'Don't you get too greedy, Herr Hackendahl. Remember you're not driving for a living now, you're driving for pleasure.'

'All right, jus' as you think. I hope it's goin' ter be a pleasure.'

By this time they had arrived at the Berlin Rathaus.

'Now then,' said Hackendahl, getting down from the box. 'Hand me out me logbook, Herr Grundeis.' He took the leather-bound volume. 'Yes, we'll feel diff'rent when we return and this book's full, what? Have a good look, boys! You c'n tell yer mothers you've seen the crazy cabby who's drivin' to Paris. Then they'll be happy that in Berlin mad people are still allowed to run around free. Now, come along, Grundeis.'

But Grundeis didn't want to go to the Rathaus.

'You are registered there already. I must do something else.'

Hackendahl had to go by himself. A town hall is not the same thing as a newspaper building; here in the Rathaus not the slightest fuss was made of Gustav Hackendahl.

'Logbook indeed! Well, hand it over! It all means more work. And that's the last we'll ever hear of you. All right – "At 11.35 on 2 April Gustav Hackendahl, cab driver, identified by his passport, presented himself here at the town hall of the city of Berlin and stated his intention of driving to Paris in his horse cab No. 7." In order, what?'

'Yes, I s'pose so,' sighed Hackendahl, somewhat disappointed by this reception. 'But when I return you'll wear a diff'rent expression.'

'Now then, off with you! We've no time for such nonsense. Here we have to work.'

'Go on!' grinned Hackendahl. 'Work? I thought you spent yer time scribbling!' And with that he left, for enraged officials are dangerous. 'Chaps like that!' he muttered. 'They're arf asleep. Wait till I come back.'

His anger subsided when he got down. Outside, however, a lot of people were standing about and the police had to clear a space for him. Grundeis, rushing up, leaped into the cab.

'Off you go!' he cried. 'But hold the horse in!'

And hardly had the cab started when there broke out a deafening honk, howl, screech all over the square; every car was hooting, apparently in rhythm.

'The Berlin drivers bring you a serenade,' bawled Grundeis into Hackendahl's ear. 'Listen! "And must I, must I leave my little hometown?"'

'Not on yer life,' shouted back Hackendahl. 'It's "The man who in God's favour stands". You c'n hear it distinc'ly. Why, where's yer ear for music?'

The noise was contagious. The trams rang their bells madly, boys whistled on their fingers, people yelled to one another, laughing. Snatches of the marches being played by the band mingled in the noise. Furious, the police ran to and fro shouting at the taxi drivers, who were the ringleaders.

Brandishing his top hat, old Hackendahl drove through the tumult.

Gradually the noise died away behind them. The band played another flourish. Hackendahl gave his brown horse a little touch of the whip. Grasmus broke into a trot, and Hackendahl, turning round, asked: 'Well, Herr Grundeis, how about it? You comin' with me? Up to the present you've bin me guest but from now on . . .' And he pressed the lever of the taximeter and the 'For Hire' sign vanished. And they drove through the town as in an ordinary cab. The old man had driven like that a thousand times. Now there was a bit of foliage on the car, and behind a sign people couldn't see or could only see too late.

'You have to get to Potsdam today, you know,' said Grundeis in a warning tone.

'Potsdam? I'm goin' to Brandenburg, Herr Grundeis,' said Hackendahl, contemptuous of any shorter distance. 'I'd definitely be late in Paris, if I already kipped down in old Potsdam.'

The chestnut trotted more briskly.

'He thinks he's going home. And you are going home, Grasmus, but then a little bit further. Ever heard of Paris, Grasmus? Nasty place! Horses are only supposed to get maize there, Grasmus!'

'Why exactly did you call the horse Grasmus? What does it mean?'

'I dunno. It was written on the seller's label.'

'Grasmus?'

'Of course! Have you got anything against it? It's made up of grass and mush.'

'Hold on, Hackendahl! I'm not feeling too good. Erasmus would surely have been better.'

'No idea! What does Erasmus mean?'

'Erasmus was a very holy man.'

'Ah, no, Red-top! Let's stick to Grasmus. Holy and going to Paris – you can't have that! Herr Grundeis, the cab don't look like makin' a sensation. Not a soul's lookin'!'

'They're accustomed to cabs here. As soon as you get in the country . . .'

'No, no, we have ter look the part. I know what I'll do.'

And, stopping outside the Widow Quaas's shop, he bought up her entire stock of flags and streamers. 'You'll have ter pay, Grundeis. It's expenses as per contract. Well, Frau Quaas, what about a dance like when Father-in-law married Mother-in-law?'

'Herr Hackendahl, you, as a serious man . . .'

'Not today. I'm travellin' today. I'm goin' to Paris. Heinz here? O' course not! T.t.f.n! – always on the go. Say hello to 'im, and tell him to see things change around here by the time I come back. Irmchen gone ironin'? Works like a Trojan! You c'n give her my regards as well. No, I can't wait any longer, I'm in a hurry ter get ter Paris. Fix those flags firmly, Red-top! They have ter last quite a while. An' every town I come to I'll buy a town flag as well. That'll look attractive. You got to have a feelin' for such things. Picture pos'cards! Who wants a pos'card of the mad cabby on his way ter Paris an' back? For a few groschen? A few groschen for a bucketful of baloney and whatever goes with it!'

'The man is beside himself,' piped the widow.

'Let's get on,' admonished Grundeis. 'You want to reach Potsdam today.'

'Brennabor, you mean, Red-top!' said Hackendahl. But he went nevertheless.

'Herr Grundeis,' he said as they approached his home, 'I do wish I'd got this business with Mother behind me. She thinks I won't be able ter do it. You'll never come back, she says – heavens, there she is!'

Yes, there sat Frau Hackendahl by the kerb on a sack of oats which was to be taken aboard, so to speak, as iron rations for Grasmus. And there was quite a crowd round her. And behold! Five or six other cabs were waiting there too. It's not as though it was the Red Town Hall. It's just Wexstrasse in Wilmersdorf. And quite all right too.

'Mother, what're yer doin'? Here in the street an' all!'

'What's it matter, Father, when you've brought us so into the limelight. There, eat something . . . Grasmus must eat, too, there's no doubting that.'

And Gustav Hackendahl, now a public character, sat in a corner of his cab and ate pigs' trotters, sauerkraut and pease-pudding, while Frau Hackendahl in the opposite corner wept and entreated him to keep warm, have plenty of hot meals and not drink too much.

'Oh dear, I shan't see you again,' she lamented.

Now and then, Gustav interrupted his meal and sold postcards. Grundeis, however, sat on the box, notebook on his knees, composing his first verse. It was perhaps hardly a poetic sight; not quite the place for a sonnet, an ode or a tercet. But he felt he was alive, involved in something indestructible. The old married couple in the cab behind him, with their wine and food, and their worries and talk of sweet nothings . . . (Of course, they'll cut out all my best bits!)

Finally, it was already past three. The cab moved off, westwards out of Berlin, towards Paris.

§ X

Cab No. 7 had driven through Berlin and was far away.

Many had seen it pass, had laughed and pointed at it, and had almost immediately forgotten it. Hardly anyone who was there on that afternoon or evening would have said: 'Did you see the old cabby who was setting out for Paris? The old chap's certainly got courage.'

The old chap certainly had. They had now left Berlin. Grasmus was trotting along happily. They were going towards Potsdam, and then were in Potsdam, at the police station, to have his arrival entered

in his log. 'You'll soon be fed up with it,' they laughed there. 'Where
are you putting up for the night?'

'Here, you mean? I only stay in the best towns. I'm drivin' on to
Brennabor.'

'Then you'll have to hurry a bit – give your horse a bit of wellie.'

'Will do, Chief Superintendent – and thanks very much. Here's a
pos'card; you c'n pin it up to prove you've had Iron Gustav here.'

He drove on. Twilight, evening, then night fell. He crossed the
River Havel and came to Werder. Only on a few occasions had he
driven as far as this. Those had been prosperous times, when such a
trip brought in twenty marks – and twenty marks had been worth
something then. On the way home everyone would be drunk and
you had to be careful not to get drunk as well, or you'd never bring
your cargo safely back. Well, he'd always got back properly – so far!

And when he now looked back, he saw a bright reflection of light
over Berlin, as if light were shining from the clouds onto the town.
Where he was driving, and also where he was driving to, was dark.
But he knew that he was not only driving away from the light, but
that he was driving towards another light, and one which was supposed to be even brighter than the one behind him.

In Berlin only a few were still thinking of him . . .

His wife sat at the window looking into the almost deserted
street. The gas lamps were burning, and only a few people were to
be seen. She had always been a tearful and discouraged woman but
tonight she was utterly wretched. She sat in her chair, the hours
crept on, and she would have liked to go to bed but she dared not,
and grew more and more unhappy. Nothing was actually different
from usual – Father had so often been out all night with his cab – nor
was it the feeling that there was no man about the house. No, it was
something sadder than absence or loneliness.

When the ride to Paris was first mentioned she had thought him
mad and had hoped that Heinz would manage to stop it somehow.
Then when Father fell ill she had believed it would all fizzle out . . .

And now it had come off, he had got his own way once more.
During the whole of her married life she could not recall a single
instance when he had not had his own way or she had not been compelled to yield. And that was something horrible, something utterly

wretched. She did not reproach him – he had always been good to her – nor did she wish anything to go wrong with his journey; no, she grudged him nothing. Only . . . she would have liked to have had her own way once in her life. She had joined up with the children against him and had never taken his part, and yet he had always won. A hundred, no, a thousand times he had been stubbornly in the wrong, and yet he had always got his way. How had that come about? Life was unjust.

She sighed. She sat there miserably, staring at the ever-emptier street. She hadn't put on the light, and sat in the dark – sat for ever and a day in the front room and never switched the light on. She just couldn't manage it.

This was one person thinking of old Hackendahl on his way to Paris.

Irma and Heinz were having supper. Otto, their child, was already asleep.

'Father was here with his cab,' Irma reported.

'So what did he say?' asked Heinz.

'I wasn't here. I was doing the ironing. He bought all Mother's paper flags from her and decorated his cab with them.'

'He was completely crazy,' squeaked Quaasin, already in bed, from the next room, which lay in the dark. 'He wanted to dance with me in the street! I've never seen him like that before.'

'Well, he was as good as his word,' said Heinz. 'It was perhaps quite right that we let him have his way.'

'Of course it was,' agreed Irma. 'Father's at last happy again.'

'But when he comes back? What'll he do then? Will he go on driving his cab, and where will his happiness be then?'

He broke off, deep in thought.

Such were two other people who thought about old Hackendahl.

The evening papers carried, of course, a short notice about the cab journey to Paris and back, so after all there were more than a few people still thinking about the old man. One or two of his former drivers: 'Yes, Mother, that's old Hackendahl, Iron Gustav we used to call him. I worked for him before the war . . . you remember? He had thirty cabs on the streets then and now he's doing a thing like that. Well, you never know, do you?'

Or Rabause, in charge of the horses belonging to a brewery. Though he was old now his memory was still good. There you are, he thought. He never stopped preaching to Otto about work and doing your duty, and now he plays the fool himself. If only Otto could know.

Or his daughter Sophie, the Matron. Smoothing down the news-paper, she thought: thank heaven I'm only known here as the Matron. No one knows my name is Hackendahl. It was lucky I got rid of him when I did. Obviously it's a symptom of senility. Heinz ought to look after him better; he ought to be in an institution.

No, taking it all in all, if the old man had known in what manner they were thinking of him in the big city he wouldn't have derived much satisfaction from it. However, things – whether small or big – are not achieved because of the belief others have in us, but only because of the belief we have in ourselves. If you believe strongly enough in yourself, others are bound to follow you. At some stage they will simply be there (and claim that they believed in you all along).

But there is one person who does in some sort believe in the old man. She who had been his favourite, so pretty and so neat – though not for many a long day – she now sat in a tavern in the Alexander-platz, not worrying tonight about earning money. That was not important. She had seen the notice in the newspaper and had been in the crowd that morning at the newspaper building; she had got a lad to buy her a few postcards. 'The oldest cabby in Berlin – Gustav Hackendahl, called Iron Gustav . . . Berlin – Paris – Berlin.'

Then she followed the cab to the Red Town Hall. She heard the car claxon serenade, and went beyond the cab to where the band playing music barred her way, and she heard it disappear at a trot. Her father had not seen her – but she had seen him and something akin to enthusiasm, akin to pride and confidence, had flamed up in her. Something that might have been expressed thus: it is all up with me but the old man is still alive; the old man is indestructible; he'll rescue us all.

God, how he sat up on that box with his great red-blond beard, how he laughed, cracked jokes with the young men, sold his postcards, and how he took the reins in his hands, and the horse responded immediately – he was inimitable, indestructible.

He'll rescue us all . . .

Something of that sort; no excuse for herself, no self-pity – things had gone too far for that. She was used up, finished. In a few months' time Eugen would be coming out of the penitentiary, a day for which she longed and yet trembled. At Brandenburg on the River Havel she would stand at the penitentiary gates hoping that he'd not reject her.

He was blind, yes, and she had lost her looks; she had no hope that she could prevent him from discovering this. In spite of blindness he would sense that she no longer represented an income for him, but had her work cut out to earn her own living. Nevertheless she hoped he would accept her. Yes, he'd find some use for her, he'd think of some way to make her of value to him – till she became of no value at all.

Well, it wasn't so important either way; the end was probably not far off. But she had lived to know that, despite everything, the Hackendahls went on. Though the branch might be broken the tree itself had not perished but was green, and this thought consoled her.

A man sat down at her table. He wasn't welcome – not tonight – but she dared not offend him, since she owed a small sum to the landlord. The man treated her to a liqueur and a beer, then another drink; he wanted to get her going – he himself was in full swing. But it was money wasted; the girl didn't liven up.

'That's my father,' she said proudly, showing him a card.

'Well, you're lucky,' he said, gazing foolishly at it, not quite understanding what all this was about – the tart and her postcard.

'Let's be happy!' he shouted. 'For the money I've got we may as well be more happy than sad. Come on folks, landlord! Chuck a groschen into the accordion! Come on, girl, get dancing!'

And because she was still staring at the silly thing he tore it in two, upon which arose a fight, a screaming and a scratching, and yet more screaming when a policeman took them both to the station.

This then was one other person who had thought of old Hackendahl on his journey. Not that it would have helped him much to know about it. Perhaps it was her thoughts, however, that made him, on entering Brandenburg, look up at the tall, gloomy walls of the jail, though Eugen Bast – his son-in-law so to speak – did not occur to him. Must be a hospital, he decided. Or was it a prison? Fancy a small town like that needing so large a prison! Well, you never knew. Everything dark already. I must make sure I get into town, otherwise I'll find no place for me and Grasmus. And it's damn chilly, like a cold day in May. My paws are frozen stiff. Oh, well. It will be warmer in Paris.

And on he drove.

There was one last person thinking of him, however, and this with all his heart and soul, full of the sincerest wishes for his welfare.

Young Grundeis could have gone home at five o'clock. His article had been set up long ago and was already in the page; indeed he had read through the galley and, as was to be expected from the ignorance and envy of his beloved superiors, there had been cuts of course. So that he might very well have gone home.

However, that was the one thing he could not do. He was too restless. He ran about the huge building, losing himself in dark, unused rooms; he disturbed night editors until they threw their blotting pads at him; he hung about the composing room hindering everybody; he got in the way of the men round the great rotary press which with a rush and a clatter was printing the morning edition, that edition which would serve up his first big article at Berlin's breakfast tables. The first article signed by his own name, Grundeis, printed at the bottom.

Didn't it look splendid? 'Grundeis.' There it was in print.

'Have you read it?' he asked the foreman casually.

'Don't stand around here, Herr Grundeis,' the man shouted. 'Read it? You expect a damned lot for the measly wage you pay. It's bad enough having to print your bourgeois rot without expecting us to read the muck into the bargain.' For the foreman belonged to another party, unfortunately, and only printed his adversary's stuff holding his nose.

So young Grundeis wandered on, thinking about the old man who, when Potsdam would have been quite far enough for the first day, intended at all costs to reach Brandenburg. Through the dark streets his own career and success were now bowling along in that cab, and should anything happen to the old man, however undeservedly, then he, young Grundeis, would certainly never be given another chance, not in this firm.

He pictured old Hackendahl falling ill (he had just been ill anyway) or run into by a car (such accidents happened every hour) or drunk (he had a suspicious-looking nose) or losing a wheel (the consequences would be endless) or transgressing some traffic regulation (and land-ing himself in jail instead of Paris) or the horse getting colic . . .

The more he cursed himself for his folly in imagining all this instead of spending the evening comfortably with a glass of beer and his colleagues, the more restless and lunatic he became. Why had he been fool enough to choose so exceptionally villainous a profession and, on top of all else, afflict himself with this damnable Paris exped-ition? Why couldn't he simply say: fate, do your worst?

He rumpled his hair, he rattled the change in his pocket; as if hounded by furies he rushed through corridors and rooms, and when he thought how long it would be before Herr Hackendahl had the grace to complete his journey, and that during all those days and nights he would be in this same state of anxiety – then he really felt he was going mad.

Be calm, he told himself. Calm down, my lad. A reporter has to keep cool. A newspaper man must be able to take notes at a murder without turning a hair. You show too much excitement, Grundeis. You must cool down.

He went into the editorial office, rummaged (how pleased they'll be in the morning!) among piles of manuscripts, picked out one, read half a page, said 'Bilge!' – took the next, read ten lines, and said 'Tripe!' The third he opened not at all, but groaned with anguish: 'Oh rot, oh bloody rot! Who'd be able to stand it?' But this time he didn't mean the manuscript . . . he had let that drop – and it had fallen into the wastepaper basket into which, as is well known, manuscripts never fall in well-ordered newspaper offices. Leaping up, young Grundeis – leaving the light on of course – rushed out.

Ten doors further along he looked for a timetable. Those words of his: 'Who'd be able to stand it?' had given him the hint that there wasn't the slightest need for him to stand it; at this hour there was bound to be a train to Brandenburg (Havel).

And of course there was. Like one distraught, although he had plenty of time, Grundeis rushed into the street and jumped into a taxi. 'Potsdamer Station,' he panted. Greatly impressed, the chauffeur reached the station in four minutes. Obviously the fare was on his way to a deathbed.

Grundeis ran to the booking office, raced up the stairs, stormed a still-empty train, settled himself in a compartment, jumped out again, went for a drink, bought a newspaper, jumped in again, out again, bought some fruit, jumped in again, out, in . . . And at last the train departed.

For an hour, for nearly an hour and a quarter, he sat imprisoned in this confoundedly slow train stopping at every station, Potsdam included. He had told Hackendahl not to go beyond Potsdam tonight, but age of course never listened to the wise counsels of youth; the man had set his mind on driving to Brandenburg – overdoing it the very first day! Gloomily he stared at his ticket. It told him that the distance between Berlin and Brandenburg was sixty-two kilometres, and he had arranged with the stubborn old fool to drive on an average thirty-five kilometres a day. His life's happiness had been entrusted to an idiot like that!

He was gripped by a feeling of profound despair. Everything was bound to go wrong. Everything he ever touched went wrong for sure. Already at school, his fat teacher had told him: 'Grundeis, you only have to know something and it's definitely rubbish.' And when his mother dressed him in his white suit with the blue sailor collar, and put him on the revolving piano stool so that he was sure not to get dirty before going out, who tried to make the stool go round, and did so till the wooden thread ran out and he fell to the ground with stool, tread and white suit?

Him. Always him! Nothing ever yet went right for him in this life. His motto seemed to be: 'Grundeis versus Grundeis'.

Dolefully he slunk through the dark and uneven streets of Brandenburg. Dolefully, timidly, he pressed the night bells at the hotels, waiting patiently and humbly till some half-awakened creature threw her 'No, not here' at him, when he would slink on to the next.

Hopeless indeed. If there was a bench, he would rather sit on it, be sorry for himself, and patiently await the only thing of which he was certain – his own collapse.

However, there was no bench. Instead, he happened upon a kind of nightwatchman, and this man informed him that the cab driver from Berlin had arrived and had been piloted by him to the Black Horse.

'A lively old boy but perished with the cold. Just around the corner, sir. I'll show you the way.'

Rather miserably, Grundeis ambled after his guide. The whole thing must be a misunderstanding, or else his competitors must have sent another cab driver out. His man must at least be in Potsdam, if he hadn't already fallen down a ditch in the road. He accompanied his worthy guide just so as not to disappoint him. He never even thought he would ever reach the Black Horse; he couldn't possibly pull a fast one on the competition! It wasn't remotely possible. Fat Willy from the evening paper was bound to be already there.

From the porch of the Black Horse Grundeis heard roars of laughter.

'The gentlemen are in splendid high spirits,' remarked the head waiter, and chuckled likewise. 'Our Berlin cab driver greatly amuses them!'

Hardly waiting to press a tip into his guide's hand, he burst into the bar parlour . . . and saw him sitting there surrounded by the local notables, an old man with a stately beard, his tanned face glowing with warmth and grog. 'An' I calls to the nag, me Blücher, Gee-up an' the bloomin' horse starts ter back, not half he didn't, gentlemen.'

And seeing him thus Grundeis felt the need to break out – he the only person who took a real interest in him – felt that he wanted to fling wide his arms and declaim: 'O godly old man, vessel of my longing and hope, sail happily to harbour!'

What he said was: 'Well, Hackendahl, managed it after all? You must be the most iron Gustav of all Berlin!'

§ XI

The old cabby was driving through Germany. April (wet, cold and stormy) had turned into warm, serene May. And the farther he got from Berlin, leaving behind the bleak, gloomy plains of the Mark, and approaching the merry Rhineland over the provinces of Saxony and Hanover, the more tempestuous and enthusiastic did his welcome become.

In Magdeburg it had been regarded as little more than an attempt to set up a record, and a speedometer was presented to him and was attached to his cab so that this record could be established – the record-breaker, old Hackendahl, meanwhile wondering if Grasmus would stay the course. And in Hanover it had been an affair of endurance, nothing more. Rainstorms chilled and soaked him. Will I be able to stick it? was his secret anxiety. Gratefully he received the gift of a mackintosh.

April, however, had turned into May. Dortmund and Cologne approached. People became more relaxed and happier. The record-breaking drive, the affair of endurance, became a triumphal procession.

Criers went through the villages, swinging their bells and proclaiming: 'Tomorrow the Berlin cabby drives through here on his way to Paris. Receive him, welcome him, honour him.'

And they received, welcomed, honoured him. On that day no peasant took his team to the field, the schoolchildren were given a holiday and they and their teachers lined the road, waving flags, while small girls with nosegays anxiously repeated to themselves the verses they had learned to welcome the strange old traveller.

Dusty, but covered with flags and decked with flowers, his cab rattled through the cheering village. The old driver sat on top. People waved to him and cheered him; more verses were recited, greetings pronounced and equine libations poured. Everyone felt highly honoured when the old man descended and took his meal at the village inn, while the chestnut, tied to a ring before the door, nuzzled an abundant feed of oats. They thought up special gifts for the driver. They couldn't exhaust their surprises for him. During the meal, his cab would be thoroughly greased by the most respected of the villagers, and Grasmus newly shod at the smithy.

As in the villages so in the towns. Hackendahl's entries into Dortmund and Cologne resembled the triumphant processions of victorious generals. Overnight the unknown cabby had become an almost legendary figure whose every word was greeted with laughter, whose every anecdote passed from mouth to mouth. In the city of Dortmund a hundred and fifty thousand people assembled in welcome and the entire police force was called upon to regulate his passage, notwithstanding which the traffic was brought to a standstill. And, so that the telephone girls could at least glimpse the old man from their windows, no calls were accepted at the exchange for two minutes. The local cabs provided an escort and outside all the inns stood landlords with foaming glasses of beer or bowls of wine. Inside the cab were gifts of cigars, wine, liqueurs, great cheeses, tubs of pickled herrings, while bouquets covered the back seat. One determined man suddenly drew a rope across the street so that the traveller had to stop outside his house.

Old Hackendahl showed himself equal to everything. Grundeis was lost in amazement. He, the successful one, who couldn't send in enough articles about the triumphant journey, watched a man even more successful. Such enthusiasm he would never have expected even in his wildest dreams.

But not the self-assuredness of the old man either. He always did what the people expected of him, or at least the people were always delighted by whatever he did.

When he went past Cologne Cathedral, and the people looked at him and expected him to do whatever he could, what in heaven's name could an old cab driver do in front of thousands of people, when he drove past Cologne Cathedral? He looked at the cathedral, then at the crowd, at the cathedral again, and then the expectant crowd . . . then he stood up and waved his glossy top hat – mother's milk jug – and shouted: 'Long live Cologne Cathedral!'

And everyone cheered. Everyone was delighted.

However, when a publicity-minded iron factory solemnly presented him with four brand new horseshoes for Grasmus, he looked at them and then at Grasmus and at the boss in his frock coat, shook his head and said: 'No, take 'em away. They don't fit Grasmus. He needs much smaller shoes!'

Then he pressed the iron shoes into the boss's hand and drove off.

And once more the people cheered and were again delighted.

What did they see in him that made them so delighted, that in town and country they poured in to see him, and found everything he did so wonderful? They worked themselves into ever bigger displays. Why did they do it?

Well, here was a man of seventy who had undertaken something which would not be easy for a man of thirty or forty.

But it was not only that.

Well, here was one of the last cab drivers. In his person a dying era travelled through the land. In him they cheered what their fathers had been.

Certainly. But there was more than that in it.

After prolonged hatred people were beginning to feel friendliness towards the 'sworn foe' beyond the Rhine, towards whom Hackendahl was travelling. He went to the French like a consoling angel, and they rejoiced in him – but that was not all. In him they were acclaiming their own indestructible will to live. This old man, from the middle of the last century, had been through it all. You only had to look at his face, lined like a ploughed field, repeatedly sown with new disappointments, worse defeats and bitter deprivation. But the eyes were bright, the lips ready. Whatever had happened had been unable to change him; he was truly Iron Gustav and had not forgotten how to hope. Even though ninety-nine of his plans had miscarried, the hundredth might still succeed. We travel. We laugh. We never give up hoping. Maybe we will fall into the mud one day, but we don't have to stay there. We mustn't give up if we do fall. On we must go.

Thoughts like these stirred the crowds to acclaim him.

But how was he affected, the old man, who, from the quiet obscurity of a completely private life, suddenly found himself at the centre of a whole people?

He did not lose his head. He was neither megalomaniac nor intimidated. He was far too sensible for that. He had never been a dreamer. 'Lor, the people!' he said. He didn't understand them or their enthusiasm. On the sly he fed their bouquets to Grasmus and sold their gifts to the people he stayed with; and he never forgot about selling his postcards. Too often things had gone badly with him; now that he saw a last chance of scraping together a bit of money for himself and Mother he took it. One mustn't be

squeamish about making money out of anything that amuses
people, and indeed it never entered his head to be squeamish. (And
this in its turn pleased people.)

But he was not so thrilled as they were. After all, he carried the
responsibility of the journey and really was old. For one thing, the
farther he went the closer came the frontier, a strange people, a foreign language – it secretly made him uneasy. But he didn't breathe a
word of this to anyone, including to the solidly red Grundeis. The
more enthusiastic people were, the more impossible it was for him
to go back.

And he was already homesick for Berlin. He hadn't ever left the
city since his early adolescence. And the Berliners, their ways of
thinking and talking, their streets and squares, the stands for the
cabs, the police – all that had become the air he breathed, the nourishment for which he now longed. Once, when they struck up some
Berlin hit song about Unter den Linden coming into leaf again, he
had to run into Grasmus's stable to hide his tears – he who could not
remember ever having wept.

But this passed, and what remained was the applause. He drove
through it all. He was old; he looked at it from afar. Dimly he felt
that it acknowledged the purpose in his life. Despite his descent from
employer to driver, despite the failures with his children, the wreck-
ing of his hopes, and despite the fact that they were young and he
old, they cheered him, cheered him because he had carried on,
because he was of iron, because he had never given in, even when
things had gone badly.

They had affirmed his life, and he theirs.

They had cheered him – and he had driven on.

And now he was nearing the border.

§ XII

At Diedenhofen he, for the first time in his life, left German soil. And
lo! There he was again, Grundeis, the young fellow from the newspaper. 'Well, Father Hackendahl, today's the day, what? Can I report
that we're crossing the border?'

'Yes, why ever not? Of course! What the devil else?'

'You're not afraid? You won't see me again before you have reached Paris!'

'Afraid? Afraid o' what? Nobody'll bite me. But I have ter ask you ter buy me a curry-comb an' a horse brush an' charge it to expenses.'

'Why, is it going to be as bad as all that?'

'Lor no! But the last village where Grasmus an' me put up for the night the pigs ate 'em. Scoffed 'em up, that's the livin' truth! You feed yer pigs in a damn funny way here, I told the people: if you ever slaughter that pig, I told them, you needn't give me any of it.'

Laughing, Hackendahl drove towards the little house with the French soldiers and Customs officers. There was no question of nervousness – he had shown that young man.

'Bonjour!' he said to the French, after long and careful preparation.

They laughed. 'Guten Tag,' they replied. 'Guten Tag.'

Grundeis was watching from the barrier. And had immediately to intervene, for linguistic abilities were exhausted on both sides. Customs duty also was not so easy to arrange. A sum of money had to be deposited as guarantee that carriage and horse would leave France within six months at the outside. Undertakings had to be signed, and Iron Gustav shouted over the barrier, 'If I kick the bucket before then you'll have ter bring the cab back yerself, Grundeis.'

'I'll do it. But you're immortal, Hackendahl.'

And Grundeis watched the cab roll on into France. Grundeis was no longer a newspaper apprentice. He had shot up like a shooting star. Someone else must now write the little fillers . . .

However, compared with what had to be achieved, little had been. Grundeis prayed fervently that the old man would reach Paris. The Paris reception, his articles about Paris, would outstrip anything ever written. If only we get to Paris! Please! Please! Grundeis begged fate, staring at the cab disappearing into the distance.

Hackendahl drove on and on. One needn't have worried. The people here were Lorrainers. They spoke German. They would understand him. None of the jubilant receptions that there had been in his own country of course – all took place in a minor key as if the war lived on here ten years after it had finished with greater might than in Germany itself, which was said to be the vanquished.

Not alone in the faces of the inhabitants did Gustav Hackendahl see how much more present the war was from Conflans-Insray to Châlons-sur-Marne. For days on end his cab rolled over battlefields, through shattered villages, between unending cemeteries. Verdun. Once that name had been mentioned every day in the newspapers of the world; that place, Verdun, was etched in the hearts of all as the site of unparalleled striving and sacrifice. And now it was only a townlet of twelve thousand souls. But around the living still dwelled the dead. Five hundred thousand graves now threatened the dwellings of twelve thousand living souls.

He drove on. Day after day. By now he knew that the black crosses were German graves, the white crosses the French. Cemeteries lined the roads. Wherever he looked the graves spread over hill and valley. And how many black crosses there were!

It was inevitable that he thought of Otto, who had once been his son. He too had fallen here, was resting in this foreign soil . . . And he tried to recall the place. Many were the names impressed on his memory by the war communiqués – Bapaume, Somme, Lille, Péronne . . . But the name of Otto's burial place he could not remember – if ever he had known it.

Sometimes he stopped Grasmus and, climbing awkwardly from the box, over the ditch, went into one of the cemeteries, any one, and walked along the endless intersecting alleys, it did not matter which. Occasionally he was approached by gardeners who tried to discover what grave he was seeking, but he shook his head. His son had never been so dear to him that there must be an individual grave for him to find . . . All of them lying here were much younger than he when they had to die. He was infinitely older than them. And now they had become immortal, and he was still mortal. And he almost wanted to ask why?

As he stood there, tourists came past him in droves, led by guides, speaking in all languages. And when he drove off again, the cab swaying along the grey ribbon of road, great charabancs raced past packed with English and Americans, their guides trumpeting through megaphones. In bands, or solitary, the inquisitive drifted by, the mourners, the vacant, the ones absorbed by their grief . . . The widow's veil still caught the breeze, mothers still knelt at the graves of their sons.

He drove on and on. He drove through ruins, artificially preserved ruins, because the tourists should have something to look at other than graves. On the signposts it says: 'To the battlefields'. And, so that the mourners could stay near their dead, hotels had risen alongside the cemeteries, near ground that was still being combed for weapons and shells; and dead bodies were still being found, skeletons which entailed the further enlarging of the cemeteries. By the wayside squatted hawkers selling pencils, vases, and ashtrays made from cartridge- or shell-cases. Here there was no ploughing, sowing or harvesting done – for the dead supported the living, supported an entire province which lived on a war that was over and yet not over.

Here the people did not prepare a joyous reception for Hackendahl. They scarcely looked back at the Berlin cab – they were used to the oddest figures, visitors from all over the world, sightseers from Australia, mourners from Asia, dark faces from Africa.

In the inns, Hackendahl had to muck in like any other visitor. It was often difficult to find a stable and food for Grasmus. He had to pay like everyone else.

Frequently he met Germans and they nodded to him. Yes, one had read about the old man. And how long had he been on the road? Well done! Yes, and now they had to move on, they had to look for their dead. It was so difficult to find a particular man among all these graves so alike. Had he anyone here? A son? Yes, of course. Hardly a family had been spared. Had he found the grave? Well, he'd find it all right; the people here readily answered enquiries.

However, he didn't look for it any more. What did it matter now? thought Hackendahl. All graves look alike. Dead men were all alike. His sadness came from the infinite number whose courage and sacrifice had resulted in nothing but collapse, misery and strife.

Slowly he drove on. Never before had he felt so old and worn-out as now, an old man still living amid the millions of young men long dead.

§ XIII

On 4 June, two months and two days after his departure from Berlin, Gustav Hackendahl made his entry into Paris, and Paris, repeating the enthusiastic welcomes of Germany, received him like a prince. The jubilation of his journey through Germany repeated itself. The Parisians could not do enough to honour the old man. The streets were full to overflowing; the cab drivers hailed their Berlin colleague; the Paris students unharnessed Grasmus and pulled the cab in triumph through their city. Enthroned on the box was old Hackendahl and in the seat of honour at the back sat young Grundeis.

Everything was joyous, vibrant, intoxicated. It wasn't like that in Germany! Here, they didn't greet an old man who had survived bad times without losing courage; here it was like a game between brothers. What was celebrated was the journey itself, and a foreign people. There were splendid banquets; some dignified, some lively; Grundeis had been hard at work. Reception at the Embassy, reception by the Anglo-American Press, addresses of welcome. And also light-hearted student feasts. The presentation of the Order of the Golden Horseshoe to be worn on a chain round the neck, with Grasmus permitted to stand in the large hall and look on, a many-course dinner of oats meanwhile served to him in a porcelain manger . . .

Hackendahl blossomed out. The melancholy of old age vanished, his fame shone anew. He composed the couplet: 'What Lindbergh accomplished with his aeroplane, Gustav with his cab brought equal fame.'

But he was outdistanced by Grundeis, photographed sitting in Cab No. 7, with this caption: 'How do you get from Berlin to Paris? Take a cab!'

Laughter, cheers, excitement. Bouquets – two hundredweight of them – in the hotel bedroom. Present upon present. Souvenirs for Frau Hackendahl. Regiments of champagne bottles. A flight for the seventy-year-old in an aeroplane. He took part in everything with unquenchable good humour.

How about something special? Something quite special?

So, at a very convivial lunch was born the idea of a race between the oldest Berlin and the oldest Paris cab driver. The course to be three hundred metres long.

Splendid!

Splendid? There were doubts. Who would win? Who should? Susceptibilities were so easily hurt. Was the German to vanquish the Frenchman in the capital of France itself? Impossible! But was it permissible to defeat a guest of seventy years of age who had just performed so blameless a feat? Equally impossible!

Endless deliberations. Schemes. Missions. And at last the solution, sealed by vows of strict secrecy, the opponents bound on their word of honour to arrive simultaneously at the goal.

'Understand, Hackendahl, we can't do it otherwise. Don't embarrass us! Rein in Grasmus! Think of our ambassador . . . the French nation . . . there could be tensions which might harm diplomatic relations which have officially improved a little . . . Don't you see?'

Hackendahl understood. He gave his word of honour.

The other gave his word of honour too.

The Champ de Mars is roped off. In their thousands the spectators are kept in order by the police, including many students with their girlfriends. As the two competitors drive up in their ancient vehicles everybody breaks into a cheer. The one raises a black top hat, the other a white top hat. Then the two cabs draw up side by side. Hackendahl's opponent has a long-legged white horse. Betting favours Germany . . .

'You remember what you promised?' Grundeis once more implores Hackendahl.

'You should have talked ter Grasmus, Herr Grundeis. He's frisky. They give him so much to eat and he's hardly left his stable. I can barely hold him in.'

'Don't let us down, Hackendahl, I beg of you.'

'I'll do what I can, Herr Grundeis. You c'n depend on that.'

Both drivers are handed a glass of champagne. They wave to one another. Reaching over from their boxes, they shake hands. Grasmus sniffs his rival, not so much out of curiosity as out of greed – he would like to eat the other's garland. But the white horse flattens his ears and bares his long yellow teeth.

Cheers.

The starting shot rings out. 'All right, off you go, Grasmus,' says Hackendahl, holding the reins tight, so that the chestnut shan't get away too quickly.

The Frenchman is also holding back his horse. Each driver keeps an eye on the other so as not to get in front, but equally so as not to be left behind; the race couldn't be slower.

Laughter and shouts, cries of encouragement . . .

I don't trust him, thinks Hackendahl, his eye glued on the Frenchman. Later on he'll sprint an' I'll win second place. Take it quietly.

The enemy thinks just the same and thus there ensues a competition in slow motion.

Cries . . . 'Get on with it! Foul play! Put-up job!'

Grundeis, red in the face, appears beside the cab. 'Get on, Hackendahl, you'll have to get a move on. Drive, man!'

'I don't dare. Once Grasmus starts . . .'

'Trot, just trot, Hackendahl, I beg you.'

'There he goes!' A student has thrown his cap at the eyes of the white horse, which gives a surprising bound and then races forward at full speed.

'Scoundrel!' cried Hackendahl. 'Cheat!'

Grasmus now feels the whip. Hackendahl is standing up. 'That's certainly not the bet we took. We Germans are damned if we'll let ourselves be beaten by you lot! Go on, Grasmus!'

Blow on blow, from Hackendahl, from the Frenchman. Forgotten is the plighted word. The drivers urge on their horses, the people urge on the drivers. 'Come on, Hackendahl,' Grundeis shouts, 'Germany to the fore.'

And his antagonist, the other contracting party to a word of honour, shouts furiously in Hackendahl's face: 'Vive la France! En avant la France!'

'Germany!'

'France!'

'Come on!'

'Faster, Hackendahl. Give it him!'

How the old cabs jog and sway! With what courage they rush

along, the horses straining at their harnesses, the drivers standing up flourishing their whips! The chestnut gains ground, the white horse slackens . . .

'Don't you see, you lying oaf!' shouted Hackendahl angrily.

Now they are neck and neck, the winning post at hand . . . The white horse has had enough, the chestnut's going to do it, Germany will win the race . . .

Crash!

The two drivers, with eyes only for one another and not for the track, have collided. Wheel locked in wheel, they sway, are about to fall and save themselves by clinging each to the other.

And so, thus embracing, they pass the winning post simultaneously, faithful to their pledge.

§ XIV

Before Gustav Hackendahl again approached his native Berlin it was autumn. The reddish beard had turned grey; his top hat, white on its departure, was now entirely covered with autographs and stamps, and looked a dirty black. The man himself, too, was hardly recognizable. Full of amazement young Grundeis walked round him. 'Gustav, man, how you've changed! You've become really slim.'

'Two stone I've lost. Mother'll go on about it. She never did like the idea o' this journey.'

'But it couldn't have been the food, Hackendahl. You've been treated like a prince.'

'The food! Oh, it's the everlastin' people! Lor', Herr Grundeis, I can't tell yer how sick I am of people. I don't want ter see any more of 'em. Wherever I could I've gone round the other way. Always cheerin' and always Iron Gustav . . . And what's it amount to in the end? Nothin'! A flop!'

'Now wait a minute, Hackendahl!' Grundeis became energetic. The reception in Berlin, which was to be the climax, appeared in danger, so tired and bad-tempered, so worn-out was the old man. Grundeis therefore spared no pains. Hackendahl was just travel-sick and that was understandable. But he had achieved things – if he

didn't think so, let him have a look at the newspapers. The whole of
Berlin was looking forward to welcoming him.

'Lor, the Berliners, they always want ter see the latest. Show 'em a
monkey painted green an' they'll run after it jus' as they do after me.'

'Rubbish, Hackendahl. You know quite well what you've
achieved – the great things you've been able to do in the last months!
And you won't have to worry about your old age.'

'Bother me old age. What do I care about it? I'll be glad to be
drivin' me cab again. Properly – as I used ter. Incogniter, you know.
I'm sick of cogniter.'

'Hackendahl, old fellow, Iron Gustav, where's your iron gone?
Have a look in the papers at the programme of welcome; you'll
change your mind then.'

Hackendahl shot an angry glance at him. 'Don't you talk about
newspapers ter me. I'm on bad terms with newspapers. The stuff
they write about me!'

'What stuff? What have they written about you?'

'Don't let's talk about it. But it knocked me properly.'

'Well, what is it? Out with it, Hackendahl.'

'I'm s'posed to have become too big a swell for a cab, I'm s'posed
to have come back from Paris in a car, that's what the dirty dogs have
written about me. Not you, but the others. I'll tell you how it was.
I'd settled down to a beer an' the boys didn't want ter let me go. An'
so another driver offered to take me cab along for me so's I needn't
miss me drinks an' we all followed later in a car. An' now I'm said to
be too stuck-up fer a cab. Me who was two hours in a car and over
five months in a cab! That shows how hateful people are. You ain't
got the heart to do anythin', it's not appreciated anyhow.'

Young Grundeis felt like laughing and crying over an old man
who was not so much tired as suffering from wounded vanity. The
old man was behaving just like a boy, he sulked. But this was no time
for laughing or crying. The great reception in Berlin – for which they
were keeping the front page open for him – was at stake. In his present mood Iron Gustav was capable of showing his iron will by
sneaking off home, leaving the people to wait for him.

So Grundeis talked with the tongue of men and angels, soothed
the old man's wounded vanity and at last succeeded in cheering him

up, not with the lure however of the great honours in prospect, the bands, the banquet, the toasts, or the reception by the mayor, but with the reminder that his expedition would end up at the place he had started from, that town hall where an official had most unamiably stamped the first entry in the logbook. This thought consoled him enormously – it would be the finest event of the whole trip.

'Grundeis, you're right. I'd be a fool to let the fellow off. Snap at me about work an' foolin' around! I'll show him. I pay rates and taxes, don't I? Well, he's livin' on me, that chap. I'll show him how to treat me. Yes, I'm lookin' forward to seeing *him*.'

§ XV

And it would indeed have been a pity if Hackendahl's mood had deprived him of his Berlin welcome. The Berliners had read how their citizen had been received in Dortmund and Cologne, in Paris and Magdeburg, and they, of course, couldn't be behindhand. Quite naturally therefore they overdid it somewhat. Three hundred thousand people, not one of whom would have dreamed of spending even a mark on the cab six months before, were on their feet for half a working day waiting for its driver, while the police were out in full force for the purpose of regulating traffic and keeping the crowds in order – it was really a fine sight. Old Hackendahl would have been sorry afterwards had he gone home by another route.

As it was he drove right into the midst of it. The Charlottenburger Chaussee was black with people. At the Grosse Stern they formed a dense mass. Unter den Linden gave passageway only for one person and that person was Gustav Hackendahl.

Along he drove, up Unter den Linden – everybody cheering him. In his wildest dreams, in the days of his prosperity, he could never have dreamed that his native town would ever cheer him thus.

As he passed the French travel agency he stopped, made a gesture, stood up. The band ceased playing, he waved his top hat, then roared out: 'Vive la France!'

And they roared with him: 'Vive la France!'

Yes, cheers for the country which had received their fellow citizen so hospitably but, above everything, cheers for the fellow citizen. He's a splendid old boy, one of us, a Berliner – we're cheering ourselves when we cheer him. Magnificent, indestructible, immortal – we Berliners!

And Gustav Hackendahl drove on, past the Schloss. In the König-strasse the press became dangerous and if Grasmus hadn't grown accustomed to crowds it might have been serious, but they got through safely and drove up to the town hall.

In the same moment all the motor cars started their honking and wailing – this time no zealous Grundeis incited them to it, this time no indignant policeman interfered. Standing on his box, old Hackendahl's voice accompanied their honking. He had no trouble in distinguishing the melody. It was 'The man who in God's favour stands'.

Outside the town hall they were waiting for him. A mayor was there to welcome Iron Gustav and in a neat speech to honour this plain man of the people as a reconciler of two nations, and to pres-ent him with the ceremonial drink of the city.

Gustav Hackendahl was used to ceremonial drinks. He drained the goblet. But when they awaited a speech in reply, he merely said: 'Excuse me a bit, gentlemen,' and hurried into the town hall.

He ran along the corridors. Thank God he remembered the num-ber of the room. Yes, he had his logbook in his pocket. Well, he wasn't going to spare that fellow. You wait, me lad!

Ah, here was the door. He rushed in. What's this? 'Where's the chap who used to be here?'

'Whom d'you mean? What d'you want? What's the idea of rush-ing in like this? Lord, it's Iron Gustav! I know you from the newspapers. Well, this is an honour, Herr Hackendahl. What can we do for you?'

'I'd like to have me return to Berlin certified in this book. Yes, it's full now. But I'd like the same gentleman who was here at the time o' my departure. Isn't he here now?'

'Herr Brettschneider? Did you know him personally? Yes, a charming man . . . Unfortunately, Herr Hackendahl – influenza, you know – as long ago as May. He would come to the office – and six days afterwards, how shall I put it? – gone like that. A pity, don't you think?'

'A great pity,' said old Hackendahl, deeming it a pity indeed that his opponent had decamped like that. A bitter drop in his cup of joy. The human heart is strange – the whole of Berlin was there to cheer him, yet he missed one dead Berliner.

Then the drive went on. They were expecting him at the great newspaper building, where they wanted to celebrate the return of their successful traveller, which they duly did. Managing directors and directors, editors and sub-editors (among whom the now bright-red Grundeis now ranked), all were awaiting him, celebrating him.

And after the many honours there everyone went to a banquet of pigs' trotters, sauerkraut and pease-pudding – his favourite repast was set before Berlin's famous citizen, on whose right hand sat a film star and on whose left sat his wife. Yes, they had dragged Mother to the banquet, Mother who no longer went out anywhere. Clad in a new silk dress, she welcomed her Gustav tearfully. 'Thank God you're back, Father. People are knocking the house down asking after you. And they're all bringing things – the whole flat is full of paper and presents and cardboard boxes – where am I to put all the stuff? And yesterday, someone came who wanted to bring you a canary, some special breed, but I sent her packing. Who knows what she meant by it? "Who sings like a canary round here, that's our business, not yours," I told her. But I don't think you'd do that, Father. People are sometimes so nasty!'

But she was not the only one to make a speech that day. Director Schulze rose to his feet and gave an address which sounded as if it had been ordered from the same firm as the mayor's. Next rose Iron Gustav, to announce the toast: 'Berlin – Paris – Berlin. Thought out, done!'

Cheers and applause.

Further toasts, merriment, shaking of hands. Not only that. Opportunity was found to slip an envelope into old Hackendahl's pocket. No need now for the old man to worry overmuch about making ends meet . . .

It was night now and Frau Hackendahl was urging a departure, in anxiety about the flat and the many handsome gifts in it. There was a further argument too – they were bent on driving him home in a car, leaving somebody to follow on with Grasmus.

But no. With his old stubbornness Hackendahl refused to go by car. His wife, yes, she could if she liked but he'd drive home in his cab.

'Don't be so silly, Mother. If I got back safe an' sound from Paris surely I'll be able to manage the little stretch to the Wexstrasse!'

Naturally, he got his way. He saw her off and went to his cab. A couple of compositors helped him stow the garlands, the flags and streamers, the placard on the back of the cab, the presents, in one of the offices.

'I'll come an' fetch that stuff sometime. I want to rattle home incogniter. A proper cabby. I've had enough o' crowds.'

He set forth. At first he looked warily at people, to see if they recognized him, but it was night and all were in a hurry, they hardly glanced at the cab rolling slowly along the street.

How comfortable it was on his box. Nice to be driving through Berlin once again as a real cabby. Click-click went the taximeter – it sounded so homely. It was good that he had made that trip to Paris, but best of all was to be driving again down the streets – the old streets he had driven down hundreds of times before.

A policeman, whose profession gave him better eyes than the ordinary townsman, recognized Hackendahl and, remembering the honours of the morning, saluted him in army fashion.

'Hey,' called out Hackendahl, 'that's all over an' done with. D'you want to do that ev'ry day when I'm plyin' fer hire? I'd drop all that lardy-da if I was you.'

And, very pleased with himself, he drove on. If they thought he was going to give up driving now that he had a bit of money they were mistaken. Driving was the finest thing in the world; that is, driving in Berlin as a genuine driver, of course.

Now he had only one wish – and hardly had he framed it when it came true.

'Hi, driver! Help me get this hamper in your cab. To the Zoo! I wanted to go by tram but they told me the basket was too big. But don't make it expensive, driver.'

'No, no, it's not goin' ter cost yer a fortune. Well, gee-up, Grasmus!' And he drove to the Zoo very cheerfully indeed. His wish had been granted. Berlin had given him earnest-money that life would go comfortably in the future.

Now and then he turned round and stole a glance at his fare. Didn't he realize he was being driven by a famous man? But the fare, a weedy fellow much too small for his heavy burden, showed no awareness. Dejectedly he was staring into space, probably wondering how much the cab ride would cost him, and thinking how cheap the tram would have been. Well, he'll get a surprise!

It was old Hackendahl, however, who got the surprise.

At the Zoo Station he helped the little man lift his basket out of the cab. Then he asked, proudly happy: 'D'you know who's bin drivin' you? Well, you've bin ridin' with Iron Gustav, you know, who made the famous tour from Berlin ter Paris an' back.' And the little man replied: 'Oh, shut up! What do I care? Look after my basket for me, please, I must catch the train to Meseritz. Paris! The mere mention of the place! You just mind your own business! One mark twenty for just round the corner! Why, it wouldn't have cost fifty pfennigs on the tram.'

Here the sorely tried little man vanished; without batting an eyelid he left the famous cab driver to guard his hamper. And the people rushed past. They were in a hurry to catch their trains, they bumped into Gustav Hackendahl, but they did not look at him – they had practically forgotten him already – forgotten the famous Iron Gustav.

The Beer Glass

It started when he was helping his wife to tidy up the flat. The place was really inconveniently crowded by presents from all over the world, which the two old people untied and unwrapped and put away, and there was many a thing there that ought to have pleased Mother, yet did not.

'Do look, Mother,' said old Hackendahl. 'It's really a handsome beer glass the Pasewalk Cuirassiers have sent me with the barracks painted on it. You c'n almost see the room where I used ter live when you met me. Nice, ain't it?'

'Put it away, Father,' she said. 'What's the good of that to us? Nice! Why, the monkey in the Zoo thinks the carrot nice you push through the netting, but all the people want is to see how a monkey eats a carrot.'

'You mean me, Mother?' asked Hackendahl. 'Are you comparin' me with a monkey an' this beer glass with a carrot?'

'Don't start an argument, Father. I feel so strange in the head. I'm all confused. And then you go and talk of monkeys.'

'It's bein' in all day, Mother. You never go out now. Wait a mo, I'll harness up Grasmus an' we c'n go for a quiet drive in the Tiergarten. Now we c'n afford it, we may as well.'

'You do what you like, Father. I've always done what you've wanted, you can't deny that. For once I'd like . . .'

'Well, what, Mother? I c'n see you're not feelin' well . . .'

'Get out of the cab, Father. You won't do anything I'd like, you never did.'

'Well, speak up, Mother. What d'you like? I'll do it if I can.'

'You won't do it, Father.'

'Course I will. What is it?'

'Well, then – throw away that old beer glass from Pasewalk.'

'What, the glass the Pasewalkers sent me! Mother, yer can't really meant that. Yer can't be feelin' well. Shall we go fer a drive? Would yer like to, Mother?'

This sort of thing happened many times but the little trips into the fresh air did not cheer her up, and when he did her bidding for once it counted nothing against the many occasions when he had had his own way. Waking up in the night, the old man would stretch his hand out to the other bed. It would be empty, and by its coldness he could feel that it had been empty for some time.

Then he would rise, get a light and look for her. As often as not she would be sitting in the dark, sitting on the bed from which he had driven Erich. Or standing in the kitchen at the sink, with the tap turned on so that the water dripped over her hand.

'Come, Mother,' he would say gently, 'come back to bed. You'll get a chill.'

And readily enough she would go and lie down.

'What makes yer wander about like that, Mother?' he said in the end, having blown out the light. 'You still in a rage with me because of the journey ter Paris?'

'Something's pressing against my heart and then it rises. Then it comes down again and I think it's Otto. Do you remember Otto, Father?'

'I do, Mother. I remember him perfectly.'

'Sometimes I think it's only me who remembers we've had children and that I brought them up just like the other children – and now they're gone and nobody remembers anything about it, nobody at all.'

'Only Otto is dead, Mother. All your other children are alive.'

'And why I let the water drip on my hand . . . no, Father, I can't explain it to you . . . I don't know myself. But I can't get away from the feeling that they've given Otto a bad coffin made of rotten wood, Father, and the rain's dripping on his face. And so I hold my hand in between so that I can do something for him, Father.'

After a long while old Hackendahl said: 'You must have dreamed it. Otto's at peace, he sleeps soundly, Mother. There's no rain can disturb him.'

And a little later: 'Tomorrow I'll fetch the doctor, he mus' give you a prescription. You've got water in yer legs, Mother. That's pressin' against your heart and gives you all those ideas which are out o' the natural. You mustn't take any notice of them.'

'Just as you like, Father.'

So the doctor was sent for and confirmed what old Hackendahl had said – there was water in the legs and it was rising. He prescribed drops which helped for a while, and when they were of no further avail, then he tapped the water. That gave her some relief, and when the young people came (as they did rather frequently now), she couldn't recount too often how much water the doctor had taken away – it became a little more every time.

'Well, Father, what d'you think?' said Heinz one day in the passage, on his way out.

The old man shook his head and looked at his son. But he said nothing.

Heinz made up his mind. 'Shall we look in again after supper, Father? The doctor thinks . . .'

'Leave me alone with her,' whispered the old man hoarsely. 'What's got to be done with Mother I've got to do, you understand? You children never think that she was a girl once and me young wife. You always think of her as Mother.'

He was gazing fixedly at his son, his eyes gleaming as though they were about to fill with tears. But those old eyes would not weep whatever the circumstances. 'I'm seventy, Bubi, but when I think what she was like as a girl!' And he pushed his son out of the door. 'Leave me alone with her when she dies. P'r'aps it'll come back to her too, what she once was.'

She was sitting up in bed, struggling for breath. Her eyes were wide open, empty eyes, and she was gabbling to herself about many, many things.

He tried to take hold of her hand which she kept on withdrawing. 'Mother!' he begged. 'Auguste!'

She did not hear him. She did not even know he was there. All the others were, but not he. She wasn't with him, she was with the others. In a high-pitched voice she cried out: 'Evchen, is the soup ready? Make haste, Father'll be coming up from the stables – Bring me another cup of coffee, he won't notice it – Sophie, lay the table quickly. Get it ready before Father comes – Bubi, tell Erich to finish dressing, Father can't wait.'

She hurried them up, she worried, she scrutinized the room, dim in the light of a solitary candle. She was back again in the Frank-furter Allee preparing the breakfast table.

'Evchen, put the crusts so that Father gets one too. He always wants us to eat the hard bits. Let him try as well.'

'Mother,' begged the old man groping for her hand. But again it was withdrawn.

She was staring into the darkness towards a shadow. 'Where's Ottchen? Is he still in the stable? Ottchen is to come at once, I can't bear it when Father shouts at him.'

She leaned back and closed her eyes, speaking now only in a whisper.

'Mother! Mother!'

'Are you there, Father? I see so badly. I must have been dreaming. Why had you only a candle burning? Put on the gas – you can spend a little money on me in my last hour.'

He climbed on a chair, lit the gas. But when he returned she was already wandering again.

'He thinks he's somebody because they blame him for being of iron. But he's nothing at all. He's done nothing. The way he ran my father down because of his slovenly stable and so on, and what kind of a stable has he got himself? Always making a row and ordering about – he thinks he's someone then – but we've fooled him!' She sat up in bed giggling.

'Fooled him! All of us. The cab drivers and the children and me more than anyone. And then he thinks he's somebody!'

'Auguste, do listen! Will you listen?'

Awake now and alert. 'Yes, Gustav?'

'D'you remember how you got the first prize at the Cuirassiers for the best-cooked luncheon? D'you remember, Auguste?'

'Yes, Gustav, I remember. A fat cookery book it was, only some-body stole it right away. They were all so jealous!'

'Auguste, d'you remember how at the ring-stickin' you had the most rings on yer sabre? An' how Colonel de Pannwitz danced the first dance with you? I was wonderful proud!'

'Yes, Gustav, I remember that, too. I had on my white dress with the pierced embroidery and a blue silk scarf round my waist.'

'An' Auguste, d'you remember when you had Otto, an' the midwife praised you because you didn't make a sound?'

'Yes, Gustav, yes. You sat beside the bed and held my hand. Give me your hand, Gustav . . .'

Yes, he had succeeded. He had managed it once again. He had summoned her back to himself, to their common youth, away from enmity and the shameful league with her children, the cab drivers, everyone else . . . And yet he knew that all she had just said about him were her real thoughts. He knew her.

But this he would not suffer. No one must die like that. And he summoned her back again and yet again. In that endless hour between two and three in the night some idea always occurred to him by which he won her back. Already the shades of death were settling on that old, weak face and the breath rattled in her throat, but he said: 'An' d'you remember, Auguste, yer little bird, yer Hänsecken? How he'd perch on yer finger but wouldn't ever come ter me?'

Over. Finished. The End.

The old man rose, passed his fingers over her eyes, but he did not look into her face. Climbing on the chair, he turned off the gas. That left only the candle burning.

Without looking at his wife he went out of the room, taking the candlestick. He had seen many a man die, had looked in the face of many a corpse, and he knew how the features which show for a time traces of the death throes change once the struggle is over. Peace has come. Often a child's face long vanished, oh how long vanished, looks out of the dead face.

It was then that he would see his wife.

He entered the small kitchen and started to search in the cupboard. Finally he found the beer glass and examined it by the light of the candle. It was a very nice glass indeed . . .

While he had been reminding Mother of all the old happenings of their youth in Pasewalk he had remembered this glass which the Pasewalkers had sent their famous fellow citizen; he had remembered that she had asked him to smash it. And that he had half promised to do so.

He looked at the sink. All he had to do was to strike the glass against the cast-iron basin and Mother would have had her way.

For a while he stood thus, glass in hand, seeing not the glass but his long, long years of married life. He was not thinking now about their youth, but of what had come later – many things – and how he had been always in the right. Even death couldn't change wrong into right.

Iron Gustav shook his head. 'It wouldn't help you, Mother,' he said quite loudly in the empty kitchen, 'it wouldn't help if to please you I smashed this glass so you could have yer way fer once. It's a handsome piece o' glass . . .'

Putting it back, he picked up the candle and returned to the bedroom, to look at his wife's face.

THE END

*Contemporary ... Provocative ... Outrageous ...
Prophetic ... Groundbreaking ... Funny ... Disturbing ...
Different ... Moving ... Revolutionary ... Inspiring ...
Subversive ... Life-changing ...*

What makes a modern classic?

At Penguin Classics our mission has always been to make the best
books ever written available to everyone. And that also means
constantly redefining and refreshing exactly what makes a 'classic'.
That's where Modern Classics come in. Since 1961 they have been an
organic, ever-growing and ever-evolving list of books from the last
hundred (or so) years that we believe will continue to be read over and
over again.

They could be books that have inspired political dissent, such as
Animal Farm. Some, like *Lolita* or *A Clockwork Orange*, may have
caused shock and outrage. Many have led to great films, from *In Cold
Blood* to *One Flew Over the Cuckoo's Nest*. They have broken down
barriers – whether social, sexual, or, in the case of *Ulysses*, the
boundaries of language itself. And they might – like *Goldfinger* or
Scoop – just be pure classic escapism. Whatever the reason, Penguin
Modern Classics continue to inspire, entertain and enlighten millions
of readers everywhere.

'No publisher has had more influence on reading habits than Penguin'
Independent

'Penguins provided a crash course in world literature'
Guardian

The best books ever written

PENGUIN 🐧 CLASSICS

SINCE 1946

Find out more at www.penguinclassics.com